Reap the Whirlwind

REAP THE WHIRLWIND

Luanshya Greer

ROWAN

This book is a work of fiction. Any
resemblance between the characters
portrayed and real persons, living or dead, is
purely coincidental

A ROWAN BOOK

Arrow Books Limited
20 Vauxhall Bridge Road, London SW1V 2SA

An imprint of the Random Century Group

London Melbourne Sydney Auckland Johannesburg
and agencies throughout the world

First published in Great Britain by Century in 1991
Rowan edition 1992

3 5 7 9 10 8 6 4 2

Printed and bound in Great Britain by
Cox & Wyman Ltd, Reading, Berkshire

ISBN 0 09 990010 6

For my family:
John, whose love and encouragement never failed,
and Ben and Suzanna – for being there

CONTENTS

ACKNOWLEDGEMENTS

The author wishes to thank the following people, without whose generous help this book could not have been written: Elsie Mabille-Verdier, the original Huguenot, for the delight of her memories spanning several decades of mission work in Africa; the uniquely talented writer, Johann Potgieter, for his insight into the peoples of Africa; John Hind, for his vast historical knowledge; Jane Hill, my editor; Mr and Mrs Piet de Wet; Suzette and Gilbert Colyn; Dr Jan S. Marais; Elizabeth and Peter Maname; Themba Nyati, Katherine Bennet, and the Monday girls, all of whom contributed in no small way, even if unwittingly.

L.G.

'You were sold for nothing,
and without money you will be redeemed.'

Isaiah 52. N.I.V.

PART ONE

1820-44

Chapter One

The scorpion darted between the flames and the basket. Its tail flicked madly over its back.

Jean Jacques, a barefoot seven-year-old half-caste boy, balanced precariously on the upturned basket. The basket was in the centre of a circle of fire. Within the circle was the scorpion.

'Push him off, Suzanne! Go on. Push him!' Clara screeched in a fervour of excitement.

'You push him, Clara. I'm afraid.' Suzanne turned her face away from the small boy. His chin stuck out defiantly though tears rolled down his cheeks.

'He's afraid. Look at him!' Clara screamed again. 'You're afraid of a little scorpion, aren't you!' Jean Jacques tilted his chin higher. He tried to wipe away the tears with the back of his hand. 'Don't think your tears bother me. Don't think crying will help,' Clara taunted and pushed the basket again. Jean Jacques almost fell off. 'If you jump, the scorpion might miss you.' Clara smiled. 'But then of course it might not.'

'Prudence. Tell her to stop!' Suzanne cried.

Prudence was just nine years old. She looked from Suzanne to Clara warily. Clara was twelve, the eldest of the three sisters and not much older than she was, but at this moment she seemed older than any grown-up. Prudence remained silent.

'Jump! Show us how you can jump, boy!' Clara hadn't even noticed Prudence. 'Shall I help you?' She began thrashing the stick at his bare feet.

Prudence and Suzanne glanced at one another. This was no longer a game. Clara wasn't just teasing the small boy. They turned to run at the same moment but stopped in fright. Their father, Jacques Beauvilliers, pulled up his horse sharply as he

3

reached them, the firm line of his jaw rigid with anger. He leapt down from his horse and strode to Clara, snatching the stick out of her hand.

'What in God's name are you doing?' He trampled the fire, kicking sand over the red-hot embers, then ground the scorpion into the dirt with his boot. 'You could have killed him!' He pulled the terrified child into his arms and held him gently but firmly, wiping the tears from his eyes. 'Are you all right, Jean Jacques?'

'We were only playing with him, Father.' Clara's face flushed red as Jacques turned his look on her.

'Playing? With fire and a scorpion? This is not the first time, Clara.' Jacques lowered the small boy to the ground and safety. 'He's a baby and you do nothing but torment him.'

'Then his mother should take more care of him,' Clara countered swiftly. Involuntarily she pulled back as Jacques swung round on her. His eyes threatened her but she held his look. 'Or perhaps his father should.'

For a moment Clara's words stung Jacques to silence; but he held his gaze, forcing her to lower hers. He spoke quietly but firmly. 'You will go to your room. All of you.'

Clara's eyes darted, straight to the small boy. Again he tilted his chin up slightly as she did.

'And him? Where will he go, Father? Back to the hovel where bastards belong? To the slave quarters and his slave mother?' The tears of fear and anger were held back in her throat but could be heard.

'Your tongue does not befit a girl of your breeding, Clara. You will learn to curb it, or you will remain in your room out of the hearing of the rest of the family.' Even as the words left Jacques' mouth he knew he had just witnessed the truth of his daughter's feelings. They were not feelings that could be contained in words, or curbed by his anger.

Suzanne tugged at Clara's skirt. Clara kept her eyes on her father, challenging him to go on. Jean Jacques watched in terror.

'Come, Clara. Please,' Suzanne begged in a whisper. Prudence, as small as she was, took up her sister's challenge and moved to her father, looking up at him directly. Her words were plain, not spiked with the razor edge of Clara's.

'Who is he, Father?' Prudence tilted her head to one side as his

4

eyes moved to her. 'Do you know who he is?'

'He's the son of a slave, Prudence! Isn't he, Father?' Again Clara's words pierced Jacques' heart.

'He is the son of a slave. Yes.' Jacques' voice kept its even tone.

'They say he's illegitimate.' Prudence said the word with all the innocence of a child who had no idea what it meant. Jacques took her hand and knelt down in front of her. The hard dry earth under his knees dug into him.

'Do you know what that means, Prudence? Illegitimate?' he asked.

'That he's a bastard!' Clara said sharply.

Jacques kept his eyes on Prudence, staving off Clara's constant challenge. "He is illegitimate, yes. He is the son of a slave. But who told you this, Prudence?" His voice was gentle, encouraging an answer.

'Clara,' Prudence said simply.

Even without turning to her, Jacques could feel Clara's eyes on him. He could feel the demand behind her words as she said again, 'Then who is his father, Father?' Before Jacques could answer her she turned her attention to Jean Jacques coldly. 'Who is your father, boy?'

In a sudden blind rage Jacques swung round and slapped her hard across the face, immediately regretting it as the force of his hand jerked her head back. But she faced him still, her head erect, though tears smarted in her eyes. Her cheek burned red with the imprint of his hand, and her heart screamed with the pain of her father's anger. Why didn't he understand what he had done to her?

'Never let me see such cruelty again!' Jacques found security in the words of an indignant father. 'Go to your room. All of you!' He turned his back on his daughters and his attention to Jean Jacques as he lifted him into his arms. 'Come.'

Prudence touched Clara's hand then turned towards the house. Suzanne moved away with her, head bowed. For a moment Clara didn't move. Prudence looked back at her quickly and whispered, 'Clara.' She waited as Clara moved to her, and the three girls walked obediently towards the house. But as they went Clara's defiance raised its head again in a murmur.

'I hate him.'

Jacques watched his daughters. Like three little monks, with the hoods of their cloaks pulled up to cover their shame, they walked slowly towards the house. It was his shame they were covering. But what shame? Could there be shame in the small boy who clung to him now? His tiny brown-skinned son whose mother, Eva, he loved so deeply? Not in the same way as he loved his wife Emily, mother of his daughters, but with love rising from the hidden depths of his soul; a love that embraced the red earth under his feet. The earth in which – apart from Eva and Jean Jacques – he found his only comfort in this foreign African land.

As he walked towards the slave quarters with his son in his arms, Jacques looked at the house which was his home: a beautiful white gabled house set in a fold of the surrounding mountains. Mountains across whose slopes the vines he cared for so deeply stretched themselves, reaching across to one another in a low canopy of green, heavy with bunches of cloudy-dark grapes. The juice of the grapes, borne from the earth of Bonne Esperance, was at last attaining the perfection of a wine fit for the most discerning palates. Bonne Esperance. A portion of the earth, built with his sweat and labour, tended with his care and pride, and blossoming now in its prime of life to be one of the finest vineyards in the Cape of Good Hope. But somehow, like his daughter, Clara, Bonne Esperance held him at bay. It was as if it knew his heart still lay in France.

The girls reached the side of the house and Clara ducked quickly behind the huge whitewashed arch from which the slave bell hung still and silent.

'Don't say anything to Mother,' she whispered to her sisters. 'I'm coming now.' With a quick glance to check that her father was still moving away in the direction of the slave quarters, Clara ran behind the house. Titus was there, as she had known he would be, and his dark-brown eyes lowered the moment hers lighted on him.

'Did you see what happened? Did you?' As she spoke Titus kept his eyes away from Clara. It was a sign of respect among his people, and though Titus was a grown man, he was a slave. He must show respect even to this young girl. She was his master's daughter.

'Next time I'll get you a bigger scorpion, Miss Clara. I'll build

6

you a bigger fire.' Titus spoke with enthusiasm and the anticipation of the final victory.

'Next time I'll tell Father it was *you* who told me!' Clara cut him short.

Titus's face crumpled as if it had only ever been held together by a few delicate sinews of pride. His dark eyes, the yellow frame of eyeballs standing out, rolled back in shame as if never to look forward again.

'No, Miss Clara no! It would be bad for you to tell the master, very bad,' Titus pleaded in a sad melody of humility. 'Miss Clara mustn't tell the master. No.' But even now, a man pleading with a child, the dignity of his race showed through.

'Then you lied? When you told me my father was that boy's father, you lied?'

'I don't lie. No, Miss Clara. It's true what I told you.' Titus lifted his head with the denial. 'You remember. You were there, Miss Clara. When you were a little girl you were there. You saw.'

All her life Clara had been fighting the memories that Titus was forcing forward now; memories which came and went at the most unexpected times and always left her devastated. She could see him now. She could see her father. Her stomach heaved involuntarily with the images thrown up by memory.

The day had begun with such excitement. The kitchens were alive with activity. Clara remembered clearly how she'd stood at the kitchen table as the suckling pig was prepared by Maria, the cook and housekeeper. Being just six years old, Clara's face had been level with the surface of the kitchen table as she stood on tiptoe, her eyes in direct line with the eyes of the pig. She had wondered if it was still alive. It seemed to look straight at her. As Maria sliced a large butcher's knife down its stomach to prepare it, she had laughed at Clara's shrieks of protest.

'You think it hurts, Miss Clara? You think I do this to a poor little pig without it be dead?' Maria bent her round black face down to Clara's and grinned. 'But if you don't get out of the kitchen now, Miss Clara, I use this end of the knife on you, see.' She had held the handle of the knife out in playful aggression. Clara had giggled with glee at the thought of Maria, all of Maria which was a lot, chasing her round the kitchen. Clara often encouraged such chases for the sheer enjoyment of watching Maria's great bosoms bounce up and down. They jumped and shivered like jelly, and Clara never knew where they would settle. Up, down, right or left. But there wasn't a moment to be wasted on such an exciting day as this and most certainly not on Maria's bosoms. That was a game she could play any day but today was special. It was leading to tonight, and the banquet.

Clara hadn't really known what a banquet was. All she'd gathered was that many people would come to their house that night, dressed in their finest clothes, and would eat of the best, and drink of the best Bonne Esperance wines. They would dance through the night, and most important of all, her father would be dressed in his dark tail coat.

She had fingered the coat as it lay with the rest of his clothes ready for him to put on. It smelt of her father. That wonderful smell which always comforted her, yet also, in a curious way, excited her. It wasn't the smell he had when she ran to him as he worked in the vineyard. Not the strong smell of sweat and horses, earth and vines. It was the smell of a man who could chase a ghost with the snap of his fingers. Who would look at her with his melting brown eyes and his wide mouth tip-tilted up at the corners in a smile, all for her, and with his firm strong hands holding her tiny body with such certainty would say in his funny French accent, 'And how's my little girl today?'

'Would you pass me my hairbrush please, Clara?' Her mother had shaken her from the dream woven into her father's coat. Clara had immediately fetched the brush. She loved her mother too, but it was different. With her mother she felt the roles were almost reversed. Clara protected her. She had picked up the hairbrush with its beautiful engraved silver back and had called to her mother brightly,

'I'll brush your hair for you. Can I, Mother? Can I brush it?'

'No! It's my turn,' Suzanne had interrupted as she stood defensively in front of her mother at the dressing-table. Brushing their mother's hair had always been a pleasure to be fought over, but Clara had decided that today Suzanne could do it. She was too young to have any idea how special tonight was, so she might just as well brush her mother's hair. Clara would do it tomorrow. She tossed the brush at Suzanne, who missed it and bent down with a small petulant stamp to pick it up.

8

'You dropped it.'

'You did!' Clara called back as she ran out of the room in search of something more exciting.

'Keep your fingers off it!' Miss Thurston's voice had been as stern as ever as Clara touched the beautiful crystal goblet. 'Look what you've done, child. Look at the marks your fingers have left.' Miss Thurston had been right. There were two small splodges on the gleaming glass: one the print of her forefinger on the inside of the glass and the other the large smudge of her thumb near the stem. Miss Thurston had continued her grumbling at the glass; as if it was partly to blame for Clara's fingerprints. 'You shouldn't be here at all. You'll break something, or worse still you'll break yourself on something. Go outside if you want to play.'

Clara had always been fascinated by the way Miss Thurston managed to hold conversations with things. When Clara had done something really bad during prayers, Miss Thurston would accuse the Bible of Clara's misdemeanour. She would then pause a while, looking directly at the Bible, as if waiting for it to answer. Clara had often wondered if it would answer her back, but she doubted it. For if what Miss Thurston said was true, she and God were always in complete agreement. But this time God was not involved, since the Bible was not at hand, and Clara had slipped away knowing she had offended only her governess.

That evening she'd got herself bathed and ready for bed before being told. She'd known that once the nightly routine was out of the way she'd have more time for important things. Things like watching the guests arrive in their carriages, watching the finishing touches being put to the large dinner table, and best of all, watching her father.

He had stood at the open door of the house with her mother and bowed as he greeted the ladies. How the ladies' colour seemed to rise as he did. They liked him. But what they didn't know, Clara had thought, was that he belonged to her. He was her father. Nothing would ever change her position of singular importance in his life. She was his first child and eldest daughter. As she watched him with her mother beside him, Clara had known that the small space between them was filled by herself.

'Clara! Come here at once before your father sees you.' Miss Thurston's voice had always grown even more clipped at times like these. When people visited the house she ensured they knew that she was the governess and in strict charge of all discipline in the household. It was an asset she did her best to make visitors envy in the Beauvilliers family. 'Go to your room and I'll be with you for prayers.' Her firm hand had pushed Clara through the door.

The Lord's Prayer had seemed to take for ever that night. If only Miss Thurston wouldn't wait for Suzanne to say each word. Suzanne never got it right and always had to be corrected. It meant they said the Lord's Prayer about ten times in all. Thank goodness the baby wasn't involved yet, Clara had thought. By the time Prudence was old enough, Clara would have found some reason not to join in the children's nightly prayers.

'. . . thy will be done, on earth as it is in heaven . . .' Clara had glanced over Miss Thurston's shoulder at the bible in her lap. She'd wanted to see how long the psalm for that night was. Miss Thurston had stopped her with the slightest irritated, yet very reverent, shrug of a shoulder. '. . . for ever and ever, Amen.' At last, Clara had thought. But Miss Thurston went on. 'And may God bless our mother and our father, keep them in health and . . .'

Music! The strains of music had seeped into the bedroom from the hall! The people would be dancing soon. Clara had to see. But the music died in her ears as Miss Thurston raised her eyes from prayer and pinioned Clara with them.

'May God bring a blessing on our home and land that it will bring forth the labours of our father and help us to live in a manner befitting a Christian person. Amen,' Clara had finished the prayer obediently.

At last Miss Thurston had reached the door with the candle in her hand. Clara and Suzanne were tucked neatly into their beds and the baby Prudence gurgled in her crib.

'And now, children, you will stay in your beds till the morning. Good night Suzanne.'

'Good night, Miss Thurston.' Suzanne's voice had been muffled by the bedclothes tucked under her chin and sucked into her mouth.

'Good night, Clara.' Clara had kept silent, her eyes squeezed as tightly shut as her mouth. Miss Thurston stood over her with the candle. Clara had opened her eyes to the stern face made sterner still by the flickering light of the flame. 'I said good night, Clara,' she had repeated.

'But it isn't a good night, Miss Thurston,' Clara had argued.

'And what's not good about it, Clara?' The candlelight shone angrily in her eyes.

'That we're in bed while Mother and Father dance. It's not fair.'

'Are your mother and father not allowed to entertain their friends?'

'But I want to watch them.' Why couldn't Miss Thurston understand? Clara had wondered. Because she was old?

'You're a spoiled child.'

'But Father said I could watch!' The gleam those words had brought to Miss Thurston's eyes was brighter than the candle-light.

'Fortunately I am in charge and not your father. Good night, Clara.' She had moved to the door and turned back. 'But let me assure you, child. If I discover you out of your bed it will be your father who will do the punishing. Good night.' And Miss Thurston had gone. She had evaporated in the darkness left behind by the candle as it vanished with her.

Into the darkness Clara had dangled her bare feet as she swung her legs over the edge of the bed. The floor had squeaked as she stood on it and she'd tensed.

'Clara!' Suzanne's whisper was filled with terror.

'Shh,' Clara had dismissed her as she tiptoed to the bedroom door. 'Oh!'

It had been too beautiful for Clara to keep the exclamation to herself. The chandeliers sparkled and flickered on to the highly polished shoes of the men as they ordered the movement of the delicate ladies' slippers before them. Clara had peered between the shoes from her position crouching on the floor, partly hidden behind the half-open door. She had searched among the feet to find her father's. Her eyes had moved from his shoes up the dark trousers, over the black coat, the thin black tie in a half bow, and on to his face. He had smiled at her mother as they passed one another in the dance. How handsome he was. Her mother was beautiful, yes, but how handsome her father was. They were talking as they danced but Clara couldn't hear what they said over the music. Black slaves played extraordinary music on the strangest hand-made instruments, and Clara had become a part of it all.

What was M. Claudelle doing? Clara had wondered as she noticed him move to her father and excuse himself to her mother. She had craned her neck to hear what he said but couldn't. Before she knew what had happened her father had moved off the dance floor with her mother. He had made his way with M. Claudelle towards the main door, and gone out into the night.

Quickly Clara had ducked back from the door and through the kitchens. Maria was so busy she hadn't noticed as Clara slipped behind her to go outside.

The African night had grabbed Clara in its warm arms. The familiar sound of the slaves' copper-warm singing replaced the light music of the ball, and the scratching crickets punctuated her thoughts. Where was her father going? There must be something wrong? Something only he could put right.

M. Claudelle, the wine-maker of Bonne Esperance, had left her father, who strode alone across the grounds towards the slave quarters. Clara waited for a brief moment, knowing that even her father would be angry if he saw her now. Outside, to be seen by slaves in her nightdress. But she had not cared. He must not disappear from her sight for a moment. She had run after him, her bare feet silent on the damp grass. She'd ducked behind a tree as he'd turned, looking back before going on. Why had he done that? Did he know she was there? She'd waited until he was safely inside the slave quarters. Yes. There must be trouble, she'd thought. Trouble with the slaves had always been something only he could see to.

The outside wall of the slave quarters had felt rough to her hands. It was cracked and flaking. She'd instinctively rubbed her hands down her nightdress. It had to be dirty. She'd stopped as she walked around the building looking for a way of seeing inside without herself being seen. What was that sound? Someone was moaning. It was a deep painful moan. Almost that of an animal.

She'd pulled back slightly as the light from a small crack in the wall greeted her. She'd peered through it and shapes had moved in front of her. A fire was burning. A large pot of water bubbled on it. An elderly woman, black as the night that surrounded Clara, sat in front of the fire and pot, watching them both. Her head was erect and her body poised even in tattered rags. Again Clara had heard that moan. Quieter. More frightening for that.

'Eva.' It had been her father's voice. Gentle. Loving. The same voice she'd heard so many times as he comforted her. 'It's all right, Eva.' Clara had twisted her neck to see where his voice was coming from. She'd seen and recoiled.

Her father was beside a Malay woman. A beautiful Malay woman. A slave. Her father was stroking this woman's head. Her father was holding this woman's hand. Her father had bent down and kissed this woman's forehead.

And the woman had screamed.

Clara had pulled back sharply. Her eyes had snapped shut and her hands had covered her ears. But she couldn't bear the darkness and silence she'd plunged herself into and had turned back to look again. She'd stopped quite still. Another sound had come from the room. A strange, unfamiliar sound. A bleating sound, yet not. What was it?

Clara had peered through her private crack in the wall of mystery again. The shape blocking her view had moved slightly and there, holding a tiny brown scrap of baby in his arms, had been her father. He'd lifted the baby up to his face. Its tiny fists clenched, then opened as if in a sigh as it looked at him, and her father had whispered just two words.

'My son.'

Clara hadn't remembered running. She hadn't remembered anything except a feeling. Death. Her father had spoken two words and killed her. He had held a small brown baby in his arms. He'd looked at him with more love than Clara had ever seen in his eyes before, and he had said, 'My son.'

'No! I don't remember!' Clara shouted at Titus now, as though shouting might drive away the memories. Might drive Titus away. He represented those memories. But Titus wasn't going anywhere. His dark hand stretched out to touch and calm her. She pulled her arm back sharply.

'Don't touch me!' she spat at him. Titus dropped his hand. His acceptance of her rebuke was unquestioning, although he knew he had to prevent her from telling her father, his master. There was only one way to do that.

'Next time I'll build you a bigger fire, Miss Clara! I'll find you a bigger scorpion!' Still his eyes didn't settle on hers as his head held the slightest genuflection. 'Then his mother will take him away.' He smiled, allowing his white teeth to shine. Clara looked at him keenly. Her head was tilted to one side with the only thought that might keep the memories away.

'You're sure his mother will take him?' she asked.

Titus nodded confirmation. 'Yes, Miss Clara. If her child frightened, she frightened. She take him away.'

'Where to?' Clara's directness surprised him.

'Away. Far away. You never see her again. Never see him again.'

'And my father?'

'The master too. He never see them again.'

Clara allowed his words to sink in and quieten her racing heart. It was all she needed to hear. But this time she would need to plan more carefully.

'I'll send for you when I need you.' She spoke the words with the authority of a woman, and then was gone. Into the house, through the kitchens and into the bedroom to which she'd been ordered. Freed from the trap of her presence Titus glanced towards the slave quarters. His master was inside with the beautiful Eva whom Titus longed to have as his own.

'They're only children, Eva. Little girls who don't know what they're doing.' Jacques looked down at Eva as she scrubbed the ragged cuffs of her son's shirt in a small bowl. Jean Jacques stood away, deeper in the dark room, his small figure moulded into a corner as he watched his mother.

'They hate him.' Eva spoke with an uncompromising simplicity. 'There is nothing you can do.'

Jacques knew Eva was right but he couldn't accept it. He didn't want to. With it came the risk of losing Eva.

'Do you want to ride, Jean Jacques?' Jacques had deliberately changed the subject and was using his small silent son to gain his own ends. 'You could ride up in front of me.' Though all he longed for was the dark warmth of Eva's body in front of his own.

'You can't.' Eva needed no more words.

Jacques looked at her questioningly. 'I teach many of the

small boys to ride, Eva. It would not be unusual.'

'He is not just one of the small boys.'

'Eva. My Eva.' Jacques moved to her and wrapped his arms around her. His body ached as the comfort of hers reached him. Her long black hair shone and fell like silk down her back in a heavy coil. 'I love you.' His words mingled with her hair. He lifted the dark hair away, exposing her slender olive-brown neck and kissed it gently. His teeth suddenly sank into her skin and Eva caught her breath, turning to him quickly as her eyes darted protectively to Jean Jacques in the corner. Jacques understood.

'Come on, Jean Jacques.' Jacques moved to him quickly and took his hand. 'You will ride on Shiva.'

'Shiva!' Jean Jacques could hardly contain his excitement and moved to the door before his mother could say no.

'It will be all right,' Jacques said as gently as he could and looked into her eyes. He smiled, and Eva's mouth flickered with a smile which even she could not hide.

'Yes, master.'

Titus watched from out of sight until Jacques had moved far enough away with the small boy. He reached the door of the slave quarters and leaned against the wall. The beads of perspiration standing out on his forehead were not from the heat of the sun.

'Eva. I must speak with you.' Titus hoped she would hear the urgency in his voice.

'I know, Titus. The master told me.' Eva stepped out, raising her hand to shield her eyes from the bright sun glaring down on them. She glanced towards the stables as Jacques moved into them with her son. 'They won't hurt him again.'

'Miss Clara will hurt him. You must go away from here. Come with me.' His eyes pleaded with her as his voice did.

'Titus, I will never be your woman.' Eva had answered the question he had never dared ask.

'It is you I fear for.' Titus would not let her answer that question. 'Your life is in danger here.'

Eva looked at him kindly. Her hand touched his cheek gently. The palm of her hand opened on his skin. 'I know.' She slipped lightly as a breeze back through the low dark door of the slave quarters.

As Eva wrung the water from the sleeves of her small son's

shirt into the basin, her eyes settled on the soapy water. Her place was not to question Jacques. He was her master. Many young slave women were taken by their masters for sex, and bore their master's demands in silence. But Eva had no need to silence herself. She loved Jacques. More than that she sensed that he never took her in any more demanding manner than he took his own wife. More passionate perhaps, but never with less respect. How could Titus understand that Jacques' white skin held no threat for her? It covered a man no different from any other. Except to her.

Her head moved with her thoughts in the direction of the large house further away. A safe distance from the slave quarters. Inside that house was Mrs Emily Beauvilliers, Jacques' wife and mistress of Bonne Esperance. A delicate woman. As pale as Eva was dark. With a skin of fine porcelain, highlighted by tiny blue luminous veins which accentuated her fragile beauty. Where Eva's hands were strong, lithe and brown, hers were as delicate as the spread of a bird's wing. They had never been dipped in soapy water. Never scrubbed her children's clothes. Had they ever dug into her husband's back as he forced himself deep inside her?

Eva shook the shirt to dismiss the last drops of water and her thoughts. She was a slave. Her body belonged totally to Jacques Beauvilliers. Her soul she had given to him as a gift; but for her son's safety, she must ensure Jacques never knew he owned it.

'May I have a bible please, Mother?' Emily Beauvilliers looked up as Clara asked politely from the sitting-room door.

'You have a bible in your room,' Miss Thurston answered before Emily could.

'I want the family bible. It's the best way to learn French.' Clara was not afraid of Miss Thurston any more. She hadn't been since she had heard her father tell her to remember her place. She had realized then Miss Thurston's place. She was a servant of the Beauvilliers family. The governess was there to serve the Beauvilliers children.

'Mother? May I?' Clara deliberately turned her back on Miss Thurston.

'Of course. I'm pleased you are learning French, Clara. Father will be most especially pleased.' Emily picked up the large Huguenot family bible and moved to Clara with it. 'Are you certain you can carry it? It's very heavy.'

'Yes. I can.' Clara took the bible and made as if to go. The moment her mother had turned away from her, she plucked a large key from its hook on the wall and ducked out with it and the bible.

Miss Thurston turned to the window and pulled the curtain back very slightly. It was as much to keep from facing Emily as anything else. It was difficult to hide her feelings about Clara, and this was most certainly not the time to show them.

'What is it about that little child?' Miss Thurston asked quietly.

'Which child?' Emily moved to the window beside her and looked out. As she did she took a deep breath. 'It's so hot today. Do drop the curtain back. I can't bear the sun streaming in on to the furnishings. It fades them so.'

Emily knew which child Miss Thurston meant. The slave child. The child her husband was teaching to ride outside at that very moment. The child of the very beautiful young slave girl, Eva.

'There's no harm in the boy, and your husband is uncommonly kind to him,' Miss Thurston continued, dropping the curtain back in its place.

'He's kind to all the children.' Emily was not certain how much Miss Thurston knew. 'Why should there be something special about that child?'

'Nothing at all. But it seems the girls don't like him. Clara especially. I've seen her tease him wickedly.' Miss Thurston was unaware of the hurt growing in Emily as she listened. 'The way she behaves one can't help but wonder if she has some reason.' Miss Thurston lowered herself into a cane chair.

'Perhaps she simply does not like him.' Emily moved back to the window and lifted the curtain again. Her eyes immediately fixed on her husband Jacques in the distance. He was riding around the edge of the vineyard. He was on the horse Shiva and in the circle of his arms was the slave boy. Emily turned away quickly, dropping the curtain. She didn't want to look deeper and see more. 'You've been Clara's governess since she was able to talk. You should perhaps know the reason better than I, Amy.' Emily held her blonde head erect and her eyes, pale blue and as delicate as a duck's egg, looked at Miss Thurston without malice. The use of her Christian name was enough. 'Oh,' she sighed, 'how I wish the sun would stop beating down.'

'Are you well, Emily?' Miss Thurston genuinely cared. She had known Emily since she was a child.

'I'm fine. The heat simply drains my strength. But I'm fine.'

'Is that really what it is, dear?' Miss Thurston moved to her.

'You know I dislike the sun. Ever since we've been in Africa I have never felt quite well.' Emily steered the conversation away from that small boy to the certain ground of her health. It always ensured Miss Thurston's concern and attention.

'Indeed, you haven't been well and it disturbs me. Like everything else about this land. I don't know why, but it breeds a hostility I find difficult to understand.' Miss Thurston placed a hand on Emily's forehead as though she were still a child. 'You're quite warm. Are you certain you feel all right?'

'It's spring at home now, Miss Thurston!' Emily's voice lifted the shroud of illness. 'If I close my eyes I can see the carriageway leading to the house, lined with cherry blossom. The palest of pink. So soft. Do you remember?'

'Indeed I do. The bluebells. The buttercups.'

'And the incessant rain.' Emily chuckled. 'Just imagine those poor souls who have come from home to settle here. Do you know, Jacques told me they had no idea what to expect? They were told the eastern frontier was as gentle as England.'

'And I hear say that no mention was made of the Xhosa warriors massed on that frontier! It's a disgrace. What is becoming of the British government? Sending innocent hard-working folk out here as a human wall of defence for the Cape!' Miss Thurston was on her favourite subject and Emily feigned interest, though her mind was still on her husband. 'They are good people trying to make a life, come what may. People who deserved the truth about what they would find. Not at all the same as those convicts shipped to Australia. These are fine upstanding folk giving meaning to the Empire. It's not right. Not at all.' Miss Thurston raised her head as if having just been personally reassured.

'But God will protect them as He has us.'

'Even in a land where so much hatred has taken root among children?'

Emily turned her pale-blue eyes directly on to her. Miss Thurston looked down at once. To her, Emily was still a child but she had been taught to respect her employer.

'It was not my place to speak. I'm sorry.'

'I love my husband.' Emily pushed her fingers gently into her temple, as if fixing that knowledge in her mind. 'Enough to give me the strength I need now.'

'No. You cannot.' Miss Thurston was horrified. Even a spinster knew what was in Emily's mind. But Emily smiled in the face of her horror.

'Why not? His vines bear him fruit every year. Must I be less to him than this African vineyard he left his native France for?' She paused. 'I love him.'

Miss Thurston's tension showed in her back, which she'd turned on Emily in defence.

'I must be honest with you, Emily, I must.' Emily waited silently until Miss Thurston turned to face her. Fear clipped her words. 'Does he love you?' Emily turned away and Miss Thurston's words moved after her. Forcing her to listen. Knowing it was not her place to speak, but feeling she had to. She would speak.

'Your husband's ancestors left France to escape Catholic persecution, Emily, but he did not. He came here for all this. For Bonne Esperance, not for love! He's here now for this and not for you! When he met you he needed money to revive this estate left to him by his uncle – and that is all!'

'I won't listen to you.' Emily moved away.

'Because I speak the truth?'

'It's not the land you find hostile.' Emily swung round on her. 'It's my husband!'

'Yes. God forgive me but yes!'

'Jacques has suffered enough without you –'

'His ancestors suffered!' Miss Thurston interrupted. 'They came to this land as oppressed people and built this place from nothing! Not him.'

'He came to save it when they died with nothing!' Emily's voice was desperate in his defence. 'Don't you think he misses Europe as we miss England? Don't you know how he longs for the heavy skies of winter and light skies of summer as we do?' Emily paused. 'As he longs for a son?'

Miss Thurston had no words to answer. She looked at Emily as a mother might look at a child about to step off the side of a mountain, with too big a distance between them to stop her.

'I love him.' Emily spoke into the silence between them and her words were followed by the crackle of Miss Thurston's stiff skirts as she moved to the door. The grind of the door handle turning. The swish of the door opening, and the click of it closing behind her.

Emily looked at the closed door through which Miss Thurston had gone. She turned away and moved to the window. Her husband, Jacques, was still riding with the small slave boy in front of him. She leaned her head back and closed her eyes.

'God grant me a son and Jacques an heir.' A moment's silence. Her head dropped in humility. 'But thy will be done.'

Clara sat cross-legged on her bed. Prudence and Suzanne lay on their stomachs across the bed, their legs bent up behind them and linked at the knees. Their bare toes touched as they listened to Clara reading from the bible. Not the large family bible which sat on the floor with the large key on top of it, but the bible Miss Thurston used during prayers.

'And Sarah saw the son of Hagar the Egyptian, which she had borne unto Abraham. Therefore she said unto Abraham, "Cast out this bondswoman and her son: for the son of this bondswoman shall not be heir with my son, even with Isaac." '

Prudence twisted her head and glanced down at the bible on the floor. 'I thought you were going to read from that one.' She stretched her foot down to the key on the bible and picked it up with her toes. 'What's this?'

'Don't!' Clara leapt off the bed and snatched the key from between the bare toes. 'How can I read to you from that one? You don't understand French.'

'Nor does anyone but Father.' Prudence shrugged.

'Then you should learn it,' Clara retorted.

'Why? He talks English.' Prudence wasn't disturbed by Clara's authority as the older sister. She didn't understand much of anything about her. She'd decided it must be because Clara was turning into a woman, and her eyes moved casually to the bodice of Clara's dress. She definitely had two bumps. Small, but definitely there, and Prudence wondered if Suzanne had them. She herself didn't. Nothing had changed about her body at all and she was happy about that. But those bumps would inevitably arrive on her chest one day and she couldn't help wondering what it would be like. She wouldn't be able to see her toes any more without bending down.

'Are you listening to me, Prudence?' Clara pushed her knee into Prudence's side as she climbed back to her cross-legged position on the bed. She placed the large family bible in front of her and held the key up. 'This is the key our father's ancestors brought to this land when they ran away from the Catholics in France. It's the key to the home that belonged to the Beauvilliers in Nîmes. It's a home that we will claim one day as our right.'

'Where's Nîmes?' Suzanne asked.

'In France,' Clara said.

'And there's a key missing there!' Prudence chuckled and rolled off the bed with amusement at her own joke. Clara put her foot on to Prudence's chest as she lay on the floor.

'If we are to claim our ancestry in France we must prove our worth as a Christian family, Prudence.' Clara was stern.

'As Protestants?' Prudence looked up at her agog. 'They don't like Protestants, you said. Catholics kill them.'

'Will you listen to me?' She waited. Prudence nodded and Suzanne leaned forward. She was listening as always. Frightened as always but listening.

'Go on, Clara,' Suzanne whispered.

'The problem is we can't claim it now. Not while that boy Jean Jacques is alive, because he's a heathen!'

'Well.' Prudence rolled over on to her stomach and stood up, pulling the bodice of her dress down. She climbed back on to the bed, lying across and on top of Suzanne. 'We only have your word that he's our father's son, Clara.'

'God knows he is! God says . . . "the son of a bondswoman . . . he must not be heir . . ." You heard it,' Clara argued.

'He was talking about an Egyptian,' Prudence interrupted, and pushed Suzanne's hair out of her face.

'I'm talking about us!' Clara was angry. Prudence knew she must be quiet and Suzanne's quick look reinforced it. 'We are our father's real children. Like Isaac. We must swear allegiance in a pact of blood.'

'Blood?' For the first time Suzanne pulled back from Clara

and sent Prudence toppling off her back.

'What blood?' Prudence asked, wide-eyed.

'Ours. The stain of that boy must be removed from this family!' Clara dug her hand into the pocket of her pinafore and Suzanne followed her every move. Clara pulled a small blade, a blade without any handle but as sharp as any Suzanne had ever seen, from her pocket. She laid it on top of the family bible beside the key, and lifted her eyes to them speaking very quietly. 'The blood from our wrists must mingle in an oath.'

'Why?' Prudence instinctively tucked her hands underneath her for safety. Suzanne sat totally still, unable to move. Clara took Suzanne's hand and looked into her eyes.

'It won't hurt.' She slid the small blade over her own wrist. 'See!' Drops of blood trickled against her white skin and Prudence watched in fascination. Suzanne held her hand out, wrist up. She was in a trance and under Clara's spell, Prudence decided. 'Prudence?' Clara's eyes were fixed on her. 'You're not scared, are you?'

'Of what?' Prudence took a breath and let it out in a huff. 'I've cut myself worse than that on a wine barrel. Here.' She stuck her hand out, wrist up, beside Suzanne's. But her eyes were closed.

In two swift movements Clara slipped the knife across Prudence's wrist and then Suzanne's. She held her own wrist up and placed it against theirs. Prudence was fascinated. It didn't hurt yet they were all bleeding. Perhaps they would bleed to death all over the bible. Clara's voice interrupted her fantasies.

'We swear . . .' She waited for her sisters.

'We swear . . .' their voices followed her lead, 'on the holy family bible . . .' Prudence watched as a drop of their blood fell on to the key then slid slowly down the rusty metal stem and dripped on to the holy family bible. She froze. Clara nudged her to go on. '. . . that the son of our father, the half-caste boy Jean Jacques, will no longer be a stain on our family.'

Prudence couldn't take her eyes off the blood on the bible. Suzanne was also looking at it. Suzanne was shaking.

'We promise together . . .' Clara went on, looking fiercely at her sisters as she waited for them to continue. They followed quietly. '. . . to rid our family of that boy. Or to die if we break this oath.' Suzanne pulled her hand back sharply without speaking the last words. Clara looked at her and repeated slowly, 'Or to die if we break this oath.' Suzanne's eyes moved back to the blood as it spread darkly over the bible. Her words could hardly be heard.

'Or to die if we break this oath.'

'When?' Prudence asked simply.

'If we . . .' Clara began.

'When do we do it?' Prudence repeated.

'In time,' Clara said calmly. She picked up the bible and held it to her chest with her arms crossed over it.

'Why do you hate Father?' Prudence asked suddenly.

'I don't.' Clara looked at her sharply. 'I don't hate him. I . . .' She stopped. She lowered the bible into her lap and looked from Prudence to Suzanne carefully. 'We took this oath because we love Father and must protect him.' She smiled.

Chapter Two

The slightest sea breeze took the hard edge off the summer sun without the brutality of the south-east wind, and the sky was so blue that the mountains stood out in sharp contrast. It was a beautiful day and the earth a warm red. Just the faintest swirls of powdery ground mist hovered above it. Up ahead was a cloud of red dust which Jacques watched excitedly. He sensed tension in Eva as she stood beside him and put his arm around her shoulder.

'He's all right. He's going to make a fine horseman, Eva,' he said proudly.

'He's so small.' Eva held a breath in her throat. Her eyes didn't move from the dust cloud as the sound of hooves thundered close. Her tiny son Jean Jacques was riding towards them on Shiva. He was at one with the horse. His small body was part of the horse. As the horse's legs stretched out in a gallop Jean Jacques galloped in the air just above its back. Flowing with it.

'You see!' Jacques' face was alive with excitement. 'He was born to it.' The horse, with Jean Jacques aboard, raced past them. Jacques cheered. Eva waved and Jacques tightened his grip on her shoulder.

'I told you not to be afraid. He's fine.'

Suddenly Eva screamed. She watched helpless as her son flew off the horse's back. His delicate body somersaulted through the air and spun in helpless circles as it fell until it landed in a small heap.

Eva ran after Jacques as he raced to the spot. Neither spoke. No sound came from Jean Jacques. The horse Shiva had stopped further away and looked back, puzzled as to what had happened to his small passenger.

Eva turned away, unable to look as Jacques bent down and

touched her son's tiny arm lying extended in the dirt. The small boy's face was buried in the sand and Jacques moved his hand to his hair carefully. He spoke quietly.

'Jean Jacques?' Jacques looked up at Eva, but she kept her eyes away. He turned back to the child. 'Jean Jacques?' He gently lifted the boy's head and turned it towards him. Jean Jacques opened his eyes and grinned, cracking the coating of sand on his face.

'I nearly didn't fall off, master.'

If only he had died, Clara thought as she ran away from the clump of trees which had hidden her. Any animal stupid enough to let someone ride on its back had to be dangerous. Why hadn't the horse killed him!

'I help you, Miss Clara.' Titus's voice came from nowhere. Clara spun round and looked for him among the vines. He was bent low, ensuring he couldn't be seen. Clara stopped as she spotted a bare black foot between the vines. The toes were spread wide and the sides of the foot dry and cracked. The yellow colour of the sole crept through the cracks towards the black arch of the foot.

'Go away.' Clara turned to run. She no longer cared if her father saw her. 'If my father sees you spying on him he'll have you hanged!'

'Fire, Miss Clara!' Titus whispered secretly. Clara stopped. She pretended it was to untangle a vine from her skirt.

'Yes?' she asked cautiously. 'You have something to say?'

'Tell Eva the master said for her to go, Miss Clara. I'll help you. I give you the fire to make her go.' Titus didn't look at her as he spoke.

'She wouldn't believe me.' Clara snapped off the offending branch of the vine, deliberately tearing its bark. 'You tell her to go!'

'I will, Miss Clara. I will make her go,' Titus promised.

Clara turned around in a small half-circle and looked at him. She was interested in his offer. 'Will you go too, Titus? Do you like her too?'

'I will go too, Miss Clara,' he answered. He was crouched low as he squatted among the vines. Clara's body quivered.

'Do you do things with her?' Curiosity turned to revulsion as she waited for his answer. She could smell him from where she stood. 'Do you do things to her, Titus?'

'No, missy,' he denied quickly. 'No.'

'Then you should.' Clara spoke as though she knew exactly what he should do. She'd once watched slaves do it. Their black bodies had shone as they writhed against one another. The only sounds were sharp breaths, groans and tiny screams from the woman. They'd been by the river and she'd watched them. She felt a rush of heat to her face as she remembered it. To her face, and between her legs.

'I don't want to talk to you!' She threw her dismissal at him and ran. Running was the only way to stop the feelings churning inside her. The same feelings she'd felt as she'd watched those two slaves making love – doing what she knew her father must have done with Eva. She didn't stop running until she reached the barn.

Safely inside in the semi-darkness Clara dropped down on to the straw. She flung her arms back and lay quite still, legs wide. The hot throbbing between her legs was still there. She lifted her arm and laid her hand on the small, hot, pulsing mound. She strained her neck and looked down. The two rising mounds of her breasts felt suddenly hard as she looked at them. Her other hand moved to her breasts and brushed over them as if by accident. She caught her breath. Her nipples were hard. Her finger pressed down on the delicate flesh in the valley of her legs and a shudder rippled through her body. She opened her mouth. Still warm air filled her lungs and she held it there. Her head dropped to one side, her eyes closed as her breath came out slowly and she cried silently.

Prudence didn't move as she sat wide-eyed watching her older sister from her special and secret place in the barn.

That night, as Prudence lay in bed she kept her eyes on Clara's shape under the bedclothes. If Clara so much as turned in her sleep Prudence would be suspicious. She'd been with Clara and Suzanne as they compared bodies a few weeks earlier. Suzanne had behaved differently to Clara even then. She'd had an air of total wonder about her as she looked down at her young body, and the magic of yet another new discovery. Suzanne had looked as if she was standing on the threshold of a miracle. Even her face had looked different. Her cheeks had been pink, bright round circles of pink, and her eyes had been alight, as if lit from behind. Or inside.

But Clara had looked different. Intense. Her voice had been deeper than Prudence had heard it before. Her eyes had gleamed instead of shining as Suzanne's did. They had spent hours examining one another and Prudence had found it all rather silly. Not least because none of the things they examined could be found on her. Why on earth they stood over a mirror and looked for a hole between their legs she would never understand. If she ever found one she hoped it would heal over quickly. Prudence had decided then that it might be better if she ignored them. And, better still if she ignored her own body from now on just in case the same disasters happened to her. But what had Clara been doing in the barn? It didn't bear thinking about.

The door opened and Miss Thurston poked her head around it as if entering Prudence's thoughts. Prudence confessed at once, feeling very guilty.

'I was just thinking, Miss Thurston. But I'm going to sleep now,' she said.

'Good girl, Prudence. Good night.' Miss Thurston left the room.

Prudence's eyes opened just once more to check nothing was going to happen in Clara's bed. Or Suzanne's. They were both asleep. At last she could go to sleep herself and forget.

Jacques was tired. It had been a hot day and he'd worked in the vineyards since early morning. M. Claudelle, the wine-maker, had been encouraging him to plant a new cultivar, Pinot Noir. Jacques had resisted though he knew M. Claudelle would be right and would finally do just what he wanted.

M. Claudelle had been with Jacques at Bonne Esperance for many years, but Jacques felt he didn't know him at all. He was older than Jacques; reserved. A singular man who kept himself to himself. One thing Jacques was aware of, though it was never referred to, was M. Claudelle's disapproval of his relationship with Eva. It was a silent condemnation. But, despite that, M. Claudelle did not allow his feelings to interfere with his work for Jacques, and Jacques admired him for that.

He'd come to Bonne Esperance from France on the suggestion of a distant cousin at home. Although Jacques still regarded

France as home he never expected to see it again. What he envied about M. Claudelle was that one day he would return to France. Though never stated, the fact had always been accepted by both.

They often talked of the changes that had taken place in France. Charles X had been overthrown by Louis Philippe, the so-called 'Citizen King'. M. Claudelle had decided he would see how things turned out. He was a Protestant himself and in Africa, almost as if to keep the threat against Protestants alive, Catholics had been given equal rights with all Christians in the Cape Colony.

Africa itself was changing rapidly. The press had been freed from control by the Governor and council, and there was much talk of emancipation. It was doubtless coming and would affect Jacques financially, although it would affect him emotionally much more. He didn't approve of the bondage of any human being and had had many disagreements with his neighbours in the surrounding community about their right to their slaves. Nowadays Jacques tried to keep his silence on the matter. For the moment at least, although his humanity abhorred it, slavery protected a part of his life which he valued deeply: Eva and his son.

Jacques wanted to forget about cultivars, emancipation, anything except sleep. He turned down the lantern and moved to the bedroom. It cast his shadow on the ceiling as if he was watching himself. He expected that Emily would be asleep as she always was, she was not a well woman. She was delicate and totally unsuited to Africa. It saddened him, but he accepted it; leaving his conscience some freedom to enjoy Eva. He cared deeply for Emily, although he was aware Miss Thurston thought otherwise. But he and Miss Thurston might be from different galaxies. She amused him in her dry English way. He'd even sensed a certain warmth behind her grey eyes on occasion. Though more often than not they were like stones set in a mask when directed at him. Each time Emily had become pregnant he had suffered the permanent set of those eyes on him. Accusing, condemning and finally ignoring until the child in question had been born without killing her delicate charge, Emily, his wife.

In days long past, Jacques and Emily had laughed as they made love with her already pregnant. The sin had been committed, so far as Miss Thurston was concerned. Once was enough. How they'd enjoyed all the other occasions in that first flush of romance. But the romance had gone, had been replaced by tender care. Jacques had not slept in the same bed as Emily for many years. She needed rest, and must sleep peacefully. He opened the bedroom door and glanced toward Emily's bed although he couldn't see it in the dark. He moved quietly past it to his own. He stopped as Emily's finger ran gently down the back of his leg. He turned. Emily smiled up at him from the warm dent in her pillow.

'I thought you were asleep,' Jacques whispered. 'Can I get you something?' Emily closed her eyes with a slight smile.

'I want you, Jacques.' Her hand ran up the side of his leg until it found his hand. Her fingers threaded through his, then curled around his hand. Her grip was gentle. Warm and caring. Emily made love with the same gentle care.

The doctor had called to see Emily in the morning, before work had begun in earnest. Jacques had not stayed, since Emily had assured him she was fine. It was no more than a little too much sun, she'd said. Jacques was not at all prepared for the stony gaze of Miss Thurston when he returned to the house.

'Pregnant?' He'd never even considered the possibility of another child and realized he didn't want one either. His longing for a son had been satisfied by Jean Jacques, but Emily didn't know that and the doom in Miss Thurston's thunderous face forced him to show his gentle Emily that he was happy. That it didn't matter if it was a son or a daughter. That all he wanted was that both she and the child were well.

'It will be a son.' Emily smiled at him confidently from the bed. 'I know because,' she stopped and her smile widened, 'I know.'

'So?' Jacques leant over her and held her in his arms. 'It doesn't matter. Another daughter? Why not another daughter as beautiful as you?'

'But it does matter, Jacques. You need a son. Someone to carry on after we've gone. A son to be . . .'

Jacques covered her mouth with his hand. 'I need my wife well and healthy. That is all I need.'

'I am.' She chuckled slightly. 'How was Miss Thurston?'

'I don't believe she will ever speak to me again,' Jacques laughed.

'Well then?' Emily's eyes revealed that she wanted him again.

'We will take care of our child,' he said, and tapped her on the nose gently. The sexual longing in her eyes stirred nothing but his guilt.

'But Miss Thurston will have no idea. Oh, Jacques.' She pulled him down to her and held him tightly. 'I will give you a son. I will.'

'Mother! Father! Is it true?' It was Suzanne calling to them in great excitement as she burst into the room. 'Is it true you're having a baby?'

'And how did a young girl know that?' Jacques asked with a smile, moving away from Emily a little.

'Because Miss Thurston's very cross. She's talking to her teacup and her saucer. I swear she will break them at any moment. Is it true?' she begged.

'And what is she telling her teacup and saucer?' Jacques asked as if he didn't know. 'That your father is a bad man?'

Suzanne nodded quickly. 'Very bad, she says. Then she said to the saucer, before she put the cup back on to it, "Another child! Didn't I tell you before? Yet another child he has forced on to my darling Emily. The . . ." ' Suzanne stopped.

Jacques raised his eyebrows at her questioningly. 'The what?' he asked.

'She didn't know I was listening or she wouldn't have said it, Father.' Suzanne looked at Emily wide-eyed and hopeful. 'Is it true?' Emily nodded. Suzanne threw herself on to the bed and wrapped her arms around her mother's neck.

'Careful, Suzanne,' Jacques chided. 'You don't want to suffocate your brother or sister, do you?'

'Brother!' Suzanne said firmly into the soft folds of her mother's neck. Emily chuckled as she looked up at Jacques, pushing Suzanne's thick blonde hair away.

'There's no question about it, Jacques,' Emily said quietly.

'What's happening?' Prudence was at the door. Clara stood slightly behind her watching her father. 'Why is Suzanne so happy? Did you give her something?'

'No, my little Prudence with the calculating mind. People are not only happy when they are given some "thing". But some "body".' Jacques moved between Prudence and Clara at the door. He put an arm around each one and Clara responded immediately, leaning into him. 'There is another one of you.'

'Of us?' Prudence asked in amazement. 'A baby?'

'A boy?' Clara's face was brighter than Jacques remembered seeing it. It was older too. One day it would be very beautiful.

'Your mother says it's a boy.' He looked from one girl to the other. 'I think you should kiss your mother.' They both pulled away from him at once and jumped on either side of Emily on the bed. Suzanne immediately covered her mother completely with her body and arms.

'Suzanne,' Clara grumbled. 'Go away.'

'I can't see you, Mother. Suzanne, move!' Prudence squealed. But Suzanne wouldn't move. She stayed firmly in place covering her mother with herself and keeping her for herself. Emily chuckled with the delight surrounding her. What a day it would be when her son was born, she thought. At last pure joy would fill their home again. Her thoughts paused. God willing.

Jacques warmed as he watched the bundle of people who were his, covering one another with love. But, even now, as he soaked in the warmth of it, his mind turned to Eva and Jean Jacques, and back to the earth from which they'd come. The red earth of his personal peace.

Whether it was the briefest flicker of sadness that crossed her husband's eyes at that moment, or the slight lowering of his chin, Emily didn't know why but she knew he felt excluded from his own family. Although she hoped his heart would be brought home by a son, there was the slightest doubt. Like a small pin pricking her bubble of certainty, there was a sadness in Jacques which she could never heal.

Clara ran out of the house looking for Titus. Titus was in charge of the slaves and seldom worked so she knew where to find him on a dull day.

The river was in full spate. The winter rains had come early and the air was moist as she ran along the bank. The mountains were shrouded in mist and hiding behind cloud. At this distance Titus's shape resembled a tree dipping down into the water. His dark skin accepted no light and looked darker still.

Clara skidded to a stop as she suddenly spotted two children with Titus. One was a boy of sixteen or so and the other was a small runny-nosed girl. They were his children, she presumed. She'd never even wondered before if he had any. She knew Titus owned some of the slaves and they were usually children. He was a good business man and leased his slaves to her father. Clara had heard three grown-up neighbours arguing the rights and wrongs of slavery, but Titus might have arguments of his own, she'd thought. Slavery meant the same to him as it did to Jacques. Eva. It was his means of gathering together enough money to buy his own freedom. Into that freedom he would take Eva.

The sixteen-year-old boy had spotted Clara before she'd seen him. He moved behind Titus on the river bank and leaned towards him. Titus immediately pulled his fishing line in, lowered his head, and made his way to Clara.

'You come to see me, Miss Clara?' He averted his eyes from hers. But Clara wasn't looking at him. She couldn't take her eyes off the sixteen-year-old boy. He was very dark. Ebony skinned. He had strong features and dark sombre eyes. He was looking directly at her. It was not something she was accustomed to from a black person. She could feel his look burning through her dress and moved away, ignoring him as she turned to Titus.

'Come away from these children.' Clara moved back the way she had come, indicating he should follow with a toss of her head. Titus followed. So did the boy. But only with his eyes.

'You said the woman Eva would go with you.' Clara turned her head slightly in order to keep the boy in the tail of her eye. 'Is that true?' Titus nodded. His head dropped further with each nod in servitude.

'Yes, Miss Clara. If you tell her. Yes.' The boy's eyes were still on her. Perhaps he was more than sixteen. He was tall and well built.

'Tonight?' Clara drew her glance away from the boy temporarily and fixed it on Titus.

'Yes, Miss Clara.' Titus nodded and his head lowered still further. 'When everyone is asleep.'

'Who's he?' Clara flicked her glance over his shoulder. Titus looked around.

'My son.'

'What's his name?' she asked innocently.

32

'Sunday.' He turned back to her and lowered his eyes quickly. 'Would Miss Clara like my son to work for her?'

Clara intuitively pulled herself to her full height. 'What do you mean?' she asked. 'Doing what?'

'In the house? Maria says Sunday is a good boy. If you say then he could be in the house. He would be there when you wanted.'

'How dare you!' She glared at Titus. 'Tell him not to look at me like that. Tell him!' Titus shrugged and Clara's fury rose to new heights. She screamed, 'Keep your black son away from me! Keep his black eyes off me!' She turned away sharply and Titus looked at his son. There was the briefest unspoken communication between them. The boy moved away in the other direction down the river bank and Titus turned back to Clara.

'I am sorry, Miss Clara.' He bowed his body as well as his head. 'Tonight. I will be ready.'

Clara looked at him coldly. Her head was held as high as possible. She noticed secretly that Titus's son had stopped a little further off.

'Good.' She turned away and walked back slowly towards the house along the river bank. She knew the sixteen-year-old boy was watching her. She could feel his eyes on her. She walked as slowly as she could. Why shouldn't he look hard at something he could never have?

Prudence was in the cellars when Clara found her. All day she'd spent with M. Claudelle as he worked, and he seemed to enjoy it. With no interest shown in what he did by anyone except Jacques, to be talking to Prudence about this one love of his life was good.

'Think of the people who came here before us, Prudence,' M. Claudelle had begun. 'Think of the hardships for them. A hostile land.' He'd smiled with slight pride. 'Of course most of them were not good farmers.' He'd chuckled. 'Vineyards? I doubt they had any idea what they were doing. I even doubt they ever tasted wine.' He'd breathed deeply and his voice had quietened with excitement. 'To witness such a miracle as the juice from the grape performs! Such a mysterious metamorphosis! It is an honour, Prudence. That first natural process of fermentation is a miracle.' His breath had come out slowly. 'How they must have wondered at it.'

'But how does it happen?' Prudence had asked with bright inquisitive eyes.

'Ah!' M. Claudelle had hidden behind the mystery of wine with much pleasure. 'The same process has been used for thousands of years, Prudence, but even now we . . .' he shrugged, 'we begin to understand now perhaps.' He had moved to a large barrel and touched it, almost tenderly.

'Does the secret lie in the casks? In the cultivar?'

He'd shaken his head at Prudence. 'It is in the hands of the wine-maker. And,' he'd smiled proudly, 'even the wine-maker does not truly know.'

'You don't know how you do what you do?' Prudence's eyes had grown even bigger.

'I pretend perhaps,' M. Claudelle had shrugged. 'It's a mysterious balance between instinct and intelligence, Prudence.'

'Then you can't teach me?' Prudence's face had fallen with his admission.

'I am beginning to doubt you need it, little girl. You're like your father.' He'd patted her on the head. 'When you get bigger perhaps I can teach you some things. The practicalities. The hygiene. Background perhaps.'

'Now! I want to know now,' Prudence had pressed him. How M. Claudelle envied the enthusiasm of youth. The strength of purpose in a child who knew what she wanted; who had little idea how to achieve it but set out regardless.

'Yes, little girl. I will teach you. One day.' M. Claudelle had wanted her to leave then. She'd already taken enough of his time. Time he enjoyed most being alone with the grape. 'When you are older.'

'But I am older now. Older than when I first asked you . . .' Prudence stopped as Clara moved into the cellars.

'Good,' M. Claudelle thought. Clara had interrupted at the right time. Little girls were a pleasure only for a while.

'Why are you in here, Clara?' Prudence was angry with the interruption and tilted her head back. 'You don't like the cellars. You told me that.'

'And Father told you to stay away from here.' Clara's nose twitched. She hated only a smell. The scent of magic the cellars held for Prudence was only a smell of rotting grapes to Clara. 'I've got to speak to you.' Clara took her arm firmly. 'Now.'

'I'll be back,' Prudence called to M. Claudelle as Clara led her out.

'Oh, yes.' M. Claudelle almost sang his pleasure as he smiled to himself, nodded to himself and disappeared back into his private world among the barrels.

'Why do you always come for me when I'm busy?' Prudence grumbled at Clara. 'It's important when I'm in here: important and private.'

'What I want is important,' Clara answered, dragging her out from the dark coolness of the cellars and into the bright sunlight outside. 'Very important.'

'There's nothing more important than learning about wine,' Prudence grumbled again. 'It's why we're here.'

'And Mother?' Clara stopped and nailed Prudence to the cellar door with her eyes. 'Is wine more important to you than our mother?'

Prudence had no answer.

Suzanne was where Clara had left her. Waiting obediently for what Clara had said was 'a very important meeting'.

'Why is Suzanne here?' Prudence asked as she spotted her leaning against the tree on the grass to one side of the house. She stopped and glanced at Clara suspiciously. Her ankle suddenly wobbled as her foot was tripped by the cobbles of the courtyard between the cellar and the house.

'I won't take my clothes off!'

'Don't be silly, Prudence.' Clara ran away towards Suzanne and sat on the grass in front of her cross-legged. She nodded at Suzanne to do the same, and glanced up at Prudence as she reached them. 'I want to talk to you before our lessons. It's a secret.' She patted the ground beside Suzanne. 'Sit down.'

'If it's a secret, why are we sitting here where everyone can see us?' Prudence asked looking towards the window of the front room. She didn't want to be there at all. 'It's stupid. Why are we here?'

'Because!'

Clara was as irritating as Miss Thurston, Prudence thought. Because what? Because why? 'Because' meant nothing on its own yet it was used with such finality by people. Usually grownups. Clara would be exactly like most grown-ups when she grew up, Prudence decided.

'Do you remember our blood pact?' Clara asked quietly, her eyes fixed on the house. She smiled and waved at someone suddenly. Suzanne and Prudence jumped as she did and then turned guiltily towards the house. Their mother stood on the small veranda, waving back at Clara. Her blonde hair looked like a halo in the sun. Prudence and Suzanne instantly waved back at their mother. They were filled with guilt. What was Clara doing? How could she talk of that pact made in blood in front of their mother?

'Mother needs our help. When a woman is having a baby she needs all the peace she can get. She must not be allowed to get upset,' Clara answered their thoughts.

'I know that,' Prudence said. 'So why do you want to talk about it here? It's wrong. She'd be upset if she knew about it.'

'She won't know. Mother won't know anything at all about that boy. That's why.' Clara glanced up as their mother disappeared back into the house. 'We're going to do it tonight.'

'Do what?' Suzanne's face paled.

'We're going to scare them. We'll chase them away. Tonight!' Clara leaned into them. 'They'll go!'

'But they can't go,' Prudence said simply. 'They're slaves and they can't go.'

'They will,' Clara said with certainty, and she lay back on the grass. 'Say nothing to anyone. But when we go to bed tonight you mustn't go to sleep.'

'Sleep?' How could they ever sleep again, Prudence wondered.

Clara pushed her full skirts down as she slid her heels towards her and her legs bent. She pulled a long juicy strand from the lawn and sucked it. Prudence and Suzanne watched her. Suddenly Suzanne leapt to her feet, pulling her skirts up and flapping them wildly.

'Oh!' She brushed her legs quickly, jumping up and down. 'Go away! Go away!'

'It's only a grasshopper,' Clara said quietly as she looked at Suzanne.

'It's horrible.' Suzanne watched the grasshopper intently as it hopped with its angular legs tucked up beside its back. It waited as it considered where to jump next. On to her! Suzanne knew it would. Everything in this wild place jumped on to her, and everything nasty pretended to be a grasshopper. She moved backwards, away from her sisters and the grasshopper. 'I'm going inside. Miss Thurston will be waiting for us.'

'You won't forget tonight?' Clara called without even looking up at Suzanne as she ran off to the house. Prudence moved to the grasshopper and tickled it, making it jump.

'Isn't it sweet?' Prudence said, almost to herself.

Clara rolled over on to her stomach and looked at the grasshopper. It was motionless, uncertain where to jump next. Clara pushed herself up on to her feet with her hands on the ground. She moved her hands down her dress and swung her right leg forward, holding it just above the grasshopper.

'No,' Clara said; and brought her foot down suddenly on top of it. Its green body squelched into one with the juicy green grass. Clara lifted her foot and looked at the small mess with cracked legs splayed flat around it. She turned to Prudence as though nothing had just died.

'Don't forget tonight.' She ran away towards the house.

'Clara! Prudence!' It was Miss Thurston calling from the house. It was time for lessons. Arithmetic. Prudence hated arithmetic. All she wanted to know was how to put that poor little grasshopper together again.

The only good thing about the fact that tonight had come at last, Prudence decided as she lay in bed keeping herself awake, was that arithmetic was over.

'Are you still awake, Suzanne?' she called quietly.

'Yes,' came Suzanne's small voice.

'Shh,' Clara whispered.

How silent the night was. As silent as it was dark. Nights in Africa were almost solid. You could feel them, Prudence thought. It was as if the night swallowed everything as it came. Only the crickets survived, chirping loudly from wherever they were not. Sometimes a hyena laughed on nights like this. Very occasionally the children thought, or hoped in terror, that they heard a lion. Better still it could be a leopard. But they had been reassured by their mother that the wild animals had moved away. They'd gone further into the wilds of Africa as yet un-tamed by man. Prudence decided that one day she would go there. In there. Up there. To the wilds of Africa. To the place she'd never seen behind the mountains surrounding Bonne

Esperance. What was further than the mountains? Every time she looked at them she wondered. People had even been there and other people lived there, she'd heard. Not people like them, and not black like the slaves either. But strange people. Little people with yellow skins. She knew about them because once, men her father knew had gone out hunting them on horseback. They called them bushmen. She didn't understand how they could hunt men even if they were small and yellow. She jumped with fright as she dozed off thinking about the small yellow men and planning how one day she'd go over the mountains.

'Are you awake, Suzanne?' Prudence had to hear her own voice to prove that the night hadn't swallowed her too.

'Yes,' Suzanne called back through the dark.

'Shh,' Clara ordered and Prudence fell fast asleep.

Suzanne stood back nervously with her cloak covering her nightdress, hood already up, as Clara shook Prudence. Suzanne hadn't slept at all and wanted to go back to bed.

'Wake up, Prudence, wake up,' Clara whispered. Prudence grunted as she struggled to stay asleep. 'Wake up!' Clara shook her harder.

'What is it? What's wrong? It's still night.' Prudence tried to lie down but Clara grabbed her by the shoulders and held her body up as her head lolled backwards.

'Here's your cloak. Put it on.' Clara pushed the cloak on top of Prudence's head.

In the cuddle warmth of sleep Prudence knew there was something special she had to wake up for, but she'd forgotten what. Was it Christmas morning? What was it? Prudence remembered and pulled the cloak off her head.

'Now?' She stared at Clara in horror.

'Put your cloak on,' Clara snapped, and moved to the door.

The house was dark as the three girls crept through it towards the back door. The floors squeaked, but they knew exactly where the loose boards were and avoided them carefully. The front door of the house was bolted. They knew it took their father's strength to unbolt it, so they had decided to make their way outside through the kitchen.

Propped up against the low garden wall was a lit beacon. It burned brightly in the night and Clara hurried to pick it up.

'Who put that there?' Prudence asked in amazement.

'Shh,' Clara replied turning back to Suzanne who didn't look as if she was following. 'Come on.'

Eva was asleep with the small boy Jean Jacques beside her. Lit by the flickering light of the beacon, the room looked even smaller than in daylight. Everything was stacked as neatly as it could be. Firewood. Dried meat. Dried fish. Pots. Pans. Each in its place.

The bed in which Eva lay with her son was small. Though the walls were dirty, the covers on the bed were crisp and clean. Even the small boy Jean Jacques looked clean, Clara thought. As clean as a half-caste could ever look. But she stopped herself thinking about that quickly. It meant remembering how Jean Jacques had come into being.

'Perhaps we shouldn't bother to wake them,' Clara whispered as she shone the beacon around the small, quiet room, and the flame licked its tongue out. 'Nobody would know what caused the fire.'

'You didn't say we'd set fire to them!' Suzanne tried not to scream. Clara silenced her with a kick. Eva stirred with the voices, then was suddenly wide awake. Her large brown eyes squinted at the light and instinctively she pulled Jean Jacques towards her.

'Father sent us,' Clara said coldly.

Eva said nothing. She made no sound at all.

'He wants you to leave,' Clara went on.

Jean Jacques woke, rubbed his eyes and leaned into his mother's breasts. Then, as if picking up a signal from the beat of her heart, his eyes flew open and he saw Clara.

'He says you must go. Now.' Clara spoke as forcibly as she could, though her voice quivered with tension. 'Can't you hear me? Didn't you hear what I said? Our father says you must leave. You must take your child with you!'

'I am not free to leave.' The simplicity of the slave woman's words and the calm in her voice enraged Clara. She held the flame closer to Eva and raised her voice a little.

'He said you must go.' She nodded at Jean Jacques. 'And him. He wants you gone by morning. He wants you gone before anyone is up.'

'When the master tells me, I will go.' Eva's voice was still soft.

'You question what I say? How dare you! I told you my father

39

says you must go!' Jean Jacques pulled back with Clara's anger. Eva didn't change the tone of her voice.

'When the master tells me.'

'Leave her, Clara. It's not right.' Suzanne tugged at Clara's sleeve.

'Right?' Clara fixed her glare on Suzanne. 'Look at him! Look at that dark-skinned bastard and tell me it's not right, Suzanne!' Prudence turned away to the door. Clara spun round shining the light on to her.

'I'm going,' Prudence said.

'You're going to leave them? To hurt our mother?' Clara kept the light on Prudence. 'For him to hurt the baby?' Suzanne joined Prudence at the door. They faced Clara together in silence then turned and fled. Clara swung back on Eva.

'My father will get rid of you! You'll see!' She ran out after Prudence and Suzanne. Jean Jacques looked up at his mother through the darkness left behind them and found comfort simply in her presence.

'It's all right, Jean Jacques,' she whispered.

'Now she'll never go! You don't care about Mother!' Clara ran after Prudence and Suzanne as they moved back to the house. Suzanne turned back to Clara as the light she carried caught up with them and engulfed them.

'You wanted to kill them,' Suzanne murmured.

'I didn't,' Clara snapped back.   .

'You did.' Prudence joined Suzanne. 'You did.' She and Suzanne ran on into the house quickly. Clara dropped the beacon on the ground and followed them. The discarded flame spluttered in the sand as if fighting for its life. Titus stepped silently out of the surrounding darkness, which his black skin seemed to make him a part of, and picked up the beacon. He turned and looked towards the slave quarters, then padded quietly towards them.

Back in the safety of their beds, Prudence and Suzanne had hidden themselves under the bedclothes. But Clara wouldn't give up. She pulled the covers off Prudence and then off Suzanne.

'You will come back with me now! We must make her go!' Clara ordered them.

'No.' Suzanne tried to grab the bedclothes to pull them over herself again.

'You will.' Clara pulled them back.

'Then I'll scream!' Prudence challenged her. Clara moved to her bed and looked down at her. Prudence tightened her mouth, and Suzanne pulled the bedclothes up over her face.

'Very well.' Clara returned to her own bed. Her attitude had changed. She climbed into bed and smiled at her sisters through the darkness. The smile sounded in her voice. 'Just remember you can never break an oath taken in blood,' she paused, 'unless you die.'

'You must, Eva!' Titus couldn't understand why she wouldn't come with him. 'They will kill you. This you see!' He held the light up. 'She will use the fire next time. I know.' He lowered his eyes with the lie on his lips. 'I stopped her now. I stopped Miss Clara this time.'

As Eva's eyes moved away from him to Jean Jacques, Titus watched her. She was too beautiful to leave to his master. She would suffer nothing but humiliation with a white man.

'I will take care of you,' he persisted.

Eva looked around the four rough walls which made the only home she knew. Four close walls. But walls which disappeared when Jacques was with her, when she felt the weight of his body on hers and his warm breath moistened her neck. She felt such fear for Jacques. She'd never feared for herself yet she did for him. He was an outsider among his own people. Strong in so many ways but different from other white people she had known. His strength was balanced by a compassion which could be used against him. When she cried, he did. When she laughed, he laughed and they seldom needed words to understand one another. Two people with such different beginnings and opposing stations, the master and slave, had become as one.

She looked at her son. He had so much of Jacques about him, but he didn't have the protection of a white skin. Jean Jacques needed her more than Jacques. Titus was right.

'If they catch us?' she asked him.

'No,' Titus shook his head, 'they will not. No.'

'If they do?' she asked again.

'I will take you far away from here. Far, far away,' he

promised.

They had gone quickly. They had no possessions to weigh them down. Only the clothes they wore and their pride. Nobody would ever take that from Eva or her son. But, even as they walked through the night away from Bonne Esperance, Eva felt a deep need to turn around. Instead she stopped. Keeping her back to Bonne Esperance, invisible as it was in the dark behind her, she could see it. An image of Jacques flashed into her mind and she whispered a private goodbye before walking on with Jean Jacques' small hand in hers.

'Fast. We must be far away before sunrise,' Titus urged, as he saw Eva's hand tighten around her son's.

Clara had tossed in her bed restlessly and flung her arms out over the bedclothes. She'd glared at the darkness and found no relief in challenging it. She didn't know Jean Jacques was already a long way away.

Morning rose over Bonne Esperance like any other. Jacques went straight into the vineyards without noticing Titus was missing. He'd long since given up trying to instil a sense of time into these people. Deep down he thought perhaps they were right. A day was as long as you made it. And a night. If these people, whom he'd grown to care for deeply, could still smile so spontaneously as his eyes lit on them in greeting, what did time mean? Their smiles wiped out a lifetime of slavery in a moment. How could the hours in their day be counted against them?

For Emily, breakfast was the same as usual. She herself didn't eat anything, morning sickness saw to that. But she insisted on being at the table with her three daughters. The morning was the only time of the day cool enough to be comfortable and breakfast the one meal at which she had the children to herself. Miss Thurston didn't attend breakfast. She didn't believe in it.

'And what are you doing today, children?' Emily asked as she spooned the fresh fruit Maria had chopped so neatly on to their hot oatmeal porridge. Prudence yawned as she stood with her plate out to her mother. 'Didn't you sleep well, Prudence?'

'I don't want any breakfast, Mother,' Clara said quickly before Prudence could answer. 'May I leave the table?'

'No, Clara. If you don't feel hungry you may go without

42

breakfast. But you know you are not to leave the table until the meal is over.' She had filled Prudence's bowl to the top. The fruit juice made deep crevices in the porridge and Prudence watched the sides cave in as they always did. 'You can sit down now, Prudence,' Emily interrupted her dreams.

'Yes, Mother.' Prudence was too sleepy to look at Clara or Suzanne. She knew how she felt and hoped they did too.

'The baby moved last night.' Emily's words hung in the air for a moment.

'Where to?' came Suzanne's response. Emily smiled as she looked at the three girls who were all now looking at her.

'It kicked me. Just slightly, but it kicked.'

'Because boys kick,' Prudence said with a smile.

'They do,' Emily nodded, and breakfast continued in the secure way of any household; in the knowledge that tomorrow would supply breakfast again, that the family was safe and happy, and the baby boy had kicked. The entire world was a cocoon of warmth.

'Quickly. We must move quicker now. The sun is here,' Titus urged Eva as she hung back with Jean Jacques. The child was tired. His small legs were beginning to give way after an entire night of walking. The ground they had travelled was rough. They had to keep away from the highways with so many carriages moving back and forth to Cape Town, Titus had said. Sharp edges of stone peeped out from the hard ground digging into Eva's bare feet and Jean Jacques dragged on her arm as he lagged behind.

'You can't rest, boy. Hurry.' Titus pulled him forward by his collar.

Eva wondered whether Titus's fear was for himself or them and was about to question him when suddenly she saw something. Far, far away in the distance it shone. It was silvery blue. It went on and on, absolutely flat, on and on until it reached the sky.

'What's that?' she asked herself quietly. Titus turned back to her, hurrying her on with a nod of his head.

'The sea. Where we are going.'

'The sea,' Eva whispered. 'Jean Jacques, look!' She lifted him in her arms. 'Look, Jean Jacques. Do you see the sea?'

'Come.' Titus moved to them. Eva lowered Jean Jacques to the ground and began walking on with him. Her eyes stayed on the sea and she felt absolutely safe.

'You can go back now, Titus,' she said without looking at him.

He shook his head. 'You need me. I take you. I look after you and the boy.'

'Go back,' Eva said simply. Her eyes had not moved from the sea in the distance. 'I am able to look after myself and my child.' Titus peered into her eyes as they stared ahead at the sea. He was still there. The master, Jacques Beauvilliers, was still in Eva's eyes.

'You will face the future alone? That would be better than being with me?' Titus asked. Eva nodded, without looking at him; just once she nodded, and Titus knew. The angle of her head, as she gazed at the sea, was set. As her mind was. His white master had won.

'How will you protect your child?' He still wouldn't give up.

'I will,' she answered.

'From his father also?' He could not hide the resentment in his voice and for the first time Eva turned away from the sea and looked straight at him.

'From his father also,' she replied.

Titus backed away slightly. He raised his arms and dropped them against his legs, in a gesture of disbelief.

'They will kill you. If they find you they kill you.' Eva kept her eyes on him as he backed away. 'I see death on you. And on your child, I see death.'

'Then go!' For the first time Eva's voice was raised, but it calmed just as quickly. 'Go, Titus, before they have seen you are gone.' She looked back at the sea and held Jean Jacques' small hand tighter. 'I am not your woman.'

Clara went to the slave quarters the moment breakfast finished. She would show the woman that she hadn't been beaten. She hadn't given up. She stood outside and sang quietly to herself, especially for Eva. She used the melody of three blind mice but she changed the words. 'Two black slaves.' It amused her and Eva would understand. She leaned against the wall with her head back and sang quietly with her eyes shut.

'They're not there.' The voice interrupted her and Clara's

eyes flashed open. Standing in front of her was the sixteen-year-old boy, Sunday.

'My father has gone also.'

'When?' she said quickly to hide her fright. Sunday shrugged. Clara watched him. This time he looked down. Clara moved round the corner to the door and pushed it open with her foot. The room was empty. She went inside quickly, forgetting that the boy Sunday was witnessing her excitement. They were gone!

Clara spun around and dashed out of the room. She passed Sunday without seeing him. She ran across the cobbled court-yard, past the stables, on past the cellars and towards the house. She turned and ran past the slave bell, around the house and in at the kitchen door. Maria looked up as Clara brushed past the large pot of stewed fruit on the table.

'Mind yourself, missy,' she called happily. Clara didn't wait to see the movement of her bosoms. At last she was inside the bed-room. She was alone. The window was wide open and the gentlest breeze blew the delicate lace curtains against the wall. She ran to the window. She looked out and up towards the sky. Her face was alive.

'Thank you for answering my prayers and sending them away.' She spoke into the height and breadth of a bright blue sky. Triumph stood firmly behind each word.

Throughout the day Eva kept her eyes ahead and towards the sea as she walked. Occasionally as she and Jean Jacques moved down a rise, an arm of mountains in front of them would hide the sea. Then she would walk faster, carrying Jean Jacques, until she could see it again. The small boy protested continually. It was hot. He was tired and hungry. Please couldn't they go back. He was thinking about the horse, Shiva. He would never see him again and it was more than he could bear.

'I'm not going any more.' Jean Jacques let his weight fall as she gripped his hand. He hung like a rag doll as she tried to pull him upright. His feet dragged across the ground refusing to take his weight. 'I don't want to go. No!'

'Must I tell you again what will happen if we're caught?' she threatened.

'The master wouldn't kill me!' Jean Jacques fixed her with his innocent eyes. Eva's control snapped and she slapped him hard across the face. The force of the blow surprised him and he dropped his feet to the ground, standing up. He looked at her with tears of anger smarting his eyes. He was filled with hatred for her, knowing only that she was dragging him away from the horse, Shiva.

'The master wouldn't kill me till I'd won at the races!' he shouted. Eva held her hand out to him firmly. He looked at it, knowing that once he took it his past life with Shiva was over. The promise of racing on Shiva would be gone for ever. She kept her hand held out to him. His little head dropped and unwillingly he allowed her to take his hand.

Jacques didn't like the sound of the piano being played by Clara, but as always, he kept up the pretence of pleasure. Each ivory key she touched only confirmed that, unlike the slaves outside – people who created an orchestra with their voices or built one from tin cans – Clara had no music in her at all. So he sat back with a fixed smile, and tried not to listen. A knock on the door saved him and he called quickly, 'Come in.'

Maria stepped into the room with a small curtsey. 'Titus wants to see you, master.' Clara looked around from the piano and her fingers banged the wrong notes.

'Excuse me.' Jacques was on his feet and at the door in an instant, turning back to Clara to say, 'Continue, Clara. Please.'

Clara sat tensely in front of the piano. What was Titus doing back? Why had he sent for her father?

'Excuse me, Mother. I'm going to bed.' Clara stood up from the piano quickly and kissed Emily. 'Good night.'

'You haven't finished the piece, Clara,' Miss Thurston chided, but Clara was gone.

'Children.' Emily was tired and seized the opportunity of bringing the evening to an end. She turned to Prudence and Suzanne, who sat engrossed in their books in the corner. 'It's time to say good night, children.'

'Oh?' they wailed.

'Yes,' Emily replied.

Suzanne moved to Emily and kissed her, touching her stomach gently.

'Good night, Mother,' Suzanne whispered. 'And the baby.'

'Good night, Mother.' Prudence followed Suzanne.

'And?' Miss Thurston waited with her face held out for a kiss. Prudence knew the sooner done, the sooner over. She quickly kissed the dry lips with the faint moustache.

'Good night, Miss Thurston,' she and Suzanne said as they raced out. Emily looked at Miss Thurston.

'I think I'll retire myself.' She moved carefully to the door.

'You *are* feeling well, are you, Emily?' Miss Thurston asked as always.

'Yes.' Emily turned back at the doorway. 'Very well.' She smiled. 'And happy.'

Screams suddenly engulfed the house. Cries of terror clawed their way through the walls and into the room, shredding the peace of the moment and gripping Emily in a brace of steel.

'What's happening?' She rushed to the window, pulling the curtains aside, and her breath caught in her throat. A slave, his head pulled back and throat as wide as an open grave, screamed as Titus brought a whip down on his back. Beside him stood her husband, Jacques. His face reflected nothing. No sign of mercy or glimmer of compassion melted its hard lines.

'Where are the woman and the boy? Where?' he shouted. The slave looked at Jacques with wild, terrified eyes. Jacques nodded at Titus and he brought the whip down again on the bare, bleeding back. 'Tell me where they've gone!' Jacques demanded.

Emily dropped the curtain back.

'Bring the children in quickly,' she shouted at Miss Thurston and ran to the door. 'Maria! Maria!'

'What's happening?' Miss Thurston was about to pull the curtain back as Emily spun round on her.

'I told you to fetch the children!' She moved back to the door as Maria ran in. Maria's eyes were large with fright. 'Lock the windows, Maria. Then go outside and close the shutters.'

'Outside?' Maria's entire body shook. Emily pushed Maria towards the windows.

'The children, Miss Thurston!' she said again desperately as Miss Thurston brushed past her on her way to the door.

'No, master! No! Master!' The scream of the last word was brought to a sudden crescendo by the thrash of the whip as it tore his flesh wide, letting loose a howl of anguish.

Emily's hands covered her ears, trying to keep the noise and confusion outside from her inner world. Suzanne burst through the door as Miss Thurston reached it.

'Mother!' Suzanne cried, and ran into Emily's arms, followed by Prudence. 'He's killing them!'

'No, child.' Emily pulled Suzanne and Prudence to her. 'Where's Clara? Find Clara, Miss Thurston!'

'What is it?' Prudence strained to see her mother's face. 'Why is Father having the slaves whipped? What have they done?' she asked.

'It's all right. It's all right, Prudence.' Emily tried to calm her child though she couldn't calm herself. Maria locked the last window and ran out to close the shutters. She chattered nervously as she went. A babble of words, unrecognizable except in their panic.

'Our Father, who art in heaven, Hallowed be thy name. Thy kingdom come, thy will be done, on earth as it is in heaven.' Prudence and Suzanne looked up at their mother as she began, very calmly, to say the Lord's Prayer.

'Forgive us our trespasses as we forgive them who trespass against us. Lead us not into temptation. Deliver us from evil. For thine is the kingdom, the power and the glory.' The girls joined their mother though their eyes were wide open in terror.

'Clara! Come away from the window!' Miss Thurston said firmly as she stepped into the room.

Clara turned with a challenging smile. 'Can I not even look out of the window?'

Miss Thurston grabbed a curtain to pull it closed. But, as she did, she looked out, in an effort to see the source of the uproar. She watched as Jacques strode to the small door of the low flat building which housed the male slaves. He kicked the door in. His head turned in a sharp movement to Titus then back to the door. Titus, in response to his master's silent command, bent low as he moved through the doorway. He reappeared dragging a young man with him.

'Where are the woman and her child?' Jacques demanded. The young man cowered. Jacques snatched the whip and Miss Thurston dropped the curtain before the lash bit into the flesh.

'Your mother wants you with her.' Miss Thurston moved to the door but Clara didn't follow. The governess raised her voice against the arrogant smile on Clara's face. She seemed untouched by the horror outside. 'Do as you're told!' Miss Thurston stood back by the door, pointing determinedly through it. The slightest glimmer of amusement flashed across Clara's eyes.

'Why are you frightened? Father has to punish the slaves sometimes or we'll be murdered in our beds.' And Clara had gone, forcing her to follow.

Miss Thurston closed the door firmly behind her, shutting off the sound for a moment before it found its way in elsewhere and at last, amid the circle of safety Emily had created with the Lord's Prayer, Miss Thurston breathed again. The word 'Amen' brought silence. Prudence looked at her mother questioningly. The silence was outside too.

'Has he stopped?' Prudence asked as Maria rushed back into the room.

'The master's riding out. He's going. There could be trouble . . . Oh!' Maria wailed, as in the background, Clara poked sharp notes from the piano.

'Calm down, Maria.' Emily moved to her with the assurance of one who had been completely reassured herself. 'Everything will be all right now.'

'But the slaves . . . the master says they could . . . it's bad, ugly . . .'

'Maria.' Emily held her soft black shoulders tightly. 'Peace.'

Suzanne glanced at Prudence. How could their mother talk of peace at a time like this? How could Clara sit so calmly at the piano picking at notes? Clara's eyes lifted to Suzanne as if she'd heard her thoughts, and they both understood why.

Eva and Jean Jacques must have gone.

Jacques mounted his horse as Titus led it out of the stable. His leg swung over its back before it had come to a halt.

'Bring Shiva!' Jacques shouted down to Titus. Titus looked at him, puzzled by his request. 'Shiva!' Jacques commanded again. Titus lowered his head and backed into the stables. Jacques looked towards the group of slaves who huddled together, still weeping from the pain he had inflicted on them. Not with his own hand, not at first, but through one of their own kind, on his orders.

Titus ran out of the stable leading Shiva. The horse tugged reluctantly, then did a small high-stepping dance backwards on the cobbles as if picking up the atmosphere.

'Come, Shiva,' Titus urged. Jacques snatched the lead from him. He indicated the slaves with a nod of his head, unable to face seeing them again.

'Lock them up. Look after the women.' He dug his heels into his horse and raced into the night without looking back.

Titus stood quite still, watching. The dust hung behind Jacques in a thundering cloud that disappeared gradually into the dark night air, leaving behind only the sounds of horses' hooves. Just an echo of the nightmare Titus had found himself in.

'It's good now, Madame. The slaves have been locked up.' Maria's statement held nothing but questions for Emily. She tried to ask them reasonably.

'Did you discover what happened?'

'A woman has run away. The master's gone after them!'

'Them?' The question mark in Emily's voice stopped not only Maria. Clara, Prudence and Suzanne had heard it just as clearly. Only Miss Thurston as she sniffed at a small bottle of smelling salts hadn't noticed.

'Was it the young woman with the child?' Emily asked. The moment hung suspended in the silence. Maria knew then, as did the children, that Emily understood the secret they had tried to keep from her. As though answered by each one's silence as she looked at them, Emily turned to leave the room. 'I am suddenly very tired. Please put the children to bed.'

Emily moved down the passage towards the bedroom, blindly following the route to sleep. It was all she wanted. Her inner voice suddenly rose.

'God. Help me, I beseech you. The pain I feel now cannot be right, Lord. If you have not turned your back on us, grant me a son of my own.' Having reached the safety of her room, Emily finished the prayer in pen and ink.

'God grant me a son of my own,' she wrote on the crisp white paper of her diary. 'If that is not your will, please give my family the courage to accept it. And myself the gift of forgiveness.'

'Stop that, Suzanne!' Clara's voice broke through the quiet sobs coming from Suzanne's bed. 'At least it's an end to that boy – or do you want him for a brother?' she challenged through the dark.

'*You* stop it, Clara!' Prudence accentuated her words with a pillow which she flung across the room. 'You're cruel. I'm never going to listen to you again!' She turned away as the pillow missed Clara and fell to the floor.

'Aren't you?' Clara's voice rang out like a hard brass bell. She picked up the pillow and moved to Prudence's bed with it. 'You're still part of our pact, remember. You can't run away from it now.'

'No we're not!' Suzanne cried out. 'We didn't do anything. We aren't part of it.'

'But it was made in blood, Suzanne,' Clara replied calmly.

'We don't care!' Prudence retorted. 'Do what you like!'

'Me?' Clara tossed the pillow on to the bed and turned away with a laugh. 'But it was made on the bible!'

The fear of God, bred into them since the day they were born, held Prudence and Suzanne silent.

As Jacques rode through the night with the horse Shiva behind him, the possibilities of what could happen now loomed in his mind. He pushed them back. He would examine them another time when he'd found Eva and his son Jean Jacques. With each solitary tree which appeared suddenly from the dark, slightly bent by the persistent wind, Jacques called hopefully, 'Eva? Jean Jacques?' But he knew that even on foot, they would be far away by now. He pushed his horse on and Shiva followed. Jacques' eyes canned the ground for any clue to their whereabouts. A dew drop clinging to a dry blade of grass glistened in the early morning light. They would need water. 'Eva! Jean Jacques!' His voice echoed among the mountain but brought no answer on its tail. He rode on through the morning and pushed the horses against the midday sun. 'Eva!' he called continually. 'Eva!'

She looked back as his voice reached her. Jean Jacques' eyes were large and puzzled as he listened to Jacques' call. But she dragged him on. Farther. Faster. On towards the sea which had not come closer, no matter how long they'd walked. He could have gone ten times faster on Shiva, he thought. Shiva? Had they remembered to feed Shiva? Did Shiva think he wanted to leave him?

'Eva!' Jacques' voice was closer and Eva panicked. Ahead of

her lay the sea which she sensed held some strange comfort, but behind her came the man she loved.

'Here, Jean Jacques.' She pulled him ahead of her into the thickening bush which covered the rising mountain on whose skirts they were treading. 'You must keep quiet.' She pushed her small son into the rough spiky bushes and followed behind. She bent low to avoid the sharp thorns lurking on the branches above.

'Come!' she urged her son on.

Jacques followed the natural track around the base of the mountain and his eyes searched constantly. It was a persistent search for something he was uncertain of finding.

'Whoa.' Jacques' voice was quiet, but his horse stopped instantly. Jacques' eyes had settled on a bush beside him. A silk thread hung, caught by a large thorn on a branch. He recognized it. It was from the scarf Eva always wore over her head and pulled across the lower part of her face, hiding that beautiful wide mouth. His hand moved over it, down to it, curled and clutched it. He pulled it free and looked at it. He peered into the dense thicket beside him as it spiked its way up the mountainside.

'Eva!' His voice rang out clearly, knowing that this time she would hear him.

Eva pushed Jean Jacques further into the bushes and looked about for another way. There was a narrow cleft in the land below. It spread out beneath them, gradually widening into a valley. She ran as fast as Jean Jacques' small legs would allow. If she could get into the valley they could hide more easily. He might not be able to see her from behind the jutting rock they'd just rounded.

Jacques walked the two horses slowly: he knew he was close, but his mind forced him to listen. What would he do when he found them? If he took them back he would be expected to discipline them. With feelings running high, as emancipation loomed, his neighbours would expect him to hang her. Not only as an example to the other slaves, but also to the British government. It would be a clear statement from the people that the slaves belonged to them. That they could do with them as they wanted. Jacques dismissed his thoughts. He would have to solve that problem when he met it. But there was Emily. As far away from her as he was, she was right beside him. Whatever happened now, she would know the truth of his relationship with Eva. The harder he pushed Emily out of his mind the faster she rolled back into it.

It was at that moment he saw it. Just a flash across the valley below and it was gone. There was no movement anywhere. He wasn't certain he'd seen anything, and moved his horse on. Quite suddenly, Shiva reared, pulled his lead from Jacques' hand and galloped towards the valley below.

'Shiva!' Jean Jacques couldn't hold himself back, and he ran out.

'No, Jean Jacques,' Eva whispered, but she couldn't stop him.

Shiva reared, neighing his joy at discovering the small boy. Jean Jacques leaned his face on Shiva's flank and stroked him. Eva stepped out and looked up. Jacques was riding towards them.

Eva had listened as Jacques begged her to return with him. Jean Jacques rode around them on Shiva, as if enclosing them in his own circle of love. There was no way but the truth and he must face it with her.

'If you want me to return why don't you kill me now, master?' Eva lifted her head, looking straight into Jacques' eyes. Her simple words, as always, drove straight to his heart. Jacques argued that nobody need ever know, and held her by the shoulders firmly.

'I love you, Eva. I can't live without you.'

'And what of him?' Eva turned her gaze to the small boy on the horse. 'Must he suffer for the rest of his life? He would be better dead.' Quite suddenly she snatched the musket from the horse's saddle and pointed it at Jean Jacques as he rode. Jacques froze. Jean Jacques reined in Shiva, and his eyes settled on his mother and the musket. Eva's finger moved slightly on the trigger and Jacques leapt at her, grabbing her and knocking the musket out of her hands. The shot banged uselessly against the surrounding mountains and Eva screamed, her control completely gone.

'Have pity . . . don't leave us to suffer any longer, master . . . please,' she begged at his feet.

'Master?' The child's voice drew Jacques' attention immediately and his eyes met the large innocent brown eyes fixed on him. 'Are you my father, master?' Jacques felt Eva tense at his feet. He looked down at her then up at Jean Jacques who sat high on Shiva's back, his steady gaze never faltering.

'Yes. I am your father,' Jacques replied.

'Then I'm not afraid.' Jean Jacques smiled.

Clara rounded the corner of the cellars and spotted Titus. He was sitting under a tree further away. She knew he'd only come back because there was nowhere else to go; and she intended to ensure he never forgot his precarious position. She moved to him swiftly but quietly. She'd been searching for him all day.

'Titus!'

He didn't look round. His head was down, his body curved and melted into the bark of the tree behind him. Clara dug her toes into the earth beside him.

'I need you to do something,' she said flatly. Titus looked up at her slowly, his sad eyes still not meeting hers. 'I want you to go to our neighbours, the Bothmas. You must tell them my father needs them. I want you to tell them what has happened. Tell them there's trouble with the slaves and my father needs help.' Her voice was matter-of-fact.

Titus's eyes moved up and met hers in horror. He knew what she was after and shook his head slowly.

'You'll go!' she ordered.

'Your father won't bring them back.'

'Our neighbours will bring them back, and then they'll hang them! It will be a warning to the other slaves!' Clara had uttered her deepest wish. She repeated it. 'They'll hang them!'

'No.' Titus spoke very quietly.

'You refuse?' Clara smiled at his fear.

'The woman would kill herself and her son before she would come back here.' Titus peered at her as if looking into the face of the devil himself. 'I see darkness.'

'Yes,' Clara cut in. She stood over him fiercely, forcing him to lower his gaze. 'Now, go!'

Chapter Three

They thundered towards Bonne Esperance. Horses, wagons, carts and men. The iron wheels churned a path as they dug into the earth. The wagons creaked, wood against iron, and the horses galloped in clattering strides.

Clara felt the flush of excitement as they approached. She turned and ran towards the house, taking a secret way across the vineyards. Nobody must know she had sent for Mr Bothma.

'What in heaven's name is that?' Miss Thurston was the first to hear them as they swung into the dirt road which wound towards the courtyard in front of the house.

Emily moved to the window and looked out. The house was suddenly surrounded by horses, men, carriages and wagons. The dust they had raised seeped under the doors and between the windows, threatening to choke them.

'Mr Bothma?' Emily said with query and fear mingled in her voice. She lifted her head along with her courage and moved to the door. 'I'll see what they want.'

'You can't go out there!' Miss Thurston argued, following her quickly. 'They're rough men, Emily. I will deal with them.'

'They're our neighbours.' Emily held the warm brass of the door handle tightly.

'Neighbours!' The distaste with which Miss Thurston marked the word touched Emily's own conscience.

'I'll find out why they're here,' she said firmly, pulled the brass handle and left the room. Miss Thurston moved straight back to the window. She had guessed why they were here and was uncertain what to do. Some of the men on horseback circled the courtyard slowly. Others looked at the house blankly from their wagons. Their mood was ugly, and Miss Thurston could feel it entering the house with the dust.

'I am certain my husband will be able to cope, Mr Bothma.' Emily spoke to him from beside the front door of the house. She spoke politely and looked into his eyes openly, determined not to reveal her true feelings. 'It's very kind of you to have come to help. However, I can assure you there's no need.'

'But he must expect trouble when he gets back.' Mr Bothma spoke English with a strong accent. He was Dutch but chose to call himself an Afrikaner. A Boer. 'Where are the other slaves now?' His eyes skirted the ground between them and the slave quarters as if looking for rats.

'My husband ensured they were locked up before he left.' She smiled. 'You see, we have no need of your assistance. All is well. My husband saw to everything. Thank you for calling.' Mr Bothma's keen eyes searched her face. Behind her politeness he could sense something else. She had a way of making him feel inferior. The cool English voice, the tilt of the pointed chin, everything about her made him feel less of a man. So he persisted.

'Your husband sent for me, Mrs Beauvilliers. He must have needed help.'

Emily's face grew puzzled. 'But I don't understand. He has been gone all night, Mr Bothma. How could he have sent for you?'

'One of your slaves brought the message.' He looked around as if to prove he had not lied. Titus stood further away beside the slave bell. 'That one. Here, boy.' He spoke to Titus in Afrikaans but Emily understood the meaning from his tone. Titus looked at him with feigned innocence. 'You. Here!' Willem Bothma repeated.

Emily watched as Titus approached cautiously, his head held low. Willem Bothma waited till he'd reached him and then spoke in Afrikaans again, turning away from him as he did so.

'You said your master sent for me.' Titus nodded in silence. 'Speak up,' Mr Bothma shouted in English. Clara watched from the side of the house and tensed. What if Titus did speak up? 'Did the master Beauvilliers send for me?' Mr Bothma said again.

'Yes, Mynheer,' Titus answered, still without looking up, but very respectfully.

'My husband has not been here for two days,' Emily argued gently. She smiled at Mr Bothma again. 'I'm afraid you must be wrong, Titus. Some mistake?' Titus looked towards her. He was trapped.

'I went with the master to help him find the slaves. He said to get help. He said for me to get Mynheer Bothma.' Emily fell silent. Clara breathed again and Mr Bothma signalled abruptly for Titus to move away. He hadn't liked his word being put to the test against that of a black. He would not suffer much more indignity at the hands of this Englishwoman. He turned to her squarely. He was a large man. A proud man. A man who might have been chipped out of the rocky mountains which surrounded them.

'Your husband knows there will be trouble when he brings them back. We will wait for him.' He moved away, dismissing her with a nod and a touch of his hat as he rejoined the crowd of men waiting beside their horses and wagons.

Emily watched Bothma as he spoke to the young boy holding his horse. It was his son, Thys. A handsome young boy. A child who sometimes played with her own children. Mr Bothma whispered to Thys and moved away with a laugh. Emily felt the stab of his quiet laugh and her eyes passed briefly over the sea of faces filling their courtyard: faces deeply lined by the harsh African sun or, more likely she thought, by the strain of resentment towards her. She had hardly acknowledged them and they had noticed. She turned to move back into the house. She knew what they were thinking and couldn't look at them since what they thought was true. She found them coarse, and yes, inferior. She spoke quietly to Suzanne and Prudence who were standing behind her in the doorway.

'Come inside, girls.'

'But, Mother,' Suzanne argued. Her eyes were fixed on the young Thys Bothma as he stood watching her. Emily gently turned her by the shoulders back into the house.

'Please, Suzanne.' It was only then that Emily spotted Clara at the side of the house. She leant calmly against the outside wall, watching the men in fascination. 'Clara!' Emily's voice was brittle. 'Come inside at once!'

Reluctantly Clara obeyed, following Suzanne and Prudence, and Emily closed the door firmly on the world outside.

'You'd think she'd be pleased we were here,' a man commented to Bothma and anyone else who cared to listen. Bothma didn't, and moved closer to his son, Thys. They would wait for the return of Jacques Beauvilliers, he told him. Even if not for the reasons they'd come. As Maria moved out of the house and nervously began closing the shutters, he knew just how distasteful the Englishwoman found their presence. He knew also how deeply it angered him. But he would stay. It was a neighbour's duty at times like these.

'Your mother's quite right, children. You must stay inside until those men have gone.' Miss Thurston was as uncomfortable, or perhaps more so, than Emily.

'But what's wrong with them?' Suzanne asked. 'They're our neighbours and they've come to help us.'

'Their mood is dangerous, Suzanne,' Emily said quietly. 'Have you no lessons today?' She looked from the children to Miss Thurston.

'But Thys is our friend. His father is our father's friend. I don't understand,' Suzanne went on.

'They're common and rough,' Clara butted in.

'Clara!' Her mother was about to scold her.

'Just because Thys Bothma is your friend, Suzanne, doesn't mean he's any different from them!' Clara said, licking the words off the ground like a snake.

'*Tace!*' Suzanne flushed with anger as she moved to Clara and met her eye, pronouncing his name phonetically again. 'T-A-C-E. That's how you say it.'

'Thys.' Clara pushed her tongue between her teeth forcing the name into an ugly heavy lisp.

'No!' Suzanne stamped her foot. 'It's short for Matheus, and you know how to say it. Tace!' Her voice lowered as the love she felt was carried in the full vowel sound of a long clear 'a'.

'It still doesn't mean he's any different from them!' Clara countered.

Emily picked up the dismissal in Clara's use of the word 'them'. No matter her own feelings, she'd always tried to instil a sense of neighbourliness in her children.

'I think perhaps it is time for the children to do a little studying, Miss Thurston,' she said. Miss Thurston knew Emily wanted to be alone. She could understand it and touched Prudence on the arm as she gathered up Suzanne and Clara.

'Why don't we do a little geography?'

'Geography?' they moaned simultaneously.

'And why not?' Miss Thurston ushered them out of the door and Emily closed her eyes. She needed time alone with God.

Willem Bothma and the men had spread out in the shade of the trees away from the house. Maria had brought them a large cool jug of freshly squeezed lemonade. They had drunk it very carefully from the fine glasses and Bothma had ensured they collected the empty glasses together and returned them to the house undamaged. The day was passing slowly for him. His son Thys had moved away from the others and stood looking towards the house. Framed in a window was Suzanne Beauvilliers. Bothma knew his son liked the girl. He could understand it in many ways. She was already very beautiful. They were both still young children, but Willem had spotted the seeds of love between them. He didn't like it. Suzanne was a stranger in Africa, where Thys's roots went deep.

'I can't wait here all day.' The gruff Afrikaans spoken beside him drew Willem Bothma away from his worries. 'I've got work to do,' the man went on.

'We must stay,' Bothma said, though he didn't know why.

'Why?' another man asked. 'Because you don't trust Beauvilliers any more than we do?' Someone laughed.

'Perhaps we should look for his woman slave ourselves!'

'Use her as he does!'

Thys listened as their coarse laughter rose. He found it strange that they should say they were there to help Suzanne's father, yet insult him. Thys had often heard the hushed whispering of his parents as they talked of Mr Beauvilliers with disgust. They'd talked of Suzanne, too. She was leading their son on, they said. Teasing him with her fine clothes and manners. It would be surprising if a child as winsome and slight ever grew to be a woman at all, let alone a woman capable of bearing children. She did not fit and was not for their son. But even now, as Thys watched her at the window, and she watched him, Thys knew Suzanne was the only person in the entire world with whom he would ever feel complete.

The darkness created by the closed shutters pleased Emily. Her mind was a chaos of competing thoughts as her fear rose of what was yet to happen. But then the baby inside her moved just slightly and reminded her that God had heard her prayer. Even if His ways were not hers, she trusted Him.

The sound of a horse galloping towards the house caught her attention and she moved quickly to the window, listening through the closed shutters. Jacques' voice was gentle as he spoke to Willem Bothma. Almost welcoming.

'Willem. Hello.' Emily quickly left the sitting-room and moved towards the front door. She knew her husband needed her support if only by her presence. He must wonder what his position was in her eyes now. It was beside him, as always.

'Then I'm afraid you've been put to a lot of trouble for no good reason, my friend.' Emily stepped out as Jacques climbed down from his horse beside Bothma. She noticed the slight lowering of Bothma's head before he lifted it questioningly to Jacques.

'You couldn't find them?' Disbelief rounded his words.

'I did,' Jacques answered coldly. He caught sight of Emily at the door and looked back at Bothma quickly. 'They were already dead. The woman had killed the child and slit her own throat.' Emily closed her eyes and turned away. Willem Bothma kept his look on Jacques as though he had said nothing at all, and Jacques turned to lead his horse away, avoiding his eyes.

'Thank you for coming but I'm afraid your time has been wasted,' he said as casually as he could. But he stopped. Bothma's eyes were still on him, and so were the eyes of every other man. 'Is there something else, Willem?' Jacques looked round as they watched him silently. 'I don't need you, I said. Thank you for coming.' Jacques turned to go again.

'If you'd brought their bodies back you could have used them as a warning to the other slaves, Jacques,' Bothma said quietly.

'Yes,' Jacques agreed. 'But I buried them where they were.'

'Why?' Bothma asked flatly.

'Why?' Jacques moved closer to him. His emotions were already in turmoil, and his anger was rising. 'Did you expect me to carry corpses on my horse in this heat? What are you trying to say, Willem?'

'I think I have said it.' Bothma remained cool but the rage had risen to boiling point in Jacques. He moved abruptly to his horse and took the bag strapped to his saddle. He pulled wide the top of the bag, which was gathered with a leather thong, and tipped it on to the ground.

'Is this good enough for you?' he asked as a small, blood-stained child's shirt fell. 'And this?' He pulled at a bloodied scarf which clung to the bag, glued to it with blood. 'Is this enough to satisfy you?' He threw a bloodstained knife into the ground at Bothma's feet. The blade juddered with the impact but Bothma didn't even look at it. Emily turned away, unable to bear it. Jacques gestured to them all and yelled, 'If you want to go back and dig their bodies up, go!'

He grabbed his horse's lead and moved away towards the stables. As he did, he caught sight of Titus trying to disappear among the men.

'Titus!' he yelled at him. 'You could sniff the bodies out for them, Titus! Show them the way to the graves, and then never come back!' He turned and moved on again in one movement. Titus ran after him quickly, his voice creeping as low to the ground as he did.

'But, master!'

'Get off my land. Go!' Jacques strode to the stables without turning back. Titus stopped. He stood quite still between Jacques and Bothma; caught in the space of hatred between them, and with no space of his own.

'Maria!' Emily suddenly shouted, breaking the moment. 'Burn those things!' She swung round to return to the house as Maria rushed to obey, but then Emily stopped. She turned slowly back to Willem Bothma and the other men with as much control as she could find.

'My husband has said he doesn't need you.' Emily took a short breath. 'Neither do I.' She turned away and disappeared into the house.

Willem Bothma moved to his horse, mounted, and indicated that the others should do the same.

'Thys!' he called.

Thys looked at the window and at Suzanne, holding her in his look for the briefest moment, her face outlined by her golden hair. She was crying. 'Thys!' his father called again and he leapt on to his horse obediently, riding out behind the others. But all he wanted to do was comfort Suzanne.

Jacques stayed in the stables until night fell. He needed to collect his thoughts and emotions before seeing Emily. The only image in his mind was of Eva and Jean Jacques. Two solitary figures on a broad landscape as they had walked away from him and gone from his life for ever. He had told them that with their freedom, he would kill their memory. That he would never see them again. That to him they would indeed be dead. Eva's eyes had settled on his at that moment, in a way which he'd never experienced before. It was as if she were drinking him in for the last time. Jean Jacques had looked up at him curiously and asked him the only question he needed answering.

'What about Shiva?'

'He's yours.' Jacques had given his son the horse because it was the strongest bond between them. And then he'd repeated his words to the child, knowing it had to be so. 'You go now, Jean Jacques, and you remember. To me you are dead.' Jean Jacques had nodded. The nod of a child eager to please but with no idea of what was really happening. That Jacques was mentally killing them was something he could not understand, but he sensed it was the only way his father could return to his family, and offer hope for their safety at the same time.

When Jacques had dropped the bloodied pieces of clothing on the ground, they had represented the death of Eva and Jean Jacques. It had been a new beginning. But as he sat in the dark, as his mind leapt back to Eva and Jean Jacques, he knew that a large part of himself was as dead as their memory.

'Missy Clara!' Titus called as he ran through the vines looking for her. He knew she always came here when she was troubled. It was the place she had run to as a small child, when Jean Jacques was born. 'Missy Clara!' Titus called again.

'My father told you to get off his land.' Clara's voice reached him tersely from somewhere among the leaves.

'Yes, Miss Clara,' he said as he searched the laden vines until he spotted her. She was sitting on the earth, her knees pulled up in front of her like a small child. 'But I want you should talk to him.' Titus bent down to her. 'Missy Clara? Please?'

'What about?' Clara stood up and dusted down the back of her skirts. She was not a child. Nothing about her was a child, he realized.

'You must tell him Titus can't go. Where Titus go? Titus will die,' he pleaded. Clara looked at his face. Perspiration ran down his temples into his eyes and the black skin gleamed with fear. His skin fascinated her in a curious way, yet it repelled her at the same time. 'You talk to your father? Please? Beg him for Titus to stay.' His eyes cried without tears, Clara thought. How strange.

'Why should I?' She turned away slightly. 'You should have thought of that before,' she added, like a small kick of sand in his face.

'Then Titus must tell the master. Tell him it was you who sent me.' The words dried in his mouth as Clara turned her look slowly back on to him. Her eyes were as cold as ice and Titus backed away. His lips trembled and he murmured, 'I saw death over them! It's you.' Clara's eyes flashed, and he backed away faster. 'Death is on you as a mother suckling her child!' He turned and fled down the narrow path between the vines. Further off he stopped and called back at her in his own language, but Clara understood every word. 'I curse you with their deaths!'

A chill of fear ran down her spine. Titus had done just that. She turned from him quickly as if to break his curse and looked up at the wide blue sky. Her voice crept out in whispered terror, 'Please, no.' But deep down inside, Clara knew nobody was listening.

'Father?' Jacques looked up as Prudence moved into the dark of the stables. He could just make out her shape against the night light outside. 'Are you here, Father?' She spotted him suddenly and ran to him. But she stopped and pulled back. She didn't throw herself into his arms as usual. Instead she stood back slightly, watching him as he leaned against the stable wall with his elbows on his spread knees.

'Are you all right, Father?' she asked gently, peering through the dark at him. Jacques nodded but said nothing. She stood quite still watching him, then she looked around the stable and back at him. 'Where's Shiva?' she asked. Jacques lowered his head, unable to look at her. 'Did something happen to him?' Still Jacques couldn't answer. 'You took him with you, Father.' Jacques looked up and caught a flicker of light in her bright, knowing eyes.

'It's all right. I'm the only one who noticed.'

'He stumbled,' Jacques said as he met her smiling eyes. Prudence's smile faltered.

'You had to shoot him?' she asked.

'Yes,' Jacques nodded. Her smile died and she held her hand out to him with her head bowed. 'You're dirty. You need to wash.' Jacques took her hand in his. Her small soft fingers curled into his palm and at last she smiled again.

'We still love you, Father.'

It was that 'love' on which Jacques rebuilt his life. Love fed to him by Emily, through her children. Even Clara seemed to have regained her feeling for him. It was as if they all knew that to rebuild their father, the bricks could be made only with unquestioning love. Love fed by the forgiveness poured out on him by Emily. Then, curiously, he'd found his love for them growing deeper. His guilt began to lessen, and with it, his passion for Bonne Esperance had been rekindled.

'Not even at Constantia?' M. Claudelle laughed as Jacques tasted the wine, and praised it beyond all other in the Cape.

'You flatter me, Jacques: but I accept.' They spoke in French, as they always did when alone. Jacques looked around the cool dark cellars and the warm smell of the casks filled his nostrils. This place was part of his inner being and he a part of it.

'But perhaps even our wines will not save the estate.'

M. Claudelle knew what Jacques meant but pushed it aside quickly. 'Never!' He moved to a large cask. 'Good wine will never die,' he said as he patted the oak. 'Bonne Esperance wine will never die!'

What Jacques admired most about M. Claudelle, even more than his ability as a wine-maker, was that he had never asked what had happened that night. He knew, Jacques was sure of that, yet he said nothing.

'You worry too much,' M. Claudelle went on. 'Forget the talk of emancipation, Jacques. Too much money stands to be lost by the British.'

'It's already a fact in the West Indies.' Jacques leaned against the rough wall between the rooms in the cellars. 'The Bill goes before Parliament soon, and I agree that slavery should be abolished.'

'Hah!' M. Claudelle's retort showed his feelings clearly. 'The British have a way of making a gesture with one hand while reaping the benefits of slavery with the other. Don't let their sudden display of humanity disturb you. And you! You agree! You need these slaves too.' He grinned at Jacques wickedly.

'Have the Americans considered freeing their slaves yet? No! Take comfort from that!' M. Claudelle answered himself. 'But that's not your problem.' M. Claudelle had a way of treating Jacques as if he were a child. 'It's your neighbours, men like Willem Bothma. They consider you as much an outsider here as the British themselves.'

Jacques nodded, unable to contradict him.

'This country will never be mine, Jacques, but you have given it to your children.' M. Claudelle drew closer to him. 'And you can't live here without taking your place in it.' He was on his favourite subject. 'And it can't be somewhere between the British and the Boer.'

'No.' Jacques shook his head.

'But you are, Jacques! Perhaps there'll come a time when you will have to choose.' M. Claudelle raised his eyebrows at him, challenging him.

'I am a Frenchman. I don't choose.' Jacques moved away to the door to avoid further talk. He knew M. Claudelle was right but it was a subject he chose to avoid. 'You're certain you won't join us tomorrow?'

'No no. I have things to do.' M. Claudelle was like a spider hiding away in the cellars, Jacques thought. He wondered that the passions of any man could be entirely satisfied by his trade. Or was it in M. Claudelle's certain knowledge that one day he would return to France because he knew his place? The thought was not one Jacques liked, and he dismissed it quickly, moving towards the house and supper.

'Good night,' he said, closing the door on the conversation.

The girls' excitement as they chattered about what tomorrow would bring pleased Jacques, but not Miss Thurston. She was a little excited, but her British reserve meant that all table manners would be respected. Even on the eve of a day to be spent at the races in Cape Town.

'Prudence!' She glowered as Prudence pushed the food on to her fork with a finger to clear her plate more quickly. 'What were knives invented for?'

'Throwing at the ladies in the carnival!' Prudence chirped, and Suzanne laughed.

'Will there be a carnival, Father?' she asked.

'Perhaps.'

'Can Thys come?' Her innocent question was dismissed quickly by Jacques.

'No.'

'Why?'

'Will we leave early?' Miss Thurston asked to change the subject.

'It will be such fun spending the whole night in Stellenbosch on the way,' Clara added.

'We will leave very early. Yes. But!' Jacques rose from the table with a quick glance at Prudence to remind her about the knife. 'I must first make sure your mother is quite happy to be left alone.'

'Oh yes.'

'She is, Father.'

'She said so,' they all cried at once.

'I'll ask her for myself.' He left the room, turning back at the door. 'When you've eaten go straight to bed. We need plenty of sleep before such a big day.'

'Yes, Father,' they sang happily. Determined nothing would stop tomorrow.

'And, Suzanne?' She looked up at him. 'Tomorrow is just for us.'

Emily smiled with great warmth as Jacques stepped into the bedroom. Her eyes always carried such a bright welcome, he thought.

'I can hear the excitement from here,' Emily said as he moved to her and she touched the bed by her side. Jacques automatically moved his hand over her stomach as he sat. She was heavily pregnant, and his hand gently caressed the large rise of her womb.

'I'm still not certain we should leave you.'

'The baby's as strong as I am, Jacques, and not due yet. Besides, you can't disappoint the girls, or Miss Thurston.'

Jacques looked at her curiously. 'Miss Thurston is excited?'

'I believe she has saved her pennies for the day,' Emily chuckled.

66

'For what?' Jacques leaned his head against her breasts and her fingers wound through his hair.

'Wagers,' Emily said.

Jacques sat up in disbelief. 'Miss Thurston?'

Emily nodded. 'Apparently she has some very good tips from the garrison.' She pulled his head back towards her and he buried his face in her neck.

'On horseflesh?' He soaked in the scent of her body. It was the smell of peace.

'Besides, I have Maria to take care of me.' Emily's fingers moved through his hair again. He lay quite still, listening to the pulse in her neck. It was as steady as she always made him feel.

'In all this time you have said nothing, Emily. Nothing at all!' He pulled back slightly and looked at her.

'Forgiveness is the greatest gift of God, Jacques.' She paused. 'Accept it.' She raised her hands to his face, his strong face with the burning brown eyes and classical straight nose. The small dent in the jaw was slightly comical, but it was a face which still excited her. She drew her finger down the line of his jaw and looked at him as if trying to imprint his image very firmly in her mind.

'Go, Jacques.'

The long beach of pure white sand was alive with activity. As if they'd sprouted overnight, colourful marquees, with flags and streamers flying from them, spread in a dazzling display. Blue sheets of water rolled in incessantly, curled over themselves as they reached their peak, then crashed down on to the beach, spreading out in a froth of excited foam. Children ran screeching from them, skirts and trousers pulled as high as they could. The moment they'd reached safety they rushed back after the departing water and prepared for the next rollicking wave to catch them.

Hawkers shouted after, chased and cajoled the men, women and children who mingled together in their finest clothes. This day came only once a year and it was a day to dress up for. Already the horses and their riders had begun to arrive, although the races were to be the last event. The best was always saved till last.

Jacques walked through the noisy crowds with Clara and Prudence hanging on to an arm each. Miss Thurston, helped by Suzanne, struggled to keep her bonnet in place as the wind threatened it. Though she grumbled continually about the wind and the sand, Miss Thurston was smiling. Jacques could hardly believe it and decided she must have word on a good horse.

'Can we buy one, Father?' Clara looked up at him as they reached a young Malay boy selling watermelons.

'Nice watermelons.' The boy smiled, revealing a mouthful of gleaming white teeth.

'Sweet?' Jacques asked.

'Juicy?' Clara asked.

'Sweet and juicy.' The Malay boy's smile never left his face.

'We'll have to drive a hard bargain!' Jacques pulled a face at Clara.

'Where do we begin?' she asked keenly. Jacques bent down and picked up one of the large watermelons surrounding the boy's feet.

'By testing if it's ripe.' He banged the watermelon on the boy's head. The small brown face looked up at him, cracking wide in a grin.

'It's good?'

'No,' Jacques said as he bent down to try another. Prudence's hand went to her head as she wondered how the boy kept the smile on his face.

'That one good!' the boy said as Jacques lifted the watermelon. Jacques banged it on the child's head again and the boy looked at him from the corner of his eye as he did. 'Yes?' The large toothy smile beamed up at Jacques again.

'Yes,' Jacques said and turned to go with the watermelon. The small boy grabbed the tail of his dark coat and grinned, holding his hand out for money.

'Good?'

'Yes,' replied Jacques. The boy tugged the coat and stuck his hand out further with an even wider grin.

'Two pence.'

'What?'

'Watermelon one pence. Two tries, two pence,' the boy confirmed. Clara shrieked with delight.

'You didn't bargain hard enough, Father!' Suzanne's excited voice broke through. 'Look! Fishing boats are coming in! Come,

Miss Thurston! Come!' Suzanne rushed ahead with Prudence as Miss Thurston struggled through the sand behind them.

'Wait for me!' she called after the running girls.

Clara watched as Jacques paid the Malay boy. She watched his back. His strong broad back that she could recognize anywhere. She held her hands out as he turned to her with the watermelon.

'I'll help you.' She tried to lift the melon with him and it slipped from her hands. Jacques dropped his end and the water melon buried itself in the sand. Clara looked down at it and laughed. 'Again?' She looked up as she bent down to it and brushed the sand from the dark-green skin. Jacques bent down beside her.

'Are you ready?'

'Yes,' Clara said. They lifted the watermelon between them. Jacques smiled and nodded to her secretly at their achievement. It was a gesture of his that was all hers, and in the excitement of recognizing it she dropped her end of the watermelon and threw her arms around him. 'I'm so happy, Father. So happy.' As she clung to him, Jacques leaned his head on the top of hers for a moment.

'So am I, Clara,' he whispered. Clara knew he meant it and held him tighter as the watermelon fell back into the sand between them. Clara stepped on to it, wrapping her arms around her father's neck, and on an impulse of sheer joy which Jacques hadn't felt for years, he swung his daughter round and round in his arms.

The past had finally lost its power.

Emily enjoyed the peace of a quiet house, and Maria took care of her with the warmth of a mother. Emily watched her as she quietly tidied the room around her, picking up her diary to dust beneath it.

'Would you bring me that please, Maria?'

Maria looked at the diary curiously as she crossed to Emily with it. 'What do you write in here every day, Mam?'

'My thoughts and feelings. Would you draw the curtains, please?' Emily had noticed the lowering sun streak through the corner of the window in a hot shaft of light.

'Yes, Mam.' Maria moved to close the curtains. 'But why do

you write it down so secretly?' she asked.

'One's feelings *are* secret,' Emily said and looked up as Maria collapsed with laughter, her body shaking like a chocolate mountain. 'You don't agree?' Emily asked, catching Maria's infectious laugh herself.

'No, Mam. Feelings are to be shared.' Maria could hardly speak for laughter. Emily leaned her head back against the pillows and looked at her.

'Oh, Maria.' She smiled at the wonder of such an open spirit as Maria's. 'You and I are from different worlds.'

Maria moved to her bed and looked at her warmly. 'Is there anything else, Mam?'

'You go and rest, Maria,' Emily answered.

'Thank you, Mam. I'll come in soon.' Maria curtsied and left the room.

Emily's eyes moved down to the diary in her hands. She opened it and looked at the blank page in front of her. She felt that for some reason the page was very important, but she felt sad. The people of Africa like Maria, slaves though they were, perhaps had more freedom of soul than she had ever known. She began to fill the page quickly, trying to release a little of her soul to freedom on the blank page.

The horses raced along the beach past the crowd with the sea rushing towards them. The crowd roared as carriages raced horsemen, soldiers against bare-back slaves. Clara clung to her father, thrilled as two soldiers raced neck and neck ahead of the others. Miss Thurston was so excited she could hardly speak as her horse's nose pushed in front of the others'. Prudence glanced up at her.

'There's yours, Miss Thurston!'

'Come on!' Suzanne called.

'Move, you devil!' Miss Thurston bellowed and Jacques looked at her in surprise. The soldiers raced on. Miss Thurston's face fell as her horse was beaten into second place. Her mouth turned down at the corners, her shoulders slumped and her bottom lip moved above the top one. 'So much for the garrison's opinion of horseflesh.' She tore up a small piece of paper.

'Have you taken odds on the next race, Miss Thurston?' Jacques said with a smile.

'They're getting ready!' Prudence shouted. In the far distance a raggedy line of horses and riders had prepared for the start of the next race. The sun gleamed low on the horizon, melting the sea and sky into one sheet of shining gold.

'They're off!' Jacques shouted as he watched through his small binoculars. 'Come on,' he called. He peered over the top of his glasses and looked at Miss Thurston, 'Who do we want to win?'

'None,' she shrugged, uninterested.

Jacques looked back at the race through the small eyepiece of his binoculars. As he did so he tensed.

'May I?' Clara turned to him brightly and took the binoculars from him.

'Look!' Prudence shouted. 'There's a boy riding. He's bareback . . . Look!'

Clara had looked. She had seen and recognized Jean Jacques among the horsemen, riding Shiva. She lowered the binoculars and held them out to her father without looking at him. She was pale and silent. As he was. The crowd rose to its feet and screamed. The small boy, Jean Jacques, was pulling through the field of other riders. He was in third place and moving up. Suzanne and Prudence yelled with everyone else, 'Come on! Come on!'

Jacques turned and met Clara's gaze as the crowd erupted around them. Jean Jacques had won the race on Shiva.

'Did you see that farm boy, Father?' Prudence began. 'He beat all the . . .' Her words died as her father looked away. 'Father? What's the matter?' she asked as Clara ran off in the opposite direction. Prudence turned to Miss Thurston in confusion. 'What is it?' Both Miss Thurston and Suzanne were staring ahead in silence. Prudence turned and looked.

Jean Jacques, now clearly identifiable on Shiva's back, was waving victoriously to the cheering crowd. Shiva turned and stepped towards the crowd carrying the small boy with him in triumph. Then Jean Jacques saw his father. He saw Miss Thurston, Suzanne and Prudence and he sat quite still. His head lowered and his shoulders fell forward as Shiva did a high-stepping dance in the sand.

'Take the children home, Miss Thurston.' Jacques' voice was flat. Matter-of-fact. 'I will follow.' Miss Thurston didn't move. Jacques looked at her and repeated, 'Take the children home.'

Prudence and Suzanne took her hands and moved her away as she muttered under her breath, 'Where's Clara! Where has she gone? Why can't she stay in one place?'

Prudence and Suzanne looked back at Jean Jacques as he sat on Shiva. He was looking at their father.

'Clara!' Miss Thurston called as she spotted her further away. 'We're going home. Come along.' She led the girls hurriedly toward the carriages. A beautiful day had been ruined and she had little idea what to say about it.

'There will be no mention of this to your mother when we get home,' Miss Thurston commanded as they neared their carriage. 'We will say nothing at all, do you understand?' She nodded at the driver to help them in.

'Why did you come?' Jacques asked as he looked up at Jean Jacques. Shiva's back was gleaming with sweat, soaking Jean Jacques' tattered trousers. 'When I spared your lives, I had to kill your memory, Jean Jacques.' Jacques looked at him hard.

'I just wanted to win,' the small boy answered simply, his wide eyes fixed on his father. 'It was for you.'

Jacques looked down. Faced by his son, Jacques' thoughts had automatically turned to Eva.

'Where is your mother?'

Jean Jacques was immediately defensive. 'She doesn't know, master. She doesn't know I'm here,' he said nervously. Jacques moved his hand to Shiva's neck and touched it as if for contact. Jean Jacques spoke very quietly. 'I wanted to win for you.'

The carriage pulled away from the carnival fast, leaving behind the magic of the beach, and the shock of the past trampling through it. Neither Miss Thurston, Clara, Suzanne nor Prudence looked back.

Maria moved into the room very quietly. Emily had dozed off as she wrote her diary and Maria slipped the book gently from her hands as she slept. The page was full. She shut the diary and put it away in its place, then moved to the closed curtains to open them now the sun had disappeared. She gazed without interest through the window as she did. She stopped at a sound. It was a scream of sheer terror and it forced Maria to peer even deeper into the semi-darkness to see what had happened.

A woman's figure moved, ghostlike, among the buildings.

Slaves backed away before her and Maria squeezed her eyes to see more clearly. It was Eva! The ghost of Eva had returned from the dead, and Maria screamed.

'What is it, Maria?' Emily had woken with a fright to see Maria turn away from the window and run from the room in absolute terror. 'What is it? What's wrong, Maria?' she called after her. Emily was suddenly afraid. She pulled herself out of bed and moved carefully towards the window to look. A sudden contraction brought on by the shock convulsed her body. She held tightly on to the windowledge as the room spun around her. Her mouth opened, and a cry ripped through her and out into the night. Her body whipped forward with another sudden and unbearable pain. Eva looked towards the house at Emily's scream and saw her fall against the window just as Maria rushed away from her and from the house.

'She needs help!' Eva called after Maria. 'Mrs Beauvilliers needs help!' But Maria, like everyone else, had gone. Eva looked around, uncertain what to do. She stared at the window as Emily clung to it, trying to stop herself slipping down. Eva ran inside the house quickly; careless of everything but Emily's distress.

Eva found her way to the bedroom and entered it quickly. Emily was lying silently on the floor, her hands clutching at the windowledge and her body contracting. She was in labour and Eva's own body reminded her of the pain.

'Maria!' she called. There was no answer. 'Maria!' Eva's eyes flew back to Emily. She knew she had to do something to help but she wanted to run. She moved to Emily and struggled to lift her. Emily's eyes opened as she did so and looked up into Eva's face. Eva stood quite still, holding her across her arms. Emily smiled though her eyes were dead. Her body retched suddenly with another contraction and a deep groan filled the room. Eva carried her to the bed and laid her on it, looking around the room in panic.

She was trapped yet she still had a way out. She could go; walk out and turn her back. Her eyes moved to the door and she willed herself to walk to it. To walk through that door and away. She had only come to look for her son, who had disappeared and who the villagers had said went to race for his father. Eva had to go from this place. What was happening here had nothing to do with her. She looked back at Emily quickly. Emily's eyes were open, looking distantly into her own. Not in fear and without threat: just pleading for help.

Eva stretched her slender brown arms towards her and Emily gripped her wrists as they reached her. She hung on tightly and Eva closed her eyes in a moment's confusion. She opened them as Emily's grip tightened further on her wrists at another contraction.

'It's all right, Mrs Beauvilliers,' Eva whispered. 'I will help you.' She moved closer to Emily and breathed deeply beside her. 'Push,' Eva whispered as her eyes were drawn instinctively between Emily's legs as they pulled up and spread wide on another scream. Eva reacted. The wet, shiny crown of a baby's head was forcing its way into the world. 'Push!' Eva shouted and her strong brown hands automatically moved to the baby's head. She'd brought many babies into the world, and she tried to convince herself that this one was no different.

'Push!' Eva stopped as she felt the small hard slippery head between her hands. It was warm. A pulse beat quickly under her palms. Emily's body suddenly stretched and rose above the bed in a tense arch. 'You must push. Breathe and push.' Eva waited, concentrating on the small head held in her hands. She waited for Emily to breathe but didn't dare to look at her.

'You must breathe. Please.' Her eyes stayed on the baby's head and she listened expectantly, but a moment of eternity held her absolutely still. Emily wasn't breathing at all. The panic Eva felt disappeared and she knew she had to get the baby out fast. She forced her fingers up into the warm channel carrying a new life and gripped the head more tightly, her hands reaching into the depths of Emily's body. She pulled but the baby didn't move. Emily didn't move. Eva closed her eyes and pulled again, as though her life depended on the new life in her hands. Suddenly, with just the slightest wash of warm bloody liquid, the baby slipped down her arms and lay still in the curve of her elbows.

The baby coughed and moved slightly. It cried. Eva looked at Emily with an automatic smile.

'It's alive,' Eva whispered. Slowly the tears she'd held back poured down her face and she whispered again, although she knew Emily was already dead, 'Your baby is alive.'

*

The early-morning sun crept around the side of the mountain as the carriage carrying Miss Thurston and the girls raced on. They had not stopped overnight on the way. They all wanted to get home quickly. Hardly a word had passed between them on the long journey, as they sat with their eyes fixed up ahead, away from one another. The driver turned into the long dirt road curving towards Bonne Esperance. The oak trees were just beginning to shed their crisp, brown leaves. Leaves die quickly in Africa, Miss Thurston thought. It was easier to think of seasons than anything else.

'Autumn's coming,' she said out loud to the children. They didn't answer.

Jacques rode Shiva, with Jean Jacques up in front of him. He knew Eva was at Bonne Esperance, and he drove Shiva on. Jacques had gone to a small fishing village, led there by Jean Jacques. It was the secret place where they now lived. There they'd been told that Eva had gone looking for her son. 'To the farm she came from,' the villagers had said innocently. Jacques had to get there as soon as he could, though he didn't know what he would do. He was confused and simply needed to get home at least as soon as Miss Thurston and his daughters.

Clara, Prudence and Suzanne began to unload the carriage as Miss Thurston moved into the house. She would see their mother first. She was determined Emily would know nothing of what had happened. She marched into the hallway, her determination in her stride, then stopped to collect her breath and thoughts. She pulled her inmost self together, straightened her dress and began to remove her bonnet, calling as casually as she could, 'We're home, Emily.' She moved from the hall into the bedroom, but stopped in the doorway, looking towards the bed. 'Emily?'

It took several moments for the facts to sink in as her eyes settled on Emily. She lay absolutely still on the bed. Her hands were crossed over her chest, and her eyes closed. 'Emily?' she said again, very quietly.

'She's dead.'

Miss Thurston's breath caught in a gasp at Eva's voice. Only then did she see her. Eva was sitting perfectly still by the window, holding a small wrapped bundle in her arms.

'Get out! Get out of here!' Miss Thurston screamed in sudden fright. 'Get out!'

The girls outside looked towards the house at Miss Thurston's shout, dropped the luggage they were carrying and rushed through the front door. They ran straight to their mother's bedroom as Miss Thurston's voice screamed on.

They hadn't noticed Jacques riding into the grounds close behind them. He leapt off Shiva and ran after them towards the house, calling back to Jean Jacques, as his boots banged on the hard cobbled courtyard, 'Stay there!'

Clara was first into the room, stopping in the doorway as she saw Miss Thurston's rigid back, and Eva beyond her by the window.

'Give me that child.' Miss Thurston's arms reached out to Eva.

'Mother!' Suzanne screamed. She pushed her way past Clara, and rushed to Emily's bed.

'Your mother is dead, child.' Miss Thurston turned to Suzanne, not knowing what to attend to next in the confusion of the moment.

'No! Mother! Mother!' Suzanne and Prudence broke down over their mother, shaking her, trying to wake her up. Eva's eyes flashed to Jacques as he stepped into the open doorway. Jacques pulled his look from her and on to his daughters as they wept over their mother's body.

'Emily?' he said and looked at Miss Thurston as she took the baby from Eva. Miss Thurston looked at Jacques coldly.

'Your wife is dead,' she said in accusation.

'What is it?' Clara's voice was terrifyingly calm and rose in a straight line from the confusion of emotions surrounding Jacques. 'Is the baby a boy?' Her voice held its steady note, and her eyes were fixed on the baby.

Miss Thurston shook her head in bewilderment as she looked down at the child.

'A girl,' Eva said. Clara's eyes moved sharply to Eva, then slowly away from her and on to Jacques. Finally she turned and looked at her mother's body. Her own body was rigid and her face quite still. Suddenly she spun round and ran at the door, trying to push her way past Jacques, but he grabbed her and held her back. She swung round on him like a cat, tearing at his face. Jacques let go as her nails ripped down his cheeks. She ran out of the room screaming uncontrollably, 'I hate you!'

Complete silence followed Clara's words. Even Suzanne stopped crying. She looked at her father as he turned to Miss Thurston and held his arms out for the baby. Miss Thurston held the baby closer, resisting his silent request. Eva looked down and quietly left the room, unnoticed. Jacques kept his hands held out.

'May I have my child, please.'

Reluctantly Miss Thurston handed the baby to him and moved to Suzanne and Prudence.

'You must come away, children,' she said as calmly as she could.

'No!' They both clung to their mother.

'Please.' Miss Thurston took them firmly by the shoulders, pulled them from their mother, and led them away. As she went through the door, tears blinding her, Prudence looked back at her father as he stood at the window holding the newborn baby. Miss Thurston pulled her gently from the room.

Jacques stayed by the window for minutes which grew into hours. The scrap of humanity in his arms moved slightly. Its tiny arms pushed out of the shawl and grabbed in small useless gestures towards his face. One of the tiny fingers touched him and he looked down. The baby seemed to be looking straight into his eyes, while one tiny finger touched his cheek. His tears fell unashamedly on the baby and through the stinging wash of grief he saw Emily. Her face expressed nothing but peace and Jacques felt himself break.

At last he moved to the bed and looked down at his wife's body. The baby's hand flattened itself against his cheek. He pulled it closer, buried his face amongst the warmth of the shawl and murmured:

'Emily.'

Chapter Four

Emily was almost seven years old. She wasn't a pretty child, on the contrary, she was almost plain; but the bubble inside her held more than beauty. Her hair was very fine and she seldom managed to survive a hairbrushing from Miss Thurston without tears. Miss Thurston was the only mother she knew and Emily adored her. The old governess had found a very special place in her own heart for the little girl. She was small; much smaller than the others had been at her age, Miss Thurston thought, but her tiny frame held more love, more sheer delight at being alive, than anyone she had ever met. Little Emily was also very bright. It was a pleasure to teach her and the child had rewarded her with an exploding excitement over each new discovery her schooling revealed.

But there were problems. Emily was a lonely little girl. Her sisters were already young women with minds of their own, and little interest in their young sister. Clara was the most difficult. She didn't like the child at all, and never ceased to make her feelings plain.

'What's the matter, Clara?' Emily asked, as Clara stepped into the room angrily. 'Come and look out of the window,' Emily went on. 'Jean Jacques is riding. He's jumping fences. Look.' Clara didn't look. Instead she scolded her.

'You're supposed to be studying, Emily. Not gazing out of the window.'

'But I have!' Her smile faded as Clara placed the family bible in front of her and opened it with a loud bang.

'You will read the bible for the rest of the day!'

'I've read it. Miss Thurston always makes me read it first.'

'Then you will read it again.'

'I don't like French.'

'You will learn it. And you will read the bible until you learn to do as you are told.' Clara turned on her heel and left the room.

As Emily looked at the bible she knew she was right about her older sister: Clara did blame her for her mother's death. Why else was it always the bible? Emily obviously needed forgiveness for killing her mother. She moved towards the window, unable to bear being inside another moment. Jean Jacques was outside in the sun riding Shiva. Prudence was in the cellars where she loved to be, and Suzanne was more than likely somewhere in the vineyard with Thys.

Emily decided she would not stay inside whatever Clara said, and quietly pushed the window wider. She lifted her skirt and petticoats, raised her small foot with the delicate ankle boot, and prepared to climb out. Out into the sun. Away from the house, and down to her own special place.

The gravestone was simple. Just a cross. But the words carved into it were very special. They were the first Emily had ever read on her own. It was a week ago that quite suddenly all the teaching Miss Thurton had given her fell into place. Scribbles became words. Words created images, and images created her mother. 'Emily Beauvilliers', the inscription read. 'Beloved wife of Jacques Beauvilliers. Mother of Clara, Suzanne, Prudence and Emily. May God hold her in His bountiful arms.'

Underneath the words were dates: 1788-1827. Emily had used her fingers to count. Her mother must have been forty when her youngest was born, and when she had died. But why had she died? Even the diary Emily had found two years ago, stacked away with her mother's old things in the attic, hadn't explained that. Emily moved to a small rock a little way from her mother's grave. She was about to lift it when Jean Jacques rode past on Shiva and she looked up.

'Jean Jacques!' Emily called and ran towards him. Jean Jacques stopped the horse, climbed down and bowed slightly as Emily reached him.

'Miss Emily.'

'You ride so well, J.J. Who taught you?' she asked with a sweet smile.

'Your father. The master,' he answered, keeping his head down. Emily ducked underneath his face and looked up into his eyes.

'Look at me?' Jean Jacques obliged. She shrugged, slightly embarrassed, for she had a secret to tell him. 'Where's your mother, J.J.?' she asked simply.

'She left many years ago,' he answered and his eyes fell again. Emily realized this was something Jean Jacques did instinctively. She looked at his lowered head. His shiny black hair gleamed, his nose was fine and his eyes, under his slightly lowered lashes, were very dark. Jean Jacques' skin was darker than hers, too. A warm glowing brown.

'Why?' Emily asked. 'Why did your mother leave?'

'Your father gave her her freedom,' he answered.

'And you?'

'I will be free when I'm twenty-five.'

Emily accepted his statement of fact. She knew all slaves would be free soon because the house was always full of angry men talking about it. Arguing with one another and with her father. He seemed to be the only one who thought slavery was wrong; and Emily knew he was right. How could one person ever own another person?

'Tell me about your mother,' Emily asked Jean Jacques. 'Where does she live?'

'By the sea,' he answered simply.

'Is she beautiful?' Emily asked.

'Yes,' he admitted. Emily had known she must be, and her eyes suddenly twinkled.

'So was my mother. I want to show you something,' she said and took his hand. He pulled back, but she held his hand firmly in hers and looked up at him. He was nearly fifteen and much taller than she was. 'It's a secret but I want to show it to you, Jean Jacques.' She pulled him on towards the family graveyard. Jean Jacques stopped as they went, forcing her to stop too as her arm tugged her back.

'I can't go there,' he said.

'But you must. I must be by my mother's grave to tell you,' Emily said seriously.

'No.' Jean Jacques was firm. 'I am not allowed at the grave of Mrs Beauvilliers.'

'Did Clara say that?' Emily looked at him directly and Jean Jacques nodded. She turned away, dismissing any objections. 'I want to show you something, and to do that I must be by my mother's grave.' She stopped and looked back at him. Jean Jacques hadn't followed. 'Now I can read I know everything, J.J.' His eyes were puzzled for a moment. 'Your father is my father.' Emily smiled as his dark eyes met hers. 'Don't be afraid.' She took his hand and this time he went with her.

When they reached the graveyard, Emily moved to the small rock and lifted it carefully. Underneath it was a black book. It was her mother's diary. She opened it carefully as Jean Jacques watched her, his expression as cautious as her handling of the diary.

'It's very old,' Emily said and looked up at him with the diary open in her lap. 'It's about you.'

'What is it?' Jean Jacques couldn't understand what Emily meant.

'This was my mother's diary.' Emily looked down at the open page. 'And now I can read I know everything.' She looked around quickly and whispered, but still with a smile, 'You won't tell anyone?' Jean Jacques shook his head. His eyes had never left the diary. He didn't understand what could be in that book about him.

'The child was born this night.' She read the words on the page carefully. 'The day was the seventh of March in the year 1820.' She glanced at him and smiled. 'The night of the ball,' Emily read on, 'the child of my husband, Jacques, was born to a slave girl, Eva. He was named Jean Jacques.' Emily's eyes flashed up to Jean Jacques as he listened, puzzled. 'That's you!' Emily said with delight and pointed her finger to her place in the book as she began reading again. 'The pain I feel cannot be right. Oh God, if you have not turned your back on me, grant me a son of my own.' Emily looked up at Jean Jacques. 'He didn't.' She paused as his eyes met hers. 'My mother died when I was born because I wasn't the son she'd prayed for, you see.'

'No!' Jean Jacques spoke quickly. 'That's not true.'

'Then why?' Emily waited silently, looking at him, for the one answer she needed. 'Why did she die, Jean Jacques?'

'Emily! Where are you, child! Emily?' Miss Thurston's voice broke the moment between them and Emily quickly hid the diary under the rock.

'You won't speak of this?' she begged Jean Jacques. He shook his head, and she smiled.

'Emily! You're supposed to be studying.' Miss Thurston's voice drew closer.

Emily filled her eyes with one more look at her half-brother, then turned suddenly and ran away, calling brightly, 'I'm coming, Miss Thurston.'

Jean Jacques looked down at the rock that concealed the diary, then back at the small girl who seemed to care for him. Even to love him as a brother. His spirit leapt inside him and he ran to his horse, Shiva. At last someone apart from his father knew the truth of his identity, and had accepted it with warmth.

Jacques had not missed the special light in Jean Jacques' eyes which had recently been lit. He was growing into a fine young man and at last Jacques thought he could see something else in him. Happiness.

'I need the men with me.' Jacques indicated a slope of vines to Jean Jacques. The vines spread up the mountainside in a low mass of green. 'Sheep have got in. We must tend to it.' Jacques despised the sheep his neighbours had begun farming to prepare for full emancipation.

'I'll fetch the men, master.'

'Father!' Jacques touched his son on the shoulder.

'Father,' Jean Jacques nodded.

Jacques watched his son's strong young body as he leapt like a buck through the vines. Life was still difficult for them all, but the day Emily died Jacques had taken it as a sign from God himself. Those you loved could be taken too quickly to allow separation. But Eva had refused to stay. Jacques could keep their son, she'd said, but Bonne Esperance was the home of another woman, Jacques' wife. A gentle woman whose child she had delivered and who had died in her arms. Jacques' wife, for whom Eva had a deep respect. So Eva had returned to the village where she had found her own comfort. Her place by the sea.

Though Clara had grown colder towards Jacques as each year passed, he still hoped that one day she would accept Jean Jacques. He was mistaken. Since that day at the races, the day on which she'd rediscovered love for her father and had it shattered again in the same moment by Jean Jacques, Clara had become a vessel of hatred. It was as though the purest moment in her life had been snatched away by evil.

Clara had grown tall and slender, her face framed by dark shining hair; her eyes almond-shaped and her mouth widely sensuous. Her walk was smooth. She seemed to glide over the earth and often walked the grounds of Bonne Esperance, as she did today. But her reasons were not always the same.

Today she was looking for Suzanne. Mr Bothma and another man had ridden in to see their father earlier and Clara knew his son Thys must have come with him. He would be with Suzanne.

Suzanne had heard the bird call as she waited under a tree for Thys to arrive and called expectantly, as her heart pounded inside her, 'Thys?' The promise of beauty shown in Suzanne as a child had been fulfilled. Her hair was a deep gold. Her face, so shaped by the perfection of her bone structure, had no angle or expression which detracted from that beauty. And it was light. There were no edges of darkness to be found anywhere in Suzanne's face, as there were in her sister Clara's.

Suzanne spun round at a second bird call. The sound had come from just behind her. Thys was there. He tilted his head to one side as her face shone into his. Suzanne could hardly believe how handsome he was. How much she loved him. The breath slipped out of her gently as his arms closed around her body. Strong arms. Gentle and sure.

'Suzanne,' he said quietly, drawing the end of her name out on a breath. She buried her head in his neck. He lowered his chin on to her hair, turned his face slightly, and ran his mouth down her cheek till he reached hers.

'Is your father here?' Suzanne asked as his lips met hers very gently.

'Mm.' His lips stayed against hers, just touching.

'What about?' she asked again, her lips moving against his.

'The slaves,' he said. His mouth closed on hers, allowing no more words to pass between.

Clara had seen them, but stayed where she was, hidden from their view, and watched them. Her body was tense, as if Thys's hands were moving over her and not Suzanne.

Suzanne gripped Thys's hand as it slipped inside the lace bodice stretched tightly acaross her breasts. A tiny pearl button jumped off the bodice. A small sound of resistance crept out of Suzanne's mouth, but as his fingers found their way down the proud rise of her breast and touched her nipple, Suzanne threw her head back.

'No.'

'Suzanne.' Her name was part of Thys's breathing. 'Suzanne.' His hand closed over her breast and the nipple pressed against his palm.

'No!' Suzanne repeated as he lowered her to the ground and leant over her. With his hand quite still on her breast, the drum of her heartbeat growing faster beneath it, he looked at her. His eyes questioned hers. She shook her head. Thys smiled and nodded. He began to close her bodice, pinning it together with his fingers as Suzanne looked down at the loose thread of the missing button. Her eyes flew to his, sparkling with a laugh hidden behind them.

'Where's my button?' she asked. Thys opened his eyes wide in an expression of total innocence. Suzanne pushed him off her. He fell away and rolled on to his back, laughing as she leant over him, one knee on either side of his body. 'Where's my button?' Thys shrugged with a cheeky smile.

'I know you have it.' Suzanne laughed as Thys pulled her down into his arms, holding her tightly.

'We'll look for your button,' he said, just before his mouth took hers.

Clara turned as Willem Bothma's voice ground its way towards her. He was angry and the anger cared little if ladies might be in earshot.

'Yes, Jacques, I do question you! Is the side you take dictated by common sense or your penis!'

Jacques ignored the insult. 'I remain on the side of justice, Willem, even if it's between my legs.'

Willem Bothma lowered his voice and fixed his eyes keenly on Jacques. 'Then you will not fight for our rights? You will stand by as the British try Cilliers in the Black Courts?' Bothma's anger simmered in his voice.

'If Cilliers has not mistreated his slaves he has nothing to fear,' Jacques replied calmly.

'His slaves are his property!' The anger in Bothma exploded. 'What right have they to try him? Like the land he stands on, his slaves are his!'

'A slave is not a piece of ground to be owned! Trampled on!'

Jacques felt a hard core of indignation rising inside him. 'You cannot own a person's soul, Willem!'

'Soul? Slaves have no soul!' Willem Bothma's eyes narrowed as he looked at Jacques. 'But where is yours, my friend? Damned by the Almighty!' He moved away in an attempt to calm his anger, but swung back on Jacques, unable to. 'Our slaves were sold to us by the British, Jacques. We paid good money for them. We looked after them! Did the British educate them? Feed them? No! It was done by us.' In his anger Willem Bothma broke into Afrikaans. 'Let them take our slaves – let them take them! But. Mark my words. You too will have nothing.' He moved around in a circle with a wide gesture of his arms, and switched back into English. 'All this will *be nothing!*'

'We are talking of men, Willem.' Jacques peered into Bothma's eyes keenly.

'Slaves!' Bothma retorted.

'Very well!' Jacques yelled back. 'Slaves! But slaves for which we will be compensated!'

'Hah!' Willem Bothma had widened his circle of anger and swung round at Jacques from a fresh distance, growling across the space between them. 'You believe the British?'

'Yes,' Jacques said simply.

'We have mortgaged those slaves! Encouraged by the British we have borrowed money against their full value and now they offer us half their value. But you say it is fair! Just? We will owe them money, man! Money we don't have and will no longer earn without labour!' He indicated Bonne Esperance once again and the land which surrounded them. His gesture was wild and his look fixed on Jacques. 'Say goodbye, Jacques. Say goodbye to everything you have worked for.'

Jacques remained totally still. Whether Bothma was right, whether his arguments were valid or not, he stood firm.

'We could talk to them,' he said quietly, and immediately regretted it.

'Talk!' Bothma exploded. 'Talk?' he repeated as he looked at the man beside him and laughed without humour. 'We have talked! You were there when we "talked" to the fine British Governor. Did he listen? From Parliament in England, do they hear our voices?' Jacques looked away. Willem Bothma was right, and he knew it.

'I will not wait till they've taken our land and our language before I fight for what is mine,' Bothma went on. 'They will not take my language from me!' He turned as if he was going, then flung back to Jacques suddenly. 'Remember, Jacques. Remember! To "them" you are a foreigner like me! To them we are foreigners: foreigners in our own land!' He reached his horse and glanced at Johannes Venter beside him. 'Where's Thys?'

'With the girl,' Johannes said as a matter of fact.

Bothma's face reflected disgust and he yelled again, 'Thys!'

Thys looked up at his father's voice but didn't move to answer. He was sitting on the ground with Suzanne leaning back against his knees, and his arms wrapped around her shoulders. Soil ran through his fingers in front of her, and landed in the skirts stretched across her lap.

'It's here in the earth, Suzanne. The beauty and wonder of our country is right here.' Suzanne rolled the small pearl button over the small mound of earth tracing a path through it.

'When you talk of it I lose my fear,' she said.

'Fear of what?'

'Africa,' she answered. Thys crossed his arms over her chest and pulled her tighter against his knees.

'But it's beautiful.'

'The way you speak of it, perhaps.'

'How?'

'As if you're a part of it. As if you grew from the soil.'

'I did. And you did, Suzanne.'

'Maybe through you I will.' She leaned her head back and looked up at him. 'You look funny upside down.' She paused. 'I think I love you, Thys.' Though her words were true, her face lost its joy. 'But I'm frightened.' She looked in the direction of Bothma's voice as it called aggressively again, 'Thys! Where are you?'

She turned around in his lap, as a kitten might, and looked at him closely.

'Hatred's building among the people, Thys. Even between our fathers.'

'But we are the people, Suzanne.' Thys kissed her on the nose as his father's voice bellowed towards them again.

'We're going, Thys!'

Thys held Suzanne's face between his hands, her golden hair slipping through his fingers. 'Tomorrow?'

Suzanne nodded. Then her eyes stilled and told him she was serious. 'You won't force me, will you, Thys?' He waited. 'I love you,' she said, 'but we must . . .'

Thys silenced her with a kiss. 'When you want to, I'll know.'

'Yes, Jacques, I have listened to you.' Willem Bothma looked down at him from his horse. 'But you've allowed the women in your family to lead you in their English ways. When you have nothing left you'll see I was right.' He looked about him belligerently. 'Where *is* he?'

'I hope you're wrong, Willem.' Jacques stayed calm.

'Hope never built a nation!' Willem retorted. He looked round as Thys ran towards him. Bothma's eyes moved from Suzanne in the distance to his son.

'You've said goodbye?' He picked up Thys's puzzlement and indicated with a nod of his head towards Suzanne. 'The girl.' Bothma turned his horse sharply, raising the dust around its feet. 'Goodbye,' he said to Jacques with finality, and raced out with Johannes following. Thys took the rein and swung his leg over his horse to mount. Jacques was moving towards him, and held the horse's bridle.

'Talk to your father, Thys. Violence is not the way.' Thys felt caught between Jacques and his father as he glanced towards Suzanne. She had lifted her hand in a wave.

'I will,' Thys said and galloped out in a dustcloud after his father.

'What will you do, Father?' Jacques turned at Prudence's voice. Her hair was untidy and her clothes covered with the stains of a day in the wine cellars.

'I've asked you to stay away from the cellars, Prudence,' Jacques said as he took in the evidence of where she'd been. Prudence looked back at him with confidence. She'd grown into a handsome young woman, firm of body and strong of face, and her words were never clouded by pretence.

'Why, Father? It's what I enjoy.'

'You're no longer a child!' Jacques answered roughly, his tension releasing itself on to her.

'But I'm learning how to run the estate. M. Claudelle is teaching me . . .'

'You will stay away from the men, Prudence!' He made to

walk away but she went after him.

'And do what? Tapestry? I hate tapestry and I hate sewing.'

'You are a woman!' Jacques said as though it were an end to it. Prudence's open face reflected her amazement.

'Does being a woman stop me enjoying work?'

'It's man's work!'

'And the devil take women? No, Father.' She followed him as he kept moving away to avoid further arguments. 'I want to help you run Bonne Esperance one day.' Jacques stopped and turned to face her.

'You will leave the running of this estate to those who are qualified.'

'To Jean Jacques, you mean?' Prudence could not disguise the anger in her voice. Jacques turned to go. 'Because he's a man?' She grabbed her father's sleeve and pulled him back, but hesitated at his expression. Then she tilted her head back, challenging him. 'When men talk of impending disaster women prepare for it, Father! I will tell you now that Bonne Esperance will survive in spite of Willem Bothma or any other man! In spite of you!' She turned and ran back towards the arched cellar doors, shouting defiantly, 'And I will be in the cellars learning to ensure that it does!'

Prudence disappeared behind the large black doors and Jacques dropped his head, too tired to rebuke her again. Prudence always exhausted him more than anyone else, even more than a man like Bothma. Not yet eighteen, she was as strong as any man. But it didn't matter. She was a woman, and her body proclaimed it proudly to any male eye.

Prudence leant against the cellar wall just inside the doorway and tried to calm herself by breathing deeply. Inside her was still the small girl who shook a little when faced with her father's anger. Why was it that even though she had deliberately ignored every curve that had appeared in her body, her father found a way of using each one against her?

Unknown to Prudence, Suzanne had felt similar confusion as she faced Clara. Clara had appeared from nowhere when Thys had gone and demanded an explanation for her behaviour.

'I love Thys, and I don't care what you think of him!' Suzanne screamed at her.

'Love?' Clara scoffed. 'You hardly know the meaning of the word.'

'No, Clara. It's you that word has no meaning for. You who imagine the Bothmas are somehow inferior to us! But look at us! What makes us so superior when love is nowhere to be found among us?'

'Perhaps that is the very reason why,' Clara said.

Suzanne looked at her at a loss, raising her arms helplessly. 'Everything I say you twist. I can't talk to you.' She turned to run away, but Clara held her back with a biting grip on her arm.

'Don't you understand I'm trying to protect you?' Clara hissed from between clenched teeth, as she held the body that Thys had caressed.

'From Thys?' Suzanne pulled her arm free.

'From your feelings, Suzanne! What you feel for Thys is pity, not love.'

'Oh no.' Suzanne had never dared challenge Clara before but she was in a position of strength when she talked of her love for Thys. 'I love Thys with every part of me. I can't think without those thoughts being of him. When he touches me . . . when his hands move over – '

As if her body had been violated, Clara slapped Suzanne hard across the face.

'I saw you with that Boer! I saw you behaving like two animals consumed by lust!' Clara screamed.

'I love him!' Suzanne cried.

'As our father loved that slave?' Silence fell between them. Clara had achieved what she wanted. Her voice softened as if to comfort Suzanne. 'It's no different. Try to understand that.'

'You consider Thys no more than a slave?' The words crept out of Suzanne's mouth as if she'd seen the real Clara for the first time. Clara ran her eyes down to Suzanne's bodice and smiled as they settled on the piece of thread which had lost its small pearl button. Gently she pulled the two sides of Suzanne's bodice together.

'You will never change the way I feel.' Suzanne didn't allow Clara's silent comment to touch her.

'Perhaps it will be his family who does that.' Clara smiled coldly.

*

In the Bothma house, Clara's words were threatening to become a reality. The air was electric with tension, as Thys sat at the scrubbed wooden table in the centre of the room and his father leaned across it towards him, speaking quietly.

'Suzanne is not a girl I would welcome into my family.' He moved his elbows as his wife, Theresa, placed a bowl of food in front of him. 'When you grow older you will know I am right, Thys.'

'No, Father,' Thys said. 'When I grow older I will marry Suzanne.' His mother looked at her son and husband from the stove as she filled another bowl. Her young daughters, waiting beside her with their bowls until the men had been fed, looked on with their mother and waited in silent expectation of an explosion from their father. It didn't come. Instead Bothma turned the bowl on the table with his index finger.

'Then we will talk of it when the time comes.' He looked across at his son as Theresa placed Thys's bowl in front of him. Thys didn't look at the food, his eyes instead followed his mother as she filled one of his young sisters' bowls. Tarcie was a slight child. Very blonde and entirely different from Anna, her older sister. Anna was dark like the rest of the family. Thys had a soft spot for his little sisters. He thought about them as his father said grace, and he knew they were more trapped by his parents' closed minds than he was: by this small house, poor but clean; shining in every nook and cranny, as if finding something to be proud of. The house was trapped by the land outside, which his father trampled under the hooves of cattle instead of nurturing for crops.

'I don't understand why you don't like her.' Thys began eating. 'Because Mr Beauvilliers doesn't agree with you?' His father put down his fork.

'Eat, Willem,' his wife said quietly beside him, but he paid no attention. His elbows on either side of his bowl, he leaned across the table to Thys.

'Because I do not want my son to turn from his own kind and betray God's word.'

'Where does God say I should not love Suzanne, Father?' Thys couldn't hide the amusement in his voice. The bowl in front of Willem Bothma flew across the room and shattered against the wall as he swept it aside in rage.

'You query the bible?' he shouted. His wife and two daughters sank lower in their seats. 'You dare to talk to me of a girl whose father lay with a slave as though God does not condemn such sin and her with it?' Bothma moved abruptly from the table. He picked up the large family bible and slammed it down in the centre of the table. His wife and two daughters held their bowls in case they should spill as the bible landed with a bang. 'Look in there! Read well the Old Testament, Thys! Joshua, nine! Deuteronomy, oovon! Enra, nine!'

'Eat, Willem,' Theresa said as she pushed her bowl in front of him, and stood to collect the broken pieces from the floor.

'And what of the New Testament, Father?' Thys reached out for the bible and drew it closer, then opened it, finding his page. His sisters kept their eyes down, as the bible stood between Thys and their father. 'Ephesians, two.' Thys read aloud, 'For He is our peace who hath made both one, and hath broken down the middle wall of partition between us.'

'Tell him, Mother,' Willem Bothma whispered between closed lips. 'Tell your son about that family's sin!'

'I don't care about the family, Father! I care only for Suzanne.'

'You don't want the splendour and finery of the Beauvilliers?' Bothma challenged.

'I want to live at peace in this land.' Thys paused. 'With Suzanne.'

'And you think the English will let you? Chosen as we are by God to live in this land, do you think the English will allow us?' Willem Bothma pushed his hardbacked wooden chair away and crossed to the corner of the room, pulling down a musket. 'That is why you're coming with me.'

'I'm not part of your fight, Father.' Thys went back to his food.

'You're not?' His father moved to him and leaned over him. 'It is not your fight too?'

'No,' Thys replied. Willem Bothma stood up straight. He looked down at Thys. His wife and daughters waited in terrified silence. Finally Bothma moved to the door, stopped and turned back as if giving Thys another chance. Thys didn't take it.

'Then you are no longer a part of this family.' Willem Bothma walked out and the door banged shut behind him. Tarcie and

Anna watched their brother, wishing he would go after their father.

Their mother broke the silence. 'Go to your father, Thys.'

He shook his head.

Jean Jacques liked Suzanne, and remembered that even as a small child she had been the reluctant one when Clara tormented him. At first he hadn't known how to answer when she asked him to meet her in the stables later that night and take her to the Bothma farm. She was going to run away with Thys, she said.

'I understand now about Father and your mother, Jean Jacques. There is nothing you can do to stop love.' When Suzanne said that, he knew he had to help her.

As Jean Jacques moved into the stables through the dark of midnight, he was not aware that Clara was waiting around one side of the building, hidden from him and from the house.

'Hello, Shiva,' Jean Jacques whispered, touching the horse as he passed him. He moved to another horse to prepare it for Suzanne, and led it into the centre of the stables. Shiva watched and neighed to get his attention. 'Yes, you can come.' Jean Jacques carried a saddle back towards Suzanne's horse. 'You like the nights as I do, hey Shiva.' He stopped. He thought he'd heard a noise. 'Miss Suzanne?' he said quietly, and moved to the stable doors to look out. Nobody was there.

Shiva lifted his feet in his high-stepping dance. He was agitated, but Jean Jacques ignored it as he tightened the girth on Suzanne's mount. Another horse, beside Shiva, reared quite suddenly and kicked out. Jean Jacques moved to it quickly, grabbed its lead and held it. 'What is it? Calm down.' He tried to hold it still but couldn't. Shiva picked up the growing tension and reared. Jean Jacques looked around between the horses' feet in case a snake had got into the stables, but stopped as he smelt something. He heard something behind him, a crackle, and turned round. Tiny flames were secretly creeping under the straw, thin streams of smoke spreading above them. Jean Jacques ran to Suzanne's horse, grabbing its lead and that of another horse, rushing to the door with them. 'Come on . . . come on,' he encouraged the horses, smacking them hard on their rumps.

'Jean Jacques!' He froze at Suzanne's hushed cry of horror when he reached the doorway. Her eyes were wide, her face framed by the dark hood of her cloak. 'Look out, Jean Jacques!'

He spun back as flames suddenly leapt to the ceiling in tall fiery arms. They were grasping at the open thatched roof. He turned to run back into the stables, but Suzanne held him back.

'No! You can't!' She stumbled as he broke free.

'Shiva!' Jean Jacques ran in, disappearing into the smoke and flames.

'Jean Jacques . . . ?' Suzanne screamed after him.

With an arm across his face Jean Jacques pulled the horses out, clapping for them to go. He moved to Shiva and the intense heat hit him like a blazing shield. He clapped. He shouted. He screamed.

'Go, Shiva!' Shiva didn't move. Jean Jacques tried to push him. He wouldn't budge. With the flames snapping round him, streaming in sparks and exploding, Jean Jacques grabbed Shiva's lead and tried to pull him out but Shiva pulled back, digging his hooves in and refusing to move. 'Shiva!' Jean Jacques pleaded as tears rose in his throat. 'You must come! Please!'

'Leave him!' Suzanne tried to peer through the smoke and heat as it forced her back. 'You must come out!' she screamed. Then she saw him. His back was in flames but still he didn't move from Shiva. 'Jean Jacques!' Suzanne shouted.

'Please, Shiva.' The tears in his voice choked him. 'You've got to come . . . please . . .' Shiva yanked the lead out of Jean Jacques' hands, sending him reeling backwards with his own weight.

'You must get out!' Suzanne shouted, not noticing Clara slipping away behind her through the darkness and dropping a burnt-out beacon. Near the house Clara stopped and a smile rose on her face. She moved away quickly as the front door swung open and Jacques ran out to the slave bell, ringing it urgently.

'Joshua! September! Quickly!' He spotted Suzanne silhouetted against the flames and ran to her. 'Come away, Suzanne. It'll collapse.'

'Jean Jacques is in there, Father,' Suzanne shouted as he pulled her back.

'Your cloak!' He grabbed at it and covered himself with it,

moving into the furnace of the stables.

Inside he could see nothing. The heat was intense and smoke choked him.

'Jean Jacques!' he shouted as a wall began to crack. It was bright with heat. As Jacques looked on in horror he saw Jean Jacques. His back was dancing in flames as he pulled at Shiva's lead, though Shiva was lying down. Jacques moved deep into the heart of the fire towards his son.

The slave bell outside rang loudly and continuously as Jacques grabbed his son and tried to drag him out.

'No! Shiva's still inside. No!' Jean Jacques struggled but Jacques held on to him and pulled him away from the blaze, as slaves ran towards the stables from all directions, yelling at one another for water. Maria watched aghast from the doorway of the house, her candy-floss hair with flecks of grey standing out on end. She looked old and dazed as she turned to Miss Thurston who had come out of the house to stand beside her, pulling a gown over her nightdress.

'What on earth is happening?' Miss Thurston asked stupidly, gazing at the stables and the flames which seemed to light the entire world.

'Fire,' Maria said simply, watching as Jacques rolled Jean Jacques on the ground in Suzanne's cloak. The flames on his back were out but he was dazed and shivering.

'Shiva?' Jean Jacques' eyes questioned his father.

'He was old. His time had come, Jean Jacques.'

With the wail of a stricken animal Jean Jacques curled into a ball on the ground, pushing himself in ever diminishing circles on the hard cobbles. Jacques reached out to him. He wanted to cradle him, but he was afraid to touch the open wound of loss which bled so unashamedly in his son.

'The horses! Are the horses all right?' It was little Emily calling as she ran towards them from the house with Prudence.

'Oh no!' Prudence pulled back as she saw Jean Jacques.

'Is he all right, Father?' Emily bent down to her half-brother, who was curled up on the ground at her father's feet.

'He's in shock. We must take him inside,' Prudence said sensibly, but before they could her attention was caught as a large burning timber joist crashed among the ember ruins; and there, as if she had stepped out of the depths of the fire, stood Clara.

'Is he hurt?' she asked calmly.

'Be careful, Father,' Suzanne called as Jacques went to move him. 'There were flames on his back. I saw them.'

'You were there?' Clara's voice came through as clear as crystal and Suzanne looked at her with sudden comprehension.

'Aren't you going to ask what Suzanne and that boy were doing in the stables at this time of night, Father?' Every word was underlined with suggestion.

'What are you saying?' Suzanne's voice was quiet as she approached Clara. 'What do you mean?'

'That perhaps it isn't Thys Bothma we need worry about after all.'

It was only when Suzanne's eyes returned to her father that she realized Clara had achieved her aim. Jacques was looking at her in a way she had never seen before. Then he turned to Jean Jacques, who was now staring at the glowing ruins of Shiva's grave.

'What were you doing with Suzanne?' Jacques asked his son, and then again with even more emphasis, 'What were you doing in there with Suzanne?'

Jean Jacques turned to look at him, bewildered by his father's accusing tone. Suzanne moved across to him and bent down to him quickly.

'Tell him, Jean Jacques. It's all right. You can tell him.' But Jean Jacques said nothing. 'I asked him to take me to the Bothma farm, Father. He was taking me to Thys! I was going to run away to Thys!' she blurted out.

'Is that true?' Jacques asked slowly, but still Jean Jacques said nothing. 'Must I take your silence as Suzanne's lie?' A bitter nudge of guilt ground against Jacques' suspicion.

'But I told you, Father,' Suzanne argued. 'Why won't you listen to the truth?'

'He has a tongue in his head!'

Emily stood a little way back in her nightdress, unable to understand her father's aggression.

'Speak to me!' Jacques brought his hand down hard across Jean Jacques' face.

'No!' Emily cried out. 'Don't!'

'Listen to me, Father!' Suzanne grabbed Jacques' hand to stop him.

95

'Tell me the truth!' Jacques yelled without listening.

'Miss Suzanne told you the truth.' Jean Jacques' eyes smouldered with resentment.

'You tell me,' Jacques shouted into his face.

For the first time in his life, Jean Jacques had seen the same look of condemnation in his father's eyes as he had seen in the eyes of other white people.

'If you don't believe it, it's because you would not believe it of yourself.' Jean Jacques' eyes moved back in the direction of the stables. The fact that he had sworn on his mother's life never to tell anyone he was taking Suzanne to Thys was not the reason he kept silent now. It was the presumption of his guilt that he'd seen in his father's eyes. Though the pain in his back was intense, and his heart ached even more, his thoughts turned back to Shiva: to the soft mouth, the warm breath that smelt of hay, and the dark melting eyes which had looked at him with such trust. Jean Jacques wept silently in the prison of his own head.

Chapter Five

'How do you spell "believe", Miss Thurston?' Emily asked as she sat at the table in her bedroom writing in her diary on a crisp white page.

'"I" before "E" except after "C",' Miss Thurston recited. She was sorting through Emily's clothes to pass on to the slave children those which no longer fitted her. Their bright faces always lit further with each piece of clothing she gave them.

'But isn't it an exception?' Emily asked.

'No,' Miss Thurston answered and spelt out to the small dress she held out in front of her, 'B-E-L-I-E-V-E. Are you certain this dress doesn't fit you any more?' she asked, thinking it really was too good to give away.

'Yes,' Emily answered, concentrating on the diary. 'It's too small.'

'Are you absolutely sure?' Miss Thurston went to her, holding up the dress. 'What a shame.' Her eyes moved to Emily's diary. 'What are you writing?' she asked.

'Just my diary.' Emily returned to it quickly. 'It's nothing important.'

'It really is such a pretty dress,' Miss Thurston said to herself as she folded it and added it to the pile.

'I don't understand why Father won't believe J.J. Or Suzanne. What does he think?' Emily wrote. 'Suzanne has been locked in her room for a whole day now. I don't understand why all this has happened. What is so wrong with Suzanne and Jean Jacques being together? Why should Father be so angry?'

'These petticoats of yours are quite yellow! I must have a word with Maria,' Miss Thurston grumbled. 'These people have no idea how to wash clothes.'

*

Suzanne was pleased to be confined to her room. It meant she could keep away from the rest of the family, and most especially from Clara. She looked up from her book at the sound of a key turning the lock. But at the sight of Clara stepping into the room Suzanne turned away to the window.

'I think it's time I reminded you of something,' Clara said as though she had every right to be there. 'Do you remember the pact we made when we were children, Suzanne?' She sat calmly on the bed. 'The pact made in our own blood? The pact which could only be broken by death?'

Suzanne remained silent.

'At last we can remove the stain of that boy, Suzanne. For the first time Father is questioning his feelings for him.' Clara was smiling. 'For the first time he no longer trusts him.'

'It was you.' Suzanne's voice was very quiet as the truth came to her. 'The fire! You trapped us!'

'What rubbish!' Clara said indignantly. 'It was you who trapped him with his lust for a white woman, and you know it!'

'You wanted to burn them to death before!' Suzanne's voice was rising to hysteria. 'You'll stop at nothing!' She ran to the door and swung it open, careless of who might hear. 'Get out of my room!' she shouted.

'Suzanne, please,' Clara tried to quieten her. 'Calm down.'

'Get out!' Suzanne screamed again. Clara moved to the door at her own pace, and slipped through it with a smile.

'You'll understand soon,' she said under her breath.

The door closed behind Clara and Suzanne leant against it hard, as if to ensure Clara could never come through it again. But her heart beat faster with the truth she had stumbled on. She had to see Thys. She had to get away from Clara, for ever. She jumped as the key locked the door from the outside, and then listened as Clara's footsteps moved away. Somehow she must attract Emily's attention. Emily was the only one she trusted.

Suzanne moved to the window and looked out. She would wait until she saw Emily, then she would seize her opportunity. She craned her neck to see as far as she could. Prudence was outside the cellars with their father. She wondered about him again. Why wouldn't he believe her? How could she allow Clara, with her sick hatred of Jean Jacques, to distort the truth?

*

Even as Jacques listened to Prudence he found his inner self uncertain: his gut writhed inside him, prodding him with an image of Jean Jacques and Suzanne making love.

'But what can Jean Jacques do to make you believe him, Father?' Prudence asked, gazing up at him earnestly. 'Suzanne told you she was going to Thys, and that he was helping her. Why can't you believe it? You of all people should understand.'

Jacques looked away; he understood too much. He knew that his love for Eva threatened his entire family yet still he couldn't give her up. Passions could be roused to a point where wrong became right, and the body's demands outweighed everything else. Jean Jacques was a healthy young male. It was only too possible that he and Suzanne had found pleasure in one another's bodies. Again his mind threw up an image of Jean Jacques with Suzanne, his dark strong body pressing down on her delicate pale flesh, and he felt suddenly sick. It was the memory of himself lying with Eva.

'How can I believe him?' Jacques pushed his thoughts aside, too afraid to examine them closely. 'Why should I?'

Prudence waited a moment before replying, her eyes passing gently over his face. 'You know why, Father. Because he's your son.'

Suzanne turned from the window to the door at the sound of a soft knock. She knew it wasn't Clara. Clara didn't knock.

'Who is it?' Suzanne whispered at the door.

'It's me! Emily,' the small voice came. 'Are you all right, Suzanne?'

'I need to see Thys!' Suzanne whispered into the keyhole. 'Do you think you could arrange it?'

'But how?' Emily asked, wondering if she could achieve such a thing. 'Do you want me to get the key to your room for you? I could let you out.'

'If you go down to the river you'll see Thys where I always meet him.'

'Shall I bring him to see you?' Emily asked.

'No. I can't see him, Clara would –'

Emily interrupted her quickly. 'Clara wouldn't know, Suzanne. I'd take her away so that she didn't spot him. I'd find the key and let Thys into your room.' Emily's whispered voice shook with the excitement of such secret planning. She felt a part of Suzanne and Thys's adventure. Even of their love. 'I'll go now. I'll go and get him.'

'Emily?' Suzanne called, but she had gone. 'Emily?' Suzanne stood up straight. Her breathing had eased for the first time with the sense that somehow her little sister would bring Thys to her. He would understand and hold her tight in his arms.

The rocks on the banks of the river were spread with sparkling white washing. The women in their bright clothes were bent in curves over the surface of the brown water, pounding clothes against the rocks as their voices reached up in song towards the surrounding mountains. Mountains which were purple now but would at any moment darken as if they had turned their back on the sun.

There was nobody coming from the direction of Thys's farm, but Emily would wait. She didn't mind. There were many games to play down here among the women. Their faces always shone when they saw her, and they called brightly,

'Missy Emily. How's missy Emily today, missy Emily?'

'Fine,' Emily called back. 'I'm fine. How are you?'

'Good, Miss Emily,' came the warm response, as it always did. Emily wondered how the babies strapped to their mothers' bent backs didn't slide over their heads and straight into the river. Their tiny brown faces looked so serious, Emily thought, as she moved close to one and tickled it under the chin.

'Hello, baby,' she said and the baby's eyes crinkled in a smile at once. Then its face smoothed into a look of open wonder as Emily ducked underneath it, peering up at it from above the water it had been so intently watching. 'Boo,' she said and leapt off the river bank, landing expertly on a rock further away. 'Watch me!' she called back to all the babies and their mothers.

'Haow!' came the friendly but slightly reproachful voice of one of the mothers. 'Careful, missy Emily.'

'Look at me!' Emily laughed as she leapt from one rock to the next, ensuring her feet never touched the laundry.

Thys was a long way off when he spotted Emily among the washing. He wasn't surprised. She was often there when he came to meet Suzanne, although Emily had never seen him. He was about to turn his horse away and take the secret route he used to find Suzanne, when Emily noticed him and called out, 'Thys!' Thys waited on his horse until Emily had hopped across the rocks to the bank of the river.

'I've been waiting for you,' Emily panted as she reached him. 'I've got to talk to you.' She looked back at the women to ensure they couldn't hear. She had a secret and she would keep it from all but Thys. 'It's very important.' Thys looked down at the grave little face as it gazed up at him intently.

'Is it that serious, little Emily?' he asked with a laugh. 'Have you seen a fish?'

'It's Suzanne,' Emily babbled. 'You've got to see her, but I'll have to get Clara out of the way first, and I'll have to get the key for you, then you'll have to be quiet because nobody must see you.'

'Emily,' Thys said gently, 'calm down. Tell me again.'

'It's Suzanne.' Emily fixed her large blue eyes on his to make certain he understood the importance of the mattter. 'There was a fire in the stables last night. Suzanne was there with Jean Jacques, but Father won't believe what she says.'

'Your father won't believe what?' Thys climbed down from his horse and knelt on one knee in front of her, holding her shoulders firmly.

'Suzanne said she was going to see you. She said J.J. was taking her to you but Father won't believe her and has locked her up in her room. For a whole day and maybe even for ever!' The words poured out. 'She has to see you.' She grabbed his hand, but a question suddenly filled her eyes. 'What's wrong?' she asked. There was something about him that reminded her of her father the night before. 'Don't you believe her either?' Thys turned away and mounted his horse.

'You do love Suzanne?' Emily asked simply. Thys nodded his answer, and Emily's face cleared in relief. 'Good. Everything will be all right now.'

'Come.' Thys reached down from the saddle towards her, and Emily put her hand in his, prepared for that moment she loved so much. Whether it was her father, Jean Jacques or Thys, it was magic. Their strong arms would lift her up and fly her through the air, swinging her up on to the horse in front of them.

She turned in the saddle and looked up at Thys, excited but more than a little nervous with the sense of danger. 'You mustn't be seen, Thys,' she said solemnly.

Thys smiled to reassure her and dug his heels in. The horse broke into a canter, bearing them on towards the house in the distance, as Emily sat in front of him, ready to complete her important task.

Thys waited behind the barn as Emily had ordered and looked at the key in his hand. His own father had turned a key on him last night. An invisible key in an invisible lock, but a key none the less. He looked towards the house which held Suzanne a prisoner. He had come to a decision last night. No matter how hard his father tried to keep him from Suzanne, no matter if it meant no longer being a part of his own family, Thys had decided that nothing would separate them. But, as he stood waiting for Emily to reappear with Clara, Emily's words crept back into his head, and scratched at his peace of mind.

'Suzanne was there with Jean Jacques . . . Suzanne was going to see you.'

But Suzanne had said nothing to him about coming to the farm to see him.

Emily stepped into the house and jumped back with fright as she met her father on his way out. He was dressed in clothes that only ever meant he was going away. His face was firm, even hard, as he spoke to Clara who was walking beside him.

'I will be back as soon as possible,' he said.

'Do you imagine his mother can discover the truth where you can't?' Clara challenged him, and moved past Emily without seeing her.

'The family is your responsibility, Clara.' Jacques ignored what she had said and strode towards his carriage where Jean Jacques waited for him.

'And he is yours?' Clara asked sharply, as her eyes settled on Jean Jacques. Her father stopped and Emily could feel the mountain of angry words waiting to pour from his mouth. But he kept them in check. Spotting Emily, he turned his attention to her.

'Help Clara, Emily. Be good.' He moved off abruptly to the carriage and Jean Jacques. Emily joined Clara and watched her out of the corner of her eye as the carriage turned around in the courtyard and pulled out into the drive.

'I've got something very important to show you, Clara. Will

you come and see?' Emily asked with a wide smile.

'I'm busy.' She turned to move away but Emily ran after her.

'Father said you must be responsible for us,' she insisted, taking her hand.

'Go away!' Clara pulled her hand free.

'But it's part of my studying. It's important for me to study, you said so!'

'For heaven's sake what is it?' Clara was angry but Emily didn't mind.

'I knew you'd want to teach me,' she said brightly, pulling the reluctant Clara away. Away from the barn and the house. 'It's about a chameleon,' she informed Clara as she caught sight of Thys running across the courtyard behind them and into the house. 'You know everything, that's why I need you.'

Suzanne stopped breathing as she heard the lock roll back. She waited across the room until the opening door revealed who was behind it.

'Thys!' Suzanne whispered, and she rushed towards him, flinging her arms around him. 'Thys, Thys, Thys.' After a few moments he held her away from him and signalled her to keep silent as he listened at the door. Suzanne watched him, her face alive with excitement, wanting to throw her arms around him again but sensing his slight reserve.

'What is it? What's wrong?' Suzanne felt suddenly insecure.

'I just want to make sure nobody is around.' To excuse the unease he felt in himself he moved to the window, looking out of it carefully. He turned back to face her and responded immediately to the expression on her face. 'Suzanne, what is it?'

'You don't believe me either,' she said. Thys moved to her but she pulled back. 'Clara knew nobody would believe the truth.'

'What truth?' Thys asked.

'I was running away to you. I wanted to go to you to be with you for ever.' Her face hardened. 'Do you believe that?'

'Yes!' Thys pulled her to him, pushing his fingers through her hair as he tilted her head back and looked into her face. 'Suzanne,' he breathed her name, as he always did. 'I believe you, Suzanne; but it would not have been possible.'

'But why?' she murmured. Thys pressed his cheek against hers and held her tightly in his arms.

'We must find another place, Suzanne.' He found her mouth with his and felt the desire in his body which had led him to defy his own father, and feel the jealousy which a hint of suspicion had aroused. 'We will find our place, Suzanne. But it is not here.'

'If he changes to the colour he's sitting on, what happens to him when he's between colours?' Emily lifted her finger with a small green dragon, which was a chameleon, sitting on it. 'You see! It's still green but my finger isn't green! So what happens if a hawk sees it now?'

'Doubtless it will swoop down and eat it,' Clara said flatly. She didn't like having a chameleon so near her face.

'I don't believe you!' Emily accused Clara, knowing that only an argument and then a scolding could delay Clara much longer. 'It wouldn't be right that something so small and clever as a chameleon could get eaten by a hawk. You're lying!'

'If you ask me a question and I answer it, it's very rude to say I'm lying. What does Miss Thurston teach you all day? It certainly doesn't seem to be manners!' Clara's scolding went on and on until, at last, Emily saw Thys slip out of the house and away. She had delayed Clara for long enough.

'I'm sorry, Clara.' Emily hid the delight of her achievement in an apology. 'What did you say?'

The foaming spray rose in glittering clouds before crashing back to its beginnings as the sea pounded against the rocks. Seagulls floated over the water, gliding on the currents of the wind, as Jacques shouted over the thundering noise.

'I need you, Eva!'

'No, Jacques.' Eva's words were, as always, plain. 'I cannot be with you.'

'Marry me.' Eva heard his words but turned and looked at him as though she hadn't. 'Marry me, Eva,' Jacques repeated and Eva's eyes moved away from him towards Jean Jacques. He stood further away on the beach with the fishermen, hauling in mussels.

'You refused to believe our son,' Eva said without looking at Jacques. 'You treated him as you would a slave.' She turned and looked at him directly. 'Isn't that true?'

'And I wanted to kill him.' He took hold of her, desperate to make her understand. 'Without you I am no good to our son.' He gripped her arm even harder and pulled her into him, forcing her body against his. 'Is there guilt in our love, Eva? Is there?' She was trembling. A smile touched his lips as he looked down at her. 'It was never the master who took his slave. You love me.'

She broke away and looked back to Jean Jacques. 'Our love brings death with it. I'm afraid for our son.'

Jacques folded her tightly into his arms from behind. 'No harm will come to him again.'

She looked at him with searching eyes. 'Will *you* not harm him again?'

Jacques let her go and moved away. He could feel her eyes on him, but he didn't look back at her.

'He spoke the truth, Jacques, and you would not believe him.' Her voice dug into him like a knife. 'You could not believe him!' Eva was deeply angry. 'You would not believe your son because you were afraid of yourself.'

Jacques' eyes moved to Jean Jacques, then he turned back to Eva. Her eyes had never left him.

'Yes.' He grabbed Eva roughly and held her tight. 'Without you I see only what others see.'

'And what of Jean Jacques?' She shook her head. 'It is only with us apart that he can be accepted. We must remain apart for his sake.'

'Eva!' Jacques' eyes bore down on her. 'Tell me you feel nothing. Tell me I took you against your will, and I will leave you.'

Eva said nothing.

'Tell me.'

'I love you.' Her words sliced through the prodding finger of accusation inside him. 'I love you, Jacques,' she repeated. A streak of shining black hair swept across her face as it escaped the silk scarf around her head.

'I accept that you will not marry me, Eva. I accept your love.' He turned and ran down to the beach towards Jean Jacques.

Eva watched as he reached him, and felt a sudden taunt of fear. She wondered if anything could protect their son from people like Clara. She knew something of the confusion inside

Jean Jacques. It was as if a light had gone out of his eyes. It had been snuffed out on the night of the fire.

Emily stood just inside the cellar doors, out of sight of M. Claudelle and Prudence, and listened intently. She wanted to know what it was about the cellars that fascinated Prudence.

M. Claudelle tasted a little wine from a tasting glass, and Emily pulled a face. She had tasted it once and that was enough.

'What do you think of it?' Prudence asked him eagerly. M. Claudelle turned and looked at her without speaking. 'Well?' she asked again. 'Tell me!'

'It is beautiful.'

'Cooling the vats was right!' Prudence beamed. Emily had never seen her so happy, and all that over a drop of wine!

'And you too are growing into a beautiful woman. Like the wine.' Emily pulled back a little as M. Claudelle's hand moved over Prudence's back and slipped down to her waist.

'Thank you.' Prudence calmly lifted his hand, holding it out to him as if giving it back. 'You are here as our wine-maker, M. Claudelle,' she said firmly, although Emily could hear a quiver in her voice. 'I think it would be best if you kept your hands around the stems of glasses and not my waist.' She paused. 'Unless of course you wish me to tell my father.'

M. Claudelle laughed. 'How that flush of temper lights your eyes! I like a woman with spirit.' Emily stepped back quickly as Prudence reached her at the door and turned back to M. Claudelle.

'How lucky that you are not a slave, M. Claudelle. My father can dispose of you immediately without waiting for emancipation!' She swept out of the cellars, and Emily raced after her, careless of being caught.

'What were you doing in there?' Prudence demanded as Emily reached her.

'Shh.' Emily pulled her along with her as they ran away. 'Are you going to tell Father?'

Prudence stopped and held Emily's small shoulders to keep her from running.

'I'm not telling Father anything and neither must you, Emily.'

'But you told M. Claudelle –'

'Emily,' Prudence interrupted her. 'Do you know how important it is that I learn about the estate?' Emily shook her head. 'It's the most important thing in the world to me. But if Father had any idea of what M. Claudelle just did, he would never allow me to go in there again.'

'Why?'

'Because – ' Prudence stopped. How could she explain something to her small sister when she herself didn't clearly understand? 'He seems to think a woman shouldn't be alone with a man.'

'Like Suzanne and Thys, you mean?'

'No. Because – Oh! How can you understand?' She paused. 'It's simply because I am a woman.'

'Yes.' Emily wondered why Prudence was telling her something so obvious.

'Father thinks only men should work. He doesn't believe I know anything about the wine.'

'Do you?' Emily asked. Prudence tilted her head up in a secret smile.

'I know more than Father would believe, Emily.'

'Had you any idea Prudence has been keeping these books, Miss Thurston?' Jacques turned the page of a ledger.

'Which books?' Miss Thurston asked the handkerchief she was embroidering.

'These are detailed accounts of the estate.' Jacques glanced at Miss Thurston as she screwed her eyes tighter in an effort to see her sewing. They had sat like this on many, many evenings since his wife's death. They had spoken only about the children or the weather; but Jacques needed the companionship of an adult, an adult who was not one of his neighbours. He took in the straight line of her mouth as she chewed the insides of her cheeks. The grey hair was pulled back tightly into a bun, and he wondered what she had been like as a young woman. Perhaps he could talk to her.

'Willem Bothma could be right when he says the abolition of slavery will bring us to ruin.' Jacques spoke as if to a total stranger.

'He would say such a thing!' Miss Thurston retorted. 'Slavery is evil.'

'And I agree with you, Miss Thurston. But what of the time

when our people could be divided by what is happening? When families could be torn apart? Perhaps even this one.'

'I hope not,' mumbled Miss Thurston, almost inaudibly.

'You've been with my family for many years, Miss Thurston.'

'Indeed.'

'And you care for my daughters. You are the one they turn to. The one they trust.' Miss Thurston deliberately kept her eyes down, but Jacques sensed she wanted to unburden herself. 'There is something?'

'You still love that boy's mother, don't you.' Jacques was taken aback by her words and Miss Thurston seized her opportunity. 'I will never understand you. But Emily did! Your wife died trying to give you a son and never blamed you. She accepted that you loved that woman as you never loved her.' Speaking of her feelings after so long brought everything back as though it had happened yesterday. She could still see Emily lying in the bed, her hands crossed over her chest. 'She forgave you.'

'The greatest gift of God.' Miss Thurston watched him, trying to hold back the emotion swelling inside her. 'Emily told me forgiveness was the greatest gift of God, Miss Thurston,' Jacques said very quietly.

'Yes.' Miss Thurston tried to wipe her tears away and talked to her sewing again to help. 'It is a shame Clara has not inherited that gift from her mother.' She looked up suddenly as if at last she could say what was really on her mind. 'She is so bitter, Mr Beauvilliers. She threatens us all with her hatred.' She stopped as she realized Jacques had turned away, and she knew he was weeping.

'I'm sorry,' Miss Thurston sniffed and picked up her sewing. 'I'm sorry, but I . . .' She hesitated. 'I have no idea what to say.'

'You're right, Miss Thurston.' She watched his back and longed to move to him, to comfort him as his mother and his wife would have. Instead she pulled herself straight, ensured her face was dry and moved to the door with her sewing as quietly as she could.

'Good night, Mr Beauvilliers.'

It was many hours before Jacques went to bed that night. When he did, his mind returned to Eva. Everything Miss Thurston had said was true and Emily's empty bed screamed at him.

*

Sleep hadn't come to anyone in the Bothma family either. The long night had begun as Thys announced to his parents that he was going to Cape Town.

'It's the other direction we'll be going in, son,' Willem Bothma said flatly. 'We're meeting in the early hours.'

'I'm not going with you, Father.' Thys tried to keep calm. His father ignored him and nodded at a musket to one side of the room.

'I've given you that,' he said, as if it would solve all the problems.

'Father. I said I am going to Cape Town.'

'There's some bread in the bag, Thys, and I've put a blanket in here.' His mother indicated a large roll by the door. 'It will be cold at night.'

'Will nobody listen to me?' Thys looked from his mother to his father. 'I said I'm not going.' His mother moved silently to the young girls and ushered them out of the room. She'd recognized the storm clouds gathering over her husband.

'Cape Town, you said.' Willem Bothma looked at Thys through narrowed eyes. 'Cape Town,' he repeated carefully.

'Yes.'

'Why?'

'To earn enough money to buy a farm of my own.'

Bothma moved towards the door as though Thys hadn't spoken. 'I'll expect you to be with me.'

'Not till you tell me what you gain by hating the English, Father!' Thys was on his feet and beside him at the door. 'Blood and more blood? Is that what you want in exchange for your slaves?'

'You no longer sound like a Boer,' Bothma said quietly.

'I am not,' Thys answered. 'I am a man of Africa.'

'And I am less?' The rage which Willem Bothma had tried to contain exploded in his son's face. 'You haven't said what you'll be doing in Cape Town but I know! You'll be selling your birthright. Selling your soul and your people for that English girl!'

'By joining the commandos?' Thys asked in amazement. 'I will be earning a wage, Father.'

'Thirty pieces of silver!' Bothma bellowed. 'Paid by the enemy!' He spat the last word out.

'The English are not our enemies.'

'You talk like one of them.'

'Then what will you and your friends do?'

'I will shoot as many as I see,' Bothma yelled.

'And they will send more British soldiers.' Thys looked at his father sadly. 'And then they will shoot you.'

'With your finger on the trigger.'

Bothma's words had hung in the air long after he'd gone. Long after he'd ridden away into the night with the others. Men who had become outlaws in their own land.

Caught between her husband and her son, Thys's mother hadn't said another word to him, not even when Thys left for Cape Town the next day.

The first day of December 1834 was the official day of emancipation, but it had passed unnoticed by everyone except the slaves. Dressed in their finest clothes, they had taken their freedom like crowns and celebrated in song.

People in England had passed a law and imagined that that was it. But Jacques Beauvilliers knew it wasn't. The country was too big for an ideal which had not taken root in the hearts of the people.

Many were already profiting from the confusion and the road to Bonne Esperance was well trodden by slave brokers. Men who offered, for a small percentage, to collect the compensation due from the British government.

'It would be in your interests, Mr Beauvilliers, if I handled the compensation for you; since I'm handling all the claims in the area.' How similar these men were one to another, Jacques thought. Every one of them determined to do him a great service.

'You'll be going to London to collect the money, will you?' Jacques asked each, and all answered in the affirmative. 'And I'll see it?'

'I'm a man of my word.'

Jacques marvelled at how suddenly the population had swelled with honourable men. He knew there would be many easy victims for them. People like Mrs Bothma who was suddenly alone on the farm with her daughters, as her husband sought revenge on the British and her son became a part of the British army. But when Jacques had gone to see Theresa Bothma, he'd been met by a stone wall of rejection. She no longer trusted anybody, and held her slaves close to her, like a family. They were the responsibility God had placed on her shoulders, and no one would ever take it from her.

Jacques knew that the conviction of people like Mrs Bothma was not something the English parliament had taken into account. Many of the slaves had gone north with their Afrikaans masters, leaving the law behind them along with everything else British.

The slaves at Bonne Esperance were working through a five-year apprenticeship and on the surface little had changed. Jean Jacques was among them, although Jacques had never considered him a slave. Nor had he considered that one day his son might want the freedom which was now legally his. Other changes in their surroundings were of more immediate interest to Jacques. They had new neighbours.

The Westbury family had been late settlers from England on the eastern frontier. They had worked hard but found both the land and the Xhosa nation hostile. Looking for a better life, they had come to the more peaceful environment of the Cape of Good Hope and taken on a small vineyard, abandoned by its Afrikaans owners. The Westbury family had determined to build a great vineyard like Bonne Esperance to secure themselves a place in Cape society. Mrs Westbury was in charge of their social climb.

Pauline was their only child. She was nineteen years old and her English looks intrigued Emily at once. Her skin was fair and her cheeks freshly pink, as if she had never been out in the sun. She wasn't beautiful like Suzanne, or statuesque like Clara, but she had a curious individuality about her and Emily was old enough to notice how her eyes lingered on Jean Jacques from the moment they met.

'I'm Emily, and this is Jean Jacques,' Emily had told her brightly as her father accompanied Mr and Mrs Westbury into their house.

'Hello, I'm Pauline,' she'd said warmly, without looking at Emily at all. Her husky English voice stroked Jean Jacques. Emily noticed him pull back slightly. It was the first time a woman had looked at Jean Jacques as if he were a man.

Tea was served from fine English china. Emily noticed the blue writing on the base of each cup and saucer and wondered where Worcester was. The care with which Mrs Westbury handled the china showed how much she valued it. Emily noticed that Mrs Westbury had only called her and Pauline in for tea. Jean Jacques was obviously not to be served. It made her very uncomfortable and she swallowed her tea quickly, but Pauline gulped hers down even faster and vanished outside. Emily decided to stay where she was and allowed her gaze to wander around the room, rather than listen as the grown-ups talked. Though there wasn't much furniture, what was there reflected the very English qualities of the family. The armchair Emily sat in was covered in chintz and she noticed it had been patched. She could hardly see where the patch began or ended, it was so carefully done. Invisible mending was something Miss Thurston had tried hard to teach Emily.

'No, I haven't taken on any labour,' Mr Westbury answered Jacques. 'I'm not one for leaving things to others.' He had a strange flat accent, Emily observed.

'You can never trust them you know,' Mrs Westbury said with complete confidence in her judgement. 'Another cup of tea . . . ?'

'Jacques,' he smiled, holding out his cup.

'Jack.' As she took the cup it rattled on the saucer and she steadied it. 'I have a cousin named Jack.'

'Jacques,' he smiled again.

'Oh.' Mrs Westbury looked at him wide-eyed. 'My name is Mary and my husband is John.' Emily hoped they wouldn't get around to the pronunciation of Beauvilliers. Just then John Westbury looked outside, straight through the wall of the house. It amazed Emily how grown-ups did that. She peered at the solid wall as Mr Westbury talked of Jean Jacques as though he could see him through it.

'Working out his apprenticeship is he?' he asked.

'Who?' Jacques said. Emily was relieved her father couldn't see through the wall.

'Your slave.'

'Oh? Yes.' Jacques added quickly, 'Perhaps he could help you. He knows all there is to know about the land in these parts.'

'Excuse me.' Emily curtsied to Mr and Mrs Westbury. Her father had allowed them to think Jean Jacques was a slave! He had not told them he was his son and she suddenly had to get away from them all.

'What a charming little girl,' Mary Westbury said. 'So well mannered.'

Emily reached the hall outside the sitting-room and stuck her tongue out. If they could see through walls then her tongue would not be missed either. So much for good manners. But once outside, Emily wasn't at all sure she wouldn't rather be back inside.

Pauline was talking to Jean Jacques, as he held the horse he had unharnessed from the carriage. Pauline was looking at him in a way Emily had never seen before. Her eyes seemed to peel off his skin. He looked very dark as he stood beside her. Perhaps that was why Pauline was intrigued.

At last Jacques came out of the house.

'Excuse me,' Emily said to Pauline as she moved between her and Jean Jacques. 'We're ready to go,' she called brightly to her father, trying to hurry every moment. She wasn't sure if she wanted to get away because Pauline's interest in Jean Jacques embarrassed her, or because the Westburys might try and pronounce their surname at any moment. Whichever, Emily wanted to go as soon as possible. It was only later that night, as she wrote her diary, that Emily expressed her true feelings.

'Father corrected their pronunciation of his name but he did not correct their conclusion about Jean Jacques.' She paused, staring at the flickering candle on the small desk. 'Jean Jacques seems keen to work for them. Does he like Pauline, or is it because Father has made it impossible for him to see himself as anything but a slave?'

It was because Jean Jacques wanted to be near Pauline, Emily realized as she watched him preparing to go to the Westbury house some days later. He was washing. He washed not once but three times, then he put on his best shirt.

'Lunch!' Mary Westbury's voice attracted John Westbury and Jean Jacques as they worked in the small vineyard on the hill overlooking the Westbury house. 'Where's Pauline?'

'I don't know,' John Westbury called back. 'Haven't seen her.'

Jean Jacques had seen her, and could still see her. She was in a small clump of trees just to the left of the vineyard. He kept his silence.

'Lunch,' John Westbury said to Jean Jacques and moved

away towards the picnic his wife had spread on a rug at the bottom of the hill.

Jean Jacques had his lunch with him as usual. Mr Westbury looked back suddenly, surprising him.

'Are you sure you have enough to eat? There's plenty here.' The gentleness in his voice struck Jean Jacques.

'Yes. I have enough, thank you, master.'

'Pauline, where are you?' Mary Westbury's voice drove solidly across the open space and up the hill to Jean Jacques as he walked away. He didn't look up although he'd noticed Pauline's blue skirt flash in amongst the trees ahead of him. A sudden surge of excitement raced through his body as she stepped to the edge of the trees and smiled at him.

'My mother told me I must stay away from you.' Her green eyes sparkled.

'Yes,' Jean Jacques said simply as he opened the small bundle of food wrapped in a white napkin and sat down under the trees. He tried not to look at her.

'Maybe she knows what I feel when I'm with you.' Pauline brushed his back with her skirts. 'If you move back here with me she won't be able to see us.'

'You should obey your parents.' Jean Jacques' body was tense.

'Why?' she asked and dug her foot gently into his spine. 'Please move back here a little.' He moved back among the trees, but still he didn't look at her.

'They can't see us now.' Pauline allowed her body to brush his as she sat on the ground beside him. 'Don't you want to know what I feel about you?'

'No,' Jean Jacques said quickly, and Pauline chuckled. It was a warm husky sound which seemed to bubble in her throat. Everything about her was like that husky laugh, Jean Jacques thought.

'Unfortunately I can't change what my mother feels,' she went on. 'I think it's because you're dark.' Her nose wrinkled slightly and then she smiled. 'You're nervous.' She ran her finger down his arm, leaving a thin white line on his brown skin. 'You feel as I do. Even a little afraid, as I do.' The white line vanished in the solid brown of his skin.

'Pauline.' Her mother's voice was closer. Jean Jacques looked up and saw Mrs Westbury struggling up the hill towards them.

'She hasn't seen me. Don't worry.' Pauline slipped deeper into the cover of the trees. 'Pretend nothing has happened at all and I'll see you tomorrow.'

'I won't be here tomorrow,' Jean Jacques said without looking back at her as Mrs Westbury puffed her way closer.

'I know you're there, Pauline.'

'I'll be waiting for you,' Pauline whispered, and was gone in a rustle of leaves.

'Have you seen my daughter Pauline?' Mrs Westbury asked officiously, keeping a respectful distance from Jean Jacques.

'Your daughter?' he asked.

'You want me, Mother?' Pauline was running down towards the picnic spot.

'Your mother's up there, Pauline,' Mr Westbury called, and Pauline looked back up the hill in amazement.

'What are you doing up there, Mother?'

Mrs Westbury turned away from Jean Jacques quickly. 'Your father will be having a word with you, my girl!' she muttered, as she started back down.

Left alone with his food, which he no longer wanted to eat, Jean Jacques glanced down to the picnic of which he was not a part.

'What possessed you to look for me there, Mother?' Pauline laughed. 'What do you imagine I'd be doing with him?'

Jean Jacques bit into the hard crust of bread. The sound in his head as his teeth crunched it blotted out his thoughts and he lay back on the ground looking up at the canopy of green leaves above him. He wouldn't come tomorrow, he decided.

But Jean Jacques went every day.

What had begun as idle curiosity on Pauline's part had grown into something else. The slight tease with which she'd begun had turned serious. The game had changed, and Mrs Westbury knew it. Jean Jacques was involved in something outside his understanding, but he no longer looked for an escape.

Emily was the only one who had noticed, and she noted in her diary: 'Jean Jacques is in love with Pauline Westbury. It's dangerous. The Westburys think he's a slave.'

What Emily didn't know was that whether Jean Jacques was her half-brother or a slave, it made no difference. All Mrs Westbury saw was the colour of his skin.

Chapter Six

The day of the ball had arrived. It was to be held at the castle in Cape Town in celebration of the coronation of their new queen, Victoria, and already Miss Thurston had covered every empty space on the walls of the house with pictures of her. Jacques was not impressed.

Emily was too young to go to the ball. She was twelve, but it seemed to her that each year she reached, the most interesting things were postponed for another.

'It takes so long to grow older,' she'd said to Miss Thurston, who had pointed out that she herself was too old to go to the ball and Emily should enjoy her childhood before it vanished. She did. Nothing dampened her spirits; neither Miss Thurston being too old nor herself too young.

She had watched Miss Thurston teaching her sisters the gavotte. Prudence wasn't very good at it at all, and Miss Thurston had told her she had two left feet; Prudence had replied that in that case she'd better not go to the ball since it was unlikely there would be a soldier with two right feet to match hers.

The three ball gowns, ordered six months before, had hung on the bedroom wall covered in white sheets for weeks. Emily had peeped at each in turn. What intrigued her most was the small label sewn inside each dress: 'Made in England'. It reminded her of Mrs Westbury's china. The dresses were part of a distant land she only ever heard talk of. The golds and shiny whites of the material dazzled one another in competition, and the tiny waists were accentuated by the miles of silk in the flowing skirts. The bodices were trimmed with the most delicate lace she had ever seen. It was from France. The other distant land, of which her father often talked.

As she watched them, Emily noticed a special sparkle in

Suzanne's eyes. Tonight Suzanne was certainly the most beautiful of her sisters. Even her father, in his black suit and high white collar, looked more handsome than she could remember having seen him before.

Emily waved happily as they drove away in the carriage. She waved until the carriage was far out of sight, then ran back to the house to imagine herself a part of it all.

Jacques turned to Suzanne as the carriage rumbled on towards Cape Town. She looked a little nervous he thought, and he touched her hand as she sat looking out of the window blankly.

'You will be the most beautiful girl at the ball Suzanne.' His eyes moved to Prudence and Clara, opposite him. 'My daughters will be the most elegant young ladies ever to set foot in the castle.'

'Good evening, Mr Beauvilliers.' The major bowed politely. 'Charles, Lord Marsden, Fifth Dragoon Guards.' Although introducing himself to Jacques, Lord Marsden had noticed Clara.

'And may I introduce my daughters, Lord Marsden. Clara, Prudence and . . .' Jacques looked around, wondering where Suzanne had got to.

'She's powdering her nose,' Prudence whispered.

'My daughter, Suzanne, will be here soon,' he added.

Lord Marsden's attention centred on Clara, but he talked to Jacques. 'I can't pretend not to have heard of your daughters, Mr Beauvilliers,' he said. 'In fact, I doubt if there is a man in the garrison who has not heard of them. And your wine.'

Clara had registered Lord Marsden's reaction to her and she studied him with more than a little interest. He was older than she was and his features were fine, almost effeminate. Beneath them she could sense an unusual self-confidence. He was an aristocrat. Clara had not come across it before and it attracted her immediately. Her eyes moved from his face and over his body, encased in a bright red jacket with gold braid. The neat white trousers disappeared into tall leather boots, the uniform accentuating his authority. He was a man whose presence commanded respect and the well-bred tone of his voice demanded attention.

'May I have the pleasure of the first dance, Miss Beauvilliers?'

he asked with a slight bow. He didn't look to Jacques for permission, Lord Marsden needed permission from nobody.

'I would be delighted.' Clara moved with him on to the ballroom floor, under the shimmering light of the chandeliers. Lord Marsden bowed again, and the orchestra began to play a gavotte. He held out his arm, and Clara laid hers on it gently, looking up into his eyes. He reacted immediately. Never before had Charles Marsden seen such sensuality in the eyes of a woman. As her body brushed past his in the dance, the promise in her eyes was confirmed.

Suzanne stood outside the main door to the ballroom looking into the castle square below. Steps ran down on either side of her and she was not sure which way to go. Table Mountain loomed out of the moonlit night sky in front of her, threatening everything at its feet.

The gavotte played behind her incongruously as the open space of the military square beckoned in front of her. Before she could decide which way to choose, she heard Thys's bird call and peered in the direction the sound had come from. She could see nothing in the deep shadow of the low buildings across the square. Forbidden cloisters, protected by white pillars.

The bird call came again and Suzanne looked about her instinctively. She was nervous. She was where she ought not to be, and she was afraid.

'Thys?' she whispered in terror, and ran down the steps to her right before someone could jump out at her from the dark. Holding up her white skirts to run faster, she suddenly stopped, trapped in the maze of pillars with Table Mountain bearing down on her menacingly.

'Where are you, Thys?' She was afraid that he was not there at all, although they had planned this meeting so carefully.

'Suzanne.' Thys's voice touched her from the dark of the veranda where she stood. She turned as he stepped out from behind a pillar and he swept her into his arms. 'Suzanne. Suzanne.' His warm breath covered her bare shoulders as he spoke her name. His hand felt for hers, took it firmly, and led her away into the depths of the cloisters' shadow.

At last Suzanne was snug in Thys's arms. As their bodies melted into one another, it was as though they had never been apart.

'Shall we dance?' Thys held his arm out graciously. She looked at his arm, looked up into his eyes, and flung herself back into his embrace.

'I thought I would never find you.' She buried her face into his chest, smelling the leather of his jacket as he held her close and they danced slowly, among the pillars. 'I've missed you every minute,' she murmured. 'I love you so much, Thys. Thys?' Suzanne hesitated. His expression had changed and he was looking towards the ballroom. 'What is it, Thys?'

'Is your father in there?' he asked.

'No, Thys. You can't – ' she began, but he silenced her with a kiss.

'I shall ask your father now for your hand in marriage.' He turned to lead her to the ballroom. 'Come.'

'But you can't go in there, Thys.' She tried to pull him back. He held her hand more firmly and led her on towards the steps.

'Come,' he grinned.

Prudence had refused every man who had approached her to dance and Jacques wondered what was wrong.

'You must dance, Prudence. You are here to enjoy yourself.'

'I don't know the gavotte,' she replied.

'But surely Miss Thurston has taught you the gavotte? No?'

'Have you ever danced with Miss Thurston?' She tilted her head to one side with a grin. 'Miss Thurston's gavotte is a little different from this.' Prudence turned her attention back to Clara and Lord Marsden. 'But how well Clara dances, Father. Look at her.'

'Where is Suzanne?' Jacques was slightly concerned.

'I'll go and look for her,' Prudence said quickly, grabbing an escape from the soldier approaching her. 'I must find my sister. I'm sorry.' She turned to go but stopped. Thys and Suzanne had stepped into the ballroom. Prudence sensed disaster as she made her way across to them. 'What are you doing here?' she demanded of Thys as she reached them. 'Father's looking for you, Suzanne.'

Thys ignored her and moved on towards Jacques, and Prudence held her breath. In his leather jacket Thys was totally out of place.

Lord Marsden spotted Thys before Jacques did and excused

himself to Clara. Commandos were not invited to the ball, and Thys must be removed before his presence impinged on the occasion.

'What's *he* doing here?' Clara had followed him.

'Excuse me.' Lord Marsden signalled to a soldier nearby to remove Thys.

'Mr Beauvilliers. May I speak to you?' Thys reached Jacques but was immediately grabbed by a soldier.

'Excuse us, sir,' the soldier said to Jacques, who had only recognized Thys when he saw Suzanne with him.

'My sincere apologies, Mr Beauvilliers.' Lord Marsden arrived beside Jacques as Thys was pulled unceremoniously away.

'But Father, Thys wanted to speak to you,' Suzanne pleaded. 'You must stop them, Father!'

'That is enough, Suzanne.' Jacques was afraid of further embarrassment.

'Is that a British soldier, Lord Marsden?' Clara said quickly.

'He is a member of the local commando, attached to the British army,' Lord Marsden replied, hoping that was an end to the incident.

'Thys Bothma is attached to the British army?' The amazement in Clara's voice didn't pass Lord Marsden by.

'My apologies. You obviously know him.' He glanced at Suzanne, slightly confused.

'Know "of" him, yes,' Clara answered. 'And therefore I must admit to being a little puzzled.'

'Clara!' Jacques' voice was firm as he turned to the door taking Suzanne's arm. 'Would you send for our carriage, please, Lord Marsden.' Lord Marsden quickly dispatched a young soldier to attend to it.

'May I not ask Lord Marsden a question, Father?' Clara defied Jacques and turned back. 'Is it normal that the son of a Boer rebel is attached to the British army, Lord Marsden?'

'Father said we were to go to the carriage.' Prudence smiled at Lord Marsden. 'Excuse us, please. It was such a lovely evening.' She led Clara away, whispering as they went, 'You cannot bear to miss any opportunity, can you!'

'It would appear it is Suzanne who misses none.' Clara smiled as she allowed herself to be led away. 'Perhaps you would care to visit us at Bonne Esperance one day, Lord Marsden. I am sorry about this,' she called back with a helpless gesture.

'Stop attracting attention to us,' Prudence said through clenched teeth.

'I think the attention is already on us, Prudence.' Clara was enjoying every moment as the large gathering watched them leave.

Jacques held Suzanne's arm tightly as he led her down the steps towards the carriage. She was crying, and he had never found a way of handling his daughters' tears.

'Suzanne,' he said as the driver opened the door for them, 'stop that.' He looked back as Thys's voice reached them.

'Mr Beauvilliers, please!' Thys called as he struggled to get to the carriage but was held back by the soldiers. 'You must listen to what I have to say!'

'Clara! Prudence!' Jacques ignored Thys and ushered the girls into the carriage ahead of him.

'Why don't you let me explain?' The carriage door slammed shut and it pulled away. 'I want to marry your daughter, Mr Beauvilliers! I love Suzanne!' His words were drowned in a clatter of iron wheels. The carriage swept around the centre square, through the gates and out into the night, beyond his reach. Thys gave up his struggle, but turned as the clipped voice of Lord Marsden demanded his attention.

'I shall expect you in my office at eight a.m., Bothma.'

Lord Marsden's office smelt of leather and polish. Deep red velvet drapes hung at the windows, held back by ropes of gold braid. The desk, drinks cabinet and every other piece of furniture in the room gleamed, as did Lord Marsden's boots. Thys was studying them carefully as he kept his head down.

'You were aware, were you not, that commandos were not invited to attend the ball?'

'Yes, sir.'

'Yet you paid no heed? You entered regardless?'

'I had to speak to Mr Beauvilliers, sir.'

'Ah yes. The little scene.' Lord Charles Marsden turned away from Thys for a moment and moved to the window, looking out. 'Is the problem that he doesn't find you a suitable match for his daughter?'

'It is more his relationship with my father, sir.'

'Mmm. Yes.' Lord Marsden turned back to Thys. His mouth was straight. It accentuated the deep lines which ran from his nose to his chin. 'I've made enquiries about your father. It would appear Miss Clara Beauvilliers is right. He is known to have joined a group of rebels. Outlaws.'

'Yes, sir.' The directness of Thys's answer surprised Lord Marsden but he went on.

'Don't you think that is reason enough for me to wonder that you have joined the commando?' He smiled suddenly, but the tone of his voice didn't change. 'Slightly puzzling?' Thys didn't answer. Lord Marsden moved closer to Thys and spoke more quietly. 'Why is your father rebelling? Against what? Against whom?'

'I cannot speak for my father, sir.'

'But you can speak for yourself.'

'Yes, sir.'

'Then why have you joined the British army?'

'I am here to serve my country, sir.'

Lord Marsden nodded thoughtfully. He turned away and moved to his desk. He sat down, and then looked up at Thys as though in need of vital information.

'Does your father know you've allied yourself with the British, Bothma?'

'My future doesn't lie in my father's past, sir.'

'Then you do see a future for your people under British rule?'

'I see a future for all the people. Prosperity, peace and independence for all.'

'That prosperity would not by any chance include the Beauvilliers girl as a wife?' Lord Marsden waited with his eyebrows raised quizzically. 'They are a wealthy family, Bothma.'

'Suzanne is not why I wear this uniform, sir,' Thys said simply.

'Then why *do* you wear it?' Lord Marsden's question was direct.

'Because I believe that unless we live as one people, the people of Africa, there will be nothing but scorched earth left behind us.' Thys looked at Lord Marsden directly. 'May I speak on behalf of my father, sir?'

Lord Marsden shrugged.

'The slaves were the tools with which he and his forefathers built this land, sir. It's not so much their emancipation which has driven him to become an outlaw. It's because they are to be placed on an equal footing with Christians, contrary to the laws of God and the natural distinction of race. That is why he will fight to the death.' Thys stopped speaking and waited. Lord Marsden doodled on the pad in front of him, as though nothing Thys had said was of any interest.

'How many things are placed at the feet of God!' He looked up quite suddenly. 'And you?'

'I believe in the freedom of all God's people.'

'You believe in God?'

'Yes.'

'You have joined us because God is British?'

'As He is Boer.' Lord Marsden nodded with a slight smile and Thys cleared his throat. 'But I find it difficult to forget who sold the black people into slavery in the first place, sir.'

Lord Marsden's eyes lit up in a sparkle of humour. 'The British you mean?' He watched Thys keenly and leant back in his chair. 'I see you have not lost the directness of the Boer.'

'If I thought joining the British army meant losing any part of my origins, I would not have joined, sir.'

'And if your father were to attack your commando, Bothma?'

'I would fight against him.'

'That is all I need to know, Bothma.' Lord Marsden stood up and Thys saluted, preparing to leave. 'There is just one thing,' Lord Marsden stopped him.

'You have known the Beauvilliers family all your life, from what I gather.'

'Yes, sir.' Thys knew why he asked. Lord Marsden took a breath and smiled, turning to the window.

'I think I shall visit Bonne Esperance soon. I should reassure them about you.' He turned back to Thys and the mask of authority returned to his face. 'But I will be keeping an eye on you, Bothma.'

'Yes, sir.' Thys saluted and left the room smartly.

'I love him, Father.' Suzanne spoke through her tears as she sat on her bed, fingering the patchwork bedcover. 'I love Thys as I've never loved anyone.'

'I know that, Suzanne.' The arguments had gone on all the way back from the castle, and Clara had been vicious in her attacks on Suzanne. Prudence had, as always, stayed quiet, yet she'd expressed her disgust with Clara more clearly than any words could have done.

'Then why were you so angry?' Suzanne pleaded with her father. 'Why did you drag me away from him?'

'My daughter had been hiding in the dark in the arms of a man and you ask me that, Suzanne?'

'How else can I meet him but in the dark? Clara despises him! She talks of Thys and his family as if they were lower than animals.'

'My feelings have nothing to do with Clara.'

'Then what *do* you feel, Father?'

Jacques didn't really know. He knew only how uncomfortable he'd felt in the castle. Although the British appeared to have accepted him as one of them, he still felt out of place. As out of place as Thys had looked.

'As a father I care only for the happiness of my daughters, Suzanne,' Jacques answered, instead of explaining his feelings.

'But Thys is my happiness!' She stopped with a thought. 'Is it the choice he made that disturbs you?'

'He has chosen a side, as his father has.' Jacques looked away.

'Have you made a choice?' As soon as the words were out of her mouth Suzanne regretted them. She got up off the bed and ran to her father. 'I'm sorry.'

'No, Suzanne.' He rested his head against hers, and her hair rose and fell with his breathing. 'You're right. I no longer know who I am. My instinct lies with the Boers, but my reason with the British. I know why Willem Bothma and his kind are afraid of being enslaved themselves. Persecution leaves an imprint on the memory of generations.' He wiped a tear from her cheek gently. 'But one thing I am sure of, Suzanne. My feelings for you.'

'Then you will know that without Thys I have no reason to live!'

Jacques' mind leapt to Eva. In many ways he had no reason to live without her.

'I would understand,' he said simply, and turned to the door. 'I will speak to Clara.'

*

Jacques found Clara in the garden, tending roses which she herself had ordered to be planted and grown. He was angrier than he had been for many years, and his anger was directed at himself as much as at Clara. She refused to come inside, so Jacques faced her in the garden, regardless of who might hear.

'No. It's not something which can wait till later, Clara.' He watched her as she clipped a rose. 'It's about your attitude and the unhappiness it is causing Suzanne. That cannot wait!'

'I would have thought Suzanne's attitude would be of more concern to you, Father.'

'Suzanne is my concern and you will respect that.' Her detached arrogance was something he could not handle. 'Do you understand me?'

'Not entirely, Father. Respect is earned and very soon this family will have none.' She clipped another rose.

'Then you may leave it, Clara.'

Clara pricked her finger on a thorn as his words hit her. 'Because I make you feel uncomfortable? Because I remind you of Mother?'

'May God forgive me but no part of you reminds me of your mother!' Jacques had spoken the words he had held back for years and they struck deep into Clara, detonating as they reached her gut.

'Do you think God forgives you for everything you do? That He forgives your lust for a slave? Christianity sits as uncomfortably on you as a saddle on an ox!' She swung away, clutching her pricked finger, the roses dropped to the ground.

Jacques' anger was raised to a level he'd never felt before, but he held himself back. 'My son, Jean Jacques, will be apprenticed to M. Claudelle. He will no longer work in the vineyards or live apart from my family.' Clara spun round, her eyes glistening with fury. 'He will live with us in the house, and he will attend both table and prayers.'

'Never.' Clara's voice was as quiet as her father's.

'I demand your obedience, Clara.'

'And if I refuse?' Her chin was tilted up aggressively.

'I will forget you were ever my daughter.' Jacques knew his words had been heard, and he knew it was because at last he had faced the truth himself.

*

Jean Jacques spent the night of the ball with Pauline. Night had turned to day as he waited for her to come to their secret place. It was the slave quarters of the Westbury farm, the only place Pauline and Jean Jacques could be certain her mother would not look for them. Pauline knew her mother would never set foot in the small building. She would never touch anything which had been touched by black people.

At first her mother's attitude had done no more than amuse Pauline.

'Mother,' she'd laughed. 'You're frightened they'll curse you!'

'Curse, be damned!' Mary Westbury had answered quickly as she scrubbed the kitchen floor. 'I'm talking about disease!'

'What disease?' Pauline had laughed.

'You might well laugh now, my girl,' Mary Westbury had chided without looking at her. 'But mark my words. Nothing but the evil they practise will ever come from those people.'

'What evil?' Pauline always enjoyed getting her mother worked up. 'Witchcraft? How exciting.'

'Don't!' Her mother had looked up at Pauline, a little afraid. 'There's no need to discuss it. Your father will be destroying the building as soon as possible.'

As Pauline slipped away from the house towards it, she wondered how such a derelict place, 'the home of so much evil' as her mother said, could contain the bubbling joy she found within it.

'I'm here, Pauline,' Jean Jacques called as she peered into the dark of the room from the low door. His face was bright as he looked at her. 'I've cleaned it up.'

Pauline stepped in, narrowing her eyes until they adjusted to the light. All the rubbish had been moved into one corner, and on the floor was a rug. She looked at the rug and then at Jean Jacques.

'Where did you get it?'

'I stole it.' He smiled.

'Good.' Pauline moved to the rug and squatted down on it, looking up at him as her fingers ran over it. 'It's soft.' She picked up a corner of the rug and held it to her face. 'It smells of sheep.'

'How do you know what sheep smell like?' Jean Jacques stood beside her.

'Because in England we farmed sheep, silly.' She yanked his hand, pulling him down beside her, laughing as he rolled on to his back. She jumped on to him, straddling him with her legs, and held his shoulders down on the ground. 'Don't think animals only live in Africa! We have them in England, too. Cows, sheep, goats.'

'Snakes?' he grinned at her.

'Yes.' She rolled off him on to the rug. 'Grass snakes. Adders. I remember when I was small, my uncle took me fishing and . . .' She stopped as she felt his eyes on her. 'You're looking at me.'

'You're beautiful.'

'Nonsense.'

'You are beautiful,' Jean Jacques repeated.

'"Pauline is the plainest of all the girls,"' my aunt used to say. "Quite plain and really rather . . ."' Her words disappeared in the mystery of the look coming from Jean Jacques.

'Beautiful,' he said.

For the first time in her life Pauline felt beautiful. She didn't move as he leaned on his elbow and looked down at her. She didn't know what to do. She'd lain beside Jean Jacques like this often. They played like puppies at the least opportunity, but this was suddenly different.

'Do you really think I'm beautiful, Jean Jacques?' He nodded. She grabbed his shoulders and wrestled with him playfully, as they always had, as if trying to recapture the innocence of what had been. But everything had changed. As their bodies rolled across the rug together, it was entirely different. She looked at Jean Jacques in sudden fright.

'No,' she whispered.

What was she saying no to? Pauline asked herself. Jean Jacques turned away suddenly, but as he did his arm brushed her breasts. She felt them suddenly swell and burn, and she looked down at her bodice quickly, certain that what she felt must show. Then she felt something else. A warm moisture was seeping between her legs and she jumped up, moving into the furthest corner of the small room.

'No.'

Jean Jacques had still not said a word. He stood across the room from her. It was a long time before either looked up. But when they did, when their faces shone across the room to one another, Pauline ran to him.

It was the most natural thing in the world when it happened.

As they held one another, as their hands moved over one another's bodies, neither had to be told what to do or what to expect. It was as if their bodies had known before they were born. Their playful puppy fights had melted in a moment into passionate love.

As Pauline lay in his arms, her head tucked into his neck, he felt a tear on his chest.

'Are you all right?' He was terrified he had hurt her. 'Why are you crying?'

'I don't know.' She laughed through her tears. 'I don't know.'

Emily had waited for Jean Jacques to return all day and she was bored. She looked down at the small pointed toe of her boot as it scuffed over the ground. The shiny black leather tip hid under a blanket of dust. She lifted her foot, twisted it among the folds of her skirt and rubbed the toe clean.

Everyone else in the family had something to do or somewhere to be, but once her lessons were over, there was nowhere for her. Even Miss Thurston, as she snored through her afternoon nap, didn't seem concerned. She paced the ground in front of the house, glancing up as she went. The beautiful white gable above the front door had tiny trickles of mildew running down towards the arched window beneath it. The two large windows on either side of the door, with their small, perfectly square panes, looked out keenly for new arrivals.

There were thirty small panes in the lower window, and twenty-four in the arched window above it. She'd counted them so many times in her short life she knew exactly. She could see a smudgy streak where Maria's dusting cloth hadn't finished its work.

Maria's daughter Rosita often played with her on days like today when the world was empty; but today she was busy helping her mother and Sunday to clear out a room for Jean Jacques. It was her father's orders. But why wasn't Jean Jacques back? He'd gone to the Westburys' to work the day before, but he hadn't come home. Emily pushed her anxiety aside and wandered to the farthest edge of the house.

With her right leg thrust forward and her toe pointed, she flung herself forward taking an enormous stride. Quickly her left leg took up the challenge and she strode across the front of the house. On her thirty-first stride she had reached the other side of the house and stopped, looking diagonally across the cobbled courtyard in front of the house. The enormous black arched door was firmly closed, and the long white building looked solemn. She thought back to the last time she had paced her way diagonally across the courtyard to the cellar door. It had taken seventy-three very long strides, and she wondered if her legs had grown longer. She took a deep breath, and noticed her boot had covered itself with dust again. She threw her weight forward and began counting her way to the cellar door. The long avenue leading to the front of the house edged into her line of vision. The oak trees lining it spread their shade generously, and she wondered at the miracle of such a tree coming from an acorn.

Seventy-one strides. She had grown. Her breathing was fast and she leaned over, gripping her knees as she panted. Her dusty boots peeked out at her from under her skirts, promising punishment, and quickly she looked up and back at the house. It stood white and secure at the foot of the dark-blue mountains behind it, with the green of the vineyards all around it.

She suddenly wondered where she had been before she was born. The house had been there. Her mother, father and sisters had been there.

Her nostrils tightened and she held her breath as the smell of fermenting grapes crept under the cellar door. It was something she'd never grown accustomed to. She looked across to the far end of the large cobbled courtyard.

The thatch of the stables ran steeply down to cover the low flat building beside it. Emily shuddered. It happened every time she looked at the slave quarters. There was one small low door and no window. It was as if the thick walls had secrets they were too ashamed to reveal.

Fifty-three paces it had taken her last time. This time she would do it in fifty. As her leg stretched out to take its fortieth stride, Emily let the breath slip out of her body and her stride shortened. She could smell the hay. She could hear the horses kicking against the stable walls as they waited impatiently for Jean Jacques, and she knew that was exactly what she was doing. She was suddenly nervous. Perhaps Jean Jacques was still with Pauline. She turned and ran towards the house without counting her strides.

'Emily!' Her father was walking his horse towards her, its hooves clattering on the hard cobbles. 'Has Jean Jacques come home yet? Has Rosita seen to his room?'

'I'm going to help her now.' She stopped as her father turned his horse. 'Where are you going?'

'I'll ride over to the Westburys' and find him.'

'No!' Emily held the horse's reins and smiled to cover her fear. 'Why don't we make it a surprise? Let him come home and find all his things moved into the house?'

'Jean Jacques has been working there long enough.'

'But they think he's a slave, because you didn't say he wasn't.' Emily stopped breathing as she realized what she'd said. She could feel her father's eyes on her.

'A son lives in the family house. Not a slave, Emily.'

Emily felt a smile spread across her lips and reach for her ears. She touched her father's hand and Jacques looked closely at the child whose life had begun as his wife's had ended. It was as if she had taken her mother's life as her own.

'You love Jean Jacques, don't you?' Jacques pushed the fine blonde streaks of hair from her forehead as she nodded seriously. He waited, allowing the light from inside her to warm him. 'Yes. We will keep it as a surprise for him.'

Jean Jacques looked around the small attic room carefully and tension gripped him as his eyes settled on the small bundle of his things. Emily could feel his tension and bounced on the bed trying to break it.

'I'm going to bring some of my things in here when Clara's not looking and I'll make it nice for you,' she chattered happily. 'This is the room I found my mother's diary in. Did you know that?'

'Clara doesn't want me here.' Jean Jacques moved to stand beside her. 'I can't sleep here.'

'You mustn't worry about Clara.' Emily jumped off the bed and wrapped her arms around his waist. 'This is your room. Father ordered it and there's nothing Clara can do about it.'

Jean Jacques took her arms from behind his back and freed himself, moving to the small gabled window. A long stem from the climbing rose outside waved its small pink flower at him. He'd never looked down on Bonne Esperance from the house

130

before. It was beautiful.

'I can't live here.'

'Why?' Emily placed herself between him and the door quickly. 'Why is everyone afraid of Clara? Why?'

'I'm not.' Jean Jacques tried to reach around her to the door, but she stood firmly in front of it. 'Emily. Please let me go.'

'Do you really want me to, Jean Jacques?' she asked with a meaning to her voice he hadn't heard before. 'Let you go?'

'I know my place, Emily.'

'In the slave quarters? You're not a slave, J.J.!'

'I am not ashamed of what I am!' Jean Jacques reacted aggressively. 'I am not ashamed of my mother.'

'Then it's Pauline?' Jean Jacques turned away and she ran around him, standing in front of him. 'You can still see Pauline, J.J.' She put her arms around him again. 'I'm very good at keeping secrets.'

Emily had spent the rest of the early evening out in the vineyards. There was so much she didn't understand and she needed to think about it. 'I know my place.' Jean Jacques' words bounced around inside her head. What did he mean by that? Was it because the colour of his skin marked him as a servant even in his own eyes? Perhaps it *was* Pauline. Emily had guessed they were in love but she hadn't seen love before, except in Suzanne, and that was terrible! She couldn't even talk to Suzanne. Emily wondered why love changed people so much when they caught it.

She looked up as she heard a bird call. She knew that sound as well as Suzanne did.

Thys waited beside his horse as Suzanne raced along the river bank towards him. When she reached him he lifted her in his arms, then brought her down against his body until her face was in front of his. Her feet didn't touch the ground. Her face was radiant.

'Father understands, Thys! He understands!' She kissed him gently and Thys responded, lowering her to the ground as the kiss grew in passion.

'Come.' He lifted her on to the horse's back and leapt up behind her.

'Where are we going?' she asked.

'Nowhere.' And Suzanne leaned back against him as Thys moved the horse on along the river bank.

'You'll fall off,' Thys said gently.

'Then you'll catch me.' Her hair had fallen out of the clips which held it up and the golden mass of curls fell over her face.

'Are you under there?' he asked. Suzanne laughed and leaned closer. She could feel the movements of the horse through his body.

'Father will say yes, Thys. When will you ask?'

Thys knew what she meant. When would they get married? When would they be together? He'd thought about it himself, constantly.

'Tomorrow?' he asked quickly.

'My father will want a grand wedding. We'll have to wait a little for that.'

'Next week,' Thys said. Suzanne turned herself around on the horse and dropped her legs one on either side of its back as she faced Thys. He was so handsome. Even the red band around his hat, the only 'uniform' which marked him as a commando loyal to the British army, suited him.

'We can wait.' He kissed her on the nose. 'Say my name.' She looked into his eyes.

'Suzanne?' he breathed, with a question at the end, and she nodded gravely. 'Suzanne,' he breathed again and she felt his voice run through her.

'How do you whistle the way you do?' she asked suddenly.

'My father taught me.' For the briefest moment Suzanne saw a glimmer of sadness in his eyes. She knew that what had happened between Thys and his father still hurt.

'Can you teach me?' She tilted her head cheekily. 'Come on!' She pushed his mouth into the shape of a whistle with her fingers. 'Show me.' Thys whistled. She moved her head back in surprise and her eyes laughed. 'Do it again.' Thys whistled again.

'Now you,' he said. Suzanne tried but no sound came out. 'Like this.' Thys whistled again and she watched him very carefully. She pursed her lips together and tried. A small trickle of spit crept between her lips, but no sound. Thys kissed her lips dry.

'You just come when you hear it,' he said, and he whistled again.

The same whistle had been answered many miles away.

The army messenger was very young and Lord Marsden watched him carefully. He was exhausted and his face was caked in mud. His trousers were ripped, the tatters held together with dried blood, covering what appeared to be open wounds.

'How long did it take you to get here?' he asked.

'Four days, sir.' The boy swayed on his feet but stayed at attention.

'Are you all right?'

'Yes, sir,' the boy answered, his body held together by military training.

'Can you tell me what happened?' The young messenger's eyes clouded with the memory, as if drawing a blind on it. 'Later.' Marsden put his arm on his shoulder. 'You need medical attention.' He was about to move to the door when the boy's voice pulled him back. It was a flat monotone.

'They came from nowhere. There was no sound. Not when they killed the watch. Not when they slit their throats.'

'It's all right,' Marsden tried gently, to stop him talking.

'They came from nowhere. Part of the night. Animals. They made no sound but they slit their throats from ear to ear.' The young messenger's voice cracked, but he went on. 'His head wasn't there – my friend. He was beside me but his head wasn't there. They walked over me. Their feet.' He looked at Marsden and screamed, 'They were so quiet!'

'Were they black?' The boy shook his head violently. 'Boer?' Marsden persisted.

The boy nodded and threw his head back, mouth wide open. 'They were so quiet!'

Marsden moved to the door, calling to the guard outside, 'Take this man for medical attention, Sergeant.' The messenger was murmuring again and again, 'So quiet.' Marsden returned to his desk quickly as the sergeant helped the messenger out. He waited for the door to close before he sat down in his chair and looked at the official letter again.

It had been written in a great hurry. The handwriting was a scrawl. 'Before sunrise. Twenty-one men dead. Boers. They – '

The letter finished in a long line which led nowhere.

Lord Marsden folded the paper carefully and laid it on the desk in front of him. His eyes rested on it and he whispered, 'Now we will see your true colours, Mr Thys Bothma.'

British troops rode fast into the grounds of Bonne Esperance and the earth seemed to shake under them. Their bright-red uniforms stood out sharply against the white of the surrounding buildings, the grey of the mountains and the green of the vines. Jacques had seen them coming for miles as they made their way down the mountain and through the valley towards him. He had not paid much attention. Troops often passed in the distance and they were always easy to see. It was only now, as he stood in the courtyard with soldiers milling around him on horseback, that he realized something was wrong.

Lord Marsden had dismounted immediately. He had met Jacques with his usual perfect manners, but when Jacques spotted Thys among the regular soldiers, he knew this was not a courtesy visit.

'I'm sorry to trouble you, Mr Beauvilliers,' Lord Marsden said. 'I'm afraid we must search your premises.'

'Why?' Jacques' eyes moved back to Thys. He looked ashamed, Jacques thought. 'Isn't that Thys Bothma?' he asked.

'It is indeed.' Lord Marsden indicated that Jacques should move a little distance away with him.

'What's happening?' Prudence called from the cellar door, and Jacques turned to her uneasily.

'Keep your sisters inside.' He turned back to Lord Marsden as Prudence crossed to the house quickly. 'Perhaps you could tell me why you need to search Bonne Esperance?' he asked. 'It seems most unusual.'

'It is.' Lord Marsden's voice was cold. 'And it is not something I enjoy, Mr Beauvilliers. But I am afraid I can make no exceptions. A British troop has been brutally murdered.' He pursed his lips. 'It was a group of Boer rebels.'

Jacques looked back to Thys where he sat quite still on his horse. 'You have my permission to search.' He turned to walk away and Lord Marsden signalled his men to dismount. Thys climbed off his horse and moved towards the barn as ordered.

Clara and Suzanne came running out of the house, even

though Prudence and Miss Thurston were shouting at them to stay inside. Emily had heard the noise outside as she sat in the barn with a lamb. She could feel it trembling in her arms.

'It's all right,' she said gently as she snuggled her face into its soft white coat. 'Those are noisy people. We'll just pretend they aren't there.'

But Emily could pretend no longer. Two men pushed the door open roughly and stepped into the barn. One of them was Thys.

'Thys!' His name came out before she could stop it. 'You gave me a fright,' she said.

'Would you come outside please, ma'am,' Thys said as though he didn't know her.

'Why've you got a gun?' she asked as she saw the gleaming musket in Thys's hand.

'Outside, please,' Thys said.

Emily stood up, holding the lamp close to her, and looked at the stranger she remembered as Thys. 'Does Suzanne know you're here?'

'Bothma,' the soldier with Thys said sharply, and Thys moved deeper into the barn with him as Emily departed. Red uniforms glimmered in the sun. They were all over Bonne Esperance, like rats.

'Why are all these soldiers here, Father?' She ran to him quickly.

'It's just routine,' Jacques said.

'Hardly routine,' Clara added coldly, as she joined them. 'Boer rebels have murdered some British soldiers, Emily. That is why they are here. They are looking for murderers!'

'Here?' Emily asked. 'Why?' She swung round as Thys came out of the barn and approached Lord Marsden.

'Barn clear, sir,' the other soldier said.

'Thank you.' Lord Marsden looked towards another soldier who rode towards him from the cellars. He was laughing and M. Claudelle was running after him, waving his arms and shouting in French.

'Keep away from my cellars! You're fit for nothing but your English ale, you British mongrels!' M. Claudelle turned abruptly and ran back to the cellars, after a well-aimed streak of spit had chased the offending soldier.

'My apologies, Mr Beauvilliers.' Lord Marsden nodded at the

soldier in question. 'Give your name to the sergeant.' He glanced at Clara. 'This is not the manner in which I expected to be calling on you.' He bowed. 'I look forward to our next meeting.'

The soldiers began moving their horses out at Marsden's signal to them to leave. Thys mounted his horse, his eyes on Suzanne, who had not spoken or moved. There was desolation in his eyes and it stretched between them like a desert.

'Surely it is his father's farm you should be searching,' Clara called to Lord Marsden. 'The Bothma farm!'

'That is where we are going,' Lord Marsden replied as he turned his horse to ride out.

'With him?' The sneer in Clara's voice caught Suzanne but was drowned by the thunder of hooves. Jacques took her arm. 'Inside, child.'

'Come, Emily.' Miss Thurston wrapped an arm around her. 'It's all over.'

'What will they do if they find the rebels, Father?' Emily asked.

'Hang them!' Clara said simply.

Mrs Theresa Bothma stood totally silent, with a daughter on each side of her as she watched. The red-coated soldiers were searching every inch of the farm and her silence confused Lord Marsden. He felt more confused as he watched Thys searching. It was as though he had never been there before, as though it wasn't his own house.

Lord Marsden's eyes passed over the Bothma house. It was strange that the Beauvilliers and the Bothmas had ever been friends, he thought. They were from entirely different backgrounds. The Bothma house was small. Smoke snaked out of the chimney, which protruded unceremoniously through the thatched roof. It was a sad, misty stream, reaching up to the blue and never getting there. Wiped out in the clarity of the African skies.

As Thys stepped out of a rundown barn further away, chickens scuttled around his feet.

'Nothing, sir,' Thys reported to the sergeant.

Lord Marsden looked at Thys as his words reached him. How did it feel to say 'Nothing, sir' when he was looking for his own father? Lord Marsden turned quickly to Mrs Bothma, a slight woman who stood like a giant guarding the doorway of her house.

'If you know your husband's whereabouts, Mrs Bothma, it would be best if you told us,' Lord Marsden said as kindly as he could. She said nothing. Marsden noticed the two slips of girls on either side of her look away from him quickly. 'I am sorry to have disturbed you.' He moved to Thys where he stood beside his horse. His eyes were on his mother. 'You may speak to your mother, Bothma.'

Black faces suddenly appeared, peering nervously from behind the house. Their eyes were enormous. They disturbed Lord Marsden almost as much as the sight of Thys moving towards his mother.

'Are you all right, Mother?' His mother looked ahead. 'Have you enough to eat?' he asked, glancing to his two sisters. The little blonde girl, Tarcie, smiled up at him. It was like a ray of sun driving through dark rainclouds. Thys returned it quickly then turned back to his mother, taking some money from his pocket. 'I'll bring you more each month.'

His mother looked at the money in his hand. Her eyes settled on it briefly, before they moved up to his face.

'What will you do if they find your father?'

'He knew what he was doing,' Thys answered.

'And you know what you are doing?' Her words cut through him, and her eyes moved back to the money in his hand. 'I do not want your money.' She turned the two small girls and pushed them into the house ahead of her. Thys stood still. His hand stayed out with the coins he had offered lying in its palm, unwanted; as he was. A stabbing pain in his back moved around him into his chest. Just at that moment a black man waved to him secretly from behind the house. As he met the black face smiling at him with his eyes, tears rolled freely down his cheeks. It was old Petrus. Thys had known Petrus all his life.

'What will they do when they find the Boer rebels?' Pauline asked Jean Jacques in a terrified whisper as she sat beside him in their secret place.

'Are you frightened?' Jean Jacques had seen Thys riding in with the soldiers and had deliberately stayed away. He'd gone quietly to the Westbury farm, instinctively running until he'd reached the security of their secret place. As he'd waited for her he'd wondered why the soldiers had not come to the Westbury farm. Then he'd known why. The Westburys were British. He remembered how, when anything went missing, the slave quarters were searched, but not the white house.

'Soldiers have always frightened me,' Pauline said. Jean Jacques hadn't known anything frightened her.

'Why?' he asked. Pauline laughed at him suddenly.

'But I'm not as frightened of them as you are of me!' Pauline would never tell him that the last time she had seen her grandfather alive he had been wearing the British uniform. She'd been tiny, but she still remembered the day her mother had told her the Turks and Egyptians had killed her grandfather. She could hardly imagine Turks and Egyptians, and decided it had been the uniform that had killed him.

'Should I be afraid of you?' Jean Jacques asked.

Pauline laid her hand on his. 'Does it disturb you?' she asked as she looked at her white hand against his brown skin.

'No,' Jean Jacques said, slipping his hand over hers and turning it until he gripped it in his.

'My mother asked me about you again.' The tease in Pauline's voice had returned. 'Again today, she asked me about you.'

'What did you say?'

'I pretended I didn't know what she was talking about.' Pauline laughed. 'When I do that she gets so cross she spits! Have you ever seen a cross woman spit?'

'Why?'

'They're so angry they can't keep the spit in. That's why. Like this.' She imitated her mother hissing and spitting, but Jean Jacques didn't laugh.

'Why?' he repeated.

'Because I think you're frightened to make love to me again.' Jean Jacques looked away and she brushed his cheek with hers. 'Are you?'

'I want to marry you,' Jean Jacques said simply.

'Are you?' Pauline repeated in his ear and ran her tongue inside the shell it formed. 'I'm not.' Jean Jacques turned, forcing her down with him into a deep pool of wonder.

It had started out as a wonderful evening: Emily's favourite kind. The day had begun with a howling north-west wind, and although it was still only March, the rain it brought with it seemed neverending. It came down in sheets and the sky was still dark and promising more. The family sat around the fire and Emily took covert looks at Jean Jacques. He always sat beside her now. She could smell hot oatmeal scones cooking in the kitchen. There was always a little cheese in them and it trickled down the edge of the scones.

'They're warm and crispy on the outside, but inside they're squidgy,' she told Jean Jacques as he took one. He'd never been a part of these evenings before, and she wanted him to enjoy them as she did.

It was at that moment that the door opened and M. Claudelle stepped in. He'd been in Cape Town for the day and heard that Mr Bothma had been caught.

Suzanne cried out and ran out of the room sobbing. Emily looked at Jean Jacques, and he at her. They said nothing, and their scones went cold, ignored.

'He's been arrested?' Jacques moved to M. Claudelle. 'You're certain?' M. Claudelle nodded.

'That's good,' Clara said as she chewed her scone with great pleasure.

'Clara!' Jacques could hardly believe his ears.

'At least we won't be bothered with soldiers searching the farm again.'

'What will happen now?' Emily asked her father. 'Does Thys know?' Thys was all she could think of at this moment. 'Where did they find Mr Bothma? Is he all right?'

'Keep quiet, Emily!' Clara turned on her. As she did she let her eyes pass over Jean Jacques quickly. Since he'd been moved to the house, Clara had behaved as if he didn't exist. 'Go to bed, Emily,' she said curtly. 'Where's Miss Thurston? What's she doing?'

'She's sick,' Emily said and ran to her father quickly. 'Will they hang him?'

'No,' Jacques said.

'No?' Clara's voice was raised in a question.

'He will have to be tried,' Jacques said. 'Please go to bed. It is the kind of night better spent in bed.' He went to M. Claudelle, going out with him. 'Clara! See to Emily.'

'I can see myself to bed.'

'Wait!' Clara followed her.

'Suzanne is unhappy.' Emily stopped at the door. 'She needs someone to talk to.'

'It will not be you!' Clara took her by the hand and led her out. A lovely wet and windy night which should have been spent around the fire with scones and Jean Jacques had been ruined.

'Good night, J.J.,' she said sadly.

'Good night, Emily.' Jean Jacques got up. He hadn't touched his scone and put it back on the plate before he moved to the door. 'Good night,' he said to Prudence.

'Jean Jacques.' He stopped at Prudence's voice and turned back to her. 'Do you enjoy the work you're doing with M. Claudelle?'

'Yes, Miss Prudence.'

'If you'd like I'll teach you all I know, too.' She looked down. 'If you'd like me to.'

'I didn't ask to be apprenticed to M. Claudelle, Miss Prudence.'

'I know,' she said. 'Father insisted because you are a man. His son.' She smiled warmly. 'And please don't call me "Miss Prudence".'

'Good night, Prudence,' he said and left the room.

In the hall Jean Jacques glanced at the front door. The rain and wind battered it, threatening to destroy the door, the house and everyone inside it. He wondered if Pauline had heard the news. His soul was clouded by loneliness as he thought of Thys. He ran quickly towards the back of the house and up the stairs leading to his attic room. He could hear Suzanne crying as he passed her door and covered his ears as he ran on to his room.

'Leave the candle, Clara,' Emily said. 'Please.'

'It's time for sleep.'

'They won't hang Mr Bothma.' Emily was not looking for re-assurance, she was telling her. 'What will happen to Thys?' she asked, more quietly.

The candle lit Clara's face from underneath as she turned to her sister from the open doorway and shrugged. A second later she had closed the door behind her.

Clara's silent answer hit Emily hard. She leapt out of bed and ran to her small table, where she flicked open her diary. She couldn't see. She didn't know what date it was or which page was open in front of her, but she wrote in the dark.

'Clara shrugged Thys Bothma out of our lives.'

Chapter Seven

'Yes.' Lord Marsden sat at his desk without looking at Thys as he stood to attention in front of him. This was not something Lord Marsden had been required to do before, and he was not enjoying it.

'The trial is over, Bothma.' He got up from his desk and moved to the large bookcase behind him. His eyes ran up and down the spines of the books without reading the titles.

Thys waited. His face was drawn and there was no life under his skin.

'Your father has been found guilty, Bothma.' Marsden turned to face him with the words. 'He will be hanged.'

'Yes, sir.' Thys's response unsettled Marsden. There was no sign of emotion as he saluted ready to leave.

'Bothma,' Marsden said. 'The local commando is required at the hanging.' He caught the flicker of surprise in Thys's eyes. 'I am certain you can be excused on compassionate grounds.' He turned back to the books, to the rigid leather spines which gave him security. 'It would be understandable,' he added.

'You said the commando would be there, sir.' Marsden turned to him slowly, and his face filled with a mixture of amazement and curiosity as Thys spoke. 'I will be with the commando, sir.'

'Would you like to see your father?'

'May I ask one thing?' Thys looked into his eyes. Marsden waited. 'Did my father admit to the charges against him?'

'He said he hadn't killed enough British soldiers.' Marsden paused and moved back to his desk, speaking as casually as he could. 'He said he hoped you were among them.'

Thys stood silent for a long, long moment. Again Lord Marsden waited.

'I would like to see my father,' Thys said.

*

It was as if all the lights in Thys's life had gone out at once. It was not because the donkergat was dark; a small dark hole in which prisoners were held during trial and before sentence was carried out. It was because the hope he had always felt for the country was beginning to fade. The depth of darkness into which his father had been thrown represented the pit Thys found himself in, and without a lamp to lead him out.

Willem Bothma didn't look up as the guard pushed open the iron door.

'Bothma,' the guard said roughly, 'your son wants to see you.'

Thys held back the door as his eyes adjusted to the almost total darkness and the shape of his father slowly formed. He was sitting on the floor, knees up and head bowed. Willem Bothma didn't acknowledge his son was there.

'Is there anything you want me to say to Mother?' Thys knew his words were meaningless, but so were any others. He watched the shadow that was his father. It didn't move. 'This isn't what I wanted, Father.'

Willem Bothma looked up and the small shaft of light from the open cell door lit the right side of his face. His look and voice focused on Thys.

'You're crying,' he said to his son, then lowered his head and disappeared into his own shadow. 'You have reason to cry.'

Thys turned away from the open door quickly, and pressed his back flat against the cold stone wall. The tears rolled down his face unchecked.

'I must be there, Father!' Suzanne begged. 'Why are you trying to stop me?'

'Because it is no place for a young girl,' Jacques said, trying to close the subject and unable to answer her truthfully.

'A hanging is no place for anybody!' Suzanne shouted. 'But it's to be a public hanging! Thys is to be there when his father is hanged and I must be with him.' She ran to Jacques and broke down in his arms. 'Please, Father.' She wept uncontrollably. Her words were jumbled in a confusion of emotions. 'If I were not with him . . . if I left him now . . .'

Jacques didn't know how to comfort her. The dolls from her childhood stared at him with glassy eyes as they stood impassively around the bedroom.

'I understand,' he said, though he didn't understand how a public hanging could return the lives of British soldiers. No more than he understood how Willem Bothma could have killed those soldiers in cold blood. 'You must be with Thys.' That was the only thing he did understand.

Prudence turned her back on Clara and climbed into bed.

'You can talk all night, but you will not convince me I should be at the hanging any more than you should be. Excuse me and good night!' She pushed her legs down the bed as Clara was about to sit on it.

'It's a public hanging for a reason, Prudence! It's to show these people what happens when they break the law.'

'Then why on earth do we have to be there?'

'To show that we support law and order.'

'Go away, Clara!' Prudence lay down. 'Do as you wish but please go away.'

'I can only assume that you care little if justice is done!' Clara had no intention of giving up. 'That justice matters little to you, Prudence?'

'Perhaps I'm not certain whose justice you have in mind. Now please leave me. I'm tired and I want to sleep.'

'Sleep?' Clara sneered. 'Should we sleep while our soldiers are slaughtered by Boers? It is only the British who can bring order to this land. The British are our hope.'

'To hell with the British!' Prudence flung the bedclothes back and glared at Clara as she sat up. 'To hell with everybody!'

'That's a fine way of looking at things.'

'You're talking to me of politics? Of British politics, of Boer politics? Am I right, Clara?'

'Yes.'

'If politics ever grew a grape and turned it into wine I might be interested. Otherwise I am not. Good night, Clara!' Prudence threw herself back on the bed and pulled the clothes up, turning her body away from Clara.

'I see,' said Clara knowingly.

'What?' Prudence didn't turn to her.

'Nothing.' Clara moved to the door.

'I'll tell you what I see, Clara!' Clara turned back as Prudence sat up in the bed again. 'I see that all you are doing is trying to impress that Lord Marsden with your British support.'

'I have no need for that.'

'No?' Prudence smiled. 'But he would be so impressed if you were there as the rope breaks Willem Bothma's neck!' Clara tensed at the door. 'Am I right, Clara?'

'I have no fear of showing my position, if that is what you mean.'

'Then you show it to him!' Prudence lay back on the bed holding the bedclothes in her hands 'Just don't try to drag the rest of the family behind you.' She covered her face with the blankets and her voice was muffled. 'But I will not be there!'

'Father said that only Suzanne was to go to the hanging, but Clara said it was her right to go too. Prudence left the room, and I said nothing.'

Emily looked up from her diary at a scratching at the window. The talk of hangings for the past few days had made her afraid of the slightest noises. She stood away from the window. She couldn't see anyone outside. The candle in her hand lit only her own face reflected in the window pane.

'Who's there?' she asked nervously as her own reflection looked back at her. 'Jean Jacques, is it you?'

'It's me.' Emily recognized Pauline's voice and opened the window. Pauline stood outside in the dark looking very afraid. 'I have to see Jean Jacques.'

'I can't get him now. It's too late.'

'Please.' Emily had never heard such fear in Pauline before. 'It's very important. Please.' Emily looked back into her room without knowing why, then turned to Pauline again and whispered, 'Wait for him in the barn.' She closed the window and moved to her bedroom door, opened it quietly and padded silently up the stairs to Jean Jacques' room.

Pauline looked around the barn from the door very carefully, shining the candle she carried in a glass mantle. It was one of her mother's most prized possessions and she'd stolen it from the dining-room table on her way out of the house. The base was silver, 'solid silver' her mother always said, pointing to the hallmark on its base. All Pauline cared was that the glass mantle would stop the candle from being blown out as she ran to meet Jean Jacques.

She saw the small lamb Emily had been taking care of asleep in a corner. It was still a baby. Her mind leaped back to what had happened in her house that evening.

Pauline had been changing for supper. She had taken off the cotton daydress her mother made her wear outside and was reaching for the smarter one her mother had laid out, when the bedroom door had opened behind her.

'Pauline?' Pauline had instinctively turned away from her mother.

'I'm dressing,' she'd said aggressively. Not wanting her mother to come in further and look closer.

'I wanted to talk to you about tomorrow.' Mrs Westbury had moved into the room and sat herself down on the bed as Pauline slipped her change of dress over her head. 'They say that the promenade is the best place to meet the young men of Cape Town. It's apparently where they all go on a Sunday.'

Then she'd stopped. She'd said no more. Pauline had looked around at her mother as she tried to button her dress.

'Go on, I'm listening.'

'Have you put on a little weight, Pauline?' Her mother had tried to pull the dress fastenings closed. 'You *have* put on weight.'

'Leave me alone, Mother!' She had tried to move away from her, tried to hide, but she was crying and she couldn't hide that. 'So I'm fat,' Pauline had said through her tears.

'And you cry for that?' Mrs Westbury had said suspiciously, and had crossed to Pauline's chest of drawers, pulling out the second from the bottom. It was the drawer in which Pauline kept the sanitary napkins her mother prepared for her every month. Mrs Westbury had stopped, the drawer wide open in front of her. It had been full of sanitary napkins. Those she'd prepared for her daughter last month were there, and those for the month before.

She had turned towards Pauline, slowly, white as a sheet.

'Pauline?' Jean Jacques' voice grabbed her from her own thoughts. 'What's happened, Pauline?' he asked as he hurried to her. 'What's wrong?' Pauline turned away from him.

'Isn't it sweet?' she said, looking at the lamb. Jean Jacques put his hands on her shoulders and turned her towards him. Her eyes were swollen with tears.

'What's happened?'

'I'm going to have a baby,' she said quickly and then ran further into a corner of the barn, looking back at him wildly. 'Why do you look at me like that? It's your child! Your baby! You did it to me!'

'Pauline,' Jean Jacques said gently as he followed her. He smiled as he reached her, and touched her. 'I love you.'

'No!' she shouted. 'You don't understand!'

'I understand. I am glad.'

'No! My parents won't accept it! They know, and they won't accept it!'

'It makes no difference if they accept it. It's our child.'

'No!' Pauline said, and the 'no' was final. Jean Jacques' face grew puzzled. He waited for her to go on but she didn't.

'The child is ours, Pauline. We'll get married and there will be nothing anyone can do about it.'

'Listen to me!' Pauline begged suddenly. Jean Jacques fell silent as he saw the terror in her eyes.

'I am forbidden to see you ever again.' Each word was crystal clear. 'It is to be as if I'd never met you.' Jean Jacques was silent. 'Do you understand what I am saying?'

'The child is mine. There is nothing they can do to change that,' Jean Jacques said slowly.

'They intend to.'

The sound of rain pouring down outside was drowned by the thunderous silence between Jean Jacques and Pauline. Her last words had lodged in his heart like three nuggets of lead.

The rainbow spanned the entire range of mountains ahead of Jacques Beauvilliers as he rode towards the Bothma farm. The morning after a night of rain often brought a rainbow with it and this was the most exquisite he had seen. Purple fused into bright green, orange into yellow and yellow into pink. Gaudy strips of colour formed an arc which lifted the earth where it met it, hanging the horizon like the base of a swing.

Jacques had no idea what he would say when he saw Mrs Bothma. It had been decided that he would go to the hanging with Suzanne. M. Claudelle had advised that he had no choice. The choice which M. Claudelle had warned he would one day have to make would otherwise be made in his absence. Jacques knew he was right. But his presence at the hanging could only have meaning if he went with Mrs Bothma's blessing. The entire community knew that she herself would not be there.

'Yes, Mr Beauvilliers. I would like you to go.' Mrs Bothma's simple words, words he had not expected, touched Jacques deeply. But he had to ensure that they weren't built on a vain hope.

'You do understand there cannot be a reprieve, Theresa. There would be nothing I could do.'

'You were Willem's friend?' she asked, needing an answer. Jacques nodded. The slightest smile crossed the little blonde Tarcie's sad eyes. 'If you are there I will know at least that his sentence will be carried out decently.'

'Theresa.' Encouraged by her faith in him, Jacques found courage to speak. 'Do you know what you are asking of me?'

'I have nobody else to ask,' she said honestly. Her body tightened as though a corset had been laced around it and her chin trembled but her eyes shone. 'I ask you to ensure my husband is given a Christian burial.' She turned sadly to go into the house, but hesitated and the two young girls stopped with her. No one looked back as she spoke. 'Please tell my son there is no room for him with me, Mr Beauvilliers.'

'Theresa.' Jacques waited but she didn't turn to him. 'Is there anything else I can do for you?'

'I have God.' At last she faced Jacques. 'I am going north and our slaves will be coming with me.' As she looked at him her face changed. It was as though quite suddenly she was looking at Lord Marsden himself. 'Though my husband is hanged, though I am unable to stop that, I will not be stopped from walking away from British laws that are against the laws of God.'

'The British are Christian people too, Theresa,' Jacques argued sadly.

Theresa Bothma put an arm around each of her daughters and looked at him with complete calm. 'The family is the centre of my Christian faith and the British will not destroy my family.' She looked across at three slaves who were building a wagon from roughly hewn wood. 'Any of my family.'

'They are freeing people from bondage,' Jacques said. 'That's all.'

'Can they free those given to us by God?' She shook her head.

'Hanging my husband will not force me to break my vow to the Almighty, Mr Beauvilliers.'

The beat of the drum was slow with the rhythm of death. Five prisoners stood on a wagon pulled by oxen behind the drummers, whose red coats and gold shoulders blazed under the bright sun. The five prisoners stood like shadows, manacled hand and foot. The crowd stood in a semi-circle around the roughly prepared gallows. To one side, separate from the red-uniformed soldiers, was a group of mounted Boer commandos, their muskets held at their sides. The plain khaki of their uniforms was relieved only by the red band around their hats. Thys was one of them.

Across the open ground, away from the soldiers and commandos, was Lord Marsden, his aide and a colonel. The colonel was immaculate. His name was Drummond, and his look was fixed on the wagon in the distance. Lord Marsden's attention was held by Clara.

She was holding a beautiful mauve parasol over her head, at a jaunty angle. Her dress was dark purple, just a hint that she did acknowledge death was calling. Her eyes caught Lord Marsden's and he looked away, although he could have looked at her for ever. Jacques Beauvilliers stood next to her in a dark suit. His head was bowed, and his arm was around the shoulder of Suzanne. Suzanne was watching Thys. She had a shawl over her head and wore a simple black cotton dress.

Lord Marsden's attention was snatched away as the sound of the rumbling wagon wheels announced that it was close. Willem Bothma was looking directly at him.

Colonel Drummond nodded to the soldiers, indicating they must move the prisoners down and walk them to the gallows. As the men were led past Thys, Willem Bothma, hobbled by his manacles, looked at his son and said quietly, 'No more tears?' Thys's eyes flashed away from his father and stared ahead as Willem Bothma spat at him. A soldier pushed him in the back with his musket.

'Move.'

Colonel Drummond dug his heels into his horse and his mount moved towards the gallows. He watched as the men were led up to five swinging nooses. Colonel Drummond nodded to the soldier beside the gallows. The first Boer prisoner was led up and the soldier placed a noose around his neck. One at a time, he did the same to each man. None showed any fear, regret or resistance. Their faces were passive.

Colonel Drummond turned towards a priest nearby. He was robed in the cloth of the Anglican Church and accepted Colonel Drummond's silent permission to move towards the gallows with his bible. As he approached, a roughly dressed man stepped out from the crowd and Colonel Drummond's look darted to him. 'He is their dominee, sir,' Marsden said quickly. 'Their church man.' Colonel Drummond reluctantly nodded that he could proceed to the gallows.

'Although you have been found guilty by the English court, and in the eyes of God, the Lord will still listen to your pleas of forgiveness.' The preacher hesitated as the dominee beside him began to speak in Afrikaans. He was reciting the 23rd psalm. The priest turned back to the gallows and continued in English, the two voices mingling in a strange unearthly way.

'O heavenly Father, on this day we beseech you to hear our cry for forgiveness of our sin,' the priest said.

'Though you walk in the shadow of death yet you will fear no evil,' the Afrikaans voice answered.

Colonel Drummond brought his gloved hand down sharply and the drums rolled, drowning out both preachers' voices. The colonel drew his sword in a smooth elegant movement and held it up high.

Thys's eyes moved from the sword to his father and his eyes closed.

The colonel's sword sliced through the air, soldiers kicked the boxes from under the men and the bodies swung forward, ropes snatching at bare necks. Time froze with the forward swing of the bodies, then, as though God had slowed the world and everything in it, four bodies swung back and the fifth, Willem Bothma, flew forward.

The rope around his neck had broken.

The scream which rose from the crowd died to utter silence. Then slowly an amazed babble took its place. A woman gasped, another cried.

'God be praised!' another shrieked to heaven.

Thys opened his eyes. His father was struggling to his feet at the base of the gallows. The crowd erupted and ran towards him, out of control.

'What's happened?' Suzanne murmured without looking. The crowd were singing and shouting praises to God.

'He's alive,' Jacques said in amazement and looked towards Thys. 'By God's hand.'

A sudden shot brought silence and Colonel Drummond regarded the crowd through narrowed eyes as he called, 'Prepare a fresh rope.'

'No!' the crowd screamed.

'He will be hanged by the neck until he is dead!' Colonel Drummond yelled over the outcry.

Lord Marsden spun his horse and galloped to him. 'Excuse me, sir.'

'Order your men to keep the crowd back,' Colonel Drummond spat.

'Keep them back!' Lord Marsden shouted quickly to his men, then turned to the Colonel again. 'You can't do it, sir.'

'Can't, Major?'

'No, sir. It's against the law. There was an occasion before when such an action brought about a riot!'

Colonel Drummond ignored Marsden and glanced at the crowd, which was almost breaking through. He gestured to a soldier to aim his gun at Bothma and immediately the crowd fell silent.

'The people have never forgiven us, sir.' Marsden spoke earnestly. 'It cannot happen again!'

'If they didn't learn then, Major, they will learn now.' He pointed to the gallows. 'Replace the rope! Prepare the man!' The drumming began again and a woman ran out of the crowd.

'You British bastards! God has set that man free and you set yourselves above His judgement!' The soldier with Colonel Drummond obeyed his order and brought his musket down across the woman's back.

Jacques felt a surge of anger rise in him. He let go of Suzanne and raced towards the colonel, shouting up at him, 'That woman is right, sir. God has seen fit to free that man!'

'You question my command?' Colonel Drummond said coldly.

'I question your justice!' Jacques shouted back at him.

'Get back to your place before I hang you with him, Boer!'

Jacques' anger erupted and he grabbed at the sword in the colonel's hand, yanking it towards him, trying to pull him off his horse. A soldier struck his rifle across the back of Jacques' head and he fell to the ground. Suzanne screamed and rushed towards him.

'Keep that woman back!' Colonel Drummond shouted. The confusion was beginning to threaten him.

'There'll be a riot, sir,' Lord Marsden warned.

'Move that man!' the colonel ordered, indicating Jacques as Suzanne knelt beside him.

The drums rolled louder. The colonel raised his sword once again, and Willem Bothma, with a fresh rope around his neck, looked ahead unseeingly as though he was already dead. Thys still hadn't moved.

'No!' Suzanne screamed as the sword flashed down above her and she spun low to the ground towards the gallows. Willem Bothma's feet dangled in mid-air. The rigid legs kicked out.

'No!' Suzanne cried out again, burying her face.

The only sound was the creaking of saddles, of horses' hooves as they moved restlessly. Through the silence Thys's voice rose on wings, ringing out to the furthest reaches of the land. It was a blood-curdling cry which tore at the solid blue sky above. He broke ranks, pushing his horse through the other soldiers. He rode straight towards the colonel, his musket held high in one hand.

Colonel Drummond glanced at the soldier beside him nervously. The soldier pulled back as Thys rode on towards them with his scream racing ahead of him like a piercing wind. He reached Colonel Drummond and brought his musket down on his shoulders, knocking him off his horse into the dirt. Tears of rage filled Thys's eyes. His horse reared as it picked up the electric tension in the air.

'If it takes me the rest of my life,' Thys yelled, 'I'll kill every Englishman I see. I'll kill you until there's not one of you left to stain our land with your heathen ways!'

'Aim,' Marsden said quietly to his small company of men. They raised their guns and glanced at one another uneasily as Thys looked back at them. Suddenly he turned his horse and raced away, with the guns firing after him.

'Thys!' Suzanne screamed and ran after him. 'Thys!'

Lord Marsden suddenly saw Suzanne in direct line of fire. 'Cease fire!' he ordered.

A British soldier broke ranks and rode towards Lord Marsden. 'The girl could be hurt, sir.'

Colonel Drummond pulled himself to his feet, slightly dazed, and looked around him in confusion. He turned to Marsden the instant he noticed the soldier riding after Suzanne and Thys. 'What is that soldier doing? Fire! Order your men to fire, damn you!'

'Shall they shoot him or the girl first, sir?' Marsden asked calmly.

The soldier reached Suzanne and swept her up on to his horse. He looked back for a moment, then turned and rode on after Thys with Suzanne.

'Arrest that man!' Colonel Drummond yelled at Marsden, pointing after the soldier. He had lost control and he knew it. Marsden climbed down off his horse and walked to where Jacques Beauvilliers lay on the ground, holding out a hand to help him to his feet.

'After we have seen the results of your hanging, sir,' he said calmly. 'Perhaps we will have to arrest everyone.'

'I will report you, Major,' Colonel Drummond threatened.

'And I you, Colonel,' Lord Marsden said quietly. He turned to one of his men. 'Cut down those bodies.'

'Leave them!' Colonel Drummond's voice was pure ice. 'They will hang until their corpses rot!'

'In hell, sir?' Lord Marsden paused. 'Along with yours and mine?'

There was a long silence, the crowd watching in hushed expectation. Then Colonel Drummond looked around in bewilderment.

'You will pay for this, Major Marsden!'

'Doubtless we all will.' Lord Marsden's eyes moved to the cloud of dust following Thys, Suzanne and the soldier.

Thys rode fast, mumbling through his tears. He'd seen the soldier with Suzanne following him. 'Leave me . . .' He kicked his horse and rode on faster. The soldier carrying Suzanne in front of him galloped on in pursuit. Suzanne's thoughts were on nothing but Thys up ahead.

Thys reached a rock outcrop and leapt off his horse, moving to the rock edge where he would be above the soldier and Suzanne. He could hear them rounding the corner below him and lifted his musket. He primed it and aimed it.

'Thys! I want to come with you!' Suzanne's voice called before she appeared below him. Thys's grip on the musket loosened as he saw her and the musket touched the rock, making a slight sound. The soldier looked up and reined in his horse. Suzanne saw Thys at the same moment. She jumped off the horse and began climbing up the rocks towards him.

'Stay where you are, Suzanne.'

'I've got to speak to you, Thys,' she shouted at him and kept going.

'I'm not coming back.'

'Then take me with you!'

The soldier waited at the foot of the rise, looking away as their voices reached him. Thys aimed his rifle at the soldier who had brought Suzanne to him.

'I'd rather you killed me than him,' she said quietly.

'You belong with your own people. Suzanne. As I belong to mine. Go to them!' he pleaded, though his voice was firm. 'I will always love you. Always. Now go.' He turned from her and moved towards his horse.

'Thys!' Suzanne cried as he mounted. 'I'll never stop trying to find you.' His back was straight as he rode slowly away.

'Goodbye, Thys,' she called desperately. He didn't look back.

The soldier climbed up to Suzanne as she sat quite still, staring after Thys. He held out his hand to her to help her down.

'I'll find him.'

It had taken three hours in the burning midday heat to bury the dead. Jacques had erected a rough wooden cross on Bothma's grave; watched by Clara as she stood in the shade of the trees. She had distanced herself from him.

After Suzanne had been brought back by the soldier, Lord Marsden had offered to take both her and Clara back to Bonne Esperance, in the Beauvilliers' carriage. Jacques had refused any medical help for the gash on the side of his head, and Marsden sensed the gulf which had widened between them. Between all the people. Though Jacques had said he wanted to be alone, he looked into the distance where he knew the sea to be. Eva to be.

As the carriage drove back to Bonne Esperance, with Lord Marsden and the two women inside, Suzanne had watched, without seeing, the soldier who rode beside it, leading Lord Marsden's horse.

'It's very kind of you to see us home, Lord Marsden.' Clara smiled. 'Very kind.'

'It's the least I can do.' As always there was a slight bow of the head when Lord Marsden spoke to her and Clara liked it.

'Did my father say where he was going?' she asked casually.

'He said nothing.'

Clara nodded and looked out of the window at the soldier riding beside them. 'Why did he do that?'

'I beg your pardon?'

'The soldier.' Clara indicated him with a daintily gloved hand. 'Did he know Thys Bothma? Were they friends?'

'No,' Lord Marsden said as he looked at the soldier himself. 'I think he was taking Suzanne to the man she loves.'

A silence fell. Suzanne hadn't listened to them and didn't hear the silence either. She was in a world far away, with Thys.

'You were disturbed by the hangings, weren't you?' Clara eventually asked Lord Marsden.

'As many of my men were.' He looked out at the soldier again. 'He expressed the feelings of many of us.'

'But you don't deny he deserved to be hanged. Those British soldiers were most brutally murdered.'

'I've often wondered,' Marsden paused, 'when one is murdered: would the method make any difference?' He smiled.

'Those Boers are very cunning. It would not be out of their realm to have tampered with the rope,' Clara went on.

'I hardly think so.'

'Perhaps when you get to know these people a little better.' She smiled sweetly. 'But I think you can rest assured that re-hanging Mr Bothma did not challenge God's word.'

Lord Marsden returned Clara's smile. He sensed she was not all sweetness and suspected she had a rod of steel running through her. But there was something about her which aroused him. As for the hanging, he could forget it now. These things happened in Africa.

*

During the time Jacques and his two daughters had been away Miss Thurston had kept Emily busy, even though the small girl's mind had been many miles away, with Thys and Willem Bothma.

'I have an idea!' Miss Thurston said brightly. 'Why don't we go outside with your net and catch ourselves some butterflies.'

'It's unkind.'

'But you've caught so many beautiful butterflies. It helps you to study them. Come along.'

'No,' Emily refused. 'I don't want to kill any more.'

'But there are plenty of them.'

'As there are plenty of Mr Bothmas?' Emily looked down sadly. 'What will happen to Thys and Suzanne?'

'I don't know, child.' Miss Thurston had run out of answers, and looked at the upside down watch pinned to her bodice. 'It's late.' She crossed to the window and gazed out. 'No butterflies today. Look. More rain. Where has Prudence got to?'

Prudence had been in the cellars all day, watching M. Claudelle. It was the stage in the process of wine-making she enjoyed most: the blending. M. Claudelle fascinated her, he was a master wine-maker and she wanted to learn everything she could.

As she stood very close to him she hadn't noticed what was happening. Her concentration was on other things. M. Claudelle had tried to ignore her closeness, he had even walked away from her several times during the day, but suddenly he could hold back no longer. The small girl who'd been close to him all her life was suddenly a fully grown woman and her body was touching his.

Prudence moved away slightly. 'I'm sorry,' she apologized.

'Isn't that why you work here in the cellars with me when your father is away?

Prudence didn't understand what he was talking about. 'Since Father doesn't think I should work here, I can only do it when he's away.' She smiled. 'But one day he'll allow me to, because I will have proved I can!'

M. Claudelle moved closer and gazed at her keenly. Prudence reacted to something in his look which frightened her.

'Jean Jacques will be back soon,' she said quickly.

M. Claudelle smiled. 'Jean Jacques is not here, Prudence. And your father is not here. You should not be, but you are. You find it exciting here? No?' His hand ran down her hair and she pushed it away violently.

'No!' She turned to run. All her instincts told her to go, but he grabbed her arm, and swung her back to him, pulling her against his body. Prudence felt a hard lump against her pelvis. She gulped as M. Claudelle put his hand roughly over her mouth and looked down at her, lowering her to the floor. He looked mad.

She kicked, trying to free herself, but his hand pushed up her skirt. She screamed and bit his hand as he held it across her mouth. He pulled back and fumbled with his belt, tearing it off as she opened her mouth to scream again. He lashed the belt across her face, sending her falling back on the ground, and forced himself on to her. Into her. She tried to scream with the pain and his hand grabbed her mouth, his shoulder jamming her chin hard against the floor. He was heaving up and down on top of her, sweating profusely, his face in a taut grimace.

His heaving went on and on. On and on. The pain grew worse and Prudence thought she was being torn apart. Ripped from between her legs up through her body. She felt sick. She choked as vomit poured from her mouth, but he kept on pounding her body under his. Kept tearing her in two from the inside. He was hideous and terrifying.

Suddenly his body slumped on top of her and for a moment Prudence thought he was dead. She hoped he was. She lay absolutely still, afraid to move. Then a low moan came from him, as if from his soul and he pushed himself away from her and ran out of the cellars.

Prudence didn't move for a long, long time. She couldn't. Her back ached and her legs didn't belong to her. She was covered in her own sick, which mixed with the tears running down her face in torrents.

'No!' she wailed, curling herself into a ball on the floor and pushing herself sideways across the hard flagstones to hide amongst the vats. Hiding from the world. From the terrible pain, and the deep shame.

It had been hours after that that the rain had come, and Miss Thurston had commented so casually, 'More rain.' It was storming now. Thunder crashed and lightning sneaked inside the cellars as Prudence lay among the vats longing for it to reach out a little further and strike her. Every fibre of her being lay in pieces around her as she begged the lightning to find her and destroy her.

'Go and look for her, Emily.' Miss Thurston had decided Prudence really was late. Emily ran out happily, glad of any excuse to go out in the storm. 'Put your coat on,' Miss Thurston called, but Emily didn't listen. She leapt across the rivers now running over the courtyard and looked up with delight as lightning lit the heavens in sheets. She waited in mid-stride for the thunder. It came, shaking the earth under her feet. She got more of a fright than she had expected and tore on towards the cellars, calling Prudence's name for comfort as she opened the heavy door into the cellars.

'I'm soaking wet! Miss Thurston will be so cross. Prudence! Where are you?' She moved inside, peering around. Lamps were lit but it was still dark. 'It's supper time,' she said. 'Miss Thurston was grumbling about you being in here again.' Emily stopped. She could see Prudence's feet sticking out from underneath the row of vats strapped up on their huge wooden supports.

'What are you doing?' Emily jumped back as she saw Prudence clearly. Her face was bruised. She was bleeding, and there was blood on her skirts. There was blood on the floor. 'What's happened?' Emily asked in terror, imagining she was surrounded by blood.

'It's all right, Emily.' Prudence spoke calmly as she crawled out. 'I was just trying to reach under the vat.' She looked at Emily, who obviously didn't believe a word she had said. 'I was trying to get behind that vat,' Prudence tried again. 'I know it was silly. I cut myself.' Prudence stopped. Emily's eyes were large, terrified pools. Prudence moved to her quickly and wrapped her arms around her as her body began to shake.

'Don't say anything.'
'You're hurt.'
'Don't say anything. Please, Emily.'
'But there's blood.'
'Emily. I'm begging you.'
'But you need help. I must get Miss Thurston.'

'No!' Prudence shouted. 'Forget about it.'

'Forget!' Emily looked at her in horror. 'Where's M. Claudelle?' she said, casting a look around the cellars. It was only as she saw Prudence turning away at the mention of M. Claudelle, that Emily sensed something.

'Him?' Emily said meaningfully, but not really knowing what she meant. A crack of lightning and thunder shook the cellar.

'What has happened must be forgotten.' Prudence's voice rode on the tail of the thunder. 'Father must never know.' She wiped a trickle of blood from her mouth. 'Do you understand what I'm saying, Emily?'

'It's why Father doesn't want you to work with men,' Emily said, although she didn't understand.

'Do you think you can help me to the house without Miss Thurston seeing us? You could tell her I'd gone to bed, that I had a headache.' Prudence needed to change the subject and was afraid. Emily smiled her yes. She wanted to help Prudence. She liked her very much, and maybe even more now she could see she wasn't as strong as she appeared.

Jean Jacques was also out in the storm: outside the Westbury barn, following Mr Westbury closely as he hurried towards it.

'I've got to talk to you about Pauline, master.'

'We no longer need you to work here,' Mr Westbury said, moving away from him deliberately. Jean Jacques looked after him as Mr Westbury entered the barn and began to groom a horse, though it didn't need it. 'Come inside.' He turned to Jean Jacques. There was a softness in his eyes, but his voice didn't reflect it. 'Do you care for Pauline?' he asked.

'I love her.'

Mr Westbury looked away immediately.

'I love her,' Jean Jacques repeated.

'Then leave her alone.' Mr Westbury leaned his head against the horse's flank. 'Take your freedom and go.'

'Where to?' Jean Jacques asked. A crash of thunder drowned his voice and he said again, 'Go where, master? What freedom?'

'Anywhere. Find yourself a new life.'

'Why?'

Mr Westbury moved up close to him quickly. His face was tense and harsh.

'Listen to me, boy. I love my daughter. I care for Pauline more than I care for anything, and I will not have her hurt.'

'I would not allow her to be hurt.'

'Damn you!' Mr Westbury stared at him. 'You have no control over your own life, how can you control my daughter's?'

'I am not a slave, Mr Westbury.' As Jean Jacques spoke, he realized that that was not the problem. It was something he could do nothing about. His colour. He was suddenly desperate, and it sounded in his voice. 'I will take her away. We will find a way together.'

'And us?' Mr Westbury looked lost. As though he was speaking someone else's words, and didn't understand them properly. 'We deserve a decent future in this country. We've worked hard for one.'

'As I have!' Jean Jacques walked away, and the second he stepped outside the rain covered him in a silver shroud. 'Pauline's future is with me.' He ran on into the sheets of rain.

'Pauline has never met you!' Mr Westbury shouted after him, stepping into the rain himself. 'Do you understand what I'm saying?'

Jean Jacques stopped, and turned back. They looked at one another through a wall of water.

'She's carrying my child,' Jean Jacques' voice called through it. 'There is no freedom for me without Pauline and my child!'

Mrs Westbury moved away from the window in the house. She had seen and heard most of what had been said, and realised that her husband couldn't handle the problem. She pulled her bodice straight, and decided she would face him with the only solution. If necessary, she would organize and carry her plan through on her own.

Chapter Eight

Clara, Suzanne, Lord Marsden and the soldier arrived back at Bonne Esperance in the morning. Emily rushed out to greet her father, but skidded to a stop on seeing Lord Marsden. He helped Clara down from the carriage with such elegance. Suzanne did not wait for him to help her, but ran straight into the house.

'Perhaps I could call on you again, Miss Beauvilliers?' Lord Marsden asked.

'I would be delighted, Lord Marsden.' She smiled invitingly. 'You will join us for breakfast perhaps?'

He agreed, and soon they were sitting at the dining-room table eating kippers. Nobody commented on the fact that neither Suzanne nor Prudence had joined them. Miss Thurston had been most impressed by Lord Marsden, rushing around to ensure breakfast was exactly right. She'd complained to Maria that the silver was not perfectly clean; she could not see her face in it. Lord Marsden hardly noticed; he hadn't seen her face himself.

As they sat around the table, conversing politely, Emily decided human beings were decidedly odd. They could talk, with great conviction, about nothing. They'd discussed *for hours* the proposed voyage of the first English steamship to New York. What had that to do with anything happening around them? What amazed Emily most was the manner in which Lord Marsden disposed of his kipper bones. With incredible sleight of hand, just a dab of the napkin to his mouth, they had gone. Up his sleeve? Emily noticed that Clara was very impressed, and concluded that was why he practised such a fine art at the breakfast table.

'The hounds have a wonderful head when on a jackal,' Lord Marsden said. 'The brush is not as fine or as full as a fox, but the scent is better.' Although Lord Marsden obviously disapproved of the pink being worn for a jackal instead of a fox, he finished by adding, 'As long as one shoots like a gentleman, perhaps it is equally acceptable.'

Was it possible to kill anything like a gentleman, Emily wondered? Jackal or fox? Even as the breakfast pageant ended, she still hadn't heard about Mr Bothma, Suzanne, Thys or even where her father was.

'Perhaps you might hear news of Father in Cape Town,' was all she had heard Clara comment to Lord Marsden. He had replied that he was certain to, and would inform her as soon as he did.

Then at last he left, riding off with the soldier, who had eaten his kippers outside. The soldier would have enjoyed his more than anyone, Emily decided. He'd have been able to put his hand in his mouth to pull the bones out.

When Emily had at last heard from Clara what had happened at the hanging of Mr Bothma, she spent hours outside Suzanne's door, trying to get her sister to let her in. But Suzanne had not opened the door, or said a word.

Prudence had gone back to the cellars as soon as she could. M. Claudelle had been working and turned away sharply as she stepped in. He hung his head and backed away as Prudence moved towards him calmly.

'Good morning, M. Claudelle.' Having no reply, she'd gone on, 'Is it not a good morning, M. Claudelle?'

'Good morning.' M. Claudelle took comfort from her smile and nodded.

'It is good?' Prudence repeated.

'Yes. It is good.'

'Good.' Quite suddenly she had swung a hard wooden pole from behind her back and smacked it up between his legs. He'd screamed with pain and fallen to the floor in agony as she had left the cellars with a last threat. 'If you ever so much as look at me again, I will kill you myself.'

M. Claudelle stayed in the cellars all day. He would have to leave as soon as he could without raising suspicion. Until then, he would never know when Prudence might tell her father what had happened. He decided he would have to find some reason to return to France.

Jacques had walked all night and most of the following day, covering many rough miles to reach the Malay quarter of the small fishing village which Eva called home. She'd been startled when she'd found him outside, with scrawny dogs yapping at him and running in circles around him. The wound on his head had dried in an ugly crust. His clothes were torn and his legs shook, unable to carry his weight another step. She had never seen him so desperate.

'Our people have been divided for ever,' was all he said.

He lay totally still in Eva's arms that night. The next and then the next. She comforted his fears with love until, at last, Jacques found his identity anew. It was with her, and his inner world was at peace again. Until he talked of marriage.

'You will be mistress of Bonne Esperance, Eva. Jean Jacques will take up his rightful place as our son.'

'Please don't force me to live there,' Eva said gently.

Jacques wrapped his arms around her from behind, as she sat on the edge of the bed. 'We have to protect Jean Jacques, and if we marry he will be recognized as my legal son and heir. I would sign the official papers and it would be a fact nobody could dispute.'

'Please don't ask me to live in another woman's house.' As she spoke, an image of Jacques' wife, Emily, filled Eva's mind. She would always be mistress of Bonne Esperance. Eva remembered holding that small slippery baby as it had snatched its first breath of life; and she asked Jacques, as she did every time she saw him, 'How's the little one? Little Emily?'

'She's fine.' Jacques kissed her on the shoulder tenderly and lay back. His body still ached but he was happy. 'I have heard you, Eva. In time I will make you see there is no reason for your fears.' What Jacques didn't know was that fear didn't keep Eva away from Bonne Esperance. It was respect for his wife.

'Bonne Esperance is your place. With me,' Jacques said to himself.

'And Jean Jacques? You talk of people being divided. He has no people.'

'He has us.'

'Not if we want him to be truly free.' Eva turned and looked into Jacques' eyes. She loved him deeply and felt aggressively protective. She knew how much he needed the security of her love. She smiled, pushing his hair away from his face. The quiet strength in his eyes was still there. 'I will marry you, Jacques.' She needed the strength she saw in him. 'I will marry you, but I will not live at Bonne Esperance.'

In Jacques' absence, Prudence had taken over the running of the estate, and M. Claudelle kept away from her. Although she had discovered Jean Jacques had an instinctive understanding of the process involved in wine-making, she also found he was not working as well as before. It was as if he was lost.

'Is there something the matter?' she asked him as she walked with him from the cellars to the labourers' quarters.

'No,' Jean Jacques assured her.

'There is with me.' She nodded towards a group of men sitting under the shade of one lonely tree. 'They won't do anything I tell them. They won't move.' She shrugged. 'Because I'm a woman.'

'They will only take orders from the master,' Jean Jacques told her.

'But you will take orders from me?'

'Yes.'

'Thank you.' Prudence smiled as a bond of understanding stretched itself between them. 'I need the men in the vineyards. I'm planting roses.'

'Roses?' Jean Jacques looked at her curiously.

'It's an idea I have.'

'Roses shouldn't be among the vines,' Jean Jacques said.

'Nor should the little greenflies. If we plant a rose at each end of each row of vines, we would be warned early.'

'Warned of what?'

'The greenfly attack roses first.' Prudence explained. 'Don't you see how simple it would be, Jean Jacques?' He nodded. She was right and it didn't surprise him. Prudence had never surprised him; but then he'd never presumed women were lesser beings than men.

'I will get the men to the vineyards,' he smiled.

'Thank you.' Prudence was about to move away when she stopped and turned back to him. 'For the first time I think I understand how you've felt all your life, Jean Jacques.' She glanced at the workers. 'Nobody sees further than the colour of your skin, as they see no further than my sex.'

Jean Jacques turned away quickly to the workers, in case his desperation led him to tell Prudence what had happened. He knew that when the Westburys looked at him, they didn't see the father of their daughter's child, or even the disgrace of their daughter having lain with a man before marriage. They saw only his colour.

'He loves her,' Mr Westbury said simply as he faced his wife.

'You call what he has done to our daughter, love?' The arguments had gone on and on. Pauline had kept herself away from her parents, and from Jean Jacques. She was confused and beginning to lose control of her own life.

'She's carrying the child of a man she loves, Mary. It's what she wants and we must accept it.'

'He's a slave!'

'He is the son of Jacques Beauvilliers.'

'The bastard son borne of a slave! Do you think that makes him any more acceptable? No! Less!' Mary Westbury moved away from her husband to the other side of the room. She had decided she must take the entire matter in hand herself.

John Westbury looked at his wife across the room and acknowledged the truth. No matter how polite she was to Jacques Beauvilliers, the day she had discovered that the boy she considered to be a slave was his son, his wife's politeness had become no more than the formality due to a wealthy man.

'There is no way I will allow our daughter to bear the child of a slave. I will not suffer the shame it will bring on this family, and that is final,' she said.

'You talk as if there will not be a child.'

'Not for Pauline.' She held the silence brought by her words as long as she could. 'I will be the one to give birth.' Pauline stepped quietly into the room at that moment and her father looked at her but said nothing. Her mother hadn't seen her.

'It will be perfectly simple,' Mary went on. 'I will ensure that it appears I am carrying a child. Pauline will be kept at home. Away from public life. People will believe she is caring for me.' John Westbury had seen panic grip Pauline's face as she listened to her mother. 'It is our duty to protect our daughter,' Mary finished.

'It's impossible.' He spoke almost to himself. 'You can't.'

'It's the only way.'

'No one will accept it, Mary. How can you ever think of such a thing?'

'I will not allow my daughter to bear the child of a half-caste!' she interrupted sharply.

'You can't deny it! It is a fact!' Mr Westbury's voice rose.

'And I will do everything in my power to keep that fact from destroying us!' His wife kept her face away from her husband and Pauline. 'It will be *my* child and that's an end to it.'

'And if it is not white?' Mr Westbury asked.

There was a very long silence. His words were words nobody wanted to hear. Not even Pauline.

'There will be a miscarriage.' Her answer cracked the glass wall of protection Pauline had built around herself.

'No!' she screamed. Her mother swung round with fright as Pauline ran to her, hitting at her. 'You want to kill my child!'

'Pauline.' Mr Westbury moved to her and pulled her back. She collapsed in his arms, breaking down.

'You won't let her kill my baby, will you? I want my child. I love Jean Jacques.'

'You're too young to know what you want, Pauline.' Her mother had regained her control and moved to her daughter firmly. As she reached out to touch her, Pauline pulled away, closer to her father. 'You must trust us to know what's best, Pauline.' As his wife's eyes sought his, insisting he add his own assurance to her words, John Westbury lowered his head and looked at his daughter. He took her hand and led her from the room.

'You can trust me, Pauline,' he said, wondering as he spoke if it was true.

Clara had received a secret message from Lord Marsden. She'd read it with a mixture of anger and shame. Immediately she'd sent for Prudence. There were matters to discuss, she'd said, concerning their various responsibilities during their father's absence.

'Jean Jacques helped me to get the men to work and everything's running quite smoothly,' Prudence reassured her. 'Father will be pleased.'

'I doubt he is bothered,' Clara said, and handed her the message at last. Prudence was puzzled. The message was on army paper.

'Who found him in the Malay quarter?' She turned the official message over, looking for a signature. 'I'm not sure I understand why he was being looked for in the first place; and especially by the army!'

'Lord Marsden found him.' Clara held her head high arrogantly.

'Ah.' Prudence understood. 'So he has his uses – other than neatly disposing of kipper bones.'

'What are you talking about?'

'Emily told me.' Prudence laughed as she remembered what Emily had said. 'She was most impressed, but I'm not certain it would be a sound basis for marriage!'

'You are so stupid, Prudence.' Clara glared at her. 'Can you imagine what he thinks?'

'Father? Yes. I'm sure he wasn't at all pleased at being searched out by the entire British army.'

'The Malay quarter is hardly a place Lord Marsden would expect to find our father!'

'If it bothers you so much you should have gone looking for him yourself.'

'I would not set foot in such a place.' Clara's body wrapped itself tightly around the core of steel inside it. 'I simply wished to inform you that I will be taking over the running of Bonne Esperance from now on.' She turned away as she took the message back from Prudence and added casually, 'Jean Jacques will be moved out of the house.'

'I beg your pardon?'

'I am concerned for the family.'

'But not for him?'

'The presence of that boy in this house is an insult!'

'Oh.' Prudence went to sit down. 'When will you be seeing Lord Marsden again, Clara? I can only presume this is to impress him, though I don't understand how removing Jean Jacques will wipe Lord Marsden's memory of our father in the Malay quarter!'

'I shall reassure him.' Clara was quite calm.

'Ah! So you are seeing him! He has not dropped you in the Malay quarter along with Father?'

Clara approached Prudnce slowly. Her sting was over her back, like a scorpion.

'Talking of men, Prudence. I would like to enquire whether you are still flaunting yourself in front of M. Claudelle?' Prudence tensed. She wondered if Emily had not kept her silence.

'I don't have to flaunt in front of men, Clara.' Prudence smiled. 'Do you?'

'Then why do you spend so much time working with him? You must admit it seems a little odd.'

'Everything seems odd to you, Clara.' Prudence moved to the door, unsure she could control the trembling she had felt at the mention of M. Claudelle. 'But let me assure you of one thing. Driving Jean Jacques out of the house will not change who he is or where he came from. Not one jot!' She closed the door behind her, then opened it again, poking her head around it. 'It would surely be easier for Lord Marsden to accept that he is our brother than the inference that we still keep slaves!'

'Never!' Clara hissed as though she had stung herself. Her blood boiled as she glanced again at the message in her hand. It was a threat to her future life and she strode to the door in agitation. 'Maria! Rosita! I need your help to remove some things!' she shouted.

As Jean Jacques' things were being hurled out of his attic, he was trying to keep hold of the only part of his life which mattered to him: Pauline and the child she was carrying. For a long time Jean Jacques had been trying to speak to Pauline. She had always run. This time he had hidden in the bushes along the path she walked every day. He had waited until she passed, and then grabbed her, pulling her into the bushes with him. She screamed but he silenced her quickly.

'I have to talk to you.' He removed his hand from her mouth carefully. She wasn't going to scream again. 'I want you to come away with me, Pauline. I want us to start a new life together.'

'Where?' she asked. 'How?'

'We'll find a way. There's always a way.'

'Listen to me, Jean Jacques.' Her eyes searched his face. 'We can never see each other again. Never!' Jean Jacques let her go, wondering why he was here. She was so cold. He could have been a stranger.

'And that's what you want, is it?' Pauline looked away. 'Tell me,' he said firmly.

'Yes.' Still she wouldn't look at him and Jean Jacques swung her back to him, holding her face firmly between his hands.

'Tell me again. Look at me and tell me it's what you want.'

'Our child has only one chance, Jean Jacques.' Tears filled her eyes. 'Without us! We have no choice any more.'

'Your parents?' Jean Jacques whispered. 'Is it them?'

'If we want our child to live, we must let him go.'

Jean Jacques couldn't remember running away from the Westbury farm and Pauline, nor could he remember how he got back to Esperance. He didn't react, or wonder what it meant, when Emily met him at the door, her face red with crying. Beside her was the small pile of his belongings.

'Clara's pushed you out of the house, J.J. But I'll fight her. I'm going to make her take you back.'

Even when Clara herself faced him he felt nothing and heard nothing.

'I have found your presence in the house uncomfortable. You will live where you belong and you will not enter this house again, unless your work as a labourer demands it.'

How could a place to live mean anything when his child might not be allowed to live at all? Jean Jacques wondered.

He went back to his old room without complaint. He cared little if he was a slave or a brother; he was a man about to lose part of himself. Emily chattered on with her plans for his return to the house, as she helped him put his things away in the labourer's quarters.

'When Father comes back he'll insist.' But he couldn't hear her. All he heard was the cry from his own heart.

'My child.'

Thys had ridden many miles since his father had been hanged by the British, but the miles had travelled in a semi-circle. He was aware the soldiers would still be looking for him but there was something he had to do before he took his own freedom.

He approached his home from the other side of the mountain,

and looked down at the small house. There was no familiar wisp of smoke from the chimney. He rode towards the house, his trepidation growing with each stride his horse took. The closer he got, the more clearly he could see that the farm had been abandoned. The few cattle they had were not there. No chickens were scratching for food. There was nobody there.

Thys climbed down from his horse and walked towards the house. The door swung back and forth in the breeze, and he stepped inside, holding it back with his shoulder. Dust had been blown into a sand dune against the back wall. He turned as he heard a sound outside. He went out, but he could see nobody, so he crept to his horse and took his musket from the saddle. When it was primed and loaded he moved in the direction of another sound coming from the barn.

The door was closed. He listened against it for a moment, then glanced up towards the mountains surrounding him. Soldiers could be waiting to trap him. He pulled back as something moved inside the barn. In a sharp movement he kicked the door open and threw himself in, spinning back as someone moved to the door. Catching sight only of a shadow, he leapt at it, pulling a man to the ground with him.

'Don't beat me . . . please don't beat me . . .'

It was Petrus, the old slave Petrus, under whose care Thys had grown up. Petrus was bleeding. He had obviously been beaten but his face lit up when he looked at Thys.

'Master Thys!' Petrus hugged him roughly.

'What's happened to you?'

'Soldiers came. They look for you they say. They not believe Petrus.' Thys moved abruptly out of the barn. He kicked the earth and glanced back at the old man who had been beaten instead of himself. Petrus smiled.

'I all right,' he assured Thys. 'You all right?'

Thys felt the comfort Petrus always brought with his toothless smile and looked towards the house for the comfort of his family. Petrus answered before any question had left Thys's lips.

'She gone. Your mother gone away. In the wagon. With cattle and chickens. She said she never come back.'

'And the others?' Thys meant his sisters.

'She took little missies. Took the slaves.'

'Why didn't you go?' Thys asked him. 'You should have gone

with them, Petrus. It would have been safer for you.' Petrus's face crinkled with laughter.

'Me? Too old! Your mother went far, master Thys. Far far away.' Petrus pointed to eternity and shook his head, but still the crinkle of joy remained. 'Petrus too old to go there,' he said, knowing it would not be long before he went much further.

'But you must get away from here. It's not safe for you.'

'I was born here. I die here.'

'Then go to Bonne Esperance. They'll take care of you.' As Thys said 'Bonne Esperance' he knew he had not only come back to find his mother. He wanted to know about Suzanne.

'They kill the old master?' Petrus snatched Thys's thoughts back. Thys nodded and Petrus shook his head slowly. 'It's bad.'

'Will you go to Bonne Esperance?' Thys repeated. 'I can't look after you, Petrus.'

'Ah! You still have the look of the small boy. The one I teach to hunt.' Petrus's eyes shone from his black face. 'Do you remember?'

'But times have changed, Petrus.'

'Yes,' the old man agreed. 'And broken our family.' He looked up at Thys. 'I will go to Bonne Esperance. It is what you want. Yes?' Thys nodded. 'But promise, young master Thys, promise one day you come back, you stop at my grave.'

As Thys left the home that held the magic of boyhood but was now the graveyard of memory, the old man waved. Then he turned, planted his stick in front of him, and began his walk towards Bonne Esperance and Suzanne.

Though Thys felt his heart deny it, he knew he must ride away to a future which could not contain Suzanne.

'You see, Suzanne,' Miss Thurston said to the patchwork bed-cover as she fiddled with it. 'Shutting yourself away from the world will cure nothing. Even at my age I know that. There have been times in my life when I've thought it not worth living. Even now. This special time I've had as part of this family must come to an end one day, but I've prepared for it. Are you listening, Suzanne?'

Suzanne nodded absently. She had never heard Miss Thurston talk like this before.

'I loved somebody once, too, you know.' Miss Thurston

turned her attention back to the bedcover. 'He's dead and buried in England. That young upstart Napoleon saw to that. But my life had to go on then, as it must now. And I still have plans. Would you like to hear them? I've told little Emily and she is so excited for me. I won't, of course, carry my plans through until her education is complete.' Miss Thurston smiled brightly and looked at Suzanne instead of at the bedcover. 'I've decided to open a school for young ladies in Cape Town! I shall teach countenance, manners, grace and charm. The things Cape Town ladies need to know.'

Suzanne got up and moved to the window although she was listening.

'You've had a good British upbringing. Even out here in the colonies you have lacked no instruction. But not many young girls have been so fortunate.' She paused and turned her lecture back to the bedcover. 'And it shows! But there you are. This old lady plans to step out into a new life and I think you should do the same.'

She reacted as Suzanne ran from the window to the door. 'Suzanne?' she called, but she had gone. 'Well,' Miss Thurston said to herself, 'at least I've got her to leave her room at last!' She didn't know that Suzanne had left because she'd seen a familiar face outside. The face of the old slave Thys loved so much, Petrus.

'It is you!' Suzanne's eyes shone as she looked at him. 'Oh Petrus! What's happened to you? You're hurt!'

'I'm not hurt, missy. Young master Thys. He send me to you.'

'Thys? Where is he?' She spun around as if he might be just behind her. 'Where is he, Petrus?'

'He gone. Away. Like everyone gone far away. He says to tell you.'

'What? What did he say?'

'He say to tell you not to worry your heart, Miss Suzanne.' Petrus paused for a moment, preparing for the lie he wanted her to believe.

'He say, he be with you one day. He say, he love you.'

Miss Thurston still believed the change in Suzanne was entirely due to her. She hadn't hidden in her room since she'd talked to her, and her face was bright. But as she watched the long line of starving slaves pouring on to the estate, her face, like everyone else's, fell.

'Dear God.' Miss Thurston's hushed words crept from her thoughts.

'Where is He now, Miss Thurston?' Prudence said flatly as she looked at the line of broken humanity. 'Where is God now?'

'We must help them,' Suzanne said.

'I'll get some food.' Emily ran away quickly.

'Tell them to find somewhere to sit,' Prudence called to Jean Jacques, who was watching from further away. 'Tell them we'll see they are fed.'

It was only when Clara noticed the activity in the kitchen that she had demanded an explanation.

'We are going to feed the slaves,' Prudence answered.

'You know as well as I do that we can't afford to feed every abandoned slave in the Cape!' Clara retorted.

'The people outside are starving!' Suzanne argued.

'They are the slaves whose Boer masters have run away from British law and order! It has nothing to do with us.'

Miss Thurston looked at Clara curiously. 'What happened to the rules of Christianity you learned as a child?'

'Those slaves will not be fed by us!'

'They *will* be fed!' Miss Thurston challenged, and Clara exploded,

'Have you forgotten your place, Miss Thurston?'

'My place?' Miss Thurston's cheeks burned. Emily looked down, unable to bear it. 'Perhaps you should inform me of my place, Clara.' Prudence noticed Miss Thurston was shaking.

'You are a servant!'

'Clara!' Emily shouted.

'I see.' Miss Thurston tried to retain her dignity. 'Perhaps that is why I have never been able to teach you manners befitting your breeding. One cannot learn from someone one regards as a servant!' She turned to the door. 'Excuse me. People shouldn't starve while we argue.' Suzanne left with her.

'You will tell those people to go, Prudence.' Clara took her temper out on her instead.

'I have no intention of telling them any such thing.'

'You will not do as I say?'

'No.' Prudence followed in Miss Thurston's wake. 'I agree with Miss Thurston.'

Clara fixed her look on the last one left. Little Emily. 'Will you also run after an old woman with ideas above her station?'

'No.' Emily looked straight at her and Clara smiled.

'Good. Order Jean Jacques to get rid of them.'

'No.'

Clara turned back. The line of Emily's mouth had straightened. She'd just watched Clara trample on the pride of the only woman she'd ever thought of as a mother. 'If you want to send those people away to die: then you do it. And if you do, Clara, it will be you who has no place in this family! Not even as a servant!' Emily dashed out before Clara could stop her.

The thanks which shone in the eyes of the people as they took their small bowls of soup and crusts of bread lit up the night. They had been feeding them for weeks and the Bonne Esperance soup kitchen had become well known in the area.

'You eat now, Petrus.' Suzanne held a bowl out to him.

'I'm all right, missy.'

Suzanne sat beside him and together they conjured up the memory that they loved so much.

'Tell me again about Thys when he was a small boy.'

Jean Jacques moved to Emily the moment he was sure no one was watching him.

'Our father wants to see us.' He nodded at a man standing further away from the rest. 'He sent a message.'

'Where is Father?' Emily asked excitedly.

'He's with my mother.'

Her face lit. She had never met Jean Jacques' mother and now, at last, she would.

'Will you take me, J.J.?' she asked eagerly. He nodded. 'When?'

'On Thursday. He said on Thursday we must go.'

'Thursday.' She looked around nervously. 'Where will we say we're going?' She suddenly smiled. 'Miss Thurston goes to Cape Town often now, planning for her school. I could meet you there and then nobody would know!' Jean Jacques glanced at the house and she took his hand. 'Clara is always out and about with

that Lord Marsden.' She chuckled. 'He's teaching her to promenade.' Jean Jacques looked puzzled. 'He obviously doesn't think
she walks quite decently.'

A military band played in the background and ladies twirled
their parasols as they strolled along a wide avenue between
newly planted trees. Their wide skirts swung with each step, and
they would look up occasionally at the man beside them and
smile to show off their perfect white teeth.

Lord Marsden wasn't interested in Clara's teeth. His eyes had
been drawn towards the extraordinary cleavage which her
natural shapeliness, a tight bodice and a cleverly fashioned
undergarment had ensured was on view. It was a mystery tour
down the secret lane between her rounded breasts, pushed up
against the pearl buttons fastening her dress and threatening to
burst out at any moment.

'I think, Miss Beauvilliers, you are a stronger woman than I
have taken you for.' He wondered how those breasts would feel
cupped in his hands. They would most certainly fill them.

'There have been times when I have doubted if I could go on.'
Clara took a deep breath, designed to swell her bosom. 'Sometimes I'm not sure I can cope with the problems of the farm
much longer.'

'How is Suzanne, Miss Beauvilliers?' he asked, his eyes drawn
back involuntarily to her breasts.

'Do please call me Clara.'

'Clara.' He pulled his eyes away. 'Clara,' he said again. 'How
is Suzanne, Clara?'

'Difficult. And on top of it all Miss Thurston is planning to
leave us. She's thinking of opening a school for girls, or some
such thing.'

'What an enchanting idea,' Lord Marsden surprised her.

'We will miss her so terribly, but I must, of course, encourage
her regardless.'

'You still find time to concern yourself with an old lady?'

'It is only right.' Clara met his eyes, smiling, as they lifted
from her breasts, letting him know she had seen, and didn't
mind. 'She has been with the family so long she is a part of it.'

'What a tower of strength you are,' he said as they walked
back the way they had come, through the parasols, uniforms and

swirling ladies' dresses. What a wife she would make, Lord Marsden thought. A wife his parents would accept. His eyes moved back to their favourite place and his loins warmed.

'Emily.' Jacques held her hands across the table. 'You are so like your mother.'

'In what way?' Emily loved hearing about her.

'You see with your heart, as she did.'

Emily looked away, shy for a moment. Her eyes moved around the strange room in which her father was so clearly at ease. Bolts of silk stood in one corner. Detailed embroidered cloths covered small round tables, and the bed had a lace cover, woven from the silk of a spider web, Emily thought. There was a curious smell and her nose twitched.

'What is it?' She sniffed.

'Incense.' He paused. 'I'm going to marry her, Emily.'

'Eva?' Emily's eyes locked on to his. Eva had been waiting on the beach for Jean Jacques when they arrived. It had been obvious that Jacques wanted to speak to his daughter alone, and now Emily understood. She squeezed his hands.

'I love you, Father.'

'Do you love him?' Jean Jacques asked his mother, as they walked barefoot along the beach, the wash from the sea stroking their feet.

'Nothing's changed,' Eva answered. 'Yes, I love him.'

He looked at her long neck stretching up from beautiful smooth shoulders, her black gleaming hair in a heavy plait down her back. She had a dignity which her life as a slave, and the tragedy of her love for Jacques, had not even dented.

'Will you marry him for my sake?' he asked again.

'Because I love him. But it will ensure you are legally registered as his son.' She looked at the strong young man beside her. When he was a small child, she had always known, just by the sound of his feet approaching, that he had been hurt by Clara. She could sense a change in him now. The aura around him had darkened. 'What's wrong, Jean Jacques?'

'There is nothing.'

'What makes you so sad?'

'There is nothing,' he repeated.

'You can tell me.' She turned, looking out to sea. 'You must trust that, Jean Jacques.'

'There is nothing,' he said yet again. But his eyes were still sad.

Emily did not go to the mosque for the wedding. Women were not allowed. Instead she sat with Eva while her father and Jean Jacques attended the ceremony.

The smell of incense and Eva's excitement intoxicated Emily. In her lovely white and gold dress, she was the most beautiful woman Emily had ever seen.

'Must you really sit here for seven days?' Emily suddenly asked. She'd heard that was part of Muslim marriage ritual.

'That is tradition. But this is a family celebration.' Eva moved to the corner of the room gracefully and came back with a package wrapped with pink and white ribbons. 'This is for you.'

Packages were always exciting to open, but this one held mystery within it. The mystery of why Emily felt so close to Eva. Her fingers carefully undid the ribbons and the paper fell open.

Inside was a lace petticoat, and Emily held it up with delight.

'Did you make it?'

'A long time ago. I think now, it will fit you.'

'Why did you make it a long time ago?'

'I'd been thinking of you. I'd seen you.' Eva smiled.

'Then it's true you were there when I was born?' Emily had at last put the question she had wanted to ask for so long but hadn't dared. 'Is it true?'

'I was the first person ever to see you.'

'You saved my life.'

'But not your mother's.' She reached for Emily's hand.

'You can't blame yourself. No!' Emily suddenly found herself in the arms of this woman she'd waited so long to meet. 'It wasn't your fault. Don't say that.'

'There's been so much pain.' Eva rocked the young girl in her arms. The baby she'd pulled out of her dead mother's body. 'Too much pain.'

Emily cried, but not because she was unhappy. She had found a friend.

'I'm glad you're my father's wife,' she said as the petticoat was crushed between them.

*

Jacques greeted his youngest daughter Emily with their secret just a twinkle between them.

'Jean Jacques.' He looked over at his son, who was leading his horse into the stables for him. 'I want to see you with the others.'

Emily ran to Jean Jacques, taking his hand to lead him into the house as Prudence ran out to welcome her father with Suzanne close behind. Clara didn't come out and Jacques noticed M. Claudelle move away quickly. He wondered why, but responded warmly to Prudence as she hugged him.

'I've planted roses, Father. Roses among the vines.'

'Roses?'

'Shall I tell you why?'

'Later,' Jacques laughed as they all moved into the house together. Suzanne looked happier than he'd expected. 'Are you all right, Suzanne?'

'Yes, Father.' She smiled at him in adoration. She remembered clearly how he'd gone for Colonel Drummond. How he'd stood up to the entire British army, and been stopped only by a vicious blow to the head. 'I'm glad you're home.'

Clara had waited in the sitting-room with no intention of greeting him as the others had. But as she'd waited, erect and determined, she'd felt a small shiver run through her. She was still never quite herself when face to face with her father.

'I have legally recognized Jean Jacques as my legitimate son,' Jacques said now. 'He is one of the family, even in the eyes of the law.' He noticed Clara's colour rise. 'Something bothers you, Clara?' She made no reply. 'Good.' He accepted her silence. 'Then I trust you will treat him with the respect a brother deserves. As you will respect my wife.'

'Your wife?' The look of horror on Clara's face said more than words.

'You want that woman to live here? In my mother's place?'

'No.' Jacques' eyes narrowed as he looked at her. 'My wife has chosen, for reasons of her own, not to live in this house. But, as my wife, you will speak of her with respect.'

'Respect?' Clara's voice rose in a screech. 'What respect will there be from our neighbours?'

'My neighbours' opinions do not concern me any more than yours do, Clara.'

'Of course not. No more than my mother's might!' Clara ran

out of the room. Jacques made no move to go after her, but crossed to stand beside Jean Jacques.

'Bring your belongings back into the house, Jean Jacques.'

'Yes, master.'

'Father,' Jacques corrected him.

'I'll help you, J.J.' Emily rushed to him. Jacques turned to Prudence and Suzanne. He could not be sure they felt differently from Clara.

Suzanne smiled. 'It's good to have you home.'

Prudence moved to him and looked him straight in the eye, hiding nothing, meaning everything.

Emily laid Jean Jacques' clothes in the drawer, chatting as she arranged each piece.

'Now everyone is happy except Clara, and she doesn't matter. Your mother was worried about you. Why was that?' she suddenly asked. Jean Jacques set down the small box in which he'd carried the only possessions he had, apart from his clothes. Books, which he had read over and over again since Emily had taught him how to, so many years ago. 'She seemed to think there was something wrong,' Emily went on.

'There is nothing.' He made for the door but Emily ran and stood in front of him.

'If you can't tell your mother it must be serious, J.J.' Jean Jacques kept his head down; he never lied to Emily and he couldn't now. He looked up and took a shallow breath.

'Pauline is carrying my child.'

'A baby? That's wonderful, J.J.!' she said quickly, before she could think.

'My child is to be taken from me.' Jean Jacques moved around her and opened the door.

As it closed behind him, leaving Emily alone with the words she'd just heard, her head dropped forward and she wept. She didn't know if she was crying because Pauline was having a baby, or because Jean Jacques was to lose it, but she cried for hours, staring into the open drawer at his clean shirts.

Emily visited the Westbury house the next morning and was told, as she had been told often before, that Pauline was not available.

'Her mother is expecting a baby,' Mr Westbury explained.

'And Pauline is too busy looking after her to join you for tea, I'm afraid.' As Emily saw Mrs Westbury move through the hall, she looked again at the 'lump' which she had, until now, believed was Mrs Westbury's baby. Jean Jacques was right. It seemed his child had been taken from him even before it was born.

That night she wrote in her diary, so that no one would ever forget, most especially herself:

'I vow this day to keep a secret watch over Jean Jacques' baby. For ever. Amen.'

She was not aware that Clara had made a vow years before. In blood, and on the Bible.

'I have no interest in all that childish rubbish!' Prudence moved away from the bible which Clara had laid on the bed with the large key on top of it. 'Don't listen to her, Suzanne. She's talking nonsense.' But Suzanne was listening. The night they'd made their pact had lived with her perpetually.

'The marks of our blood are still on this page.' Clara held the book up. 'Our blood.'

'No,' Suzanne murmured and ran to the door, but Clara had locked it.

'We are not children any longer, and it is no longer a game, Suzanne.'

'Because Jean Jacques stands to inherit Bonne Esperance? Why should you care? You don't care about Bonne Esperance at all!' Suzanne shouted.

'I care for what is rightfully mine!'

'Yours!' Prudence yelled, and moved to Clara with a strength she had never seen before. 'Give me that key!'

'When we have finished.'

'We *have* finished!' Prudence grabbed Clara's arm and pulled the doorkey out of her hand, throwing it to Suzanne. 'Go, Suzanne!' She wrestled with Clara to hold her back. 'I'll listen to your lies. So, if you want to talk about blood on bibles! About Jean Jacques! Tell me!' Prudence yelled in her face.

'Suzanne!' Clara shouted as Suzanne disappeared and the door closed behind her. 'Take your hands off me, Prudence!'

'I will, Clara! We all will!' Prudence moved to the door, removed the key and put it in the lock on the outside of the door. 'You're obsessed with keys. Try getting this one out!' Prudence slammed the door shut, and locked it quickly from the outside as Clara banged on it.

'Shall I send for Charles Marsden? Tell him his damsel is in distress?' Prudence laughed.

'Let me out!' Clara shouted from behind the locked door.

Prudence didn't know that Suzanne had not just left the room: she had left altogether. She had run out into the night, away from what she could no longer bear; Clara's hatred seemed to kill everything around it and Suzanne was looking for love. For Thys. Impossible as it was she must find him. If not she'd have no reason to live.

It was not until morning that everyone knew Suzanne had gone.

Miss Thurston had been the first to worry, after she'd looked for her in her bedroom and noticed her bed had not been slept in. She knew that when the rope had broken Bothma's neck it had also broken Suzanne. She went straight to Jacques.

Every member of the family and staff had searched the grounds. Even M. Claudelle had come out of hiding. But not Clara.

Prudence decided it was her fault. She had thrown the key to Suzanne and had helped her run away. But she kept her own feelings back.

By midday, every inch of Bonne Esperance had been combed. The barn, cellars, stables and even down by the river. Emily had said they must look on the river bank, as it was where Thys and Suzanne used to meet.

'His house? Perhaps she's gone to the Bothma house.'

Jacques looked back down the slope at the Bothma farm, and suddenly felt cold. As Suzanne could be. He rode out of the Bothma grounds quickly, back to Bonne Esperance. Suzanne would surely have stumbled home by now, he thought.

But neighbours had begun appearing at the door to help find her. Mr John Westbury was one of them.

'Are you certain you can leave your wife at a time like this?' Jacques asked. He remembered the time he'd left Emily during a late stage of pregnancy.

'The child isn't due yet,' Mr Westbury assured him. 'Besides, Pauline is with her.' Emily looked away. She wasn't sure he would miss the accusation in her eyes. She watched her father, with Jean Jacques and five other men, ride out. Prudence stood on her own looking disconsolate, and Emily moved to her.

'They'll find her, Prudence. I know they will.' She was trying to reassure herself, too, but inside her head she prayed, 'Find Suzanne. Please.' And as always she added, with finality, 'Amen.'

Jacques looked down the sheer drop at one side of the rough track they were riding. He indicated for three of the men behind to keep moving along the track, while he and the others searched higher up the mountain. Fear of what he'd see prevented him from looking down again.

The men spread out and Jean Jacques stayed with his father. Should they discover the worst, he hoped he could help him through it. All day they searched but found nothing. By the end of the next day they had still found nothing.

The days turned to weeks. Every evening they would recomb the areas they had searched before. Then, on a branch, on the edge of the ravine Jacques had avoided, he suddenly saw a piece of Suzanne's dress. It was held in the gnarled claws of a dead tree which clung to the sheer side of the mountain.

John Westbury offered to climb down. He knew it would be to look for a body. Jacques insisted he would go himself, and they were all to leave; even Jean Jacques. But Jean Jacques stayed.

The climb was difficult and slow. Made more so by the certain knowledge that if he found anything it could only be Suzanne's body. It was a ritual. Perhaps a form of cleansing before accepting the inevitable. Jean Jacques watched him from above, until he had reached the bottom of the narrow valley beneath. He could hardly be seen, the shadow was so dark. Jean Jacques wondered what he would say to Jacques, and he wondered about his child.

Jacques pulled himself over the edge and back to where he had begun. It was dark. His climb had taken him far into the night. Jean Jacques led his horse to him but neither said a word. They rode all the way home in silence. They had accepted, in silence, that Suzanne must be dead.

But, for three months, although nobody ever admitted it, every member of the family spent every spare moment in a secret search for Suzanne. There was no way she could be alive. Even if she had survived an impossible fall, she would not have survived nature. Leopards had been seen once or twice. Lion had been reported. Snakes were everywhere. It was Africa. Despite white houses and tended vineyards, Africa was all around.

Eventually Jacques organized a memorial service for his daughter. He was reluctant to, but in a way it was a relief. The torture of hope was finally over.

Lord Marsden asked if a soldier might be allowed to attend with him. The soldier who had swept Suzanne off her feet and carried her to Thys stood gravely remembering a young girl he had never known, as the Beauvilliers family said goodbye to Suzanne. But not Emily.

No matter how hard she tried to silence it, a small voice inside her head repeated continually,

'Suzanne is alive.'

Chapter Nine

'**H**old her down!' Mrs Westbury shouted at her husband John, as Pauline screamed and pushed herself up the bed with another violent contraction. 'I need your help!'

John Westbury couldn't move. Every ounce of strength had drained out of him at Pauline's first agonized scream. He moved away, faced the wall and dropped his head against it. He wanted to smash it.

'You know what we have to do!' His wife's voice banged against the wall and echoed inside his head. Sweat poured from his face and body, his clothes clung to him, and his body shook in despair at his own inadequacy. He pushed himself away from the wall, out of the room, through the front door and out of the house. The midday sun glared down on him accusingly, leaving him nowhere to hide from himself.

'Push, Pauline!' His wife's voice chased him across the space between them.

'No!' his daughter's voice rose against his wife's, 'I can't go on . . . no!' Her scream wrapped itself around his heart. Instinctively he moved under a tree, as if its shade would keep the sounds out. At last the screaming stopped.

John Westbury turned cautiously and looked back at the silent house. The lace curtain at Pauline's window licked out with a breeze and wiped the windowledge clean. He didn't move. His eyes stayed on the window. He didn't breathe. It was an eternity. Suddenly his body snatched a breath against his judgement and he swung away further, moving still deeper into the shade. He pressed his body against the hard bark of the tree trunk which stretched up between his arms, opening into a protective umbrella of leaves. He held on, as if drawing comfort from its age.

'Look at him.' His wife's words tapped him on the shoulder. He turned, and saw her moving towards him from the house. In her arms she held a small bundle, wrapped in a shawl. The tree stood rigid behind him, refusing to let him back away.

'Look at him,' Mary Westbury's voice commanded, as she stopped in front of him. He shook his head stupidly. He was crying. 'Look,' she said again, and pulled the shawl back. John Westbury's eyes snapped shut and his head spun with memories. Tiny new-born kittens, legs and claws splayed in terror. Blind eyes and pink noses, struggling to stay above the water. He could feel them as they fought for life in his hands as he pushed them deeper into the barrel. Quite suddenly their tiny bodies were limp in his hands.

'No,' he wept openly, 'please, no.'

'John,' Mrs Westbury's voice threatened. He opened his eyes, he couldn't see through the wash of tears in front of them. Through the haze he saw only a blur of his wife's hands, and the shawl. A low gurgling sound came from the mist and he looked up at his wife's face hopefully. His tears cleared. He could see her face. It told him nothing and left him no choice.

He lowered his eyes, back to the shawl and on to the baby. The baby was white. With a surge of joy he reached out and took it, holding it close to his face. The scrap of humanity cried, and its mouth sucked instinctively at his cheek.

'John.' He looked at his wife in response to his name.

'We'll call him John Westbury,' she said, 'after his father.'

News of the baby's birth didn't reach Bonne Esperance for a month. Emily knew the time had come but Jean Jacques never spoke of it. When Emily suggested the family should perhaps visit, to see if Mrs Westbury was all right, she was told it would be better not to. At Mrs Westbury's age there could be problems with a child. Only Emily and Jean Jacques knew the real danger was something altogether different. But at last the Beauvilliers family were invited to meet the Westburys' new son.

'Wait for me,' Emily called as she ran inside to collect the booties she'd knitted for the baby under Miss Thurston's keen instruction.

'Aren't you coming?' she asked the old governess, as she dashed to leave.

'I have things to do.' Miss Thurston found it hard being treated as a servant by Mrs Westbury. More so because she knew the woman was from a far lower social position than herself.

Jacques drove the carriage, with Jean Jacques up in front beside him. Emily sat with Prudence, and looked at Jean Jacques' back. How did he feel, knowing he would not be allowed to touch his own child?

'He's so tiny!' Emily said as she peered at the baby. 'What's his name?'

'John.' Mrs Westbury smiled. 'After his father.'

'Oh,' Emily said flatly.

Prudence didn't want to show too much interest in case the baby was handed to her. 'He looks exactly like him,' she said, unable to think of anything else.

'Who?' Mrs Westbury asked, a little too quickly.

'His father,' Emily cut in. 'Where's Pauline?'

'She's resting.' Mr Westbury changed the subject. 'A drink, Jacques? To wet the baby's head?' He was nervous, and couldn't help showing it.

Emily's eyes never left the baby. She wanted to be able to describe him in detail to Jean Jacques, once they were alone.

'Jean Jacques has become an expert at grafting,' Jacques said suddenly, without sensing the tension his remark induced. 'Perhaps I could send him over to help you one day. We could arrange it now.' He moved to call him.

'No,' Mr Westbury said sharply. He handed Jacques a glass of wine, covering himself quickly. 'I've had the help of a man from Constantia.' He raised his glass. 'Good health.'

'*Santé.*' Jacques held his glass towards Mrs Westbury and the baby. 'May he bring you much joy.' Emily turned away to the window. She couldn't bear it and she felt very hot. Jean Jacques was staring towards the house. He looked very alone.

'I'll go and say hello to Pauline,' Emily said quickly.

'She really isn't well today,' Mrs Westbury said to try to stop her.

'I won't stay with her long.' She ran out, knowing Mrs Westbury would not be able to follow her. The baby had begun to cry.

'Pauline? It's Emily. Can I come in?' She waited outside the bedroom door for a moment. 'I've got to see you, Pauline.' There was no answer. Her hand moved to the door handle. She tried it, not expecting it to open. She stopped in surprise as the door swung open and she saw Pauline's back at the window.

'Go away,' Pauline said very quietly.

'I had to come.' She watched Pauline's back. She was looking out at Jean Jacques, and Emily knew it. 'He's so sad, Pauline.'

'What do you mean?' Pauline swung round on her and Emily pulled back, startled by the fear in Pauline's eyes. 'What do you mean?'

Emily moved closer to her, afraid but determined. 'You and J.J. have a beautiful baby.' Pauline tried to turn away but Emily prevented her. 'I won't tell anybody, Pauline. Nobody will ever know.' Pauline kept her eyes away from Emily. 'But you must tell J.J. you still care.'

'No.'

'You must.'

'No.' Pauline's face reflected only the firmness of her refusal.

'But I don't understand.' Emily realized how much less Jean Jacques must understand. 'There has to be a way.'

'Was there a way for your father and Jean Jacques' mother?' Pauline asked coldly.

'Yes!' Emily's chin stuck out boldly. 'They are married now. Jean Jacques is our brother and he's been accepted into the family. Even the law accepts him!'

'Accepts him?' Pauline's eyes flashed at Emily. 'Why should my child need laws to be accepted!'

'Do you accept him, Pauline?'

There was a long silence. Emily could see the deep cut her words had made in her and didn't know what to do. Pauline's shoulders heaved with emotion. Then, as the sound of the baby crying ever louder broke into the room, her hand moved to her bodice. It was wet with milk.

'He cries and my milk flows. But I must wait until it is safe, to feed the lie my mother has built around him.' She moved closer to Emily. 'Can you imagine what it's like? To hold him close as he sucks. To look down into his eyes as they gaze up at me.' She spoke in a daze. 'I feed him.' She nodded as if reminding herself. 'She brings him to me when he cries, if nobody is here, and I feed him.' She looked directly at Emily. 'Then she takes him! Drags

187

him away, snatches him from me!'

'Oh, Pauline!' Emily threw her arms around her. 'Please don't cry!'

'Tell Jean Jacques,' her hands gripped Emily's shoulders more tightly, 'if we want him to live we must forget him.' She lowered her face. 'Tell J.J. that I've lost my child, too.'

The journey home seemed neverending and Emily's head buzzed with the confused emotions she felt. The baby depended on Pauline for his life; not only on her milk but on her silence. She glanced at Jean Jacques and her mind turned to her own mother. How had she herself been fed? Her mother had died in childbirth. It was something Emily had never thought about before, but suddenly it was very important. Was there a bond between a baby and the woman who fed it? Was that bond between Pauline and her child?

'I just wanted to know,' Emily said to Miss Thurston as casually as she could when they got back. 'Babies have to have milk from their mothers and I just wondered what happened to me.'

'It seems a very strange question to ask out of the blue.' Miss Thurston turned away, embarrassed.

'Why?' Emily was even more puzzled by Miss Thurston's attitude. 'Someone fed me!'

'What on earth do you mean?'

'Somebody must have.'

'Really, child! If visiting Mrs Westbury and her new baby has aroused you to such extraordinary curiosity, perhaps it's best you don't visit again.'

'What's so curious about wanting to know who fed me?' Emily persisted.

'Just be thankful you were!'

Miss Thurston left; she was not going to be drawn any further on the subject. Emily moved to the window and looked out. She still couldn't talk to Jean Jacques on his own, her father was with him, so she went to the kitchen. Maria was with her daughter Rosita. Rosita was Emily's age and they'd often played together when they were small. Emily leant against the door as Maria showed her daughter how to prepare vegetables, without wasting too much in the peeling.

'Did you feed Rosita, Maria?' Emily asked brightly. Maria

chuckled as she looked at the small nick on her finger.

'You nearly made me cut my finger off, Miss Emily. Why? Does she look hungry?'

'When she was a baby, I mean. Did you?'

'How else you think she grow big enough to work like me!'

'Who fed me?' Emily asked, and Maria's broad smile vanished. Her gleaming white teeth disappeared behind closed lips. 'Do you know?'

'Out of the kitchen! I got to teach Rosita how to work!' She chased Emily with a large broom. Emily stood outside the back door to the kitchen and wondered why nobody knew or, if they did, why they wouldn't tell her. She saw Sunday sitting under a tree preparing his fishing rod and she ran over to him. He knew everything. Sunday would tell her.

'Hello,' she said with a smile as she leaned against the tree, watching his nimble fingers attach a handmade hook to the line. 'Are you going fishing?'

'Do you want to come?' he asked her, looking directly into her eyes. Emily noticed how he did that to her, although he never looked directly into the eyes of anyone else in the family. He treated her differently. 'It's a good day for fish,' he added.

'Did you see me when I was born, Sunday?'

'You?'

'After I was born. Did you see me?'

'I don't remember.' He bit through the line around the knot he'd made for the hook. 'Why?'

Emily slid her back down the tree trunk and drew a pattern in the sand with her finger. 'They say I was fed by one of the slave women.' She hoped her guess would elicit the truth.

Sunday got to his feet to check on his fishing line. 'I didn't hear anything.'

'Your father Titus?' Emily looked at him keenly. 'You said he told you everything, Sunday. Everything that ever happened here, you said.' Sunday shrugged and moved to go.

'Who was it?' She forced him to stop and look at her.

'She didn't tell you?'

'Who?'

'Then you not supposed to know.'

'Who? Please. Please tell me, Sunday.'

'Maria.' He looked around quickly. 'Don't say!'

'Maria?' Emily whispered.

'They say it was because she had a baby. Rosita. They say she fed both babies.' Emily stood absolutely still. 'You must not say I told you.'

'Thank you,' she said. 'I'm glad.'

Emily ran back to the house, looking for Jean Jacques. There was a bond between herself and Maria, and that meant there would always be a bond between Pauline and her baby.

'That's why they didn't tell me, J.J.!' Emily held his hands tightly in hers and looked excitedly into his eyes. They were in his small attic room. It was late at night, and the only time she could talk to him alone. 'There is nothing Mrs Westbury can do to make the baby hers because Pauline is feeding it.' Jean Jacques looked away, and Emily ran her finger down his back. 'Look at me.' He turned to face her. 'He even looks like you. He's beautiful.' There was no reaction, and Emily was disturbed by the sadness in his eyes. 'He'll be all right, J.J. You must believe that.'

'And Pauline?'

'It's hard for her, too. That's why you must understand.'

'I don't understand!' Jean Jacques' face was on fire with anger. 'I stood outside while everyone else looked at my son! I waited outside with no way to reach him! To touch him!'

'But he's still yours!'

'He's theirs!' He stood abruptly and left the room. She listened to his feet padding softly down the stairs.

'One day everyone will know the truth,' Emily wrote in her diary that night. She wiped her pen and put it in its stand. Then she picked it up and dipped it in the inkwell again. 'Amen,' she added.

'I'm not entirely certain why you ask.' Clara looked up at Charles Marsden as they walked across the rise above the vineyards of Bonne Esperance.

'Is it so extraordinary that I should want you as my wife, Clara?' He turned her to face him. He'd been preparing for this moment for nearly three years. Their courtship had been carried out with the decorum bred into him through generations. He had written to his family in England mentioning Clara, and they had responded that perhaps he should return home. He had done no such thing. He had deliberately not told them Clara's family was wealthy. Although his own was in dire financial straits, like many of the English aristocrats, they looked on marriage into the rising classes of the *nouveaux riches* with great suspicion. Clara was quite simply a mongrel, and French at that. They chose to ignore him until he came to his senses.

'Haven't you known all along that I would want to marry you?' Charles asked gently.

'No.' Clara removed her gaze coyly from his face and looked out across Bonne Esperance. It stretched for miles, nestled in the spreading arms of the mountains. 'Only when I look at all this. Your reason for wanting my hand in marriage.'

'Clara, I want nothing else when I look at you. Nothing.' She was aware that his eyes were on her body, and she liked it.

'It's not possible. No. I cannot believe it.'

'I love you,' he said, and she turned away as if unable to bear the burden of his words; but knowing, as he did not, that they had risen from the longing in his loins. The power she had over him gave her a secret thrill of pleasure.

'Is my love for you wrong, Clara?'

'You can't possibly!'

'Must I speak to your father first? Would that make you believe me?'

'My father?' Clara turned back arrogantly towards him. 'He is part of our problem.'

'Problem?' Charles Marsden lifted his head with all the dignity he could muster. 'I am not acceptable to him?'

'You?' She looked at him in amazement. 'It is I! I am unacceptable to a man like yourself, Charles. It is I who have nothing to offer you but a dowry which rattles with deceit . . . with lies . . .' She stopped. 'I have nothing.' Each word was a whisper.

'It is you I want, Clara.'

'And what of our future? Our children's future?' She swept her arm angrily across the panorama of Bonne Esperance. 'All this should be mine; yours through our marriage; our children's through inheritance. But,' she paused, looking back at him, 'I have nothing.' She moved away as if unable to face him. 'Try to imagine the agony I feel, Charles. I can't live without you, but cannot accept your proposal, knowing my life is a lie! I couldn't insult you so deeply.' She looked down over the vineyards, drawing him to look with her. 'Unless justice can be done, our love will be stolen; as my inheritance has been.' She pointed sharply towards a group of labourers in the vineyards. 'He is the one who stands between us, and he is the reason I cannot marry you. My father's son and heir, Jean Jacques.'

Her voice quietened and her expression softened. She touched his face. She touched his face gently, looking deeply into his eyes.

'How I wish I had never been forced to speak those words to you!' She lowered her eyes and allowed a tear to run down her cheek. 'That is why I cannot accept what I want most desperately. To be your wife.'

'Clara.' Charles lifted her chin and wiped the tear from her face. 'Do you imagine I would allow anything to stand in the way of our marriage?'

Clara's mouth spread into the most sensuous smile he had ever seen. Her eyes shone with greed for him. She raised her face and her lips touched his. 'The depths of passion I have for you are more than you have ever dreamed, Charles,' she whispered against his lips and stirred the agony of lust she knew she roused in him. 'I *will* marry you.' Her tongue parted his lips and forced its way into his mouth with promises of ecstasy to come.

'Don't move, please.'

Emily bit her lip as she looked at Pierre Justine, the artist ordering them to remain frozen to the spot. They were posing for a wedding portrait. 'Have my buttons popped, Prudence?' she asked between clenched teeth, terrified to speak but more afraid not to.

'Yes.' Prudence pulled the back of Emily's dress together. 'But if we have to stand here much longer I can't promise to keep you decent.'

'Please, ladies!' The artist glared at Prudence through insulted eyes.

'Sorry,' Prudence smiled quickly.

Emily glanced down. Her bodice was bursting in an effort to contain her in a dress made without consideration of her approaching womanhood. Clara and Lord Marsden had been married six months earlier, but the wedding portrait had continued one day a month ever since. With every day her budding breasts seemed to grow larger. In order not to think about it Emily turned her mind to Jean Jacques. He used these days to escape and she knew exactly where he would be. Hidden among the bushes close to the Westbury house, happy just to catch a glimpse of his son and Pauline.

'Enough. I have work to do,' Jacques said suddenly and moved away. The artist tossed his brushes into the air, and they spiralled down like wooden birds.

'How shall I ever finish?'

'Without me!' Jacques retorted. 'I have a vineyard to run.'

'You must be in the family group for our wedding portrait,' Clara argued crossly.

'Should I?' He had no wish to be a part of the charade being played out one day a month. 'It is you he has married, not me! And my family is not entirely present.'

'Father's right!' Prudence seized her opportunity and ran off quickly.

'And my dress no longer fits,' Emily added, running after Prudence.

'And now?' The artist looked at Clara and Lord Marsden from wide eyes, astonished at their strange behaviour. 'I do what?'

Charles Marsden picked up a paintbrush and offered it to him, secretly pleased. 'Use your imagination.'

He took Clara's hand and moved towards the house, leaving the irate artist at a loss. He had only a short time to spend with Clara before returning to the castle. 'You have no other plans?' he smiled at her questioningly.

Charles could still hardly believe the incredible world she had led him into. One he had glanced at in dreams, and been ashamed of in daylight. He looked at the beautiful full breasts as she allowed them to fall free of her bodice and his body surged with excitement. Her eyes met his and she ran her hands lightly over her breasts. Encouraging him.

'How I've missed you.' She moved to him and stood in front of him, brushing her naked breasts across his face. Her nipples were erect. Dark and hard. 'Feel me,' she purred, taking his hand and passing it gently over her breasts, over the nipples, and down until it reached the gentle rise of her stomach under her petticoat. 'Take it off,' she said. He obeyed her, totally bewitched. His hands fumbled behind her with the drawstrings as she pushed her breasts against his face, and his tongue reached for them. She laughed and wriggled herself free of the petticoat. Underneath she had nothing on at all.

'What would you have done if you had known I was naked out there in front of everyone?' She took his hand and slid it down the line of her stomach between her legs. She leant her head back as she forced his hand against her and shivered, moving her body rhythmically as his fingers reached into the moist warmth of her being. Her back arched, and she pulled his hand against her slippery mound with a gasp. She looked down at him, her eyes moist and blurred: beckoning, tempting, teasing, drawing him on.

'Do you want me?' she asked, and Charles snatched at her buttocks, pulling her towards him and burying his face in her dark pubic hair. 'Yes?' she whispered. Her hands ran up her own body to her breasts and she looked down at him. 'You made a promise, Charles. Remember? Before we married?'

'Yes.' He was desperate.

'You will keep it?' Her eyes smoked from under her lashes.

'Yes!' With his lust for her at its height, Clara lowered herself on to him with a passionate cry as he slipped deep inside her.

Emily looked back at the house warily. She had grown accustomed to the curious noises which came from Clara's bedroom whenever Lord Marsden was there, and she ran towards the cellars to escape.

A man she had never seen before was with her father and M. Claudelle.

'This is my youngest daughter, Emily, Mr Wagner. Emily, this is our new wine-maker. He's from Germany.'

'Hello.' Emily held her hand out politely and he kissed it. She glanced at M. Claudelle. 'Are you leaving us, M. Claudelle?' she asked innocently, and he kept his head down.

'I must go back to Europe. My mother is growing old and frail.'

Emily nodded. She knew the real reason. Time may have passed, but she knew M. Claudelle was still afraid. 'Then you must go, of course.' She turned to Mr Wagner. 'You speak English, do you?'

'A little.' He shrugged. 'I will learn.'

'I will teach you.' She smiled. She had grown into a gentle young woman.

'All we need is your expertise,' Jacques said. Emily spotted Prudence standing in the cellar door and turned to her father quickly.

'May I take the carriage out today, Father?'

'Where are you going?'

'To see little John Westbury. Rosita will come with me.'

'Again?'

'I am his godmother.'

'Of course.' He moved away with M. Claudelle and Mr Wagner. 'Be careful, Emily.'

'I will,' she called back and sprinted towards the stables.

Prudence watched them carefully. She was glad M. Claudelle was going but she would have to ensure Mr Wagner knew the cellars were hers. She would teach him English, but without the words she so despised.

'The vineyard is not the place for a woman.'

Charles lay on the bed looking down at Clara curled in his arm half asleep. Even asleep she was in command, for he was the slave of the lust she had roused in him. He moved carefully to get up without waking her.

'Have you come to any decisions yet?' Clara asked, surprising him.

'I have hardly been thinking about Jean Jacques,' he smiled.

'But you must, Charles.' She stretched her body. 'Did you enjoy yourself?'

'Yes, Clara.' He looked away quickly to break her spell. 'I have an idea.' He sat down, pulling his breeches on. 'I think the army might be an excellent career for him.' He slipped his foot into a boot and tugged it on.

'The army enlists half-castes?' Clara asked with some interest.

'The Cape Mounted Riflemen.' He yanked the boot up to his knee. The taut leather gleamed.

'And they have to fight?' Clara rolled on to her stomach and watched him from the bed. The tease was in her eyes again.

'Yes.' He shut his eyes as she rolled over on to her back. 'I must go.' He felt excitement and guilt building inside. Guilt was a part of the passionate web she spun.

'The sooner you speak to Jean Jacques about the army the better.' Her hands moved over her breasts, stroking her nipples. 'Perhaps then you will have more time to spend with me.'

'Clara.' He was captivated again and moved to her. Quickly she rolled away across the bed and looked at him with a scolding behind her simmering eyes.

'You must talk to Jean Jacques first, Charles.'

Emily had asked Jean Jacques to wait for her in the stables after he had prepared the carriage for her visit to the Westburys. He'd sensed that she was planning something and waited nervously.

'Good day, Jean Jacques,' Charles Marsden said from the doorway.

'Good day, sir.' Jean Jacques lowered his eyes as he always did and hurried to fetch his horse for him.

'I've been wondering about you.' Charles watched him with a faint smile as he untied the horse's rein. 'About your future. Your plans. Have you any?'

'My father wants me to stay here, sir. He's preparing me to take over the estate.'

'Really!' Charles allowed his amazement to show as he took the rein, without saying thank you. 'And you believe him?'

'What do you mean, sir?'

'No matter.' Charles was about to mount but stopped and turned back. 'One day I should perhaps take you to Cape Town with me. You could make your own decision.'

'I have, sir.'

'To take over Bonne Esperance?' Charles Marsden's raised eyebrows expressed his amusement. 'I see.'

'It is my father's wish, sir.' Jean Jacques wished he would leave before Emily appeared.

'And yours?' Jean Jacques didn't answer. 'I am not sure you should turn your back on everything else in the hope he will fulfil his promise to you.' He ran his eyes over Jean Jacques' face. 'Unless!' He looked at him with sharp curiosity. 'Unless your father's promise also offers respect as his equal!'

'I have his respect.' Jean Jacques kept his eyes averted.

'You can hold your head up with pride and demand all that is yours?' Charles threw his leg over his horse with the disdain his words expressed. 'There are no marks of servitude in the British army, Jean Jacques.' He walked his horse out of the stables, calling back casually, 'And a good wage to be earned.' He knew Jean Jacques was listening and looked back as he ducked his head through the door. 'We need men like you.' He held his head up proudly. 'Unless, of course, you are no more than the servant they treat you as.' With that, Charles Marsden dug his heels in and rode out. Jean Jacques closed his eyes. For the moment he had more important things on his mind.

Pauline had seen Emily approaching in the fly carriage with Rosita before her mother had. She was accustomed to Emily's visits, but still felt a little nervous. She looked at her son as he sat on the floor tossing small handmade toys around with glee. He was two years old.

'Mother!' she called.

Emily was aware of Pauline's uneasiness and hoped her constant attention as fairy godmother had earned Mrs Westbury's trust. She rapped on the door and waited, smiling quickly as Mrs Westbury opened it with the child in her arms.

'Hello, Emily.'

'My but he's grown!' Emily held out her hands to take him. 'How's my godson today?' She held him above her and he giggled.

'I do believe you'd be a better sister to him than Pauline!' Mrs Westbury glanced at her daughter, who had moved into the doorway behind her.

'Hello, Pauline.' Emily smiled sweetly but turned to Mrs Westbury quickly. 'We have a new colt at home. I wondered if I could take little John to see it?'

'No,' Pauline said immediately.

'Of course you may,' Mrs Westbury contradicted.

'Thank you.' Emily returned to her carriage before she could change her mind, handed the baby to Rosita and climbed in beside her. 'I'll have him back soon,' she called as she drove out. Mrs Westbury waved to Emily and spoke to Pauline quietly.

'It would appear strange if I refused such a simple request.' She moved back inside. Pauline stood in the doorway watching the carriage drive back to Bonne Esperance. She knew where Emily was taking her son.

Jean Jacques looked up sharply as the light from the opening stable door reached him.

'Here we are, little John Westbury. Your father would like to meet you.' Emily stood against the light with the child in her arms and looked at Jean Jacques. He was motionless.

'Take him,' Emily encouraged. She waited until he lifted the child from her arms, very carefully. He stared at the toddler in his hands; then quite suddenly he pulled him into his body and held him tightly against him. The blond curls of the small child pressed against Jean Jacques' brown face, and broad moist tracks of tears lit his cheeks. Emily quietly left the stable.

It was the first time she had seen Jean Jacques cry. All the hatred and humiliation he had suffered, and yet he wept now only with joy.

Jean Jacques had gained fresh courage from the moment he held his son in his arms. He had gone to the Westbury farm the next morning and waited in his usual place to catch a glimpse of Pauline and his child. But this time, he chased Pauline, his hands gripping her arm tightly.

'Why are you afraid of me?'

'You know what I'm afraid of.' She tried to pull away. 'You know you shouldn't be here.'

'No. I don't know any more.' He pulled her out of sight amongst the bushes. 'Do you know how long you've avoided me, Pauline? How many years it's been since you spoke to me?' She pulled herself free and glared at him.

'Our son has been accepted. He has a life ahead of him and that is a good enough reason for everything.'

'No!' The determination in his voice surprised her, but she held her head up firmly.

'Then we have nothing to talk about.' She made to go, but he snatched her arm. She looked down at his hand accusingly.

'You're hurting me.'

'And I've wanted to kill you!' He let her go. 'I love you.' She didn't pull away. She didn't look away either. 'When we met I wondered if it was me you wanted, or if I was just a challenge to your parents. But now we have a child. I've held that child in my arms!'

'A child with a future,' she said.

'Without parents? What future is that?' He watched her. 'Pauline,' his voice was very soft, 'if I can prove to you there is a future for us together, will you come to me?'

'There is none!'

'You aren't listening to me!' His voice rose in desperation as he held her shoulders and shook her violently. 'You and my son are my life!'

'No!'

'You love me!'

'No!' She turned away and he wrapped his arms around her from behind, holding her close, leaning his head against her hair. 'You feel the same as you always have. Nothing has changed.' He felt her body tremble against his. 'Yes?' he whispered.

'Yes.'

Jean Jacques closed his eyes and held her tightly as Lord Marsden's words rolled in his head. 'In the army you'd be your own man. You can hold your head up with pride and demand what is yours.'

Jacques glanced at his son with a fond smile as he spoke to Günther Wagner in the cellars.

'M. Claudelle seemed to think Jean Jacques would soon be ready to take over.' He hadn't noticed Prudence. She was keeping out of sight in the shadows.

'I think soon. But is more still him to learn,' Mr Wagner said politely and added, 'Like my English.'

'Are you ready for more learning?' Jacques put his arm around Jean Jacques warmly.

'I'm not sure.' Jean Jacques was uncomfortable.

'Isn't this what you want?'

'I've been thinking about a military career.'

Jacques stood back and looked at his son.

'No. I don't think a military career,' he said.

'Lord Marsden has been telling me about it.'

'And the uniform suits him very well! But not you. This is yours. Bonne Esperance.'

'What about Prudence?' Jean Jacques asked. 'The wine-making is her life.' Prudence pulled back quickly in case she'd been seen.

'Women's lives revolve around babies,' Jacques said predictably; and Prudence felt her colour rise in anger.

'But she knows more than anyone about wine.'

'She knows. Yes. But.' Jacques looked at him with raised eyebrows. 'The army is not for you.' He glanced at Günther Wagner with a smile. 'You will prove that to him, I hope.' Jacques left the cellars to avoid further confrontation, but he turned back as he went. 'I need you,' he said.

Prudence remained quiet as her father left. She too would have to fight for her future.

Jacques sat on a jutting rock that hung suspended over the valley beneath. He had heard Jean Jacques clearly, though he didn't want to believe what he'd heard. His children would all make their own ways soon. Except Suzanne. The pain he'd lived with since she'd gone was one he could not accept again. If Jean Jacques joined the army it would be as if he too had died. Though Jacques tried not to think about it, he couldn't stop himself. No more than he would ever stop thinking about Suzanne.

Chapter Ten

Over eight hundred miles away the mission station was a speck of civilization in a landscape of dense bush, sudden scrubland and rock outcrops through which death prowled continually. It was a small mission but grew daily as mud and wattle huts were erected to accommodate orphaned children and wounded soldiers.

The Reverend Phillip was a quietly spoken man who had been running the mission for ten years. What had begun for him as a calling to preach the word of God in Africa had developed into something far more. His mission had become a sanctuary, not only for men's souls but for their broken bodies. The constant 'kaffir' wars had taken their toll on hundreds of British soldiers posted to the eastern frontier, and he had tried to do his part to relieve the suffering.

It had been the need for another doctor to help him which had led him to make a journey three years earlier, to Cape Town. He had gone to collect Dr Steven, a young surgeon who had asked to be posted to Africa. As they had made their way back from Cape Town, through the night, with miles and weeks of travelling ahead of them, they had been stopped suddenly by a sight neither would ever forget.

A young girl, with a mass of golden hair, had suddenly appeared from the surrounding darkness and run across the path of their wagon. The wagon was sixteen feet long and made of rough wood, held loosely together. The oxen were reined by their horns and inspanned in pairs. A yoke of heavy wood ran across their necks. They had been moving down a hill, and the weight of the heavily loaded wagon defied anybody to stop it as it rolled straight towards the girl. But, impossibly, the wagon and oxen *had* stopped, just in time. Rev. Phillip felt immediately that God had played a part.

Dr Steven clambered down and rushed to the girl, who stood quite still in front of the lead oxen. He screamed at her, in shock at her appearance and the nearness of her death at their hands.

'Are you mad? You could have been killed!' Dr Steven berated her for many minutes before realizing that she had not reacted at all. She'd simply looked up at him, in a dream.

'Who are you?' Rev. Phillip eventually asked quietly, but there was no reply.

'She must come from nearby,' Dr Steven said, and then regretted his stupidity as he remembered the miles of open country through which they'd passed. 'Are there any farms around here?' he added quickly.

Rev. Phillip moved close to the girl and put his hands on her shoulders to ensure she didn't run. Also to make sure she was real. He hadn't been certain.

'Are you from one of the wine farms?' She immediately pulled away from him.

'What do we do?' Dr Steven asked.

'Take her to the nearest farm.'

'Is there one?'

'No!' The girl's voice had their attention instantly. She backed away into the bush and peered at them in terror. Rev. Phillip moved after her cautiously.

'Then tell us where you are from.' She said nothing.

'What's your name?' She said nothing.

'You can't stay out here alone.' With that the girl ran into the surrounding night, forcing them to chase her. When they caught up with her, she was standing perilously close to the edge of a ravine with a long drop beneath her. She looked at them from eyes filled with fear and whispered, 'If you won't take me with you I will jump.'

As they helped her back to safety, away from the ravine edge, a thread of her dress had snagged on a thorny bush.

Jacques Beauvilliers still kept the piece of torn fabric with him at all times.

'Suzanne?' Rev. Phillip called as she moved ahead of him across the dusty ground. She had a tiny black baby in her arms, and several other small children trailed behind her.

'I've got to feed these little ones or they'll eat me,' she laughed as she turned back to him. She was sunburnt, and had gained a strength in the fragile and delicate line of her body. She was different in many ways from the girl they had stumbled on that night. She'd learned to nurse, learned the Xhosa language, yet no one had learned anything about her at all.

'Don't you want to see the new bibles?' Rev. Phillip asked, holding one up. 'They're in Xhosa.' He joined her and opened a bible. 'You see?' He watched her as she examined the open page. She was still a mystery to him. He wasn't even certain her name was Suzanne. He knew nothing about her. Except 'Thys'. She had said the name Thys in her sleep many times on their journey. 'You look at that bible almost with fear.' He saw the tension in her face and regarded her curiously. In the years she'd been with him, he'd never missed any opportunity to find out about her. 'Why? What does the bible mean to you?'

'Nothing.' She turned to go to the children. 'I have work to do. Excuse me.'

'Perhaps you would find what you're looking for in this book, Suzanne.' He walked with her and the children towards the small mud building which they used as a kitchen. 'You should look among its pages.'

'Not in that book.' She called a straying child, 'Nensa! Here!'

'Why, Suzanne?' Rev. Phillip persisted. She stopped as the child reached her and she took the small black hand in her own.

'Today I read in the bible that man is made in the image of God. I read it to the children.' Her eyes held his steadily. 'I don't think they believed it any more than I do. It is difficult to believe anything written in the bible when I see these children starving: when soldiers are brought to us with their lives bleeding away into this barren, dry ground which God supposedly created with love!'

'But they listen, don't they, Suzanne? The children?'

'And I am beginning to wonder if it is right they do.' She tried to move on again but Rev. Phillip stopped her with a hand on her arm.

'When I see the compassion in you, I know man is made in the image of God, Suzanne.' She looked at his hand on her arm. 'I know there is hope.' He removed his hand and she turned to go. 'Who broke your heart? Was it Thys?' Suzanne spun back to face him, challenging him to continue. 'These children have merely rattled the pieces. Who broke it?'

She had not, as always, given anything away at all. Rev. Phillip looked at the bible still open in his hand. Nothing but a fear of the bible, he thought.

The sound of horses and carts driving into the mission attracted his attention. A small group of roughly dressed soldiers raced into the centre of the dusty grounds, leapt off their horses and moved quickly to the carts, calling, 'They're badly hurt, Father. Can you help us?'

Rev. Phillip hurried over to them, shouting for Dr Steven and Suzanne. Two young soldiers were strapped to the cart on rough stretchers. The arm of one of them was hanging by shreds of skin, his young body covered in deep gashes made by assegaais. The soldier's eyes stared at Rev. Phillip as if still seeing the terror he had been a part of. 'Would you prepare for surgery, Suzanne.' The second soldier was dead.

As Suzanne sat outside the rough building in which they had operated, she was still shaking. Rev. Phillip and Dr Steven at last came out and stood before her.

'Will he live?' she asked.

'I think you need a drink, as we do, Suzanne,' Rev. Phillip said shaking his head, and she went with them into the small hut used as a church on Sundays. Rev. Phillip poured some wine into a glass for Suzanne and she closed her eyes. She didn't want to remember Bonne Esperance now, any more than the young soldier's face. It was a time in her life which was over and as dead as the soldier.

She took the glass from him quickly and raised it, trying to dispel the depression which fell with the early hours of the morning.

'Here's to those we couldn't keep alive. They will, of course, be with your God.' Suzanne smiled and drank.

Dr Steven glanced at Rev. Phillip. Neither said anything. The crickets were the only sound.

'Good night,' Dr Steven said, as he moved away having finished his drink.

'Mmm.' Rev. Phillip couldn't take his eyes off Suzanne. She looked different. He could feel the anger she always hurled at the bible, at his God, but that was not the real issue.

'Who's Thys?' Her wide blue eyes settled on him, but she said nothing. 'When we first found you his name was often on your lips as you slept.' Suzanne looked away. He moved to stand beside her and looked down at her. At last she spoke; so quietly, he could barely hear.

'He could never love me again.' Rev. Phillip felt his heart jump. He had never heard her use the word love before. 'The British hanged his father,' she added.

'To love someone on the other side is very hard, Suzanne.' As the words left his mouth he regretted them. Suzanne's eyes were alight with anger.

'What other side, Reverend?' she spat. 'Surely we're all just people trying to live in this God-forsaken country! Has he forsaken it? Your God? Has your God turned his back on this land, Reverend Phillip?'

'No, Suzanne.'

'But love is wrong? Love is doomed, if it's for someone on the other side, you say?'

'In this world perhaps.'

'This is the world we're in!' she screamed and ran to the door.

The sun was about to pull itself over the flat horizon, her eyes passed over the country waking with dawn. Its threatening bleakness melted for a moment into the green beauty of Bonne Esperance and she could see Thys riding along the river's edge towards her. She could see the proud purple mountains behind him, and the babbling water beside him. She could hear him call her name on a breath, 'Suzanne.'

She turned to Rev. Phillip suddenly, her eyes shone with determination.

'I will find Thys! I will find him in *this* world! Not in the next, Reverend Phillip!' She moved out and into the light of the rising sun. Rev. Philliip didn't know how he could convince her that the Kingdom of God was to be found on earth.

Thys looked up suddenly as he poured coffee into a tin mug. He thought he'd heard his name called. Gerrit Malan, a man of nearly forty-five, with deep weather-driven lines scored on his face and piercing green eyes, watched him as he prodded the fire that crackled between them.

'What's wrong?' he asked Thys in Afrikaans.

'Nothing,' Thys said, dismissing the call he thought he'd

heard in the far reaches of his mind. Their wagon was parked a little way off. It was covered with strong canvas, held up on bamboo frames, forming a tent on the wagon base. They slept underneath it. Thys had shared Gerrit's wagon since he'd joined this small group of trekkers in his search for his mother. Gerrit treated him as though he were his own son. The son who had been murdered, with his wife and three daughters, by a group of marauding blacks as they travelled north.

'I heard news of another group moving further upcountry.' Gerrit's voice was deep. 'They said your mother was with them. At least, a woman by the name of Bothma, and two girls.' Thys moved closer to him. A chicken scratched round his feet and he pushed it away.

'Where?' he asked.

'Two weeks ahead. That was the word I heard.' Gerrit glanced up from the fire at Thys. 'She'll be safer now the Matabele have been moved out.'

'Is what we're looking for – what my mother's looking for – is it worth the price, Gerrit?'

'Freedom doesn't come cheaply, son. You should know that.' Gerrit was referring to Thys's father.

'But is it freedom or running away?' Thys asked suddenly.

Gerrit chuckled and stood up, giving the fire a kick as he did. Sparks flew as a red-hot log cracked open. 'We can't fight the British army but they can't stop us walking away from them.' Gerrit held a hand out for coffee and Thys passed him a tin mug. He looked into it before drinking, swirling the coffee gently in his cup. 'I have no quarrel with the British but my heart needs to sing its own song.' Gerrit looked out over the land. It looked beautiful at this waking time of day, he thought; when the dew glistened on the flat red earth, with climbing aloes suspended from sparse trees.

It was the most beautiful country he had ever seen. The country God had led his people to, as though He had created it for them. When the rains came, jasmine would load the air with perfume, and the ground would be spread with a carpet of delicate flowers. He still marvelled at it.

'I will guide my people,' he quoted quietly, 'to the land I have promised them.' Gerrit knew he'd found that promised land, and he turned to Thys brightly. 'This is where I will settle.'

'Here?' Thys was surprised by his sudden statement.

'I will come with you to find your mother but then,' he looked back over the domain he had claimed for himself, 'then I will come back here. And you?'

'I will go with my mother.'

'Of course.' Gerrit tossed the dregs of coffee into the fire. It sizzled, sending up a thin stream of smoke. 'And you will still think of the English girl.' He handed his empty cup to Thys. 'There is no harm.'

Others in wagons close by were beginning to prepare for the day's travelling. They called and shouted to their oxen, outspanned in the surrounding country. The black slaves who had elected to go with them moved to the oxen with long rhinoceros whips, beating them to move, yelling and whistling as they did.

Thys's mind leapt back to the 'English girl'. Suzanne. Why had he thought he'd heard her calling him? He would never hear Suzanne call again, and he would never again make his bird call to her. He moved quickly towards Gerrit's oxen and whistled for them, blotting the sound of her name from his mind. But many weeks and miles of rough country later, Thys was confronted by her name again.

'Suzanne!' Theresa Bothma glared at her son where he stood beside the ox wagon she sat in. His two sisters, Tarcie and Anna, sat obediently beside their mother, looking at him, but they said nothing. 'You chose the English woman. There is no place for you with us.' His mother's words cut the last strand of the bond between them. Thys lowered his head, feeling her eyes on him. 'We have no need of you. September!' she shouted at the driver who stood at the head of the oxen; and September laid his whip smoothly down the brown hide ox backs. As he pulled the twisted hide trek rope fastened to the yokes he glanced at Thys. Thys caught his look. He was from the past, one of the slaves Thys had played with when they were both children. He was Petrus's son, born in September.

Thys stood still beside his horse as the wagon rolled away after the others, carrying his mother out of his life. Tarcie, his blonde sister, waved to him as the wagon broadened the distance between them, but turned away quickly, forced to turn her back on Thys as his mother had.

Gerrit came silently up to him as the wagon disappeared in its own dust.

'You asked once if I would join you,' Thys said quietly, without turning.

'I had begun to think you were lost, son.' Gerrit allowed his green eyes to cover Thys with welcome, stretched out his hand and laid it on Thys's shoulder. 'Our land is waiting for us. Our roots are crying out to be put down.' Gerrit walked with Thys to their horses, wagon and cattle. 'And you still love Suzanne.' Gerrit paused for the slightest moment, then winked. 'If you have it in your mind's eye, it will be.'

PART TWO

1844-62

Chapter Eleven

The sun hadn't yet woken to reach up to the small windows set high in the wall and the stables were still dark. Jean Jacques was as quiet as possible as he led his horse to the stable door. Its hooves were muffled with cloth to tread the cobbles of the courtyard in silence. He reached the stable door, and stopped. Emily stood very quiet and still, a cloak covering her nightclothes.

'You were going without saying goodbye to me.' Her words were soft, but hurt was engraved on each one. She ran her hand down the horse's nose, keeping her eyes away from Jean Jacques. 'Will I ever see you again?'

He raised his head and looked at her. He could not allow himself to give way.

'When we were young and you taught me to write, I promised that one day I would write a letter to you,' he said.

'Will I see you again?' Emily lifted her face to him.

'Yes.' Emily wrapped her arms around his neck and held on to him tightly, her delicate body clinging to his.

'Would you give this to Father?' Jean Jacques dug a letter out of his pocket and handed it to her, trying to break the moment. 'I was going to send it when I wrote to you.' His voice warmed the damp dark air between them.

'Can't you face Father? Not even him?' Emily's eyes were moist. 'Please don't go, J.J.!'

'I must.' He held her hands between his and Emily watched him. She remembered the night he'd first told her about the army. It had been late and she'd sat on his bed in the attic room, unable to believe what she was hearing.

'Because in the eyes of the world I'm not worthy of my own son, Emily, I have to prove myself worthy of being his father,' Jean Jacques had said.

'But you *are* his father!' Emily had turned away. 'It's Clara's husband. Lord Marsden has talked you into it!' Emily had swung back. 'You don't need to join the army to prove yourself, J.J. You can do that here, running the estate the way Father wants you to.'

'Father doesn't know about Pauline and my child.'

'Then we will tell him.'

'And then?' He held her shoulders, to impress her with the facts. 'We cannot reveal the truth. You told me that.'

'You could go to Cape Town. You could work to earn enough money to find your own way. How much will you be paid in the army?'

'A shilling a day.'

Emily's eyes had closed. One shilling a day to prove himself. Was dying worth only one shilling a day?'

Although Emily had grown into a woman, she was still as unsure of herself as the little girl who had read to him from her mother's diary. She was a small bird, tipped too soon from its nest, and Jean Jacques ached as he remembered the bright face of that small girl at her mother's grave.

'Your father is my father.' The same little girl was the woman looking at him now. The same love and complete acceptance, but tinged with adult fear.

'A uniform renders all men the same colour, Emily.'

'And bullets are colour blind,' she'd said as she'd run out of the room.

He could still see the fear in Emily's eyes as he looked at her now. The mist of early morning, before night gave way to day, swirled around him.

'Take care, J.J.,' Emily whispered as he melted into the mist outside and silently led his horse away. Emily stared at the empty doorway. Then she turned and looked wildly around the stables. Even though they had been rebuilt after the fire, they still held terror within their walls. She hurried out and strained her eyes in the direction of the road leading away from Bonne Esperance to Cape Town and the army. She could hear nothing, and through the mist she could see nothing.

An idea Prudence had had which could improve the grafting of cuttings on to rootstock had worked in practice, and she'd been looking for her father since early morning to tell him. She asked the labourers where he was and then at last she found him. He was higher up the slopes of the vineyard.

'I wanted to tell you about the grafting, Father,' Prudence panted as she reached him. Her hair, as always, was a tangled mess around her face. Her clothes were untidy, and marked with wine stains.

'Your appearance is a disgrace, Prudence.' Jacques turned away coldly.

'What?' She looked down at herself, brushing at her dress. 'I've found a better method of grafting, Father, and I . . .'

'Don't you care what you look like?' His voice cut through her excitement.

'Does it matter, Father?'

'You are a disgrace!' Jacques walked away, but her anger was roused and she wouldn't let him go.

'Aren't you going to listen to what I have to say?' Jacques kept walking in silence as she ran after him so she grabbed his coat sleeve, pulling him round to her. 'Do you think what I look like makes a ha'p'orth of difference to the way I graft?'

'It makes a difference to you, Prudence. Have you no pride? Must you insist on insulting your womanhood constantly?' Her face fell as his angry eyes bore into her for a moment, then he walked on to put an end to their conversation.

'What is it, Father?' Prudence chased after him again. 'This has nothing to do with the manner in which I am dressed. Tell me what's wrong!'

He put a hand in his pocket and pulled out Jean Jacques' letter. He handed the letter to her abruptly and watched her expressionlessly as she read it.

'I presume it was your idea,' he said flatly.

Prudence turned the letter over as though she might find the answer to her confusion on the other side.

'You've always wanted to run Bonne Esperance!'

'You imagine I talked Jean Jacques into this?' Prudence had never before been hurt so deeply. She didn't hear her father's voice a she ran towards the house.

'Prudence!' he called. She kept running, and her anger rose with every step she took.

*

'Have you forgotten to knock before you enter my room?' Clara asked as Prudence burst in and the door slammed back against the wall. Clara was at the mirror, brushing her hair.

'Do you want me to knock?'

'Perhaps you came to borrow my hairbrush?' Clara smiled, but turned in surprise as Prudence marched back to the door, swung it open and slammed it closed on herself. She banged on it loudly from the outside, then opened it and marched inside.

'Was that good enough?'

Clara went back to brushing her hair with silent disdain, but Prudence snatched the brush out of her hand.

'I want to ask you a question, Clara, and I want an honest answer!' Clara took a slight breath and picked up a silver hair comb. 'What have you got to do with Jean Jacques enlisting in the army?' Prudence demanded.

'Me?' Clara smiled as she pulled the comb through her long dark hair. 'I have no interest in anything he might choose to do.'

Prudence seized the comb and threw it to the floor. 'Swear to me you know nothing about it!'

'Charles did mention it.'

'It was his idea, wasn't it? He persuaded Jean Jacques to join his toy soldier army! Didn't he!' she yelled.

'He's a soldier himself,' Clara paused, 'and not a toy one.' She got up and calmly retrieved her comb. 'He was concerned about Jean Jacques wasting his life as a labourer and . . .'

'Concerned?'

Clara stopped in front of Prudence and held out her hand for the brush. 'I'm surprised you don't know more about men, Prudence.' She took the brush from her. 'You of all people should know what men want.' She sat down at the dressing-table again.

'What women offer them!' Prudence challenged.

'Is there something you're trying to say, Prudence?'

'It was your idea,' Prudence blurted out.

'Mine?' Clara laughed.

'You forced your husband to do your dirty work for you! To get rid of Jean Jacques!'

'I forced my husband?' Clara's words were round with amazement. 'I have no need,' she smiled.

'No?' Prudence leaned forward and glanced at Clara in the

mirror. 'You hold sex in front of him and use it like a weapon! Jezebel!'

'Jezebel?' Clara laughed falsely. 'You talk to me of Jezebel? You who choose to work with men under the pretence of caring for the estate? It is you who uses sex, to try to get control of Bonne Esperance!'

Clara's words stirred all the pain, anger and humiliation Prudence had suffered at the hands of M. Claudelle. She could neither see nor hear as she grabbed a handful of Clara's hair.

'Let go!' Clara screamed, trying to pull her hair out of Prudence's grip. 'How dare you!'

'It's not because he's a half-caste, is it, Clara! It's because he's our father's son!' She yanked Clara by the hair. Clara screamed, lashing out with her nails. Prudence tried to hold Clara's hands by the wrists, away from her face, but Clara's nails tore down her cheek.

'You hate him because he took Father away from you!' Prudence pushed Clara away, sending her reeling back on to the floor. She leapt forward, jumping on Clara who struggled and kicked, but Prudence was stronger and held her down. With one leg across Clara she pinned her arms down on the floor.

'Now tell me the truth!' Prudence yelled.

'Stop this!' Clara screamed.

'Tell me!'

'Clara! Prudence!' Jacques was standing in the doorway. 'Leave the room, Prudence! Go!' Prudence glared down at Clara. She wanted to kill her.

'One day,' she whispered menacingly and stood up, pushing past her father at the door. Jacques kept his eyes on Clara as she got to her feet, straightened her dress and moved back to the dressing-table.

'She's an animal. It's time you spoke to her, Father. She's quite wild and it's because she works with men!'

'I need to talk to you.'

'She attacked me,' Clara went on. 'I assume you will punish her.'

'Clara!' he said firmly and she finally turned to him. 'I want to ask you about your marriage to Charles.'

'Suddenly everybody is asking me about Charles,' Clara laughed. 'I know very well you don't like him.'

'Are you happy?' The warm tone of his voice caught her by

surprise. She looked into his eyes for the love she had seen in them when she was young.

'You care that I am happy, Father?' Clara's words were measured by amazement.

'I have cared since you were a child.' Her eyes shone. Edges of joy touched her lips and softened the line of her mouth. 'But you're no longer a child, and I'm not certain I know the woman you are.' He walked over to the window. He needed space for truth to move between them. 'Perhaps it's because your husband is not a man I could know.'

'I'm happy, Father.' She moved to him, and tentatively stretched out her hand, as if she were reaching back into her childhood. 'Father.'

'Do I have no reason for the uncertainty I feel?'

'About what?' She longed to throw herself into his arms. She yearned to be his child again. The little girl who had died as she'd watched her father cradle a newborn baby with such love. 'I have something to tell you. Something very important.' Clara ran her finger down his arm and curled her hand around his, lifting it to her face. 'What would be the best news I could give you?' Her attitude confused Jacques. She kissed his hands as she held it against her cheek.

'I'm having a baby, Father.' She clasped his hand between hers. 'You are to have a grandson.' She gazed at him in excitement. 'Smile?'

'I am pleased,' Jacques said, but he couldn't smile. 'Congratulations.' He removed his hand from hers and went to the door. She waited expectantly for him to turn back to her and reveal his happiness. But when he did turn, his face was as set as his voice. 'When did you know?'

'You are the first to know, Father.'

'When did you know about Jean Jacques?'

Clara swung away as the name burned her. Her voice was brittle as she looked at him in the mirror.

'We will never understand one another, Father. Would you leave my room, please.'

Prudence's feelings were in as much of a mess as her hair and dress. She pulled the bodice of her dress open, sending the buttons flying, and tugged at the skirt.

'I should care how I dress! Care that I work with men!' she muttered in rage. 'I'll show you how much I care for such nonsense!' She ran to the door and pulled it open. 'Maria!' Her hands wiped away the blood which welled from the scratches on her face. 'Maria!' she shouted again, with blood smeared across her cheeks.

'What you done to yourself!' Maria's great bosom shook as Prudence pulled her into the room and closed the door behind her. 'What you done?'

'I need your help, Maria.'

'You need water for your face!' Maria tutted.

'Did Jean Jacques take all his clothes with him?'

Maria's mouth opened in puzzlement.

'Did he?' Prudence made her sit on the bed beside her. 'Will you go and see?'

Maria was uncomfortable sitting on the bed, and shrugged her shoulders. Her chin pushed forward determinedly. 'Why?' She tilted her head back a little and her eyes settled on the ripped dress on the floor. 'You done that?' Maria used the clothes as an excuse to get up off the bed. She picked up the torn dress and examined it. 'You don't like it?' She held it up to Prudence. 'It's a pretty dress.' Maria pushed the cloth together as though she could mend it by magic.

'Yes, Maria. It's a pretty dress, but I'm not.' Maria's wide face folded as she looked at her. 'Please help me, Maria.' Prudence moved to her, wrapping her arms around her and leaning her head on the soft dark shoulders.

'Why you spoil your dress, child?' Maria's arms came up around Prudence and held her head against her shoulder. 'What wrong?' Her strong black arms were wrapped around her as though Prudence was still the young girl she had often comforted. 'Maria not cross, child.'

The horses tossed their heads and struck out with their hooves at the hard cobbles of the courtyard, both restrained firmly by the straps of their harness. The carriage was prepared and ready to leave. The driver, in a dark suit and tall hat, opened the carriage door as Jacques approached.

'We're leaving, Emily,' he called back impatiently. He stopped, his attention caught by a line of Malay labourers across the courtyard near the cellars. They wore cone-shaped reed hats, three-quarter-length dark trousers and full white cotton shirts and were passing heavily laden baskets of grapes along the line and into the cellars. Jacques reacted sharply as he noticed one of the reed hats duck and hide behind the others, then run. Jacques chased after the Malay as he disappeared around the corner.

'Come here!' he shouted. 'Don't think you can laze the day away in sleep the minute I'm gone!' He turned the corner, close behind. 'Wait!' he commanded.

The figure stopped, cowering under the tall reed hat as he crouched against the cellar wall.

'Are you sick?' The silence puzzled him and he bent down to see what was wrong. 'Speak to me.' The hat was pulled down further over the face. 'Why are you afraid?' Jacques asked gently, then his expression changed. He could hear laughter. The body under the hat was shaking not from fear but from laughter. 'You're not sick. Get back to work,' Jacques ordered. 'This is no time for games.'

'Father.' Jacques looked startled as the hat lifted and long blonde hair tumbled out from beneath it.

'Prudence!' Emily collapsed with laughter as she turned the corner and saw her. 'What on earth are you doing?'

'He didn't recognize me.' Prudence stood up and Jacques' eyes passed over her in amazement. She was dressed like the other workers, in a shirt and trousers. 'You didn't know me, Father!' She smiled. 'This is no time for games!' she imitated his voice.

'It is not,' Jacques said severely. 'Not at all.'

'But you thought I was a man! Tell the truth.' Prudence turned to Emily. 'He didn't recognize me! I know he didn't!'

'I'm not surprised, you look very strange.' Emily tugged at the calf-length trousers. 'These are Jean Jacques', aren't they?'

Prudence plonked the reed hat back on her head and looked up at her father. 'Do I look better than in a dress? Less untidy and more suitable for man's work?' she asked.

'We must leave, Emily.' Jacques turned to go and Prudence followed him quickly, hanging on to his arm.

'You're not angry with me are you, Father?' she asked.

'No.' Jacques glanced at her as they walked across to the carriage. He couldn't prevent a smile as he put an arm around her shoulder. 'But I think I prefer you in a dress.' The fresh stark simplicity that was Prudence was something he could not resist.

'You are too much a woman ever to be a man.' He pulled her tightly under his arm and they moved on together to the carriage. The Malay workers giggled, enjoying the moment to its full and dropping baskets of grapes all around them.

'You laugh?' Jacques shouted, with slight amusement. 'Perhaps women can work better than you! Remember that!' He turned to Prudence as the driver held open the carriage door for Emily. 'Take care of things while I'm away, Prudence.'

'I will, Father.' Prudence caught his hand. 'Please give my love to Jean Jacques.' She paused. 'And thank you, Father.'

'What for?'

Prudence could never tell him how ugly she'd felt since M. Claudelle had attacked her. How 'unlike a woman' she'd wanted to be since that day. She made no reply, but released his hand and ran towards the house.

Jacques glanced after her, puzzled, as he closed the carriage door. He looked back at the workers, who were still watching them in fascination. 'If the harvest isn't complete when I return I shall replace you all with your mothers, wives and sisters!' He sat back in the carriage beside Emily and broke into laughter. Emily laughed with him as, at the command of the driver, the horses stepped out and picked their way around the courtyard into the oak-lined driveway.

Miss Thurston stood back as Emily looked around the room in amazement. A tiny Malay man of fifty-four, as thin as a reed and without a tooth in his head, pointed proudly at the hand-painted frieze below the cornice.

'You see it?' Miss Thurston asked. 'Raphus Jeremiah and I restored it ourselves.' The small Malay man nodded his whole angular body, and his mouth widened in a smile. 'I've always loved a frieze on the wall. It's very much a part of England,' Miss Thurston went on.

'Raphus Jeremiah?' Emily asked as she looked at the tiny man. 'Is that his name?'

'Caesar,' Miss Thurston added. 'Raphus Jeremiah Caesar.'

Emily couldn't help smiling as she looked at the tiny frame which bore such an enormous name.

'The whole house has become a small part of England, Miss Thurston.' She moved to a chair and ran her hand down the velvet arm. 'You must be exhausted.'

'No more than Raphus Jeremiah.' Miss Thurston smiled at him and he replied with another toothless grin. 'He's very bright, you know. Once I told him how to plumb, plumb he did!'

Emily saw the pride swell in the small dark frame as he moved to the silver teatray with an extra bounce in his step. He was totally out of place in the English surroundings, but somehow he completed them, Emily thought. She turned to Miss Thurston in wonder. 'There's nothing of him!'

'Once or twice I nearly lost him down a drainpipe!' Miss Thurston patted a cushion on a chair and waited for Emily to sit in it as Raphus Jeremiah nodded confirmation and handed her a cup of tea. 'For a man who has spent his entire life in such an insanitary place as Cape Town, I have managed the impossible! He no longer spits!' She passed the tea to Emily and the dark hand held out another to her with a slight bow of his thin body.

'Tea, mama,' he said.

'Tea, Miss Thurston,' she corrected him.

'Yes, mama.' He squatted in the doorway with his grin as wide as his spread knees.

'I doubt I shall ever stop him calling me "mama",' Miss Thurston confided to Emily.

'You're incredible! When you bought this house at the auction I wasn't at all sure you'd done the right thing.' Emily was impressed and Miss Thurston was pleased.

'I've met the auctioneer since!' she chuckled. 'Would you believe, he still imagines I fiddled him.'

'You did!' Emily noticed Raphus Jeremiah nod his agreement.

'I simply used his bad arithmetic to my advantage.' Miss Thurston added, 'Besides, he had not told me about the fixture!'

'He's a fixture?' Emily's eyes opened wide with amusement at the thought of Raphus Jeremiah being a fixture.

'And one the auctioneer thought devalued the property! If he had but known what lay behind that string of names! A veritable champion!' She turned to Emily innocently. 'But I was not to let him know that, was I?'

'Instead you made him offer you more money before you made your bid!'

'It was his harebrained scheme to offer people money to bid for the house in the first place. Surely he should know that if a person manages to double the money that's on offer for bidding, that person is most likely to then halve the offer they plan to make! It's quite simple,' Miss Thurston assured her.

'And you've got your house, you've got your school, and Raphus.'

'. . . Jeremiah Caesar,' Miss Thurston added.

'I'm so happy for you I could cry!'

'Please don't,' Miss Thurston smiled at her, 'it would upset him most terribly.'

Emily took her hand. 'But you do look tired. You must promise me not to strain yourself.'

'Nonsense!' Miss Thurston's eyes gleamed with life, though her face showed every one of her three score and ten years. 'I've spoken to a great number of people in town and it appears I shall hardly have room enough for all the pupils.'

'Are you sure?' Emily's face grew sad as she looked at the old woman she loved and couldn't bear to see hurt. 'You really must take care of yourself.'

'My dear child,' Miss Thurston squeezed her hand, 'you worry so! There are several young ladies in Cape Town who are waiting to learn the finer graces of English manners. I will not let them down.'

'From the talk around town all they want to learn is the hornpipe,' Emily said.

'The hornpipe?' Miss Thurston's face reflected her disgust, as Raphus Jeremiah's did, in instant agreement. 'Why, most of the sailors "hornpiping" on those convict ships ought to be dropped off in Australia themselves. But the gavotte, the waltz! Now there, my dear, are the dances for young ladies.'

'You'll be teaching them the waltz?' The question in Emily's voice did not escape Miss Thurston.

'I do believe you think I would not be able to demonstrate the waltz?'

'I didn't say that!'

'Stand up!' Miss Thurston stood in front of Emily. Emily mouthed the word 'Me?' Miss Thurston held out her hand and said firmly, 'You.' She put one arm around Emily's waist, took her hand and looked at her determinedly. 'Ready?'

Raphus Jeremiah rose from his squatting position in expectation.

'One two three, one two three.' Miss Thurston swung Emily around the room in a beautiful careless waltz and Raphus Jeremiah ran ahead of them, moving pieces of furniture out of their path. He was alive with fun and his slim lithe body moved with the music he felt in the air though it couldn't be heard.

'I can't waltz for too long!' Emily cried as she was whirled around the room. 'Father will be collecting me to visit Jean Jacques soon.'

'I could waltz for ever,' Miss Thurston chirped as she saw a delicate chair whipped out of their way just in time by the dancing imp in front of her. 'Thank you.'

'I'm exhausted!'

Miss Thurston allowed Emily to drop back into her chair. 'So you are!' She held herself upright. 'And what do you think now, young lady!' She sat down in her own chair, straight-backed, holding her breath. 'Do you think I'm capable of teaching the waltz?'

Emily nodded as she breathed deeply, watching Raphus Jeremiah restore the room to English order. 'I am certain you could, Miss Thurston.'

'Good.' Miss Thurston glanced at the small but proud man who was again squatting at the door. 'Thank you, Raphus Jeremiah Caesar. Thank you very much.'

As the carriage approached the castle, with the sea curving in a white frill right up to its wall and Table Mountain standing guard behind it, Emily touched her father's hand.

'Don't worry.' She leant her head on his shoulder. 'Please let Jean Jacques find his own life. As Miss Thurston has.'

'She is well?'

'And very happy.' Jacques looked away. 'And Eva?' Emily asked.

'Yes,' Jacques nodded but said nothing more. He looked at the sea washing gently towards the sides of the road their carriage travelled and his mind turned back to Eva. She had known nothing of Jean Jacques' plans to join the army, but she'd accepted the news in the calm way she always accepted facts. She had simply tried to impress on him that their son must find his own way.

Jacques closed his eyes as the carriage rumbled up the cobbled drive towards the castle gates and moved through the deep brick arch into the castle itself. He could still hear Thys shouting after him in desperation and Suzanne crying that she loved him. It had been a night Jacques would never forget.

'Don't think of Suzanne,' Emily said as if reading his mind.

The carriage door was opened by a smart, red-uniformed soldier. He stood to attention beside the carriage and saluted as Emily stepped out ahead of her father.

As she looked about her Emily could at last place Lord Marsden. He was a part of these surroundings. The formality of the low square buildings and the rigid line of white pillars was his background. The entire castle seemed to stand to attention. Above it, Table Mountain rose in folded pleats of silver granite. It was as if Queen Victoria herself sat on its flat top.

'Good morning,' Charles Marsden greeted them, stepping out of the building and into Emily's mind. 'Jean Jacques is waiting for you in my office.'

Jean Jacques looked incredibly handsome in the green uniform of the Cape Mounted Rifles and Emily suddenly understood what he had meant about uniforms. She turned to Lord Marsden. 'Is there somewhere you and I could wait while my father and Jean Jacques speak?'

'After you.' He stood back indicating that she should leave with him.

Jean Jacques didn't look at Emily as she departed, nor did he look at his father, although he was alone with him.

'You look very smart,' Jacques said.

'Thank you, sir.'

Jacques stiffened at his propriety and moved away from him slightly. 'You're enjoying it?' It was as if Jean Jacques was a total stranger. 'The army?'

'Yes, sir.'

Jacques' eyes sought his son's in an attempt to break the formality between them.

'I'm sorry I didn't tell you myself, sir.'

'Were you afraid?'

'I was afraid you might change my mind.'

'I would have tried.' Jacques walked away a little then turned

223

back to his son. 'I have seen your mother.' Jean Jacques looked up at him, waiting. Jacques nodded. 'She says your life is your own, but I don't agree.' Jacques walked away again. He felt very uncomfortable faced by his son in a uniform which separated them completely. 'How long before they send you to the frontier?' This was the question in the forefront of his mind.

'I will go when I am ordered.'

Jacques looked at him intensely. 'Have I given you so little, Jean Jacques?'

'Perhaps you tried to give me too much.'

'You're my son!'

'A son doesn't need to be reminded who he is.'

Jacques knew how often he reminded both himself and Jean Jacques that they were father and son. How he continually reminded everyone, everywhere, that Jean Jacques was his son. 'I was told you have changed your name to Villiers,' he said.

'I want no special treatment, sir.'

'Lord Marsden's idea?'

Jean Jacques allowed his eyes to settle on his father. 'Now I'm no longer with you will you still love my mother?' he asked abruptly. The words cut Jacques and a sudden anger rose inside him.

'Do you imagine I married your mother for *your* sake?' Jacques watched him. 'Do you?' he pressed. Jean Jacques nodded.

'Then you are very wrong!' Jacques' face hardened.

Charles Marsden was after all as real as anyone else, Emily thought as she watched him over the tea they'd been served in his office. He looked up quickly as a soldier arrived with Jacques.

'You'll join us for tea?' he asked Jacques. 'Sit down, please.' He pulled a chair out for him.

'I have to get back to Bonne Esperance.' Jacques held his hand out to Emily. 'Come, Emily.'

'But I have something to tell you.' Charles moved to him. 'Please.' He held out the chair again.

'I know Clara is expecting a child,' Jacques said flatly. 'Congratulations.'

Charles Marsden crumbled. It was as if Jacques had pricked the puffed red chest and it had slowly caved in.

'That's wonderful news, Charles,' Emily cried, to cover her

father's disinterest. 'And thank you so much for the tea. It was lovely.' She had seen Charles Marsden's damaged pride and was afraid.

Chapter Twelve

'**P**rivate Villiers!' Jean Jacques looked up as he pulled a pail of water from the well between the main courtyard and the rear yard of the castle. 'May I speak with you.' Jean Jacques saluted while wrestling with the pail of water and snapped his heels together sharply.

'Sir.'

'If you have an assignment I won't interrupt you.' Charles Marsden glanced at the pail in his hands.

'I'm feeding the horses, sir.'

'Carry on.' He nodded for Jean Jacques to pass in front of him, moving after him to the barracks across the yard. 'I hear you spend a great deal of your time with the horses, Private Villiers.'

'I'm in charge of them, sir. Yes, sir.'

'But not riding yet.' Charles kept his tone warm.

'No, sir.' Jean Jacques slowed his pace so that Charles Marsden was not behind him. The insecurity he had always felt in the presence of Lord Marsden was heightened by his position as a senior officer. 'Do you wish to speak to me, sir?'

'Carry on with the horses.' Marsden followed him to the stable doors. A horse immediately stretched its nose out to Jean Jacques and nuzzled his neck. 'I see you haven't lost your way with horseflesh,' Marsden commented quietly.

'They're good horses, sir.' Jean Jacques went into the stable. 'Excuse me.'

'I hear your company is due to go to the eastern frontier,' Marsden said casually from outside the stable door.

'Yes, sir.' Jean Jacques moved back to the door and stood to attention again. As Marsden looked into his open face he felt the slightest unease.

'I might, of course, be able to ensure you do not go, but I can't be certain of it. You do understand that.'

'I will go with my company, sir. I ask no special conditions.' Jean Jacques saluted.

Marsden turned and walked away towards the officers' mess. He stopped and looked back at Jean Jacques. A quiet dignity ran right through his being. It was something Marsden had never come face to face with before and it moved him deeply.

Charles Marsden formed a circle of silence around himself as he sat alone in the officers' mess. He gazed deep into his glass of port, puffed on his cigar and allowed the smoke to curve slowly out of his mouth and up over his face in a swirling white cloud. He was bound by his desire for Clara. But he knew he could never carry through her plans.

'And if Jean Jacques was sent to the frontier there would be nothing you could do to stop that happening, would there, Charles?' He could hear Clara's voice. He could feel her as she pressed her breasts against his back and leaned into him. 'It would be so easy, Charles!' He could feel her fingers as they stroked the inside of his thigh.

'Charles?' The voice snapped him back. He looked up as Colonel Stringer from the Indian Horse Artillery came up to his table. 'May I join you?' He was older than Charles, a professional soldier with an air of continual excitement.

'Yes, yes.' Charles pulled himself together as the colonel sat down at the small round table.

'What a country!' Colonel Stringer announced. 'I envy you!'

'I thought India was your second home. The jewel in the crown, with you wearing it.' Charles smiled.

'It is indeed.' Colonel Stringer leaned back in his chair and glanced up at the broad beams of the yellowwood ceiling. 'But this is where it will all happen.' He grinned at the ceiling.

Charles puffed on his cigar and peered at him through crinkled eyes. 'The war you've been looking for?'

'These bloody kaffir wars? No, no, no. They will be put down soon enough.'

'Ah!' Charles smiled. 'New enemies? Your kind.'

'A kind never met before!'' Stringer removed his gaze from the ceiling and leaned forward. 'I have a nose for it.'

Charles looked into his empty glass. 'Can I get you another?'

Colonel Stringer slid his glass across the polished table to

Charles. 'Can you imagine what will happen if they should ever get ideas above their station?'

'The kaffirs?' Charles nodded for the black waiter in his starched white uniform to refill their glasses.

'The Boers.' Stringer glanced around nervously and lowered his voice. 'They'd murder every last one of 'em.'

'Murder who?' Charles asked without particular interest.

'The mother's boys who come out here with handkerchiefs in their pockets thinking they're joining a picnic in the sun.' He aligned his backbone against the hard-backed chair struts. 'I have a mind to take them on myself.'

'The Boers?' Charles was intrigued.

'Our troops!' His voice dropped to a confidential whisper. 'A bunch of staff officers who'd do better guarding our Queen, God bless her. It's bush warfare should be taught, not parade drill. If I had my way, I'd send one of these dark fellows here back home, and have him teach them a thing or two before they even stepped off the boat!'

His words had touched Charles with a fresh idea.

Colonel Stringer leaned back as he took his drink from the waiter without seeing the smiling black face at all. 'Here's to your learning that dockside Flemish language, Major Marsden!' He raised his glass. 'For if I have half an eye at all, this rebellious nation of Boers will one day fight back.'

'I doubt such an indolent and apathetic being as the Boer will ever be a major threat to the Empire.'

'Mark my words, Major.' Stringer downed his drink smartly and set his empty glass on the table with a flourish. 'Mark them!'

The large square sundial above the arch connecting the castle courtyards showed ten o'clock. Charles automatically added forty minutes in his head as he looked at it, and moved on towards a small troop of Cape Mounted Riflemen as they drilled. The sundial was a relic of the Dutch Administration in the Cape. Being made in Holland, the lower angle of the sun in the southern hemisphere had not been allowed for and it always irritated Charles. He remembered Colonel Stringer's warnings about the Boer and smiled to himself. There would never be a danger. The Boer would always be forty minutes late.

He stopped close enough to the drilling riflemen to see the

lieutenant in charge of them clearly. It was Lieutenant Duncan Shaw: a young officer who had promised a brilliant career in the Colony yet had not gained his due promotion. Charles knew the reason. Shaw was an extremely handsome man, blond and blue-eyed. A man with a past.

'Lieutenant Shaw!' Charles called as he reached him. 'My office in ten minutes.' His eyes singled out Jean Jacques among the troops and he turned smartly away. Colonel Stringer's words played among his thoughts. 'If I had my way I'd send one of these dark fellows back home.' Charles had decided he might have the answer to Clara's demands.

'No, Lieutenant Shaw, you will not be going to the frontier.' Charles looked across his desk at him. 'You are not pleased?' Lieutenant Shaw was obviously not pleased. 'You enjoy action?' Charles glanced at a piece of paper on his desk in front of him. He didn't read it, but he looked at it as if it was vital. 'You have a Private Villiers in your command, have you not?'

'Sir?' Lieutenant Shaw obviously had no idea.

'They all look alike do they, Shaw?'

'Sir.' Lieutenant Shaw cleared his throat. 'I believe there is a man of that name, sir.'

'And?' Charles leaned back in his chair. 'Is he a worthwhile member of the British army?'

'They are not best fitted for army life, sir.'

'They?'

'He is a half-caste, sir.'

'Oh,' Charles nodded, forcing him to go on. Making him as uncomfortable as possible.

'They have the worst of both white and black, sir. Not to be trusted in the least.'

'I see.' Charles returned his look to the paper on his desk. 'Then I am to take it you consider him unfit for service?'

Lieutenant Shaw looked at Charles curiously, uncertain where the conversation was leading. 'Have you a particular interest in Villiers, sir?'

'No more than yourself, Lieutenant.' Charles leaned back in his chair. 'There's been a suggestion that one of the men, one of our darker compatriots, a man perhaps like Private Villiers, should be sent home in order to acquaint new recruits with what to expect in terms of bush warfare.'

'A man like Villiers would be entirely out of place with English customs, sir.'

'As out of place as we with Africa!' Charles stood up and moved to the door. 'Thank you, Lieutenant Shaw.'

'I think I could find a better man, sir.'

Charles smarted at Shaw's arrogance. 'Very often the best do not achieve their full promise, Lieutenant Shaw – as you well know.' Charles laid a slight threat behind his words. 'They make small mistakes which, though concealed, will never entirely disappear.' Charles released him temporarily from the threat of the past which Shaw suddenly knew he held over him. 'Good day, Lieutenant.'

John Westbury bubbled with the mischief of a healthy five-year-old as he bounced up from behind Emily's chair.

'Boo!'

'Oh!' She pretended to be very afraid. 'Come here.' She grabbed the small boy and pulled him into the chair with her.

'Let me go!' He struggled ferociously.

'I'll take him out.' Mrs Westbury took his hand. 'You're being a very naughty boy, John. Not at all the way to impress your godmother.'

'I want to play with Emily,' he called as he was carted out.

'Aunty Emily,' Mrs Westbury reminded him, using the term used for all grown-ups, and Emily wondered if she had truly forgotten the truth of it. She looked at Pauline as at last they were left alone. Pauline tensed and crossed to the teatray.

'Tea?'

'I have some.'

'Are you sure it's not cold?' Pauline felt the teapot. 'The pot is cold.' She moved to take Emily's cup. 'I'll get a fresh pot and you a fresh cup.'

Emily touched her hand. 'I'm not here for tea, Pauline.' Pauline turned away without taking her cup. 'He seems to be enjoying army life.'

'How's your family keeping?' Pauline asked. 'Are they all well?'

'He writes of you always in his letters, Pauline.' Emily looked up, startled, as Mrs Westbury came back into the room.

'Did you know Clara's baby is due soon, Mother?' Pauline

said quickly.

'Your father will be pleased,' Mrs Westbury assured Emily.

'Why?' Emily challenged her silently with the truth, which Mrs Westbury avoided unthinkingly.

'A grandson is such a blessing!'

'Yes,' Emily agreed. 'He is very pleased.'

'More tea?' Mrs Westbury asked.

'Pauline says the pot is cold.' She smiled graciously at Mrs Westbury.

'Then I shall warm it up.' Mrs Westbury hurried out of the room again carrying the teapot.

The moment her mother had gone Pauline's façade dropped. 'I want to see him, Emily.' She spoke very quietly. 'I need to see Jean Jacques.'

Emily had used Miss Thurston as an excuse to go to Cape Town to see Jean Jacques, and she used the same excuse to take Pauline.

'If you cared at all for Miss Thurston, you would tell her to forget that school! The idea is entirely ridiculous,' Clara snapped as Emily prepared to leave the house with Pauline. 'I am quite certain Pauline is not in the least interested in what she is doing.'

'But I am, Clara,' Pauline protested.

'I can't tell Miss Thurston to stop dreaming.' Emily took her parasol from the stand. 'Are you feeling a little sick with your pregnancy, Clara?' She twirled the parasol. 'Is that bile in your mouth?'

'She is too old to open a school!'

'But not to dream, Clara.' Emily had gone before Clara could answer.

'Does she know?' Pauline asked nervously as Emily climbed into the carriage, and – as she asked repeatedly during the journey – 'Are you sure he wants to see me?'

'Clara is only interested in herself, Pauline.' Emily touched her hand to calm her. 'And you have other things to think of.' She squeezed her friend's hand. 'Yes, Pauline. He wants to see you.'

Houses stood tall in proud terraces on either side of the cobbled road. Their windows were like rows of gleaming square eyes, their open eyelids flattened in green shutters against the white walls. It was as if they were watching out for Pauline and Jean Jacques.

'He'll come to the top of the street,' Emily assured Pauline as she climbed down from the carriage. 'This is Miss Thurston's house and I'll meet you here when you're ready.' Emily enjoyed the secrecy. She glanced back at Pauline conspiratorially as she climbed the steps to Miss Thurston's door. 'Make your way now and you will see him.' The door swung open immediately she rang the bell and Raphus Jeremiah Caesar stood grandly in its frame.

'Good day, Miss Emily.' He bowed and swept his arm back in an expansive gesture indicating Emily should enter. He was dressed exactly as an English butler might be.

'Raphus Jeremiah!' Emily exclaimed in surprise.

'You like?' He looked down at his smart suit shyly.

'I like.' Emily went inside. Just before the door closed she glanced behind her into the avenue and prayed silently that Jean Jacques would come.

Pauline walked slowly towards Jean Jacques as he sat on his horse at the far end of the avenue. Jean Jacques dismounted and stood facing her, but they didn't touch. She could hardly breathe as she looked at him. He looked different, but so handsome. His shoulders were broad and his waist tiny in the green uniform with gold braid epaulettes. He removed his plumed hat and held it neatly under his arm.

'Are you allowed to take it off?' Pauline asked, not knowing what else to say.

'No.' His eyes communicated a million words. 'Emily said you would be here. Are you well?' He waited. Her eyes met his and her lips trembled as she smiled.

'I've missed you so much, Jean Jacques.'

As though his deepest fears had been assuaged by her assurance, Jean Jacques' face spread wide with joy. He held his hands down forming a step to help her up on to his horse. 'She's never carried a woman before.' Pauline placed a hand gently on his shoulder and a foot in his joined hands. She straightened her leg, allowed her weight to fall on his hands, and he lifted her. She looked down at him from where she sat side saddle on the horse's back. His hands gripped her ankles and his face was against her legs. Slowly and with inexpressible tenderness she ran her fingers through his hair.

'I'll get wet!' Pauline shrieked with laughter as Jean Jacques chased her over the hot white sand of the beach. Breaking waves rushed around their feet as they reached the shoreline, threatening to drag them back and out to sea. Jean Jacques pulled her down on to the wet sand and a froth of white foam swept over them.

'I *am* wet!' she laughed.

Jean Jacques rolled her on to her back and kissed the water from her face. 'Very wet.' His mouth tasted hers. 'And salty.' He spoke against her lips.

Holding his face between her hands, Pauline looked up at him. 'Our son is so beautiful, Jean Jacques. Just like you.' His lips passed gently over her eyelids, her nose, her cheeks, and she gripped his face tighter between her hands as their mouths found one another.

Pauline screamed as an enormous wave crashed over them, dragging them under the water, rolling them in the sand. She sat up in confusion as Jean Jacques struggled to his feet and moved quickly to her. 'Your uniform!' she laughed as he pulled her to her feet and they ran away from the waves. 'You'll be thrown into the dungeon!' She dropped to the ground as they reached dry sand and he fell back beside her.

'What are you thinking about?' she asked quietly.

He pushed back the wet strands of hair that clung to her face. 'We're going to be together, Pauline.' A moment later he was kneeling in the sand in front of her. He paused a moment, staring intensely into her eyes. His own were filled with tears. 'Will you marry me?'

'Yes?' he urged, when she made no reply. She nodded. 'When?' he persisted.

'Now.'

Jean Jacques leapt to his feet and raced down to the water's edge. He pulled a long snake of seaweed out of the waves as they deposited it at his feet, then ran back dragging the green monster behind him.

'I have the ring!' She yelped with laughter as he wound the length of seaweed around her, tying her in a knot and pulling her

233

back into the sand. She laughed but didn't resist. 'I pronounce us, man and wife,' he said seriously, and looked at her where she lay beside him, entwined in seaweed. 'Where would you like to go, Pauline?' He watched her as she unwound the seaweed. 'England?'

'England?' she smiled. 'How?'

'Somebody understands.' Jean Jacques grabbed her in his arms and rolled over with her, the white sand clinging to their wet clothes. 'Somebody cares!'

Pauline felt a deep peace. She had heard two words which could change their lives. 'Somebody cares.'

'That is not what I had in mind at all and well you know it, Charles!'

'He will be gone, Clara. Jean Jacques will no longer be between you and me.' He caressed her shoulder, then stroked the back of her neck. 'I have spoken to his commanding officer and he will add his recommendation.' She allowed him to turn her head to face him and he felt the power he held in the army slip away.

'Take your hand off me!' Reluctantly, Charles dropped his hand. 'Do you care nothing for the child I am about to bear, Charles? You might yourself take our son's future and throw it aside before he is born.' She took a deep breath and lowered her head. 'Would you leave me, please.'

'Are you all right?' Charles was immediately nervous.

'No. You said Jean Jacques was to go to the frontier!' She paced to the window in agitation.

'The orders were changed.'

'By whom?'

'A Lieutenant Shaw.'

'Lieutenant Shaw?'

'Clara.' Charles moved to her quickly. 'What more can I do?'

'Have I not satisfied your desires in ways which you had not even imagined possible?'

'You have bewitched me!'

'Then assure me, Charles.' Her eyelids lowered and her head tilted back. 'That you did not find your way into my bed on false promises.'

'I cannot send a man to his death in cold blood.'

Charles's emotions were thrown into sudden confusion as Clara doubled over and screamed in pain.

'Get out!' she hissed as her hands gripped her stomach and she looked at him with hatred. 'Get out until you have fulfilled your promise!'

Emily and Prudence stood in the hall and looked on in astonishment as the midwife rushed around ordering boiling water, clean towels, hot tea and gin.

'Gin?' Prudence pulled a face. 'I think I shall remove myself from this madhouse.' She turned to Emily as she moved out of the chaos of the hall to the front door. 'I'm sure you have better things to do, too.'

'Yes. But perhaps we should be here to help,' Emily said. They both started at a loud banging on the front door.

'Doubtless a doctor! One dragon of a midwife would not be good enough for Clara!' Prudence went to open the door as the midwife accosted Emily.

'Where are the towels?' the strict, starched woman demanded.

'I'll see what I can do.' She moved towards the kitchen and called, 'Maria!'

'I will not have her touch them!' the midwife stated.

'Emily.' Prudence approached her gently. She had a note in her hand.

'If we don't have any towels the baby cannot be born!' the midwife insisted. 'And boiling water! I asked for boiling water!'

'Yes. I'll see to it.' Emily turned back to her, wondering if newborn babies were dropped in boiling water by this midwife.

'Emily,' Prudence tried again. 'There is a message for you.'

'If you don't mind, young lady, I have asked for towels!' the midwife snapped at Prudence.

'Then get them yourself!' Prudence took Emily by the arm and led her hastily out of the house.

As they stepped outside and she took in the expression on Prudence's face clearly for the first time, Emily's blood ran cold. She knew the contents of the small note Prudence held in her hand without reading it.

'Miss Thurston?' Emily asked, not needing an answer.

'Do you want me to come with you?' Prudence took her hand and held it tightly. Emily shook her head.

'I thought I ordered gin!' the midwife's voice rose from the house, and Prudence closed her eyes.

'I'll drown her in it.' She looked at Emily as she gazed out across the mountains. 'Emily?'

'I would like to go to her alone.'

The room was dark, the heavy curtains drawn tightly closed as if to shut out life itself. Emily held Miss Thurston's cold pale hand in her own.

'I do believe there will be a long queue before you know it.' Her eyes beseeched the old lady as she lay quite still on the bed. The sagging skin on her face had the look of death already, but her eyes, the palest blue, were fixed intently on Emily's face. Her breathing was regular, short breaths held for a moment, before passing slowly out of her body.

'You must get well so that everything is in order for the pupils.' Emily hesitated as the pale-blue eyes flickered with a question. With slight fear. Another short sharp breath was snatched and slowly released. Emily glanced anxiously at the doctor who stood quietly at the bottom of the bed. At the door, Raphus Jeremiah squatted, his arms crossed over his spread knees. Tears ran in streams down his dark cheeks and on to his smart new butler's uniform. Emily turned back to Miss Thurston. There was so much she wanted to say and so little time left to say it.

'You always told me it is God's will that the truth be brought to light, Miss Thurston. But there are many truths which I must keep to myself for ever.' Miss Thurston gasped another breath and Emily waited as she released it.

'You didn't like Jean Jacques at first. You couldn't quite accept him, but you learned he was a good person. I think you even began to care for him. Didn't you?' She followed Miss Thurston's eyes as they pulled away from hers and moved to a picture of England on the wall.

'You always said that if I went to England it would be as if my mother had gone home. But that's not true, Miss Thurston. Not for me.' She waited for the familiar short breath. She waited for its release. 'As Jean Jacques is my brother, so Africa is my home.' She leaned her face beside Miss Thurston's. 'It's your home, too,' she whispered as her tears came. 'It's yours too.'

Emily waited for the short sharp breath to come.

'Miss Thurston?' Emily sat up and looked at her. The pale eyes stared back like two pebbles in shallow water. The doctor moved to the bed and took Miss Thurston's wrist. He shook his head. Emily stood up, looked for the last time at the only woman she had known as a mother, and kissed the cold brow. Then she turned and moved to the door. She stopped beside Raphus Jeremiah, who looked up at her, his face one big question.

'Mama is dead, Raphus Jeremiah,' she said

Charles paced the room, fear, inadequacy and resentment fighting to control him. He'd been locked out and totally cut off as Clara had gone into labour. She'd made it plain she wanted nothing from him. He pulled his fob watch from his waistcoat pocket and looked at it, then hurried out to the hall as he spotted the midwife going past on her way back to Clara's room.

'She's been in labour for forty-eight hours. There must be something you can do,' Charles demanded.

'Childbirth is a long and difficult process, Lord Marsden, which is doubtless why it is left to women.' The midwife moved on abruptly with her brace of gin and a glass, disappearing into Clara's room. She snapped the door shut behind her, locking him out once more.

Charles returned to the sitting-room, at a loss. He felt tired and completely out of place. Bonne Esperance had never become his home. It was Clara's; her inheritance. He moved to a chair and sat in it, crossing one leg over the other. A dull ache in his lower spine reminded him of the tension throughout his body. Suddenly Clara's voice rose in a long violent scream. He got up from the chair and paced the floor again. Throughout her labour her voice had carried the same vicious rage he'd aroused in her.

Charles was torn between his anticipation of the birth, the beauty of what it meant for a child to be born, and the guilt which his lust for Clara caused. An image of Jean Jacques rose in his mind, and he pushed it back quickly rather than face it. And even in the hour of her confinement Clara's sensuous and demanding body tugged at his thoughts.

'Is it not yet over?' Jacques' calm voice interrupted the turmoil of his thoughts. 'You should go out and breathe some fresh air, Charles. Sitting inside is not good for you.' Jacques came into the room and spoke as if nothing unusual were happening.

'It appears these things take quite some time,' Charles said as though he knew, as though he were a part of it. Wishing he was.

'Then perhaps you could do with a glass of wine.' Jacques took a bottle from the cabinet and prepared to open it. He stopped and smiled. 'Silence.'

Charles got up then hesitated at the door. Instinctively he listened for a baby's cry.

'Go and see your child,' Jacques encouraged him. For the first time Jacques thought he could understand this outsider at Bonne Esperance. As Charles was about to obey, the door opened in front of him.

'Mr Beauvilliers?' The midwife's voice was brusque. Her eyes passed over Charles without seeing him and settled on Jacques. 'Come.'

'Pardon?' Jacques said in slight confusion.

'Is my child born?' Charles asked eagerly.

'Your daughter would like to see you,' the midwife repeated to Jacques, and turned to go. Charles grabbed her arm. She swung round, her eyes demanding he remove his hand.

'Has my child been born?' he asked.

'You have a son.' She pulled her arm free and turned deliberately away from him. 'Your daughter is waiting for you, Mr Beauvilliers.' She threw Charles a dismissive smile.

'Excuse us.' Jacques halted as he reached the midwife at the door. 'Shall we go in?' He took Charles's arm.

Clara looked straight at her father as he entered the shaded room with Charles behind him. Her hair had been brushed back and her face was scrubbed clean. She held the newborn baby in her arms, but when it made a slight sound she looked down at it as if it didn't belong to her.

'It's a fine healthy boy,' the midwife stated flatly. She was in command in this room and would not have it otherwise. 'I am not at all surprised it took so long for him to enter the world. Particularly when one considers the utter lack of help I have had in this household!'

'Your grandson.' Clara smiled up at Jacques, ignoring Charles completely.

'Charles.' Jacques stepped back, allowing his son-in-law to see the baby. 'You have a fine son, Charles,' he said. 'Look at him.'

'You look at him, Father. Look at your heir!' Clara said, as though Charles was not in the room.

'I have an heir.' Jacques spoke quietly but firmly. 'My congratulations to you both. You have a fine son and heir, Charles.' He moved to the door, deliberately removing himself from the position Clara had tried to place him in. He stopped as he passed the midwife, who stood tightlipped at the end of the bed.

'I presume your work is over now?' Jacques asked with a kind smile.

'And not before time.'

'Then I would be obliged if you left my house immediately.' He picked up the bottle of gin standing half-empty on the dresser and handed it to her with another polite smile. 'You may remove this as well.' Jacques left the room.

'Take the child!' Clara snapped at the midwife, holding the baby out like a parcel. 'I'm tired.' She turned away, leaning her head against the pillow. 'Send everybody out.'

'You heard your wife,' the midwife said, clutching the baby to her and glaring at Charles.

'And I believe you have been released.' Charles held out his arms. 'My child, please.'

'Never in my life have I come across such an ill manner!' she complained as he took the baby from her. 'It's quite unbearable.'

'Then I suggest you remove yourself and return to your bottle of gin!'

'Will you allow this, Lady Marsden?' the midwife spluttered.

'Go!' Charles said loudly.

The door slammed shut behind the midwife. 'Thank you, Clara,' he said simply, as he gazed at the baby in his arms.

'When I am able to thank you, perhaps I will accept your thanks.' Clara twisted her head further away from him.

Charles looked back at the baby and tears filled his eyes. His voice was full of wonder.

'My son.'

'We will call him Jacques,' Clara whispered, laying the foundations of a solid wall between them.

Chapter Thirteen

The thin black hands under the glass face of the half-hunter pocket watch pointed to half-past four. It was the morning of 23 July, the year, 1843; the day on which Jack Marsden was born at Bonne Esperance, some eight hundred miles away.

'You will walk your horse in six directions of sixty degrees from your starting point. You will walk your horse for half an hour in each direction.' An arrogant English voice carved its way through the thick dark air, not yet lit by sun. Thys sat quite still on his horse.

'When the hands on my watch reach the half-hour, I will fire and you will mark your position with a stake.' Thys's horse reared as a gunshot ripped through the darkness around them and exploded in a noisy crackle of rebounding echoes.

'Like that.' The Landrost lowered his rifle to his side and leant on it, gazing at the wall of darkness from which there was no response. He looked down at Gerrit for some approval, but Gerrit continued to stir the pot of coffee on the fire in front of him, and gave none. The Landrost's ruddy face, lit by the flames, grew puzzled. His colour deepened as he looked back into the deaf night wall before him.

'When I fire,' the English voice rose, as if trying to find its way across an unknown distance, 'you will return to your starting point before moving in the next direction.' The Landrost turned back to Gerrit. 'Are you certain he can hear me?' he asked.

'Thys!' Gerrit's voice blasted through the still black space between them. 'Did you hear what the Landrost said?' Gerrit's voice ran after its own trail and disappeared into the dark.

'Yes,' the lower note of Thys's voice found its way back to Gerrit clearly.

'He can hear you,' Gerrit said quietly as he glanced towards the East. His accustomed eyes had caught the first glimmer of sunlight as it nudged the solid black sheet above it. Day was about to lift night on its shoulder. 'The sun will be up soon and it will be a hot day.' Gerrit urged the Landrost to hurry his instructions.

'You will mark the six furthest points you reach with your stakes, and the circumference of the joined markers will be the boundaries of your land.' The red cheeks of the Englishman glowed with achievement as he finished. He turned to a young field cornet who sat further away, his hat pulled over his eyes and his body bent like a bow as he slept under a tree.

'Riaan! Wake up!' he shouted, before settling his huge frame on the ground beside Gerrit. 'Do you understand the rules?' he asked, as though everyone barring himself was a fool. He didn't notice that his young cornet hadn't stirred under the tree.

'I think so.' Gerrit allowed himself to appear uncertain of such official procedures. 'Thys must walk his horse to the furthest point in six directions, and our land will be within the joined markers of those six points.' He smiled, 'Yes?'

'That's right.' The Landrost sounded surprised that he had understood. 'But he must walk his horse.'

'Yes,' Gerrit agreed with a twinkle in his eye. He glanced into the pot of coffee. 'It's good and hot. You'd like some?'

'It'll pass the time.' The Landrost laid his pocket watch face up on the ground in front of him, dusted a spot of sand from the glass and looked over at the cornet still asleep under the tree. 'Riaan!' his voice boomed. The field cornet woke with fright as the voice bounded at him a second time through the dark, and from several directions at once it seemed. 'The rifle! Take it and prepare.'

'Yes, sir.' The painfully thin young man stood, pulling up his trousers as they dragged below his hips. He peered into the darkness and moved towards the small glimmering fire. 'Is it coffee I smell?' he asked Gerrit in Afrikaans.

'Thick, dark coffee,' Gerrit replied also in Afrikaans, but reverted quickly to English as he caught a gleam of irritation in the Landrost's expression. 'I have, for later, some good Cape smoke,' he tempted him. The Landrost's eyes shone as Gerrit indicated a barrel of peach brandy beside him.

'A rank spirit.' The Landrost's attention was held by the small but promising barrel. 'Though I have been known to enjoy it, once the first taste has worn away!' He held his rifle out to the field cornet where he stood beside him, still half-asleep. 'And there's the watch.' He nodded at the pocket watch. 'Keep an eye on him and the time.'

'Yes, sir.' The field cornet took the rifle and glanced enviously towards the barrel of peach brandy as Gerrit filled two mugs with hot coffee.

If I get my way, neither of you will have eyes fit to keep on Thys and his horse, Gerrit thought.

'Coffee?' Gerrit's warm, innocent smile belied his intentions.

Thys's horse shifted nervously beside the hewn stick planted in the ground as a marker. The horse seemed to sense that the day for which they had practised so long was about to dawn. Thys ran his strong suntanned hand down the horse's neck.

'We'll do it for Gerrit,' he whispered.

The Landrost eyed the horizon as a pale yellow glimmer spread like thick liquid into an orange splash of colour. Gerrit watched the Landrost, his leathery face warmed by the light of the rising sun. The field cornet stood like a tall blade of grass, with his rifle aimed at the dark sky above but his eyes fixed on the Landrost, awaiting the order. At the nod of his thick neck, he tightened his finger on the trigger and fired.

The gunshot heralded the day. Thys dug his heels into the horse's flanks and the horse plunged forward. Thys held the reins tight and forced the horse to walk.

'Do you play cards?' Gerrit asked the Landrost as he watched Thys and the horse in silhouette against the rising sun. 'It'll pass the time.' He pulled a pack of well-worn cards from his pocket.

'I like a game.' The Landrost turned to the field cornet after checking, by a cursory glance, that Thys was walking his horse. 'Keep your eye on him, Riaan.'

'Yes, sir.'

'This is good coffee,' the Landrost complimented Gerrit as he sipped it, 'but it could do with a touch of your peach brandy to sweeten it perhaps.'

Gerrit hit his forehead as if he had forgotten the most important ingredient of coffee. 'Of course.' He took the steaming mug the Landrost held out to him and moved to the barrel with it, glancing as he did towards Thys as he walked his horse away into the dark which had yet to meet the light spreading thinly on the ground from the East. Gerrit handed the sweeter, and now very powerful, mug of coffee to the Landrost. 'Your coffee sweet enough?' he asked the young field cornet in Afrikaans.

'He's too young to drink.' Despite the foreign words the Landrost had spotted the nod of Gerrit's head towards the barrel of peach brandy 'None for him.'

'It's no more than honey water,' Gerrit confided in the Landrost. 'It will serve to keep his eye on the clock.'

'A little then,' the Landrost agreed.

The field cornet drained his mug of coffee and held it out to Gerrit. 'Fill it up,' he said in Afrikaans.

'Walk!' the Landrost yelled as he spotted Thys egging his horse into a trot.

'His horse can't walk,' Gerrit said very quietly. He handed the field cornet his well-laced mug of coffee. 'For months he has been training the horse to walk.' He shrugged his shoulders in despair. 'A horse can't stand still long in these parts without being eaten alive.' He noticed the Landrost swill the last dregs in his mug. 'More?' he offered.

With each step his horse took across the hard brown earth, Thys was claiming a piece of the world for himself and Gerrit. He had spent months preparing himself and his horse for the event. The time before that had been spent selecting the exact portion of land best suited to their cattle.

But time meant nothing in the space of Africa, only the seasons counted. He and Gerrit had waited patiently on each season. They had watched the glorious swell of the river after rain. It was a sight the Landrost would not believe possible as he looked at the dry riverbed now, scoring its way across the parched land like a healing scar. There was no sign of the moisture just beneath its sandy bed.

'You think this land will sustain your cattle?' the Landrost asked, as his mind conjured an image of the gentle green hills of England, with gleaming, fat cattle spread over them. He licked the peach brandy disguised as coffee from his lips and nodded towards the rough wooden cattle kraal further away. 'I hope they survive the dry season.'

'We'll manage.' Gerrit ensured there was no hint in his voice to betray the magic he knew the earth stored just one inch under its surface. 'Would you like to deal?' He passed the grubby pack of cards with their corners turned up to the Landrost and took his empty mug to refill it with peach brandy. 'The cattle have grown used to the sparse grazing.' He handed the powerful yellow liquor back to the Landrost.

The Landrost picked up the cards he'd dealt. 'Ah!' he exclaimed as he studied them. 'It is my day today!'

While the Landrost's attention was fixed on his own cards, which he held secretively in the cupped palm of his hand, Gerrit indicated to the field cornet to help himself to more peach brandy. He needed no encouragement.

Thys glanced over his shoulder as his horse walked. It was tugging for rein to ride out but Thys could still see the shapes of the Landrost and Gerrit in the distance. He could also see the movement of the field cornet as he returned to his tree. Thys dug his heels into the horse's flank just a little and loosened the reins. The horse stretched itself gently into a canter, striding out with ease across the dusty plain and stealing more ground with every stride.

'Walk!' the Landrost's voice called out from the far distance. Thys tightened the reins and the horse reluctantly shortened its stride back to a walk. Thys raised his hat in a wave of apology but his face was alight with the joy of the stolen land now left behind him.

'Hah!' A note of triumph in Gerrit's voice as he examined his new card attracted the Landrost's attention. Gerrit shook his head from side to side with a small hum of pleasure and held his hand out for a second.

'Another?' The Landrost looked at him in surprise. Gerrit opened his eyes wide and nodded at the Landrost's mug.

'Another for you? Why not!' Without waiting for a reply Gerrit took his mug.

Over by the tree the field cornet pulled his hat down over his eyes and the peach brandy seeped comfort and security through his body. The Landrost waited till Gerrit's back was turned then quickly peered at Gerrit's hand. He took a deep breath of defeat, replaced the cards and looked back at his own in dismay.

'There.' Gerrit held out the fresh peach brandy with a bright smile and sat down again to his cards. The Landrost dealt him another.

'What time is it?' The Landrost looked about in agitation for his pocket watch, though it sat right in front of him. 'Riaan!' He turned round, slightly dizzy and unable to see him. 'What time is it?'

'Ten minutes to go,' Gerrit assured him as he picked up the pocket watch and looked at it.

'Ten minutes?'

'Yes,' Gerrit nodded. 'See.' He leaned closer to him with the watch.

The Landrost clutched his cards close to his chest and challenged Gerrit, 'What's your wager?'

'An extra five minutes.' Gerrit laid the watch casually back in the sand beside him, its polished face down.

'Prepare to fire, Riaan!' the Landrost shouted, without seeing him. 'Five less is my wager.'

'Done!' Gerrit glanced at the immobile field cornet asleep against the tree.

'Let's see then!' the Landrost demanded.

With a flourish Gerrit spread his cards on the ground in front of him. The Landrost focused on them with difficulty.

'Are you sure these cards aren't marked?'

'See for yourself.' Gerrit leaned back on one elbow and looked out at Thys. He was now a long way away, with a vast plain of scrub and thorn trees behind him. Gerrit smiled with satisfaction as from the corner of his eye he saw the Landrost peer closely at each of his cards. He noticed the slight waver of his hand as he adjusted the distance from his eyes. Gerrit had prepared the peach brandy with great care. Each drop he'd distilled to perfection. It was the most powerful peach brandy he'd made in his life, and its effects were already written on the Landrost's face.

'What time is it?' The Landrost glared at Gerrit accusingly as he momentarily found his way through the alcoholic haze he was slipping into.

'Time?' Gerrit asked carelessly as he picked up the pocket watch again and wiped the sand off its face. The large hand pointed accusingly to eight minutes past the official half-hour. 'Time,' Gerrit nodded. 'Including my winning five minutes, of course.'

'Fire!' The Landrost struggled to his feet looking around for the field cornet. 'Fire!' he yelled as he walked unsteadily, his direction wavering as he spotted him under the tree. 'Fire!' He bent down and yelled into the field cornet's ear.

'Sir?' The field cornet looked up in confusion for a moment, then suddenly sprang to his feet and looked around in a daze. He was not quite certain where he was, or why.

'Fire the gun, you fool!' the Landrost yelled at him.

'Yes, sir.' The field cornet thought he remembered what he was there for. 'Yes, sir!'

'Where's the damn rifle?' the Landrost snarled and his huge body swayed forward dangerously.

'There, sir!' The field cornet snatched the rifle to himself from its position against the tree, as if he'd just found a lost child. He looked around, squinted into the distance and spotted Thys. He was just a small glimmering mirage on the horizon, engulfed in a cloud of dust, but he'd found him. The field cornet raised the rifle, butted it against his shoulder, lowered the barrel and aimed it at Thys.

'Not the man, fool!' The Landrost knocked the rifle barrel firmly towards the sky. 'Now fire!' he shouted.

The field cornet pulled the trigger and it blasted heavenwards. Gerrit chuckled. Another three minutes had been gained. He watched with pride as Thys plunged his stake into the ground, turned his horse in a swirl of dust and raced back to the starting point. Thys leaned out of his saddle, low to the ground, scooped up a second hewn stick and Gerrit cheered. Thys turned the horse, faced it at a new angle and walked the horse away. Gerrit threw his hat on the ground and jumped on it.

'You did it, Thys! You did it, my boy!'

'Sixty degrees?' the Landrost called suspiciously.

'Yes,' Thys shouted back. 'Sixty degrees.'

'Half an hour from now?' Gerrit asked.

'Half an hour,' the Landrost agreed.

'Go, Thys!' Gerrit cried happily as he looked at the pocket watch and held it out to the Landrost. 'Thirty minutes from now! You see the time!'

'Yes.' The Landrost collapsed in a heap beside Gerrit. He leaned back on his elbows and his stomach rolled over the leather belt where it dug into the pink flesh exposed by his gaping shirt. 'Have you any more of that peach brandy?' he asked. 'It's very good.'

'Of course.' Gerrit made sure the field cornet had gone back to his position under the tree and refilled the Landrost's mug with more mind-sapping spirit. 'Go on, Thys!' he shouted in Afrikaans as he looked out at the huge area of land rapidly becoming theirs. 'Go on, boy, claim it all!'

'What did you say?' The Landrost pushed himself up and accepted his fresh supply of brandy.

'I told him to slow down.' Gerrit picked up the watch. 'Shall I keep an eye on the time for you?'

'That's Riaan's job.' The Landrost pointed at the cards still lying on the ground between them. 'I expect you want another game,' he said, as his eyes at last found Gerrit and brought him into focus.

'If you like.' Gerrit sat down beside him. 'For ten minutes this time,' he smiled warmly. 'Don't worry about a thing. I'll see to it Thys keeps the horse to a walk,' Gerrit placed the watch firmly in front of himself, 'and my eye on the time.' He glanced at the field cornet, who was sound asleep with his hat over his eyes. 'I'll make sure of everything.'

Thys pushed his sweating horse faster in the last minutes left. The sun was still low in the sky but already it was burning hot. His own face poured with sweat. His skin gleamed and his eyes shone. Gerrit yelled, cheering him on as he stood beside the sleeping field cornet with the rifle in his own hands. He cast an eye at the pocket watch, which he'd looped over the barrel of the gun. The large hand hit the half-hour. Gerrit pulled the trigger and the gun fired. Neither the Landrost nor the field cornet stirred. Their snores broke through the following silence.

He smiled warmly as Thys raced back towards him having plunged in the last of the six markers. Gerrit dug his boot into the Landrost's chubby shoulder.

'It's over, sir.'

'What?' The Landrost closed one bleary eye as if to straighten his vision out. 'What's over?'

'The time is gone.' Gerrit held the pocket watch under the Landrost's nose.

'What?' He pushed the watch away and glanced towards the field cornet. 'Wake up, you lazy bastard!'

'Yes, sir.' The young boy leapt to his feet. He looked around in a panic for the rifle, he knew he had to shoot something.

'I've got it.' Gerrit held it out to him. 'And we have our land!'

'Let me see that watch!' The Landrost grabbed the pocket watch and peered at it. He turned to Gerrit in amazement. 'You haven't stolen time!'

Gerrit nodded. 'Just my winnings.'

'And the horse walked!' The Landrost shaded his eyes with his hand to see Thys as he galloped closer.

'He did his best, sir,' Gerrit smiled. 'But as the sun moves higher, the kraal flies get more vicious.' Gerrit shrugged. 'Perhaps he sometimes didn't walk. Would you with that sting in your backside?'

Thys pulled up his horse and leapt down with a broad smile, wiping his hat over his face. Gerrit winked. 'You've done well, Thys.' He turned to the Landrost. 'Shall we eat before you record our claim?'

A large antbear was roasting on a spit over the fire. Gerrit turned the stick driven through its middle and the fire sparked as fat dripped into it. 'The crackling is fine. Like my brandy.'

The Landrost needed food and time to sober up. 'Yes.' His eyes calculated unwillingly the miles of dusty plain he must travel. 'We will eat first.'

Gerrit and Thys, their stomachs full, and warmed by peach brandy themselves, lay back under the shade of the tree. The field cornet had gone with the Landrost around the perimeter of their claim. Even their horses seemed to droop underneath them when they finally pulled up beside the tree. The sun was setting in a dazzling display over the horizon and the crickets were just beginning their scratchy chorus.

'At least four thousand morgen!' The Landrost slid off his horse and dropped to the ground between them, pushing off his boots. Thys grinned across the Landrost's great sweating body at Gerrit. 'If you've any argument speak now!' He passed a piece of paper to Gerrit. A pencil line joined six marks in a strange squared-off circle. Gerrit passed it to Thys. 'Then tell me what you want to call it.'

The Landrost held his pencil point on the paper, ready to write.

'Doornfontein,' Thys said with a glance at Gerrit.

'It's the name of my father's old farm in the Cape,' Gerrit explained.

'Doornfontein,' the Landrost wrote. 'What does it mean?' He screwed up his eyes as he struggled to see in the fast disappearing light.

'The fountain among the thorns,' the field cornet translated. He'd forgotten the Landrost didn't like him even understanding Afrikaans.

'I know you speak kitchen Dutch, you fool, and I've seen the thorns!' The Landrost chuckled at his own joke.

'You're lucky.' The field cornet looked out over the country and deliberately spoke in Afrikaans. 'My uncle lost his land in the East.'

'How?' Gerrit got up and moved away to relieve himself, joining him in their own language. 'What happened?'

'The English government tells him he must forget about it and start again. He lost four thousand in livestock but they say he must start again.'

'What did he say?' the Landrost asked suspiciously, looking at Gerrit. Gerrit watched his urine as it formed small rivulets then ran in a broad yellow stream across the dry ground. He pulled his trousers together and turned to the Landrost.

'He says your English government stole his uncle's land in the East.'

'Hah!' The Landrost allowed his belly to ease further over his belt. 'He might not like our English government, but he likes our English women well enough!' A deep rumble of wind broke. 'I beg your pardon.' He wiped his mouth with the back of his hand. 'I've never seen a man so happy being nursed from death's door as this one.'

'She was different,' the field cornet argued. 'Not like an Englishwoman at all.' He leaned on one elbow and looked across at the younger man, Thys, as though he would know what made a woman special. 'She was like an angel. So gentle. Her hands were so soft. And her hair. Gold like the sun itself it was.' Gerrit noticed the slight movement in Thys's body as he listened.

'She was just a nurse at a mission station on the frontier,' the Landrost stated flatly. 'No angel!'

'Not just a nurse!' the field cornet contradicted him.

'What was her name?' Thys asked quietly.

'Suzanne.'

Gerrit's eyes rested on Thys as the name flew at them both.

'Suzanne?' Thys breathed. His entire body leaned forward. 'A nurse?'

The Landrost stood up and moved to the barrel with his mug.

'They don't know where she came from,' the field cornet went on, unaware of the tremor of excitement the information he'd given had caused. 'She was special.' He smiled as he remembered. 'I think she was an angel.'

Suzanne held the struggling body of the soldier down under her weight, but turned her face away. She'd learned to nurse both the dying and the survivors, but still she could not bear the violence of amputation: the horror of limbs shattered by carbines and sawn off to leave just part of a man behind. It was something she couldn't accept. She blotted out the sound of the saw tearing through bone and closed her ears to the screams of the writhing young man, whom she had to keep still, no matter how hard he fought.

The wars on the frontier had grown bloodier each year. Soldiers poured in from the Cape daily and daily they were slaughtered. The British army had turned to the mission for help. Suzanne could see no point. There was nothing in the dark shadows of death around her which offered any hope for man, or God.

'Try to hold him, Suzanne,' Rev. Phillip reminded her. She had accidentally eased the pressure as she escaped into her thoughts.

'I'm sorry,' Suzanne murmured guiltily and opened her eyes as she pressed her weight harder upon the young man's shoulders. He screamed and pulled to get away. She held on, averting her eyes quickly as she caught a glint of the saw pulling back through the flesh and bone. She felt sick and fixed her attention on the tall triangle of light in the tent opening. As she did, she felt the earth move under her feet.

'Suzanne!' Dr Steven said aggressively as he operated. 'Hold him down!'

Suzanne couldn't move. Thys was standing just four feet away from her, outside the tent.

'Do you want him to die?' Dr Steven yelled again. 'Hold him before he rips this wound further and bleeds to death!'

'Yes. I'm sorry!' Suzanne tore her attention away from the tent flap and back to the man in her care. She pushed her weight down on him, her entire body shook. Tears ran down her cheeks carelessly and she buried her face against the soldier's chest. 'Thys,' she wept. She didn't know how much time had passed when she opened her eyes. Nobody was there.

'Suzanne.' She stood up straight, bewildered and distressed. 'It's all right now, Suzanne.' Dr Steven's voice had quietened. 'He's unconscious.' Suzanne looked down quickly at the soldier.

'It's all over,' Rev. Phillip said kindly. 'In your secret world again?'

Suzanne looked at him in a daze. Her large blue eyes blinked in confusion. 'Is he dead?'

'No.' Rev. Phillip looked at her curiously. 'Are you all right?'

'Excuse me.' Suzanne turned to go and stepped into the light of the tent opening. The light in which she had seen Thys. It stared blindly down on her.

'Where are you going?' Rev. Phillip was by her side.

The mission had spread into a sprawling mass of temporary abodes. Army tents stood like sharp khaki ant heaps. Mud and wattle huts, like beehives, sprouted on every inch of the brown valley at the foot of rugged cliffs. The huts were filled with orphaned black children.

Suzanne moved automatically towards her own hut. She walked with her head down, telling herself she had been dreaming. A horse stood alone in the centre of the mission square. It was knee-haltered and Suzanne's breath caught in her throat. Two simple half-stitches had been taken around the horse's foreleg with a strong rein. They were attached to the neck strap and held the horse's head forward towards the ground so that it couldn't move.

The only horse Suzanne had seen knee-haltered in this way belonged to Thys. She spun round as she heard the familiar sound of a bird calling.

Thys stood at the far end of the mission.

For a long moment neither moved and every sound around them died. Suzanne couldn't see Thys's face, but she could feel him. She could feel the warm tingle his presence had always given her and she began to walk towards him. He was walking towards her. When they reached one another they stood quite still. Their eyes locked and they stared deep into one another's being.

'Suzanne,' Thys breathed, and she felt her skin rise taut on her arms. His face was firm and brown with the sun. His grey eyes were flecked with blue. The line of his mouth was straight, the lips parted just slightly revealing his fine white teeth. His hair fell across his forehead in a warm brown fold. Straggling curls ran down his neck, and rested on the stiff leather collar of his jacket.

'Thys.' Suzanne looked at his strong wide hand as it stretched towards her. She leaned her cheek against it as his palm opened. 'It is you,' she murmured, and the six long years that had separated them dissolved.

Thys could hardly breathe as he looked at Suzanne. Her face was stronger than he'd remembered, but no older. Her hair was pushed up under a white cap. A few strands trailed like gold thread down her slim neck. The sun had kissed her nose and cast a glow across her high cheekbones. Her bright blue eyes shone as they drank him in.

Rev. Phillip could only see Thys's back but he knew who it was.

Preparations for the wedding had been underway for two days. It was to be a most unusual festivity. The black children had prepared their own songs and dances, the soldiers Suzanne looked after had prepared theirs, and Rev. Phillip had prepared the most important service of his life.

As he watched Suzanne, led towards him by Dr Steven through a hushed but excited crowd, Rev. Phillip felt a lump rise in his throat. He'd married many people inside the cold stone churches of England, or outside in the green of the countryside under sombre skies. But never before under the blue sky of Africa when destiny had seemed set against it. He looked at Thys as he stood in front of him, waiting for Suzanne to reach his side. Thys met his look with bright clear eyes and smiled. His smile spoke volumes and Rev. Phillip knew he was witnessing the second part of God's plan for Suzanne.

'Do you, Suzanne Beauvilliers, take this man, Matheus Stephanus Bothma, to be your lawful wedded husband?'

'I do.' As Suzanne answered, her hand brushed against Thys's leg. She seemed to hold her breath as Thys drew a gold ring from his jacket pocket. It was the Reverend's ring, his mother's wedding ring. Something he'd kept since she'd died when he was a small boy. A band of gold, representing the union of a man and a woman in a neverending circle.

'And let no man put asunder those whom God has joined together in Holy Matrimony.' Rev. Phillip's words carried authority and were confirmed by a sudden swell of African voices as they lifted to the sky in song. Clear bright voices slipping easily one through the other, the children's voices running melodies like dancing beacons over the dark warm tones of the men. The harmony included the earth they stood on.

Alone in the hut at last, Thys slipped the white cotton robe from Suzanne's shoulders and ran his eyes from her face, down her neck and on to the gentle curve of her breasts. His hand touched her shoulder and a spark ran through her. It was the same spark she had always felt when they touched. She looked down at his hand on her flesh, the tanned smooth skin stretched across its wide back, with just the faintest soft rise of a vein. She leant her cheek on his hand as it held her shoulder. He turned his hand upward and ran his fingers across her cheek and up through her hair. Golden strands wound their way around his hand, twisted their way between his fingers, and hung like shot silk over his wrist.

Suzanne's lips parted as she looked up at him. Thys gently held her head, pulling her forward until her lips met his. Her mouth opened and lovingly his tongue pushed its way between her lips, searching. A sudden surge of desire ran up through her. Her hands gripped his shoulders and she pressed her body hard against his. He could feel the length of her thighs, the soft curve of her stomach and the hard rise of her breasts against him.

'Suzanne,' he breathed against her skin. 'Suzanne.' She leant her head back and his mouth ran down the arc of her throat, on down towards her breasts. The edge of her white cotton gown stretched taut across them, the soft white mounds reaching towards him. He buried his face in the soft cotton. Her nipple pressed at his lips under the cloth. He ran his tongue lightly around it until it pushed proudly through the wet cotton.

'Thys!' Suzanne's voice cracked as her body arched back over his arm. He caressed her, his heart pounding as he pushed away the white cotton, baring her full, perfectly rounded breasts.

'Suzanne . . .' Thys ran his mouth over the swell of her breasts, on down through the folds of white cotton over her body until he buried his head in the warmth of soft hair between her legs. His hand ran down the arch of her back and gripped her round firm buttocks as she pulled his face closer into her body. She could feel the warm moisture soaking down to Thys. He looked up at her and his eyes blazed with love.

Suzanne couldn't speak, her body was screaming for him. She slipped herself down through his hands in front of him, pushed the white cotton robe down and wriggled out of it. 'Thys,' she begged and he eased her on to her back.

Suzanne felt the weight of his body on hers, as he pushed himself deep inside her, and a hungry moan crept from her. Her hands gripped his back, her nails dug into his skin, and she pulled him closer, deeper into herself, wanting only to become a part of him, to disappear inside him until they were one. She felt his breath, hot against her neck. She turned her head as he lifted his face to hers. Her mouth opened wide in a cry as she sucked him into her and his passion exploded inside her. Her body rose in a rigid arch, forced itself against him and took all of him.

'Suzanne?' Thys kissed her eyelids gently and her eyes opened. Her mouth tilted up at the corners and spread into a wide beautiful smile.

'Thys,' she whispered.

'He could build your church,' Suzanne said to Rev. Phillip as she stood beside Thys, holding his hand and leaning her head on his shoulder. 'You've always said that one day you'd build a real church here, and Thys could help you do it.'

'Would you?' Rev. Phillip asked. Thys held Suzanne tightly against him. 'Though even the Lord would say permanent hospital buildings are more necessary than a church at the moment.'

'I'll build both.' Thys moved closer to Suzanne. 'I'll build anything you want.'

'And then?' Rev. Phillip looked from him to Suzanne. 'And then what?'

'We'll go to the farm Thys and Gerrit have in the North,' Suzanne said brightly. 'In time,' she added.

'What time?' Rev. Phillip hoped she couldn't see he was curious. 'Although I would like very much to have Thys help us, why don't you go now to the farm? Why don't you begin your lives together now? Away from the bitterness of these wars.'

Although Suzanne and Thys had told him everything that had happened, all that had led to their being with him at the mission, Rev. Phillip instinctively knew it was not all. Something else still stood between them.

'There's something I must do first.' Thys looked down as he spoke. Rev. Phillip glanced quickly at Suzanne. She had also looked down.

'My mother.' Thys looked straight at him. Suzanne's eyes flicked quickly from Thys to Rev. Phillip.

'Thys needs his mother's blessing. She has never accepted me.'

'Then you must get her blessing,' Rev. Phillip said simply. 'You know where she has settled?'

'I have heard.'

'Then go.' Rev. Phillip looked from Thys to Suzanne. 'You will go to your mother when the time is right.' It was not the time to force a decision. 'In the meantime, Thys, yes,' he nodded warmly, 'I would like it very much if you could help. There are often wounded men out there.' Rev. Phillip turned and glanced up at the vast cliffs above them. The granite edge was fringed with thick dark bush lit by bright strelitzia. 'They die because we can't reach them in time.'

'It's dangerous,' Suzanne whispered. 'No.'

Rev. Phillip looked at her keenly. 'But it must be done.' He walked away without turning back.

'He's right, Suzanne,' Thys said gently.

'And you must go to your mother,' Suzanne said, pleading for him to answer 'no'. Instead Thys held her tighter and his mouth ran down her neck in dry kisses.

'I will go to my mother, Suzanne. One day.' She smiled as his lips brushed hers and he spoke quietly against the soft, tempting mouth. 'My mother will add her blessings to those we already have.'

'I know,' she whispered and pressed her lips against his.

A group of tiny black children turned and ran towards them with shrieks of delight, their scraggy black legs throwing up clouds of red dust.

'They think we're strange,' Suzanne laughed.

'Are we?' Thys held her face in his hands and looked into it. 'When Gerrit sees you he will know it was not his peach brandy talking when the field cornet said you were an angel.'

Rev. Phillip looked back and watched them walk away, their arms around each other's waist. He knew it would be a long time before Thys could bring himself to leave Suzanne again.

Chapter Fourteen

The bizarre effect of the red coats of the British soldiers lit by the bivouac fires of the camp contrasted strongly with the pitch dark around them. The effect had escaped Charles Marsden entirely. The incessant hum and buzz of hundreds of voices, interspersed occasionally by the shrieking laughter of a Hottentot, and confused with the shrill neighing of horses, didn't interrupt his thoughts either. As he stood before his tent he thought back to the day two years earlier when his son had been born. He could still feel the insecurity aroused in him by the casual way Clara had announced, 'We will call him Jacques.' She had behaved as though the child had nothing to do with him. His son was merely a weapon to be used in her claim on Bonne Esperance. He had tried to find his way back to her; to the delights of her body. But she had refused him.

'You sent for me, sir?' Lieutenant Shaw stepped out of the dark. He snapped his heels to attention and saluted. Even in the dim light afforded by the bivouac fires, Charles could detect the edge of superiority in the lieutenant's handsome face. He knew why it was there, and as always it caused a surge of anger within him.

'Yes.' Charles nodded abruptly that Lieutenant Duncan Shaw should move into his tent. He waited until he had passed him and then glanced back over the camp. Phantom figures shrouded in mist glided ghostlike between the fires and tents. The air was heavy with the threat of a storm. He followed Shaw into the tent, pushing back the memories as he did, but they would not be dismissed.

Clara was in his arms. Clara was making love to Lieutenant Duncan Shaw.

Charles slammed the shutters of his mind on the image

thrown up at him and pinned his eyes on Shaw instead. But the memory pricked him again. He pushed down the rage of jealousy swelling in his gut and walked up close to him. The lieutenant's strong young body stood erect. Challenging him.

'I've been looking through your record of service in this country, Lieutenant Shaw.' Charles spotted the slightest flicker of fear in Shaw's eyes. 'It's very interesting. Quite a career you had here on the frontier in your previous command.'

'Yes, sir.' Lieutenant Shaw's voice revealed nothing.

'It seems strange that your career was so suddenly brought to a halt.' Charles allowed a smile to cross his lips. 'It's the only reason you're here now with the Cape Mounted Rifles, of course.'

'I requested transfer, sir.' A look of disdain passed over Lieutenant Shaw's face as he looked at the man whose wife he had stolen.

'How interesting.' Charles turned away, permitting a silence to develop between them. 'It has always seemed strange that a man of your calibre should be with such a lowly regiment as the Cape Mounted Rifles. But, of course . . .' Charles moved to a chair in front of his temporary army desk. A lantern burned on it and it was piled high with army dispatches. He riffled through the heap of papers, and held one sheet up, between two fingers. 'How did you convince them? A little family persuasion?'

Lieutenant Shaw's mouth tightened in a line of enforced silence. Charles allowed the piece of paper to slip out of his fingers and drop on to the pile again. He tipped back in his chair, digging two of its square wooden feet into the sand.

'It was a severely embarrassing situation for Her Majesty's Government, I believe. It still is. Yes,' he tipped his chair forward and leant his elbows on the desk, 'it is still a thorn in the side of our diplomatic relations with the Xhosa people. You are aware of that, are you?'

'I don't know what you're referring to, sir.' Shaw's confident attitude sparked embers of hatred inside Charles and his eyes narrowed.

'I'm talking about an eight-year-old child! A black child! A child murdered by you in cold blood, Lieutenant Shaw!'

'No, sir. You are wrong.'

'You didn't murder him?' Charles peered up at him. He got to his feet and moved to him. 'I'm afraid, Lieutenant Shaw, no matter how high the price paid by your family to protect you, the truth has a nasty habit of lurking somewhere.' He paused. 'The British army is very fond of records! Buried they might be, but never destroyed.'

'Our orders were to kill, sir. To arrest any black caught without a pass, sir. To shoot if they ran, sir. To set an example, and strike terror into the enemy, sir. It was our duty and a standing order on the frontier.' Lieutenant Shaw could feel the flush of anger rise in his cheeks. 'Sir,' he finished.

'Your orders were to kill children?' Charles's voice rose in mock amazement. 'A child of eight was your enemy?'

'I didn't see him, sir. My orders were only –'

'To shoot all kaffirs!' Charles silenced him. 'You told me that. Yes.' He used the silence and walked around Lieutenant Shaw in a small circle. He stopped behind him. 'But this was a particular kaffir! The son of a Kaiser Chief!' He completed the circle and looked into his face. 'His people are still waiting for justice, Lieutenant Shaw.' Charles paused. 'I am not sure which you would prefer. Disgrace or black justice?' He shook his head. 'I believe there is not much left of a man after that.' Charles played his trump card. 'Or perhaps you would like my justice.'

Lieutenant Shaw said nothing. Charles had gained the upper hand and continued quickly.

'Perhaps we could come to an arrangement. I need something done. Something rather in your line of business. You don't care for half-castes any more than you care for blacks, do you?'

'Sir?' Lieutenant Shaw waited. His eyes stared straight ahead. Charles watched him for a moment in silence, then smiled and dismissed him.

'I will give you details when I am ready.'

'Sir.' Lieutenant Shaw saluted and left the tent quickly. As Charles watched his broad back disappear into the night outside, his mind raced back to the reason he was on the frontier at all. The reason he had spoken to Lieutenant Shaw as he had. Clara.

'Do you love him?' Charles had asked, terrified of the answer he might get but demanding it.

'I love him as I have never loved any man.' Clara's words had stung him, bloating his entire being with poison. He had stood by silently for so long. For so very long, as Clara had thrown herself into the social life of Cape Town. He had stood by as she had abandoned their son Jack to the care of Maria, Rosita, Prudence, Emily, or anyone else who might look after him. Installed in Miss Thurston's house, which Emily had inherited, Clara had convinced everyone it was because she wanted to be closer to her husband. She had passed her time in continual parties. There was always an excuse to be found for celebration in Cape Town, and Clara had found them all.

She had also found Lieutenant Duncan Shaw. At first she had set out to find him. To see this man Charles had told her was in charge of Jean Jacques. She'd wondered if perhaps he could help where Charles had proved useless. But Clara's initial interest in Lieutenant Shaw had quickly changed. What had begun as a useful contact had been turned on its head by sex. Clara had found herself confronted by a man as sexually in command as herself. A man who demanded her body and took it with an authority Charles had never had. Her passion for him had grown so deep she'd no longer cared when Charles discovered their relationship. Instead she had tormented him with it.

'But how will you take your wife and son to England, Charles?' Clara had allowed the sneer in her voice to sound clearly the day he'd informed her of his plans.

'I will keep my wife at any cost!' Charles had tried to keep calm but failed.

'But how?' Clara had turned her eyes on him and revealed nothing but the contempt she felt. 'You would have to sell your commission to pay the fare. And then what? What more have you to sell? Your soul?' She had pushed him away from her as he had tried to hold her. She had laughed as he'd spelt out his desperate need.

'There's nothing you can do, Charles,' she had purred with pleasure as he poured his suffering out at her feet. 'If you had kept your promise to me regarding Jean Jacques, things might be different. But now you are nothing but a title which echoes with emptiness.'

Clara's words still banged uselessly inside his head. Charles tried to stamp out the bitterness he felt, but could not. Clara was right. He had nothing. Without her he was nothing.

Charles stepped out of his tent and into the night, trying to escape Clara's persistent voice as it speared at his memory. His eyes settled on a hazy figure in the distance among the horses. It was Jean Jacques. Charles took a deep breath and looked up at the sky where dark clouds were gathering. A sheet of lightning suddenly lit the camp and thunder cracked after it, wrenching the vault of heaven wide. A first heavy drop of rain fell to the ground in front of him and quickly disappeared. It left no trace except the earth's thirsty smell. At once the clouds opened and let go their store of torrential rain. A solid wall of water covered Charles but did nothing to dampen his need for revenge.

Emily knew exactly why the two-year-old boy was crying as he wandered back and forth, all alone in the courtyard of Bonne Esperance. She knew why she herself wanted to cry every time she looked at him.

'You thought we'd all gone and you were alone, did you?' She scooped the child up and felt the warm wet tears as his face rubbed against hers. 'I'm here, little Jack. Aunt Emily is here and about to find you something to do.' She walked with the child in her arms towards the stables. 'How would you like to sit on a great big horse's back?' she asked, chattering to take his attention from his unhappiness. 'It'll make you tall like your father.'

'Mama!' the small boy cried loudly. 'Mama!'

'Your mother will be home soon,' Emily lied as she stepped into the stables with him. 'I promise you.'

'Mama!' he cried again.

Emily lifted him on to the back of a tall grey horse. The horse reminded her of Shiva. She held him up and regarded him anxiously as his small body crumpled in a heap on the horse's back and he grabbed its mane in his tiny clenched hands.

'You don't like the horse?' Emily lifted him down and held him to her again. The little body heaved in her arms and tears of rage poured down his bright red cheeks.

It had been just six months after his birth that everything had changed. Clara had persuaded Emily to allow her to live in Miss Thurston's house in Cape Town. Although Emily had sensed it was wrong, she'd found it impossible to resist Clara's constant appeals. She could understand that Clara wanted to live in Cape Town to be closer to her husband, but why must she abandon her son? Charles seldom came to Bonne Esperance any more and Emily had presumed it was the demands of army life. She had since learned that she was wrong.

Raphus Jeremiah had been the first to worry her. He was unhappy with Clara in the house. Emily was forced to wonder why and had gone to Cape Town unannounced.

Clara was not available, Raphus Jeremiah had repeated continually, his head down, as if checking the buttons on his butler's uniform.

'But her cloak is here and her carriage is outside,' Emily had coaxed him. 'Is she perhaps upstairs?'

'No, Miss Emily.' Raphus Jeremiah had turned away quickly, as though he needed more protection than just a lowered head. 'She out.'

'And Lord Marsden?'

'He not here. He gone too.'

'Gone where?' Emily had taken his thin shoulders and turned him back to face her. 'Where?' His bony shoulders shrugged under her hands. He still hadn't looked at her. 'Raphus,' Emily had tried to be firm, 'if there is something wrong you must tell me. I have left you in charge of the house and you must tell me if something is wrong.'

Emily had been stopped by a long passionate cry from upstairs. It was one she remembered well; the same sexual cry had rung around Bonne Esperance in the first days of Clara's marriage to Charles. Emily had cleared her throat, let go of Raphus Jeremiah's shoulders and stood back from him. Finally he had looked at her.

'Raphus Jeremiah not want to stay here any more, Miss Emily.' All she had wanted to do was run out of the house with him. 'Raphus Jeremiah want to go.'

On that day, 3 December 1843, Emily had written in her diary, 'Father's lack of interest in Clara's child, the heir apparent, has revealed a side of her none of us knew existed. She is prepared to risk everything for Duncan Shaw: or is it simply to strike back at her husband? Her affair, about which we knew nothing here at home, is common knowledge in Cape Town.' Now, when Emily read that entry again, she was terrified. Jean Jacques was with the Cape Mounted Rifles on the frontier. So was Duncan Shaw. And Charles Marsden was in overall command of them both.

'Dear God,' Emily prayed. 'The evil man plans, turn to your good, Father. Please.' She picked up her pen and dipped it into the ink. She glanced at the window as the lace curtain curled into the room and wrapped itself around the pink velvet curtains held back by braid rope.

'Little Jack bears the guilt of his mother like a cross. But still he cries for her. He calls for her, he looks for her every day.'

'Emily?' Emily closed her diary quickly as Prudence came into the room. 'I need to talk to you.'

'No,' Emily said flatly and moved to the window. She pulled the lace curtain away and closed the window. 'I told you I couldn't help you, Prudence.'

'But what else will you do with the money Miss Thurston left you? Bonne Esperance needs it.' Prudence plonked herself on Emily's bed. 'Father won't listen to me so I must come to you.'

'Perhaps Father is right.' Emily returned to her desk and her diary. She wanted to be alone.

'Even the Westburys are farming sheep now, Emily,' Prudence argued. 'It's practical.'

'Father hates sheep.'

'And so do I!' Prudence moved to her at the desk. 'I hate sheep more than I hate greenfly, but I'll use them if it means saving Bonne Esperance!'

'From what?' Emily looked into Prudence's open face, which looked back without pretension of any kind. There was no trace of make-up on the tanned skin or her well-shaped mouth. Though her clothes were tidier these days her hair still escaped attention and hung in a dishevelled blonde mass around her face.

'Have you thought of wearing your hair up?' Emily asked.

'The only reason our wines are selling so well now is by favour of the British government, Emily,' Prudence stated flatly, ignoring mention of her hair. 'Because they tax French wines.'

'Then perhaps we should say thank you.' Emily glanced at her diary. 'Can we talk another time, Prudence?'

'Don't you understand we are at the mercy of every whim of the British Parliament?' Prudence paced away and turned back with her hands wide in appeal. 'We have to protect ourselves!'

'With sheep?'

'If necessary!'

'Then it will be without my money.'

'Then what is your money for, Emily? What on earth is more important than Bonne Esperance?' She moved closer to her. 'Tell me what happens if France ever forms an alliance with England.'

'They never will.'

'Never?' Emily sat down at her desk but Prudence leaned over her shoulder. 'What are you keeping that money for?'

She turned in her seat. 'It's personal.' Prudence looked at her curiously and Emily sighed. 'No. It's not a man.' She flicked the pages of her diary across her thumb. She longed to open it. To write her thoughts down while they were clear.

'And it's not Bonne Esperance?'

'No.'

'Then I think you'd better note it in your diary, Emily. Write down what is more important than Bonne Esperance.'

'People!' Emily's voice halted Prudence on her way to the door. She looked back curiously. 'Little Jack,' Emily said, trying to hide the whole truth. 'Perhaps he'll need it.'

'He has a mother. He has a father.'

'And where are they?' There was a catch in Emily's voice. 'Have either of them shown any care for him at all while they destroy each other with him in between?'

Prudence stayed quite silent. She could see the hurt in Emily and she knew it wasn't over Jack. 'None of us has the privilege of choosing our parents, Emily.'

Emily turned away. She had allowed Prudence to see too deeply into her feelings.

'Please go now,' she said quickly.

Prudence twisted the door handle, then she let it go and watched it slowly turn back. She spoke gently. 'Jean Jacques will be safe.'

When Prudence had gone Emily opened her diary. She lifted her pen and wrote, 'Jean Jacques will be safe because I will give Pauline the money for their fares to England. I will make their dream come true. Jean Jacques will escape.' She looked at the last word carefully, crossed it out and wrote instead, 'buy himself out of the army', as she remembered the last time she'd seen him.

He had run to her as she walked through the vineyards carrying Clara's small abandoned child.

'My son is well,' Jean Jacques had said, smiling at them both. 'Pauline says he's grown so big.'

'He has, Jean Jacques.' Emily had let him go and stepped back a pace. 'He's like you. And you look so happy. Why?'

'Can you keep a secret?' Jean Jacques' eyes sparkled.

'I hope so, after so many. Tell me.'

'Pauline and I have made a decision. We are going to England when I get back. Major Marsden says . . . '

'When you get back from where?' Emily had moved away from him slightly. 'Where are you going?'

'When I've served my time in the army, then we'll leave,' Jean Jacques sidestepped the question.

'Where are you going?' She'd touched his arm. 'The frontier?'

'Yes,' he'd admitted. 'And then we will leave.'

'No!'

'It's all right, Emily.'

'Don't go to the frontier. Go now, with Pauline, Jean Jacques. Take your son and go.'

'It's impossible.'

'I've got Miss Thurston's money. I've kept it safe for you. It's what she would have wanted me to do with it.' Emily had stopped, seeing a look on his face which she'd never seen before. 'What's wrong?'

'You're asking me to turn the only success I've had into a failure.'

Lieutenant Shaw rode out of camp with Jean Jacques and two British soldiers, Privates Pym and Moore. Charles Marsden watched. He had arranged with the commander of the Cape Mounted Rifles to take his place on this frontier excursion. He had to be there for diplomatic reasons and Charles intended to use the power he'd borrowed on every level in order to carry out his plan.

Everything had proved easier than he'd expected. Lieutenant Shaw had understood immediately why Charles Marsden wanted Jean Jacques dead. He was happy to oblige him. In fact it amused him greatly that Charles could think he would ever get Clara back. Not even the death of Jean Jacques would achieve it.

'His being of mixed race will of course make it fairly easy for you, Lieutenant.' Charles had been calm. The knowledge of Duncan Shaw's past which Charles held over him ensured he could be very calm. 'Go well.'

Lieutenant Shaw glanced at Jean Jacques as they rode out together. He knew exactly how to kill him without leaving a trace. Many British soldiers had been found dead in the bush, mutilated by the blacks. Assegaais were driven through their bodies and left there on display. It would be easy, and it would satisfy Marsden enough to bury his past record.

Jean Jacques rode well, he had all the nimbleness of a black in the bush, Lieutenant Shaw decided. Take that uniform off and he was no different from the naked savages who were their enemies.

'I'll go ahead, sir,' Jean Jacques called to him and spurred his horse on, disappearing into the dense bush. Lieutenant Shaw addressed the two privates riding beside him.

'I'll ensure he eats and sleeps separately. Don't worry,' he assured them.

'Yes, sir.' Francis Pym and Stanley Moore exchanged a look. It seemed Major Marsden had been right when he suggested they keep an eye open for any trouble between Lieutenant Shaw and Jean Jacques.

Charles strode across the camp grounds towards his desk. It had been placed in the shade of a tree, outside his tent.

'The dispatches are waiting, with your other papers, sir.'

'Thank you, Fraser. That will be all.' He returned the young soldier's salute and settled down to study the papers. Among them was the record of Lieutenant Shaw's murder of a black child of eight. An irrefutable statement that Shaw was the man the Xhosa people demanded be released to them. Charles sat in his chair and gazed at the thick bush surrounding the camp; bush into which Shaw, Jean Jacques and the two witnesses had disappeared. He looked forward, with growing anticipation, to the moment they would return. It would be with sworn evidence that Lieutenant Shaw had tried to attack and kill Private Villiers. That Jean Jacques had fought him off and they had stopped the fight themselves.

Charles couldn't help a smile. It spread its way over his face and into his eyes. He had no need to fear for Jean Jacques' safety. He'd seen him fight many times. He was strong and never taken by surprise. There was no way in which Lieutenant Shaw could ever harm him. To ensure that, Charles had also warned Jean Jacques to be on his guard. All that could happen was that Lieutenant Shaw would tie the noose even tighter around his own neck. And then – Charles's smile widened further at the thought – Lieutenant Shaw would be dismissed and returned to England. In the meantime Charles could relax. He would be seen by Clara as having attempted to fulfil his promise to her, yet he would not have harmed a hair on Jean Jacques' head. It was something he could never do.

As evening fell Lieutenant Shaw stopped his small troop at a deserted farmhouse. The farmhouse could be reached only with great difficulty. It lay at the bottom of a rocky ravine, carved into great jutting steps by the torrential rains. Shaw had decided they would spend the night in the farmhouse, resting the horses before moving on to the post they were to relieve in the morning.

Every sound was exaggerated at night, Francis Pym thought, as he gazed out of the broken window towards Jean Jacques, who was alone on guard duty. Pym closed his eyes and tried to sleep, pulling his blanket over his head. The minutes passed. All of a sudden the sound of footsteps startled him out of a doze. He lifted the edge of the blanket and took a peep. Lieutenant Shaw was making his way quietly out.

'Hey!' Pym whispered the moment he had gone. He crept over to Stanley Moore where he lay spread out carelessly and sound asleep. 'He's gone outside.' Pym shook the sleeping soldier. 'Come on.' He crept back to the broken window and looked out.

'What the hell do you think he's going to do?' Stanley Moore scratched his backside and yawned. 'These bloody mosquitoes.' He slapped one into a brown mess on his arm.

'Look!' Pym silenced him quickly and gestured for him to come closer. The night was lit by a full moon, he could see the shape of Jean Jacques as he stood guard.

'What must I look at a tree for?'

'A walking tree?' Pym indicated the shape of Lieutenant Shaw as he moved towards Jean Jacques at the edge of the clearing then disappeared into the bush.

'What's he got in his hand?' Pym asked. 'What was it?'

'An assegaai. It's a kaffir assegaai.' Stanley Moore was suddenly wide awake.

'Jean Jacques?' Jean Jacques looked around. 'Here, Jean Jacques. Come.' Jean Jacques' hand moved automatically on his rifle and tightened its grip.

'Who is it?' he asked carefully.

'Come.' The voice came from behind a tree, deep in the bush. It was a silver tree which glimmered mysteriously in the moonlight as it reached up from the dense growth around it. 'Jean Jacques!' The voice seemed to slither up the tree.

'Is it you, sir?' Jean Jacques asked, looking around cautiously. Lieutenant Shaw never used his name. Villiers was as personal as he got.

'Quickly. I need you!' The voice expressed urgency. Jean Jacques moved closer and held his gun ready.

Pym pushed Stanley Moore down and back behind the wall as he watched Jean Jacques move into the bush. He leapt up as a bloodthirsty yell tore its way through the dark bush. Startled birds woke and swooped into the night sky in a flurry of wings.

Jean Jacques looked up in horror at Lieutenant Shaw, standing above him on a bank of earth, holding an assegaai high over his head.

'Come on, Villiers!' Shaw spat. 'Come on!'

Jean Jacques' hands instinctively held his rifle tight, ready to swing it up and knock the assegaai aside. He'd been taught how to do it. He knew exactly how to do it. But as he looked up into the white face, Jean Jacques faltered, he saw every white man he'd ever seen in his life. They were all Duncan Shaw. They were all superior and demanded subservience. Jean Jacques lowered his rifle. For a moment Shaw hesitated then with all his strength he plunged the assegaai deep into Jean Jacques' chest.

Jean Jacques had handed him his own life, as if it was his by right, as a white officer. Lieutenant Shaw had taken that right.

'Lieutenant!' Shaw turned at Francis Pym's voice. Pym ran to Jean Jacques and bent over him. Jean Jacques looked up at him from deep dark eyes, his hands gripping the shaft of the assegaai in his chest. He was trying to pull it out, but the harder he pulled the more it twisted, the deeper its angular metal head screwed its way inside him.

'It was an accident,' Lieutenant Shaw said to Pym quickly. 'I thought he was a kaffir.'

'For God's sake, help him!' Pym screamed.

'There's nothing we can do.' Lieutenant Shaw was calm. 'Put him out of his misery.'

'No, sir.' Pym stood up and faced him.

'You question my orders?'

'Yes, sir. I saw you come out here looking for him! I saw you attack him.'

'Come on, Pym.'

'And I saw you, sir,' Stanley Moore said as he approached.

Jean Jacques could hear a murmur of voices above him. He heard Pauline calling his name. She was laughing. She was holding a baby boy. He heard Emily speaking very seriously. 'My father is your father, Jean Jacques.' He squeezed his eyes tight to focus the image above him. White faces. Luminous in the moonlight. He didn't know who they were. They began to move backwards, down a long dark tunnel. They were going away. They mustn't go. No. A man was kneeling down beside him. His father was looking down at him. He smiled. His mother was beside him. She was crying. 'You mustn't cry,' Jean Jacques wanted to tell his mother, but he couldn't.

'He's dead.' Pym leant over Jean Jacques. His eyes were wide open and stared blindly up at him. 'You've killed him, sir.'

'Bastard!' Marsden's voice shook the tent canvas stretched above him as he demanded of Pym and Moore, 'Tell me again what happened! Tell me!'

'He had an assegaai, sir, and he must have called Private Villiers to him. He was in the bush, we couldn't see exactly what happened.'

'Didn't Villiers fight?' Charles interrupted and looked from one to the other in desperation. 'He must have fought. He had his rifle with him.'

'Yes, sir. He was on guard. He had his rifle.'

'Then why didn't he fight?' Charles stared at them both. 'Shaw couldn't have killed him in a fight. He could not have. Why?' Charles's voice soared in disbelief.

'Perhaps it was something else, sir.' Charles looked at Pym, waiting for an explanation. 'He was white, sir.'

'What are you talking about?'

'I don't think he even raised a hand in self-defence, sir.' Pym shrugged and Charles moved closer to him. 'I think Private Villiers let it happen, sir.'

'What?'

'He was faced by a white man, sir. A white officer.'

Charles felt sick. He glanced at Stanley Moore, unsure what to say next. 'Thank you.' Charles's voice was as dry as his throat. He moved away to his desk. Pym nodded at Moore and they saluted, ready to leave.

'Just one thing,' Charles looked up at them, 'you will be prepared to state exactly what happened at the court martial of a fellow white soldier?'

'Yes, sir.'

When the men had gone, Charles dropped his head into his hands. His fingers pushed hard against his temples and he sat absolutely still. Jean Jacques had been born a slave, born less than white, and he had died obedient to white masters. It was the only factor Charles Marsden hadn't taken into account.

As the guard left the small mud hut which served as an impromptu prison cell, Charles Marsden's eyes travelled the length of the wooden pole in its centre. It was dug deep into the hard ground and Shaw was chained tightly to its base. The lieutenant's former arrogance had gone, replaced by a cowering terror. A curve of fear running through his spine.

'You should thank God I'm not allowed to serve punishment on you myself.' Charles stood above him, his hands on his hips, his expression grim. 'In public at least.' Charles had ordered his men to stay clear of the hut. 'Have you anything to say in your defence?' His hand went to the scabbard at his side.

'I didn't know Pym was there, sir. I didn't see them.' Shaw's voice rose to the high pitch of someone pleading for his life.

'But he saw you!' Charles stepped closer. His hand remained on his sword, its knife edge hidden in the scabbard but known well by Shaw. Charles's eyes flashed with anger, fed by the futility of all that had happened. 'You murdered a man in cold blood, Lieutenant Shaw. Your crime was witnessed.'

'But, sir!'

'There are no buts, there are no excuses. This time you stand condemned by your own men.' His voice was hard.

'You told me to kill Villiers,' Shaw shouted. 'I obeyed your orders!'

'I told you what?' Charles curled his fingers through the hilt of his sword. 'What did I order you to do, Lieutenant Shaw?'

'I gained nothing from Villiers's death. I can prove it was you who wanted him dead!' Shaw's words died in his mouth as Charles drew the sword and whipped it high above his head.

'How will you prove that, Shaw? Tell me how you will convince a court that you are innocent, a man who killed once before without gain, a man who hates blacks, a man who thinks nothing of shooting black children! Tell me how you will prove anything but your own guilt!' The sword trembled in his hand and his voice rose suddenly. 'You will pay the price of lying with my wife!' Charles whipped the sword higher over Shaw's head in a sudden slash, cutting through the air with a hiss. Shaw tugged at the chain restraining him. He was held firmly in the line of the sword as it hung in the air about to drop and his imagination raced ahead.

He saw the sheet of silver light above him as the sword sliced down towards him. He felt its edge bite deep into his skull and split his head in two, falling apart as it dropped on the ground in front of him.

'No!' Shaw screamed. But the sword had not dropped.

'Private Villiers was in chains too.' Charles slipped his sword back into the scabbard. His voice was calm again. 'Though I doubt you would have seen his chains.' He turned away.

'Bastard!' Shaw's terror was heightened by shock. 'Lying bastard!'

'You will face a court martial.' Charles spoke quietly, his back turned.

'Then I will be returned to the Cape! I must be tried in the province, by Her Majesty's command!' Shaw fought to regain some authority.

'You will be tried in Grahamstown by Her Majesty's command. Among your own men, of mixed race. All soldiers of our Queen.' Charles walked to the door, bringing the meeting to an end, but froze as Shaw spoke very quietly.

'I will be tried for your crime as your wife bears my child?'

Silence held the world still.

'My wife will confirm your claim?' He turned to Shaw, the question in his eyes and in his voice. 'My wife has already denied your claim. Publicly.'

Lieutenant Shaw knew Charles Marsden had his life under his arm and had walked out with it. The sword might not have dropped, but he was already dead.

'Has the priest arrived?' Charles called as he stepped outside, and caught sight of two soldiers digging a grave at the edge of the camp.

'He's been seen approaching, sir.' The guard saluted.

'Good.' Charles forced his eyes away from the grave. He had to keep his mind on practicalities. There were dispatches to prepare. The Beauvilliers family must be told at once. He must ensure he could tell them Jean Jacques had been given a Christian burial. He strode out, crossing the ground quickly towards his tent. Then he stopped.

Jean Jacques' body lay under a tree. It was tightly wrapped in faded canvas. Charles looked at it and felt himself step out of his own body. He watched himself, as if he were a total stranger. He heard a major of the British army scream at the soldier close by Jean Jacques' body, 'You will use a coffin!' He watched himself stride angrily up to the soldier. He watched himself swing the soldier around by his arm and yell into his face, 'You will use a coffin!'

'It is not practice on the frontier, sir,' the soldier replied nervously.

'Did you hear what I said, Private?' He shook with rage.

'We have no coffins, sir,' the soldier argued, although he was afraid.

'Then you will use the British flag!' Charles heard a screech of madness rise in the voice of the stranger who was himself.

'We have no flag for burial, sir.'

'You don't?' Charles looked at the erect body of the Major Marsden, clad in bright red. He saw the veins stand out on the neck above the high collar. He saw ripples of tension run through the thighs, held tight in crisp white trousers. He looked with him to the pole in the centre of the camp, from which the Union Jack fluttered. He saw the sword whip out of its scabbard.

He saw it gleam in the sun as it pulled back through the air and sliced across the flagpole ropes. He saw his country's flag fall in a folding heap of red, white and blue.

'You have a flag!' he heard his own shrill voice.

Charles felt suddenly that he was in fragments and that the small pieces were being examined by a sea of staring faces around him. He realized he had just witnessed his own insanity.

'See to it, Private.' He embraced the security of orders and strode away from the Union Jack lying in a crumpled heap at his feet.

Rev. Phillip was riding with Suzanne and Thys towards an army camp with a soldier leading them. The trail was narrow and dense bush to either side of them clawed at the horses' legs.

'No, I do not imagine the entire British army has suddenly been set on fire with God, Suzanne. More's the pity.' He smiled as he looked at her. She sat in the saddle in front of Thys, leaning back against him, as though they were one. 'But I can't pretend I'm not pleased that a Christian burial has been asked for.'

'Who is the soldier who's been killed?' Suzanne asked. 'What's his name?'

'I don't know,' Rev. Phillip said. 'That he's been killed is enough.'

'And was it a Christian death?' Suzanne asked with a smile.

'Suzanne,' Thys whispered to silence her and rubbed his chin on top of her head.

'He'd miss it if I didn't tease him after all this time.' She looked across at Rev. Phillip, whom she adored; whose faith she envied but would never understand. 'You would, wouldn't you?'

'I would,' Rev. Phillip smiled. 'For then I would know you had stepped out of reach.'

'Out of reach of what?'

'Reconciliation,' Rev. Phillip said simply.

'There, sir.' The soldier leading them pointed towards Marsden's tent. 'The Major will be in that tent, sir.'

'And that is the man to be buried?' Rev. Phillip indicated the group of soldiers who had moved under the tree beside Jean Jacques' body. They were about to wrap it in the Union Jack.

'Yes, sir.'

'I'll be with you in a minute.' Rev. Phillip rode towards them and looked down at the body. It lay unwrapped and in full dress uniform. The faded canvas was pushed away in a pile as two soldiers lifted the body on to the flag spread out on the ground beside it.

'What is his name?'

'Jean Jacques!' Suzanne's scream blasted through the clergyman's question and echoed around the camp. 'Jean Jacques,' she cried again and jumped down from the horse. She pushed Rev. Phillip aside to get to the body, and fell to the ground murmuring, 'No, no.' She lifted Jean Jacques' body in her arms, buried her face in his neck and rocked as she held him. 'No!' Her voice rose again in a howl of anguish, tearing at the silence of the watching soldiers.

It reached Charles Marsden as he sat alone in his tent. He was staring at the formal words of the dispatch he had written in his stylish calligraphy: '. . . to inform you of the death in action of Private Jean Jacques Villiers.' On his desk lay an unopened letter, addressed to Jean Jacques. The handwriting was Emily Beauvilliers'.

Charles lifted his head in the direction of the voice. It was familiar, but not at once known to him. He pushed back the canvas flap and looked out. Thys was holding Suzanne. He was trying to drag her away from Jean Jacques, but she clung to the body desperately.

'She's killed him!' Suzanne screamed.

'Suzanne, please.' Thys couldn't reach her. She was lost in a crowd of images from the past. A small boy cowered in the light of a beacon and clutched his mother tightly in fear. A small brown boy looked down in terror at a scorpion as Clara's voice broke through the images. 'If you jump, the scorpion might miss you. But then of course it might not.'

'No!' Suzanne screamed, seeing the family bible open in front of her and a drop of blood falling on to the page. Clara's voice intoning, 'We swear on the holy family bible,' Prudence's voice joining Clara's, 'that the son of our father, the half-caste boy Jean Jacques, will no longer be a stain on our family.' Flames from a stable fire on Jean Jacques' back. An image of Charles Marsden stepped forward and rose up in front of Suzanne, looking down at her. He had Clara's eyes.

'You killed him!' Suzanne screamed at the memories, the

voices, the past. She didn't remember Lord Marsden was not a part of those memories. He was standing beside her, looking down at her. He was there and he had Clara's eyes. 'It was you!' she whispered.

Thys pulled her out of the nightmare and into his arms. He held her head against his shoulder and whispered on a breath, 'Suzanne.'

'Is there somewhere she can go?' Rev. Phillip was looking at Charles. He had noted the shock of recognition which had flashed between them all, and realized that the death of this young half-caste, Jean Jacques, had opened a past as wide and as deep as the grave he would be lowered into.

'Sergeant,' Charles nodded at Sergeant Forbes. 'Would you show them to my quarters, please.' He indicated Thys and Suzanne. Thys lifted his eyes momentarily from Suzanne and looked at Charles. Charles caught his look.

'She's wrong,' Charles said quietly to Thys. Thys turned without a word, wrapped his arm tighter around Suzanne and followed Sergeant Forbes across the camp.

Rev. Phillip waited, as Jean Jacques' body was finally covered by the Union Jack. 'Is this normal?' he asked quietly. 'To use the flag?' He glanced at the bare flagpole in the middle of the camp. 'What happened, Major?'

Charles felt himself step closer to the edge of a deep crevasse of guilt. 'Private Villiers was murdered,' he said.

'Why?' Rev. Phillip's simple question threw a million reasons forward in Charles's mind but he shut them all out. The clergyman's white collar was like a belt of truth, but still he resisted.

'The man responsible is to be court martialled.'

The sun burned down relentlessly on the scorched earth. A buzz of dry heat and the ache of parched land accompanied Rev. Phillip's prayer.

'Take this your son, Jean Jacques Villiers, in your wide and bountiful arms, we beseech you, Lord, our God and our Father. Your arms in which he will gain so much more than he has lost to move between. Your arms, which will hold him beyond the reasoning of man, and in whose shelter he will find peace. Amen.'

Thys felt a silent cry of pain rise in Suzanne as she stood close

beside him. He saw the long lashes lower on to her cheeks and
darken with tears. He watched the British flag, tightly bound
around the shape of Jean Jacques, as it was lowered on ropes
into the dry bowels of the earth. He bent down and scooped a
little of that red earth into his hand, then took Suzanne's hand
and tipped some into her palm. She didn't move. He turned back
to the grave and sprinkled a few grains on to the wrapped cocoon
enclosing Jean Jacques. Suzanne opened her hand and allowed
the earth to fall in a stream of dark red dust. Rev. Phillip lowered
his head as his thoughts slipped gently into a prayer.

'Help her to forgive them, Lord.'

'You will be staying for supper?' Charles's voice intruded into
the silence surrounding the grave as he looked at Suzanne and
Thys. 'There are many things to discuss.'

'I don't think there is anything to talk about,' Suzanne said
simply, her eyes directly on him and her tears gone. 'May we
go?' She turned to Rev. Phillip.

'Of course, my dear.' Rev. Phillip moved away towards their
horses. Thys was about to follow with Suzanne when he turned
back to Charles.

'Will you be going back to Cape Town, Major Marsden?'

'I will be going to Bonne Esperance,' Charles said. 'As soon as
possible.'

'You will be telling them you have seen Suzanne?' Thys asked.

'No!' Suzanne's voice was cold. 'To my family I am as dead as
Jean Jacques. Tell them I never wish to see Bonne Esperance
again.' Suzanne ran after Rev. Phillip towards the horses.

'Tell them, I'm sorry,' Thys said quietly and followed her.

Charles watched as the three figures rode out of the army
camp and along the trail which wound narrowly into the dense
surrounding bush. The trail on which he'd last seen Jean
Jacques alive.

Rev. Phillip rode slightly ahead of Thys and Suzanne. His mind
had travelled back to the night she had stepped from the dark
and into his life. In the years she had been with him at the mission, without ever allowing her to know, he had enquired of
anyone who came from the area if they knew of a missing girl.

All the stories he'd heard were confused. Because no body had
ever been found, myths had arisen surrounding a young girl's

disappearance. She was an angel. A witch. A goddess. Finally Rev. Phillip had come to his own conclusions. Suzanne must be the girl from the estate Bonne Esperance. In all the years that followed he had never allowed even a hint of what he suspected to reach Suzanne or the people of Bonne Esperance.

As he thought back to the burial of Jean Jacques, and Suzanne's reaction, he knew he'd been right to keep his silence and rest in the word of God.

He glanced back at the couple he had married, their bodies swaying together with the movement of the horse, and he knew that they too had buried the past in silence.

Chapter Fifteen

'Come on, Prudence!' Emily called as she stood by the carriage ready and waiting to go. The small child Jack tugged at her hand. 'I want to go.'

Emily looked up as her father emerged from the cellars and came to her. He'd assumed a tremendous dignity with his years.

'Are you going to see Clara?' he asked.

'And her new baby boy.' Jacques shrugged and turned to go.

'Father. Does it matter?' she asked. She knew how he hated the gossip surrounding the birth of his second grandchild.

'Perhaps it matters to Charles.' He glanced at Jack. 'Perhaps it does matter. Yes.'

'You can't hold what Clara has done against her child.' Emily moved him away from the carriage and out of the hearing of the small boy, but he followed and tugged at her skirts. 'Please, Father, be kind,' she pleaded, taking the child's hand.

His face softened as he looked at her. 'You have kindness enough for us all.'

Just then, a horseman in army uniform appeared at the far end of the road leading to Bonne Esperance. All that was visible was the cloud of dust raised by the flying hooves.

'Perhaps it is a letter from Clara telling you not to bother to visit her,' Jacques smiled.

'My apologies. I'm ready.' Prudence rushed out of the house, pulling a bonnet on to her head and tying it roughly under her chin. Her hair fell out of the bonnet as fast as she pushed it in. 'You'll be proud of what I'm going to buy in Cape Town today, Father. A crinoline! They have just arrived from England.' Emily watched the rider as he approached. Something about him disturbed her.

'A crinoline?' Jacques' face was puzzled as he repeated the strange word.

'It's like a cushion made of horse hair.' The rider came closer. Jacques watched him, as Emily did. 'One wears it under one's skirt, along with several hundred petticoats. One wears a bundle of horse hair in order to look like a tea cosy!' Prudence laughed. 'And that is what being a woman is all about.' She turned to the carriage. 'Come on, Emily. Fashion waits for nobody!'

'Mr Beauvilliers?' The rider pulled up as he reached them and hurriedly dismounted. He saluted and held out an official envelope. 'A dispatch for you.'

'You were right, Father,' Emily laughed. But as she examined a second envelope which the soldier held out, her laughter died. It was the last letter she'd sent to Jean Jacques. It was unopened. 'I believe that's mine,' she said and moved to take it from him. The small boy tugged at her skirts. 'Go away,' she said, pushing his hand away.

'What is it?' Prudence saw the envelope which Jacques held in his hand but didn't look at. His eyes were on the soldier.

'Where is it from?' Jacques' voice was flat.

'From the frontier, sir.'

Jacques turned away and his hand clutched the envelope tightly. Emily moved to him, her own letter crumpled in her hand.

'Father?' Her insides were knotted and she could hardly breathe.

Prudence looked from them to the soldier and felt her heart skip a beat. 'Do you want me to read it?' Her voice was soft. Jacques said nothing. Emily looked away as tears filled her eyes. Prudence took her father's hand and she felt the hard edge of his knuckles as he gripped the letter. She took the corner of the paper between her fingers.

'Father?' she said. Jacques' hand opened. Prudence took the dispatch, turned it over and pushed her finger under the seal. She opened the crisp white army parchment and read the words penned in stylish calligraphy. She closed her eyes. When she opened them Jacques' eyes sought hers, asking for what was in his mind not to be true.

Prudence held the paper out to him and Jacques took it. His eyes passed over the words though he wasn't reading.

'Thank you,' he said, and walked away without looking back. He walked away from the house, away from his daughters.

Prudence looked at Emily as despair caught in her throat.

'I've always known,' Emily whispered. 'Always known.'

The small boy, Jack Marsden, stood alone and totally forgotten. He looked at his aunts as they wept. He looked at his grandfather as he walked away towards the vineyards. He couldn't understand what had happened, but he could feel the grief all around him and his little chin trembled as a huge tear rolled silently down his face. He wanted his mother.

Eva looked up at Jacques as he sat on his horse high above her on the cliffs. She knew why he was there and turned away to the sea as the outline of his horse began moving down towards her. With every sweep of white foam that raced towards her and lapped around her feet, a voice deep inside her told her that she must accept whatever had happened.

'Jean Jacques is dead, Eva.' Jacques was standing beside her. Eva said nothing. Her eyes and her thoughts stayed out among the waves. 'Eva?' He reached out to her and her unspoken grief tore at his heart. She lifted her head and he could see she wasn't crying. Her eyes reflected nothing.

'Where is he buried?' she asked.

'On the frontier.' Eva tried to turn away but Jacques' hands gripped her shoulders, preventing her. 'Look at me.' There were still no tears. He couldn't understand her passivity. Her lack of resentment and anger. 'It's my fault,' he prodded for a reaction.

'Death is not the fault of anyone, Jacques.' Eva's eyes grew puzzled as she looked at him. 'Death comes of its own accord.'

'Not to Jean Jacques.'

'To us all,' Eva said simply. 'As love does,' she added, expressing, in the simplest words, the quality of her people.

Jacques pulled her into his arms and held her close. Their passionate, consuming love had matured into a deep understanding. He could feel the gentle beat of her heart against his body. 'Weep, Eva!' He held her tighter. 'Our son is dead, Eva. Weep.' He felt his own tears break. His throat closed and his voice faltered. 'You must!'

Eva gently wiped the tears from his cheeks, her dark eyes skimming across his face. His eyes were streaked with grief, yet still she could see her son in him.

'Our son is dead, but he lived.' Eva smiled. 'He lived.'

'How did you hear?' Charles moved into the sitting-room of Miss Thurston's house and sat on a velvet chair. 'You've seen your family?'

'Emily wrote to me.' Clara moved to a chair beside his and sat down. Her hair was swept up in a chignon, her eyes were bright and hard. 'I wasn't certain you had it in you, Charles.'

'Oh?' He rested his head against the high red back of the chair and looked at her from the corner of his eye. 'To do what?'

'Fulfil your promise.'

The sound of a baby crying reached them from upstairs. Charles took a breath and cleared his throat.

'I assume your father paid for the usual quota of nursing staff?'

'It is normal for a family to take care of one another. Especially when the husband is not there.'

Charles felt his face flush with anger and stood abruptly, moving to the far side of the room. His eyes flashed sharply to the door at the baby's renewed crying. 'May I see it?'

Clara got up and tugged a gold braid bell pull on the wall. 'I had no idea you were interested in babies, Charles.'

'What have you called it?'

'His name is Geoffrey.' A young Malay girl stepped into the room. 'Bring the child in, please.'

'Yes, ma'am.' The dark eyes dropped in obedience as she turned and left the room.

'What happened to the little butler?' Charles asked suddenly. Clara looked at him in wide-eyed innocence. 'That man with the long name whom Emily employed. Where is he?'

'He went.' Clara moved back to her chair. 'You can't trust people at all. They are totally unreliable. Ah!' She crossed to the door as the young girl returned, carrying a small bundle of baby. 'There he is.' Clara glanced over at Charles. 'You wanted to see him.'

Clara was on edge, but she decided to keep on playing the strange game he had dealt her. She ran her fingers delicately over the fontanelle of the tiny baby's skull. A sheen of invisible hair lit the edges of its head. Clara could feel Charles mentally step back. She sensed he was weakening in the face of Lieutenant

Shaw's child. 'What's the matter, Charles?'

'Have you seen Jack recently?' His eyes whipped from the baby and on to her. 'Our son. Have you seen him, Clara?'

'He's being taken good care of, I'm sure. It's better for a young boy to grow up in the country.'

Charles stepped forward, suddenly in command. 'You will be coming to Jean Jacques' memorial service with me,' he stated.

'Charles, really!' Clara indicated to the servant that she should leave with the baby.

'I have a carriage waiting outside.'

'I will not be attending,' she said coldly.

'No?' In one movement Charles was beside her. His hand gripped the collar of her dress tightly and he pulled her towards him.

'Let go of me.' Humiliation gripped her as tightly as his hand.

Charles loosened his grip immediately and went to the door. 'I will wait outside until you and the child are ready to leave.'

'Coward!' Clara yelled. 'You haven't even the courage to question that child!' For the first time Clara was confused. He disturbed her.

'I have no questions about that child!' He added quietly, 'I have my wife. And I will wait for her outside.'

The sky was heavy with rain but it didn't fall. Moist dark clouds shrouded Bonne Esperance, and the mountains too, as if they were not there at all: as though Bonne Esperance never was. The group of people in the small family graveyard stood in a huddle of black. The harmonious voices of mourning from the labourers melted into the mist and became a part of it. The priest's voice mingled with the singing, and the whole swelled with the gentle throb of Africa.

'We bless this stone in the name of Jesus Christ and in memory of Jean Jacques Beauvilliers, and commend to you the soul of this our child, our brother, taken so silently and so swiftly by you.'

The coffee warm tone of African voices rose through the mist and disappeared, reaching up to God himself.

Jacques looked at Eva as her lips moved in a silent Muslim prayer. Prudence wrapped an arm around Emily's heaving shoulders.

282

'Our memory is of his body but your joy, o Lord, is in his spirit.'

Emily pulled away from Prudence and ran. Maria, her eyes sunk deeper by age in her black face, her fuzz of hair edged white and her body as wide as the land of her birth, moved after Emily. She clasped her, her voice still rising in African song, and led her away.

Jacques looked at the grey stone. Engraved on it were the words, 'Jean Jacques Beauvilliers. 1820-1845.' Jacques had insisted the name was not shortened. He was his son. Beauvilliers.

'And as his spirit is reunited with you now, our Heavenly Father, we rejoice in your glorious name.' The priest's 'Amen' was echoed by a multitude of voices. It swelled in song, and hung over Bonne Esperance among the clouds.

Clara's position as heir to Bonne Esperance had been established through Jean Jacques' death, but she had to ensure that Charles was reconciled to her. The comedy of manners in which he'd been bred had so far assured his silence. She slipped out to the barn as the family gathered in the house after the memorial service, making sure Charles knew where to find her. She'd sensed there was something very different about him. If it was only her involvement with Lieutenant Shaw she knew she could dismiss his fears.

Clara undid the buttons which ran down the front of her black dress. The smell of hay was exciting. Death was exciting. She looked at her breasts as they rose, smooth and pale against the black of her dress, and ran her hand over them. In her thoughts was not her husband, but Lieutenant Duncan Shaw. She remembered his hard, demanding hands running over her body and gripping her hips as he arrogantly pulled her to him and forced his way inside her.

'Clara?' Charles's voice intruded upon the desire which flooded her body as she thought of her lover. He stood in the doorway.

'You do want me, don't you, Charles?' Clara let her breath out slowly. Her lips parted slightly as he entered the barn and made his way to her.

'I will accept your child as my own, Clara.' Her eyes lit. He did want her. He was prepared to buy her. 'He will bear my name. Geoffrey Marsden. Is that what you want?'

'I want you.' Clara's voice dropped to a whisper. 'I want you as I have never wanted you before, Charles.'

'Show me,' he said. Clara was surprised, but whatever had changed him excited her as much as it disturbed her. She shrugged her shoulders free of her bodice and took his hand, holding it to her lips. He watched her as she moved his hand gently over her skin. 'All of you, Clara.' Charles stepped back and looked at her. 'All,' he demanded.

'You go over there,' Clara whispered and gestured towards a corner of the barn piled high with bales of hay. 'You can watch,' she purred. 'And enjoy.' She knew he enjoyed her sexual tease.

Charles moved away, sat down and leaned back against the hay. Clara loosened the fastenings of her skirt and stepped out of it, turning her back to him. She looked over her shoulder as she pulled the drawstring on her petticoats and they tumbled to her feet. She was naked.

'You see, Charles. Naked under the black of mourning, I waited for you.' Charles lifted his pocket watch and glanced at it. Clara noticed and laughed. It was a deep, sensuous laugh. 'There's plenty of time, Charles.' She moved towards him. The dark shadows in the barn stroked her slender, womanly body. She was still extraordinarily beautiful. Bearing children had only added a fuller curve to her sensuous lines.

'It's been a long time,' Clara said as her hands reached towards him. 'You'll just take me? Here in the barn?' An excited husk entered her voice as she remembered Lieutenant Shaw doing the same at the barracks.

'I have just seen the time.' Charles felt himself tense as her hand caressed his inner thigh and moved higher.

Clara smiled. 'Jean Jacques' death has excited you too.'

'I was thinking of the father of your child.' Charles glanced at his pocket watch again. 'He is facing a firing squad at this very moment.' He put the watch back in his pocket.

He saw the shock run through her body, and suddenly her nakedness meant nothing to him. The trap she'd held him in for so long broke into pieces around him and he stepped out of it.

'What have you done?' she hissed after him, as he moved to go. Her hands stretched out to his face, fingers splayed like claws. He grabbed her wrists and held her back, his eyes filled with disgust at her naked body struggling to free itself. All he saw was used flesh. Flesh which had lost its power to control him.

'The father of your child has been executed for the murder of Jean Jacques.' He pushed her back, sending her reeling across the barn floor. He looked down at her coldly. Naked, on her hands and knees, she would once have aroused a powerful lust in him. Now, he stepped out of the barn and out of her reach.

Charles moved in long determined strides across the court-yard and straight to his carriage. As he did so, Prudence emerged from the low white cellars further away with Jack.

'I didn't think it was good for him to be inside with so much unhappiness,' she said, taking the toddler's hand.

'Hello, Jack.' Charles bent down and Jack hid behind Prudence's skirts. 'I want to speak to you.'

'I'm not certain he knows you.' Prudence looked at the small uncertain boy. 'Say hello to your father.' The large brown eyes turned slowly from Prudence to Charles. They were the eyes of a fully grown man. Thinking eyes which balanced what they saw on their own scales of justice.

'I want Mama.'

Charles stood up stiffly, as if he was in pain.

'I am leaving for India.' He cleared his throat. 'But there is something I must tell you before I go.' At the edge of his vision Charles noticed Clara in her black dress of mourning run towards the house. 'Suzanne is alive, Prudence.'

'Suzanne?' Prudence was bewildered. 'Suzanne?' she repeated.

'She is at a mission on the frontier. She is well.' Before Prudence could question him further, Charles strode away to his carriage and climbed into it. Jack had seen Clara run to the house and tugged at Prudence's hand.

'Suzanne!' Prudence's face lit with joy as the reality dawned on her. 'Suzanne's alive?' She swept the small boy into her arms and raced towards the house. 'Suzanne's alive,' she told him as she pushed open the front door. She ran into the sitting-room with the child still in her arms but stopped in horror as Clara's voice met her in a scream of rage.

'Get that black woman out of this house!' Clara was closing on Eva.

'Clara stop it!' Emily tried to hold her back.

'Get her out!' Clara lunged at Eva as she stood calmly beside Jacques. Jacques grabbed Clara's hands as they reached for Eva and swung her away. His hand lashed out with tremendous force as years of anger exploded in a hard crack across her face. As the sting of the blow jerked Clara's head back, she saw more hatred in her father's face than she'd ever seen before.

Eva walked out of the house into the breath of freedom and Jacques called, 'Come back, Eva.' She turned back. Her dark eyes glowed as they searched his for understanding.

'There is no place for me here,' Eva told him quietly. Her slender brown hand covered his as he touched her shoulder. 'I thought Jean Jacques was the greatest price we could pay for our love. But it isn't!.' The black scarf wound tightly around her hair added dignity to the inner quality that was Eva. 'Leave me to my own world. Please.' She turned away to her carriage. Mixed with the rumbling of the carriage wheels Jacques could hear Clara's obscene screams still ringing from the house.

'Suzanne is alive.' Jacques thought he felt movement under his feet as the mountains slipped somewhere among the clouds. Prudence's voice was clear as she repeated, 'Suzanne is alive, Father.'

As the carriage drove Eva away from him towards the place she called home, Jacques' sadness was swamped by sudden joy. The mountains were still in place. One part of what held his life together had not died.

'Go now, Pauline.' Mr Westbury held the reins of the small fly cart as she climbed in quickly with her son, John. He was seven and a half years old. Slim and blond, with deep blue eyes that questioned the man he thought of as his father.

'Aren't you coming, Father?' he asked.

'Your mother has a headache!' John Westbury glanced at the house and caught sight of a lace curtain dropping back, witnessing his lie. But there was nothing that would stop him helping his daughter.

'Don't be too long, Pauline.' He smacked the horse's rump.

Mr Westbury had suffered almost as deeply as Pauline when he'd heard of Jean Jacques' death. He had known there was no way his wife would allow Pauline to go to the memorial service being held at Bonne Esperance.

'For what reason? Why would Pauline attend the service of a slave she hardly knew? People would wonder!' Mr Westbury had realized then that his wife would never give up the lie they lived. She would never waver in her determination to keep John Westbury's true identity a secret.

As he stepped through the doorway of the house Mrs Westbury pushed past him.

'Where have they gone?' she challenged him as the small cart bobbed its way into the distance.

'For a ride,' her husband answered and moved past her into the house.

'They've gone there!' she shouted at his back. 'Why are you lying to me?'

'Yours is the lie!' He turned on her. 'John is their son and they will stand together for a moment in memory of Jean Jacques.'

'Have you told John?' Her face tensed into hard lines and her temper flared. 'I'll never understand you!'

'Because you don't understand our daughter! You have denied her love, Mary!'

'Love?' Her voice expressed the insult she felt. 'And you would have stood by, while her entire life was sullied by disgrace? By filth?'

'What filth?'

'That man!'

'She loved him!' The arguments which had raged so many times in the Westbury house sparked again as she attacked him bitterly.

'And you are still prepared to face that child with the shame of who he really is?'

'Perhaps one day he will have to face it.' Mr Westbury tried to move away. 'But not in shame.' He hated arguments. 'The shame is in you, Mary!' He hated the violence they aroused even in him. 'In the lie we live!'

'Never!' The finality in his wife's voice arrested him. He looked back at her. Every inch of her taut angular body denied him. 'So long as I draw breath the only truth will be that I gave birth to that boy. God help you if your weakness today should threaten it!'

*

As she drove towards Bonne Esperance with her son beside her, Pauline knew that an argument would be raging between her parents. She had heard them many times before and she was always the focus. But as she saw Bonne Esperance, with heavy clouds folding over it, all she could think of was Jean Jacques. She looked at the envelope of money she held in her hand, opened it and pulled it out. It was Emily's. Money she'd given for them to go to England and live in peace with their child.

'What is the money for, Pauline?' John Westbury looked at her from serious blue eyes. 'And why was Father trying to get us away from Mother?'

'I don't know.' Pauline slipped the money back into the envelope. 'Mother doesn't think we need to go to the memorial service.'

'Who was he anyway?' he asked. Pauline looked at her son as the lie her mother had woven around them tightened with his words.

'You don't remember Jean Jacques at all?'

'No.' He glanced at her. 'You do, though.'

'Yes.' Pauline looked away. 'He was someone I knew.'

'Then why didn't Mother want you to go?'

'He was not white.' Pauline wrapped up the truth in four neat words and wished she could make him understand. 'You would have liked him.'

'Why?'

'Because he was a good man.'

'And he's dead.'

They reached the low stone wall which marked the perimeter of Bonne Esperance. On the other side of the wall was the grave-yard.

'Jean Jacques will never really be dead,' Pauline said as she climbed down from the fly cart. Emily was standing alone beside Jean Jacques' memorial stone. 'Emily,' she called gently. Emily looked up at her. Her eyes moved from Pauline and back to the stone.

'It's over,' she said quietly.

John smiled at Emily and nodded in a polite half-bow, not sure what to say.

'Hello.'

'Hello John.' Emily came over to him, and as she drew nearer

288

the empty space left by Jean Jacques seemed to close a little. She was stepping out of one era and into another. He noticed her eyes peering into his and felt suddenly uneasy.

'Pauline says Jean Jacques was a friend of hers.' He smiled at Emily, trying to break free. 'He was your brother, wasn't he?' Pauline looked at him in surprise. Nobody had told John anything about Jean Jacques. Pauline's mother had seen to that.

'He was my brother, yes.' Emily held her hand out to him. 'Do you want to climb over the wall?' John shook his head. He still had no idea why but he felt safer with a wall between himself and whatever that gravestone really meant.

'I'll stay here,' he said with a shy smile. It was Jean Jacques' smile. Emily turned away from him quickly, and helped Pauline over the wall and into the graveyard. As they approached the stone, Emily's hand automatically dug into the deep pocket of the pinafore she wore over her dress and touched the letter she'd written to Jean Jacques.

Though Pauline stood erect, her face was wet with tears. She held out the envelope containing the money to Emily. 'Thank you.'

John Westbury was puzzled. What was that money really for? Why was his sister giving it back to Emily on the day a total stranger called Jean Jacques was put in the ground?

'He's just like him,' Emily said quietly with a quick glance at John.

'Are you ready to take your sister home?' Wiping her eyes, Pauline moved away from the stone and returned to him.

As Emily watched their fly cart drive across the open country and back to the security of the name Westbury, she recognized that Jean Jacques' death had brought something else with it. John Westbury's identity would be hidden for ever. Not just by Mrs Westbury but by Pauline herself. She felt the letter in her pocket again and remembered the words she had written.

'Your success is in yourself, Jean Jacques. You are no less than any other man. You are more, because what you are grew from love and blossomed with the birth of your son. None can demand your obedience except One!'

Emily turned back to the house and, as she walked, the words came to her that she would write in her diary that night.

'Jean Jacques is dead but his son must not be buried with him.

He is the truth of the past.' Emily completed the entry in her diary and put out the lamp. She glanced out of her window at the moon as it passed behind the clouds, and prepared herself to face a new era. John Westbury would be at its centre instead of Jean Jacques.

But it was the strange little boy, Jack Marsden, crying so continually for his mother's love and never getting it, who climbed into Emily's thoughts, and remained there: standing firmly beside John Westbury, in the heart of the future Emily was trying to imagine.

Dominating them all loomed Clara. Emily had seen Clara's face as her father had hit her, and the corset of hate that had clamped itself around her. She had lost her husband and her lover. She had nothing left to lose.

Chapter Sixteen

The white church stood proudly in the centre of the mission. It dwarfed the mud huts erected on every inch of spare ground around it and reached up from the valley in which the mission lay. Bare roots of trees groped down the sides of the high grey cliffs, looking for a hold and bright orange strelitzia stood out like nature's beacon along the dramatic line of rocks above.

Suzanne looked away from the church Thys had built for Rev. Phillip and down at the letter in her hand. It was from Emily. They had been writing to one another for almost three years.

'Everything seemed to stop as New Year dawned, Suzanne. While all around us the past is pushed back by the future, as it moves into Africa, we remain trapped in time. I'm glad that at last a little peace has been achieved in your part of the world. What a bloody war it was. They all were, with the bloodiest not even a part of war. Yes, Jean Jacques' death still haunts us. And you, Suzanne? How's Thys? I long to hear you have a child.'

Suzanne folded the letter in her lap. She looked back at the church and wondered if there was anything in Rev. Phillip's beliefs. If there was, why did the God he worshipped not give her a child?

She saw Thys coming out of the church and walking across the mission grounds with Rev. Phillip and Dr Steven. Thys wanted a child as much as she did. She watched his easy stride, the leanness of his body slightly more muscular now and still provoking in her an excitement. Suzanne longed for his child to complete their love and wondered again what prevented it. She pushed the thought aside, as she and Thys had done so often, and finished reading Emily's letter.

'No, Suzanne. I don't think Father will ever get over his death.

He walks over the land which he used to call "the mother who never dies", he looks at the vines, but he doesn't see them any more. His heart is no longer here. I've often wondered if perhaps it's France he longs for, even with Europe in the midst of Revolutions. But then there is Eva.'

Suzanne had to speak to Thys. She could feel the living death reaching out to her from the pages of Emily's letter. Thys must get his mother's blessing on their union or they too might be trapped in time.

'I know why you don't want to go, Thys.' Suzanne ran her fingers down the side of his face as she lay beside him, curled in the crook of his arm. She'd miraculously turned a small hut into a house. A loving home. 'You must go to your mother,' she said.

'Yes.' Thys didn't open his eyes. Suzanne leant on one elbow and looked at him. She ran her finger down his straight nose. 'Are you listening?' He nodded, his eyes still closed. 'The church has been complete for a long time, Thys.'

'I promised Reverend Phillip I would stay on for a while.'

'No, Thys.' He opened his eyes and looked at her. 'You know you must go.'

He pulled her to him and wrapped his arms around her tightly. He spoke into her neck, his warm breath against her skin. 'Suzanne, why so much fear?'

'I won't listen to you any more.' She drew away from him. 'I love you and I want to bear your child, Thys.'

'Going to see my mother won't achieve that.'

'Thys.' She looked into his eyes keenly. 'Tell me you feel nothing for your mother. Tell me you don't care that her last words to you were a curse.' Thys regarded her in silence. 'I'm as afraid of being parted again as you are, Thys.'

Thys turned his head away. Suzanne leaned over him, forcing him to look at her.

'You know where your mother has settled, don't you.' Thys nodded. 'You've known for years.' Thys nodded again. 'So have I, Thys. In Natalia.'

'And now moved on to Transorangia, away from the British again.' There was a catch in Thys's voice.

'Thys,' Suzanne whispered, 'go to her.'

Thys took a long deep breath which expired slowly from his

lungs. He pulled her into his arms again. 'I would be gone a long time.'

'We said that when you had built the church, when you'd seen your mother, we would go to Gerrit. To your farm.'

'You'll like Gerrit. His peach brandy you'll like too.'

Suzanne relaxed. For the first time they were facing what each had been afraid to face alone.

'With your mother's blessing we will have a child, Thys.' She rubbed her nose against his. 'We will.' Her mouth moved to his and she gently parted his lips with hers. She knew every part of his body. As she slipped her leg across him, his skin warmed to hers in familiarity and she tried not to think of his leaving.

Thys looked down into the pass. Successive torrents of rain had washed bare the precipices leading to it. The brown river winding through the pass was swollen, its banks carved wide by the force of the water. The last time Thys had seen the river it had been so narrow his horse had leapt over it in an easy stride. Now it ran wide with rains, and its strong rippling currents challenged anyone to cross it.

He saw the debris of an ox wagon spread over the rocky outcrops below. Still inspanned, the white skeletons of the oxen had been cleaned by scavengers and bleached by the sun. In death they tried to warn him, it seemed, and his horse moved backwards in small nervous steps. Thys ran his hand down its sweating neck and climbed off its back. He could see a narrow winding path, a path more suitable for a goat than a horse. He rubbed the horse's nose.

'It's all right,' he said in gentle Afrikaans. The horse tugged at its rein, flared its nostrils and resisted with stamping hooves.

'Come,' Thys insisted and led the horse to the beginning of the winding trail.

A baboon barked at Thys from a large rock which overhung the pass. It bared its long yellow teeth as it dared him to invade its territory.

'Go away!' Thys shouted at the baboon on its rock throne, looking down at him from close-set eyes. Immediately a troop of baboons ran to the king and squatted round him in a semi-circle. They barked with him, echoing his authority over their domain.

The horse pulled back on its rein and neighed its fear. It had seen the sharp, threatening teeth. Thys unstrapped the gun on his saddle, slid it out, and raised it. A shriek of appalled terror filled the air as the troop turned as one, showed Thys their itchy red behinds and ran. Thys smiled as he lowered his gun. He was reassured. The baboons knew what a gun was.

'Come,' he encouraged his horse. 'They say it's safe.' He led his horse, picking his way carefully down the narrow trail. The horse's hooves clattered on the rock, slipped and scraped. Gradually the baboons returned to their position and sat in silence watching, as if waiting for disaster. A stone dislodged itself under Thys's foot and he stepped back quickly, pushing the horse's neck back with his arm as the stone bounced down the rocks until it reached the bottom with a thud. Thys waited for the echoing to die away.

He held the horse's rein tighter and went on. His mother must have made this journey, as many of his people had. He thought of the document they had left behind them with the English: 'We are now quitting the fruitful land of our birth, in which we have suffered enormous losses and continual vexation, and are entering a wild and dangerous territory, but we go with a firm reliance on an all-seeing, just and merciful Being, whom it will be our endeavour to fear and humbly to obey.' And he wondered why people used God to separate themselves from others. Why Suzanne separated herself from Him, and others revelled in derision.

'You have reason to cry.' He remembered his father's last words to him, and his mother's, 'You chose the English woman. We have no need of you.'

The bark of the baboons was suddenly distant. Thys's concentration had been so fixed on the path he took he hadn't noticed how far he'd gone. He looked back and up at the barrel-chested baboons, standing on spindly back legs as they peered down at him from a great height. The roar of the river drowned their calls and Thys moved down to its bank.

There was no fording place. The banks were high and the water a bubbling swirl of brown. Thys knew there was only one way to cross it. He stripped off his clothes, rolled them into a bundle and tied the bundle on his head.

'It's safe,' Thys comforted his horse and led it to the bank. He crossed the stirrups over the pommel of the saddle and waded into the water, pulling the reluctant horse behind him. He allowed the horse its head and guided it by the snaffle as they sank together into the water.

The only way to cross the raging torrent was to relieve the horse of its weight, float alongside it and guide its head. The current pulled them fast downstream, and the horse held its head high, its spread nostrils just above the water. Thys swam beside it, his naked body allowing the water to sweep him with it.

He felt the hard edge of a rock thud against his hip. The horse pulled his arm as it was swept on. He gripped the snaffle tighter and flowed with it. They were being pushed to the bank on the opposite side, which was bordered by tangled vegetation overhung by the mountain rock. Thys grabbed the gnarled root of an ancient tree and the horse struggled and splashed to find a foothold. Its hooves at last gained purchase on the slippery stones under the water and Thys shouted encouragement. It pulled its shining wet body out of the water and stumbled its way up the bank.

Thys fell back on the dry ground beside it and laughed as the baboons sat watching him in silent amazement from the other side.

'Come on!' he shouted at them. He was answered by the familiar flash of angry raw behinds as they scampered back up the rock face to their kingdom.

Thys stood up, naked skin gleaming light brown, sprinkled with droplets of water. The rocks before him beckoned and he climbed them nimbly. Suddenly, as far and as wide as the eye could see, the land opened out in a carpet of tiny flowers, each bright colour competing with the one beside it. The whole was the most incredible display of vivid beauty. He heard the plaintive coo of a ring dove, the incessant chirp of crickets and the twitting of a multitude of birds. The thickets around him sheltered a swarm of animal and insect life, while ahead of him a startled duiker leapt away and a small herd of griesbok looked about in silent curiosity. There was plenty of food for the pot.

He felt very small as the vast expanse of Africa stretched before him towards his mother, hundreds of miles on.

Rev. Phillip could hear Suzanne. She was throwing up. He moved away from the low doorway to her hut towards the church. As he entered it the sudden cool air wrapped around him in a shadow. He looked up. It was a glorious church. A gallery of yellowwood ran around the rear, and the altar stood high and proud, covered in a white cloth embroidered by Suzanne. An enormous cross hung suspended over it. It was carved from hard African stinkwood. He remembered the months Thys had spent on it. He'd poured his own sweat into it as he carved and shaped it, each shaving of wood scraped with great effort from a tree formed over hundreds of years.

Rev. Phillip remembered Paul's words to the Galatians: 'I am crucified with Christ: nevertheless I live; yet not I but Christ liveth in me', and he stopped in front of the altar. His head bowed instinctively as he turned away, moving into the small vestry to prepare communion.

As he lifted the silver chalice he wondered at the way in which African people accepted the ornate ceremony of the Church with such simple faith. He rubbed the soft polishing cloth across the silver skin. His own face looked back at him, distorted by the curve of the cup. He wondered if the silver itself distorted the simplicity of Christ's message. The light step of feet in his church disturbed his reverie.

'I'm in the vestry, Andreus,' he called to the young Xhosa boy who always came to help him. He set the chalice down and turned to the door, expecting Andreus to step in with his usual bowed, curly head. But the doorway remained empty. Curious, Rev. Phillip stepped out of the vestry and into the church.

Suzanne knelt among the rows of wooden pews. Her eyes were closed, and her face was lit by the most glorious smile he had ever seen. As if knowing he was there, her eyes opened.

'You were right, Reverend Phillip,' she said quietly. He remained silent, afraid that any word he said might halt this first tentative step Suzanne had taken. 'God has answered my prayer.' Her eyes rose to the cross and shone. 'I am with child.'

'Suzanne is expecting a baby, Father.' Emily made her way to her father as he sat where he always did: beside the stone which commemorated Jean Jacques and among the graves of his wife, Miss Thurston and the crumbling stones of his forebears. 'I have a letter from her.' She tried to force away the gloom which always surrounded him now. His fifty-nine years showed clearly in the rounded curve of his shoulders, the deep crevices scored across his face, and the silver hair at his temples. But underneath the mask of age Emily could still see the strong jaw and the inquisitive dark eyes.

'Is she coming home?' he asked. 'Will Thys come home with her?'

'She has other things to do, Father.' Emily had hidden what she had sensed from Suzanne's letters; that she would never come home. 'Thys has gone to find his mother. They need her blessing.'

'Why?' Jacques' eyes narrowed slightly. 'It is their life.'

'You often speak of Mother's forgiveness, Father.' Emily's eyes moved to her mother's grave. 'You said she told you forgiveness was the greatest gift of God. That only if we forgive others will we find forgiveness.'

Jacques turned away. Away from everything. The graves, Bonne Esperance and Emily.

'Prudence is right, Father. Bonne Esperance is dying, and you're dying with it.' She waited anxiously for her father's reaction. It didn't come. His silence was even more frightening. 'Jean Jacques is dead! He has been dead for more than two years. I loved him as I've never loved anyone but *I've* accepted it.'

'Why?' The flat denial that there could be any reason struck at Emily as it always did.

'Because I want my father back,' she answered.

Jacques turned to look at her. In her face he saw his wife. 'You have a remedy for what I feel, Emily?' His voice was bitter. Challenging the goodness of his wife which glowed from Emily. 'What remedy is there for the emptiness he left behind? And what right do I have to happiness?'

'You mustn't think that, Father.' She went on quickly before she lost courage. 'Bonne Esperance doesn't need you as you are! We don't need you like this.' She could see the look of a hurt child behind his eyes. 'But Eva needs you.'

Jacques turned away again and Emily knew why. Eva had gone to her place and left him in his. The only thread which joined their worlds, Jean Jacques, had gone.

Emily looked round at a child's frustrated shout, 'Wait for me!' She saw the figure of a small boy clambering over the cobbles of the courtyard. Little Geoffrey was chasing after Jack Marsden and was, as always, left behind. At almost twice his age, Jack's strides were long and he used them to keep a distance between himself and the small brother who had claimed his mother's love.

'Go away!' Emily could hear the anger in Jack's voice as he turned on his small brother. 'Leave me alone.'

'What about your grandchildren, Father?' Her thoughts included John Westbury; but she couldn't tell him. 'What of their future if we allow it to die before they grow?'

Young Jack Marsden stepped into the small dark room and his body tingled with the excitement of the forbidden. He had been told time and again by his mother not to go there. He was not to mix with 'those people'. Fear always lurked behind her words. At first he'd obeyed in an effort to please her and only watched them from a distance. He'd watched the gleam of dark skin as they tipped water over their bodies. He'd watched the outbursts of violence which flared between them in an instant and died just as quickly. He'd watched their open gestures of appreciation of women like Rosita, Maria's daughter. But most of all he'd heard their music. It stirred something inside him which he couldn't identify, yet seemed to be part of himself.

Sunday smiled up at the young white boy as he stepped into the unfamiliar dark of the labourers' quarters. Jack saw the gleam of Sunday's white teeth and smelt the musky scent of his sweat. He felt the same excitement he always felt when he stepped into this alien world.

'This hook is one like my father made,' Sunday said quietly. Jack's eyes found their way through the dark and settled on the slim black fingers with cracked tips. 'This hook catch the clever fish one day, my father said.' Sunday smiled to himself.

'Are we going fishing today?' Jack said keenly. 'Where your father Titus took you?'

'Yes,' Sunday nodded. Jack noticed the pale palms of the black hands as they cupped the hook, and his eyes moved to the bare feet. The soles were pale like the palms of his hands. As pale as Jack himself.

'Go away!' he grumbled as Geoffrey's small figure appeared in the doorway.

'Please.' The little boy waited nervously at the edge of the darkness which enclosed his big brother in a world he was always shut out of.

'Mother will get cross. Go away,' Jack scolded him. The small boy stepped across the threshold into the darkness and stood firm.

'I want to fish.'

Emily saw Geoffrey disappear into Sunday's hut and knew there would be trouble. Clara was already calling as she emerged from the house.

'Geoffrey? Where are you Geoffrey? Have you seen Geoffrey?' Clara called across to Emily.

'Where's Jack?' Emily answered and avoided further questions by walking away.

Clara's eyes went straight to the labourers' huts. 'He is entirely disobedient,' she muttered. 'Geoffrey!' she shouted as she moved towards the hut.

Emily watched Clara's stiff skirts brush through the dust as she moved closer to the forbidden area. Since Charles had gone to India, without a word to the rest of the family, she had seen Clara pour all her attention on to her younger son, Geoffrey, the child of her dead lover.

'Come out of there at once, Geoffrey.' Clara stood back from the dark entrance to the hut. She remembered Titus and she remembered his boy, Sunday: but she would never allow herself to acknowledge him. She grabbed Geoffrey's hand and spat condemnation at Jack as he stood nervously behind him. 'I have told you not to bring Geoffrey here! You will never do it again.' She swung away, dragging the small boy with her. Jack stood alone in the doorway. His mother had dismissed him yet again.

He turned back into the black world his mother had abandoned him to and his eyes, still accustomed to the dark, rested on Sunday. Sunday noticed a swell of tears filling the boy's eyes, held back as always.

'Tell me again,' Jack said, moving to Sunday. He sat down beside him on the ground and looked up at him longingly.

'About the fish?' Sunday asked hopefully. Afraid of being dragged back into the secrets of Bonne Esperance.

'About what happened here.' Jack's lips formed a straight line and he looked hard at the source of all his information; information he was gathering in an effort to understand. 'Tell me what your father told you happened here a long time ago.'

'No.' Sunday shook his head and held the hook out. 'It's just stories.'

'Tell me the stories.' Jack stared at the tight black curls as Sunday lowered his head. The flat nose spread wide beneath his downturned face. 'Tell me what your father told you about the slave girl. About the baby. Tell me what Titus said.' Jack's voice trembled.

Sunday lifted his head and looked into the determined young face. 'Maybe it's not true,' he said evasively.

'Tell me.' Jack's eyes didn't blink.

'You want trouble?' Sunday peered into the unblinking eyes. He knew Clara's kind of trouble. His father Titus had told him.

'I want to know the truth.' Adult eyes set in a child's face challenged Sunday with all the authority of a white master. 'Tell me.'

'It was a long time ago,' Sunday began obediently. 'The girl was beautiful, my father said. Her name was Eva.'

As Sunday led Jack into the past, Geoffrey sat in the centre of a circle his mother had spun around him. He was trapped.

'We are called to take on certain tasks in life, Geoffrey. And you have been called to a great responsibility.' Her words went over the small boy's head. 'It is you who will restore the family to the dignity it once held.'

Jack and Sunday would have crept down to the river by now, Geoffrey thought. Sunday would have his fine hook for catching the clever fish. John Westbury might even join them at the river. He was his hero and almost grown-up. Geoffrey's attention was snatched back as Clara held a very large and very old key in front of his face. He'd often wondered what that key was for. It hung alone on the wall, as if it held some special meaning. Yet it couldn't open any door in the house. Jack had discovered this and told him.

'It is you who will one day turn the lock. With this key, you will return to this family what is rightfully theirs in France. But to do that the family must prove itself worthy. Untainted.'

Geoffrey was none the wiser about the key.

'It is an honourable calling, Geoffrey. A calling which

demands the highest from you in everything you do. Do you understand?'

'Yes,' Geoffrey nodded, hoping his mother would think he had.

'Now go to your room and say your prayers.'

Geoffrey's heart sank. There was only one prayer in his head at the moment: to be magicked outside with Jack and Sunday. He prayed it earnestly. But as he felt his mother's hand take his firmly in hers, and lead him to the door, he knew the prayer he had to make.

'God help me wash away the stain of sin upon this family.'

'What are you thinking about, Prudence?' Emily asked. Günther Wagner had told her that Prudence was in the vineyards.

'Do you know what's happening in Cape Town?'

'And what is?' Emily asked.

'The whole town is protesting against the landing of convicts from the ships bound for Australia. Did you know the Government plans to turn the Cape into a penal colony?' Prudence walked on, examining leaves and buds.

'Should we welcome the convicts, or wave them goodbye, Prudence?' Emily followed her.

'I want to see them.' Prudence turned to her. 'I want to see some people who come from somewhere beyond the boundaries of Bonne Esperance. Somewhere that's still alive.'

'I spoke to Father,' Emily said quietly.

'And he ignored you.' Prudence stopped beside the low wall that ran around the edge of the vineyard. 'There's a whole world still living out there, Emily.' She dug her toe into the wall and it crumbled.

'And you want to go to that new world?'

'Perhaps I just want to breathe a little.' She looked at Emily suddenly. 'Do you see how it's crumbling, Emily? Do you see how soon our land will be swallowed by weeds? I can't bear it.'

'What is it, Prudence?' Emily could sense her sister was looking outside Bonne Esperance for the first time. 'Tell me.'

'I've told you,' Prudence lied. The truth was that she could no longer bear to watch Bonne Esperance slowly die as her father was. 'Our mother's money won't last for ever, Emily, but he won't listen to me.' She paused. 'I don't know what to do.'

'Did I tell you Suzanne was expecting a child?' Emily asked, moving closer to her.

'And she won't come back here.'

'Do you know why?' Emily asked.

Prudence thought she knew the real reason Suzanne would never come back: the oath they had taken under Clara's guidance. 'Because Thys Bothma quite rightly has little time for us,' she said instead.

The settlement was as quiet as the grave and Thys's eyes passed over the clearing filled with hastily built wattle houses. Avenues and side-streets had been worn between the houses by many feet, yet none walked them now. Well-used wagons sat ghostlike among them. Cattle and oxen stood around idly under the shade of sparse trees, and flies buzzed incessantly in the hum of dry heat. A sudden gust of wind led a spiral of red sand in a dance between the buildings. Thys felt his body tense. He was looking into a place in which people had settled to live, yet there was no sign of life. His horse tossed its head uneasily and lifted its feet off the ground, as though unsure of what lay underneath it.

Thys walked down into the settlement. As he passed an open door he heard a faint groan. He pushed the door back and peered inside. The sun streaked through a dusty windowpane, and illuminated the shape of a man. He lay shivering in a heap in the far corner of the room.

'What's happened?' Thys spoke in Afrikaans as he moved to the body. It shook continually. He touched the man's shoulder and the flesh burned under his hand. The man curled into a tighter ball and Thys leaned over him to see his face. His lips were swollen, his eyes glazed and his mouth moved in constant unidentifiable jabbering.

Terror skipped through Thys.

'Theresa Bothma. I'm looking for Theresa Bothma!' The man's eyes rolled back and dry cracked lips moved faster in a silent stream of words.

Thys ran to the door. He ran down the trodden paths between the houses, pushing open doors as he went.

'Mother!' he called. 'Tarcie! Anna!'

He jumped at the sound of horses. Men were riding into the settlement, their bodies one with their horses in a shivering mirage of dust. Thys turned and ran towards them, waving his arms. A man dismounted and approached him. He wore a scarf over his nose and mouth. Thys looked at the other men. They all wore scarves over their noses and mouths.

'What are you doing here?' the man demanded in Afrikaans. His voice was muffled by the scarf. 'Don't you know this place is restricted?' Thys heard fear in the voice.

'I'm looking for my mother. She was here. Her name's Theresa Bothma.'

'Bothma.' Thys didn't know which of the masked men had spoken.

'Bothma. Theresa Bothma,' he said to all of them. They looked over their scarves in silence. 'Is she here?' he pleaded.

'Yes.' A man pushed between the others and nodded in the direction of a house further away. 'The rest of the family is already dead.'

An image of his two younger sisters suddenly flashed into Thys's head. The beautiful delicate Tarcie would have been a woman by now. She might have had a family of her own.

'What family?' Thys asked in terror.

'It was a big family.'

Thys grabbed the man by the collar of his jacket suddenly, forcing words out between clenched teeth.

'Was?' His voice grew into a shout. 'What happened?'

'Disease.' The word held the terror of the unknown in it.

'What disease?' Thys demanded.

'These people brought it from Natalia with them. A fever,' an ownerless voice said.

'It kills like the blacks kill. It swamps like the blacks swamp,' another voice came at Thys.

'Your mother was still alive yesterday.' At last a man's voice broke through the others with the news Thys needed to hear. Others soon undermined it.

'Every day we come to bury them.'

'We must contain it.'

'The disease must not spread.'

The men stood together in a sudden silence as Thys walked to the house they'd indicated. They watched him as he went into it, and then a voice shouted, 'Don't go in there!'

'Keep away or it will kill you too!' another followed, but it went unheard. Thys's eyes had picked out a tiny lump under rough bedclothes. It was his mother.

As Thys moved to her carefully his eyes passed over familiar pieces of furniture. The chair on which his father had always sat. The family bible. The table at which they ate, at which they prayed and over which they'd fought.

'Mother.' Thys reached out and took her hand in his own. He could feel the heat rise from her and placed his hand on her forehead. It was burning. Her hair stuck out in grey tufts against the pillow, which was wet with perspiration. Her eyes were closed, sunk deep into a hollow face. Her lips were cracked in dry sores and her tongue moved between them involuntarily, searching for moisture.

Thys bent quickly to a bucket of water on the ground beside him. He pulled the scarf from around his neck and dipped it into the water, then squeezed it into his mother's mouth. Her swollen tongue pushed out to take the liquid.

'It's Thys.' He leant over her further and felt the fragile bones under the blanket. Her rasping breath carried the rattle of death. 'Mother.'

Theresa heard her son. He was calling her from somewhere outside the furnace she was locked in. He was running towards the house as she stood waiting for him at the door. His hair fell in a shining tumble over his eyes and his body was young and strong. He'd grown into a fine boy. Why was he fighting with her husband? She could feel the bitterness between them. She could see her two daughters standing nervously beside her. She felt something in her hand and heard her own voice. 'I don't want your money. I do not want you.' Red-coated soldiers stood around the farm. They were looking for her husband and her son Thys was with them. His eyes looked into hers. They were dull. Theresa felt a sudden longing. She wanted to hold her son and tell him how much she loved him.

'Forgive me, Thys.'

Thys felt his heart lurch as the voice crept out from the dry cavity which was his mother's mouth. Her mouth stayed open, as her voice failed in mid-sentence. But breath passed through her; she was still alive.

'Come out of there,' a disembodied voice called from the doorway. 'We've buried the dead. Come away.'

Thys kept his back to the man who stood at the door. 'I am staying with her.' He didn't know that as he spoke, he was no longer a part of her dreams.

The earth was rock hard as Thys dug into it. There had been little rain the season before and the land was scorched. In the heat of the sun Thys dug the grave and only as the sun dropped below the horizon did he finish. He climbed down into the grave with his mother's body. It was light. So light.

He felt ice run through his own body, then fire. He ignored the pain and crawled up out of the grave, the sides crumbling as he did. Deep into the night he filled it in. He didn't know where his sisters were buried and he was too weak to look. There were newly dug graves everywhere. Unmarked graves.

Thys marked his mother's grave. On the wooden cross he carved, 'Bothma family.' It was in memory of them all. Thys pushed the cross into the loose soil at the head of the grave. He couldn't see it. The sun was rising but he couldn't see. His eyes were burning. His mind was spinning and his head began to throb as his tongue licked his lips for moisture. He turned his head towards the small house his mother had lived in. The sharp pain of an axe drove through his head and blurred his vision. He knelt on the ground and crawled his way blindly across the rough dry ground towards the house and the water he knew it contained.

Thys didn't know where he was or how long he'd been there. Darkness had come and gone repeatedly, and flames were eating at his body. Flames seemed to be eating away at the walls of the house. He heard voices. Afrikaans voices. Muffled voices.

'He's dead.' Thys felt a hand on his head.

'Burn the house.'

'We can't.'

'Do you want our families to die too?'

The flames leapt higher up the walls around Thys.

He heard the thunder of hooves outside. He strained to open his eyes, but couldn't. He tried to move. He couldn't. The hooves died away and he heard the indrawn breath of fire crackling through the thatched roof over him. The roof was being eaten by fire as his body was. Sparks shot down towards him and confused him further. He couldn't move. He was on fire and he couldn't move. He felt himself being lifted. He was being carried.

305

He was moving over the ground fast, cool night air was sweeping over his body, then he was put down. He could smell the earth. He was on the ground. He felt something on his lips. He could taste nothing. His senses blanked out with his mind.

Light flickered in the blackness surrounding Thys. Small flames licked up close by him and he heard voices. Laughter. He heard a strange word, 'Tshepo'. It sounded with a sharp 'tsssay', and melted into a soft hypnotic 'O'. Thys forced his eyes to open. From black he saw black. A black face was looking at him, dark eyes examining him intently. Thys felt himself slip back into the comfortable dark of unconsciousness, but before he did he heard the strange word again, 'Tshepo.'

It was cooler. The sun was shining but Thys felt cooler. He could hear cattle. He could hear horses. He could hear a mixture of languages, black languages which he didn't recognize. Thys turned his head and opened his eyes. He could see. A group of black men sat in a huddle further away. They sat around one particular man. He was a young man. A large man. He had a wide face and laughing eyes. He laughed as he looked at Thys. He got up and moved towards him. Thys felt a numb wash pass through his head and he slipped away into nothingness again.

It was night and Thys was being carried again. Horses were moving all around him. Dust choked him. Cattle were nearby, moving with him. It was day. It was night. Thys was floating through air, suspended.

Hard ground was under his body again and the sounds of horses and cattle had gone. He could no longer hear voices or laughter. He was surrounded by silence. He was cold. He could see a sliver of moon above him and he looked at it. He didn't know what it was. He fixed his attention on it, trying not to slip back into unconsciousness. He heard a curious sound. A dog barking. He could feel its hot breath on his face as it barked. He felt the tread of feet on the ground beneath him.

'What is it?' He heard an Afrikaans voice. 'Quiet!' The dog kept barking. Its breath was foul.

'What's this?' The man's voice was closer. Two large shoes halted beside Thys and the dog stopped barking. Thys looked from the shoes up the legs and on to the face. It was lit by a small flame. It was a wide, weatherbeaten face with puzzled eyes.

'Rizza!' the voice suddenly called in amazement. 'Rizza!'

Rizza helped Thys to the table and held a bowl of soup out to him. She was a round, comfortable woman.

'This will do you good,' she assured him as she spoonfed him. 'It's time you eat properly.' Thys allowed his eyes to move around the room. It was a room he'd never seen before. Ten children, all blond and blue-eyed, stared at him in silence from solemn faces.

'Where am I?' he asked in Afrikaans. They were the first words he'd spoken.

'You are Boer.' Rizza smiled. 'Hendrik!' she called towards the open doorway where a man's square bulk was silhouetted against the glaring sun. 'He is Boer.' Hendrik turned and looked into the house. The sun lit the outline of his huge body in a yellow glow.

'Boer,' he repeated. The ten children watched their father in silence.

'Boer,' Thys confirmed. He wasn't sure why it was so important.

'Where did you come from?' Hendrik's Afrikaans was guttural. He came into the room and crossed the floor to the scrubbed table at which Thys sat. 'It's strange I've never seen you before.'

'Not from here,' Thys said quickly. 'I don't come from here.' He felt his head spin and closed his eyes, forcing it to clear.

Rizza held the spoon to his mouth again. 'It's good,' she encouraged. 'You must build your strength.'

'How long have I been here?' Thys asked. It could be a day or a year.

'Four weeks.' Hendrik sat down and leaned forward on the table, looking at Thys keenly. 'You were not from there?' The fear in Hendrik's eyes touched Thys and he recognized the look. It was the same look he'd seen in the eyes of the masked men at his mother's settlement. Men who had burned the village to the ground when they'd thought he was dead. 'Well?' Hendrik persisted. 'Are you from there?'

'Hendrik,' his wife scolded him. 'He's not yet well.'

'How did I get here?' Thys asked as unidentifiable memories ran through his mind. Flames, Afrikaans voices, black faces, horses, and the word 'Tshepo'.

'We found you,' Rizza said calmly. 'You were left on our land.' She glanced at a large buffalo skin to one side of the room.

'You were on that.' Two long sticks were bound down either edge of the skin, forming a stretcher.

'What's your name?' Hendrik asked and Thys looked at him blankly as he heard the word 'Tshepo' again. 'You don't know your name?'

'Leave him, Hendrik,' Rizza said. 'Outside.' She clapped her hands and the children silently left the room. Thys felt suddenly threatened.

'Rheno Potgieter,' he said.

'Potgieter,' Hendrik tried out the name, 'where are you from?' Thys felt the trap of his lie tighten. He couldn't tell them he was from an English mission, that he was married to an English-woman.

'The Cape,' he said. He thought of Suzanne, and felt a sudden urge to be free.

'What are you doing so far from home?' Hendrik would not give up. 'And without a horse? With a gun but without a horse?' Thys felt Hendrik hold a gun on him, and the room closed in on him. He couldn't breathe. The room began to spin.

'I told you he wasn't well.' He heard Rizza's gentle voice buzz as it reached into his brain. He felt her hand on his face. 'He's still not well and all you do is question him.'

'We must know,' he heard Hendrik say, and he forced his eyes open. He forced them to focus on Hendrik, and he forced words out.

'When I have worked for what I owe you I will leave,' Thys said.

'You owe us nothing.' Rizza's gentle voice was like a caress. 'Only to get well.'

'I work well,' Thys said. He looked at Rizza. 'I am well.'

'Thys is dead, Suzanne!' Rev. Phillip's words echoed around the church but she stared at him as though he had said nothing. 'He is dead.' He pulled her into his arms and held her tightly. She struggled to pull herself free, stood back and faced him, holding herself erect.

'How?' Suzanne asked flatly. 'How do you know?'

'I sent a message to him about your child, Suzanne.' She waited and her eyes searched his face. 'The entire village, the vil-lage his mother was in, was wiped out by disease.'

'Who told you?' Suzanne's voice was brittle. 'I don't believe you.'

'I've checked in every way I know how, Suzanne.' Rev. Phillip had been checking ever since the transport rider had returned with the news that the village in Transgriep where Thys's mother had settled had been ravaged by disease and then burned down by blacks who had stolen the cattle. Rev. Phillip had said nothing to Suzanne then; he'd waited and sent more messengers. They too had enquired everywhere for Thys Bothma. They had visited all the surrounding farms. There was no Thys Bothma anywhere. The only Bothma anyone knew of was the name on a grave. One had remembered Thys Bothma being there. He had died, he said. He had seen his body before the blacks had burned the village to the ground and stolen the cattle.

'The entire Bothma family is dead,' Rev. Phillip repeated. He was waiting for Suzanne's reaction, for some sign of the grief she must feel. He had lived alone with the secret knowledge of Thys's death until he was certain it was true. As he looked into her eyes, he saw that their usual bright blue had turned pale as ice.

'And now you are going to tell me of God's love? You are going to tell me where He was when Thys was killed? When the Bothma family died? If you can tell me that, perhaps I will listen to you about God!' She slowly turned the gold ring on her third finger, slipped it off and handed it to him. She still hadn't broken.

Leaving the church she moved across the mission yard towards the hut in which she had made a home with Thys, and stopped at the door. Joanna, a young black girl, ran after her.

'Suzanny! Suzanny!' she called. The thin dusty black legs froze in an awkward, angular stance as Suzanne turned back to her coldly.

'Leave me.' Her head lifted as she looked back across the space she'd made between herself and Rev. Phillip. 'And you tell your God to leave me alone!' She ducked into the hut.

Rev. Phillip saw her body slacken as she did, as though her spine had been cut, and he felt lost for the first time in his life.

'Where were you?' he demanded inside his head. 'Have you turned your back?' His voice echoed against the bone of his skull.

'He has,' a quick bright voice answered in his head, 'he's not there.'

Rev. Phillip looked up at the beautiful church Thys had built. Uncertainty swelled in him. He felt the warm gold of his mother's ring in his hand and clutched it tightly, looking up at the sky. 'Abba!' he whispered.

Suzanne was wet. She was very wet. The edge of the bed she sat on was soaking.

She had sat there for weeks since she'd been told Thys was dead. She'd refused to see either Rev. Phillip or Dr Steven and had taken food only when it was brought to her by the small girl, Joanna, but she was suddenly very afraid.

'I'm wet,' she said.

'Yes, Suzanny,' the child grinned at her. She had no idea what she meant. 'You want water?' Suzanne looked down at her stomach. She was nearly eight months pregnant and the bulge of her child seemed lower. It was too low and quite still. The gentle movements and kicks she'd felt over the last months had stopped. She ran her hand over the lump that was her child. She could feel the bony outline of a baby, even through the cloth of her dress. It was totally still. Her eyes moved down to the floor. Liquid poured between her legs and fell in a pool at her feet.

'Get Reverend Phillip, Joanna.' Suzanne's throat was parched with fear. 'Get Dr Steven.'

'The waters have broken,' Dr Steven said quietly as he looked at Rev. Phillip, who stood beside the bed holding Suzanne's hand.

'Is the baby all right?' Suzanne asked quietly.

'Do you feel any contractions, Suzanne?' Dr Steven avoided her question. 'Is there any pain?'

'No.' Suzanne shook her head and glanced up at Rev. Phillip. 'Is my baby dead too?' she asked. 'Don't leave me!' she shouted as Dr Steven moved to the door.

'I'm here,' Rev. Phillip said quietly.

'We will have to bring the child on, Suzanne.' Dr Steven came back to her. He had a jug of mixture and a small tin cup. Pouring a little into the cup he held it out to her. 'Drink.' Suzanne retched as the foul smell invaded her nostrils. 'It's a laxative. Drink.' Dr Steven put the cup to her lips. She held her breath and swallowed. It quickly came back in her throat but she forced it down. Her child would live.

'It still hasn't turned.' Dr Steven's face glowed with sweat as he worked between Suzanne's spread legs. He had gripped the child's head. It was facing up and he knew he had to turn it before it could pass to life.

'Push!' he shouted. Suzanne gripped Rev. Phillip's hand tightly and pushed with every ounce of strength she had. The pain was searing, her back ached, and nothing happened.

'Again!' Dr Steven shouted as he held the slippery head in his hands. 'Again!' He had to turn it. He had to pull it to life soon.

Joanna's eyes shone in enormous black pools. She wiped Dr Steven's forehead. She'd seen women give birth many times before and it had been easy. They had squatted and a baby had popped out.

'It's here.' Dr Steven's voice was quiet and silence followed it. A long silence. Suzanne heard the beats of her heart and counted them as she listened for a cry that didn't come.

'He's dead!' Suzanne suddenly shrieked and her head thrashed from side to side on the pillow. 'He's dead!' She pushed Rev. Phillip's hands away as he tried to hold her still. 'He's dead!'

'Listen, Suzanne!' Rev. Phillip shouted over her screams.

A strange noise rose against his voice. A small indistinct gasping. A bleating sound. Suzanne closed her eyes in case the sound wasn't real.

'It's a boy.' Dr Steven's voice carried a smile with it.

Suzanne felt something very soft and warm against her cheek. It was moving. It was crying. Her child was alive. She turned her face to it and Dr Steven smiled down at her as he placed a wrinkled pink scrap of living baby beside her.

'It's a boy,' he said again.

Suzanne looked at the baby lying on the pillow next to her. Its face was puffed and red, its eyes squeezed shut and its red mouth wide open as it cried. Great slow tears poured down her face and on to the baby as she pulled its tiny shaking body against her face and her grief broke in waves.

Thys turned over on the huge wooden bed. He'd been dreaming of Suzanne and he ached for her. The feather mattress underneath him shaped itself to his body again and he wished it could swallow the longing he felt for her. He pulled the quilt over his head and the cotton print danced against his eyes in the early morning light.

Thys felt good. He was strong and healthy at last. He'd worked for six months on Hendrik's farm in return for their care and food and purchased a good horse from him. In all that time he'd managed to keep his identity a secret.

People still talked in a deadly hush about the village of death where whole families had been wiped out. They talked as if the disease still lurked outside their windows. They talked as if the whole Bothma family were dead. He didn't contradict them.

Thys remembered the arrival of a man at the Hendrik farm. He was looking for someone last reported to have gone to the village. Someone called Thys Bothma. He had believed him when Thys had shrugged.

'They say nobody survived.' Thys had been unable to ask why the man was looking for him. It could be that people were still suspicious; still afraid of the disease. Even Hendrik. It was then that Thys had made his decision. When he had worked out his time for Hendrik and Rizza he would move on. He was moving on today, and he would send a message to Suzanne with the first transport rider he met. Africa was too large to allow time to race between those you cared for. He must go and see Gerrit and tell him to prepare for his return with his English wife, Suzanne. He must make sure Gerrit was all right; he was an old man. If he had not put off seeing his mother, things might have been different.

As he threw his legs over the edge of the bed Thys felt happy. Though he wanted nothing but to be back with Suzanne and hold her in his arms, he would wait until he had seen Gerrit. For the first time he would do the right thing.

Suzanne looked down at the small face with the nose flattened against her breast as the baby's delicate pink lips pulled in a continual sucking movement. Clear blue eyes gazed up into hers and she lifted one of the tiny fingers which pressed rhythmically on her breast. The baby stopped sucking for a moment and its eyes peered up into hers. Suzanne smiled. The little mouth seemed to curl up around her nipple, as if it had caught her smile, and suck harder in contentment.

'Suzanne.' Rev. Phillip stepped into the small hut. 'They're here.' Suzanne didn't cover herself or the child as she stared across the room at him. Her look was not cold, it was empty. Rev. Phillip could be a stranger, and he felt it. 'The Pieterses would be glad if you went to their farm.'

Suzanne looked down at the baby as it ceased sucking. It was falling asleep, but its mouth still held tight the source of sweet warm milk.

'Have you decided on a name for him yet?' Rev. Phillip asked.

'Pieter,' Suzanne said simply. 'Tell them yes. We'll come.'

'Don't you want to meet them?' Rev. Phillip moved closer to her. 'Their son is with them.'

'He is partially blind you said.'

'Yes.'

'Then there is no need for me to see him any more than he will see me. I will take their offer of work, and I will look after their son. In exchange, I want nothing but a home for myself and my child.' She paused for a moment. 'Away from here.'

'How many more times can you turn your back on any place which brings grief with it, Suzanne?' Rev. Phillip asked.

'Tell them I am ready to go with them.' Suzanne closed her dress over her breast: the baby had fallen asleep and let go. 'I will come now.'

'You are trying to walk away from God, Suzanne.'

She looked at him, sharply: got up and moved away from him with the sleeping baby, laying it in the small wicker crib the African people had woven for her.

The mission retreated, left far behind in the valley by the rolling iron wheels of the wagon, and Suzanne didn't look back. She kept her eyes on the baby in her arms.

'He's a healthy child,' Mrs Pieterse said to Suzanne in Afrikaans. She was a woman of fifty, a strong woman who wore the deep lines of hard work with dignity. She glanced at her own son Johan where he sat beside her husband, who was driving the wagon.

'Johan is pleased you have come,' she said.

'I thought he was a young boy.' Suzanne spoke in English as

her eyes ran over the back of the young man in front of her.

'He is thirty years old.' Mrs Pieterse spoke in Afrikaans. She knew Suzanne understood, as she understood her English. 'But he's still a child to me.'

'Yes.' Suzanne looked back at her own child.

The whip came down across the backs of the oxen pulling the wagon and Jan Pieterse turned his thin face and dark eyes on to his wife behind him, and then on to Suzanne, in silence.

'Is she a believer?' he asked in Afrikaans.

His wife silenced him with a glance at the woman and child at her side. Was she the answer to her prayers? Were they driving back to their farm with a wife for their son and a child already born? A perfect child?

Suzanne turned around in the wooden seat and looked back. The mission was out of sight.

'Have you thought about coming with me?' Dr Steven asked Rev. Phillip, who was still staring into the distance after Suzanne, although the wagon had long since vanished. 'It's time you had a change, perhaps.'

'Yes.' Rev. Phillip took a breath as he walked away with the doctor. It was time to leave Africa for a while. 'Yes,' he repeated, and looked at the church which suddenly seemed as out of place as he felt. His fingers traced their way around the small circle of gold wedding ring in his pocket. 'I will come with you.'

Chapter Seventeen

Prudence had woken that morning with a feeling of dread. It sat like a hard lump in her stomach and pricked her awake. It was the knowledge that she had to face her father yet again with the inevitable ruin of Bonne Esperance if the British government abolished the tax on French wine. To still her nerves her mind sifted through the wealth of knowledge she had harvested since first she could question M. Claudelle about wine-making, and the call of the African seasons sounded in her heart.

In the second winter month of July her body always tingled. The earth was waiting for the cycle to begin again, as a woman waited for the cycle of fertility. The labourers would dig to a depth of three feet while the soil was still soft from the winter rains, and then, as it was cleared of weeds and stones ready for planting, Prudence would push her hands deep into the red earth, exhilarated at the feel of it under her fingernails. If a vine had died she knew it must not be replaced by a new one. Even in death the old vine had possession of the ground. Instead of replacing the old, the new vine was planted next to it and grew alongside it until the second year. The earth itself had schooled her in her relationship with her father.

But although Prudence had grown tall beside him, waiting her turn, she knew her time had not come even yet. Jacques seemed determined she would never move into the root space he had claimed as his own.

'If you refuse to listen to me you are blind, Father!' Prudence's hands clutched at her skirts as she shouted across the room at him.

'Then leave me blind!' Jacques kept his back to her as he sat at the desk, and did what he always did when these arguments began: buried his head in the books and allowed figures to convince him he was right, though deep down he knew Prudence was. 'Bonne Esperance is thriving. It will be passed down from generation to generation and never be turned over to sheep!'

'Then it will not be passed on to anybody!' Prudence glanced across at Emily. She sat in silence looking out of the window. Emily hated the arguments which flared between Prudence and her father and tried to keep herself at a distance from them. 'Tell him, Emily. Explain it to him!'

'Not even when I die will Bonne Esperance die!' Jacques slammed the books shut on his desk.

'And if the British government decides it no longer cares to protect our wines in the marketplace?' Prudence flung the challenge at her father and Emily tried to shut their voices out of her head.

'There are no "ifs" in the land!'

'Even when Disraeli says we are no more than a millstone around the neck of the English people?'

'I do not need the English government to survive!'

'You talk like a Frenchman!'

'Yes!'

'And you think you can live in this grand European house while Africa swallows our land!' Prudence wanted to reach out to him and make him understand why she argued with him. 'Don't you see it's because I care, Father?'

'Care?' Jacques was white with rage. She had touched on the truth again. 'If it is true that you care, Prudence, then perhaps it is time you cared for something else. Your obsession with this estate is unnatural.'

With words which always hurt Prudence more deeply than any others, Jacques departed, and Emily felt the air sucked out of the room as the door closed behind him.

'Prudence?' Emily spoke for the first time as she moved to her sister. 'Father didn't mean that.'

'Perhaps he's right.' Prudence turned away. 'Perhaps it is unnatural for me to care.' Emily saw the curve of Prudence's neck as her head dropped forward. 'Clara will win. She will!'

'Clara?' Emily was puzzled.

'Don't allow her to convince you she has changed, Emily. Don't ever forget what Clara is.' Prudence turned back and confronted her. 'She will destroy everything to achieve her revenge and Father is helping her do it.'

A tingle of fear ran through Emily's body. She knew Prudence was right.

'If you still need money, I have it.' She was referring to the money Jean Jacques had not lived long enough to use. 'You wanted money before, to buy sheep. You can have it.'

'It's too late. Before has gone.' She put her hand on her younger sister's arm. 'But I will take your money.' Emily was surprised, but Prudence went on quickly, 'There's a continent out there beyond Bonne Esperance! There's life. There's the whole of Africa.'

Emily remembered the last time Prudence had talked of life. Life was always outside Bonne Esperance, and Emily could feel the ties which held the family together being stretched across a continent.

'Where are you, Geoffrey?' From outside the house came Clara's familiar call.

But Emily shut Clara's voice out. She thought instead about the unanswered letters she'd written to Suzanne. Letters returned without comment from the missionary, just a statement of fact. Suzanne was somewhere in the big continent Prudence talked about and now Prudence wanted to disappear into it herself. Emily felt slightly sick. She still hadn't shaken off the cold she'd had for so long.

'I'll give you the money you need.' Emily looked at her keenly. She had decided that she too must take to her wings, and find a life for herself beyond Bonne Esperance.

Jack Marsden looked away from the river and back towards the house as he heard his mother calling for Geoffrey.

'She wants you!' Jack was nearly nine years old and still hoped that one day his mother might come looking for him. It had never happened. 'Go on!' He pushed Geoffrey away, while Sunday teased a struggling fish on the end of the line. 'She's looking for you.'

'I want to see the fish.' Geoffrey hated being singled out by his mother and hated her constant lectures. He knew he could never be as good as she demanded.

'Geoffrey!' Clara shouted again.

'Go on!' Sunday urged as he held the shaking rod in his hand, his eyes on the silver curve of the fish's back as it leapt out of the water, fighting for its life.

'Go!' Jack insisted.

'Geoffrey!' His own name dragged him away from childhood to his mother. He didn't know why Jack could be bad and his mother didn't seem to care.

'Coming!' he called at last and reluctantly ran away from the excitement of fishing, back towards the solemn future his mother was preparing for him.

The silver body of the fish flew through the air and landed behind Jack and Sunday. It was huge; its fleshy body encased in silver armour. But it was useless against the hook Sunday had been taught to make by his father, Titus.

'Is this the clever fish your father talked about?'

'It is his son.' Sunday sensed Jack was about to delve into the past and he looked around quickly. 'We need a rock.'

'I'll get one.' Jack ran and picked one up. He paused a moment as he held it above the fish's head and Sunday saw a curious look in Jack's eyes. The rock smashed down on to the fish with more force than was necessary.

'It's dead,' Jack said as the rock dropped out of his hand beside the fish. Its eyes had popped out of the flattened head.

'I take it home now for Rosita to cook.' Sunday picked up the fish and moved to go.

Jack watched the black man who'd become the trustee of his thoughts and said suddenly, 'Why?'

'To eat?' Sunday shrugged. 'When you marry you do as your wife she say.'

'Do women know what men should do?' Jack challenged. He resented Maria's daughter, Rosita. Since Sunday had married her he didn't have time to talk to him. He didn't tell him the stories he'd told him before. Stories which hinted at a truth he knew was in the past. 'Women don't know anything,' he said. But he was questioning Sunday. 'Do they?'

'They know.' Sunday pushed a sharpened stick through the fish's mouth and held it up for a moment before swinging it over his shoulder. The fish eyes hung out, but still they seemed to look at Jack in horror. Women know,' Sunday added.

'Then tell me what my mother knows that I don't.' Jack

followed Sunday as he walked away. 'Is it about my father?'

As much as Jack had learned about the past from Sunday, he still knew nothing about his father, except that he was an English aristocrat and had gone to India with the British army. Nobody ever talked about him. He didn't write to them and his mother never mentioned him at all.

Sunday turned away and gazed at a horse that was riding towards them from the other direction. 'It's Master Westbury,' he said, glad of an excuse to leave Jack. He had heard the servants gossip that the English Lord was not the father of the boy Geoffrey. But it was something Sunday would never tell Jack. His new wife Rosita had warned him not to. 'I go,' Sunday said and moved away quickly as John Westbury reined his horse in on the ridge above the river bank.

'I see you caught the clever fish,' he called down to Sunday, who was walking away with the fish swinging on his shoulder.

Sunday turned his head and smiled in pleasure at the young boy who had saved him from Jack's continual questions. 'Yes.' He walked on. 'It's the son of the clever fish.' He smiled again. 'Like me.'

Jack looked up at John Westbury as he climbed off his horse and clambered down the bank towards him. John Westbury was nearly fourteen and he spent a great deal of his time at Bonne Esperance. Jack wondered why.

John reached the rocks and looked into the water. The river was low. 'It's dry,' he commented. 'Where's Geoffrey?'

'He's with my mother.' Jack looked at him with a question in his eyes.

'Where's your mother?'

'My mother?' Jack had a way of asking strange questions. It fascinated John but also disturbed him. 'She's at home.'

John glanced at his young friend. 'What are you thinking about?' he asked, noticing the pensive look in Jack's eyes.

'I was wondering.' Jack kicked a small stone and it landed in the water with a gentle plop. He watched the brown circles on the surface of the river as it swallowed it. 'Did you know my father?' he asked the circles.

'No.' John Westbury shook his head. 'I saw him once.' John squatted on the ground beside him and fiddled with a blade of brown grass. 'Has Sunday been telling you stories again?'

'I've heard things,' Jack said quietly. John met his eyes. They were threatening eyes, yet at the same time they were lost.

'Sunday's father was a slave at Bonne Esperance. His name was Titus and he knew everything,' Jack said.

'What does he tell you?' John Westbury had wondered about many things as he grew older. He remembered the secret knowledge which was shared by his sister Pauline and Emily. It was something to do with a stone commemorating a man he knew nothing about, called Jean Jacques, who was Emily's brother. The son of a slave, like Titus, whose son seemed to know so much. 'I'd like to know.' John leaned back on his heels and dug them into the hard ground beneath him. 'Tell me what he says.'

'He can't tell me why my mother doesn't like me.' Jack threw another stone into the water and John watched the circles form to drown it.

'Perhaps it isn't true,' he said. 'What did he tell you?' Jack turned away, saying nothing, and John Westbury watched his lean boyish body as he looked into the distance towards the house and his mother.

'Don't you ever wonder about things?' Jack's voice was hesitant.

'About what?' He was trying hard not to let Jack disturb him, but he did.

'Who you are?' Jack said.

'I know who I am.' John lowered himself on to the ground and stretched out, looking up at the sky. He decided he'd been wrong. Jack's questions were simply those of a child being deliberately provocative.

'He knows,' Jack insisted. 'Sunday does.'

John felt strangely insecure. Puberty was already forcing him to question his identity. He sat up and stared at Jack's slim tense back. 'What else has the slave told you?'

'He's the son of a slave.'

'What else has he told you!' John Westbury couldn't hide the irritation in his voice. 'Perhaps he's lying to you. Have you thought of that? They do.'

'Who does?' Jack asked.

'Them.' John shrugged, dismissing all black people as liars. 'You don't like them, do you?'

'No.' John looked at Jack. 'What did he tell you?'

'You said he lies.' He peered at John. 'Why are you angry?'

'I'm not angry.' John stood up and dusted himself down. 'I think perhaps you listen to him and then you talk nonsense.'

'Then why do you come here to find out what I know if it's nonsense?' John moved away to his horse, and Jack followed him. 'You're angry.' He had sensed unease in John Westbury and tugged at it. 'What could he know about you?'

'I'll tell you what you don't know, Jack Marsden! Why your mother doesn't like you!' John Westbury glared down at him. 'Because you lie!'

'Lie?'

'Like the blacks!' John Westbury threw his leg over his horse. 'You make things up.' He rode off quickly. He had to get away from the past in which they had both been digging.

'Sunday doesn't lie!' Jack called after him as he rode away, but his voice came back at him unanswered. Jack's small heart pounded. His questions still screamed for answers.

He flung a stone into the water, bent down grabbing a handful, and flung them quickly one after the other into the ever-widening circles. He knew one thing about John Westbury. He had a mother, a father and love. Jack hated him.

Emily's familiar fly cart stood outside the Westbury house and John led his horse behind the house as quietly as he could. He knew Emily would be inside with his sister but he didn't want to see either of them. He walked the horse towards the field of sheep in the distance. He could see his father and he had to ask him something. It was urgent, because the only time he felt at peace was when he thought about it. When he was a safe distance from the house he mounted his horse and galloped towards his father.

'Why school in Cape Town?' Mr Westbury whistled at the black and white dog which raced low to the ground, herding the sheep. 'Isn't the education you get now good enough?'

'I want to study law when I grow up.' John watched his father for a reaction. He often wished his father was younger; surely then he would understand.

'How do you know something like that at your age?' Mr Westbury replied without looking at him. He knew the boy was intelligent and he also knew it was an intelligence beyond his own. The dog darted back and forth around the sheep. 'Wait till you're a little older.'

'I'm nearly fourteen, and I know what I want, Father.'

The name 'father' disturbed Mr Westbury as it always did. He walked his horse towards his grandson and looked at him.

'You want to study law?' John nodded. 'In Cape Town?' Mr Westbury added.

'I would work hard. I'd pay you back every penny it cost.'

'Yes,' Mr Westbury nodded as he looked at him, 'I believe you would.' He thought of the debt he could never repay his grandson. The accumulating debt of a lie. 'I'll think about it.'

'And Mother?' John knew his mother would not agree to his leaving. Not even in a few years. 'Will you speak to her?'

'Not yet.' He turned away deliberately as he saw a few sheep scatter. He knew he could never speak to his wife honestly about John. He whistled and the dog ran quickly in a zig-zag trail, herding the sheep back to the rest.

'Did you say hello to your godmother?'

'Is she here?' John asked innocently.

'Yes.' Mr Westbury turned back to him, 'I heard what you said, John.'

'Is there something else, Father?'

'About?' Mr Westbury looked at him curiously.

'Jack Marsden says strange things.' He paused. 'He spends his time with blacks.'

'He's an odd boy. You shouldn't listen to him.' He longed to know what Jack had said. 'I don't know why you spend so much time at Bonne Esperance.' He concentrated on the dog. He had witnessed again the contempt John felt towards black people. 'I'll speak to your mother,' he said, knowing he would not.

'Are you certain you can drive home, Emily?' Pauline was concerned as she walked with her to the fly cart. Emily didn't look well. 'I could drive you in our carriage.'

'I'm fine, Pauline.' Emily felt a numbness in her legs which contradicted her but she wouldn't give in. Her strength seemed to have been sapped from her body. 'Think about what I asked you. Please,' she urged.

Emily had asked if she could tell her father who John Westbury really was. If she could tell him he was his grandson and that Jean Jacques had not died leaving nothing behind him. 'He would tell nobody else, I promise,' she'd said.

Emily felt a wash of weakness run though her body and steadied herself on the side of the cart. Her arm was weak. She forced her legs to lift the weight of her body as she climbed up into it. She took the reins in her hands but couldn't feel them between her fingers. She looked down at Pauline.

'I know what it would mean to you. But please.' Emily tried to flick the reins on the horse's back. She couldn't, so she called instead, 'Go on, Shaban! Take me home.' The horse obediently moved forward, as if it understood something was wrong.

'Is Emily all right?' Pauline's mother joined her from the house. 'She looks very pale.'

'She says she's fine.' Pauline watched the fly cart drive out of their grounds towards Bonne Esperance.

'And what did you talk about today?' Mary Westbury asked. Emily's words came back to Pauline: 'The truth has got to be spoken.' And then her own: 'It's impossible. You know that as well as I do.'

'We talked about Prudence. She's gone to live in Cape Town,' Pauline lied. Emily's voice sounded in her head again: 'I know the reasons for keeping your son's identity a secret but it can't go on, Pauline.'

'Perhaps Prudence will find a man in Cape Town,' Mrs Westbury interrupted her thoughts. 'Emily should be married by now, too.'

'So should I, Mother,' Pauline said quietly. Emily had insisted: 'There is no longer anything more important than for the truth of your son's birth to be spoken aloud, Pauline.' 'Why is it suddenly of such importance?' Pauline had argued. 'Because he is the true heir to Bonne Esperance and if it is not revealed, two more young lives will be destroyed by Clara!' 'And how many will the truth destroy?' Pauline heard her own final words.

'Pauline?' Mrs Westbury looked at her daughter anxiously. 'You're miles away. What are you thinking about?'

'I was thinking perhaps it's right,' Pauline said. 'That Prudence has gone.'

The pages of the book ripped as Geoffrey tried to snatch it away from his older brother.

'It's mine! Mother said it's mine!'

'Look what you've done!' Jack's body swelled with rage as he saw the pages of the book he prized ripped apart. He lunged at his brother and grabbed him by the throat. 'I hate you! I'll kill you!' Jack saw Geoffrey's small face contort as he squeezed his neck. He wanted to kill him.

'Leave him *alone!*' Clara strode up to Jack. She hadn't seen her two sons, she'd seen Charles Marsden killing Duncan Shaw, and she was already out of control when she snatched Jack sharply away from Geoffrey. Jack caught the look in her eyes and heard the venom in her voice. 'You're the one who should be killed!' she screamed.

Jack felt himself disappear; made invisible by her hatred. His head jerked back with the force of her hand across his face.

'Bend over!' Clara shouted at him.

'Don't!' Geoffrey ran after his mother as she moved to the long rhinoceros whip. It hung on the wall as an ever-present threat to Jack. 'He didn't hurt me, Mother. It was my fault. I tore the book.'

Clara pushed him away and closed on Jack with the whip in her hand. Her eyes were like stones. Jack knew, as always, that it was more than punishment, whether or not he deserved it. He felt her hand grab the top of his trousers and pull them down. He heard the swish as the whip was pulled through the air behind him and he felt the shame of his nakedness. He clenched his teeth as the familiar stroke of the whip cut deep into his soft skin and tears burned behind his eyes. The whip came down again. It was humiliating. It was agony, and it went on and on as Clara paid back the humiliation she'd suffered at his father's hands.

'No!' Jack heard his small brother shout again. 'You're hurting him!'

She wants to kill me, Jack thought, as the beating went on and his body shivered with pain. At last the whip lashed his raw flesh for the last time and he saw it drop to the floor, his own blood soaking into the long strip of woven hide. He heard his mother's heavy breathing above him.

'You will remain in your room for the rest of the day.' He heard the squeak of her shoes as she turned away. 'Come along.' He heard his brother's obedient footsteps as he followed her to the door. 'He's evil and you will stay away from him, Geoffrey.'

Jack heard the door close behind them and despair and humiliation consumed him.

He tried to pull up his trousers but his body was shaking. He gritted his teeth and pulled harder. His face contorted with the pain as the rough cloth chafed his fresh wounds. He closed his eyes and willed his body to accept the pain. To enjoy it.

His eyes moved to the book where it lay broken-backed on the floor. The diagonal tear across the pages seemed to symbolize what Jack felt. He picked it up. It was the predictions of Nostradamus, written in French. Jack tried to fit the pages together. His effort to learn French and prove that he was worth something had been torn apart. He took the edge of the pages between his fingers and pulled hard, completing the destruction himself.

The fly cart moved towards Bonne Esperance out of control. Emily was leaning over to one side; her body lurching with the movement of the cart. Jacques ran quickly towards it as the horse pulled round, too fast, into the courtyard.

'Emily!' he shouted in alarm, grabbing the reins and forcing the horse to stop. 'What's wrong?' Emily looked at his hand as he held it out to her. 'Where am I?' She tried to pull her thoughts together. She was confused. 'I must have fallen asleep.' She tried to step down from the carriage, but as she felt her foot touch the ground her leg gave way under her. She dropped like a rag doll.

'Emily?' Jacques lifted her delicate frame into his arms. 'Emily?' He tried to call her back.

'Is Aunt Emily going to die?' Geoffrey's small voice stole through the dark of the bedroom towards his brother. 'Do you think she'll die?' There was a lump in his throat. 'Jack?' He sat up in bed and peered through the blackness in the direction of his brother's bed. 'Are you still sore? Does it hurt?'

Jack lay quite still on his stomach, with his face buried in the pillow, and tried to ignore the persistent voice. The pain from the whipping was still almost more than he could bear. It was something more than pain which had crushed him with each stroke of the whip.

'I'm sorry,' Geoffrey piped again. 'I didn't mean to tear your book. I didn't want her to hit you.'

'Go to sleep.'

Geoffrey closed his mouth tightly. When Jack wanted to get rid of him he either told him to go away or to go to sleep.

'What does he tell you, Jack?'

'Who?'

'Sunday.'

'What does Mother tell you?' Jack countered.

'I don't know.' Geoffrey *didn't* know and he didn't want to know. It was far more than he could understand. 'What was our father like?'

'Ask Mother.'

'She won't tell me. Is your behind still sore?'

'You're so stupid.'

Geoffrey's small soul crept back into the dark. He would never be as clever as Jack but all he wanted was to be his friend. 'I know I'm stupid,' he agreed sadly.

Silence fell between them and Geoffrey listened through it. He could hear the grown-up voices further away. They were hushed. He could hear feet moving backwards and forwards across the polished floors. He had seen the doctor arrive earlier, and he'd seen the fear in his grandfather's face. He wondered again if his Aunt Emily would die and he hoped she wouldn't. She was kind.

'Do you feel any pain at all?' The doctor's voice was matter-of-fact. 'Can you feel your legs?' He looked at Emily as she lay still on the bed. She shook her head against the pillow, unable to speak in case she cried. She'd never felt so entirely useless before. She had watched the doctor lift her legs and bend them. It was as if they didn't belong to her at all. She felt nothing. He lowered her legs and, as he did, she saw the resignation with which he drew a breath.

'Will I ever walk again?' Emily pitched her voice low in an effort to control her emotions. The doctor kept his eyes averted. 'Will I?'

'I'm sorry.'

'Sorry?' Emily turned her face away from him. He looked down at her with sympathy and she wanted to scream at him.

'Will you tell my father, please,' she said curtly, rejecting the sympathy she dared not accept.

The doctor stood up and moved quietly across the room. He stopped at the door and looked back at her. Still she hoped he might say the word 'but'. He turned and left the room in silence.

As the door closed on the prison of her own body, locked in paralysis, she looked down at her legs and willed them to move. They lay totally still. They no longer obeyed her. She bit her lip as the anger rose inside her. Her wings had been clipped. She'd been bound to Bonne Esperance for life and its shackles held her tight. She wanted to get up and run. To run away to Suzanne; or to Prudence. To free herself and live.

Jacques came into the room and looked at his youngest daughter as she lay motionless on the bed. Her eyes were squeezed shut, as if trying to blot out the truth. Jacques opened his mouth to speak but found there were no words he could say.

He moved close to the bed and stood quite still. Emily's eyes opened and she tried to smile.

'It's all right, Father,' she whispered.

He leant over her without a word and lifted her up in his arms, holding her body tightly against his as he felt her shiver.

'Yes, Emily. Cry.' He poured his love on to her and finally her control snapped. He hugged her close as she broke and wept in his arms.

Prudence knew nothing of what had happened to Emily. If she had she would have dropped her plans and returned home, but Emily had asked Jacques not to tell her. Prudence was in Cape Town trying to build a life for herself outside Bonne Esperance. It was what Jacques had said she should do and Emily had insisted he leave her free to do it.

The months Prudence had been in Miss Thurston's house she had spent very carefully. She'd mixed with as many people as possible, trying to establish where she might find a future for herself. There was only one. It was deep in the interior of Africa and it was dangerous for a woman, but it tempted her. She had begun to look for a way of circumventing the danger. Her mind was constantly active. She was a natural business woman and she had to seize her chance now. Africa was bursting with opportunity for those prepared to take risks.

She stood naked in front of the mirror and examined her face closely. It was an oblong mirror set between two oak pillars of drawers. Her eyes ran from her face down the length of her body. Her breasts were round and firm, her waist was small and her hips curved out gently. Everything about her body was feminine.

She tugged her hands through her hair and pulled it up, away from her face, firming her mouth into a straight line. She turned sideways and looked at her face in the mirror again. The straight nose helped. With the hair away from her face and her chin firmly out, her nose was her most prominent feature. It was a strong nose, not the pert *retroussée* she'd often envied Emily and Suzanne.

She thought again about her plans and her meticulous research into men. She'd bought the trousers, shirt, hat, boots and jacket that morning, telling the inquisitive lady in the shop that they were for her brother. That he was too busy to come himself and, since he was roughly her size, she had decided to buy them for him. In the shop she had simply held them against herself. She hadn't yet tried on the clothes and was excited at the prospect.

She moved to the bed and picked up the trousers, pushing one leg into them and then the other. They were tight, not cut for the fullness of a woman's hips. She pulled the shirt over her head and then put on the leather jacket, turning to admire her transformation in the mirror.

She looked absurd. The rise of her breasts showed clearly under the shirt and jacket. She was still all woman.

She pushed her hair up and plonked the brown felt hat on her head. She looked even more ridiculous. Tossing it on to the floor and leaning forward, she peered into the mirror again. Her hand touched the long blonde hair which hung down to her shoulders and her eyes moved to a large pair of scissors on the dressing-table.

The last thick braid of blonde hair fell to the floor, and Prudence looked into the mirror. Her hair was cropped short, but still she looked nothing like a man. Her eyes went to the smooth arch of her well-shaped eyebrows. She tugged the hairs away from her face, forced one of the scissor blades against her skin, and clipped. If she could destroy the feminine arch of her eyebrows, her plan would work.

Prudence waited for the tingle of pain to settle over her eyes and inspected herself closely. The skin around her eyebrows was red and puffed. She'd dug into it with the sharp scissors in her effort to remove their giveaway shape. She smoothed her short hair down on her skull and tried on the hat. She looked very different. Quite ugly. She had begun to look like a man. Her eyes returned to her breasts and she tore the jacket off as excitement built in her, pulling the shirt over her head. She grabbed her petticoat from the bed, ripped a length from its edge, and with one end firmly against her chest she wound the rest tightly around her. She ignored the discomfort in her breasts as they were forced flat against her. As she tucked the end of the material back into itself and looked at herself again she could hardly breathe. The cage in which she'd buried her breasts forced her head and shoulders back, and all the feminine curves had gone.

Her hand moved to her face and she smiled. Her hands had always been slightly too big; rough from work among the vines. But the soft skin on her face stood out against them. She would burn her face in the sun, she decided. She could easily toughen the delicate facial skin until it looked as rough as her hands.

Prudence pulled on the shirt, slipped into the jacket and looked into the mirror. With practice it was quite possible she could be accepted as a man.

As Prudence looked across the water at Table Mountain standing proudly over Cape Town which nestled on its lower slopes, she allowed the roll of the tall ship to carry her body with it. She already felt sick. Silently she said farewell to Bonne Esperance, which lay behind the blue mountains in the distance. Her body tensed as a man's arm leaned on the rail beside hers.

'Where are you going?' the man asked without looking at her.

'The interior,' Prudence said quietly.

'Like everyone else.' The man turned around and leaned against the rail. He looked straight into her face. 'You believe the rumours of gold?'

Prudence realized he hadn't noticed a thing and courage crept through her body and into her voice. 'Why not?' She turned and leaned against the rail as he had done, crossing one boot over the other. 'There must be a reason Marais has been sent to look,' she ventured.

The ship rose on a wave and slid down the other side. She tried to hold her eyes firmly on the mast to still her stomach, but couldn't. Her head spun and she turned to the man beside her. He was leaning over the rail, heaving over the side. Together they threw up violently into the foaming water round the ship, glanced at each other, retched again, and groaned as one man.

Her name was Pierre Chabrol, she told the men on board. They ate together, laughed together and again they were sick together. Only as she woke on the fifth morning and looked across Algoa Bay did she know she had at last found her sea legs.

The small town on the shoreline was barren and desolate. Untidy rows of houses were scattered along the inhospitable strand, and dangerous surf crashed in long heavy rollers on to the beach.

The 'lightering' was to be done by whale boats. They bobbed up and down in the sea around the tall ships, waiting and bargaining. The wind was blowing hard and the sea was rough. The price the boatmen demanded to take the passengers ashore was two guineas. Four times the usual cost. The high laughing voices of the fingos, waiting to carry the passengers over the surf and on to the shore, mixed with the cries of hungry gulls and Prudence felt the excitement of adventure as the boatman kept the bow straight with the waves, heading for land. A scantily clad fingo waded through the surf and grinned at Prudence.

'I take you, master.' A wave swamped him. Coming up for breath, he added, 'Two shilling and six pence.' Prudence hadn't enjoyed herself as much since she was a child. She hung on to the back of the near-naked fingo as he clambered through the waves to the shore and felt free at last.

With her feet planted firmly on dry land, and the fingo paid his two shillings and six pence, she looked again at the town. It was shut in by steep hills and bare of the green vegetation of the cape. By comparison it was ugly, but it excited her. Port Elizabeth was the gateway to Africa, and behind those hills lay her future.

Angus Macbride, an old, very old man, sat with his back against the white wall of the small trading store which stood all alone in the barren countryside outside Port Elizabeth. His hat was well pulled down over his eyes, and he watched Prudence's brown leather boots march up and down in front of him. They raised a cloud of dust which he waved away as he listened to her.

'The price of a wagon in the Cape is sixty pounds and the price of a good horse, twenty-five.' Prudence nodded towards a trading wagon which stood close by. It was covered in saleable wares. 'So how much do you want for that wagon?'

'If you stopped churning the dust into my eyes, young man, I might be able to think.' The Scottish voice was entirely out of place in its surroundings.

'Very well.' Prudence stopped in front of him. She put her hands on her hips and looked down at him, her hat pulled cockily over one eye. 'Think.' She rubbed the dust away from her mouth roughly with the back of her hand. 'My offer stands at one hundred and fifty pounds for the wagon and goods.'

'Aye.' Angus Macbride lifted his hat off and held it up against the sun as he looked at her. With a lazy smile he put it back on his head. 'Aye,' he said again. 'Your offer was best blurred by dust, sir.' He settled under the hat again.

'Then how much *will* you take for it?' Prudence had checked the prices of everything she'd need for her new life as a trader. She was also aware that she'd come face to face with a man who cared little for established prices. His was a world with no rules but his own. She watched him as he leaned back, pulling a clay pipe from deep in his trouser pocket. He stuck the pipe into his mouth and allowed the stem to balance on his lower lip. He didn't fill the pipe or light it.

'Well? How much will you take for it?' Prudence allowed her impatience to show in her voice. 'I haven't all day to waste arguing with you.'

'Then perhaps you should run your eye over the goods on that wagon, sir.'

'I already have.'

'It might be in your interests to do so again.' Angus Macbride smiled around his pipe and fell silent, chewing on the stem. Prudence turned abruptly and moved to the wagon. Her eyes passed quickly over the pots and pans, the cuckoo clocks, the packets of seed and oats, the china. Bolts of cotton cloth were stacked against the inside edge of the wagon. She'd examined them all carefully before.

'I see no gunpowder,' she said.

'That would be because there is no gunpowder,' Angus Macbride replied.

'Gunpowder is the most lucrative trade. Most especially with the Griqua people.' Prudence walked back to him.

'True enough.'

'If you were to include gunpowder,' her eyes moved past him and into the dark of his trading store, 'perhaps then my offer could be a little more.'

The old man pulled the pipe out of his mouth. 'Where did you say you came from?'

'I didn't. And since I'm tired of arguing, maybe I should return there without more ado.'

'Ado?' The man chuckled.

'Ado,' Prudence repeated, knowing she had allowed a feminine word to slip in. 'Well?' she added roughly.

The old man looked away from her as his eyes picked out something further away. He squinted against the sun as he looked in that direction and then popped the pipe back into his mouth suddenly and turned back to Prudence.

'Two hundred pounds.' He got up stiffly and went into the trading store for a few moments.

'Two hundred pounds?'

'With gunpowder included.' He tossed two large bags at her.

'The sun's addled your brains.' Prudence turned away for time to think. She stopped. A man was watching them as he leaned against a tree a little way off. Beside him stood his horse and a little further away a black man squatted with his hands hanging casually between his knees. He was dressed in nothing but a skin.

'Hey!' Prudence strode towards the odd group. 'How much would you say for gunpowder, sir?' She looked at the man.

'I wouldn't ask him,' the Scottish voice came after her.

'Well?'

'In goats or sheep?' The cockney voice was edged with humour, but the face was serious. He glanced at the black man, who remained squatting beside him. 'What do you say?'

'I asked you.' Prudence came closer and stood in front of him. As he turned and looked at her she felt suddenly very nervous. His eyes were hazel and sparkled with amusement. His face was warm and attractive. For the first time in months Prudence felt like a woman and she moved away quickly, looking back toward Macbride. 'He wants two hundred pounds.'

The man chuckled quietly behind her. There was something about him that made Prudence uncomfortable.

'Two hundred pounds!' He moved past her towards the wagon.

'Don't you try your tricks here, Jim Audsley! You've been after stealing my wagon as long as I've known you,' the old man called after him. 'And keep that flea-bitten black of yours away from here!'

Prudence watched Jim Audsley as he turned back to her after looking casually over the wagon.

'How much did you offer?' he asked.

'Two hundred pounds is what he wants.'

Audsley nodded. One definite and uncompromising nod.

'What does that mean?' she asked him cautiously.

'Angus is a canny man.'

'And I?'

Audsley looked at her, took a slight breath and moved across to the old man, sitting down beside him. Prudence was unsure of what to do next. Neither was looking at her.

'Have you nothing to say?' she asked them both. Audsley glanced at Macbride and Macbride shrugged. She felt a rage of inadequacy building inside her. 'Are you just going to sit there?' she demanded.

'It would appear to be the winning side,' Audsley said quietly as Macbride pulled on his empty pipe. 'One hundred. Take it or leave it, you thieving Scotsman!' Audsley rammed the old man's hat down over his eyes, stood up and rejoined Prudence. 'You can help me load my things. It's settled.' With that he moved away towards his horse and black friend.

'Wait one moment!' Prudence followed him quickly. 'Load what things?'

'We'll split the wagon down the middle.' Audsley calmly unbuckled the saddle on his horse.

'With my one hundred pounds you imagine you get any part of the middle?' Prudence's voice had risen in pitch in her astonishment and she lowered it hurriedly. 'I am not a party to this bargain at all!'

'No?'

'No,' she said firmly.

He nodded and began to replace the saddle on his horse.

'I'll have my hundred before you fight over it,' Macbride called across to them.

'You can go back to two hundred,' Audsley called back.

Prudence pulled her hat off and flung it on the ground. A puff of dust rose around it and she glared at Jim Audsley.

'Well?' Macbride asked, the pipe held in the corner of his mouth.

'Perhaps I was wrong.' Prudence bent down and picked up her hat; dusting it against her trousers, to give herself time. She moved towards Jim Audsley, whose eyebrows rose slightly as he glanced at the black man beside him. He lifted his eyes to heaven.

'From what I've gathered you would like to partner me on this venture.' Prudence shoved her hat on her head as she reached him. His hazel eyes glinted with laughter and she went on quickly. 'Perhaps it would be an idea. I'm new to the area. It might be a good thing.'

'What would?' His voice was soft.

'If you came in with me. As a partner.' Prudence shrugged. 'As you said.'

The old man pulled his hat down as if hiding from them both and Jim Audsley glanced again at the black man in animal skins. The bare black shoulders lifted and dropped in an indifferent shrug.

Prudence strode back to Macbride. 'We said one hundred. It's settled.'

'Whoa!' Jim Audsley ambled across the dusty ground between them and stopped beside her. His eyes ran over her face, he walked around her, and Prudence felt every curve of her feminine body.

'Is there something wrong?' she asked as he stopped in front of her, his examination complete. 'Well?'

He held his hand out to her. 'Audsley's the name. Jim Audsley.'

As Prudence felt the strong hand take hers she trembled. Her eyes moved up to his and her heart missed a beat. 'Chabrol. Pierre.' She shook his hand firmly.

'Pardon?' Jim Audsley's face was a picture of incomprehension.

'Pierre Chabrol,' Prudence repeated and removed her hand from his. 'From France. Europe.'

'Ah!' The tone of his voice suggested that that explained everything. 'You can load the skins, Themba.' The black man looked up at him without moving. 'We're moving out.'

334

'You'll load nothing till I've got my hundred.' Prudence had forgotten about Angus Macbride until she heard his voice. Her eyes settled on the rifle he'd aimed straight at her. The black man stayed down on his haunches and Jim Audsley's eyes twinkled as he watched.

'Are you going to pay the man, Mr Chabrol, or shall I shoot him?' he called. There was a laugh in his voice.

'If he'll put that rifle down, I'll pay him,' Prudence said without looking round, her eyes fixed on the rifle.

'You heard the gentleman, Angus.'

'Aye,' the old man confirmed, but his rifle stayed on Prudence.

She pulled a wad of notes out of her pocket reluctantly. 'One hundred pounds!' Prudence kept her eye on the rifle as she peeled the notes. She saw him lower it slightly as he prepared to take the crisp notes and she kicked her boot forward in the dirt, shooting sand into the old man's face. She grabbed the rifle, pulling him forward into the dirt at her feet.

'I hope I won't have the same bother with you,' she said to Jim Audsley and tossed the notes in a fluttering heap on to the old man's head. He struggled in the dirt to catch them before they blew away.

'Inspan the oxen,' she ordered Audsley, nodding towards a small herd nearby. 'Four will do me fine.'

'Oxen?' Angus Macbride looked up sharply as he snatched the last note safely into his hand. 'You said nothing about oxen!'

'Neither did you. But I have little intention of pulling the wagon myself; unless, of course, my partner here has other ideas.'

'Uh, uh.' James Audsley held his hands up. 'We don't steal the man's oxen.'

'Did I say steal, my friend?' Prudence looked at him askance. 'I'm borrowing them to move my purchase.'

'The oxen will be another fifty!' Macbride stormed up behind her, waving the banknotes in his hand.

'Have you counted the money you just picked up?' Prudence turned away as Macbride quickly did so, and she gestured towards the black man. 'Who is he?' she asked Audsley.

'My doctor.'

'There's one hundred and fifty pounds here.' Angus Macbride's voice was filled with amazement.

'Are you sick?'

'Just ensuring my survival.' Jim Audsley smiled. He was impressed that such a dandy-looking Frenchman was so sharp.

'He's a witchdoctor?' The black man sat quite passively, looking up at her. His skin was covered in a strange-smelling grease.

'Themba!' Audsley called and pointed towards the oxen. The black man rose from his squatting position in one movement and glanced at Prudence as he moved past. She caught a glimmer of amusement in his dark eyes.

'Does he ever bath?' she asked, turning back to Jim Audsley.

'Your money might buy the wagon.' He nodded towards the slightly bent figure of Themba as he whistled his way towards the oxen. 'He buys a safe passage.'

The long rhinoceros whip curved back through the air before Themba laid it in an immaculate line down the brown backs of the oxen as he walked beside them. Prudence looked ahead, toward the unknown into which they were travelling. Pots and pans clattered behind her in the wagon and the iron wheels groaned under the weight. The dry dusty air seemed to clog her nostrils. Even without looking at Jim Audsley she could feel the undeniable presence of a man beside her. A man who attracted her. She pulled her shoulders back and settled her thoughts on the vast new country that stretched ahead.

Chapter Eighteen

Emily gazed suspiciously at the strange wooden chair on wheels which stood at the foot of the bed. It had been there for two weeks and she had not moved from her bed for six. Her father had made the chair himself in an effort to help her.

'Are you going to get in it today?' The small boy Geoffrey had come just inside the door as he did every day. He longed for her to climb into the chair so he could push it for her.

'Not today,' Emily said, as she always did.

'Oh.' Geoffrey turned to leave.

'Where are you going?' Emily asked. It was something nobody could understand. People could walk away from her and when they did they left her more isolated than if they had never entered her room.

'I don't know.' Geoffrey's shoulders lifted in a shrug.

'Where's Jack?' Emily asked.

'I don't know.' The shrug came again. 'He told me to go away.'

'Then where are you going?'

'Nowhere.' Geoffrey couldn't tell her that he'd decided where he was going the moment she'd said, yet again, that she wouldn't go in the wooden chair. What he was going to do was something he couldn't tell anyone. 'When you want to go in the chair you call me and I'll call Rosita,' he said as he left. His small body slipped around the door, but before it closed behind him he said quietly, 'You shouldn't be scared.'

Geoffrey was a little scared himself as he crept towards the kitchen and then into it. Maria's wide hips swelled under the tight cotton of her dress and spread over the edges of the stool she sat on. Her fat black arms moved with the careful rhythm of her fingers as she peeled the hard skin from the twisted forms of sweet potatoes. Geoffrey liked sweet potatoes.

'You looking for your mother?' she asked.

'No.' She was so old she should be dead, he thought. His eyes ran over the tight white curls which sat on her head in a cotton wool mop. 'Aunt Emily doesn't want to use her chair.' The dark lips pursed and the fluffy white head nodded. 'Do you think she'll ever use it?' Geoffrey wanted to ask her to reach up for the big key on the wall of the sitting-room. He'd tried several times himself but there was no way he could reach it. 'Do you know that key?' he said suddenly. 'The old big one?'

'Which one?' Maria had eyes only for the sweet potatoes. She knew exactly which one.

'The one on the wall in the sitting-room.'

Maria nodded her head slowly and her breath came out in a small huff. The key annoyed her. It was old and dirty and hung there for no reason.

'Can I have it?'

'What for?'

'To clean it.'

'What for?'

'I don't know.'

'Then why?' Old people asked more questions than he did.

'Will you get it down for me?' he asked instead of answering.

'Rosita!' Maria called, and Geoffrey watched the loop of peel fall in a spiral on the wooden table. Maria didn't look up as Rosita stepped in from outside carrying a bundle of dry washing. 'Get that key for him.'

'What key?' Rosita turned her bright warm eyes on to Geoffrey. She was beautiful.

'That key.' Geoffrey gazed at her. 'You know.'

'He'll show you.' Maria nodded at Geoffrey. 'But don't tell your mother, boy!' Geoffrey noticed she had not shifted on her stool; all that had moved was her fingers. He wondered if the stool was a part of her large behind: if maybe it had been swallowed by it.

Rosita took the key off the wall and placed it in Geoffrey's hand. He had no idea what the key meant to his mother, but it haunted him. The thought of growing up only to take it back to France on some extraordinary mission terrified him. If it didn't fit any door in the house, how would he ever find one in the whole of France to fit it? He didn't want to go to France. The people didn't speak English. Jack had told him that was why he was learning French.

Because of that, he had decided he would hide the key, then, when Jack was ready, *he* would take it to France for their mother. Geoffrey didn't know that the key was a symbol, and that symbols could not be hidden.

'Thank you, Rosita.' He smiled happily as he clutched the key.

'What are you going to do with it?' Rosita rubbed her hand through his blond curls. 'Don't tell your mother I gave it to you.'

'I won't lose it.' He realized even she was afraid of his mother, and pushed the key into his trouser pocket.

'You don't tell your mother!'

Once Rosita had gone, Geoffrey crept around the sitting-room door and up the stairs which led to the attic room. It was the room in which the secrets of his father lay. He didn't know it was the room which also held memories of Jean Jacques.

His small heart rose with excitement as he pulled the bright-red jacket out of the trunk and slipped his arms into the sleeves. They hung right down to the floor. His tiny hands pushed the cloth together across him, from half-way inside the sleeves and he looked down to see the jacket covering his feet. One day he'd grow and then he would wear one just like it. He would be just like his father. He glanced at the gold crown on the shoulder; he'd be a major too! He pulled the jacket off, dug the key out of his trouser pocket and put it into the jacket pocket. His mother would never look there. He could hear someone climbing the stairs so he rolled the jacket up and pushed it back into the trunk. He stood back nervously, trying not to look at the box which held the secret of the key and of his future.

'Hello Jack,' Geoffrey said quickly as his brother came in.

'What are you doing here?' Jack's eyes moved around the room in which Sunday had told him the slave woman's child had once lived.

'Nothing.' Geoffrey shrugged.

'I know what you were doing.'

'Doing what?' Geoffrey's question was filled with innocence and guilt.

'Father's uniform.'

'It's too big now.' Geoffrey moved to Jack quickly. He wanted to tell him why he was really there. 'Do you know that key?'

'What key?'

'The one that doesn't fit any lock in the house.' Geoffrey cocked his head in the direction of the trunk. 'It's in there.'

'Why?' Jack's face was puzzled.

'I don't want it. It's yours.'

'You're stupid!' Jack left the room suddenly, and loneliness rushed to greet Geoffrey again.

'You won't say that when I'm a soldier!' he murmured after his brother.

'Rosita?' Emily's voice broke into his thoughts from her bedroom below. 'I want to use the chair! I want to go out.'

Geoffrey leapt to the door, his loneliness disappearing in excitement, and he shouted, 'Rosita! Aunt Emily wants to use the chair!' Being a soldier could wait.

The sensation of air brushing past Emily's face was the most beautiful feeling she could imagine. The squelch of grass as the wheels rolled over it and the rustle of taller grasses bending back to make a path were the most beautiful sounds. Geoffrey's young face was alive and his blue eyes shone as the sunlight danced in them.

'Do you like it? Is it good?' he asked, running backwards in front of the chair. 'Can I try?'

'It is good, Geoffrey.' Emily touched Rosita's hand as she pushed the chair. 'It is very, very good.' Rosita's dark eyes smiled down at her.

'Emily?' Jacques whispered to himself as he saw the chair in the distance. He was in the vineyards, pretending he still cared that he was alive. He climbed up on to his horse and trotted towards Emily as Rosita turned the chair towards him.

'She likes it!' Geoffrey ran excitedly towards his grandfather. 'Aunt Emily likes the chair you made her!'

Jacques slid down off his horse and knelt on the ground in front of Emily, the warmth of her smile washing through him.

'Everything is different now, Father.' Emily looked into his eyes, trying to encourage them back to life. 'Everything will be different.' She pulled him closer, and wrapped her arms around him. 'I promise.' The vow she made was to herself.

The chair had become part of the routine of Bonne Esperance. Pauline sat on the bench next to Emily and followed her look towards Jacques as he rode out. Pauline knew what Emily was going to ask, as she had asked so often before, and heard her own answer before Emily had even put the question.

'My mother has lived a lie to protect my son. If I told the truth now it would destroy her.'

'The truth destroys nobody,' Emily said. 'If my father doesn't find a reason to live, he will die.' Pauline could see the stoop in Jacques Beauvilliers' shoulders as he rode towards the vineyards.

'Now that John is at school in Cape Town, isn't it possible?' Emily's voice was filled with hope. Pauline looked at the wooden chair: her eyes ran down the plaid skirt and rested on Emily's feet planted on the small step at the base of the chair. She knew Emily had no feeling in them.

'Tell him,' Pauline said.

Emily caught her breath in surprise. She reached out to Pauline and took her hand, pleading silently for confirmation that what she'd heard was true.

'But please ask him to tell nobody.' Pauline lowered her eyes.

'Eva?' Emily asked.

'I care about my mother too,' Pauline said carefully.

Emily's heart raced. She wanted to leap out of her chair and run across the vineyards to her father. She wanted to throw herself into his arms and shout to everyone, 'Jean Jacques had a son!' Instead she bottled up her joy. She would wait until she could tell him in private.

Jacques' mind swam with confusion. He couldn't believe he had heard Emily clearly, and peered at her, trying to focus his thoughts. He wanted to believe it but didn't dare.

'Tell me again,' he said quietly as he sat on the edge of her bed.

'Pauline and Jean Jacques had a child, Father. John Westbury is that child.' Emily had told him everything and was waiting for the facts to become real to him. She saw the faintest glimmer of light in his eyes but he turned aside, got up and moved away. He kept his back to her.

'Father?' His shoulders had rounded and he'd disappeared inside himself. 'Go to Eva now, Father. Tell her.'

Jacques turned and looked at his daughter. 'Why didn't he tell me?'

'Jean Jacques had to protect his child.'

Jacques knew exactly how his son must have felt as his child was taken from him, and suddenly understood the one thing he'd never understood before. That Jean Jacques had joined the army to find a way to regain his own son and the woman he loved; the happiness Jacques still yearned for with Eva.

'I've been looking for you.' Clara's voice cracked Jacques' thoughts apart as she entered the room. 'I would like to speak to you.'

'Again, Clara?' Jacques looked at her coldly. There was only one subject Clara talked about now. His will.

'I am going to Cape Town,' he said as he moved to the door.

'Cape Town?' Clara's eyes questioned him arrogantly. 'You are going to Cape Town to instruct an attorney?'

'No.' As they faced one another it was not distance that stood irrevocably between them, it was suspicion. Jacques knew what Clara wanted and had resisted it. 'You wish me to ensure my affairs are in order?' he asked formally.

'It is only right that you see to your responsibilities.'

'I know where my responsibilities lie, Clara.' Jacques opened the door, glancing at Emily in a secret moment. 'I would suggest you look more clearly at your own.' He left the room. Clara's eyes slithered from the door to the bed and Emily. Clara's beauty had hardened. Its mask was more obvious.

'Why is Father behaving like this?' she asked.

'I'm not sure I understand you.'

'He hasn't been to Cape Town for years.'

'No.' Emily picked up her diary from the table beside her bed. 'I think perhaps it's time he did.' She opened the diary and then glanced up at Clara. 'There's nothing I need, thank you.'

Clara sensed something was different. She heard the sound of a horse outside and crossed to the window quickly. She was uncomfortable. Her mind ground suspiciously over the past few months. 'Where is he going?' she asked as she watched her father ride out from Bonne Esperance.

Emily ignored her and wrote very neatly in her diary: 'The truth has woken Father from the dead.' She looked up at Clara.

'Why should Father not go to Cape Town?' She could see the slightest flicker of confusion in Clara's eyes. 'Shouldn't he go to the woman he still loves?'

The door slammed behind Clara and left Emily alone. She took a deep breath and looked back to her diary. The words she'd written stood out on the page. She added, 'Please God keep the truth from Clara.'

As Jacques rode down the drive and out of Bonne Esperance he was watched not only by Clara, but by Jack. He, too, wondered why Jacques was leaving. He stood silently, hidden amidst the green of the vines which ran along the roadside, then stepped out of his cover as the horse galloped away and up into the fold between the mountains. Jack knew where his grandfather was going. To the slave woman Sunday had told him about. The woman no one in the family ever talked of, but who had borne his grandfather's son, Jean Jacques.

The village of Wynberg was only a few miles from Cape Town and Jacques spent the night at a small pension. He had made his decision suddenly. It was a long time since he'd seen John Westbury. He knew John had been sent to school near Cape Town: to a small school run by an Englishman and his wife. John and a few other children who lived too far to return home at night boarded with their family. Some were sickly children, sent from England to Africa for the sunshine.

Jacques walked his horse quietly through the village. It was peculiarly Dutch: houses were trim with green shutters, its formal avenues backed by the grandeur of Table Mountain. Plantations of proteas crept up its slopes, looking almost unreal as they merged with fuchsias, aloes, prickly pears and Hottentot figs. Jacques found the large white house that loomed higher than its neighbours and pulled the brass doorbell. He heard it clang behind the door, followed by the scurry of children's feet and the firm voice of a man.

'When I return I shall expect a recitation without pause.' The front door opened on to a middle-aged man. Mr James Robertson. His dark top coat was smudged with chalk. Hair fell over his face, and he flicked it back in what had become an automatic gesture. His face grew puzzled at the sight of the grown-up who had intruded into his world of children. 'Can I help you?' he asked, with the authority of a schoolmaster facing an alien.

'If you would.' Jacques tried to appear calm. 'I'm a friend of young John Westbury's family, and I wondered if I could call on him.'

'John Westbury?' the man queried. 'Is there some reason he should need a visitor?' His voice was immediately defensive.

'I was passing,' Jacques said quickly.

'I'll see where he is.' James Robertson inspected Jacques as he ushered him in reluctantly. 'A friend of the family, you say?'

'A neighbour.'

'I see.' He indicated that Jacques should sit on the chaise-longue which stood in the hall. 'I won't be a moment. And neither will you, I'm sure. We are studying.' He included himself in the activity. 'We are doing well. Oh yes. John Westbury has a bright future ahead of him.' The schoolmaster couldn't conceal his pride.

A young girl walked across the hall dressed in a school pinafore and bobbed a curtsey to Jacques as he sat on the horsehair seat. 'Good day, sir.' She moved on and disappeared quickly. Jacques could smell paper and chalk. He could hear the sing-song voices of children as they recited the *Iliad* somewhere. He heard the solid feet of the man who'd allowed him into his world with such suspicion: a world Miss Thurston had coveted.

John Westbury stepped into the hall, and stood to attention in front of Jacques.

'Mr Beauvilliers. Good day.' He lowered his head in a formal bow. His eyes were blue and the slightly curled hair quite fair. Jacques realized he'd never looked at him before and all he could see now was his son. Only his colouring was different.

'Hello, John.' Jacques held out his hand to him. The young boy on the verge of being a man took it firmly and shook it. He was tall for his age. The gawkiness of youth hadn't yet given way to manhood, yet the man was visible in the boy. 'How are you?' Jacques asked.

'Fine, thank you, sir.' John Westbury watched him curiously. He felt awkward. He hardly knew Jacques Beauvilliers and couldn't understand why he had come to see him. 'Are my parents well?' he asked.

'Yes,' Jacques nodded. 'I was in Cape Town. I decided to stop by and see you.'

'You were in Cape Town?'

'Yes.'

Silence fell between them. The moment lengthened and John felt slightly uneasy. He was aware of Jacques' eyes constantly moving over his face. He smiled quickly with relief as the young girl came back into the hall.

'Sarah.' John turned to her. She flushed immediately and John turned back to Jacques. 'This is a friend of mine. Sarah Ransome. She's from England, and lives here with Mr and Mrs Robertson.'

'How do you do, sir.' The girl curtseyed quickly. She was delicate and pale; glancing at John, she flushed again.

The schoolmaster cleared his voice. Jacques' time was over.

'That is all?' Jacques' question answered itself as Mr Robertson opened the front door for him. 'Thank you.' Jacques moved to the door and John Westbury looked after him, puzzled. Nothing had been said that warranted a visit.

'Would you give my parents my regards, please?' he asked. 'And my sister, Pauline.'

'Yes.' Jacques didn't trust himself to take the boy's hand again as he realized the depth of the lie the Westbury family had spun. 'I will give your sister your regards.' Jacques wanted to get away. His visit had made things more difficult. He'd seen the complex web of deceit woven around his grandson and knew he could not disturb it.

'Why did he come to visit you?' Sarah asked quietly as the door closed behind Jacques. 'Who is he?'

'Back to lessons.' Mr Robertson clapped his hands sharply.

'He's a neighbour,' John said, as though that explained everything.

'Oh.' Sarah allowed her arm to brush against his as they walked after the heavy steps of the schoolmaster.

The closer Jacques got to the fishing village where Eva lived, the more alive he felt. For the first time since Jean Jacques had died he had a reason to see her.

Two scraggy dogs darted out from one of the sandy streets

which ran between the rows of thatched houses, yapping excitedly at the horse's hooves. Weatherworn faces beaten by the sun and sea looked out from doors and windows curiously.

The thatch of Eva's cottage ran from the ground in a tall A shape. Jacques rested his hands on his saddle and waited, allowing the feeling of Eva to drift over him. A little while later her voice reached him above the sound of the sea.

'How are you, Jacques?' she asked, as though it was only a short time since she'd seen him. She was smaller than he remembered, warmed by years and the sea, which had formed her face into one of its own.

Jacques climbed down from his horse. His hand touched her skirt and he looked down at her small bare brown feet on the sandy earth. He looked up, and as always her eyes met his in a deep glow. The words her eyes spoke to him now were different, but as strong as they had ever been. Her hand took his. She knew he must have come to see her for a reason.

'John Westbury?' They had walked down to the beach and Jacques had told her of a miracle. Waves crashed against the rocks and fell in white, frothing spray all around them. 'Can I see him?' Her eyes darted over Jacques' face.

'No, my love.' Jacques held her close. He no longer felt the pounding urge of desire as her body touched his. It was as if he'd woken from a nightmare and found himself still warm beside her. He let the softness of her body curve against his own. 'Not yet. Perhaps never.'

'But he's there.' The wind blew a streak of black hair across her eyes and Jacques pushed it gently away. He could see the time they'd been apart written on her face in fine lines, and he wondered how the years had made her even more beautiful.

'You're hungry,' she said suddenly, gripping his hand. 'Come.'

She picked her way ahead of him across the rocks, pulling him behind her up the steep rise to the village and her small house. The brown faces watched passively as she closed the door behind them.

'He must be fourteen.' She spoke quietly as if even their grandson's age must stay a well-guarded secret.

'How do you know?'

'There was something Jean Jacques was afraid to tell me. I re-

346

member when it was.' She ran her slim brown hands down his cheeks. 'Fish?'

'Yes.' He kept her hand in his.

'Yellow tail?'

It was as if their son was alive again, as if at any moment he might step into the room with their grandson. Jacques sank into a chair as she moved away and tied an apron over her skirt. She chattered as she did, her excitement bubbling over out of control.

'Does he look like him?' She unwrapped the fish from the leaves.

'He does.'

'And?' She laid the fish in front of her. 'Is he like him?'

'I hardly know him.'

'But you've seen him. You went to his school, you said.' Eva ran the knife down the centre of the fish and opened it wide. 'And Pauline? Is she a kind person?'

'So many questions.' Jacques closed his eyes, seeing John Westbury, Pauline and Jean Jacques.

'Fourteen!' Eva turned and looked at him suddenly. 'He must be tall.'

'Taller than you.' Jacques watched her as she cleaned the fish. She was still so young. Beautiful and so warm she shone.

'It's good, Jacques,' she whispered as his presence flooded her house again.

Chapter Nineteen

The air was filled with waves of emotion carried on ululating voices. Victory wrestled with grief and pain and erupted in long shivering wails, as though centuries of denied sorrow had been released in the black people all around Emily. Then it took to the air on wings, and soared in melody. Sorrow was left behind as Maria was buried with great joy, returned to the earth from which she'd come.

Emily looked at Rosita who stood beside her mother's grave. A small black child stood on either side of her. Though tears poured down her cheeks, her face was broken by a smile and her voice rang out with the others. Sunday stood next to her, his eyes closed. He turned his voice suddenly into a rhythmic high-pitched call; he stamped his feet and dust flew around him. Soon black feet all around were pounding the earth and the ground shook under Emily's chair.

She glanced back at the house in the distance. It stood proudly, bound by convention. It was no longer the simple L-shaped house she remembered as home. It had been extended many times over the years. It was as though the walls had been built one on top of the other to keep Africa out. Her eyes moved further away to the small family graveyard. It was immaculate, still and quiet. She remembered the sombre days of family burial. She could still feel the emotion she had held back, as though it was too shameful to release. Now, the stamping feet and gyrating black bodies swept her up in the rhythms of Africa. They were disturbing. She knew how little of her father's soul had ever been contained by the white walls of that house. He was as much a part of the earth as the black people around her, and his roots were as firmly planted.

Quite suddenly Emily felt swamped by the writhing black

bodies. She was afraid and she didn't know why. She turned her mind quickly to Suzanne. She must write to her again.

'Dear Suzanne,' Emily wrote in her head to keep the sound of stamping feet away. 'I will continue writing to you until one day my letters are not returned.' She remembered the pile of unopened letters which had been returned from the mission, like the letter which Jean Jacques had not had time to open. Emily decided that this time she would enclose another letter addressed to the mission. Perhaps they might tell her where Suzanne was. And Thys. And their child.

'Your baby must be . . . ' Emily stopped and mentally deleted the words. She couldn't be certain the baby was alive. She could be certain of nothing. The stamping feet and rising voices broke into her thoughts again.

'Maria is dead, Suzanne.'

Suzanne read the words through a wash of tears and they swam in front of her eyes in bending lines.

'She died yesterday. She was so much a part of us that with her death I feel alone. You are all so far away and I'm frightened.'

Suzanne looked up as Marie Pieterse entered the small dark house. She carried a basket filled with eggs.

'Do you see how well they are laying?' she said in Afrikaans as she paused in front of Suzanne and held the eggs under her nose. 'When the chickens lay well it is a good sign.'

'Is it?' Suzanne looked at the letter while she discreetly dried her tears.

'What does it say?' Marie moved closer to her. Suzanne's eyes lifted from the paper and settled on the seven brown eggs in the basket. They were dirty, with feathers and straw stuck to the shells.

'It's a letter from my sister Emily.' Suzanne too spoke in Afrikaans as she closed the letter.

'She's well?'

'Yes.' Suzanne wished Marie would go away and leave her with the letter and the past, which called to her from its pages.

'The child's awake.' Marie responded to a baby's cry and moved on towards the kitchen. It was a small corner of the same room and had the same dank smell of poverty. The house was primitive. Four square rooms divided by mud walls and dung floors which had to be swept clean constantly against the invasion of dust. Hard wooden beds, hard chairs and bare tables added to the severity of their life.

Suzanne had become a part of the surroundings, as though trying to lose herself in them. It was punishment for being alive when Thys was dead. She heard her child cry again in the room behind her and pushed Emily's letter into the pocket of her drab brown skirt.

'Have you thought again of what I said?' Marie stopped her with the question.

'Yes.' Suzanne disappeared into the other room to pick up the child, and Marie followed closely.

'Then tell me what you feel for my son, Johan?'

'I care for him.' Suzanne looked down at the chubby kicking child. He smiled up at his mother gleefully, as if she made waking up a wonder. Suzanne's body screamed for Thys as she looked at his son, a scream which would never be answered. She picked up her child quickly and he grabbed a handful of her hair, tugging at it with a chortle. 'I like Johan. He is a good man.'

'You pity him.' Marie Pieterse stood behind her. 'He loves you, girl.'

'No.' Suzanne stepped back into the safety of her own language, and leant her head against her baby. 'Johan likes me. That is all.'

'I've watched him when he's near you,' Marie said, keeping to Afrikaans, and ducked out of the room. She knew that the messages being passed between them needed no words.

Suzanne waited, then followed Marie to the kitchen. She watched the sharp movements of Marie's elbows as she transferred the seven eggs from the basket into a bowl. Suzanne knew there would be one person who would go without an egg in order that someone could have two. Marie would do without.

'A child without a father has little hope in this land.' Marie glanced over her shoulder at Suzanne. 'Survival is battle enough.'

'I don't love your son. I have told you.' Suzanne sat down with her child on her lap. She could see Johan standing just outside the house, his shadow stretching timidly into the doorway and towards her.

'This world of ours has little place for love.' Marie wiped her hands down her apron. 'Just practicalities. What is sensible.'

Suzanne ached with the emptiness of Thys's death.

'There is no place for love,' Marie went on. 'And your man is gone.' Johan's shadow stretched further into the room, revealing the gentle giant that he was. A giant who saw only the invisible. 'Your child's future depends on you. And he would find one in this family.' Marie did not expect a reply. 'He won't expect you to love him, as he loves you.' Marie turned and stood in front of Suzanne, looking at the child. 'Another tooth,' she said.

'Yes.' Suzanne wiped the dribble from her son's chin and allowed him to chew on her finger. 'Are you offering me your son as a father for my child?'

'I am offering him hope in a land where each day is dug out of granite.' Marie held her arms out. 'Now you see to the chickens.' She returned to her private corner of poverty with the child on her hip.

Suzanne looked down the length of Johan's shadow. If she could believe there was a God to cry to, she would cry to Him now, she thought as she stepped out of the house towards the chicken coop and him.

His father, Jan Pieterse, shouted from further away. He was chasing after an ostrich, herding it into an enclosure with another ostrich, a female. The ostrich trotted haughtily in front of him, its long neck curved as it looked back at him and hissed its distrust. Its enormous black eyes warned it might kick its strong legs back at him.

'I don't think Emir wants the wife your parents chose for him,' Suzanne laughed.

'Is she pretty?' Johan ducked as she pulled his hand down, leading him after her into the chicken coop. She looked back at the ostrich being taken to its selected mate, in an attempt to supply feathers for fashion in France.

'Your mother has been talking to me again,' she said quietly.

'Don't listen to her.' Johan turned away and the chickens scuttled to the edges of the enclosure, clucking nervously.

'She thinks I should marry you.' Suzanne hauled the sack of chicken meal closer; digging her hand into it, she tossed seeds on to the ground.

'I know what my mother says to you.' He didn't turn to her.

'Is it what you want, Johan?' Suzanne tried to shut Thys out of her mind. Marie Pieterse was right; there was only space and time for practicalities.

'I would want nothing from you.' Johan's voice carried the expectation of rejection. 'But I would take great care of my wife and child.'

A gunshot blasted and they raced out of the coop in time to see Mrs Pieterse rushing out of the mud house. She yelled at her husband in anger, swelled by shock. 'Don't shoot it, Jan! Those feathers are our food!'

'Did you hear what your feathers are for?' Jan Pieterse glared at the ostrich as he lowered his gun. It blinked its long eyelashes and glared back. 'Get in with that hen or I'll shoot the feathers off you!'

'I will be a wife to you.' Suzanne's voice was a whisper, and she had closed her eyes.

'Thank you.' Johan placed his hand over hers and she felt the gentle care he offered. In that moment she had at last accepted the finality of death.

Over seven hundred miles away, across rough untamed land, with hundreds of spent days between Suzanne and himself, Thys faced Gerrit's anger and truth.

'No! I do not accept it and I still do not believe you!' Gerrit's eyes were alight as he looked at Thys. He swept an arm in an expansive gesture over the vast spread of land around him. 'We have to fight to keep our land from the predators! Lion, leopard, hyena and man! We must fence it to keep them out, then mend the fences when they break them down. We fight for each drop of water and each day is a new struggle for survival. But love? Love we have as a God-given gift.'

Thys looked at his friend in confusion. He'd explained everything to him when he'd arrived. He had travelled miles just to see him. Hundreds of hard long miles he'd come, just to do the right thing.

'Don't tell me what is right, Thys!' Gerrit went on without Thys having spoken. 'You have a wife and it is to her you go! Or is it that you have been chained by your parents' beliefs? Is it their rejection of an Englishwoman, of anyone who is not their own kind, which still binds your heart?'

'My heart is not bound. I am going to Suzanne! I have told you!'

'When?' Gerrit challenged him. His hands hung at his sides in bewilderment. 'Time separates people faster than distance, Thys. I will not accept your excuses. You must be with Suzanne!'

Thys was desperate. 'I came to see you!'

'No! You are here because you are afraid of love. But I will not accept that fear, Thys,' Gerrit walked away and looked out over the land they had claimed together: land he had fought alone to preserve for Thys and his wife Suzanne. 'You will not live here until you have your wife with you. I do not need you.'

Thys knew Gerrit was right. Gerrit carried the wisdom of nature inside him and his roots ran deep into Africa.

'I came to you because I sensed time between *us*, Gerrit. I was afraid of it!' Thys tried to explain.

'The only fear is that it wipes love out with its passing shadow.' Gerrit looked hard at him. 'Don't let it.'

'She knows where I am. She knows why I'm here. I sent word with a transport rider.'

'And you had word back?' Gerrit moved to Thys suddenly, narrowing his eyes, boring them deep into Thys. 'You can't entrust love to a messenger. Did he get to her? The transport rider? Is he alive?' Gerrit knew how many had been murdered by marauding blacks and transmitted to Thys a sudden stab of fear. Had Suzanne ever got his message?

'Practicalities have little to do with love, or love with them.' Gerrit spoke quietly, remembering his own wife and son; how they were murdered in a moment of time which had separated them. 'I will wait for you to return with your wife, and then I will welcome you.'

A curious relief filled Thys as he realized he no longer had to deny his feelings. 'I will go,' he said simply and the warmth returned to Gerrit's eyes. He smiled.

'But I thank you that you cared, Thys.'

The wagon Gerrit had made his permanent home had sunk its iron wheels into the earth as foundations. 'We will build a house for you and your Englishwoman.' Gerrit glanced at two black men riding among the cattle further away. 'Does she enjoy a drop of peach brandy?' Gerrit looked at him with a twinkle.

'Makes fine children where there were none before.' Thys smiled back at the man who had become more of a father to him than his own, and felt a great pride. Gerrit was a true Afrikaner, a man of Africa, not yet spoiled by greed.

'You will be going back the way you came?' Gerrit had achieved his objective and moved on to the practicalities. 'You will go via Thaba Nchu?' Thys nodded warmly and Gerrit repeated, 'Thaba Nchu,' hoping the young man he'd befriended would return soon. He knew how much he would miss Thys.

The narrow metal ring slipped on to the third finger of Suzanne's left hand, and the voice of the Afrikaans dominee spoke in high Dutch. The words were of marriage and with them a door was closing behind Suzanne. But through the door she could hear the voice of Rev. Phillip as he married her to Thys. It was distant, echoing from the immense stretch of time past.

'And do you, Suzanne Beauvilliers, take this man, Thys Bothma, to be your lawful wedded husband?'

'I do.' Suzanne heard her own reply and felt Thys beside her.

Johan gazed down at her and Suzanne's eyes moved to Mrs Pieterse as she held Thys's child in her arms.

'Kiss the bride, Johan,' came his father's voice, anticipating his son's pleasure. Johan's lips touched Suzanne's. His body moved closer and his hands held her tightly. Suzanne had felt nothing at all.

Thaba Nchu was four weeks behind him as Thys looked back at the narrow cleft in the dry earth with just a trickle of water in it. He remembered the sound of the swirling water he'd struggled through at this point before and realized it was not just a new season. Many seasons had passed; but the season of love for Suzanne had remained constant. A baboon barked down at him from a rock and Thys slipped down off his horse, leading it towards the narrow track. The baboon stood up on its hind legs and bared its long yellow teeth, defying him to climb further. Thys shouted, his voice bouncing off the rock walls of the pass in reverberating echoes.

'Get out of my way!' The baboon was suddenly surrounded by others, all staring down at him, listening to his echoing voice. 'This is my territory!' Thys shouted, forcing his voice to run back over itself among the echoes. 'I've come for my wife.'

Suzanne felt Johan's body edge closer beside her and his hand touch her breasts. She turned her head away on the pillow and kept her eyes tightly shut.

'I love you, Suzanne,' Johan murmured as his body moved over hers. She squeezed her eyes tighter and a tear ran down her cheek. She couldn't wipe the tear, or her mind. It was on her wedding night with Thys.

She felt Johan push himself inside her. It hurt. She wasn't moist and wanting as she'd been with Thys. She was dead to the passion growing in Johan.

'Are you all right?' he whispered. 'Suzanne?' His hands gripped her closer and he found his way deeper inside her. Her body heaved with emotion and she sobbed openly. Her thumb pushed at the cheap metal ring on her finger as his body dropped on to hers and a shiver ran through him.

'I'm sorry.' His voice was very quiet. 'I'm sorry.' He felt her hand touch his, but her body had moved away.

The church gleamed its whiteness against the sun, its high gable curved over the large carved door. Thys could still feel the slippery wet mud under his hands as he remembered turning the circular shapes of the four corners on the gable. He could feel the curve of Suzanne's breasts under his hands and smell the gentle perfume of her body. He dug his heels into his horse and galloped down the familiar slope which led to the mission.

He remembered when he had first ridden down; when he had travelled as many miles on the word of a stranger who'd talked of a nurse called Suzanne. He remembered her face as she'd looked at him from inside the tent, and the way her mouth had parted slightly as her spirit flew to him.

Children ran out from all directions as he reined in his horse and looked towards the hut which he and Suzanne had made their home. He whistled their private call and he waited.

A sea of small black faces peered up at him and suddenly it was as if he was a total stranger. 'Hello Joanna,' he said, but the small girl turned and ran. Others fled with her and Thys felt a steel clamp tighten around him. He looked back at the small hut and whistled again. Gerrit's words raced through his head. 'You cannot allow time to come between you.'

'Do you want something?' a voice called to him and Thys turned. A tall slim man was watching him from the church door. 'Is there something you want?' the English voice asked again.

'Suzanne,' Thys said as he looked at the stranger in Rev. Phillip's white collar. 'I'm looking for Suzanne.'

'Suzanne?' the Englishman repeated, slightly puzzled.

'Where's Reverend Phillip?' Thys scanned the other buildings as he climbed off his horse, moving to the man he'd never seen before. 'Where are Doctor Steven and Reverend Phillip?'

'They are not here.' The pale eyes peered at Thys curiously. 'They are in England.'

'Where's Suzanne!' The steel clamp constricted his chest as he stepped into a nightmare. 'I am looking for my wife.' He tried vainly to control his voice. 'Suzanne.'

The face in front of Thys crinkled in puzzled lines.

'Who are you?' Frederick Mortimer asked quietly.

'My name is Thys Bothma.' He watched as the puzzlement vanished and an expression of deeper confusion passed over the clergyman's face. 'What's wrong?' he asked. 'What's happened to her?' He gripped Frederick Mortimer's shoulders. 'Where's my wife?' he shouted.

'Thys Bothma?' he said flatly. 'You can't be.'

'What is it?' The black children moved closer cautiously. They knew something he didn't and panic flew at his throat. 'Tell me!'

'They said you were dead.' Frederick Mortimer kept his eyes down. 'Reverend Phillip was told you were dead.'

And all at once Thys felt death fall on him. He felt the cold clay walls of his mother's grave close in around him and he looked up and out of the grave at the priest.

'Suzanne?' he asked, and the priest's head dropped forward. Thys examined the short thick hair which ran down under the white collar around his neck as he waited for an answer. The priest's head lifted and his pale eyes regarded Thys with chilling finality.

'They said you were dead.'

Thys drove his horse on in the direction of the Pieterse homestead although he didn't know why. He had listened in silence as Rev. Mortimer told him all he knew; a silence filled with anger.

Anger that Gerrit had been right: time had stolen Suzanne, and he had allowed it to happen. Now, many miles from the mission, all he'd heard rattled inside his skull.

'Reverend Phillip was told you were dead.' The priest's voice rang like a church bell in his memory. 'It was black-water fever, they said. He asked transport riders to look for you but they all came back with the same report. Your whole family was dead. You were dead.' Thys remembered the man who had come to Hendrik and Rizza's farm looking for him, and he felt sick.

'Suzanne has married again,' Rev. Mortimer continued as factually as he could. 'I discovered where she was when I sent one of many letters addressed to her with a trader. I had received this myself.' Rev. Mortimer had handed Thys a letter from Emily.

'If you have any idea where my sister Suzanne is, please send my letter on. Try and find her, I beg you.' In black ink on white parchment paper, Emily's neat handwriting had assured Thys the nightmare was not his alone.

'Where is she?' he had asked the priest as he handed back Emily's letter. 'Have you seen her?'

'I have told you all I know, Mr Bothma.' Rev. Mortimer's tone had been gentle, but Thys had sensed his need to be released. 'All I have heard is what I have told you. She lives with her husband, Johan Pieterse. They have a child. A son.'

'They have a child. A son. She lives with her husband, Johan Pieterse.' The priest's words jangled endlessly in Thys's mind.

'It is because you are afraid.' Gerrit's words overlaid them. 'You cannot allow time to move between you.'

Thys looked ahead, trying to shut the voices out of his mind. He could see a thin stream of smoke rising from the roof of a small house in the distance. Suzanne would be cooking over the fire that made the smoke. She would be cooking for her husband and her child.

The smoke breathed itself into a sky about to bring down the shutters of night, as his reported death had brought down the shutters on his life. Thys felt his body stiffen as his eyes settled on a man digging in a circle of cleared ground away from the house. An ostrich stalked about behind the man, poking its head forward in short jabs as its long neck waved and twisted in curiosity. Thys knew who the man was.

Johan looked up at the sound of a horse. His hand ran up the rough wood of the spade handle and gripped it as he straightened his back.

'Who's there?' he called in Afrikaans towards the sound of the approaching rider.

'I'm looking for water.' Thys looked down at Johan as he pulled up his horse beside him. The bitterness which ran in his veins turned suddenly to shame as Johan's blind eyes peered around to find him. 'Do you have water?' Thys repeated in Afrikaans. He glanced towards the house at the sudden, startling cry of a child.

'Water. Yes.' Johan pointed away from the house, ignoring the child's cry. 'Down that way. There's a small stream.'

'Thank you.' Thys watched Johan as he stood beside the hole he had been digging in the ground. It was one of many holes which had been dug in a large circle. Prepared and carefully tended saplings lay nearby.

'You're planting trees,' Thys said as his eyes searched Johan's face for a trace of Suzanne.

'Pepper trees.' Johan looked up suddenly and directly into Thys's face, as if he could see him. 'My wife likes the smell of pepper trees.' He lowered his eyes. 'They are good shade trees.'

Thys was pulled back to the house by Suzanne's voice. She was singing to the crying child.

'My son only sleeps when my wife sings to him,' Johan confirmed as if reading his thoughts. Thys's horse picked up its feet in a nervous dance on the spot, as if the tension between the two men had passed itself on.

'You're a stranger in these parts.'

'Yes.' Thys could say no more. He dug his heels into the horse's side and rode off fast.

'Who was that?' Johan turned quickly at Suzanne's voice and felt suddenly trapped by his own instinctive sight.

'A stranger,' he said and took the child from her.

'What did he want?' Suzanne watched Thys's silhouette against the fading evening sky. He was already a long way off.

'Water.' Johan rubbed his face against the child's hair.

'He hasn't gone for water.' Suzanne turned to Johan. She saw the white of his knuckles under the taut brown skin of his hand as he held her son. 'Did you know him, Johan?'

'He was a stranger,' Johan repeated, though he knew he was not. 'We can begin planting in the morning.' He smiled at Suzanne, escaping gladly into the security of his blindness. 'When our son grows he will climb these trees and touch the sky.' He pulled her into his arms, with the child held between them, burying his face in the gold of her hair. 'Trees are the shade of God's right hand.'

'What's wrong?' Suzanne sensed Johan's insecurity and automatically she turned and looked after Thys. 'Who was he?'

'He was looking for water.'

Thys turned in the saddle and looked back into the past which held Suzanne, the time which he had allowed to slip through his fingers. He knew that their love had not been taken by time or chance. His parents had reached out from beyond the grave and snatched it.

'You have reason to cry.' His father's last words skipped through his head.

'I do not want you.' His mother's echoed them.

'Tshepo.' The strange word which had rooted itself in his subconscious loomed again. 'Tshepo.' Thys took a deep breath and held the night air in his lungs; as deep as the love he still felt for Suzanne. He looked away from the small homestead, away from Suzanne, and ahead into the unknown. Releasing his breath, he urged his horse on, and with each stride it took his mind took another into the future. He would build it with Gerrit.

Chapter Twenty

Jim Audsley leaned back against the buckboard of the wagon. His hat was pulled down over his face, and his crossed legs stretched over the swaying backs of the oxen. Pierre Chabrol's voice washed over him like a sleeping draught. The crack of the whip, as Themba brought it down over the team of oxen, served as punctuation to the neverending chatter of his partner.

'. . . and after I left Natalia I went back to the Cape. It was then I decided my frontiers should be pushed north, if I was to discover anything of value in this land.' The whip cracked down and Prudence paused for a moment, glancing at Jim Audsley. 'That was when I decided to trade.'

Audsley wondered again why his travelling companion and partner told so many lies. He'd heard a different version of the same story many times.

'But if I'd known all I'd get for my trouble was sheep, I'm not so certain I'd have bothered,' Prudence added.

Audsley opened one eye and glanced at the offending sheep which wandered around and behind the wagon. His horse followed the wagon wearily, watched by a tiny black boy, a loosely held together bundle of dusty brown skin and angular bones. The day after they had left the last Griqua settlement in which they'd traded, Themba had produced the boy from nowhere. Audsley never questioned Themba. Witchcraft wasn't his concern, except to ensure it was on his side.

'Are you listening to me?' Prudence's question, as always, came as a surprise to him. Why should he be listening? 'I haven't yet learned anything about you in all our time together,' Prudence complained and Audsley reflected that his partner was right. 'Have you something to hide?'

360

'No more than yourself.' He pulled his hat further over his face and shrugged himself into a more comfortable position on the hard wooden seat. Flies were buzzing around the oxen and he flicked them away, watching the tick birds perch precariously on the oxen's rocking backs: birds who rose as Themba brought the whip down, then returned to the oxen and their meal of ticks.

Prudence stole another look at Jim Audsley. The longer they were together, the more like a woman he made her feel. She wanted to be a woman again.

'Hey!' She leaned out and shouted to the boy walking solemnly behind them, carrying a stick which was bigger than himself. 'Watch the sheep, Jacob!'

Jacob's big round eyes fixed on her as he sniffed up the mucus about to run from his small flat nose. He turned his attention to a few straying sheep, ran to them, and whacked them hard across the back one at a time.

'Themba!' Themba held his whip poised. 'Tell him not to hit the sheep, Themba,' Prudence yelled in Xhosa.

'English!' Jim Audsley corrected from under the brim of his hat.

'He's not English.' She leapt down from the moving wagon and strode after Themba as he returned to the oxen. She had had to learn Xhosa quickly to gain a position of strength over Jim Audsley.

Audsley tossed his head and forced his hat back off his face, taking a sharp irritated breath as Prudence and Themba talked in a series of unintelligible clicks. Themba's behaviour was something else he couldn't understand. He treated Pierre Chabrol with respect.

'How is it you never learned to fire a gun when you learn everything else so quickly,' he asked casually. 'Are you afraid of guns?'

'I am well aware that in your opinion all men must be capable of firing a gun, hunting, fighting, drinking, brawling and behaving as no less than an animal, or you consider them less of a man!'

'Have you finished?' Audsley smiled his crooked smile. As he did, Prudence felt a flush in her cheeks.

'Yes, Mr Audsley, I have finished,' she replied and tugged harder on the trek rope. She noticed Themba's crinkled black shoulders heave slightly with laughter and moved back to the wagon, climbing up.

'You forgot one thing.' Jim Audsley spoke quietly. 'Womanizing.' He kissed the word as it passed his lips and Prudence felt the familiar tingle rise in her body.

'And that,' she added. 'Womanizing.' She felt her breasts swell, as if they were trying to push their way out of the tight binding that held them flat.

The wheels grated over stones as they rumbled on, and the wagon swayed dangerously. Prudence looked around at the country to avoid further conversation. Great rocks were strewn everywhere. Some stood in clusters; others leant over, holding one another up; and several lay flat on the dry dusty ground. It was as if they'd stumbled on a giants' battlefield frozen in time: bodies clad in solid grey armour lay spreadeagled in death as the rest struggled to get away carrying their wounded.

'As much as you talk, you never talk of women.' Jim Audsley's voice was teasing.

'Perhaps it's because you talk of nothing else and appear to think of nothing else. Like these damn sheep!' Prudence turned to look at him. He was peering at her curiously from under his hat. 'Is there something wrong?' She dreaded the day her disguise might fail, yet a part of her longed for it.

'I was just wondering why you shave twice a day.' He pushed his hat back again and glanced at the sheep. 'What's wrong with them anyway?'

'We get more every time we trade. That's what's wrong.'

'Sheep are all the Griqua people have to trade.'

'And soon it'll be all we have!' Prudence retorted.

'You should have thought of that when you laid your plans to push back the frontiers, Mr Chabrol!' Themba's whistle cut through their argument as he spotted a small herd of springbok in the distant scrub. Audsley reached back for his gun and pushed the shot down hard into the barrel. His wide straight lips pulled back over his teeth and his strong brown hands held the gun firmly. One cradled the barrel and the other ran flat-palmed down the wood of the stock, one finger curled under the trigger.

The gun blasted and Prudence closed her eyes. The explosion had happened inside her own body.

'I shot it, you skin it,' he said.

Prudence swallowed and pulled a knife from her belt, glancing back at him as she climbed down from the wagon. He had replaced the gun and prepared himself to sleep.

'Good night!' she said as she untied his horse, and galloped towards their next meal.

The knife ran down the gentle white underbelly of the springbok and Prudence felt her stomach heave. The blood was still warm and the flesh almost alive. She closed her eyes and pushed her hand inside the carcass. It was hot and sticky. She had learned that the first thing to do was remove the offal, but she could still hardly bear to touch it. She looked up as a pair of dusty black feet stopped beside her and Themba held his hand out to her for the knife.

'He is asleep,' he said in their secret language of Xhosa, and a shiver of relief ran through her body as he proceeded to skin the buck. His gnarled black face seemed to hold the wisdom of ages.

'You know?' Prudence asked quietly.

Themba peered at her from slow wise eyes. 'Mfazi?' he said. Themba knew she was a woman but quickly she denied it. 'Ndoda,' she defiantly contradicted him.

'Ndoda?' Themba's bent body rocked with laughter. 'Ndoda?' He shook his head violently and pointed at her. 'Mfazi!' The sinews in his black arms stood out like ropes as he ripped the skin off the animal in one piece. She rubbed her bloodied hands in the sand.

'Does *he* know?' she asked in Xhosa and Themba chuckled, shaking his head. 'How did you know?' Themba nudged his elbow at the bag of witchdoctor's bones which hung from his waist. 'But you haven't told him?'

The rich deep chuckle which came from deep inside Themba assured Prudence that the witchdoctor's master had no idea she was a woman.

'I skinned it. You cook it!' Jim Audsley woke with a start as the bloody springbok carcass dropped on to his head and blood dripped over the brim of his hat. 'I'll prepare the fire since you still have no idea how to handle such matters.' She walked off towards a small anthill.

'Wait!' Audsley climbed off the wagon in a rage, swinging the bleeding carcass in his hand as he moved after her. 'What are you smiling about?' he demanded of Themba, who shrugged as his smile vanished. 'That's better.'

Prudence, digging a hole beside the anthill to build a fire, asked casually as he reached her, 'Have you told Themba to outspan the oxen?'

'You tell him!'

'Outspan the oxen,' Prudence called in Xhosa and Themba immediately moved to do as he was told. Jacob ran to help, moving like a spindle puppet.

'I suppose he's taught you witchcraft too.' He stepped back as she pushed him away from the anthill.

'Perhaps.' Prudence looked up at him, suddenly confident. 'And I'll teach you how to cook on an anthill.'

'That witchdoctor is my witchdoctor!' Jim Audsley exploded as he pointed towards Themba. 'You hear me?'

'I teach you to cook, and you teach me to shoot!'

'You're going to shoot?' he asked in amazement.

'As you're going to cook.' She sliced off the top of the anthill with her knife. 'It's time the work was divided equally between us.' She nodded at the meat in his hand. 'Put it on there.' She stepped back as he dropped the carcass on to the red-hot surface. 'Do you know why an anthill retains heat?' She proceeded to tell him. 'It's impregnated with formic acid by the ants and becomes a kind of lime kiln. If you dig several holes in the top it's possible to cook five or six things at one time and it retains the heat for hours.' She looked up as she realized she was talking to herself. Jim Audsley was moving away towards the wagon, where he sat down and pulled his hat down.

'Now you can teach me to fire your gun,' she said. He tossed the gun out from under the wagon.

'Point and pull,' he said.

'Like this?'

Jim Audsley felt his hat slide back off his head. The gun was pointing directly in his face.

'What's wrong?' Prudence asked innocently.

'You're insane.' He glanced at Themba. 'And what's he still smiling about?'

'He bothers you because he smiles?'

'You bother me, Mr Chabrol.'

'I am quite simply waiting to learn how to fire that gun.' She pulled it away from him. 'Themba!' she called. Themba's old black body came after her with a spring in his step as she strode away, and Jacob followed.

'He's not touching that gun.' Audsley ran after them all. 'He'd kill us both!' Catching her up, he snatched it out of her hands.

'He could kill us with a thought.' She turned her attention back to the gun. 'I presume you are ready now.' She reached for it and her hand touched his. He held it firmly and she felt herself weaken. 'Perhaps it's best if you stick to shooting, I to cooking, and Themba to his thoughts.' She moved quickly towards the cooking anthill, and away from her feelings.

Audsley kicked the ground and cursed as the toe of his boot gathered more dust with each kick. 'I come all this way to a God-forsaken place and end up with a French pansy!' he yelled. 'Never stops talking! Never baths! Tries to steal my witchdoctor!' Themba was still smiling. Audsley marched after her in fury.

He stopped dead. It was the first time he'd seen his partner walk from behind. His partner's rear end was pear-shaped, and it swung.

His straight mouth spread into a smile, but he said nothing.

Jacob sat perched in a tree, sound asleep. His small bent figure tucked into the curve of a branch, he looked like a part of the tree itself. Themba had retired under the wagon; and Prudence, her body curled away from Jim Audsley, was sound asleep with the fire burning brightly between them.

Being awake in a world of sleeping people was unusual for Jim Audsley. As the noisy night silence settled around him, he realized how much he missed London; the bustle of people and the security of crowded city streets. He remembered the last night he'd spent with Annie on Bethnal Green. He could still feel the soft swell of her buttocks in his hands. His ears picked up the sound of scratching crickets and he remembered the creaking of the tall ship on which he'd earned himself a trip to Australia. At his first glimpse of Table Mountain *en route* he'd known there was something special about it. The Cape Colony had refused to allow the convicts to be landed, which had encouraged him. Anyone who imagined they could possess a convict-free continent must be ripe for plucking.

He had slipped over the side of the tall ship unseen and swum naked to shore, pounded by waves, taken up and sucked under by ten-foot swells, and constantly aware of sharks somewhere in the deep dark waters. He'd found himself suddenly at the base of Cape Town Castle and told the soldier who'd held a rifle on his nakedness that he was a soldier himself, blown off the rampart by the strong south-easterly wind. He had later walked out of the castle gates dressed in the bright-red uniform he'd stolen from the same soldier, and had promptly sold it to a Boer rebel. In exchange he'd got his clothes, his horse and his witchdoctor, Temba.

A gentle snore from Prudence attracted his attention and he crept on all fours around the fire towards her. As he lifted the jacket collar away from the face his partner automatically swatted his hand, keeping mosquitoes away even in her sleep. Audsley leaned closer and examined her face carefully in the flickering light of the fire. The skin looked extraordinarily smooth for a man who had to shave twice a day. A gentle line of blonde fluff ran down from the hairline in front of the ear. He blew on it, and moved back quickly before the swatting hand caught him across the face.

His eyes ran down the length of her body, well tucked into the jacket, and settled on the rise of hips. He lifted the jacket and peered at the trousers underneath, grubby and hard with dirt. It was another thing he'd noticed. For a man who shaved himself twice a day, Pierre Chabrol had never joined him in a bath. Whenever they came to a good running river, Pierre Chabrol had immediately found something more important to do.

Audsley held his hand tentatively over the buttocks, wary, but curious. He lowered his hand carefully towards the trousers, pressed it on to the hard material and felt the undeniable soft plumpness of a woman's buttocks. Blood rushed through his body with the familiarity of female flesh under his hand, and he squeezed.

'What was that?' Prudence sat up and shook him by the shoulders roughly as he feigned sleep. 'Wake up!' she yelled in his ear. 'Something touched me.'

'Mmm?' He peered up at her and was astounded. How had he ever been fooled? Pierre Chabrol was all woman. Nothing about this woman was a man. He picked up his hat, rammed it on his head and kept his new-found information firmly under it.

'I'll get my gun.' He stood up and looked around.

'You were sleeping on guard and you don't have your gun?' she shouted at him.

'I was hiding it from him.' He nodded towards Themba, who looked back blankly from under the wagon. He pulled the gun out from among a pile of skins beside him and threw it at Audsley.

'Tell me where it is and I'll shoot it,' he said to cover his embarrassment. 'Where is it?'

'Where is what?'

'Whatever touched you.'

'I don't know what touched me.'

'You don't know?' He looked down at her. 'You don't know what touched you yet you woke me up to shoot it?' He remembered her voluptuous bottom.

There was a look in his eye she hadn't seen before. 'How would I know what touched me when I was asleep!' She moved away quickly and lay down on her side of the fire, pulling her jacket around her.

'Go to sleep,' he said, lying down on the other side.

'Have you got your gun?' she asked quietly through the silence.

'Yes.' His hands tightened on it with the memory of that womanly mound of flesh he'd held for a second. 'We'll move on to Thaba Nchu tomorrow.' His voice was warm. 'You agree?'

Prudence wondered why he suddenly cared whether or not she agreed.

'Thaba Nchu is the crossroads of Africa,' he added. 'As Munich is the crossroads of Europe.'

'Is it?'

'Didn't you know?'

'No.' Prudence knew what was different about him; he was talking to her. 'Are you quite well?' she asked.

'Better than.' He smiled his crooked smile into the darkness.

'I wondered if the flames were entirely out on your back.'

'What flames?' He sat up, trying to look at his back.

'When I went to sleep you were on that side of the fire. When I woke up you were on this side. It seems you must have rolled through it in your sleep. Good night.'

Prudence pulled the collar of her jacket over her face and left him to worry about why she'd said that. He didn't. He closed his eyes and wondered how long he could keep his hands off her.

They had moved on in a north-westerly direction through Transorangia and Thaba Nchu was four days behind them. Themba had told them that the Waterboers had unusual stones to barter and Jim Audsley had immediately thought of diamonds.

'I wonder where Themba went?' Prudence said as she walked ahead of the oxen pulling the trek rope.

'Didn't he tell you?' Audsley flicked the whip over the line of oxen and ducked as it swung back at him. He always walked behind her now. The sway of her hips was a wonder.

'He said his ancestors had called him.' Prudence struggled with the trek rope.

'Oh.' As the whip swung back it caught in an overhanging tree. Audsley glanced back at Jacob. 'Get it down, boy.' The small black body shinned up the tree like a monkey, untangled the whip and threw it down.

'At last,' Audsley said suddenly.

'What?'

'We can take a bath.' Prudence glanced ahead suspiciously. A thin curling brown ribbon of water ran across the plain ahead of them.

'You could at least have the decency to undress behind a bush.' Prudence turned her back firmly on Jim Audsley and pretended to be busy checking the wagon.

'Why?' he asked, wearing nothing but his crooked smile. 'To whom would I be showing courtesy?'

'You could scare the boy to death.' She nodded at Jacob who sat watching them both quite calmly.

'Right!' Audsley suddenly grabbed Prudence from behind and dragged her over the rough ground towards the river. She screamed and kicked out at him with her boots.

'What do you think you're doing!' she yelled.

'If I have to spend all my time with you I'd prefer the air to be sweeter.'

He spun her around as he reached the edge of the river and

hurled her into the water. Prudence gulped as she surfaced and Audsley jumped into the water towards her. She waited till he had gone under, lifted her arms out of the water and brought them smacking down on his head as he came up. Then, finding her feet on the slimy river bed, she began to wade to the side.

'Leave me alone!' Prudence yelled back at him.

'Not till you've bathed, Pierre Chabrol!' He grabbed the sleeve of her jacket and pulled it. She yanked it back to free herself. He pulled harder on the sodden sleeve, she pulled the other way and her arm slipped out. She spun round on him as he let the empty sleeve go and the spongy wet leather looped through the air, whacking him across the face. She quickly pulled her other arm free and swung the jacket over her head, launching it at him. He caught it, pulled it, and she plunged face down in the water. Coughing and spluttering she surfaced, water running out of her nose, her short wet hair lying flat on top of her head.

'How dare you!' she shouted. 'What are you doing?'

'I'll show you what I'm doing, Mr Pierre Chabrol!' He lunged forward and pulled the front of her shirt open.

'Keep away from me!'

He grabbed the loose end of wet material strapped around her chest and pulled it, spinning her round in the water as the binding unwound, turning her like a top and tossing her into the water again. He pulled till the binding came free in his hand, then launched himself at her, pushing her under the water. She struggled but he held her arms.

Jim Audsley couldn't breathe. Her firm full breasts gleamed white in the sun as the water skimmed over them. His eyes pulled away on to her face as she looked up at him. It was a look he'd never seen on her before. Her lips were slightly parted and her eyes seemed to smoulder behind a translucent film. Desire pounded through his veins and he pushed her shoulders back, moving his face down to hers.

The still hot air was torn apart by a scream. Prudence screamed as his body came down towards hers, as his face became the face of M. Claudelle and the full horror of the past flashed into her mind.

He pulled away from her in the shallow water and looked down at her in confusion. Her face was twisted in terror as she screamed on and on.

The small boy, Jacob, watching from the branch of a tree further away, scratched his head in puzzlement. Sheep and oxen stared blankly towards the river as they chewed.

Audsley waded quickly to the bank and she quietened immediately. He was bewildered. When he stopped and looked back, she was crying.

'It's all right,' he said quietly. 'I'm going.'

'No!' she howled and began crawling after him towards the bank.

'No?' His mouth formed the word silently. He was totally lost and ran towards his clothes in panic. Prudence looked after him as she reached the bank. She couldn't understand what had happened, her body had ached for his for so long. She had dreamed of what would happen had he known she was a woman and she wanted him.

Pulling the torn pieces of her shirt together, she dragged herself up the river bank and ran in the direction he'd gone.

'Where are you going?' she yelled. He was dressed and untying his horse.

'Away.' He leapt on to his horse quickly.

'No!' She ran towards the wagon and snatched the gun, waving the barrels at him. 'You're going nowhere, Jim Audsley!'

'You want me to stay?' He was baffled.

'We made a bargain!'

'I struck a bargain with a man!'

'You struck it with me!'

'With a woman pretending to be a man! Do you call that a bargain?'

'Would you have struck one with a woman?'

'With a woman?'

'With me.'

'No.'

'Then what else was I to do?' She lifted the gun again as he turned his horse, about to ride away. 'Stay where you are!'

'You're going to fire that?' He began to laugh and Jacob closed his eyes as Prudence lifted the gun higher, tightening her finger on the trigger. 'Fire!' he called and dug his heels in.

Prudence closed her eyes and pulled the trigger. The kick of the gun knocked her back on to the ground. She looked up in a useless rage as he shouted back with a laugh, 'Fire again, Mr

Chabrol!'

'Damn you!' Prudence flung the gun across the ground. 'Damn you, Jim Audsley!' she threw after him, though she knew he could no longer hear. A cloud of dust surrounded him, as he grew smaller in the distance. 'Come back!' she wailed through the tears choking in her throat. 'Please! Come back!' She doubled over, curling into a broken ball on the ground.

Memory had leapt out and snatched away the first man who had ever made her feel like a woman. She rocked backwards and forwards, her face buried in her hands. The sun burned down on the back of her neck and the hard stone chips dug into her knees, but she felt nothing except a deep longing.

Jim Audsley was no more than a dot on the horizon.

She tensed as she felt someone behind her, and her body turned to ice. Each vertebra in her spine seemed to rack up a notch. Her eyes moved instinctively to where she'd thrown the gun. It had gone. She looked down as the sand beside her rose in puff balls and two black feet stood firmly next to her, the spread toes splayed on the earth. She heard the creak of dried animal skins and a sudden acrid sweet smell filled her nostrils as a hand touched her shoulder.

Themba's slow wise eyes smiled as he looked into hers.

'He will come back,' he said in clear English.

The blood ran freely in her veins again and her eyes drank comfort from his.

'You speak English,' she said quietly.

Themba nodded and handed her the gun.

Jim Audsley lay back on the flat rock and allowed the heat of the sun to burn through his body. His eyes followed a wispy white cloud as it passed in front of the sun and vanished. The stillness of midday was broken only by the hot wind stirring the long dry grass around him, and a slight movement on his hat.

He squinted up at the brim and watched a thin green tail curl its way over the edge of the brown felt. He slid his index finger underneath it and a tiny green foot stepped cautiously on to it. He waited a moment, and then gently lifted it down. The chameleon watched him with one eye and sat quite still. Bold stripes of pale blue and pink ran down the sides of its bright green body, its dinosaur neck lying flat against the line of his finger.

'Hungry, are you?' He brought the small creature to his face. 'Not many flies here, are there?' He glanced around as though looking for flies himself and the chameleon's eyes looked with him, independently.

The corners of Jim Audsley's mouth tipped into his crooked smile as he heard the sound of wagon wheels in the distance. 'I believe your next meal is on its way, Charlie.' He lifted his finger to the brim of his hat and watched the chameleon climb carefully back on to it. 'She owes me fifty per cent of that wagon, my friend, and a man doesn't turn his back on a deal.' But he knew that wasn't why he had come back for Prudence. She fascinated him.

'Whoa!' Prudence called as the oxen ploughed on towards her, their thick brown necks bent low against the wind. 'Whoa, Themba!' she called again, as their heaving bodies lumbered, threatening to tramp on and over her. Themba's shrill whistle pierced its way through the oxen's thick skulls and they came to a grunting stop.

Jim Audsley rode down the rise towards her. Themba saw him coming and led the small boy Jacob away towards the shade of a tree.

'Are you lost?' Prudence asked, tilting her head back aggressively as Audsley stopped his horse a few yards in front of her and smiled his crooked smile. 'Have you come back for your gun?' His smile grew wider. Prudence cleared her throat and tilted her chin up further, her eyes challenging him. 'You've come for your fifty per cent, have you?'

'Could be.'

'If you imagine for one moment you still have any claim . . .' Her voice died in her throat. He had climbed down from his horse and was moving towards her.

'I've learned to fire that gun since you abandoned me.' She tried to muster a note of authority, but he kept on coming. 'Themba?' His name crept out of her mouth unheeded as Jim Audsley came to a halt in front of her, his body so close she could feel him breathing.

'What do you want?' The air seemed confined, hot and tight, in the small space between them.

'My partner.' His eyes moved down to her breasts and his lips brushed her mouth, her nose, her eyelids. 'You.' His breath stroked her, and against her will Prudence reached for his mouth with hers.

'My name is Prudence.'

'Prudence.' His lips moved slowly to her mouth and Prudence felt her nipples rise hard against her shirt as his dry mouth found hers.

'Is this your normal manner of introduction?'

His hands ran down her sides and firmly gripped her buttocks. A hot wetness surged between her legs, but she pulled back sharply at a slight tickle on her forehead. She looked up as the chameleon's tail waved for a moment before curling itself again under the brim of his hat.

'You have a chamelon on your hat, Mr Audsley,' she said, moving her mouth back to his.

'Indeed I do.' His tongue licked gently over her lips.

'Why do you have a chameleon on your hat, Mr Audsley?' The chameleon had reminded her of Emily, and with that memory her mind went back into the past. At last M. Claudelle had vanished from it.

'Flies.' He lifted the chameleon off his hat on his finger and walked towards the oxen, setting it down on the wooden yoke of the wagon. He lifted his hand to stop Prudence as she moved up behind him. 'He needs to concentrate.'

Flies buzzed around the oxen. The chameleon's tongue flicked out, caught one, and rolled it back into its mouth. Its bottom jaw chewed like a toothless old man's, and its eyes rolled around in search of another as the last black thread of a fly leg disappeared in its wide flat mouth.

Themba nudged Jacob, muttered under his breath, and the small boy reluctantly looked away as Prudence and Jim Audsley moved arm in arm towards the wagon.

'What was that?' A copper kettle hanging from the side of the wagon had hit Audsley across the face as he crawled into the wagon towards her. He replaced it carefully before he sidled on, low to the wagon floor and Prudence.

'This will be more comfortable.' He pulled at an animal skin and ducked as a pile of skins fell on top of him. Prudence shook with laughter as he pushed the offending skins aside, but didn't hear the dull thud as something fell over on the crate above them. 'You're amused?' He grabbed her ankles and pulled her towards him, sliding her body under his.

She looked up at him with a rising passion which no laughter could hide and he felt the pull of sensuality in her eyes. Their lips touched and her mouth opened wide to him as his hand ran up her side and to her breasts. Her flesh rose against his palms as his lips moved down her neck in kisses.

'What's that?' He looked up as he felt a warm, wet drip on his head.

'It's honey.' Prudence's body rocked with laughter under his as she licked her lips. 'It was the honey jug you knocked over.' Her eyes sparkled with a mixture of humour and desire. 'We're covered in honey!'

He smiled, looking down at the honey dripping on to her body.

'We shouldn't waste it,' he said.

Themba looked up as another cry of delight burst through the stiff white sheets of the wagon tent and the wagon rocked noisily from side to side on its iron wheels. He glanced nervously at Jacob. He sat with his chin perched on his bony kneecap, gazing at the wagon in wonder. Themba dug his sharp black elbow into Jacob's ribs and the small boy turned his large brown eyes on to him without expression. Themba shut his eyes and leaned against the tree, indicating that the child must do the same.

After a moment's silence Jim Audsley's voice reached them.

'Partners?'

'Partners.' Prudence's voice was rich with the dark mellow tone of pleasure.

Chapter Twenty-one

Jack Marsden gripped the collar of his young brother's shirt, hauled him back, and threw him headlong towards a tree. Geoffrey's head thudded against the bark. He made no sound as his body crumpled but his arms went round the trunk. Jack leapt after him, grabbed his hair, and pulled his face back to smash it on the hard, knotted wood. But Geoffrey was already beaten. His cheeks were bruised and blood gushed from a wide cut over his eyes.

Overlooked by towering purple mountains, the peace of Bonne Esperance had been shattered. Years of childhood hatred had exploded in the body of a man. Jack Marsden was nineteen years old, lean and strong. Geoffrey was just over fifteen and no match for Jack's strength or bitterness.

'What in God's name are you doing?' John Westbury galloped towards them and jumped off his horse. 'Leave him, Jack!' Jack didn't hear or see him as he held Geoffrey against the tree with one hand and pulled the other fist back to hit him.

'I said let him go!' John's voice carried the authority of a man. He pulled his rifle from his saddle and fired a shot in the air. Jack paused and turned to him curiously, as if the blast had shocked him back to reality. 'Let him go,' John repeated quietly, and lowered the rifle, aiming it directly at Jack.

'You'd fire that?' Jack's eyes rested on the barrel. A thin wisp of smoke curled from it. 'You have business at Bonne Esperance?' he asked.

'I told you to let Geoffrey go.'

'And I asked what business you have on this land?' Jack dropped Geoffrey and turned his anger on John. His eyes ran over the clean arrogant lines of his face as he reached him. 'Do you speak as a lawyer, a neighbour or a trespasser?' There was an air of superiority about John Westbury and Jack despised him.

'I would hope as a friend.' John remained calm.

'Friend?' Jack glanced at his brother as he pushed himself up with his back against the tree. 'Did his mother order you to protect him?' He pointed angrily at Geoffrey. 'His mother's friend, are you?'

'She's your mother too.' John moved to the tree to help, but Geoffrey walked away.

'I'm not hurt. It's just a scratch. There's no need for you to stay.' The deep feelings of love he'd had for his brother as a child hadn't changed, though he still didn't understand why Jack hated him so much. He tried to wipe the blood from his eyes and smiled at John. 'I must wash.'

'That's right!' All reason in Jack had vanished. 'Wash yourself before Mother sees you! Go on! Wash yourself clean!'

'Jack!'

He fell silent at John's voice but his body shook with rage. He no longer knew at whom it was directed.

'Perhaps you'd like to talk to me.' John's voice was as practical as ever.

'About what would I talk to you?' Jack sneered.

'I think you need help.'

'I'm no longer a child, and I no longer need your advice, John Westbury!'

'Then perhaps you need this.' John held the rifle out to him. 'You could use it on your brother now you're no longer a child.' He paused as he noticed the glimmer of confusion in Jack's eyes, and played on it. 'Take it,' he urged. 'Go on.' He tested the moment. 'Use it.'

'Leave us alone.' Geoffrey moved between them defensively. John lowered his rifle, looked from one to the other, and turned to move back to his horse. He stopped, and slipped his hand inside his jacket.

'Perhaps you'd be kind enough to pass on this invitation from my mother to yours.' He held a parchment envelope out to Geoffrey. 'Your entire family is invited, of course.'

'Our family is good enough?' Jack watched the neat envelope as it passed from John to Geoffrey.

'It is my mother's invitation.' John's voice expressed no more warmth than his eyes. He turned away abruptly to his horse. Jack took in the broad shoulders and straight back in the well-tailored jacket, the long slim legs in sharply creased grey trousers. Everything about John Westbury reflected what he had become: a young man with a great future ahead of him as an attorney. He was everything Jack was not.

As John Westbury rode through the vineyards and out of the grounds of Bonne Esperance, Geoffrey watched his older brother. There was nothing in the world he wanted more than to reach him.

'It must be to introduce his fiancée, Sarah Ransome.' Geoffrey glanced at the invitation in his hand, then quickly rubbed it against his jacket as he noticed a spot of blood on it. 'I think you should give it to Mother.' He held it out to Jack.

'Haven't you ever wondered, Geoffrey?' Jack peered at him, his voice slow and quiet. 'About us? Our family?'

'No.' Geoffrey shrugged and touched his cut brow. The blood was beginning to dry.

'Do you believe what Mother tells you?' Jack's words were barbed.

'What about?'

'Do you want to know?' Jack moved closer to him and spoke in a confidential whisper. 'Do you want to know what our family really is? What our grandfather really is and where he goes? With whom he spends all his time? Do you want to know why John Westbury looks down on us?'

'Does he?' Geoffrey little cared; but Jack was talking to him. His brother had at last taken him into his confidence. 'Why should he look down on us?'

'Come.' Jack was already striding away.

'Where?' Geoffrey moved after him quickly, anxious not to lose his first contact with his brother.

Geoffrey's entire body was racked with pain as he rode with Jack towards Cape Town. He sensed a frightening darkness around his brother, but he said nothing. Jack seemed cut off from the rest of the world, locked inside his own mind, and far removed from him.

'I gave the invitation to Rosita. She said she'd clean it up and give it to Aunt Emily.' Geoffrey spoke casually, as if riding to

Cape Town without knowing why was an everyday occurrence. 'I also told her to say we'd gone fishing. All night, I said.' He glanced at Jack. 'We will be away all night?'

Jack nodded.

The throbbing pain over Geoffrey's eye drew his attention again and he held his hand over it. Jack glanced at him, and Geoffrey smiled quickly. 'It's healing,' he assured him.

Jack withdrew into his own world and Geoffrey allowed the movement of the horse to distract him from his pain as they rode on towards the mystery Jack was leading him to.

The small Malay fishing village was asleep, and the rows of tiny A-frame houses looked more dismal and meagre without the bustling life of daytime.

'Where are we?' Geoffrey asked warily as Jack got off his horse and stared at one particular door. 'What is this place?'

'You will come with me.' Jack grabbed the reins. 'You said you wanted to know about our grandfather.'

'But I don't understand. Where are we?'

'Come!' Jack grabbed him by the coat and hauled him down off the horse. A wiry-haired dog ran out from the dark between the houses and snapped at Jack's heels. Jack kicked it violently, catching it across the head with his boot, and the dog squealed, crawling away with a whimper. Geoffrey's blood ran cold. The fragile moments of tenderness which he'd tried to build between them had vanished.

Jack's boot smashed against the wooden door as they reached it and it burst open. Geoffrey fell into the room, pushed from behind by Jack.

'Look, Geoffrey! That's our noble grandfather Beauvilliers whose fine estate our mother wants us to fight for!' Jack's voice carved through the dark humidity of the small room. Geoffrey looked up from the rough floor, straining to make out the shape of someone who was stirring on the bed. He heard a voice; a woman's voice.

'Jacques?'

'Look at our grandfather, Geoffrey!' Jack's hand grabbed him by the collar again. Geoffrey's body was out of his control as he was flung across the room at the bed. 'That's the blood we carry! The blood of a man who only feels at home in the arms of a slave!

Look at them!'

Geoffrey's head was yanked back as Jack held him by the hair. His eyes were growing used to the dark and he could see his grandfather. He was in bed with a woman. The woman was naked and dark-skinned.

'That is what we are! Have no illusions, brother!'

The door slammed shut behind Geoffrey and Jack had gone. He groped in the empty space where Jack had been as he saw his grandfather rise and move towards him. He saw the dark woman pull white bedclothes around her. He felt sick. He wanted to scream but he couldn't.

'Geoffrey.' His grandfather made a move towards him and Geoffrey found his voice suddenly.

'Don't touch me!' He pulled back and away from Jacques, slipping as he fumbled towards the door. He ran outside and stood for a moment in a daze as wooden shutters and doors opened all around him. Dark faces peered at him. They were all around him. Dark, poverty-stricken faces with large hollows sunk into them instead of eyes.

'Geoffrey.' He heard his grandfather's voice, and found himself running. There suddenly was his horse, and he swung himself into the saddle.

'Go on,' he urged the horse between gulps of tears. 'I hate you!' he screamed back at his grandfather as the horse galloped away.

Jacques Beauvilliers stood in the doorway of Eva's house and watched his grandson ride away. Truth had shone a light into the dark corners of his life, and a young man had been destroyed.

Eva's hand touched his. 'Go to them, Jacques,' she said quietly. 'Go back where you belong.'

'Why?' His voice was flat. It carried death in it and Eva heard it.

'They are your grandsons,' she said.

'And John Westbury?' Jacques' eyes searched Eva's for an answer. 'Where do I belong, Eva?' he asked.

Jack walked beside Emily's chair as Rosita pushed it along the border of the vineyard. He was aware of his aunt's eyes on him. Geoffrey had convinced Clara that they had gone fishing that night, and that his injuries had been caused by a fall from his horse. But Aunt Emily appeared to believe none of it.

'Where did you take Geoffrey?' There was no accusation in Emily's voice but even so Jack looked away defensively, turning his attention to a vine. He examined the bark carefully.

'I'm not my brother's keeper.'

Emily glanced at the gnarled wood of the bare vine he stared at. 'Jack?' She cared for him deeply but had never found a way over the high wall he'd built about himself. He was so like her father, she thought. A stranger in his own world. 'Would you leave us alone please, Rosita,' she said.

'Yes, Mam.' Rosita touched Emily gently on the shoulder with a quick knowing glance at Jack. 'You will take care of Miss Emily.'

'Can you?' Emily asked as Rosita moved out of hearing. 'Can you care, Jack?'

'We were talking about Geoffrey.' Jack pushed the chair and the wooden wheels grated on the iron hubs, filling the awkward silence.

'I am talking about Geoffrey.' Emily shivered as a cool breeze ran through the lifeless vines. 'You took him to see your grandfather, didn't you?' The chair stopped. Although she felt slightly afraid she went on, 'You took him to my father and Eva. Am I right?'

'I thought it was time he knew.' Jack pushed the chair forward.

'Why?' Emily reached over her shoulder and touched his hand on the wood of her chair. 'Who were you trying to hurt?' She held his hand firmly under hers. 'Talk to me, Jack.'

Jack looked at her. Though fine lines of age had just begun to thread their way from the corners of her eyes and deeper lines of pain ran from her jaw down her neck, Emily still looked almost like a child. She reminded him of a bird with a broken wing.

'Who hurt you, Aunt Emily?' He moved around her chair and knelt in front of her. 'Who put you in this chair?'

Emily felt suddenly uncomfortable and looked away. 'I can see you have no intention of speaking to me, Jack,' she said brusquely.

'But I am speaking, Aunt Emily.'

'About what?' Emily found her temper rising against her better judgement, and she removed her hands from his. 'Perhaps you should call Rosita.'

'Can't you answer me?' It was as if Jack was trying to communicate for the first time in his life.

'You ask questions but you won't listen to answers!'

'You haven't given me one.' He turned away sharply.

Emily watched his shoulders as they bent forward in the same way they had when he was a small boy. She longed to get out of her chair and wrap her arms around him, to force his spirit to bend a little.

'Do you imagine the only way I can accept being crippled is by blaming someone else? Is that what you're trying to do, Jack?' Emily was aware of the slightest trembling in his body as he listened. 'Do you think your grandfather's love for Eva has anything to do with what you are, or what you feel for Geoffrey?'

'It has to do with what my mother feels for me!' Jack's voice had the bitter edge of rejection.

'How?' Emily had spotted a crack in the wall and tried to open it wider. 'Your mother's feelings can't change what you are.'

'What *does* she feel?' Jack turned to her suddenly. 'What is it about me she despises?'

'Oh no.' Emily shook her head sorrowfully. 'No.'

'No?' He leaned over her in the chair, forcing her to look at him. 'You know why, Aunt Emily.' His eyes were suddenly the eyes of the small boy she'd tried to comfort, and she couldn't bear it.

'Would you call Rosita back for me, please.'

'What is it about me, Aunt Emily?' he persisted.

'I'm tired. Please take me back to the house.' She wanted to pull him into her arms and tell him about his father, Charles Marsden. About the murder of Jean Jacques. About his mother's love for Geoffrey's father, Lieutenant Shaw, which was the root of the bitterness which ran so deeply in Clara. But she couldn't. It would destroy him further. 'Will you answer me one question?' she said instead. 'Can you love?'

The muscles on his jaw tightened as his teeth clenched. 'Perhaps I'm like my grandfather.' Jack's voice was dismissive. 'Not worthy of love.'

'Do you think "love" is judged by whom we love?' she challenged.

'It's true of John Westbury. Why else is his marriage to Sarah

Ransome causing such excitement than because he is bettering himself! Proving himself worthy.'

'Of what?'

'His mother. What more could she have hoped for from him.'

'And you envy him that?'

'I envy him that he is not me.'

Emily felt the breath drain from her body at the contempt in which Jack held himself. She had no answers to give him. There were no words of comfort. And to her dismay he had taken her thoughts back to the Westburys, to Pauline and Jean Jacques; to the approaching wedding . . .

The Westbury house had been in an upheaval of activity since the small hours of the morning. Floors had been scrubbed clean, windows buffed till they shone like mirrors, and furniture waxed to shimmering perfection.

Pauline watched her mother as they hung the chintz chair covers out to dry. They would receive the early warmth of the sun, and not be left out to fade as it reached its height. The day Pauline had secretly dreaded for years had arrived. Today, the girl her son intended to marry would be formally introduced.

Pauline had known Sarah Ransome since John had been at school with her. She had watched a childhood friendship develop into something far deeper as they grew, and the implications of their love terrified her. But her mother had chosen to ignore them. She had convinced herself that John was her own son, and a lie of twenty-odd years had proclaimed itself the truth.

'Aren't you at all worried, Mother?' Pauline pushed the wet covers away as the wind flapped them in her face.

'If he loves her it's quite natural they should marry. She comes from a fine English family.' Mary Westbury continued pegging the chintz covers to the rope line that stretched between two trees.

'Mother.' Pauline looked over the line at her. 'We can't pretend any more. We can't keep hiding behind a lie.'

'A lie?' Mary Westbury drew two more pegs from her apron pocket and moved along the rope.

'The only people who matter now are John and Sarah. I owe them the truth. They will have children.' A cock crowed, and Pauline waited. 'You must accept it.'

'Accept?' Mary's hand thrust another peg on to the line and it broke in her fingers. She tossed the two pieces of splintered wood to one side and turned on her daughter aggressively. 'When you brought the disgrace of a half-caste child on to your father and me, you insulted everything we stood for. You violated our very being! Now you tell me I must accept it?' She snatched another peg from her apron. 'The only truth is that I brought John up as my child, I devoted my life to wiping out your shame.' She clipped the peg to the line. 'Now I see you are prepared to insult me again.'

'Who do the lies insult?' Pauline moved to her and reached out to touch her. 'Mother.' Mary pulled her angular shoulders away. 'They insult John and the girl he wants to marry.'

Mary hung up the remaining covers then picked up the empty laundry basket and swept away to the house. Pauline followed her hurriedly.

'And they insult Jean Jacques! The only man I ever loved!' Her mother stopped. 'That is the truth John must know. That I loved his father.'

Mary turned back to her slowly and Pauline noticed the folds of ageing flesh around her neck. Her eyes were paler than she remembered them, and the lids drooped in paper-thin hoods.

'You are going to tell him?'

'Yes.' Pauline looked at her mother and met a look she had only seen once before: when she had asked her what they would do to her child if he was born dark. 'I must tell him the truth.'

'Tell him and I will deny your every word!' Mary straightened her back and tucked the laundry basket firmly under her arm. 'Yours will be the lie, Pauline.'

John Westbury had left the house the moment he awoke. He didn't like the smell of polish and soap, but he understood it was necessary. Today was a big day in his mother's life and he would enjoy it as much as she did.

'I see Mother's keeping you busy,' he said as Pauline walked past him to empty a bucket of dirty water. 'I'm sure Sarah will be impressed.'

'Does that matter?'

John caught the edge in Pauline's voice and moved after her. 'It's not my fault you've never married, Pauline.'

Pauline turned and looked at him. He reacted to the hard line of her mouth, and laughed defensively, turning away slightly. 'Very well. It is my fault.'

'We need to talk,' Pauline said quietly.

John waited. He didn't know why but he was on edge. She held the bucket out to him and glanced back at the house.

'You want to ensure I really am in love?' He took the bucket from her.

'Perhaps.' She walked with him away from the house down a gravelled path.

'I had no idea what love was until I found it with Sarah. Have you ever felt it?' He looked down. 'I'm sorry.'

'I have, John.' Pauline stopped and faced him. 'I do know what love is. Yes.'

'Who was he?' John's face lit with sudden curiosity. 'I didn't know.'

'He died.'

'Is that why you've never talked about him?'

'John.' Pauline ran her hand down his arm and took his hand. 'What I'm going to tell you is hard for me to tell and harder for you to hear. But I want you to listen with your heart.'

'You don't have to tell me anything, Pauline.' John was embarrassed by his sister's growing emotion. 'Where do you want the water?'

'We had a child, John.' Her hand clasped his. 'You are the child.'

John's hand didn't move in hers. No part of his body moved, but his eyes flickered as if a distant inner knowledge had been touched.

'You are my child but I had to let you go.' Pauline felt tears burning in her eyes. 'I even let your father go as I did you.'

'Who?' John's voice was dead. Pauline put her other hand on his shoulder. 'Who was he?'

'His name was Jean Jacques . . .' Pauline felt the water from the bucket splash on to her feet. John had dropped it and moved away. She ran after him, but as she did he ran further. 'He was the only man I ever loved, John, and he loved you!' she cried after him.

'*He was a half-caste!*' The venom behind John's words slapped Pauline in the face. 'He was the son of a slave. He was black.'

'John!' She moved to him and held him by the shoulders.

'Don't touch me!' John's voice spat hatred, and he pushed her hands roughly off his shoulders.

'But what difference does it make?' Tears poured down Pauline's cheeks as she watched her son hold himself rigidly away from her. 'I told you I loved him.' She ran after him as he walked away again. 'Please listen to me.' But he ran on without heeding, disappearing into the stables. She jumped back as his horse burst through the stable doors. 'John!' she cried, but he raced past her, his head low over the horse's back as it galloped away. There was nothing she could do to stop him.

'You bitch! You shameless slut!' her mother screamed at her as she hurried from the house. 'Now tell me you were right to put your guilt on his shoulders! It's your shame, not his!'

'Shame? Guilt?' Pauline found herself moving towards her mother, driven by a deep anger. 'Is that all my son ever meant to you?'

'Pauline.' Mr Westbury had followed Mary out of the house and now tried to step between his wife and daughter. 'I'll find him and bring him back.'

'Back to what?' Pauline shouted. 'To a woman who regards him as a cross to bear? No!' She moved in slow determined strides past her father and on towards her mother. 'I saw John's face when he heard the truth. He was ashamed. My son was ashamed because of you!' she screamed in her mother's face.

'But you never were!' her mother screamed back.

'Please! Calm yourselves,' Mr Westbury tried again.

'Of what was I to be ashamed?' Pauline's voice overrode her father's attempts. 'But now I can see what Jean Jacques had to live with. What insults he had to bear because the colour of his skin was something people like you couldn't accept. It is *you* who are less. Not my son!'

'How dare you!' Mary swung her hand and slapped Pauline hard across the face.

'I dare because you have made the wonderful man who was my son disappear among the rubbish of your prejudice!' Pauline's face was red and tears rolled down her cheeks. 'But if it's true, Mother, if it's true he is less, then it would have been best had you killed him at birth!'

Pauline stormed into the house and slammed the gauze fly door behind her.

The wood frame shut against the sudden silence.

'Pauline is right, Mary,' Mr Westbury said quietly.

'Pauline is wrong!' His wife looked at him coldly. 'And I will deny what she has told him as long as I live.'

John Westbury didn't know where he was riding to, or what he was riding from. His brain felt as if it had been squeezed like a lump of dough. The sun was directly overhead and its bright white light burned fiercely. His horse was foamed with sweat and pulled its head back as he forced it on, until he felt a desperate need to rest. He allowed it to stop and slid off its back, dropping to the ground near a tree. He hauled himself under its shade. His head throbbed. He was mentally exhausted and his identity had been torn in two.

He leaned back against the tree, remembering Jack's black friend, Sunday. The sharp distaste he felt for all blacks pressed itself between his tongue and the roof of his mouth. He remembered the day of Jean Jacques' memorial and the faint embarrassment he'd felt, even so young, that his sister had come to the grave of a half-caste. But he was a half-caste himself. That man had been his father.

John's eyes moved down to his bare arm. His skin was tanned. He scratched his fingers over it and dug in his nails. They left short sharp white marks, but he knew that was not what it was about and he felt suddenly sick.

His body heaved and his stomach ejected a burning acid liquid. He shut his eyes tightly as pain stabbed his right temple and his body shook. He could hardly see.

He tried to keep his head still. Through the nightmarish pain and distorted vision of a migraine, images loomed at him. The memory of a Malay man begging outside the solicitors' offices of Mather and Beuselinck in Long Street where he worked. As though looking in a mirror he saw the contempt in his own face as the beggar held his brown hands up to him.

'If they cleared the streets of these people, Cape Town would be a healthier place,' he'd commented to Sarah and moved past the man quickly; not wanting the man's eyes to touch her.

The migraine lifted suddenly, and in the brief clarity of the moment he knew he still felt the same way. But now he was one of them.

His head cracked as if an axe had sliced into it and the migraine returned with more fury. He closed his eyes and tried to lie still but his body shook violently. He could see himself as he lay under the shade of the tree. Another one of the halfbreeds he despised. Then he realized he was crying. The halfbreed under the tree was crying. Shudders of emotion deepened the pain in his head but he couldn't stop. He was lost in the wilderness of prejudice bred into him, and looking for himself.

A voice called to him from a long way off.

'John? John Westbury?'

He peered into the red of his closed eyelids and saw the image of a man. The man was Jacques Beauvilliers. A man whom Mary Westbury, the woman he'd thought of as his mother, looked on as the lowest and most despicable of men. That man was his own flesh and blood, his grandfather. His body jerked over and his stomach emptied itself again of the bile and acid which filled him.

'John Westbury hasn't yet returned home.' Emily dipped her pen into the inkwell as she wrote her diary in the privacy of her bedroom. 'Pauline blames herself for what's happened; for allowing her mother's prejudice to grow like a weed in her own son. She's thinking of returning to England.' Emily looked up from her diary with a thought.

'How could the colour of a man's skin change who he was?' Her head filled with Jean Jacques' voice. 'I have to prove myself worthy of being his father, Emily.' Jean Jacques' face shone in front of her for a brief moment. 'Prove it to whom, Jean Jacques?' she asked out loud.

'Emily?' She quickly closed the diary and replaced the pen. 'Are you up?' Clara called from outside her door.

'Come in.' Emily opened a book and pretended to read as the door opened and Clara stepped in. Whenever Clara came into a room, the room felt smaller. Though nearly fifty, the age at which Emily had once thought all people should die, Clara was still a striking woman.

'Is there any news of John Westbury?' she asked as she perched straight-backed on the corner of Emily's bed. The enormous rings of her crinoline stood out in front of her. They looked ridiculous, Emily thought, but she said nothing.

'I haven't heard.' Emily turned back to her book. 'Why are you interested?' She knew Clara seldom asked about anyone unless it affected her directly. 'I didn't think you had much time for the Westbury family.' She was terrified Clara had somehow found out why John Westbury had left, and remembered what she had written in her diary almost a quarter of a century earlier when he was born: 'I swear this day that Clara will never know of the child of Pauline and Jean Jacques.'

'I was concerned for Mrs Westbury.' Clara's eyes skimmed over the room as though looking for the source of a bad smell. 'He was, after all, very special to her.' She pushed the front of the crinoline down. 'What do the Boers call a late child? A laat . . .'

'A laat lammetjie,' Emily said for her.

'What an ugly language it is.' Clara's top lip curled down over her teeth as though wiping it from her mouth. 'He had, of course, proved himself beyond even his mother's expectations. It is all such a great shame. Very shameful.'

'What is, Clara?' Emily closed the book. 'Are you talking about Sarah Ransome?'

'Perhaps her family decided against it.' Clara brushed a speck of imaginary dirt from her skirt. 'After all, they sent their daughter to the Cape to clear her chest, not marry a sheep farmer.'

'John Westbury isn't a sheep farmer.' Emily tried to control her irritation. 'He is an extremely promising attorney.'

'Yes.' Clara pulled a stray hair back from her face. 'He has done very well . . . considering.'

'Considering what?'

'He is hardly from a privileged background.'

'I'm sorry, Clara, I'm really not interested in discussing it.'

'One must accept the facts of one's position in life.'

'Then what is Jack's position?' Emily faced Clara. 'Jack does, after all, stand to inherit his father's title.'

Clara dismissed Emily with a small huff, stood up and moved to the door.

'By the by, I'm thinking of having some improvements made to the house,' Clara changed the subject.

'There's nothing wrong with the house.'

'The house is run down, Emily! It might even be better to build another.'

'Clara!' Emily was genuinely shocked. 'Run down or not, this is our home!'

'You obviously haven't visited the houses around us recently, Emily.' Clara smiled from the door. 'I'm afraid your Protestant leanings towards poverty are out of date. Everyone is improving their home. The vineyards are booming and we must reflect our status. We must use the money to improve our standing.'

'Have you forgotten that the British government might soon remove its taxes from French wines? Lord Palmerston is already talking of it. And Prudence said it would happen.'

'Prudence said many things, Emily,' Clara dismissed her with the disdain she still felt. 'Too many.'

'And most of them appear to have been right,' Emily added abruptly.

'Then where is she now?' Clara allowed herself another smile. 'Trading? I believe that was what you heard of her last. In animal skins, gunpowder and sheep?'

'Why!' Emily's voice was flat but insistent. 'Do you imagine a fine house will turn this family into something it is not?'

'What this family had snatched away from it!' Clara's voice was spiked by the bitterness her years had served only to heighten. 'Dignity!'

'Do you expect Geoffrey to restore your dignity?' Emily was filled with amazement. 'Or Jack?'

Clara looked at her coldly, and turned away as though Emily's question was unworthy of an answer. She pulled the door closed behind her.

'Perhaps it will be John Westbury?' Emily said wonderingly into the silence.

Jacques Beauvilliers had not been back to Bonne Esperance since his grandsons had burst into his life with Eva. He had spent days alone on the beach watching the fishermen hauling in their catch. The nights he'd spent deep in thought.

As the sun dipped over the edge of the horizon and dived beneath the sea, he took a last deep breath of lively salt air and began to climb back up to the village, and Eva.

His head held low against the wind and his body stooped forward, he trod barefoot towards the narrow path up the cliff, trousers rolled up to his knees and the wide sleeves of his white shirt puffing out as they filled with the wind.

He stopped to get his breath and his feet sank deeper into the soft sand. He looked up towards the village and remembered how he used to run all the way without pausing for breath. He remembered the beautiful young Eva standing on the cliffs waiting for him. But the years had passed, and those years were the reason he'd been lost in thought. They could only be faced when he was certain to whom he belonged.

He lowered his head, took another deep breath and pressed on with his climb. But he stopped. An image of what he had not seen, but had looked at, replayed in his mind. A young man was standing at the base of the cliffs. The slim figure stood quite still. The outline of the body shimmered as the glow of dying sunlight reflected up from the sand around it. Jacques' mouth moved silently, and his lips parted as if in mid-sentence.

The young man walked towards him, and the closer he got, the faster Jacques' heart beat; until, as they stood face to face, he could hardly hear for its drumming.

'Grandfather?' John Westbury said. He met Jacques' dark-brown eyes and saw the wonder of a small boy trapped inside the body of an old man.

Jacques lowered his head, raised his right hand and laid it on John Westbury's shoulder without looking at him. The fingers of his hand hesitated, then pressed, and he pulled his grandson to him.

The night had been long but nobody was tired. Eva produced food and her eyes danced between Jacques and their grandson. The dignity of her youth had returned. Only the long plait of hair with grey streaks threading through it betrayed the years during which Jean Jacques' son had grown into the man John Westbury was now. Although there was nothing about the handsome blond man that resembled her son, Eva could feel the spirit of Jean Jacques in her small house again.

'You go to Sarah and you tell her.' Jacques leant away from the table and looked across the empty plates which Eva was clearing away quickly and silently. 'She loves *you*, John. Not what you're supposed to be.'

'How do I tell her?' John didn't understand why, but he felt totally at home in the small dark room. He felt as though he'd known Eva and Jacques all his life; but confusion stirred the edges of his soul.

The man he had grown up to think of as his father was his grandfather, as Jacques was. His mother was his grandmother and his sister was his mother. He lowered his head as the confusion blinded him for a moment and then he looked up towards Eva.

'Why didn't they tell me the truth?' he asked. 'Why so much fear?'

'Why?' Jacques nodded. 'Why indeed.' He sought John's eyes and took his hand in his own. 'But fear isn't always for ourselves, John.'

Eva watched the two men reaching out to one another across the table.

'Tell me about him.' John held on to his grandfather's hand tightly. There was an unexpected security in the warm hard fingers which threaded through his own. 'Tell me about my father.'

Chapter Twenty-two

The lazy Sunday-afternoon silence was broken by the clatter of horses' hooves on the cobbled Wynberg street. A ginger cat looked up, stretched its back and arrogantly padded across the road in front of the horses. Jacques Beauvilliers looked down at the cat as his horse sidestepped it and the feathery tip of its ginger tail brushed cheekily up its leg. He turned to smile at John Westbury riding beside him and remembered when he'd come to visit his grandson: unable to speak to him except as a neighbour, and unable to tell him the truth of who he was.

But now he could feel a silent bond of trust between them, as though the past was not as he remembered it. Only the backdrop of the mountain, with its halo of wispy white clouds, was the same. Jacques fancied he could detect a smile on its massive stony face.

'Mr and Mrs Robertson are Sarah's guardians.' John glanced at his grandfather as they rode. 'But they're more of a mother and father to her than her own now.' His voice was flat and practical.

'Her parents are in England?' Jacques sensed that John was diverting himself from what was to come.

'She was sent to school in the Cape for her health and she stayed.'

Jacques pulled up his horse a few houses away from the school as he felt John losing courage. He reached across and touched John's hands, which clenched the reins tightly.

'You told me Sarah loved you.' Jacques' quiet voice offered the wisdom of his years. 'That's why she stayed.'

'Yes,' John said without conviction, 'that's right.'

*

Sarah ran down the stairs two at a time as she heard the front door open and James Robertson exclaim loudly, 'John Westbury! My word!' His headmaster voice was raised in excitement as he called, 'Sarah! John's back!'

Sarah wanted to throw herself into his arms as she came down the stairs, but she held herself back. She didn't know why her visit to his parents' home had been cancelled and had imagined the worst, that John had changed his mind.

Her foot reached out for the bottom stair, she steadied herself against the banisters, terrified to take the last step. The fears of the last week leapt out and jeered at her again. He had come to tell her the truth, that he no longer wanted to marry her. Her delicate pointed chin tilted up. The tears which had flowed so continuously pricked at her eyes and nose. She set her mouth into a welcoming smile as James Robertson stepped to one side, revealing John.

'Sarah?' John's voice was timid as he came towards her.

'Hello, John.' She kept her eyes averted, certain all he could see was the plain girl he'd rejected just in time.

'Do you remember Mr Beauvilliers?' John turned to his grandfather and politely held a hand out towards Sarah. 'Sarah Ransome.' He caught Jacques' eye in a momentary pause and added, 'My grandfather.'

Jacques saw the sudden confusion in Sarah and moved to her quickly. 'We have met before.' Sarah smiled shyly as he took her hand and he saw the English porcelain looks of his first wife, Emily.

'I believe Sarah and John need time to talk,' he said to Mr Robertson as he retreated to the door.

'Must you go?' James Robertson blustered. He was out of his depth in the silent emotion around him and uncertain what was expected of him. He moved to Jacques with a clumsy gesture of welcome. Two fingers were held slightly apart as if a piece of chalk was permanently between them. 'May I offer you some tea?' His puzzled frown gave way to a quick bright smile as his eyes lit with a thought. 'My wife is in the next room. Come through, please.' He held out an open hand towards Jacques and dropped his imaginary piece of chalk.

'I'm afraid I have a long way to travel home.' Jacques glanced at Sarah and John. Their eyes were fixed on one another. 'When you are ready I hope to see you both at Bonne Esperance.' A weight dropped from Jacques' shoulders as he looked at the two young people. 'Thank you, Mr Robertson.' He smiled warmly as he turned back to him. 'Goodbye.'

'Well,' James Robertson said to the oak door with its round brass knob as it closed after Jacques. 'Well.' He moved his weight from one foot to the other as if wondering which to talk to. He was an intruder in his own schoolhouse and didn't know how to behave. 'No tea!' He looked up and brushed an imaginary chalk mark from his lapel. 'Perhaps you would like a cool drink?' He knew they were not listening and smiled politely as he backed towards the door and escape.

'The covers on these books are a disgrace!' James Robertson stepped back quickly as his wife pushed her way through the door in front of him. A precarious pile of books was balanced in her arms, held steady by her chin.

'John!' Her chin lifted in surprise and Mr Robertson watched in horror as the precious books began to slide. 'Where on earth have you been? Have you any idea how worried we were?'

'Elizabeth!' James Robertson tried to call her back with his headmaster's tone as he picked up the fallen books. 'You're dropping the books, Elizabeth!' he said stupidly. 'Don't mind us,' he muttered, trying to drag her away. 'Excuse us.' James snatched up the last of the books and bundled her into the schoolhouse.

Alone in the hallway with Sarah, John tentatively held out his hand to her in the silence.

'I need to talk to you.' His voice was solemn and it terrified Sarah.

'I'm listening,' she said quietly.

'May we go outside?'

'Perhaps you should tell me here.' Sarah lowered her head, waiting for the blow to fall. 'I'm not dressed to go out.' She fingered the delicate blue daydress she wore. John took her hand and lifted it between his own.

'Please,' he said simply.

Sarah sat up in front of John as the horse clopped slowly down the street. The green shutters against the whitewashed walls of the houses seemed to her like ears pinned back in an attempt to hear every word that passed between them.

'Whatever you want to do now, I will accept your decision.' John's voice was matter-of-fact, the lawyer's practised separation of emotion and fact. He had told her the truth of his identity in the same emotionless voice. 'I would understand if you no longer wished to marry me,' he finished.

'Then perhaps you would help me off this horse before you "let me go"?' Sarah felt her body bend into his. 'I thought you'd left me, John.' The relief in her voice conveyed her fears of rejection. 'Why would I leave you now?' John's spirits lifted at her light tone. 'When you asked me to marry you I said yes. I told you all I wanted was to be your wife and the mother of your children. You believed me then.' She turned herself around on the horse and put her arms around his neck. 'Why should my feelings be different because you tell me your father isn't who you thought he was?' She rubbed her nose against his. 'Must I jump off the horse myself?'

'But everything's different, Sarah.'

'Have your feelings changed?' She ran her finger across his mouth. 'I don't see anything different about you.' She paused and her face lost its joy for a moment. 'But I do have a bone to pick.' She pulled back and his heart froze. 'Do you know how awful it feels when the only person you've ever loved disappears without a word? I felt so silly that I had ever imagined you could love me.'

A laugh stirred deep inside John as he listened to her.

'All I wanted was to die.' She looked at him seriously, as if her life depended on him. 'You really do love me?' Her bright eyes grew perplexed as the laughter inside him spilled over. 'You're making fun of me!'

'Yes.' John held her tightly. 'I am.'

The snare of prejudice which had nearly destroyed him had sprung as wide as the freedom from which Sarah's love flowed. He'd told her he was a half-caste and it had passed over her head without touching her.

Geoffrey had seen his grandfather ride in to Bonne Esperance and had quickly ducked out of sight, hiding himself at the side of the house. The sight of Jacques had slung him back into the small close room in which he'd seen his grandfather and the dark woman on that terrible night.

He paced the ground as an argument raged inside the house and his mother's raised voice reached him.

'I refuse to believe you!' Clara sounded hysterical. 'It's a lie!'

Geoffrey's stomach churned as childhood memories were stirred by her shouts. Shouts of hatred which had lashed out at his brother Jack, as a whip did. He tried to shut out her voice but couldn't, and he walked away from the house. His walk turned to a run as his grandfather's voice chased after him.

'You will accept what I am telling you, Clara!' Jacques lowered his voice and tried to regain the calm with which he had begun as he faced his daughter across the sitting-room. 'John Westbury is the son of Jean Jacques and my legitimate heir.'

'Never!' Clara screamed and covered her ears. 'I will not listen to more of your lies!'

'Please,' Emily tried to pacify her sister. 'Father has told you the truth.' Clara turned her eyes on to Emily coldly.

'You knew about this?' she murmured.

Emily nodded and Clara felt the floor quake a little under her feet. Her mind raced back in time, back to a small dark boy in her father's arms, a dark boy racing bareback along the beach. Jean Jacques was still there in the midst of their lives.

'But he's dead,' Clara whispered almost inaudibly. 'Jean Jacques is dead!' Her voice rose on a scream of defiance. 'Dead!'

'He had a child,' Emily said quietly.

'No. It's not true.'

'Why would I lie about such a thing?' Jacques reached out to her.

'Don't touch me!' She pulled herself back into the steel cage of her body and locked Jean Jacques out of it. 'You've lied to me always!' Rejection screeched in her voice as her thoughts leapt to Eva. 'You lied to my mother. You took my mother's love, you took her money to build Bonne Esperance, and you threw it to swine!' Her voice dropped to a hiss and her eyes darted arrows poisoned by memory. 'Jean Jacques is dead.' She backed towards the door. 'Dead.'

'Leave her, Father,' Emily cried as he moved to go after Clara and the door slammed shut in his face. The light Emily had seen in Jacques' eyes when he returned to Bonne Esperance had gone, and he seemed suddenly very old. His legs were slightly bent, his back was stooped and his head low into his chest.

'Are you all right?' She wheeled her chair towards him. 'Father?'

'It's too late.' Jacques turned to his youngest daughter, his face grey and his eyes dull. 'I can remember the child Clara was.' He paused and took a breath. His mouth opened slightly and his eyes narrowed, as though he had just seen clearly into the past. 'I destroyed her.'

A small flat white stone bounced its way across the surface of the brown water as Geoffrey sat on the river bank. He took another stone between his thumb and middle finger and swung his arm back to throw it, but something made him stop. He ran the flat stone down his thumb with his finger until it fell into his palm. He curled his fingers tightly around it and looked back the way he'd come. His mother's shrill voice still rang in his ears.

He'd never spoken to anybody about the night Jack had dragged him to his grandfather, but he knew that what was happening in the house now was a part of it. A strange sense of release filled him. He stood up and looked back at the house. He had no idea why, but he knew that the reason his grandfather and his mother hated one another somehow contained his freedom.

'Your grandfather's tired,' Emily said warningly when Geoffrey returned.

'Let him be.' Jacques put his hand over Emily's and patted it. He smiled very slightly into Geoffrey's clear wide eyes. 'I think perhaps we need to talk.'

'I would like to.' Geoffrey glanced at Emily. 'I'll sit with him, if you'd like me to.'

'He thinks I'm dying,' Jacques said.

'No.' Geoffrey was immediately embarrassed. 'I'm sorry.'

'Never be sorry,' Jacques said quietly.

Emily looked from the old man approaching the end of his life to the young man on the threshold of his. She ran her hands down the arms of her wheelchair, stroking the wood, then on to the wheels and propelled herself to the door.

'I'll be with Clara if you need me,' she said.

'You ran away when I arrived,' Jacques said quietly as the door closed behind her. 'Why?'

'I was afraid.' Geoffrey raised his blue eyes to Jacques. 'What is it between you, Grandfather?' Though on the verge of manhood, Geoffrey was still a cosseted child, Jacques thought.

'Between your mother and myself?' Jacques narrowed his eyes to see him more clearly. He took a long breath and let it out slowly before he spoke again. 'She adores you. Never forget that, Geoffrey.' Jacques' fingers pulled gently on a button of his waistcoat and twisted it. He released it and watched it turn slowly as it unwound. 'What has Jack told you?'

'I want you to tell me,' Geoffrey said quietly.

Feeling the warmth from his young grandson Jacques suddenly realized why he had known such loneliness. He had alienated himself from his own flesh and blood.

'It's a long story,' he said. Geoffrey moved to a chair, lifted it and placed it beside his grandfather. 'All I've ever wanted is to ensure that my son's place in this land is never forgotten.' He paused, seemingly lost in thought. 'If you understand that, I think you might understand everything else.'

'When was the child supposedly born?' Clara had not looked at Emily at all as she had told her the story of Jean Jacques and Pauline. Her moment of near insanity had left her mind crystal clear and she rapidly assessed each piece of information Emily gave her. 'Pauline must have been almost a child herself if what you say is true.'

'I saw the baby, Clara. I held him. And it was I who took him to Jean Jacques.' Emily had her feelings under control.

'So, you were there when John Westbury was born?' For the first time Clara turned to Emily. Her eyebrows arched. 'How extraordinary!'

'Of course I wasn't there, Clara! But I know.'

'How? How do you know John Westbury is Pauline's child? Jean Jacques' child!' Clara spat. 'Tell me that.'

'I know because it's the truth.' Emily squared her shoulders in the face of Clara's disbelief. 'Pauline will tell you herself if you care to ask her.'

'And I should believe her?' Clara laughed. It was an empty laugh. 'I suppose I should believe Mrs Westbury too. A woman whose only ambition in life is to better herself would, of course, never lie in order to add Bonne Esperance to her aspirations!'

'Perhaps she would.' Emily was talking to herself as she remembered what Pauline had told her about her mother.

'Pardon? I didn't hear you.' Clara picked up Emily's mistake eagerly. 'Did you say Mrs Westbury would lie?'

'For her own reasons, I doubt she's any happier the truth has come out than you are, Clara.' The moment the words left Emily's mouth she regretted them. Clara's body had straightened with a new-found strength.

'If you'll excuse me I'd like to rest,' Clara said, and Emily felt the hard ring of Clara's crinoline brush past her. 'Would you come and get Miss Emily, Rosita.' Clara's voice was bright. 'She wishes to leave my room.'

Mrs Westbury poured the tea from the silver-plated teapot, and tried hard to steady her shaking hand. Clara's apparent interest in their well-being had not deceived her. She had come on the pretext of delivering a wedding present for John and Sarah. She'd heard, she said, that they had already married in Cape Town and that Pauline was leaving for England.

'So much has happened in the last weeks,' Clara went on. 'It is, of course, not unnatural that Pauline would want to leave now.'

The teacup rattled on the saucer as Mrs Westbury lifted it, and a little tea slopped over the lip. 'I'm so sorry. I'll fetch another cup.' Mrs Westbury glanced at her husband, who sat stiffly to the side of the room. He was keeping himself away from both women. 'Perhaps you would pour Clara's tea while I get one.' She left the room hurriedly.

'Is your wife quite well?' Clara turned to Mr Westbury, and smiled with seeming concern.

The cup and saucer clattered on to the kitchen table and Mary Westbury leaned over it, holding herself steady with one hand on either side of it. The tea had tipped over the lip and filled the saucer. She fixed her eyes on a splash of tea as it spread quickly across the red gingham check of the table cloth.

'Mary.' Her husband was at her side. 'I'll tell Clara you're unwell and ask her to leave.'

'I'm perfectly all right.' She lifted her head and rested it back against him. 'Perhaps you would bring a clean cup through for me.' She had steadied her nerves, and looked at the spilled tea as if it were his fault. 'You'd best soak the cloth in cold water.'

'You know why that woman is here, Mary.' Mr Westbury moved after her. 'Why can't you leave it be. Let her think what she chooses.'

'Do you imagine I would allow her to get away with her arrogant accusations?' Her mouth turned down. 'Oh no! She will not pass the disgrace of her family on to mine!'

'Mary.' Mr Westbury lowered his head in the face of her determination. 'There is only one truth and, for all our sakes, I beg you to accept it.'

'Yes,' she smiled, 'there *is* only one.' She turned to the door with her truth brandished firmly in front of her.

A gilt-framed painting of John Westbury as a small boy hung proudly over the mantelpiece and Clara was disturbed by it. Something about the eyes reminded her of Jean Jacques. But in another way the painting itself encouraged her. The pride of position it held in the room meant something.

'I'm so sorry about that. What with John's wedding and Pauline's aunt dying so suddenly in England, I really am a little tired.' Mrs Westbury bustled into the room and sat down quickly. 'I presume when you spoke of Pauline you were referring to the rumours which even I have heard. I'm sure you are aware they are totally without foundation.' She smiled. 'But it was kind of you to consider Pauline's feelings in the matter.'

'It's the least I could do. I'm afraid my father is an old man who has quite simply been used.' Clara glanced at Mr Westbury as he stepped into the room with the clean cup and saucer. 'You know what these people are like as well as I do.'

'Perhaps you would pour the tea, darling.' Mrs Westbury turned back to Clara. 'I do, of course. But how unfortunate it is for your family. Such malicious gossip must be very upsetting; and of course it's not the first time,' she added gently.

Clara took the cup from Mr Westbury but avoided his eyes. 'We are quite aware of the lengths some people will go to in order to destroy what they cannot have. Bonne Esperance has always provoked envy.' She looked at Mrs Westbury with a sudden thought. 'But then of course it's quite possible that it's John they are trying to destroy.' She glanced at the painting over the mantelpiece. 'I hear he is doing very well. And he's such a handsome young man. A scandal would most certainly do him no good. Or his marriage.'

Mr Westbury turned away and closed his eyes. Every word the two women said was aimed at the other, and every one found him.

'I doubt such ridiculous stories would ever reach the ears of Sarah or the people John mixes with,' Mrs Westbury bounced Clara's threat back at her. 'But it must be so difficult for your family to live here in the midst of such talk. Wineland people haven't the sophistication to know what breeds it.'

Mr Westbury left the room, barely noticed by the two women. All he could think of was his daughter about to sail to England. He had lost her and his grandson, but what hurt him most was the loss of his own courage.

'We've learned to tolerate their hunger for gossip.' Clara gazed over her cup as she sipped her tea, then lowered it thoughtfully. 'Doubtless you've heard the old stories yourself; about a young labourer who used to work for us.'

'A labourer?' Mrs Westbury opened her eyes wide in apparent curiosity. 'I have never paid any attention to gossip, Clara. Mind you, how on earth your poor father stood for such talk I shall never know.'

'Because it's more difficult for a man to disprove such things.' Clara set her cup down on the crocheted cover protecting the chair arm. 'You will, of course, be able to ensure the gossip about your son is stopped.' She paused and smiled. 'The doctor who attended you during your confinement will doubtless put a halt to it.'

'That won't be necessary,' Mrs Westbury said with more confidence. 'I need nobody to confirm the birth of my own child, Clara.'

'Of course.' Clara stood up. She had heard all she needed and could see no point in staying longer. 'I simply wanted to reassure you that there is no way my family would ever have believed such nonsense.'

'But you came to make certain?' Mrs Westbury couldn't resist one last strike and Clara looked up in surprise. 'There is no way my son would ever lower himself to make a claim on Bonne Esperance, Clara. You may rest assured of that.'

Clara straightened her dress and her full breasts pushed forward against the buttons of her bodice.

'Such a thing never entered my head. Thank you for the tea,' she smiled, as her trap sprung neatly closed around Mrs Westbury.

The screech of gulls, the loud bartering of boatmen and the calls of fishermen shouting the delights of stumpnose, roman nose and snook added to the bustle of Cape Town's docks. The tall ship stood in the offing ready to set sail on the voyage to England, and lightering boats flitted between it and the dock, bobbing in the swell beyond the harbour wall.

John Westbury pulled Sarah and Pauline back as a huge net of fish was tipped out beside them. The brilliant orange markings on the fish heads gleamed in the sunlight as they writhed in a useless effort to return to the safety of the sea. Pauline looked at the now confident young man with his arms around Sarah and herself. She knew she would never forget the look on his face when she'd told him his true parentage; but it was the memory of his simple, secret wedding to Sarah that she would cherish. It had been a symbol of the marriage to Jean Jacques which had been snatched from her.

'Pardon?' The wind howled through the docks and Pauline held on to her hat tightly as she tried to hear her son over the noise.

'He said we would write to you!' Sarah shouted.

'I still can't hear you,' Pauline called as a grinning Malay boy walked up to them with a stick strung with glassy-eyed fish.

'You want fish? Cheap fish?' he shouted, but John took Pauline's arm and guided her away from the crowds towards the boats.

'I'll look after the luggage,' Sarah called after them.

'There's no reason for you to go. You do know that.' John looked directly at her.

'You need to be free to start a new life.' Pauline paused. 'And my mother.'

'It's the same life.' John lowered his head with a smile.

'Why are you smiling?' Pauline asked.

'I have just realized how much I got away with when you were my sister.'

'She's a lovely girl.' Pauline glanced at Sarah then back at her son. 'You are so like Jean Jacques, you know.'

'I believe he was a better horseman,' John smiled, remembering the many stories he'd heard about his father from his grandfather. 'And he loved you.'

The moment between them crystallized in silence; then John pulled her to him by her shoulders.

'He loved you,' he said. 'As I do.'

A bright-eyed and keen-dealing young Malay boatman approached Sarah with a quick glance at Pauline's luggage.

'Come. I take you now.'

'No!' Sarah held on to the luggage as he tried to lift it and she waved frantically. 'John!' she called. 'Pauline!'

'You don't want a boat? You want to wait?' The Malay turned to move away.

'I want a boat!' Sarah said. 'I mean, she wants a boat.' He lingered, confused, as she waved at John to attract his attention. 'John. Pauline. A boat! Come quickly!' The young Malay lifted his reed hat and scratched his head.

John and Pauline joined Sarah hastily and the boatman tossed her luggage into a small boat.

'I think it's time to go.' Pauline tried to hide the sudden wrench she felt and looked down awkwardly at the small bobbing boat as her last piece of luggage was tossed into it. The young Malay, whose reed hat somehow managed to stay on his head in the gusting wind, held his slim hand up to her. As she laid her own hand in it and his brown fingers curled over her white skin, she glanced back at John.

'Watch where you're going,' John said.

'I will.' Pauline looked down into the boat.

'You can swim?' The Malay boatman smiled widely as his body rocked with the movement of the boat.

'No.' She gripped his hand tighter and stepped down. The boat moved away under her feet, and quickly he balanced her with his other hand, seating her firmly on the small wet wooden plank at one end.

'Are you sure this boat's safe?' She looked at the surrounding water nervously.

'All right, lady. I can swim.' He grinned and pushed the boat away from the dockside with an oar. Pauline held on to the sides of the boat as it rocked and looked back at John where he stood on the dock with his arm tightly around Sarah's waist. He raised his hand in farewell and Pauline closed her eyes.

All she could see was Jean Jacques, and all she remembered was the last time she had seen him on the day they decided to leave for England together. She turned her face away and looked towards the mountain. The grey stone walls of the castle shivered in the spray and somehow she knew the secret of Jean Jacques' death would be forever enclosed within it.

The young Malay's face was puzzled as he looked across the bobbing boat at her. 'You leave for ever?' he asked.

'Yes,' she said, 'I'm leaving for ever.' Her eyes moved back to the receding figure of her son on the dockside. 'Goodbye John,' she murmured as the water deepened between them.

The warm mellow taste of the wine was exactly as Jacques had hoped. It was a true Cape wine, heavy and fruity. He spat it out and held the tasting glass out to his grandson.

'You've done well, Jack. It's a good wine and we'll need the very best if we're to compete with the French.' He glanced at the wine-maker, Günther Wagner, who kept his back to him as he tested the temperature of a vat. 'Isn't that true, Günther? Competition is good.'

'I have need to talk of that.' Günther Wagner wiped his hands down his large white apron as he turned to Jacques. They had never become more than employer and employee, and he was aware that he had never replaced M. Claudelle in Jacques' affections. 'I think perhaps we will be unable to compete, Mr Beauvilliers.'

'With wine like this the English will be prepared to pay the extra taxes! Our wines are famous throughout Europe,' Jacques argued, but he knew British politics had touched his life again. 'If the English can offer the French only reduced taxes on wine, I doubt we need worry about a permanent alliance.'

'British soldiers fought alongside the French in China,' Jack said and moved away from his grandfather with the tasting glass. 'Perhaps they are already allies.'

'They tried to bring us to ruin before, but they didn't achieve it.' Jacques went deeper into the cellars after his grandson, and a spark of his former spirit lit his face. 'You mustn't allow politics to disturb you, Jack. Nothing must come between you and the land.' His passion for the land had not slackened as his body had. 'No matter what they do, you must fight!'

Since Geoffrey had told him about John Westbury, Jack Marsden had tried hard to prove his worth to his grandfather. He *was* fighting; not for an inheritance, but for himself. He was aware that his grandfather had been testing him.

'I think I've shown you well enough that I am capable of taking care of the land and the wines, Grandfather.' He felt Jacques' eyes on him and flushed. 'Have I?' It was the one question he longed to have answered.

'You understand the land. Yes.' Jacques peered through the dim light of the cellars and his eyes passed over the rows of wooden vats. 'And the wine it produces. You understand that well.'

'But?' Jack tensed as he waited for his grandfather to continue. The night Jack had dragged Geoffrey into Eva's house had never been mentioned and his grandfather had given no sign of resentment, but there was a slight awkwardness between them. 'Is there something else I have to learn?' he asked, cautiously.

'Yes.' Jacques scrutinized his grandson's face. 'Can you love, Jack?'

'Father!' Clara's voice cut between them, as she came towards the cellar doors.

'Try to love her,' Jacques said quietly, and turned to greet her. 'Your son has done well, Clara, you should congratulate him.'

'Would you leave us alone, Jack.' Clara ignored him and Jacques marvelled again at her complete dismissal of her eldest son. He waited until Jack had gone, then tackled her.

'There is something you have to say, Clara?' His speech was slow. 'About your son, perhaps?' He moved towards her. 'Because I do not wish to talk any further about John Westbury.'

'I'm afraid we must talk about John Westbury.' Clara wanted to shake him; to make him understand what he had done to her. 'I have spoken to Mrs Westbury.' She paused. 'She has confirmed that John Westbury is her son.'

Jacques lowered his head and shook it helplessly.

'Mrs Westbury has confirmed your lie, Father, and I insist the matter be cleared up once and for all!' A pain stabbed Jacques' left arm as Clara pushed on. 'Admit Jean Jacques died childless, and face the truth!'

Jacques' mouth dropped open as he tried to force his lungs to breathe. He was stranded on a plateau of pain and his legs were dead weights.

'Bonne Esperance is mine and will be Geoffrey's,' Clara continued without noticing the discomfort he was in. 'If you insist on believing the lies that woman Eva has fed you, then I suggest you return to her and leave me to restore the respectability you stole from this family.' She turned sharply and walked out. For the first time since her father had returned, she knew she had won.

Jacques lurched forward after her, his hands grabbed at the air and his mouth formed unheard cries for help. His chest had caved in and his ribs dug into his lungs. He leaned against the door and tried to call again. His eyes blurred and Clara's image swung back and forth as she strode away from him towards the house. He turned back into the cellars and tried to focus on the vats. He lunged towards them. Though every part of his body screamed, when his legs buckled under him he crawled.

He grabbed the metal band round the curved wood and hauled himself up against it. His face fell forward and pressed against the wood, pushing his jaw forward grotesquely. His eyes squeezed shut fighting the pain and his hand slid down the vat to the tap. He forced himself to turn it. He felt the warm liquid soaking through his trousers as it poured out and he pushed himself off the vat, rolling back against the next. Again his hand turned the tap and red wine flowed.

Jack waited around the side of the cellars until his mother disappeared into the house. The sound of running liquid and Jacques' short gasping breaths snatched his attention and he ran into the cellars. Jacques was dragging himself down the line of vats as red wine poured freely on to the floor.

'Grandfather!' Jack moved towards him but stopped as Jacques hauled his body round and leaned against the vats protectively. His eyes were wild, saliva ran from his mouth, sweat poured from his forehead and his eyes stood out from dark sockets above hollow grey cheeks.

'You want your inheritance?' The words rasped on a snatched breath. 'Take it!' His mouth locked, his eyes rolled back into his head and his body slid slowly down the vat, bumping against the metal rings before falling face-down on the floor. He lay absolutely still.

Jack moved to him quickly as the wine gathered in a dark red pool around him. He rolled him over and held him in his arms. Jacques' head lolled to one side and his eyes opened. His mouth was moving. Jack stopped breathing as he caught a sound. His grandfather was calling for Eva. Pushing his arms further underneath his body, Jack lifted the old man and turned to the door. The frail body was unexpectedly light as he carried him through the cellar, wine dripping from them both. All he could hear was his grandfather's faint call: 'Eva.'

His arms placed neatly at his sides, Jacques lay in his bed under a crisp white sheet. He had been washed clean and lay absolutely still, waiting for death. But his lips moved continually.

'He's still asking for Eva,' Emily said, trying to hold back her tears as she glanced at Jack beside her.

'You want to see Eva?' Clara ignored them both as she looked down at her father. 'Then we'll just have to wait and see how good you are, won't we?' She pulled a document from the waistband of her skirt and held it in front of his closed eyes. 'You know what I want, don't you, Father?'

Jack turned abruptly and ran from the room.

'Clara!' Emily pushed her chair towards her and snatched at the paper. Clara pulled it away sharply. Her eyes were bright.

'He can't die without signing his will, Emily.'

'Even as he dies you can't love him!?' Emily screamed in horror.

'I know what he wants!' Clara shouted.

Emily wanted to climb out of her chair, snatch the will away from Clara and throw her out of the room, but there was nothing she could do to stop her tormenting her father.

'Jack!' she shouted as she wheeled herself through the door. 'Where's Jack?' Emily barely looked at Geoffrey, who was waiting outside the bedroom, but pushed her chair towards the front door. 'Jack! I need you!'

Rosita rushed to Emily from the kitchen, her eyes round and white against her dark skin, wet with tears. She could still feel the dying body Clara had made her wash and tidy; still hear his whispered, 'Eva.'

'Master Jack is going.' Rosita moved to the front door and pulled it open. 'Master Jack!' she called. But even as she shouted, he was racing out of the stables and away from Bonne Esperance.

'Where is he going?' Emily turned away from the door and pushed her chair insistently to Geoffrey. 'Where's Jack going?'

'I don't know.' Geoffrey felt impotent.

'Your mother's tormenting my father, Geoffrey.' Her eyes pleaded with him. 'I am begging you to stop her.'

Geoffrey looked towards the bedroom. If he took a stand it would be his first step against his mother and into manhood. But he hesitated as she stepped into the doorway.

'There's no more I can do for him.' Clara moved past him through the door and the sharp edge of the document in her hand crackled as it touched him. 'He won't be with us much longer.'

Geoffrey's courage drained through the floor and he looked at Emily helplessly.

'Come and say goodbye to him,' Emily said quietly.

Geoffrey approached the bed and his eyes went over the slight body of his grandfather where it lay under the sheet. Jacques' mouth was still moving slightly and Geoffrey knew who he was calling for. He wanted to say so much to the old man who had suddenly found a place in his heart, but he couldn't. He looked back at Emily as the courage he'd lost in the face of his mother suddenly returned. He walked resolutely out of the door.

'What is it, Geoffrey?' Clara stood underneath her wedding portrait in the sitting-room. 'Is he dead?' she asked coldly.

'I don't want it, Mother.' Geoffrey's eyes moved to the document in her hand. 'I can't do what you expect of me, and Bonne Esperance is not mine to have. I'm sorry. I'm like my father. I have no place in the world you occupy.'

'Get out.' Clara's voice was little more than a whisper. 'Get out!' It rose to a scream.

The door closed behind him and her body began to shake as she turned to look at the painting on the wall. Her father seemed to gaze down at her from it, almost as if he was about to stretch out his hand towards her. Her hand tightened around the document and the rigid tension which ran through every part of her body gave way.

'Father?' She moved closer to the painting and looked up into it. 'Father!' she cried to it, and the small girl who had worshipped him so deeply wept as she reached up to him.

'You've done no wrong, Father,' Emily said as she looked down at Jacques. 'All you did was love.' She swallowed to hold back her emotion. A fine grey hair clung to her father's damp forehead and she pushed it back gently. 'I will never forget. Jean Jacques will never be forgotten.' She leaned her head on the white sheet over his chest and felt his shallow warm breaths against her hair. The bone of his arm pressed against her neck and her pulse beat against it as though it might bring him back to life. 'Forgive Clara.' The tears could be held back no longer and they spilled on to the sheet under her face. 'She doesn't know what she's done.' She felt his other arm trying to move and peered up into his face. 'What is it?'

Jacques' mouth had stopped moving. His eyes opened and he looked at her. He seemed to smile faintly, and then his hand, moving slowly with the effort, found her shoulder and patted it. He had used his last moments to comfort her.

Dawn was breaking in a warm yellow glow over the sea, and mist hung close to the ground before the sun dispersed it. Jack's hair was wet with sweat and his breathing was heavy as he banged on Eva's door. He was too exhausted to notice the small wiry dogs which barked at him as the door opened and Eva's dark eyes ran over his face.

'Grandfather's dying.' Without meaning to, Jack stepped back from her. 'He's calling for you. You must come.' She turned away into the small room, stood still for a moment, then pulled a stool from under the table. It grated against the floor, balanced for a while on one leg, then settled.

'You must come, Eva.' Jack stepped tentatively towards her, but she stood motionless beside the stool.

'He is dead,' she said quietly. 'Your grandfather is dead.' Her certainty touched him, and he was drawn by the dark pools of her eyes which held him steady.

'Why are you crying?' she asked, and Jack realized that he was. For the first time in his adult life he was crying and he turned away in shame.

Eva moved to him and touched his back. 'Cry,' she said gently. 'But cry for us, Jack. He has found his peace.' She smiled with great sadness as Jack turned to her. 'Now we must find ours.'

'He loved, Lord. Though he had not faith or hope; he loved.' Emily pulled the white sheet over her father's face, and looked at the sharp outline of his profile through it.

'Goodbye, Father,' she said. She could still feel the gentle touch of his hand on her shoulder.

PART THREE

1862-80

Chapter Twenty-three

Suzanne stood alone among the pepper trees outside the house and looked up at the low arc of green cover they already formed. She rolled the small ball of crumpled paper in her hand and clutched it tightly. It was a letter from Emily. An ostrich careered across the dusty ground in front of her, her son Pieter riding it like a horse.

'Be careful, Pieter!' she shouted in Afrikaans and ran out from the shade of the trees. The ostrich accelerated as Pieter's legs gripped its body just in front of its useless wings. 'Pieter!' she yelled after him in terror, and Jan Pieterse glanced up before returning his attention to the plough he was making.

'He has to learn to look after himself.' Marie Pieterse was approaching the house with a bundle of dry washing. 'What was your letter about?' She dropped the washing into a large wicker basket and turned to Suzanne with her hands on her angular hips. 'From your family was it?'

'My father is dead.' No moment in her life was private any more and she resented Marie Pieterse's continual questions. She pushed the letter into her pocket and watched her son leap off the ostrich's back. 'Be careful it doesn't kick you, Pieter,' she called as her imagination raced ahead of her and she saw her eleven-year-old son's head cracked wide open with the ferocity of an ostrich kick.

'You'll destroy that boy yet,' Mrs Pieterse stated flatly as she picked up the basket and moved into the small house.

Why? Suzanne thought bitterly. 'Why should my son be prepared for a hard life?' she said aloud. She had grown tired of the constant battle with the harsh African land and longed to be free of it. She was choking to death on the dust that crept up to the door of the house and found its way underneath it. She hated the

413

hot dry wind of the day and bitter cold of night and was suffocated by the perverse pleasure Marie Pieterse and her husband seemed to take in suffering.

'Did you see me, Mama?' Her son looked at her from his wide face spread with freckles. 'Did you see how fast I went?' He turned excitedly back to the ostrich as it strutted in a small angry circle, as if assuring the child his next ride would end in disaster. 'You see how angry he is!'

'Yes I do.' Suzanne lifted the corner of her skirt and wiped the dirt away from his eyes. She pulled his ears forward and peered into them one at a time, and his small face fell. 'Look at your ears!' She held his face between her hands. 'I told you to clean your ears every day.'

'I can still hear.' Pieter's nose twitched and Suzanne pushed him away quickly. She had seen Thys clearly in his cheeky face.

'Go and wash them immediately!' She watched his small body slouch as he turned and wandered reluctantly towards the stream. His hands were dug into the pockets of his shapeless trousers and his small shoulders rounded, but his tousled fair head tilted from side to side cockily as he tried to regain the pride his mother had just squashed.

Suzanne sat down on the rings of sawn logs which formed a seat, pulled the page of Emily's letter open and flattened it on her lap. The creases forced Emily's neat handwriting into wavy lines.

Her mind travelled back to her small bedroom at Bonne Esperance. She could see the delicate wall coverings in her room and the white lace curtains at the window. She could smell the eucalyptus tree just outside her window, and memory walked her to the window to look out at it. A wave of warmth ran through her body as her inner eye passed over the lush green of the vineyards with their backdrop of magical mountains and all at once she felt a deep yearning for home.

A sound interrupted her memories and she stood up quickly. Her heart raced and her mouth was dry. She'd heard a bird call. It was Thys's bird call. Her eyes skimmed over the surrounding land and searched among the thorn bushes. Common sense told her she had heard nothing: that Thys was dead. But the call came again. She ran out from the shade of the trees as though they were hiding her from the source of the call, and narrowed her eyes against the suddenly blinding sun.

'Did you hear that, Mama?' Her body tensed as Pieter ran towards her in great leaping strides. 'Did you hear?' He reached her and looked up with a grin of achievement. His small chin trembled as his mother's eyes drove fiercely through him.

'Don't ever do that again.' Suzanne snatched at the fading blue material of his shirt and pulled him towards her. 'Never!'

'Why?' His flecked grey eyes shone with hurt pride. 'It's like the birds.' He whistled again.

His head snapped back as Suzanne's hand slapped him hard across the face.

'Stop it!' she shouted, and his soul crept away from her as she turned on her heel and walked away towards the house.

Pieter kicked the ground as tears of anger filled his eyes. He had washed his ears as she'd told him to. He'd learned to whistle as the birds did. He could ride an ostrich, saw logs, wring a chicken's neck, and still his mother wasn't proud of him. His bottom lip pushed forward and he narrowed his gaze on his mother disappearing inside the house.

He decided he wouldn't speak to her for the rest of the day. He wouldn't allow her to kiss him good night when he went to bed and he would never learn English as she wanted him to.

'What else was in your letter?' Marie demanded, and Suzanne spun round with surprise. She hadn't seen her in the dark corner of the kitchen which was her private world.

'I told you.' Suzanne moved away to the broom and automatically began sweeping the dust back towards the door. 'My father is dead.' Marie Pieterse said no more, and turned back into her dark corner. Suzanne looked down at the pile of sand at her feet. 'I want to go home,' she said abruptly, staring at the sand. 'I'm going home.' She looked up as Marie moved out of the shadow.

'With what will you go home?'

'I don't understand.' Suzanne swept the heap of sand towards the door, turning her back as protection.

'With what will you go?' Marie stood behind her angrily.

'My son.'

'And mine? Johan?'

Suzanne turned and looked at her. Over the years she had

grown to despise everything about Marie Pieterse. What she had first seen as a great strength, bravery in the face of a hard land, she now saw as stupidity. The 'practicalities' with which Marie had smothered Suzanne's deepest longings were no more than obstinacy before overwhelming odds.

'My son must learn.' Suzanne ran her eyes over the thin angular body and sharp features which gazed back at her coldly. 'He must go to school.'

'Will they teach him how to survive out here?'

'Maybe it is not out here he will have to survive!' Suzanne turned away and pushed at the dust with the broom. It spread out and floated up in a small cloud at her feet in defiance. She was aware of Marie Pieterse's eyes on her back.

'I want to go home!' she cried out for understanding. Marie's hands kneaded the cloth of her skirt. She turned and walked back to her corner, disappearing into its darkness in silence.

'Suzanne?' Johan's tall figure stooped under the doorframe as he stepped into the room. 'Pieter needs you.' Suzanne moved immediately to the door but he stopped her as she reached it. 'He wants to show you something.' Suzanne felt his warm breath against her hair, the gentle grip of his hands on her shoulder, and all she wanted was to run. She looked up into his face and he smiled. 'I have told him he can drive the wagon.'

'The wagon?' Suzanne's throat tightened.

'Your son is growing up, Suzanne.' Suddenly she was deeply ashamed. She knew Johan had felt the distance which had grown between them. 'Tell him he has done well.' His hand released her shoulder and his body moved away from hers. He had turned away into the dark of the kitchen to his mother.

Suzanne sat in the wagon as Pieter drove it in a circle of dust in front of the house. She watched the sharp profile of his determined face as he concentrated on controlling the horses.

'One day you might drive me a long way in this wagon, Pieter,' she said, trying to draw closer to him. 'I had no idea you could drive a wagon.'

'Where?' he asked without looking at her. 'To the market?'

'Further than that.' Suzanne touched his hand as it held tightly on to the reins. 'A long, long way.'

'Why?' Pieter's mouth pulled up to one side as he turned the horses around the corner. 'I like it here.' He straightened the wagon. 'Will Papa go?' Pieter asked.

'No.' The wagon rounded the corner and Jan Pieterse stopped what he was doing, his blank face staring at them.

'Well?' Pieter's eyes lit as he pulled the wagon to a stop and turned to her with an impish grin of success. 'Can I drive a wagon?'

'Yes, you can,' Suzanne smiled and Pieter's grin widened. He twisted his small body around, calling brightly to Jan Pieterse. 'She says I can drive, Granpapa!'

Suzanne felt the familiar slow fall of her spirit as the invisible walls of the prison closed around her again.

'Honey, tea, coffee!' Gerrit's eyes sparkled at Thys as he sifted through a pile of goods on the veranda of their small house. Deep purple bougainvillaea flowers hung in clumps above their heads and the knotted dry stem, pushing its way along the wooden struts above them, defied explanation for the beauty which exploded from it. A spider, suspended from an invisible thread, swung perilously, seeking a new place to spin its web.

'And this!' Gerrit lifted an enormous black iron pot by the wire handle threaded through a hole on each side of it. It swung with the spider. 'All for one scrawny beast!'

'Where's his wagon?' Thys asked as he watched Jim Audsley ride away westwards across their land. Sheep scattered around his horse and Jacob, now a tall black youth, herded them together. One of Gerrit's cattle loped beside the horse, its sharp bones protruding through its brown hide. 'Where does he come from?'

'England.' Gerrit examined the iron pot proudly. He was thinking what fine peach brandy it would make and glanced at Thys with a wicked twinkle. 'The widow Heunis and her daughter will enjoy a spot of my peach brandy, I think.'

Thys turned his gaze away from the trader who'd ridden off with one of their cattle in exchange for a few unnecessary items: items which attracted Gerrit in his attempts to secure the widow Heunis for himself and her daughter for Thys. His eyes passed over their land and he could feel it aching. There had been no rain for five years. He looked up at the sky hopefully as clouds scurried across it, gathering in promisingly dark clusters. He felt the thirst of the earth under him and knew that the clouds would pass on without leaving their gift of water. It would be burnt away by the sun before it ever reached the ground.

'I think I'll start on it now.' Gerrit moved into the house with the iron pot swinging from his hand and his thoughts only on peach brandy, the widow Heunis and her daughter. 'We'll invite all our neighbours. A fine get together it will be.'

'What are we going to do, Gerrit?' Thys moved after him. 'The land's dying.'

'The rains will come.' Gerrit's eyes narrowed as he turned and looked up at the clouds. 'If not today, tomorrow.' He refused to allow the drought which had ravaged their land to deter him from his plans. 'I hear she's a fine cook. Did I tell you?'

Thys turned away and watched the figure of the trader fading against the horizon. Suddenly he envied him riding away. Riding across the dying land without thought, because it wasn't his.

'She's strong too. And she's plenty of flesh on her.' Gerrit nudged Thys in the ribs. 'Have you noticed her yellow hair and red lips?' He tried to divert Thys's attention on to the widow Heunis's daughter.

'I don't want a woman,' Thys said simply as he helped Gerrit cart his weapons of seduction into the house. Thys's body had thickened and his hair was beginning to grey at the temples. Age had added warmth to his still handsome face.

'Every man needs a woman.' Gerrit's hair was completely white and his chin lost in a frizzy beard, but his eyes still shone like those of a young man. 'It's natural to have a woman.' Gerrit looked over the land he loved but which died a little more each day. 'It's what the land needs too. A woman's touch. The tread of a woman's foot is enough.' He glanced at Thys and remembered the day he'd ridden back without Suzanne. He remembered how they had moved alone into the house Gerrit had built for her. 'He said he had too many sheep to move his wagon.' Gerrit turned his mind back to Jim Audsley as he looked in the direction he'd gone. 'He said his partner waits with the sheep and wagon when he rides out to trade.' He scratched his beard thoughtfully. 'He wasn't like an Englishman.' His beard twitched with a sudden smile. 'He's going up North for gold, he said. To the Transvaal.' Gerrit nodded to himself. 'Uitlanders see gold in anthills,' he chuckled and turned back to the house to announce a very important fact. 'His partner is a woman,' he said.

'If the rains don't come soon we'll have to move the cattle to pasture.' Thys stepped back on to the veranda and sat down on the wooden bench Gerrit had carved. The yellow grain of the wood curved around the bench unbroken. He pressed his shoulders back against it, crossed one leg over his other knee and wiped at the thick dust on his boot with his elbow. 'One of us will have to work to earn money.'

'Where?'

'I don't know.'

'Doing what?'

'Perhaps the rains will come.' Thys tipped his hat over his eyes. 'When is the widow Heunis coming with her daughter?' He took Gerrit back to the only thing which interested him. 'Theresa you said her name was?' Out of the corner of his eye Thys saw Gerrit's face relax into a smile. 'Yellow hair and red lips?' Thys questioned with a tease. 'And the widow?'

'I believe her hair was yellow.' Gerrit sat himself down beside Thys on the bench. 'And her lips? Well.' He pulled his shirt together as it spread open in a wide gap revealing his round white belly.

'Red?' Thys asked.

'Ruddy.' Gerrit glanced at him secretly. 'But I could live with them.'

Gerrit was right, Thys thought as he looked across the crowded room towards the widow and her daughter. Men filed in a long line to the kitchen and Gerrit's peach brandy, while the women stood back in solemn groups.

'You have a fine house.' Theresa looked up at Thys when he reached her. Her cheeks flushed bright pink as his eyes moved from her hair to her lips. Gerrit was right. 'My mother says we will have to leave our home soon if the rains don't come.' Her eyelashes brushed her cheeks in shyness.

'Where will you go?' Thys stepped back slightly. Being so close to a woman reminded him of Suzanne, but she wasn't Suzanne. He glanced at Theresa's mother who stood square-framed against the wall. Everything about her was square. Her mouth was square. And ruddy.

'People are talking of joining all the farms in the area together.' The widow Heunis's eyes roamed the room looking for Gerrit. 'That will be the only answer.' Gerrit was in the kitchen, pouring peach brandy into tin mugs held out by a line of neighbours. 'Are the men discussing what to do about the drought?' She turned her look on Thys and her thick eyebrows knitted. 'Is that why they're all in there?'

'Would you like some peach brandy?' Thys said quickly. 'It's the finest Gerrit has made yet.' The widow's nose twitched and her nostrils pinched as though he'd held a dead rat out to her. 'You don't like peach brandy?' Thys tried to hold back a smile as he turned to Theresa. 'Do you?'

Theresa shook her head and her yellow hair swept over her plump shoulders. 'My father did,' she said.

'And died of it,' the widow sniffed.

'Does Gerrit know that?' Thys asked with apparent concern.

'If he doesn't I will tell him,' the widow Heunis assured him and pursed her ruddy lips. 'Peach brandy is from the devil himself.'

'If you'll excuse me I would like to refill my glass.' Thys held his tin mug up with a smile and backed away towards the kitchen. He could feel the widow's distaste following him closely.

'Is she not as I said?' Gerrit's eyes glowed with peach brandy as he looked up at Thys and handed a full mug back to the thin, teetering man in front of him. 'I think you'd best move outside. There's no room in here for bodies.' Gerrit grinned at Thys as the man rolled past him as if he was climbing a mountain backwards.

'Yellow lips and bright red hair?' Gerrit shook his head to sort out the words. 'Is she not what I said, Thys?'

'But you were wrong about the peach brandy.' Thys shook his head.

'The best I've made yet,' Gerrit objected and peered into the mug he'd just poured. 'What's wrong with it?'

'The reason she's a widow.' Thys turned away to allow the next man to pass through with his mug.

'What do you mean?' Gerrit's white head bobbed around his next customer. 'What widowed her?'

'The devil, who makes peach brandy.' Thys turned to move

outside. 'But don't worry, she's certain she can stop a man from drinking it.' He ducked outside quickly.

The dark shapes of the wagons which had travelled many miles stood around the house in a defensive circle. His eyes settled on a young woman sitting outside one of them feeding her baby. The curve of her full breast pressed against the tiny baby's face shone in the light of the lamp that swung quietly above her. He felt a sudden longing to bury his head between Suzanne's breasts and hear the gentle beat of her heart again.

'How?' Thys turned at Gerrit's flat demand. 'How does the widow stop a man drinking peach brandy?' Gerrit's eyes focused themselves on him.

'She's a strong woman.' Thys shrugged.

'Do you like her?' Gerrit asked sharply.

'Who?'

'The widow's daughter.' His stocky body swayed and he parted his feet to balance himself.

'She's a good-looking woman,' Thys said.

'You don't like her?' Gerrit asked hopefully. 'I wouldn't force you.' Gerrit looked at the house as if he could see the widow and her daughter through the walls. 'I would be prepared to give up the widow if her daughter didn't suit you.'

Jim Audsley pulled his shirt over his head and looked into the wagon. Prudence was tucked into a blanket in one corner, and she curled her body tighter as she heard him. Her hair had grown long and was plaited in a knot on top of her head.

'He said it was a good beast,' James said. 'It looks fine. Mangy; but there's meat on it somewhere, I think.'

Prudence pushed the blanket back and sat up. The roll of her hair slowly unwound and tumbled over her bare shoulder, which had rounded slightly with the years, as her breasts had. 'What are we going to do, James?' It was a question she asked every day, and every day she got a new answer.

'I have an idea.' James climbed into the wagon and crawled on all fours towards her. A pillow hit him in the face and he held it in front of him like a shield. 'What's wrong now?'

'I want a baby!' Prudence pushed her hair back off her shoulder and her full breasts beckoned him. 'If I don't have a child soon it will be too late!'

'Yes.'

'And you know why I haven't yet had a baby? Do you know why?' Prudence demanded.

'No.' He shook his head as he realized he had no idea why. He had done his best to provide one. He crept towards her on his elbows. 'Tell me,' he encouraged her.

'Because of this!' She gestured around the wagon. 'I want a home! I want a house. I want a fence!'

'A fence?' He lowered his face to the floor in horror and covered his head with the pillow. 'A house?' he mumbled under the pillow, and she yanked it away hitting him with it. 'I married you!' he said in amazement. 'You were there when the Landrost married us!'

'Don't you understand?' Prudence leaned towards him and wrapped her arms around his neck. 'You leave me here alone with the sheep. You wander off on your own and leave me in a wagon.'

'Not a house. No.' His hand moved to her breast and his finger ran gently towards her nipple. He smiled as the nipple stood erect when he brushed his finger gently across it. 'Why do we need a house?' He had seen the familiar sensual glow in her eyes, and leaned his face towards her. 'I've been thinking about moving on to the Transvaal.'

Prudence yanked the blankets up under her chin.

'I'll come back.'

'Never!' She pushed him away roughly. 'If you go to the Transvaal you won't come back!'

'And if I find gold?' He leaned towards her again. Making love to Prudence was the only way he knew of distracting her and he enjoyed the games which led up to it as much as she did. 'They say there's gold in the Transvaal.'

'And they say there are diamonds here! Have you seen a diamond here, Mr Audsley?' Prudence couldn't deny the growing throb of desire in her body but her longing for a child and a home spurred her on. 'I want a house!' She held his face away from her and looked at him seriously. 'I love you and I want a house!'

'Yes,' he mumbled, nuzzling her neck.

'And I hate your sheep!'

'Our sheep.'

'They multiply every day. I don't believe you've noticed how they multiply. Every day I look there are more sheep!' She sighed as he kissed his way down her neck to her breasts. 'And more shepherds! James, if you don't build me a house, please don't come back from the Transvaal.'

'I won't come back,' he said as he felt her legs part under his weight.

'When are you going?' she asked as he pushed her wide and reached into her body. 'Even Themba has multiplied,' she whispered as her nails dug into his shoulders. 'Like the sheep.'

'And fifty per cent is mine.' He moved in deep rhythmic thrusts inside her.

'Not of the house you won't build or the land you won't claim.' Her back arched and her hips moved up to him.

'No,' he said, and decided he would leave before she woke in the morning.

'You'll be gone when I wake up, won't you?' She turned her face against his and knew he would. But she closed her eyes as he thrust himself deeper. This time perhaps she would be pregnant, and this time she would build a house for herself.

The letter had arrived three days earlier and Emily had read it several times over. She drank in the wild and wonderful news of Prudence's life and escaped the confines of her wheelchair as she lived her adventures with her.

'I don't know how many thousands of miles we've covered with our wagon but each has been a lesson in how to live with a man who finds it hard to stay in one place for more than six months. It's so curious, Emily, but I believe I love him. Everything about him angers me. He has the devil in him and our marriage is something which suits him only when he needs the comfort of a woman. It's strange. I believe I have found love.'

Emily dropped the letter into her lap and smiled. This man, James Audsley, whom Prudence wrote about with a mixture of anger and love, had discovered the woman in Prudence; though Emily wasn't certain he'd tamed it. 'The saddest thing is that I must now accept being childless. I can imagine your face. Me wanting a child! I can assure you it has more to do with the body's promptings than my own desires. But Nature's bad joke will soon be past.'

Emily tried to work out how old Prudence would be now. She must be nearly forty-four. Her breath came out slowly as the number hit her. She couldn't imagine Prudence one day older than when she'd left. But curiously, it was her age which showed in her letter.

'So, I finally decided to claim the land the sheep stood on. It seemed easier than moving them. Each time I move the sheep I gain another shepherd, and he another wife, and they more children. I've decided the house will be in the centre of the land. It won't be like Bonne Esperance, of course, but it will be a house. How is Father?' Emily closed her eyes for a second. She had no way of letting Prudence know their father was dead. The letter had been delivered to them by a passing transport rider. 'I can hear him laugh as you tell him I am running a sheep farm.'

Emily leaned back in her chair and looked out of the window. The vines were heavy with grapes and the cellars were full. But they could no longer sell the wine.

'Tell Father, Emily. Tell him that even surrounded by sheep, I still think of Bonne Esperance.'

A knock on the door called Emily from Prudence's letter. 'Who is it?' She put the letter down on her desk, folding it, as if trapping the vicarious life she'd lived amongst its pages. 'Come in,' she called.

The door opened and Jack stepped in. He looked exactly like her father as he stood slightly uncomfortably in the doorway, as if he didn't belong.

'What is it, Jack?' Emily turned her chair to him.

'My father is back.'

'Your father?' Emily was suddenly confused. 'Lord Marsden?' Her mind slipped back in time. 'Where is he?' she asked. She remembered the first day she'd seen Charles Marsden over the breakfast table, eating kippers behind a silk kerchief. 'When did he get back?'

'I'm not sure what to do.' Jack's eyes were puzzled. 'He asks if I would go to the Castle.'

'Then you must go.'

'Why?' Jack looked at her directly. 'I don't know him. He deserted my mother.'

'No, Jack.' Emily shook her head as she remembered the guilt-ridden man who had finally broken free of Clara's spell. 'He's a good man, no matter what your mother has said.' Emily had never believed Charles Marsden had killed Jean Jacques. 'And he *is* your father.'

Chapter Twenty-four

Lord Marsden looked out over Cape Town from the top of the Castle walls and the years he'd been away spread in rows of neat new houses running up towards the shelter of Table Mountain. Though the colony was suffering a severe depression the small town had developed into a hive of bustling activity as it fed the growth of settlement northwards.

New towns had sprung up in what he remembered as virgin land. Railway lines had begun winding their track of cold steel through what had been unknown territory. The long arm of the British Empire had stretched deeper into the dark continent with an open hand; snatching at each conquering footstep the Boer trekkers had taken. But Britain's African adventures had cost the taxpayer dearly and many were calling for the withdrawal of the expensive Cape regiments. Charles Marsden knew he was part of those 'unnecessary expenses'.

Relegated to a desk with the rank of Colonel, he wondered where his life had gone wrong. Why, through the many wars in which he had fought, he had remained unscathed. To him it was evidence that his entire service in the British army had changed nothing. Least of all himself.

The night he'd first seen Clara in the Castle ballroom was still vivid. His memory strode through the twenty-six years past, stopping only to examine the moments of pain and the ache of failure. Memory increased his tension as he waited for his son, Jack. He remembered him only as a small boy whom Clara had used to humiliate him. His newborn son had been handed to Jacques Beauvilliers as a human sacrifice for Bonne Esperance and then rejected: pushed aside by Clara for her second son, Geoffrey, the child of her lover, Duncan Shaw. His mind skipped suddenly to Jean Jacques' death and the sickening reality that he had been the cause of it. He forced the memory away and tried to recall Jack. The last time he'd seen him he'd been calling for his mother, as he himself had he turned his back on Bonne Esperance for the last time.

'Charles Marsden?'

The modulated English tones of the voice drew Charles's attention back to the present and he turned from the window to the man behind him. He was dressed in a rough leather jacket and his tattered trousers were pushed into worn leather boots. The lower half of his face was lost in a grey beard, and a pair of sparkling grey eyes laughed from a weather-beaten face.

'It is Lord Marsden? Charles Marsden?' The English accent was in total contradiction to the rough figure of the man from which it came. 'You don't remember me?'

'I'm afraid not.' Charles straightened his softening body in the armour of his tight red jacket. The dignified line of his straight mouth had turned down at the corners through the years. He looked again at the bright eyes of the stranger peering at him, but he was still none the wiser.

'Do I know you?' Charles said arrogantly.

'Not quite the pomp and splendour of the Raj, is it?' The man glanced back at the Castle. 'But a fascinating land with an uncertain future.'

'Major Stringer!' Charles moved towards him with the sudden security of his identity.

'Colonel.' Stringer backed away, holding his hands up. 'Not too close. Can't bathe, you understand: be tracked down immediately.' Charles shook his head in amazement as he looked at the dishevelled figure that was Major Stringer. A man whose active career in India had ridden even higher on the envy Charles had felt for him.

'When did you return to grace these beautiful shores?' Colonel Stringer looked straight through the camouflage of the red uniform beneath which Charles concealed his spreading waist. 'I see you've grown into the round comfort of a chair.'

'It happens to us all.' Charles pulled in his stomach. 'The last I heard of you you'd retired in glory.'

'What glory is there in retirement?' Stringer scratched at the growth on his face with a rough suntanned hand. 'It's the first symptom of an ignominious death.' He frowned at Charles. 'Like

427

the desk they've sat you behind! Its wood will be sawn and hammered into an even more uncomfortable coffin; doubtless draped by the Union Jack but nevertheless a dull mode of conveyance heavenward.'

'Did you chop up your desk for firewood?' Charles said lightly.

'I simply smelt excitement.' Stringer's face lit, he moved closer and Charles knew why he'd suggested he keep his distance. 'Tell me,' he spoke excitedly, 'do you remember what I said of the future here in Africa? The new form of warfare to be learned in this land?' He grinned in anticipation. 'The Boer is going to be a wily opponent.' He looked out as though seeing them.

'The Boer?' Charles Marsden smiled. 'We are not at war with the Boer.'

'You talk like the Government, who ponder the simplest way of keeping them down while they gaze at the Thames.' Stringer leaned closer. 'Mark my words, the Boer will soon decide peaceful resistance is futile.' He smiled suddenly and shrugged. 'And they have learned from the land. Like the blacks.' He flicked a grubby finger at the red cloth of Charles Marsden's jacket, its stubby tip jabbing Charles directly over his heart. 'Bull's eye!' Stringer's face spread in a wide smile. 'How they'll love your bright-red jackets, just as the kaffirs did!'

'So you're preparing to take on the Boer?' Charles asked, but his attention had been snatched away. Someone was climbing the steps that led up to the rampart.

'And asking you to join me.'

Colonel Stringer looked in the direction of Charles's attention. A man dressed in smart civilian clothes had stopped at the top of the steps and was looking towards them.

'You have company?' Stringer turned back to Charles, irritated by the civilian who'd intruded into his world of wars. 'We'll talk again!'

Jack stood still and watched his father as he moved down the broad stone wall towards him. All he saw was the red jacket which had hung so comically on the small body of his brother Geoffrey.

'Jack?' Charles looked into the face of the tall man in front of him. 'Jack?' he repeated incredulously into the face of the man who had been his small son. 'You've grown!' he smiled.

The coffin, whose disguise as a desk had been shattered by Colonel Stringer, stood clubfooted on the gleaming yellowwood floor of the smaller office Charles had occupied since his return. The grubby colonel's words stopped him sitting behind it. Instead he had pulled his chair out for Jack while he perched on top of the desk; on the lid of his coffin.

'Mother is very well.' Jack's voice had taken on a higher pitch to combat his nerves. 'Yes. She is well.' Jack looked across at his father and wondered why she despised him so much. 'We are all well.' A part of him wanted to ensure Charles knew he had not been missed: that he had been totally unnecessary to their well-being; yet he yearned to bridge the abyss of the years between them.

'And Bonne Esperance? How is it surviving the depression in the winelands?' It was as if Charles was talking to a stranger. 'I believe your grandfather has died. You are running the estate, I presume?'

'I didn't tell Geoffrey, as you asked.' Jack tossed the words at his father and waited for a response.

Charles looked away and the toe of his boot dug into the yellowwood floor.

'All Geoffrey wants is to see you,' Jack prodded, to discover why his father had not wanted to see his younger son. 'He needs your help.'

'With what?' The lines scored down the sides of Charles's face seemed to deepen, and he pushed himself up off the desk. 'I doubt if there is anything Geoffrey could need from me.'

'He wants to join the army.'

'Why?' Charles kept his voice level.

'Why?' Jack looked away for a moment and then smiled. 'Because he's your son. Because he's like you. I can see it myself.' Charles looked at him in amazement. 'As Aunt Emily says, I am like Grandfather.' Jack shrugged. He had sensed an unease.

'Yes, you are like your grandfather.' Charles moved back to his desk. 'Your mother must have told you that.'

'What is it?' The insecurity Jack had sensed in his father at the mention of Geoffrey pushed him on. 'You should be pleased one of your sons wants to follow in your footsteps.'

'Waiting for a helping hand, is he?' There was distaste in

Charles's voice and Jack heard it clearly. 'It would, of course, be what your mother wants for him.'

'No, it is not what Mother wants.' Jack's words were measured. 'She despises you.'

Charles studied the grain of the wooden desk, allowing its whirling circles to engulf his mind.

'Why?' Jack asked abruptly.

Charles lifted his eyes from the desktop and looked at his son. He could feel beads of perspiration standing out on his forehead and pulled a crisp white handkerchief from his trouser pocket.

'I'm afraid I would be unable to help Geoffrey.' He wiped his forehead. 'I will be leaving my command here.' Charles had latched on to Colonel Stringer's request to join him and side-stepped the truth. 'Please ensure Geoffrey doesn't waste his time coming to find me.'

'You haven't answered my question.' Jack's voice had lowered. 'Tell me why!' the stranger sitting opposite Charles demanded.

'Because I am not his father.' Charles handed Jack the weapon he had looked for all his life, the weapon with which he could destroy his brother, and he crumbled. He got up, turning his back on his father, and he stood quite still. Then, from across the distance Charles had placed between them, he spoke even more quietly.

'Don't ever tell him.' He turned and looked at his father. For the first time he saw the vulnerable man beneath the uniform and remembered his small brother Geoffrey standing proudly in the red jacket. 'It would cripple him,' he pleaded. He felt his father's hand on his shoulder and the tentative curl of his fingers as they gripped it.

Charles held on to the compassion he felt in his son.

John Westbury shouted over the jeers of the unruly mob which packed the square white courtroom, but his voice went unheard. The judge hammered his gavel, but chaos reigned. Law and Prejudice had met head on.

'Mr Westbury.' The judge peered over his pince-nez at John as he stood beneath him facing the angry crowd. The courage John showed and his cry for justice had not passed the judge by unnoticed. 'I demand silence in this court!' he bellowed.

The court quietened to a low disgruntled babble as the judge's keen eyes fixed on them. A slow catcalling jeer broke through the silence and the wigged judge turned his icy gaze on to the culprit.

'Perhaps, sir, you would like to take my place? As judge, jury and hangman!' A nervous laugh rippled through the crowd before they settled into an uneasy silence and the judge turned back to John Westbury, nodding for him to continue.

'Your Honour.' The black of John's robes swirled around his feet as he turned to face the court. His eyes shone with anger as they passed over the sea of hostile white faces in front of him. He could feel the ugliness pouring from them and turned his look on to the black man standing, head bowed, in the dock: the black man John was defending on a charge of murdering his white employer. 'If this man is found guilty by this court, the penalty he faces is death.' John Westbury closed his eyes as the crowd cheered.

The judge hammered his gavel again and shouted above them all, 'If you do not contain yourselves I shall have no choice but to adjourn this court!'

'And justice will have been adjourned in this country for ever!' John Westbury added. He moved to the packed benches and lowered his voice as they fell silent. 'What justice will there be if this man is tried by a jury whose only non-white member you have demanded be dismissed? I defy any man in this court to claim such a trial would be just!'

He swung round and held out his hand to the black man in the dock. Large terrified eyes stood out in his black face as he looked at John Westbury like a trapped animal. 'Is this man to be denied a fair trial by you? Or has he the equal right to dismiss the eleven white jurors?' John switched his attention to the jury and his eyes passed over each member in turn before settling on the one dark face. 'This juror has been duly elected by court procedure, yet you have dared to demand his dismissal!' He swung his attention back to the packed courtroom. 'Because the colour of his skin is the same as the accused's? Because the accused is charged with the murder of a white man, you demand that he be judged by white men. Why? Because – ' He moved towards the crowd and leaned against the rail before them – 'he is not white!' His heart pounded as he gripped the cold metal. 'If that man is dismissed from the jury I submit that British justice will have been dismissed in this country today.' He turned back to the black man in the dock whose life hung in the balance. 'I submit, Your Honour, should the wishes of this court be observed, the accused will have been pronounced guilty without due access to a court of law!'

He pushed himself off the rail and moved abruptly to his seat as the crowd erupted. He felt the sudden stab of a migraine over his right eye and pressed his fingers against his temple. He saw himself lying under a tree, throwing up the bile and acid of a lifetime as he'd come face to face with his own coloured identity.

'Silence!' the judge bellowed, but neither his voice nor his gavel could be heard above the chaos which had broken out again as paper missiles flew in all directions. John looked up as a hard ball of white paper hit him on the shoulder and he met the cool eyes of a young white man in the crowd. The man smiled and nodded at the ball of paper in John's hand.

John turned up the crumpled corner and flattened the paper on his knee.

'Nigger lover' was scrawled across it in spidery strokes.

'Katinka Westbury.' Emily smiled at the chubby baby girl she held in her arms. Fine auburn hair stood straight on top of her head and the tiniest button nose was tip-tilted in defiance as her serious eyes gazed out at the world. 'She's beautiful.'

'I'll take her from you while you have your cup of tea.' Sarah held her arms out and lifted the child from Emily's lap. The baby's eyes lit as she saw her mother and she chortled.

'I think you're beautiful too.' She pulled the baby into her and snuggled her face against it. 'Like your father.' Emily leaned back in her chair as the warmth and security of the home Sarah and John had made together in Cape Town soaked into her. It was like lying in a warm bath and her mind floated back to the day she had carried the little John Westbury so secretly to meet his father.

'It was the first time he cried,' she said suddenly to Sarah. 'I never got over the fact that the only time I ever saw Jean Jacques cry was with happiness when he saw his son.' She lifted her teacup in an effort to pull her thoughts back to the present. 'How is John? They say he's making quite a name for himself.'

'They?' Sarah smiled at Emily. 'Do you mean his family?' Emily nodded and sipped her tea. She felt slightly uncomfortable. 'I know why you've come, Emily.' Sarah looked at her as though reading her thoughts. 'But John won't go.'

'Mrs Westbury is dying, Sarah.' Emily spoke quietly and gently as though treading on egg shells.

'I know.' Sarah tucked the baby closer under her chin. 'Why is there so much bitterness between them?'

The front door opened and was slammed shut. Sarah's face clouded and she moved to the door as John's footsteps echoed on the quarry tiles of the hallway outside.

'He's home.' She opened the door. 'Look who's here, Katinka. Papa!' she said brightly.

'Hello, Emily,' John nodded politely, then kissed Sarah on the cheek. His hand gently brushed the back of the baby's head in a practised routine. His jaw tightened as he moved to Emily's chair and took her hand. 'How are you?'

'I'm fine, John. Very well.' Emily was bothered by his distraction. 'I think your daughter is beautiful.'

'And you think I should display her proudly before my grandmother! I am sorry.' He turned away and moved to the window, opening it wide as if to escape. 'I'm afraid that isn't possible.'

Emily ran her eyes down the rigid line of his back and the tension in his legs.

'Has she been assured my child is white?' John went on. His voice was cold. 'Would she welcome my child if she was black, Miss Beauvilliers?'

'John.' Sarah was embarrassed. 'Please don't.'

'It's why you're here, isn't it? To suggest we visit my grandmother?' Emily felt the peace of the small home fracture around her. 'I am sorry, but there is too much at stake to pander to the fears of people like my grandmother. I meet them every day in court.'

'She's dying, John.' Sarah held her cheek against the baby's hair.

'Sarah!' He moved to her and turned her to him with the baby between them. 'I have just watched justice tossed to one side by a courtroom of people who condemned a man because he is black, and I understood their feelings! I was brought up on them and I can't forget them! The prejudice I saw in that court today was fed to me by my grandmother!'

'And now you condemn her.' Emily's voice was cool. 'How you have grown!'

'Into what I am!' John held his head as it screamed with pain. 'One of them! Do you know who "they" are, Emily? Do you know me?'

'Then the people you despise so much have already won the battle, John.' Emily held her shoulders firmly against the wooden back of her chair. 'How delighted my sister Clara would be to see you wallowing in such self-pity.'

'Please. No.' John turned away.

'Yes.' Emily lifted her head higher. 'When you were born your father was forced to disown you. He was pushed aside, condemned like that black man you talked about!'

'Perhaps he shouldn't have stepped aside.'

'But he did! And he did so to give you a chance.' Emily looked down and noticed her hands were tightly clenched in her lap. She moved her fingers, trying to release the tension, and spoke again. 'He died for you.' She looked towards Sarah and the baby. 'For your child. Yet you are simply indignant! About your grandmother's fear? For that is prejudice, John. When we feel threatened by someone's position, wealth, or even their education, that is prejudice. But if you have the courage to turn the fire that's been lit in your belly today away from yourself and on to the injustice caused by fear, then people like your grandmother and my sister will be freed by truth. Walk right up to the Gates of Hell, John Westbury, and shake them.'

'So you waited till your mother died to lay your claim on Bonne Esperance?' Clara withdrew into the secure knowledge of her superiority and looked down on John Westbury as he faced her. 'She was at least above that.'

'It's a country I want. Not Bonne Esperance.' John pushed the legal document into her hand and turned away.

'Sarah asked if you would care to visit us on the farm soon,' he said to Emily.

'Huh!' Clara shot an arrogant glance at him. 'Don't imagine the new mistress of the Westbury household will have any more social success than your mother.' She flicked the document with a dismissive smile. 'For I still do believe she was your mother.'

434

Emily looked at John firmly as she saw how Clara's innuendo had touched his pride.

'Is there some reason you wish me to keep this document?' Clara held it out to him between two fingers. 'If you are uncertain of your identity it's quite curious you should look to this family for reassurance.' She allowed herself a calculated moment of amusement. 'I have no need of this.' Her fingers opened and the document fluttered to the floor.

Unable to hold back her anger, Emily pushed her chair straight at Clara. 'How dare you behave in such an offensive manner!'

'So this little charade was your idea?' Clara tugged her skirt from under the wheel of Emily's chair. 'How very quaint.'

'It was mine.' Mr Westbury was a shadow in the doorway which nobody had noticed. His body was frail, bent as if it had been blown by a strong and constant wind. But unlike the last time Clara had seen him, his face was firm and his eyes determined.

'I have waited for more than twenty years for this moment and it has taken every one of them to find my courage.' Mr Westbury paused and took a slow breath. 'The truth will not be buried with my wife as you had hoped, Lady Marsden.' His eyes moved down to the document on the floor. 'That is a sworn affidavit. It declares John to be the son of my daughter Pauline by your half-brother, Jean Jacques Beauvilliers.'

Clara turned away sharply. Without lifting his eyes from her back Mr Westbury came into the room. Each short step he took was measured by age. He stopped beside the document and carefully bent down to pick it up. John moved to help him, but he glanced up at him, brushing him aside with a look as his attention went back to Clara.

'When your hatred touched my daughter it touched me.' He lifted the document and the curved body regained its slight lean to the right. 'You touched my cowardice.' He took another slow breath. 'I will remain silent no longer.' His eyes grew puzzled as he looked at her. 'Even your father you denied.' His pale eyes filled with sorrow and he raised his hand with the document in it. 'Take it,' his voice rang out sharply.

Clara took the document, but didn't look at him.

'Thank you.' He lowered his head. 'I ask you never to set foot in my house again, Lady Marsden.' His pale eyes dismissed her. He turned to the door, each step as short and measured as when he had entered but with a new dignity.

From the shadow of the slave bell under which he stood, leaning against the solid white arch, Jack emerged into the sunlight as John led his grandfather to their carriage. Geoffrey stood quietly to the side of the house and watched.

'Are you pleased to be back in the country?' Jack smiled at John with apparent warmth as he reached him. 'We don't need the south-easter here to freshen the air.'

'It'll be good for my daughter, Katinka.' John looked up as a middle-aged black man moved towards him and held his hand out to help Mr Westbury.

'You remember Sunday?' Jack said quietly. 'He taught us to fish.' Jack hadn't forgotten the distaste John Westbury had had for Sunday. 'Do you remember?'

'Yes.' John glanced at Sunday and was met by a wide grin. It was the same wide grin he'd seen every time he'd caught a fish as a young man. 'How is the farm?' he asked as he moved on to the carriage, ignoring Sunday in an effort to separate himself from the past.

'Bonne Esperance?' Jack's voice was casual as his eyes swept over the grounds. Neglect and decay shouted from the crumbling walls running alongside the courtyard and the dilapidation of the house seemed worse than yesterday. 'The vines are producing well.' He smiled. 'We were prepared for the slump in the wine market.'

Günther Wagner's words, as he had left for Europe, rang in his head: 'Cape wine is dead.' Jack pushed the voice out of his mind.

'Hey, you!' Jack was surprised by Mr Westbury's call and he frowned as the old man pointed a finger at him. 'Your mother.' Mr Westbury looked at the house. 'I think she needs you.' Mr Westbury paused as he took a long breath and his head tipped back. 'Bonne Esperance is yours.'

As the carriage pulled out and rattled away Jack turned at Geoffrey's touch on his arm.

'So the lawyer isn't interested in Bonne Esperance!' Jack said.

'Neither am I,' said Geoffrey simply.

Jack thought he heard the faint cry of a dying dream. 'Suddenly, nobody wants Bonne Esperance.' He looked down at the ground.

'You do.'

'Me?' Jack's eyes flashed with sudden anger. 'Now there is nothing worth having you will walk away as if you were giving me something that is mine?' Childhood bitterness burned inside him. 'Your mother says it is yours, Geoffrey!'

'And I've never wanted it.' Geoffrey was no longer trying to buy his brother's love, but his help. 'Our father's back,' he said quietly. Jack felt his body relax as Geoffrey went on, 'He's taken leave, and nobody knows where he is, but I'll find him.'

Jack was unsure what to say in the silence that followed. For the first time in his life something akin to brotherly love had stirred and Geoffrey trembled on its threshold.

The rosewood drawer closed with a bang and the brass handle dropped back against the wood as Clara let it slip from her hand.

'If you consider the document worthless, why put it away in a drawer?' Emily asked. 'Why not burn it? You've always enjoyed bonfires.'

'There is no need.' Clara dug at a worn patch on the carpet with the sharp toe of her shoe. 'Sometimes I wonder if this carpet has ever been properly cleaned. By the by, I have dismissed the rest of the servants.'

'You've done what?' Emily shouted after her as Clara strode towards the door. 'Who have you dismissed?'

'They were hardly earning their food and we must learn thrift.' Clara turned back. 'I suggest you sell your house in Cape Town.'

'Never!' Emily spun her chair away. She felt useless. Bound to a wooden chair while everything happened around her. Her eyes ran down the brocade curtains with their age and wear streaked in bleached lines. 'I will never sell that house.'

'You will allow Bonne Esperance to die before then?'

'It is already dead! You've been fighting for a corpse, Clara.' She lowered her head as the truth of her own words came to her. 'I will not allow you to dismiss Rosita and her family.' She looked at Clara over her shoulder. 'You would be turning them out to starve.'

'And you would rather we starved together?' Clara's eyebrows reached for their arrogant arch. 'Martyrs are tedious people. Emily.'

'If you dismiss Rosita,' Emily spun her chair round and faced her, forcing the full weight of her years into her threat, 'I will ensure that document is pinned to every tree in Cape Town!'

'Do you imagine for one moment that disturbs me?' Deep lines ran from Clara's eyes down to her chin. 'Why should it?'

Emily looked hard at the woman in whom her father had said he could still see a loving child. Bitterness had worn her spirit as threadbare as the carpet she stood on, and her mouth was an open grave.

'It's taken me all this time to understand.' Emily left her comment in the air and pushed her chair towards Clara. 'It was never Bonne Esperance you wanted.' She looked into Clara's eyes as though seeing her for the first time. 'It was to destroy Father because he gave his love to another woman.' Clara tensed as Emily's chair brushed against her skirts and the sharp jab of her words pierced her. 'When you talk of restoring dignity to this family, I suggest you look to yourself, Clara.' Emily halted her chair but didn't look back. 'You have sown the wind and will reap the whirlwind.'

The sound of the chair rolling away over the wooden floor outside faded, but Emily's last words didn't. Clara's eyes moved to the top left-hand drawer of the rosewood desk. Inside it was the written evidence of everything she'd tried to wipe out, and she felt suddenly dirty. Her body cringed as though the slime of her father's love for Eva had tipped over her again. The small drawer couldn't contain it, it would seep out and stain her again.

The brass handle slipped under her fingers and she felt wood slide on wood as the drawer opened and her eyes reached for the document. Its contents threatened her, but what of John Westbury? He had said it was a country he wanted.

Chapter Twenty-five

News of the discovery of diamonds at the confluence of the Vaal and Hart rivers had spread through the southern tip of Africa in a frenzy of excitement. The economy of the country, on the verge of bankruptcy, had found a promise of wealth in the transparent stones over which the wheels of Boer wagons had rolled blindly. Men had arrived from all over the world and rushed northwards in search of a fortune. The British government hadn't been slow to recognize the importance of the find and stretched its grabbing hand deeper among the mass of burrowing humanity.

Colonel Stringer had sensed discontent brewing in both black and Boer as their land was hollowed out under their feet, and had taken it on himself to extend the military arm northwards. He sat easily in his saddle like an extension of the horse under him.

'Surely you can see the possibilities?' he asked Charles Marsden as they rode ahead of a group of ten equally filthy men. 'There's been enough trouble concerning the Basuto border with the so-called Orange Free State. The Boer republic has grown up. Found its voice.'

Charles nodded as he looked out over the hypnotic desert. The hot wind blew in his face, adding another layer of dust. Charles had always felt a sneaking pride in the cleanliness he had achieved before godliness, but had discovered something new in his time with Colonel Stringer. He was alive to the land and had become part of the dark continent of Africa for the very first time.

He glanced at the roll on his horse's back which contained his uniform. In the moments when he felt he had lost all trace of his military pride, smothered by Stringer's constant coaching in bush warfare, he would open the roll and the red of the uniform reassured him.

'Tell me about your wife,' Stringer asked out of the blue. 'She's French? Huguenot, I believe you told me.'

'Yes.' Charles finished the conversation before it had begun.

'Every man here has left a wife, Charles.' Stringer squinted as he looked out over the flat spreading land ahead of them and spat chewed tobacco on the ground. It rolled itself into a sand ball immediately. 'It has always confounded me that women spend so much energy to catch themselves a particular husband, only in order to rearrange him.' He chuckled. 'The black has the right idea. Move on to another before the first has any ideas.' He glanced at Charles. 'Word has it there's a fine brothel in Du Toit Span.' He grinned. 'I have reasoned why prostitutes are always such cheerful creatures. They change their men instead of changing their men, if you get my meaning!' Stringer snapped his fingers under Charles's nose to attract his attention. 'Come back,' he said. 'I had a wife!' he went on. 'Last I saw of her she was in Oxford Street, dressed in that American woman's bloomers!' He roared with laughter.

Charles rolled his shoulders to ease the stiffness and looked across at Stringer.

'I have a son.' He paused. 'Two sons.' He looked away as Stringer met his eye. 'If ever a soldier named Geoffrey Marsden crosses your path . . .' He stopped and looked down as though he'd forgotten what he was going to say. 'I believe he wants to follow in my footsteps.'

'Then send him that uniform.' Stringer nodded at the roll behind Charles's saddle. He knew that Marsden still dreamed that one day his country would call him back to save it.

'If anything happens to me,' Charles looked at him again and Stringer sensed the urgency in his voice, 'if you should meet him . . .' He shrugged and fell silent.

Stringer allowed the silence to continue and pushed fresh tobacco into his mouth. Charles Marsden had in some curious way tried to bare his soul to him.

The surrounding country was bare and desolate, a vast plain covered with karoo bush and scanty vegetation. As if the plain had been held up by its four corners and tipped, a huge encampment spread in lanes of wood and canvas. Everywhere, men imitated ants as sand and stone were sifted under the shade of sparse trees and worthless rocks flew in all directions, discarded by eager diggers. Men from every walk of life prowled among the diggings for easy prey while the diggers themselves clung possessively to their thirty feet of claim.

'If you want your fifty per cent, Mr Audsley, you will collect it from the barrel of this gun!'

Jim Audsley didn't know what confused him most. The sight of Prudence, dressed in an alarmingly bright red dress with a bustle, the discordant sound of a honky tonk piano behind her, or the sign which swung outside the wooden building she stood in front of. It read, 'Mrs Audsley's Parlour.'

'That's my name!' He pointed at the swinging sign aggressively. 'You have painted my name above a bordello!'

'Since you have such experience of them it seemed sensible! Besides,' Prudence aimed her gun at him as she stood on the wooden steps, 'it's my name too. Or have you forgotten?'

'I didn't marry the madame of a whorehouse!'

'You married a man!' Prudence laughed.

'That would be better!' Audsley looked up at the sign as if he was dreaming. 'Why?'

'For financially sound reasons!' Prudence pushed her full bosom forward. Everything about her was fuller than when he'd left her to look for gold. Including her lips, which were outlined in bright red rouge. 'I learned from you the most constant needs of men, Mr Audsley!'

'What have you got on your face?' His eyes narrowed and he moved closer, peering at her in wonder. 'Paint?'

'Indeed.' Prudence stepped aside as a man walked out of the building. 'We are living in the Seventies, not the dark ages.'

The man raised his dusty hat to her. 'Good day, Mrs Audsley.'

'You have paid, I hope?' Prudence fired him a suspicious look.

'Of course.'

'In what?'

'Diamonds.' The man nodded at Jim Audsley as he passed. 'She's tough, but the women are good.'

'Well?' Prudence watched her husband as he turned around, following the man with a look of wonder. His eyes passed over the rows of tents and small wooden shacks lining the sandy street. Wagons were parked for miles around, overflowing with goods for sale, and the background rhythm of pick-axes battled with the piano.

He took his hat off, turned back to Prudence and flung it on the ground like a gauntlet. A cloud of dust flew up as it landed and he coughed.

'You were sitting on a diamond field and you sold it for this!'

'This was mine!' Prudence tilted her head up. 'The house you didn't build for me but I did!' She levelled her gun at him again. 'It is my house.'

'And the land around it? There are trespassers on our land!'

'Themba said there were no diamonds.' Prudence was embarrassed. 'Besides, I had sold the sheep and there seemed little point in land for grazing!' She narrowed her eyes. 'I was not born to be a sheep farmer.'

'You sold all the land?' Amazement dripped from him.

'I've told you. Themba said there were no diamonds here. He said they were under the house.' She drew herself up to her full height. She didn't enjoy having to admit she'd made a mistake. 'And I refused to dig under my house.'

Jim Audsley looked up at the swinging sign and his breath came out slowly.

'Are we going to stand talking on the steps all afternoon or will you risk coming inside?' She looked at him comically. 'Or is it that your pockets are weighed down with gold from your escapades? Is that why your trousers are hanging from your hip bones?'

'Where is that fleabitten witchdoctor anyway?'

'His ancestors called him away.' Prudence looked over his head, as if he wasn't there at all. 'So, you will not be coming inside?'

'No.'

'Good.' She turned away. She stood still on the wooden step and twirled the gun like a parasol. 'I've missed you,' she said quietly. Behind the paint the woman he remembered lurked mischievously.

'Have I complained that your bottom is rounder?' Jim Audsley ran his hand down the soft white flesh of Prudence's back. 'Even

442

if a little lower.' He found her lips with his. He squinted and pulled back as a pillow under her head was yanked out and flew at him. He slipped off the bed as it hit him, unable to hold on to the slippery sheets. 'What are these things?' He pulled the sheet up off the mattress like a small tent.

'Silk.' She leaned over the edge of the bed and looked down at him. She'd wiped the make-up off her face, and although older, the sensual glow still lit her eyes. 'What did you say? What exactly is lower, Mr Audsley?'

'Only a little lower.' He climbed back on to the bed towards her and decided silk felt rather good. 'Your age suits you.'

'Suits me?' He felt the sudden wind of the pillow as it came at him again and backed off the bed before it hit him. 'What age?' she yelled. He grinned up at her from the floor before climbing back on to the bed again.

'I presume that's a poor little eider duck's feathers in the pillow to match the silk sheets.' He leaned over her. 'How much do you charge for such luxury?'

'I don't.' She turned her head away. She could feel her age and quite suddenly felt unattractive. 'I employ women.' The light had gone from her eyes.

'Hey!' Audsley ran his finger around her chin and on down the back of her neck. 'Because I said your derriere was a little lower?' His hand grabbed a handful of her soft behind. 'I only noticed because I remember it so well.' Prudence's eyes had regained their glow, and he kissed her.

'It was a flood.' He drew back curiously as she spoke out of the blue. 'There had been a drought for years and suddenly it rained. The diggings collapsed around the house.' He kissed her nose. 'The house collapsed – and the fence.' She kissed his. 'Temba was right.' She ran her fingers down his back as his tongue pushed between her lips to silence her.

'You've stopped talking,' he said as his mouth moved down her neck.

'There were diamonds under the house. But only surface diamonds. There were just enough to build this business.'

'Your breasts are fuller.' He paused. 'But not lower.'

She turned her head away and murmured as her body responded to the familiar touch of his mouth.

'And, of course, fifty per cent is yours, Mr Audsley.'

'One hundred per cent.' His mouth moved down the line of her stomach. 'Mrs Audsley's parlour is all mine.'

Thys whistled loudly as the oxen pulled hard against their yoke. He held on to the rough wood and his heels skidded across the dry ground as he was dragged after them until they finally stopped.

The sprawling mass of buildings, wagons and tents he'd been told was there was concealed by darkness. Only the flickering lights of fires dotted everywhere confirmed he had reached the end of his journey. A honky tonk piano banged incongruously over the sounds of people and animals preparing to sleep.

'You think diamonds you will rain, Thys?' He heard Gerrit's voice in his head and could see his stocky figure standing on the veranda as Thys had driven the wagon out to look for some means of earning a living. 'They don't want Boers in the diamond fields!' Gerrit had called after him. 'The only work you'll get is serving them! Like a black!' Thys moved towards the wagon and climbed into it to sleep. He heard himself answer Gerrit: 'They pay well for the use of wagons.'

'And with that you will buy rain!' Gerrit couldn't understand that perhaps Thys was looking for something else. 'Do you think you will buy Suzanne back?' Gerrit knew Thys had never lost his love for Suzanne, that she was still in every breath he took. But the hard edge of Gerrit's voice the day he'd left had reminded Thys of his father.

'You'll be a second-class citizen to them! Remember that! You might get bread from them but it will be crumbs!' Gerrit had expressed the growing resentment of all his people, but it was aimed at keeping Thys at home. 'I will stay here. I will die on this land rather than crawl under a British table! Hear me, Thys! Those diamonds will be the death of the Republic!'

Thys climbed off the wagon and decided he wouldn't wait for the morning to ride into town. He moved to the oxen and flicked his whip across their backs, trying to blot out Gerrit's voice.

'When will you come back, Thys?' Gerrit had asked. He had suddenly looked afraid and alone, aware of the time left to him on their piece of land. 'I'll be here.' At last Gerrit had called out the only words Thys wanted to hear before he left.

*

Smoke from the fires crept into Thys's nostrils as he looked down the raggedy lines formed by the dark shapes of tents and wagons. They seemed to grow from the earth on either side of the well-trodden street. The discord of a honky tonk piano battered his ears. He glanced at the sign swinging above the door of a wooden house with three wooden steps. 'Mrs Audsley's Parlour,' it announced in fancy letters.

'Tshepo!'

The familiar sound had come from somewhere among the dark shapes on the wagons around him and Thys moved forwards, drawn by the haunting word which still roamed his subconscious.

'Tshepo!' It came again and Thys pulled hard on the trek rope, hauling the oxen behind him as he moved towards it. He was suddenly back in the oblivion of a high fever, he was being carried, he could hear laughter, and the same sound – 'Tshepo.'

An emaciated dog growled and the African voices around him fell to the depths of silence. He'd been cast headlong into a strange new world.

'I'm looking for Tshepo,' he said to the circle of black faces peering down at him from the back of a wagon. They looked at him silently from dark, mysterious eyes.

'Do you know Tshepo?' he asked again, and pulled back as a large man dropped silently beside him, animal skins covering his body.

'Tshepo?' The man's voice was deep and Thys knew he had come face to face with the sound which had haunted him.

'You saved my life.' Thys looked into the brown eyes fringed with thick dark lashes, they were alight with silent laughter.

'Tshepo? Saved your life?' He peered closely into Thys's face. 'Why would Tshepo save the life of a white man? The black man only kills! Has your white mother not told you that?'

'You saved my life,' Thys repeated. 'You carried me from a burning village.'

'Why?' Tshepo stepped back, folding his arms as he looked at Thys in mock amazement. 'For why?' Thys could feel the deep suspicion in him.

'I don't know,' he said. 'But you did.'

'Now I own your life, am I not right?' He snatched a gun from the wagon and waved it in front of Thys.

'I want this. Not your life! You can get it for me, Boer? Fire?'

'No, but I can teach you how to use them.'

'You think I don't know?' The gun tipped up and exploded. Tshepo shrugged as boughs of the solitary tree they stood under splintered down around him. 'The Boer in the tree is dead!' He doubled over with laughter, then looked at Thys curiously before jumping back on to the wagon.

'What is your name?' The voice reached at Thys from the darkness.

'Thys Bothma.'

'Thys Bothma,' Tshepo echoed with careful pronunciation. 'Go to sleep, Thys Bothma. We will do business when the sun wakes.'

'Yes, Tshepo. We will do business when the sun wakes.' The purpose Thys had found sounded in his voice and a strange excitement crept up on him. Suzanne was a part of the lost time he'd just reclaimed.

Jim Audsley balanced on a low wall at the back of the bordello. His legs spread wide as they stretched over the picket fence and his new leather boots were crossed. He had a book in his hand and noted down payments he made as black men moved forward with piles of skins and firewood. He was completely at home and in charge.

'I want to see the lady,' a hesitant Afrikaans voice said and he looked up. A thin pale girl stood to one side of the line of black men he dealt with. Behind them all was Tshepo, watching from his wagon with an enigmatic smile. Thys sat beside him, chewing on a piece of grass.

'Inside.' Audsley nodded towards the gauze door behind him as he examined a pile of skins.

'Mangy, aren't they?' He looked into the black face of the man trying to sell them. 'How much did you say you wanted?' He leaned back and his smart new hat tipped forward a little.

'Water,' Thys whispered to Tshepo, his eyes fixed on the bordello. 'We'll sell them water.' He nodded at James Audsley in his smart clothes.

'Water?' Tshepo looked at him curiously. 'My water?'

'Ours,' Thys grinned.

*

The room was dark and hung with deep red velvet drapes. Prudence turned to the door at a timid knock and saw the top of a wispy blonde head as the Afrikaans girl dropped into an immediate curtsey.

'Good day, lady.' The pale face with huge dark eyes looked up with a hesitant smile.

'And what's your name?' Prudence narrowed her eyes to see her more clearly. 'How old are you, child?'

'Sixteen, lady.' The young girl's heavy accent made her nervousness less audible. 'Old enough, lady.'

Prudence looked at the child in front of her and turned back to her desk. She was suddenly uncomfortable.

'I'm afraid there's no work for you here.' Prudence sat down and waved her hand abruptly. 'I'm sorry.' She wanted the girl to go.

'But, lady – '

'I hardly know what you're doing here.' Prudence dismissed her again with a brusque wave; but the girl stood quite still.

'I'm clean, lady. I speak English.' The young girl moved towards her. 'I need money. Please.'

'To feed your entire family, I suppose.' Prudence looked at her coldly. 'This is a business,' she said sharply. 'I do not employ children.' The girl's large brown eyes dipped down. 'I have no work for you. Go back to your mother.'

'My mother sent me. She told me what is expected in your house.' The girl moved closer. 'I know what to do.'

Prudence looked up at her, startled. She could feel the thin girl's heart reaching out, and it touched her.

'What's your name?'

'Marianne, lady.'

'Very well, Marianne. I will give you work but it will not be the work you're looking for.' Prudence eyed her keenly. 'Can you count? Without your fingers can you count?' The girl looked at her blankly. 'Then I will teach you.' Prudence leaned back in her chair and watched the smile spread across Marianne's face. 'I will teach you the practical side of the business, but you will not work in the bordello itself.'

'Prudence!' Jim Audsley's voice called her sharply from outside but she ignored him.

'Can you make a cup of tea?' Marianne nodded with a glad

447

smile. 'Then take yourself to the kitchen and I want a cup of tea in here when I return. And, I want . . . the sum of twelve plus six?' She paused, not expecting an answer.

'Eighteen, lady,' Marianne said.

Prudence heard her husband's voice calling her again and turned Marianne gently by the shoulders to leave with her.

'I will tell Mr Audsley he will no longer be the only person able to count in this establishment!'

'Water's more valuable than diamonds.' Thys was beside Jim Audsley and talking keenly. Tshepo smiled as he watched one white man sell another white man his water.

'Your offer is not enough. But if you double it I will consider doing business with you,' Thys said.

'What is it?' Prudence pushed open the gauze door and held her hand up against the sun. Thys looked up and as her eyes met his she felt the air between them vibrate.

'Thys Bothma! I don't believe it!' She stepped forward and the gauze door banged behind her in short sharp raps. 'It *is* Thys Bothma!' She walked through the years towards him.

Jim Audsley watched in silence and Tshepo resettled himself on the wagon.

'Prudence Beauvilliers?' Thys murmured as she stood in front of him. Audsley mouthed the name Beauvilliers in amazement.

'It's not my short sight!' Prudence threw her arms around Thys. 'It *is* you!' She stepped back, holding him by the shoulders. 'And I do believe you're even more handsome! Yes! Even more handsome than I remember. It's the grey temples. And general wear and tear!' She took him by the hand and led him past Jim Audsley. 'We have many years to catch up on, Thys.'

'Water,' Audsley said quietly. 'He came to sell water.'

'Then buy it,' Prudence beamed. 'You always did enjoy a bath!' She laughed as she led Thys through the gauze door.

'Your disapproval shows, Thys.' Prudence handed him a cup of tea and looked down at him. 'Still the Calvinist Boer, I see.' She could feel his eyes on her, and she was reminded of Bonne Esperance.

'What are you, Prudence?' Thys looked up at her directly and

448

his eyes took in the thin Afrikaans girl.

'I am a business woman.' She waved curtly at Marianne to leave.

Thys watched the young girl as she slipped out like a breath of wind. 'Are young girls like that a part of your business? Afrikaans children? What's happened to you, Prudence?'

'Life!' She lifted her head high and sat on an elegant chair beside him. 'You don't believe in brothels?'

'You're not a whore!' His face was harder than she had ever seen it and his eyes were sad.

'I'm the madame, not a whore. What are you?' She settled her bustle back against the chair and felt the horsehair press into the small of her back. 'Tell me,' her voice was accusing, 'tell me where my sister Suzanne is? Where did you leave her when you ran, Thys Bothma?'

'There are other ways of earning a living, Prudence. Employing starving children as prostitutes!' Thys watched her keenly. 'You could have found another way.'

'So the Boer is going to tell me!' She couldn't hide her anger. 'What is your living, Thys? Dealing with the black renegade, Tshepo? My, how proud your father would be of you!'

The hurt which Prudence tried to cover with bravado showed clearly and Thys wasn't sure how to handle it. Under the heavy make-up of a bordello madame he could see the Prudence he remembered; and Suzanne.

'I have land, and I have love for Suzanne.' He shrugged. 'But she is married to someone else.'

'And what have you found to blame that on? The death of your father?'

Thys watched her silently but anger burned in him.

'The past is past and all I've done is earn a living!' Prudence stood up, her eyes and voice were cold. 'You're judging me, Thys Bothma: and I have little respect for your judgement.' She glanced out of the window and towards Tshepo and his wagon. 'You judge me while you sell guns to blacks?' She turned back to him. 'To kill the British, are they?'

Thys stood up and moved to the door. His footsteps were determined and she cried out as he reached the door, 'No, Thys! I'm sorry.'

He took the brass handle. 'I came to sell water.' He turned to

Prudence. 'Not guns.'

'I also am trying to make a living. And water is what I need, Thys.' Tears welled in her eyes. She wiped them away quickly and streaks of black charcoal from her lashes smudged her cheeks. 'I'm a married woman, would you believe. That man out there is my husband and I love him.' She wiped again at her eyes as the charcoal stung. 'I'm just a married woman trying to earn a living in the hope that one day my living might save Bonne Esperance. It is still all I want.'

Thys moved to her, lifted the tail end of his shirt and very gently wiped the charcoal from the corner of her eye. She blinked as the pain vanished and she touched his hand.

'I'm not surprised Suzanne loved you.'

'I'll be back soon,' Suzanne called brightly as she flicked the reins over the horse's back. She'd heard that Rev. Phillip had returned to the mission and she wanted to see him. She wasn't sure why, except that perhaps he would reassure her in some strange way. He was a part of her life with Thys, and a part of his death. She looked back at the tall young man who was her son and waved again.

'Goodbye Pieter,' she called with false gaiety.

Pieter didn't wave. He was aware of a silent drama being played out between his parents and looked towards the house where Marie Pieterse stood absolutely still in the doorway.

He had picked up the tension and was on edge. He moved to Johan as he saw him pick up a rifle, tuck it under his arm and walk away with it. He'd never seen his father with a gun before.

'Where are you going?' Pieter asked him in Afrikaans. The rifle was suddenly threatening. 'If you're taking a gun, where shall we go?'

'I'm all right,' Johan said quietly and moved away, signalling him to stay.

Pieter looked back in the direction of the small cart carrying Suzanne away.

'The wood needs chopping,' Marie Pieterse reminded him and he joined her at the door.

'Why is my mother going to the mission?' he asked. He no longer believed the story about Rev. Phillip returning from England.

'Firewood!' Marie handed him an axe. 'It'll be a long hard winter.'

Johan held the gun between his legs and pointed it directly at the empty blue sky above him. His hand dug into his pocket and he pulled out a small piece of paper. Although he couldn't see what he'd written on it, he looked at it. The blind handwriting spelt out only two words. 'Fly free.'

Johan flattened the paper on his knee and placed it on the ground beside him. He felt for a stone and put that on top of the paper. He lowered his head towards the gun and opened his mouth to take the hard cold steel. His hand ran down the barrel and stopped at the trigger. His finger curled around it.

'Fly free, Suzanne,' he said in his head, and let her go.

The log split in two under the heavy slice of Pieter's axe and birds swept up from the surrounding bush in a startled mass at the reverberating sound of a gunshot.

'Father!' The axe dropped out of Pieter's hand as he ran full pelt in the direction Johan had gone.

Marie Pieterse stepped out of the house and her body froze as the gunshot echoed through the air. The ostrich stopped and, legs splayed wide, it stared in the direction of the shot as a large round stone bumped its way down its long neck.

Jan Pieterse ran round from the back of the house calling, 'What is it?' to his wife.

'Johan,' Marie said, as though releasing her son.

The miles of dry ground which sped under the wheels of the cart as Suzanne drove towards the mission seemed to whisper a sweet promise. Each mile was a step she had longed to take for many years. Her journey was into the past and she planned how she would take her son and Johan back into it. She knew she could never separate Pieter from the man he considered his father, but also knew they had to escape if they were to survive. Survival depended on finding the courage to break through the rigid biblical laws the Pieterse family had used to imprison her. Laws which chained her to a man she cared for deeply but didn't love. Laws which rattled accusation at her as she struggled against the cold Calvinism Jan Pieterse demanded above and beyond love.

For the first time she felt that perhaps Rev. Phillip's faith offered the answers she was looking for. She lifted the reins and brought them down on the horse's back as she drove on faster in search of a way.

Marie Pieterse looked on as her husband spread loose sand over their son's grave. Pieter stood to one side and stared at the earth.

'Will you not say a prayer?' Marie was distressed as her husband turned his back to walk away.

'He took his own life.' Jan walked on without looking back.

'But you must!' For the first time emotion broke through Marie's control and she ran after him. 'Please, Jan, please. Please forgive him.'

'When you brought that woman to our home I told you I would not have a nonbeliever among us, but you didn't listen.' Jan Pieterse turned and faced his wife coldly. 'You did not listen, and our son died outside God's will.' He turned his bitter gaze on Pieter. 'Your mother has condemned him to eternal damnation.' He turned and walked away.

Through tear-blurred eyes Pieter stared at the unmarked grave, and a hard knot of resentment swelled inside him.

Suzanne looked across the scrubbed wooden table at the old man facing her. She could hardly believe he was there. It was as if he had never been away.

'You came back to Africa to die?'

'Africa has made itself my home.' Rev. Phillip's eyes shone from his luminously white face. The wisdom behind his eyes glowed stronger than before.

'Why?' Suzanne asked, taking his hands between her own. 'I don't understand.'

'You don't hate Africa, Suzanne.' Rev. Phillip studied her tenderly as he spoke. She was almost a daughter to him, yet he had never been able to touch her with his beliefs. 'Any more than you hate God,' he added.

'Then perhaps it is He who hates me.' Suzanne looked into his eyes as though the guilt which plagued her might find forgiveness in them. 'I have never loved Johan. He gave me everything but I never loved him as a wife. Thys is still with me and I can't accept that God took him.' She paused. 'Or can you tell me why he did?'

Rev. Phillip shook his head. How could he tell her the truth after all these years?

'You say He is a God of love?'

'Suzanne.' He held her hands tightly. 'I didn't just come back to Africa to die. I have unfinished business. I made a mistake.'

'Mistake?' Suzanne's eyes flickered. 'What are you talking about?' Neither had reacted to the sound of a galloping horse and angry shouts outside.

'Tell me.' Suzanne's mouth was slightly open and her breathing shallow. 'Tell me.' She felt as though she stood on the threshold of something she hardly dared to hear, but had to.

'Where are you, Mother?' Pieter's voice broke into the room.

'It's my son.' she murmured, and stood up quickly, withdrawing her hands from Rev. Phillip's. Pieter stood in front of her, but he wasn't her son: he was a stranger. He held a small bundle in his hand and stared into Suzanne's eyes as though seeing her for the first time.

'My father is dead.' He threw the bundle at her feet, carried on a wave of hatred. 'He has given you your freedom and I ask you to take it from me too.' He straightened his back, as if daring her to touch him, and shouted, 'He gave you his love and you condemned him!' He paused. 'You are not my mother.'

Suzanne moved to go after him but Rev. Phillip held her back. She tugged her arm, trying to release it from his grip as her son walked out of her life. 'Let me go!' she screamed.

'Let him go, Suzanne.' Rev. Phillip's voice was firm but her passion was too much for him. He released her arm and in the bright glare of daylight outside she was just in time to see her son riding out of the mission.

'Pieter!' she screamed. He didn't look back.

Suzanne stood absolutely still in the doorway, her body rigid, her fingers holding tightly on to the doorframe. Rev. Phillip ached as he looked at her and turned his eyes away. They settled on the bundle on the floor. It was Suzanne's life, and her son had thrown it at her. He saw a piece of paper tucked into the top of the bundle and reached out to take it, but Suzanne's voice stopped him.

'Is that what your God does?'

Desperation filled her voice. She had seen the words on the paper: 'Fly free.'

'He kills Thys! He kills Johan and he turns my son against me!' Her voice rose in hysteria. 'Is that the God you worship, Reverend Phillip?'

'Yes.' His voice was quiet as he moved to her.

'No!' She shook her head as she watched him coming. 'Keep Him away from me!' She backed through the door as though Christ himself walked beside him. 'Keep your God away from me!' Her voice rang through the mission.

'I don't understand either, Suzanne.' He grabbed her and held her by the shoulders. She struggled, kicking against his shins.

'I hate your God!'

Rev. Phillip held on to her. He had seen the gleam of the Lord's double-edged sword held high above them both, and he felt her body shiver in his hands.

'Thys is not dead, Suzanne.'

She stopped struggling and her body stiffened. He pulled her tighter, trying to still the emotion that had erupted inside her.

'Thys is alive.'

She looked up from wide bewildered eyes. She was stepping from one nightmare into another. Doors were opening and closing all about her and she was lost.

'Thys isn't dead?' Her words were filled with disbelief. 'No!' she screamed. 'You're lying!' Rev. Phillip watched the last shreds of Suzanne disintegrate at his feet.

'Abba,' he cried to God in a whisper.

'No!' she screamed as twenty lost years mocked her. 'No!' She doubled over and crouched like a wounded animal. 'Thys,' she cried out, and Rev. Phillip knew that only one edge of the sword had touched her. It had broken her in two.

He closed his eyes as the words of Isaiah filled his mind. 'For a small moment I have forsaken thee: but with great mercies will I gather thee.'

The dry dusty plains of yesterday had become a carpet of tiny flowers born on the rain of the night before. Each bent its head as the heavy iron wheels of wagons rolled over them, the wagons' flat backs covered with sleeping members of Tshepo's family.

'Who do you trade with here?' Thys called as they rolled noisily into the grounds of a mission station. It was large and well established but seemed empty. The ringing church bells reminded him of Rev. Phillip but nothing else had any connection with the mission he remembered so well.

'The very holy Reverend Unsworth!' Tshepo brought the wagon to a halt, leapt down and moved in bounds towards a portly gentleman who had stepped out of a small house beside the church. His white collar was slightly crooked around his throat and his chubby neck bright red, like all Englishmen.

'My friend! Welcome!' Rev. Unsworth's voice boomed and his plump arms wrapped themselves around Tshepo. 'Welcome, welcome!' He patted Tshepo's back and then stood back as he saw Thys.

'I see you have a prisoner?' He smiled at Tshepo but his eyes were on Thys.

'I own him!' Tshepo roared with laughter as he beckoned Thys. 'Mr Thys Bothma.'

'Come in.' Rev. Unsworth indicated the neat white manse close by, putting his arm around Tshepo as they moved towards it.

Thys followed Tshepo as he walked arm in arm with a man of God. He glanced back at the others; they had all slipped off the wagons and moved under a tree to sleep.

'My friend Tshepo tells me he owns your life.' Unsworth stood back at the door for Thys to enter. 'Come in. Enjoy a glass of wine?' Although his words were welcoming Thys felt ill at ease. He glanced at Tshepo, whose eyes darted between them, trying to place Thys's true loyalties.

'You do not know each other?' Tshepo asked, surprised.

'No.' Thys stood awkwardly in the doorway.

Tshepo hesitated as he looked at the two white faces beside him, and then towards the familiar comfort of his sleeping family.

'I speak business when you have finished your white talk.' He grinned at Unsworth, backing away towards his people under the tree. 'Talk! Talk! He talks English!' he reassured Unsworth, and loped away towards the shade of the tree.

'What business do you do with Tshepo?' Thys asked as Unsworth led him into the cool of a small whitewashed room. It was a paradise of all earthly things and Thys's eyes danced in amazement.

455

'Excuse me.' Unsworth clapped his hands and a naked black girl slid out of bed and ran out. 'One of my patients.' He moved to a tray of bottles. 'And what is your business, Mr Bothma?'

'Water. I trade in water with Tshepo.' He watched the chubby soft hand uncork a bottle of wine. 'And you in guns?'

'One has to earn a crust.' Rev. Unsworth handed a glass of wine to Thys. 'You do drink wine and not kaffir beer, I trust.'

'Why do you arm these people?' Thys's eyes settled on a dusty bible under the bottle of brandy by the bed. 'These people trust you.'

'Believe me, dear fellow, there'll come a time when those savages out there won't choose between Boer, English or God himself. But,' he dropped his huge frame into a chair and it sank till its sagging base touched the floor, 'in the meantime I encourage them to use the guns on one another. The biggest war in this pretty land will be between the black tribes, you know.' He smiled. 'Very useful to my tribe. The British.' His lizard eyes slid on to Thys. 'Though perhaps not yours.' He sipped his wine. 'You see, Mr Bothma, I serve only the Queen. And God,' he added as an afterthought.

'Tshepo thinks of you as his friend.'

'I am!' He smiled happily. 'He wants guns, and I get him guns. Useless guns perhaps, but he knows no different. Then, when the time comes, I will go home.'

'Do you care nothing for this country or its people?' The acid edge of the wine in his mouth inflected his voice. 'When you have what you want you'll walk away?'

'I will have left God's word.' Unsworth looked at Thys in mock surprise. 'A fair exchange for their land.' He smiled. 'Or do you consider it your land?' The lids of Unsworth's eyes lowered like hoods.

Thys stood up, placing his glass on the table. Everything his father had said about the British was wrapped up in one man.

'You will take our land. And our language.' Thys saw his father's hanging body surrounded by British troops. 'And then we will kill you.'

Unsworth leaned back and printed Thys's face in his memory.

'Tell your black friend I am ready to talk of guns.' He flicked his hand and dismissed Thys as he would a servant.

Thys looked at the wagon rumbling slowly in front of them. It was loaded with guns, hidden under a pile of skins.

'Why does the missionary anger you?' Tshepo was studying him intently. 'The Boer does not think the black man should have guns? You do not trust us?'

'I do not think you can trust the missionary,' Thys said quietly.

'Can he trust us!' He nudged Thys hard in the ribs and laughed. 'Can you?' Tshepo's eyes opened wide as a look of mild curiosity filled them. 'What is it the Boer wants from me? My water or my land?' He watched Thys keenly. 'Why do you ride with me? You like blacks?'

'I've told you.'

'Because I saved your life?' Tshepo shook his head. 'I don't think so.'

Thys didn't really understand why himself. He was fascinated by the dignity and humility Tshepo embodied, but what had begun as a fragment from his past had developed into something deeper.

'Remember you can't trust me either, Boer!' Tshepo rolled over the back of the wagon seat and dropped on to the flat back, pulling his shirt over his head ready to sleep.

'How many days travelling to your land?' Thys asked.

'You will know.' Tshepo's voice stirred against the edges of sleep and the grinding wheels of the wagons rolled on, carrying Thys into the depths of Tshepo's Africa.

Chapter Twenty-six

The former glory of Bonne Esperance fell away as early-morning shafts of light streaked across the room highlighting the spaces on the walls where pictures had hung. The curtains were down and the windows bare and grubby as the sun penetrated each small pane. The wood in the frames was cracked and, as Rosita took down the last curtain, paint flakes clung to the brocade as if trying to escape with it.

'My children are grown. They will be all right.' Rosita smiled and Emily saw Maria in her face. Maria would have wept if she could see them now, she thought. 'Sunday says he will find work and I will come with you.'

'There will be no other work for Sunday.' Emily closed her eyes as Jack took the curtain from Rosita and pushed it into a box. Her entire life was disappearing into boxes.

'Tell Sunday to go to Mr Westbury!' Clara stepped towards Rosita. 'Unless, of course, his ideals as a politician end where the practicalities of life begin.' She tugged at the curtain Jack had packed. 'Must you roll them like that!' She turned her anger on to him as she hauled the curtains out of the box. 'Heaven knows why we've bothered to take anything with us. Doubtless they will take the entire country from under our noses soon enough.'

'Who will?' Emily regarded Clara coldly.

'I do believe you're enjoying this! Indeed, I believe suffering has begun to suit you, Emily!'

'What suffering? There are many more unfortunate people than us. People who don't even have a small house in Cape Town to move into!' Emily turned to Rosita to avoid Clara's gaze. 'I think we should do the carpet now. Would you call Sunday, please.'

'Yes, Miss Emily.' Rosita slipped out of the room quickly as

458

she sensed a storm brewing.

'I have kept silent for long enough.' Clara looked down at Emily. 'I have sat and watched you eat mealie pap like a black and heard you preach to us all that poverty is good for the soul! You continually remind us that it is *your* house in Cape Town which will save us! That even as a cripple it is you who will lead us to the promised land!' Clara's eyes glinted, lit by anger. 'I will tell you why we're here! It is punishment for the sins of our father, which you condoned!'

'How dare you constantly lay the blame at his feet!'

'No, Emily. I lay the blame directly at yours. It is you who has gained some perverse pleasure from the poverty we've been driven to. It is you who encouraged Geoffrey to sacrifice himself in order that there would be one less mouth to feed!'

'It isn't a sacrifice, Mother. It is what I want.' Clara swung round at Geoffrey's voice as he came into the room. He was dressed in the bright-red uniform of the British army and her eyes darted over it in a moment of panic. She moved to him but stopped as Jack stepped in front of her.

'No,' he said firmly, and stood resolutely between his mother and brother.

'No?' Her voice was dry. 'You dare to tell me "no"!'

'Geoffrey is going. There is no more you can say.'

'Isn't there? Tell me the truth, Geoffrey. It was Jack who talked you into this, am I right?'

'No, Mother.' Though his body shook Geoffrey hid his fear under the cloak of his uniform. 'It was my decision.' He looked at Jack. 'He tried to stop me.'

'Because of your father?' Clara's voice was suddenly gentle. 'Charles Marsden?'

Emily looked up as she caught the tone she had grown to recognize and waited for Clara to play her last card.

'I think it is time I told you about your father, Geoffrey.' Clara's voice quietened further. It was almost seductive. 'Have you ever wondered why you are so special to me?'

The weight of Jack's hand on Clara's shoulder stopped her. 'I would like to speak to you, Mother,' he said politely and turned her forcefully towards him, indicating she should move through the door past Geoffrey.

'You dare to interfere in Geoffrey's life again?' she spat.

'I dare, Mother.'

Geoffrey stepped aside as his mother passed him and he caught Jack's eye.

'Go,' Jack whispered.

'No!' Clara swung towards Geoffrey but Jack held her back firmly, bundling her out of the room.

'Go, Geoffrey,' he repeated firmly.

Clara tugged her arm free of Jack as he pushed her into the kitchen. 'Don't imagine I'm not aware that even as Bonne Esperance crumbles around us you will push your own brother out to die simply to keep it!' She tried to push past him in the doorway but he held her back. The strength of his grip on her arm was not just to keep her there; she sensed the anger of the grown man behind it and she snatched at the only weapon she had left to use against him.

'It is you who should go! It is your father he's running to, not his own!' She waited for the weapon to pierce Jack's strength but it didn't. Her eyes flickered with momentary confusion. She could feel his fingers dig deep into her shoulder.

'Did you hear what I said?' she screamed in the face of Jack's silence. She tried to pull away again as she heard a horse riding out and reached for the door handle. Her body spun back as he swung her round to face him.

'If you ever tell him the truth of his parentage you will not only have lost your son to the army; you will have lost him to the only man he wants as a father.' He released her and moved to the door. 'I have accepted the shame of your past, but if ever you cared for Geoffrey you will tell yourself, and believe, that Lieutenant Duncan Shaw never existed.' He turned and walked out.

Clara stood absolutely still as Jack's last words banged their way around the kitchen among the stacked pots and pans. She strode to the table and swept a whole pile of plates to the floor. Her eyes fixed on a large pot of mealie pap bubbling on the open wood stove. The smell suffocated her. Her anger centred on the pot and in long determined strides she moved to it; her hand reached out to the handle, steam licked at her wrist. Her fist clenched the hot iron handle and she hurled the pot to the floor. A yellow river of boiling porridge spread across the red quarry tiles and surrounded her.

*

Geoffrey looked back at Bonne Esperance and for the first time in his life he felt totally free. He felt the snug fit of the uniform on his body and turned his horse away from the only home he had ever known. The heels of his highly polished black boots dug into its flanks, his thigh muscles stood out against the tight white cloth of his trousers and he pushed his horse on towards the future Jack had secured for him.

Jack lifted the red tunic from the trunk in the attic and looked at it. The gold braid on the padded shoulders hung in tattered loops and the red cloth hung limply from his hand. Small holes in the material marked the trail of moths. He smiled as he remembered Geoffrey standing in the doorway in his own smart new uniform. As he rolled his father's jacket to put it back in the trunk, he felt something hard pressing against his hand. He shook the jacket and something moved in the pocket. Carefully he slipped his hand in and his fingers closed round the missing key. The key to a symbolic door somewhere in France. The key which his mother had said would one day open the door on the lost pride of the Beauvilliers family.

The morning sun glinted in the mirror pinned to a tree and reflected back on John Westbury's face. He was standing outside the Westbury house, pulling the blade of his open razor down the line of his chin. He stopped as he caught sight of Sarah in the mirror. She was heavily pregnant and chasing after their seven-year-old daughter Katinka.

'Come here!' Sarah ordered as she stopped to catch her breath, and her hands held her stomach. 'Come back and put your shoes on.'

'I don't need them!' the barefoot girl called back as she ran towards the stables.

'Let her go. It's good for her.' John turned and watched his daughter. Her auburn hair was a long mass of curls flying behind her and her slim, suntanned legs stretched out in long strides.

'She's quite wild,' Sarah panted. 'I can hardly control her.'

'She's a part of the land.' John ran his eyes over the full line of her belly. 'And you've another child to think of.' Sarah turned away and John caught the slightest hint of fear in her eyes. He wiped his blade on the towel around his neck and slung it in the curve of the tree.

'You won't lose this child, Sarah,' he tried to reassure her gently.

'You're going away again?' Her voice was flat. 'Barnstorming?' She looked over her shoulder and he saw clearly the changes in her. Changes which had happened so gradually he'd missed them. 'Politics is all you live for now.' Her words were full of the fear he'd seen in her eyes. 'It takes up every moment of your time. Every tree bears the face of John Westbury for miles around us but it still isn't enough for you!'

'Sarah.' He felt her body tense under his hand. 'What's wrong?'

'I hear what they say about you around here. I see the looks they give me as your wife.' She turned to him and held on to him. 'You've stepped into another world and it frightens me.'

He rested his chin on her head. 'And if nobody dares to step into that world, Sarah? What then?' he asked.

'But why must it be you?' He saw again the gentle sweetness in her face and he tilted her chin up with his finger. 'Why?'

'Because I am able to step into white politics where others can't.'

'But do you know who the others are any more? Do you know any longer who you are, John?' Fear had returned to her eyes. 'Can't we go back to Cape Town? They understand in Cape Town. They agree with what you're fighting for.'

'That is why I'm here, Sarah. Because these are the people who have to understand their own prejudice.'

Sarah's lip trembled as she looked at him. 'They frighten me.' He pulled her closer, trying to quieten her.

'What about Emily and her family?' Her eyes pleaded with him. 'They're being forced off their land too. Have they any more rights than the people you're fighting for?'

'They have the colour of their skin.'

'Will that stop them losing their home?'

John looked around as Mr Westbury came out of the house. He was bent almost double and squinted up at the sun, as if surprised to see it once again in his lifetime. He moved slowly as he always did and sat himself down carefully on a chair just outside the door.

'I want to go to Cape Town to have the child.' She lowered her head. 'I'll go to Mr and Mrs Robertson.'

'Why?' John felt suddenly threatened and moved in front of her as she turned away.

'It's what I want.'

As Sarah walked towards the house John felt the small gap which had opened between them widen and he no longer knew how to bridge it. The young woman whose freedom of spirit had saved him had somehow been lost.

The sound of a horse attracted his attention. The rider was well dressed and obviously not used to long journeys over rough ground. He pulled his horse up beside John and climbed off it awkwardly.

'Good day.' He dusted his smart black jacket before looking at John properly. 'I'm looking for the farm Bonne Esperance. Can you tell me where it is?'

'That way.' John pointed and then moved away, dismissing what he presumed was yet another debt collector. 'About three miles.' His mind was still on Sarah. On her fears, and the destruction of her spirit.

'John Westbury!' the young man exclaimed as he suddenly recognized him. 'You were with Mather and Beuselinck, am I right?'

'Yes.' John looked at him curiously.

'I work with them now, sir.' The young man lifted his hat. 'It's an honour to meet you, sir. I've followed your career with great interest.'

'Thank you.'

'My name's Ralph Saunders.' The young man held out his hand. 'I wish you luck. Great luck.' Saunders turned back to his horse with a slight air of reluctance. 'How far did you say?'

'Three miles.'

'Honoured to have met you, sir.' He egged his horse on and lifted his behind off the saddle the moment it touched it. 'Goodbye.'

John turned and looked back at the house. He could see Sarah standing at a window. For some reason the admiration of a stranger had made him feel very alone.

'Why do I feel that death is near us again?' Emily looked around her bare bedroom and at the few boxes that contained her belongings. She dipped her pen in the ink, watched the black liquid swirl round the nib and felt herself sinking in it. She could hear voices in the sitting-room but she ignored them. 'Perhaps Bonne Esperance has finally died.'

She looked up at a sharp rattle on her door as Rosita's voice called excitedly, 'Miss Emily, you must come. Quickly!'

'The door's open, Rosita.' Emily was puzzled by the excitement shaking Rosita's entire body. Her teeth gleamed against her dark lips, which were spread in the widest smile Emily had seen for months.

'Come.' Rosita moved to her chair and propelled her hastily to the door. 'Everyone's waiting for you.'

Jack stood silently as Mr Saunders spoke. His words offered the hope he had not imagined possible and he was afraid that if he interrupted, everything would fall apart like a shattered dream.

'Our client wishes to buy all the wines you have and to purchase an option on your next three years' supply.' Mr Saunders looked at Clara as she listened without revealing anything. 'And our client has stipulated that the wines must be ready for shipment immediately,' he went on.

'That's impossible,' Jack objected. 'Surely you can see the farm is run down? It needs money to restore it before we can produce the quantity you are talking about.'

'Be quiet, Jack.' Clara's voice was sharp. She turned to Mr Saunders and smiled. 'We accept the offer.'

'We accept?' Jack looked at Clara with contempt. 'What do you know of the destruction in the vineyard, Mother? You can tell me how we turn land that has lain idle for years back to full production? Can you?'

'My client is aware of that possibility.' Mr Saunders looked up as Emily was pushed into the doorway by Rosita. 'Good day,' he smiled politely.

'Please go on,' Emily said quietly. She had caught the tingle of excitement in the air.

'My client would be prepared to advance the capital required to restore the estate, against the wines.' He looked at Jack questioningly. 'I presume it is you who will be running the estate?'

'Yes.' Jack's voice was low. 'If your client is prepared to advance the money, then of course we will accept the offer.'

'A suitable guarantor would have to be found.' Mr Saunders was enjoying his moment as the bearer of good news. 'And the estate will naturally stand as collateral against the advance.'

'Excuse me.' Emily cleared her throat and he looked at the gentle face of the woman in the wheelchair. 'I'm a little lost. This client you speak of. Who is it?'

'I'm afraid that's impossible for me to say.'

'You don't know?' Emily looked at him in surprise.

'Does it matter?' Clara snapped. 'Or are you sorry the chance of installing the family in your Cape Town house has passed you by?'

'One moment,' Jack overrode Clara. 'There is still the question of a guarantor.'

'That should be no problem at all.' Mr Saunders' face lit with a smile. 'Your neighbour, Mr Westbury, would be more than acceptable.'

'John Westbury?' Clara regarded him with horror. 'You would require John Westbury to guarantee our worth?'

'I'm certain my client would find him more than acceptable. It would be no problem, surely?' He looked at Clara quizzically. 'You know him, I believe?'

'Who is your client?' Emily persisted, while Clara seethed with indignation.

'I'm afraid I'm not at liberty to disclose the identity of the person involved.'

'That's all right.' Jack seized the chance that had been held out to him by a stranger. 'I assure you I will get the guarantees you require, Mr Saunders.' Already his mind was preparing what he would say to John Westbury. 'I will ensure everything is in order as soon as possible.'

Emily still felt threatened by the anonymity of their sponsor but she pushed it to the back of her mind as she looked at Jack. His first chance would not be snatched away by her.

The road to the Westbury farm was longer than Jack remembered. He looked through the dusk at the sheep scattering in a field behind the house and saw the small girl, Katinka, racing bareback among them. He could just make out the outline of Mr

465

Westbury sitting quite still on the chair outside the house.

'It's a simple request, John,' he practised the words he would say. 'It would benefit you to be seen to support the farmers in this area.' The words weren't right, he decided, and began again. 'It seems your guarantee would be quite acceptable,' he said in his head with surprise behind the words.

A light went on in the house ahead of him and Sarah stepped out. She took the old man by the arm and led him in, calling out into the dusk, 'Katinka! It's time to come inside.' The girl turned her horse and rode obediently towards the house and Jack Marsden.

'Do you want to see my father?' The lovely young face of Katinka Westbury looked across at Jack as he rode to the house and she reached for the reins. 'I'll take your horse for you. You're Jack Marsden, aren't you?' The delicate pink mouth turned up in a bright smile. 'I've seen you before.'

'Yes.' He climbed down from his horse. 'And you're Katinka Westbury. Am I right?'

'Jack!' It was John Westbury approaching from the house. Jack prepared his speech again in his head.

'You know my father?' Katinka smiled as she held his horse's reins. Her small body jerked forward as his horse tossed its head back. 'I didn't know that,' she beamed and walked the two horses away.

'Hello, Jack. It's nice to see you.' Jack looked at John Westbury's extended hand. 'Is there something I can do for you?'

'Yes, actually, there is.' Jack took his hand and opened his mouth to allow the words out. But as he did, all his pretence dropped under John's open and friendly gaze.

'I need your help,' he said instead.

Suzanne watched as the carriage rolled down the road towards Bonne Esperance with only one small bag on top of it. It was Rev. Phillip's bag. She had pushed into it the few items that her son had tossed at her feet. They had filled only a corner of the bag and the emptiness surrounding her belongings had closed in with the soft brown leather. She walked slowly after the carriage in the tracks the iron wheels had made. Rows and rows of unkempt vines ran alongside the road. They rustled and she heard the childish shouts of children echo among them.

'Come here, Suzanne!' Prudence called with a laugh. 'Come here and I'll tell you! Thys Bothma likes you! I think he loves you!' Prudence's giggle somersaulted over the vines and away.

'Has he kissed you?' Emily's young voice came in its place. 'Ugh! Fancy letting him kiss you.'

Suzanne started as she heard a bird whistle behind her. Her pulse raced and she had to force herself to keep going towards the house, ignoring the sound.

A shimmering sheet of flames spread in front of it as she looked and she heard herself shout, 'Jean Jacques' back is on fire, Father!'

'Perhaps it isn't Thys Bothma we need worry about after all.' Clara's voice rang clearly through the crackle of flames. Hooves thundered and the red flames became the uniforms of British soldiers. Charles Marsden sat proudly on his horse and Thys was beside him. He looked confused. Suzanne felt the thud of a kick against the back of her legs and Willem Bothma's body swung from behind her, and round till it faced her. He turned slowly like a spinning top, and smiled at her as the rope strangled him.

'Who's that?' Emily looked through the window curiously as she held the weight of the curtain while Rosita rehung it and leaned forward in her chair to see more clearly. 'Someone's here.'

Rosita doubled her large body over and bent down to look as she held the curtain up with one hand. 'It's a carriage,' she said.

'I know it's a carriage, Rosita. But nobody has climbed out of the carriage!'

Rosita sighed; she bent forward and looked again. 'Nobody has got out of the carriage,' she agreed.

Emily pushed the curtain off her lap and Rosita clung to it as the full weight pulled her down and the stool she stood on wobbled. She let her breath out in a huff and lifted the curtain with her foot to hold it as Emily pushed herself towards the door.

The carriage driver sat quite still with his top hat tilted to one side. He straightened it as he saw Emily push her way through the open door of the house.

'Evening,' he said and nodded.

'Good evening.' Emily looked at the empty carriage, saying

nothing. The driver turned his head away, as though there was nothing untoward at all. Emily cleared her throat. He turned and looked at her.

'Is there some reason you're here?' she asked with a polite smile.

'My passenger is following behind,' he said with a little embarrassment and glanced at the roof to distract her attention. 'I'll unload the baggage.' He reached back for the small bag on top of the carriage.

Emily was a little irritated by the absurdity of his carefully unloading one small bag.

'Would you mind explaining yourself, my man!' She carried the authority of her years in her voice. 'You drive your carriage up to our front door. You unload a bag . . . ' Emily stopped. A woman had walked around the sharp bend of the drive leading to the house.

'Who's that?' her voice crept out. The woman began running towards her, the darkening gold hair slipping from the top of the woman's head and falling around her shoulders as she ran.

'Oh!' Emily exclaimed, and the driver looked at her curiously. 'Suzanne!' Emily's excitement shrieked in her voice as her sister reached her and threw her arms around her in her chair.

The driver looked at the two women and his nose twitched with discomfort as they rocked in one another's arms without speaking. He dropped the small bag with a thud beside them. 'That'll be half a crown,' he said.

'I haven't got half a crown,' Suzanne turned to him and wiped at the tears running down her cheeks. 'Have you, Emily?'

'No!' Emily laughed as her own tears fell freely. 'I haven't got a half-crown.'

The driver glared at the two women, who apparently found great amusement in the fact that he was not to be paid. He snatched the small bag back as some form of surety and Suzanne laughed hysterically.

'That's not worth half a crown.' She turned back to Emily as tears of laughter poured down her cheeks.

'Have this.' Emily pulled a small pendant from around her neck and tossed it at him.

'What am I supposed to do with this?' He looked at the pendant in his hand glumly.

'Eat it!' Emily's eyes devoured Suzanne's face as if she were snatching back the lost years.

Suzanne pushed Emily's chair into the sitting-room and stopped as their impoverishment swamped her. Emily felt the shock which had involuntarily stopped the chair and looked back at her. Suzanne's face was pale as her eyes moved over the room looking for the comfort her memory held.

'Miss Suzanne!' Rosita hooked the curtain finally into place and clambered off the wooden stool, clapping her hands in delight. 'It's you!' Her voice dropped to a warm mellow note. 'Oh!' Her hands covered her mouth. 'Your bedroom! Where will she sleep, Miss Emily?' Rosita's concern had switched quickly back to housekeeping.

'It's all right, Rosita.' Emily touched Suzanne's hand.

'May I see my bedroom?' Suzanne said quietly. She longed for some contact with the past. Memory played strange tricks. She had forgotten that the sense of unease she felt now had always been there, even when the family had been wealthy.

'Where's Clara?' she asked suddenly as she remembered the source from which it sprang. She looked around sharply as though afraid Clara might appear from nowhere.

'What is it, Suzanne?' Emily asked. Suzanne was looking down the hallway towards the familiar closed door of her bedroom. She took a tentative step towards it and stretched her hand out to open it.

The lace curtains had gone. The room was bare and the delicate wall covering she remembered was brown and faded, its edges tattered and curled back as if it was trying to roll itself off the walls in shame.

'It's all right now, Suzanne. Bonne Esperance will live again. Jack has great plans.' Emily could see the deep sadness in her eyes. 'Bonne Esperance will rise again.'

'No.' Suzanne looked towards the window. 'Too much has happened.' She moved to it as if looking for a way out. 'It's not just poverty is it, Emily?' She looked at her sister as she sat quietly in her chair. Emily looked curiously old-fashioned; remote. The chair seemed to have trapped her in the past which Suzanne remembered, but which seemed to have vanished. 'Everything's gone,' she said, as she noticed the eucalyptus tree was no longer outside her bedroom window.

Emily took Suzanne's hand and ran her fingers over the hard skin that betrayed the life she had lived as a poor white. She could see the years of pain in her hands as well as her eyes.

'I told you about John Westbury,' she said. Suzanne nodded without looking at her. 'He has found his place in politics and will fight against the very thing which brought us to this. You're right. It's not just poverty.' She felt Suzanne's hand pull to release itself but she held on to it. 'He came back to where it all began. To his beginnings.' Suzanne turned and looked at Emily. 'This is your home,' Emily said. 'You can never run away from it.' She caught the slightest contradiction in Suzanne's eye, and paused. 'At least try.'

The slippery head of the newborn baby pushed into the open palms of Elizabeth Robertson's hands and she looked away. She had seen the jet-black hair and dark skin, still warm and moist from birth. She felt the soft bone of the skull and the tiny neck with her fingertips and instinctively pulled the baby towards life. She didn't hear Sarah's last cry or the baby's first gasp of breath. All she heard was Sarah's clear voice the day she'd arrived in their home.

'If it is dark, you will take it away. You will find a home and you will forget the child was born alive.' Sarah's voice had been sharp. Nothing about her was the way the Robertsons remembered her. The open young girl they had loved as their own had vanished.

'But why?' James had interrupted, almost putting his hand up for attention. 'I don't understand why, Sarah.' He'd turned in a circle and looked at her helplesssly, pale with horror. 'It's your child. What difference if it isn't white?' His arms had dropped to his sides in bewilderment. 'It's a baby. It's John's child!'

'And it could destroy him.' Sarah's voice had held the flat note of certainty. She had leaned forward suddenly, gripping her stomach at a contraction, and stared at them both from pain-filled eyes. 'Promise me you will do as I say! Promise!'

'But I've never delivered a child before,' Elizabeth argued, glancing at her husband for help, or escape. 'It's dangerous.'

'I will not allow your life to be put at risk.' James Robertson had tried to infuse his words with common sense. 'Elizabeth cannot be held responsible.' He turned away as if the headmaster's decision was final.

'Then you do not care for John.' Sarah had waited until the provocation had made him turn back to her. 'If you cared for him at all, you would not allow this child to threaten him.' She had paused and looked from one to the other, her eyes filled with betrayal. 'Promise me,' she begged. 'Please.'

They had. Reluctantly Mr and Mrs Robertson had promised that if the child was not white they would arrange for it to be cared for in an orphanage, and forgotten.

The baby's screams broke through Elizabeth's anguish and she looked down at the wriggling baby on the bloodied sheets between Sarah's legs. It was a boy. A dark boy child still attached by a long fleshy cord to its mother.

'Tell me.' Sarah's voice reached out to Elizabeth on a heavy breath. Elizabeth looked down, unable to answer. Mechanically she held the cord tight and cut it as Sarah pushed herself up on her elbows, looking down between her legs. 'Take it away!' she screamed and fell back, burying her head in the pillow.

Elizabeth turned to her husband for help as the baby cried. James Robertson stood a little way away, gazing silently at the slippery dark child whose future was in his hands. He moved to Elizabeth and took the child. He felt the tiny body writhe in his hands as the small limbs waved through the air, clutching for something to hold on to in the frightening world outside his mother's womb.

'You will look at this baby,' he demanded and carried the screaming dark scrap of humanity towards Sarah's face.

'No!' She swung her head to the other side, her eyes tightly shut.

'Look!' James Robertson demanded again. 'It's your son and he needs you.'

Elizabeth looked down as the placenta slipped out with Sarah's last unwilling contribution to the birth of her unwanted child. A son she would once have loved deeply, whose colour she would not even have noticed; but that time had passed.

James Robertson glanced at his wife helplessly as he held the baby and she lifted the placenta, dropping it into a bowl. The remnants of its birth discarded, they looked together at the dark little face, its mouth stretched wide with its pathetic cries. Elizabeth wrapped the baby in a soft white blanket without removing it from her husband's arms. James Robertson's face was confused as he looked at her. A small boy peered at her from her husband's face; a small lost boy whose head suddenly bowed with the guilt he carried in his arms.

'Go,' Elizabeth said to him. His eyes lifted to her face and a single tear formed. It rolled slowly down his cheek and Elizabeth knew it wasn't just for the child in his arms. It was for the girl they had taken into their hearts as their own daughter. A young girl who had died at an unrecorded moment when her husband John had stepped into the political arena to fight for the rights of 'non-white' people. She had been exposed to a fear she had not known existed till then.

James Robertson stood before the flaking walls of the convent, with the baby in his arms. Each step he had taken towards this place was a step away from his deepest beliefs, his belief in the dignity of man.

He couldn't remember ringing the bell, and he couldn't remember the door opening. All he saw was the nun's face peering at him from the oval frame of her black habit. Her eyes were pale and her face scrubbed till it shone. Behind her a middle-aged coloured woman leaned around and looked at Mr Robertson curiously. Her eyes moved from him to the white-blanketed bundle in his arms. She knew there was a baby in it, and she knew its colour. The guilt in James Robertson's face had told her everything.

'What is it?' the Irish nun asked as she looked at the wrapped bundle in his arms. 'What are you wanting?' She pulled back the blanket with fingers entwined by a rosary, looked at the baby's face and held out her hands as though her question needed no further answer.

'I found him,' Mr Robertson said nervously as the child was taken from him and his body moved after it protectively. He drew back and moved his weight from one foot to the other, glancing at the coloured woman beside the nun.

'He was abandoned,' he said to her.

'Yes,' the nun said quietly as she handed the baby to the coloured woman. 'What's his name?'

The coloured woman's eyes moved from the dark child to

James.

'Villiers,' James spluttered as he remembered the name Beau-villiers.

'Christian name?' The nun's face had not changed since he'd first looked at her. 'Or is he Muslim?'

'John,' he said quickly.

'Villiers is an Afrikaans name, surely.' The nun didn't smile.

'Johannes,' he corrected himself quickly. 'Johannes Villiers.'

'Johannes Villiers,' the nun repeated, and the coloured woman nodded.

'Yes.' James noticed his shoes were dirty as he looked down at his feet and examined them with great care.

'His name was attached to him when you found him?' The nun's face had still not changed expression and the coloured woman's eyes hadn't wavered.

'It is his name.' James Robertson pulled himself erect. 'All children should be named. Most especially abandoned children.'

The nun nodded and lifted her pale hand towards him. Automatically he lifted his to take it, but she had reached for the door, to close it on him.

'Goodbye,' she said.

Through the rapidly closing gap he saw the coloured woman looking at him, as though she herself had just been passed into the anonymous hands of an orphanage.

'May I come and see him?' James Robertson blustered and put his foot in the door. 'I would like to be able to visit him.'

'Why?' The nun held on to the door and looked at him keenly. The coloured woman's eyes lit with a moment's hope as if her life depended on his answer.

'Perhaps it's better I don't.' James watched the hope in the coloured woman's face die with his words. He had died a little himself.

He turned as the door pushed closed against him and heard the rattle of a key in the lock. He stepped forward and walked in uncertain steps towards the gate. He stopped, as if he was being called by unheard voices, and looked back. A crowd of small brown faces with large round eyes and noses flattened against the window panes stared at him.

Chapter Twenty-seven

Geoffrey dug deep into the hard wood of the solid door with an angular piece of sharpened flagstone. He ran his finger down the groove he had carved in the wood. It was the letter G. It had taken him days to carve one letter in the dark of the prison cell and he pressed on slowly, knowing that many days stretched ahead of him.

He heard the small shutter outside the cell open and moved himself along the wall towards it. He felt for the familiar brick and pulled it out of the wall, peering into the oblong shape of light. The lid of a metal bowl clattered as it was pushed into the space. He lifted the cover quickly, before the light vanished, and saw the familiar lumpy porridge.

'Who are you?' Geoffrey called out to whoever had delivered his food. 'Talk to me.'

The shutter slammed shut. In darkness Geoffrey felt for the bowl, pulled it out and replaced the brick in the wall. He moved down the rough damp stone with his back until he reached the corner of the cell and sat on the floor, wet from the sea just outside the castle walls. He dug into the porridge with his fingers.

The events which had torn the immaculate red uniform from his back and tossed him into the oblivion of the cell came into his mind, as they did every day and he pondered again how his dreams had come to such an abrupt end.

The red coats of his troop had stood tall and erect in a long line, their rifles ready to fire. He had heard the bawling voice of the sergeant, 'Aim!' He saw himself still low to the ground, rifle to his shoulder, waiting for the last possible moment before rising.

'Marsden!' The sergeant's voice had blasted into his head and Geoffrey had risen from the ground, snapping to attention. The grim-faced sergeant had marched towards him and the crunch of his boots still ground into Geoffrey's memory.

'Do you imagine the name "Marsden" singles you out for special treatment, boy?' the sergeant bellowed in his ear. 'Do you think the name Marsden enables you to disobey orders?'

'No, sergeant.' Geoffrey heard his own reply and felt again the anger the sergeant's ignorance stirred in him. 'I have tried to explain that we must rise as they do, sergeant. Rise prepared to fire.'

'As "they" do? They?' The sergeant's foul breath had wafted into his face. 'Who?'

'The Boers, sergeant.'

'So, you prefer to be taught by ragamuffin Boers?' The voice rose.

'They have learned from the land, sergeant. If this drill had been in the face of the Xhosas, every soldier would have an assegaai in his head. Or a bullet.'

'Ah!' The sergeant's beady eyes had fastened on to Geoffrey more keenly and the stale tobacco breath had hit him again. 'Your father taught you that, did he? Your father and the famous Colonel Stringer?'

'No, sir. The people.'

'People!' The sergeant's voice had reflected amazement that there were such things as people. 'People!' he had screamed again.

Geoffrey swallowed hard as a solid lump of porridge stuck in his throat, then he coughed and breathed again. His mind turned back to the sergeant, to soldiers being drilled as if all wars were fought according to the rules in the British army manual, and to his own stupidity as he defied orders yet again. Geoffrey could still feel the strong grip of the military policemen as they snatched at his pride and dragged him away.

'An army cannot sleep in the comfort of pyjamas! You're an idiot!'

He had yelled back at the sergeant: 'The blood of these soldiers will be on your hands when your stupidity kills them!' Geoffrey had felt his head lifting off his shoulders as he was yanked up by his hair.

'Throw him in the donkergat!'

*

475

The cold wet chill of the 'donkergat' prison cell ate into Geoffrey's bones as he ran his fingers round the inside of the bowl and licked from them the last scrap of porridge. He looked blindly into the darkness and his hand felt for the small chip of sharpened flagstone. He crawled back across the floor to the wall and his fingers ran down the cold stone until they found the wood surround of the door, and the words carved almost forty years earlier, WILLEM BOTHMA. The name meant nothing to him except the brotherhood of a fellow prisoner, and the fact that it was immediately above his own carved letter 'G'. His finger found the letter, tracing its way through its curve, and his hand moved a fraction to the right to carve the letter 'E'.

'Marsden!' Geoffrey pulled back at the blinding light which burst through the door as it was swung open. He fell forward as his balance was disturbed by the sudden light, and saw the highly polished boots in front of him.

'You have your chance to prove yourself, Marsden.' The sergeant's familiar rasp tingled with anticipation of revenge. 'You are to have the opportunity of putting your theories into practice, boy.'

Geoffrey looked up from the large boots to the square chin above him. He squinted against the unfamiliar light which still blinded him. Through the glare, yellowing teeth appeared between cracked lips as the mouth widened in a smile.

'Your father is to be promoted,' the sergeant's voice cracked with a laugh. 'At last he is old enough for an end to be put to the embarrassment he and his friend Colonel Stringer cause.' The collar of Geoffrey's shirt squeezed tight around his neck as the sergeant pulled him off the ground towards his foul breath. 'You have been selected to ride out and inform him that he has been promoted out of the British army and into the obscurity of retirement.' He paused. 'The loss of one man is all we are prepared to risk, and it seemed fitting it should be you.' Geoffrey's body crumpled as the sergeant released his grip on the shirt. He looked at the gleaming boots in front of him and he wept. At last he was to meet his father.

Marsden watched Stringer keenly and pulled at a piece of dried meat with his teeth, ripping it off the hard stick of biltong. The salty taste was something Charles had grown to enjoy. Chewing on dried meat and gristle had become part of his new life, a life in which all childhood lessons on table manners had been forgotten. His sixtieth birthday had also passed by, forgotten in the world Stringer created; one which laid no importance on time yet paid the seasons close attention. It was one in which Charles Marsden had found a strange sense of joy.

Stringer peered through the darkness towards the mission as he ground the meat between his teeth into a flat pad.

'We'll move into the mission at dawn.' He glanced at Marsden. 'When he's unprepared.'

'Has he reported trouble?' Marsden spat the slimy remains of biltong into the fire which crackled between them.

'Only the trouble he causes himself while he's feathering his own nest.' Stringer smiled as he spat his chewed remains after Marsden's. 'Strange fellows these missionaries.' He leant back on one elbow. 'This one appears to have a special arrangement with God. That he should take part in any manner of devilish things so he can report back on the enemy's success or failure!' Stringer laughed and pulled again on the dried meat. 'I asked Unsworth once why he was surprised the Boers had tried to close the missionaries' roads.' He glanced at Charles. 'They are gunrunning roads and I believe well travelled by Mr Unsworth. He answered, that the blacks up North needed protection. "From whom?" I inquired. "Themselves," he answered.' Stringer's jaw moved continually as he talked. 'The blacks have no respect for the Boers, but don't much care if the white skin belongs to an Englishman either, according to Unsworth.'

'Perhaps they imagine it's their country.'

'The Boers?'

'The blacks.'

'Perhaps.' Stringer patted Marsden's arm as he stood up and stretched his aching body, which had covered thousands of miles in Marsden's company. 'I think we'll convince them they need us.' He grinned. 'Why should we wait till the morning, old man?'

Marsden and Stringer pulled together on the mission bell rope and their eyes sparkled with the delight of naughty children as they shouted over the metallic clanging.

'I was a choir boy, you know. Westminster Abbey!' Charles Marsden beamed pleasure at Stringer as they tugged sinfully on the rope.

'And I an acolyte at St Paul's!' Stringer roared with laughter, looking down from their position on top of the church. He saw the flicker of an oil lamp as it struggled to burn itself to light. Then the door of Unsworth's small house opened, and he grinned. 'Pity we haven't still got the choir boy pitch!'

Charles looked blankly at his moving lips as the bell drowned his voice. Stringer held his hands up, cupped them around his mouth and shouted down.

'I have come for you, Reverend Unsworth!' he bellowed, moving his cupped hands open and closed to add a ghostly echo.

Unsworth stood naked in the centre of the mission with the light from his swinging lamp glowing around his large pink body as he peered heavenward while turning in a small circle.

'Who is it?' he called to the stars. He stopped and the hoods of his eyes lowered against the light of the lamp. 'It's you, you bastard kaffir!' he yelled.

'You don't know me?' Stringer boomed down. 'But I know you, Reverend Unsworth, and I have come for you!'

Unsworth looked up in terror as two figures slid down the curved white arch of the church gable and leapt to the ground in front of him.

'We've seen worse, Unsworth.' Stringer allowed his eyes to pass over the man's protruding pink belly and shrinking manhood. 'Your mission bells call us to God naked as we came surely.' Stringer paused as a black girl ran out of the house behind Unsworth. 'Though usually one by one,' he added.

'I had no idea you were coming tonight, Colonel Stringer.' Unsworth backed his mass of pink flesh away. His thighs closed together in protection, forcing his legs to bend outwards at the knees. 'I am hardly prepared for such an honour.' He bowed to conceal his wobbling pink flesh.

'Nor were we!' Stringer chuckled, put his fingers to his lips, and whistled. 'But I'm certain my men will not object.'

The band of grubby men appeared from the darkness like moths, surrounding Unsworth with roars of raucous laughter.

'We need food, sleep and news.' Stringer glanced at his men. 'Some might need other recreation.' He turned to Charles. 'May I introduce Colonel Charles Marsden. This is the Reverend Unsworth. On mission in darkest Africa for his Queen, his Country

478

and his pocket,' he smiled at Unsworth's nakedness, 'which appears to have been mislaid.'

His body clothed at last, Unsworth handed Stringer a glass of wine and turned to Charles with another.

'It's a Cape wine. Much better than I'd have thought. A luxury I purchased from a charming woman at great cost.' He sipped his own and smiled his chubby smile. 'A decent little wine in its way. Yes.' He nodded his knowledge at them. 'I need it for communion, you know.' The eyes regained their lizard look, the lids lowered and he tried to gain some authority.

'Where's it from?' Charles looked up as the taste pushed him headlong into a past he'd almost forgotten. He reached for the bottle and looked at the sticky remnants of a label. 'There's a similar wine I knew well once. Bonne Esperance.'

'I'm afraid I have no idea of its identity,' Unsworth smiled. 'I ensure the labels are removed before I purchase the wine, being uncertain where it originated, if you understand my meaning.'

'Shall we talk of news in this area rather than wine?' Stringer leaned back and pushed his boots off. His bare feet were brown with dirt and he flexed his blackened toes with pleasure. Unsworth moved away to the open window. 'What have you for us, Reverend?'

'Things are still quiet. But trouble is just around the corner I should imagine.'

'Why?' Stringer pushed a roll of tobacco into his mouth. 'Which corner?'

'The diamond fields. Ghastly places, filled with man's greed.' Unsworth took refuge in the innocence of a churchman. 'Is it not true that both the Boers and blacks are more than a little uneasy?'

'Why?' Stringer asked, knowing exactly why. 'Do you know?'

'Because of the claim our government has quite rightly made on the land?' Unsworth ventured.

'Perhaps they don't agree that it is British land.' Charles took another sip of wine. He remembered what Thys had told him of Boer aspirations: to live on their own land in peace. 'Du Toit Span and New Rush are, after all, within the boundaries of the Boer Republic.'

'But that particular land is owned by a man who wishes it to

479

be looked after by the British.' Unsworth's pride swelled against his tight clerical collar as he included himself under the Union Jack. 'Nicolas Waterboer, I believe his name is.'

'The other claimants don't seem to agree.' Stringer smiled. 'The Orange Free State, Adam Kok, the Rolong and Thlaping kingdoms. Quite a motley band of people and all laying claim to the diamond fields.' He smiled at Charles. 'Curious so many should claim such a remarkably unattractive piece of land.' He looked at Unsworth suddenly. 'You know these people, do you? Boer or black are they?'

'Both.' Unsworth drained his glass and his eyes narrowed. 'As a matter of fact, I have made myself acquainted with them quite deliberately.' He sat down for the first time and crossed his fat legs. He felt certain he could lead them by the nose to Thys Bothma, who had threatened his dealings with Tshepo. 'Have you ever known a Boer to live with blacks without good reason?'

Stringer watched Charles Marsden curiously as they walked through the mission grounds towards their horses.

'You know the Boer Unsworth talked of, this Thys Bothma?' He stopped beside his horse and pinned his eyes on Charles. 'Do you?' He had noticed the recognition in Marsden's face at the mention of the name. Charles mounted his horse and looked down at Stringer.

'I know him.'

'Yet you said nothing?' Stringer swung his leg over the saddle and the horses bumped together as they pulled their necks back and high-stepped on the hard ground.

'I don't care for that man.' Charles's eyes followed Unsworth's rotund figure as he moved across the grounds. 'He has all the makings of a politician.'

'Indeed.' Stringer shrugged but his eyes stayed firmly on Charles. 'Who is this Thys Bothma?'

'We hanged his father.' Charles turned his horse to ride out. The movement of the wheeling horse carried him back to the hanging of Willem Bothma and the disgrace he'd felt. 'Thys Bothma swore then to seek his revenge on the British,' he called back to Stringer. 'But we will see what information "the Reverend" gathers to uphold his accusations.'

*

Thys had been deeply suspicious the moment Unsworth rode into the village. He had watched him quietly, with Tshepo's small son standing beside him holding his hand. He had seen the faint smile which had passed over Unsworth's face as he took in the fact that Thys was indeed living with the black people; that a small black child held his hand so comfortably.

Unsworth glanced over the circular village of mud huts which bustled with activity and laughter. The people were dressed in an odd assortment of European and native clothes. Some men, women and children among them were not as solid black in colour as Tshepo. Their blood was mixed. Tshepo glanced back at the waterfall which thundered behind them as Unsworth and he talked.

'We deal in water, the Boer and I. Did you not know, Reverend Unsworth, how these white whores love to bath!' Tshepo waved for Thys to join him in front of the small mud hut. 'I notice you have brought me no guns?' he said without looking at Unsworth.

'It's not guns I wish to discuss.' Unsworth watched Thys walking towards them with the black child following each step he took. 'It is your trees I am interested in, Tshepo.' He turned his look back on him. 'I must congratulate you on the number of trees in your area.'

'Your God put them there.' Tshepo banged his fist on the skin he sat on, ordering Thys to sit beside him. 'It is my trees he wants now! You, my water, and he my trees.' He grinned at Thys. 'And all I want is my land with the guns to protect it.'

'It is your land.' The black child settled himself in Thys's lap and Unsworth noted the affection between them. 'The trees on your land are worth a great deal of money, Tshepo. The people on the diamond fields are cold; and there are no trees for firewood. I will pay you very handsomely,' Unsworth promised.

'So does the whore.' Tshepo glanced at Thys.

'But I will give you a guarantee.' Unsworth's huge body rolled over to allow him to reach into his pocket. 'This is a formal contract. Binding on both parties.' Unsworth held out a paper to him.

'Don't sign it,' Thys said quietly, and Tshepo caught the flicker of anger in Unsworth's eyes. He leaned back on one elbow, anticipating the spectacle of two white men fighting over his land.

'It's not the trees you want.' Thys turned to Unsworth coldly. 'You want this piece of land because it blocks the route to the diamond fields.'

'If my friend says that then I want to talk about my land, Reverend.' Tshepo looked at Unsworth, wrapping his arms around his bent knees. 'How do you answer my friend?'

'Your friend!' The lizard eyes slid on to Thys. 'Do you imagine your "friend" is capable of protecting your land in the face of Britain's claim on it? He will fight the entire British army?'

'But you will?' Thys moved the child on to his other knee. 'To protect yourself?'

'Your friend is needlessly alarmed, Tshepo.' Unsworth dismissed Thys. 'I am here only about your trees, offering to sell them for you.'

'No, my very Reverend Mr Unsworth.' Tshepo leant the tips of his elbows on his spread knees and looked at him keenly. 'When you tell me you will sell my trees, you tell me they will be "your" trees! And "your" trees have their roots in the land underneath them!' He shook his head slowly. 'They are my trees. Their roots are in my land! And I have guns, remember!' He shook his head at Unsworth as if scolding a small child.

'And help in using those guns.' As he stood, Unsworth's podgy white hand dusted the wobbling cheeks of his behind. 'So, it is only the whore you will deal with?' He moved away and nodded for the young black man who waited beside his cart. 'And the Boer!' His smile widened as he waved the contract at Tshepo. 'We will forget this for the moment.' His eyes moved to Thys. 'But I doubt the British will forget your friend.'

His short legs carried his corpulent body towards the cart and he climbed into it. He leaned against the cushioned seat as the black man drove the cart away. Unsworth waved his hand grandly.

'The British have long memories, Mr Bothma,' he called back as the cart rolled away from the village across the African plain. Aloes stood like Roman centurions guarding the passage of an emperor.

'You disturb the missionary, Thys Bothma! I think the British will know about you now.' He nodded seriously. 'Not just in memory.'

'Then they will know I have little time for them.' Thys leant back as the small black boy pushed at his face in a play fight.

'Only time for the whore's sister.' Tshepo glanced towards a slim young black girl in the centre of the village. Her naked breasts glowed with sweat and bounced with her movement as she ground corn in a large wooden tub. 'Even a Boer needs a woman,' Tshepo stated.

'I have my woman.' Thys lifted the child in his arms and stood up.

'I do not see her.' He looked around in comic amazement.

'She's in my heart.' Thys took a deep breath of the hot dry air.

Tshepo's great brown eyes had suddenly lost their humour. They passed slowly over the small village and among his people.

'What is it?' Thys crouched beside him and Tshepo's small son leaned forward to his father with him.

'I have heard on the wind, my friend.' Tshepo held a long moment of silence. 'They will take my land. The white men.'

'I will protect your land with you.'

'You?' The sadness in Tshepo's eyes deepened. 'You are white like them!'

'I am your friend.'

'And I own your life?' Tshepo's face grew puzzled. 'And when I have no land to call my land, will your life still be mine?'

Tshepo's son fitted his small hand into Thys's and Thys felt the silky softness of his skin. At once the little black face lit and spread into a smile filled with love.

'You own my life.' Thys looked tenderly at Tshepo's son, who had claimed it as his own.

Prudence sat quite still behind her desk and watched Unsworth as he talked. It was as if the room had closed in around her as his wet pink lips shaped his distaste for the Boer people and spoke with the presumption that she agreed with him.

'Gun-running? Really?' Prudence looked down her nose at him from the height of her chair. Her hands were laid carefully on the desk and the first slight twist of arthritis bent her fingers awkwardly. 'Who did you say this man was?' she asked casually.

'Thys Bothma. I believe you do business with him and his partner Tshepo, the black renegade and thief.'

'Indeed. But we deal in water.' She lifted her nose a little higher. 'It's strange.' She allowed her comment to hang in the air for a moment. 'I have heard the same tales of gun-running about you, Mr Unsworth.' She smiled. 'And theft.'

'Reverend,' he corrected her.

'What a surprise.' Prudence allowed her contempt to show clearly. 'But I'm afraid I know nothing about Thys Bothma. Except that due to him we are able to offer our customers hot baths.' She stood up and moved around her desk. 'If you'll excuse me, I have a business to run.'

'How is it?' Unsworth didn't move. 'Your business?'

'Very good.' She went to the door. 'As yours doubtless is. Goodbye, Mr Unsworth.' She rested her hand on the porcelain knob.

'I assume you know why I questioned you about your relationship with the Boer?' Unsworth waddled to the door beside her, his eyes peeling off her clothes. 'But it might, of course, be an entirely different relationship you enjoy with the Boer than a man of the Church could imagine.'

'Indeed it might.' Prudence swung the door open. She paused as she saw Jim Audsley standing outside. 'Have you heard enough, James?' She nodded for him to enter. 'You said that you'd heard I was a good business woman, Reverend Unsworth. It is because I choose carefully with whom I deal. Goodbye.'

Unsworth pushed past her and she felt the deliberate touch of his shoulder on her breast as he turned back with a crocodile smile.

'Perhaps I will see you again, Mrs Audsley?'

'Perhaps not.' She closed the door firmly behind him, breathing deeply as though at last the air was fresh.

'Who is he?' Audsley asked. She leaned against the door for a moment, closing her eyes. 'This Thys Bothma.'

'The tactics of a man like Unsworth don't suit you, James!' She moved back to her desk.

'And if he's right?' Audsley was on edge.

'About?' Prudence placed her hands on the leather desktop and her eyes ran over the swelling joints of her fingers.

'It would hardly be good for business if the British army takes it into its head to search for him here.' He paused. 'You knew him before he arrived here. True?'

'Of course I know Thys Bothma!' She looked up sharply. 'What is it to you? Have I ever questioned your past?'

'No.' Audsley moved deliberately towards a bottle of wine and she noticed the stoop of his shoulders.

'Where has the money gone, Prudence?' He turned, holding the bottle out to her with a straight arm. 'Why have these labels been removed, Miss Beauvilliers?'

'If you don't like the wine it seems strange you drink so much of it.' Prudence avoided his eyes, and his use of her name.

'Why didn't you tell me?' He came to her desk and set the bottle in front of her. 'It's your family's, isn't it? Bonne Esperance is your home, and this is its wine!'

'Does it matter?' She glanced at the bottle. 'It's fine wine: you've said so yourself. It has also increased our trade and I haven't noticed you refusing the profit we make from it!' Prudence looked at him in the silence left by her words and suddenly she felt sad. He hadn't bounced back at her. He had lost his spirit and become no more than a whorehouse pimp.

'James,' her voice softened, 'everyone talks of the gold in Pilgrim's Rest. Why don't you go there?' She moved around the desk and stood in front of him, searching his face. His eyes no longer held the sparkle of mischief she'd fallen in love with and the crooked smile seldom spread over his face. 'I think you should go.'

'You need me here,' he said quietly.

'Go.' She peered into his face, still searching for a spark of the man he'd been. 'I know what makes you happy.' She wrapped her arms around his shoulders and leant her face against the brocade of his waistcoat. 'These clothes have never suited you. Please go!'

'Did you care for him a great deal?'

'James!' Prudence looked at him, her face a picture of amazement. 'I do believe you're jealous!'

'Have I reason to be?' His jealousy showed clearly.

'Oh James.' She buried her face against his chest again and the charcoal smeared around her eyes. 'How I love you.' She smiled and her radiance lit the room. 'You take the years away! You look at me and you are jealous!'

'Have I reason to be?'

'How you would love Bonne Esperance. Oh James, how they would love you.' She took a deep breath. 'But I can't trap you any longer. You must go, so that you can come back!' She remembered the surge of warmth she had felt every time he had returned to her in the past. 'I don't own you, James. I love you.'

Thys rolled the last barrel of water towards the wagon and Tshepo stood back watching carefully. His son ran beside the barrel cheering, as though each cheer added his strength to Thys's as he pushed the barrel up the wooden ramp and rolled it back against the others. The small boy imitated the sound of slopping water and leapt on to the wagon, clambering over the barrels.

'The missionary has laid a trap for you, Thys Bothma. Don't go to the whore,' Tshepo said without moving to him.

Thys walked to him and the boy jumped off the wagon and ran after Thys, taking his hand possessively when he reached him.

'I see I have lost my son to you.' Tshepo glanced at the child.

'Hiding isn't the answer.'

'I think it is you who are hiding, Thys Bothma.' Tshepo turned and moved away. 'But my son will bring you back, this time!'

With hundreds of miles behind him, his strength had grown and Geoffrey had buried the British army as he'd buried his uniform. Each day had seemed to bring him closer to his father, but he vanished the moment he thought he had caught up with them. Tracking Colonel Stringer had proved almost impossible.

He looked across the vast flat plain, strewn with rocks and cacti. He had set his attention on two flat-topped mountains in the distance and sensed that this time he would find Charles Marsden, somewhere behind them. He leaned lower to his horse's neck, pushed it on faster, and its strides lengthened easily over the flat ground.

The street was wide enough to turn a full span of oxen and the red sand had been flattened and compressed as hard as rock by constant use. Charles Marsden stopped his horse beside a man sitting outside a tent under the shade of its spread of canvas. The sifter's table he worked at was smooth, with a rim around three sides. Stringer pulled up beside Charles and looked down at the sifter as the man pulled a lump of dirt and stones towards him with an iron scraper. With three quick motions he spread the dirt, picked out the stones and tipped the refuse off the board.

'And that's what it's all about.' Stringer glanced at Marsden and then towards the swinging sign outside the bordello. 'Will you join me in Mrs Audsley's Parlour?'

'I'll wait here.' Marsden climbed down from his horse as the sifter pulled another pile of dirt towards him.

'I do believe you're afraid of Mrs Audsley, Charles Marsden.' Stringer lifted his hat and wiped his head with his sleeve.

'Of a whore?' He looked at the bordello. 'But when she leads you to Thys Bothma himself, I will be there.'

Stringer walked with his horse towards the bordello, brushing his beard down and dusting his hat on his knee as he went. His eyes settled on two buxom prostitutes spread out in the sun on the steps outside.

'Good day, ladies,' he said politely. They watched him blankly, without reply. 'Good day, sir!' he answered himself, and climbed up the wooden steps to the bordello.

'Have you seen Mr Audsley, Marianne?' Prudence asked as she came into the kitchen. Her eyes searched among the pots and pans as though she'd lost something. 'I can't find him anywhere.' Prudence stopped. A very old black man was standing in the back doorway with the gauze door held open. He bowed and clapped his hands as Marianne handed him a crust of bread. Marianne had filled out with flesh and confidence and for a moment the old black man was hidden behind her. Prudence indicated for her to move aside and Marianne did so, glancing at the old black man nervously.

'He was hungry. I gave him a crust and told him to go,' she said defensively and waved her hands at him. 'Go on! Shoo!'

'Leave him!' Prudence commanded. There was a silence. 'Why have you come back, Themba?'

'Mfazi needed me.' Themba's wise old eyes radiated a greeting across the kitchen and his mouth widened in a toothless smile.

'Mr Audsley has gone,' Prudence said flatly, in the certain knowledge.

'He has gone,' Themba agreed.

'Good.' Prudence pulled herself straight and turned to Marianne with sudden officiousness. 'Fill a bath and put him in the room down the hall.'

'Mrs Audsley!' Marianne looked at her with horror. 'Surely you don't mean he should sleep inside?'

'Do as I say, Marianne,' Prudence demanded. 'And I will remind you that you needed more than a bath when I took you in!' She turned away abruptly, but was stopped by Themba's slow voice.

'He will come back.'

'Is there anyone at home?' Stringer's voice broke through the moment as he invaded the kitchen. 'Is the Parlour open or closed, Mrs Audsley?'

'Tell him we're closed.' Prudence kept her eyes on Themba as Marianne bobbed a rebellious curtsey and made her way to the door. She pulled up sharply as Stringer stepped into her path.

'Mrs Audsley?' He smiled and bowed to Marianne, then to Prudence, uncertain who was who.

'I am Mrs Audsley, and I'm afraid we're closed.' Prudence dismissed him quickly as she took in his grubby clothes. 'My premises are closed at noon like any other business, sir!'

'I am here on Her Majesty's business, Mrs Audsley.' He smiled and lifted his hat. 'And though her business keeps me on duty even through the heat of midday, it unfortunately does not include sampling your merchandise.'

Prudence dropped the curtain back and her skin rose in goosebumps of recognition. Charles Marsden had looked across at the window from his position beside the sifter and she had seen him clearly. She turned to Stringer with a protective disdain and moved confidently to her desk.

'So that is the man you call your respectable partner. Colonel Marsden. He looks no more respectable to me than you do.' Prudence's mind was filled by memories of Charles Marsden and Clara and she longed to examine him more carefully. To talk to him and somehow make contact with the past and Bonne Esperance. 'Is it no longer army practice to wear a uniform?' She remembered Charles in his red tunic. It had accentuated everything she despised about him. 'Well? What is it I can do for you?' she asked, though she was aware that the repercussions of Unsworth's visit had stepped into her bordello along with Stringer.

'I believe you do business with a black named Tshepo.' Stringer kept his eyes on Prudence constantly. 'In water, so I heard.'

'And firewood and skins.' Prudence sat down behind the safety of her desk. 'Would you enjoy a bath while you're here?' she asked. 'Or is it other business your queen has sent you on – business which does not require cleanliness?'

Stringer was amused by her unusually forthright manner. 'You are aware, I presume, that there could be a spot of trouble brewing in this area while ownership of the diamond fields is determined?' he asked.

'Determined to be British?' Prudence smiled. 'There is always trouble in the diggings, Colonel Stringer, and I don't remember being offered protection from the British army before.' She picked up a small eye-glass and held it to one eye, peering at him. 'It is pure dirt,' she said with mock surprise. 'I believe I should offer you that bath free of charge as my contribution to the welfare of the British army.' She lowered the eye-glass and her amusement vanished. 'Tshepo is the reason you came to see me? A simple black trader disturbs the British Empire?'

'Word has it there is a Boer with him, and we have ample reason to believe he could be stirring unrest among the blacks. He is well armed.'

'Really?' Prudence leant back in her chair as her suspicions about Unsworth were confirmed. 'Are you referring to a Boer named Thys Bothma?'

'You know him?'

'No more than your friend Colonel Marsden out there knows him.' Prudence fixed a candid gaze on Stringer. 'The madame of a brothel doesn't "work" in her own business, Colonel Stringer. It would be a little like having a dog and barking oneself, don't you think?' She raised her eyebrows at him.

'But you do deal with the Boer?'

'In water.' Prudence massaged the joint of her middle finger. 'I believe the gun-running market is already handled rather profitably by another of Her Majesty's servants.' Prudence stood up and walked slowly to the door. She was aware of Stringer's unwavering attention. 'I know Thys Bothma no better than any of the hundreds of Boers who pass through in search of work. I'm afraid I cannot help you.' She opened the door wide.

'Then I will have to talk to him myself.' Stringer stopped beside her as he reached the door.

'That would seem sensible.'

Prudence stood back, waiting for him to leave.

'When is he due?' Stringer's smile vanished. His eyebrows lifted slightly and his blue eyes sparkled. 'Your water barrels are waiting outside, Mrs Audsley: and they are empty.'

Marianne waved her arms over her head as she stood in the cart holding the reins in one hand.

'Stop!' she shouted in Afrikaans across the wide plain. 'You mustn't come today!' She waved more determinedly as the cart tore on towards Thys and the wagon which was loaded with water barrels.

'Whoa,' Thys called as the oxen pulled forward in rough heavy movements. 'Whoa!' When they finally came to a halt he held up his hand against the sun to see Marianne clearly.

'You must go back!' her Afrikaans voice warned him. The cart rattled as the horse reared away from the lumbering line of sweating oxen. 'Mrs Audsley says you mustn't come today. There are soldiers in the town. British soldiers. They are looking for you.' Marianne's voice was an urgent cry of solidarity with one of her own kind. The familiar tingle of anger rose in Thys as he looked past her and on towards Du Toit Span in the distance.

'Tell Mrs Audsley I will deliver her water as usual.' He spoke in Afrikaans and tugged at the rope as the oxen dug their heels in, refusing to move.

'But she says you mustn't come.' Marianne touched his arm. 'They are looking for you. British soldiers.'

'Why do they look for me?' Thys lifted his whip high in the air over the stubborn oxen.

'You're Boer,' Marianne said, as if that was reason enough, and leapt off the cart as he brought the whip down over the long line of leather backs. 'You mustn't go!' She suddenly noticed a small black face peering at her curiously from among the barrels. It was Tshepo's son. 'Who's that child?' Her voice was filled with distaste.

'My child,' Thys challenged her tone. 'Tell Mrs Audsley I will be there as always.' He whistled and the whip cracked down again.

Marianne watched the wagon roll past her in thundering groans. The small black face peeped again from among the barrels and the boy waved to her with a wide grin. Quickly she moved to her cart.

'Perhaps they'd be right to arrest you!' she shouted at Thys as she turned the cart overtook him at speed in a clatter of hooves. 'You're no Boer.'

Prudence watched Charles Marsden and Stringer from her window as they waited near the empty barrels in the street outside. She could see many other strangers in town, lurking among the tents or leaning against a building as if they belonged. She turned away from the window and looked back at the letter in her hand. It was from Emily.

'I'm so pleased to hear your tea parlour does well, Prudence. I would never have imagined tea would be popular in the diamond fields, but you always were a good business woman. My world has been opened by you, and by Suzanne of course. What a sad life she's led. She's still not happy here and wants to leave. Why is it Bonne Esperance holds so many fears for her? When she talks of Thys she talks as if he is dead yet she knows he's alive. I think perhaps it's Suzanne who has died.'

Prudence dropped a chair and her eyes stayed on the words on the paper although she didn't read them again. All her thoughts were of Thys. Marianne had told her his reaction and his determination to ride in regardless. She knew there was only one way she could prevent this stubborn man, who'd grown more stubborn with age, from walking into the waiting arms of Colonel Stringer.

'I will not go back to that man!' Marianne spat the words at Prudence as she faced her in her small bedroom. The room was sparsely furnished but neat. Each object had been placed with great care. 'I have to do the accounts. I must do my work!' She turned to the ledger on the table by the window and tried in vain to dismiss Prudence.

'You will do as I tell you!' Prudence slammed the book shut and snatched the pen from her hand, stabbing it into the inkwell. A blot of ink splashed on to the immaculate white tablecloth and spread in a slow black pool. 'You will go to Thys Bothma now, and tell him what I have said.'

'Never!' Marianne looked up from the black mark which had

added coal to the fire of her temper. Prudence could feel the heat of rage burning in her body as her dark eyes flared. 'He lives with blacks and he has a black child! Let him walk into the trap the British have laid. My people don't need his kind!'

'Your people?' Prudence grabbed the back of Marianne's wooden chair and swung it around till she faced her. 'What "people" were you, Marianne? When you walked in here, sent by your mother to whore! What "people" were you?'

'It's lies!' Marianne's face was rigid with anger, her mouth held in a straight line. 'How dare you!' she screamed. Her eyes had none of the innocence Prudence had first seen.

'Because it's true, Marianne. I dare because Thys Bothma's life could be in my hands, and I will not allow it to be wrenched from my sister again!' Prudence turned away in an effort to calm herself. 'You will go back and tell him that Suzanne is waiting for him at Bonne Esperance,' she said slowly and firmly. 'You will tell him to go home!'

'He has found his home.' Marianne's mouth trembled and the tears rolled freely. 'It's with a black woman and their black child!'

'God help me, Marianne, you will go!' Prudence snatched at her arm and hauled her out of the chair. 'It is the same blind stupidity I see in you which tore Thys from my sister before, and I will not stand for it again!' Prudence looked at the girl who had donned the robes of apparent righteousness and threatened everyone. 'You will go to Thys Bothma and you will tell him my sister Suzanne is waiting for him. If not, you will leave this house the "poor white" who entered it!'

Chapter Twenty-eight

Every footprint Thys left on the dusty ground was stepped into by the small black foot of Tshepo's son. Every move he made was watched by the child's father.

Thys looked from the wagon he was loading and back at the village. It bustled with the activity of people on the move. Goats and sheep were herded together with rough sticks and hurried shouts. Belongings were hauled out of huts and tossed into the large baskets balanced on the heads of a line of black women. Small children stood back, a little lost, as the mass of moving people passed behind and in front of them without seeing them.

'Where are you going, Thys Bothma?' Tshepo's question was spiked.

'Where are you going, Tshepo?' Thys turned and faced the suspicion in his friend.

'To the whore's sister, you said? That is where you are going, Thys Bothma?' There was a hard edge of disbelief in Tshepo's voice which had never been there before and he held out a piece of folded paper. 'Your Queen has told me where to go! You see!' He pointed at the red embossed crown at the top of the paper. 'Your Queen's hat! You see, she writes to me!'

'I am going to Cape Town.' Thys turned and grabbed at Tshepo's small son as he leapt on to the wagon behind him. He held the kicking boy out to Tshepo. 'Your son.'

'You give me back my son? You name him Adam, and then you give him back? Now your Queen has taken my land from me you give back my son?' Tshepo's eyes had regained the hostility Thys had first seen in them. 'You are taking your life away from me because your Queen has told you to?' Tshepo shook his head slowly without taking the child. 'You whites do not understand that the sun and moon watch over our agreements. Tell that to

493

your Queen!' He looked around at the seething mass of black people preparing to leave. 'We will be coming with you!' he declared.

'You can't.' Thys touched Tshepo but pulled back as he felt the muscles in his arm tense. 'That is not my Queen!' He looked at the paper Tshepo clenched in his hand. 'I said I am going to Cape Town. To Suzanne.'

'Then we will come to Cape Town.' Tshepo's mouth spread into a wide smile, but it was ice cold. 'Or is it the British you are going to, Boer? Why are you going? Why now?' The mistrust showed clearly in Tshepo's narrowed eyes as the destiny he'd seen in the crossing of their lives crumbled around him. 'Why?'

'I have told you why.' Thys looked at him keenly but knew he could not make him understand. 'I am going for my woman!'

'No.' Tshepo's smile disappeared. 'You told me you are going for the whore's sister.' He paused. 'But you are going to them! You came from them and you go back to them! Like God's servant Unsworth, your white skins stick together!'

Thys lowered his head and looked at the ground at his feet. He didn't know how to convince Tshepo he had not betrayed his trust.

'She is English, you told me.' Tshepo's bare black feet stepped on to the ground Thys looked at. 'You are going all the way to Cape Town for an English woman, but you wouldn't take a black woman?'

'I am going to *my* woman!' Thys shouted in desperation. 'I hate the British as you do! I am not going to them, but to my woman!'

'But you said you would fight?' There was a slow question in Tshepo's voice. It questioned everything about Thys. 'Our land is to be taken from us.' He held the paper out to Thys again. 'Why is it you are not fighting now as you said you would?' He looked down at his son, who had wrapped his arms around Thys's leg. 'Why is it only a child can touch your heart, Boer?'

Tshepo looked around the silent faces of Tshepo's people as they watched him. Their eyes were filled with betrayal.

'I'm not betraying you and you know that!' Thys felt the friendship he had found with the black people splinter, and turned away to his wagon at a loss. 'I want my woman.' He pleaded for understanding. 'She is all I want.'

'But I own you!' Tshepo laid his words like manacles at Thys's feet. 'It was you who told me I saved your life, Mr Bothma. It was you who came to me! Now I come with you and you will save me.' Tshepo waved his arms at the people around him, shouting loudly in Tswana. He lowered his head with a smile as a slow 'Ehhh' came back from them.

'Ehhh,' Tshepo imitated the sound. 'They say yes! They say yes they will go with you! Ehhh!'

Thys looked at the little black boy holding his leg as Tshepo turned in a small circle, stamping his feet and shouting again at his people.

'Ehh!' came their answer, and he swung back to Thys slapping him hard on the shoulder.

'Ehh, Mr Bothma! We will come with you to Cape Town!' Tshepo whistled into the distance and a horse cantered towards him. He leapt on its back and whirled it around, as if saying goodbye to his land. 'The white man will tell us where we live now.'

The challenge behind Tshepo's words hit Thys and his heart sank. The driving energy which had spurted inside him like a fountain when Marianne had told him about Suzanne drained into the ground.

'I've told you where I am going to live, Tshepo!' Thys turned to his wagon and reached for the trek rope. 'With my woman.' He looked back at the black man as he unrolled the rough leather of the trek rope and the small boy hauled it out for him. 'And we will live on my land.' He remembered the house Gerrit had built for them, and his mind set firm on Suzanne.

'We live in "our" land, Boer,' Tshepo said quietly.

'My, you can smell the damp!' Emily's bright voice penetrated the silence and dark of the empty room. The shutters were closed and an aura of death hung over the sitting-room of Miss Thurston's house. The furniture stood like crouching ghosts. The wooden floor was dull with a covering of fine dust, which lifted in a grey mist and resettled on the white sheets that covered the furniture.

Suzanne came into the room cautiously and her head turned sharply to the windows as a shutter banged in the brisk south-easterly wind. She looked back nervously as Emily was wheeled into the room behind her by Rosita and Katinka Westbury.

'I'll do it!' Katinka said cheerfully to Rosita and removed her hands from Emily's chair: a mass of auburn hair fell over her face as she bent lower to push it. 'Who lived here?' Katinka asked as the sombre shapes and silence of an empty house reached out to her. 'Did you, Miss Emily?'

'Open the shutters, Rosita!' Emily clapped her hands to break the grip of memory the room had wrapped her in. She could hear Miss Thurston's voice sounding the beats of a waltz. She could feel Rafus Jeremiah Caesar squatting in the doorway just behind her. 'A house without sun is one without love. Open the shutters!'

'I'll help,' Katinka offered and ran to Rosita who was struggling with the catches.

Suzanne's eyes moved around the room carefully before settling on Emily.

'You'll be happy here, Suzanne,' Emily said. 'You'll be close to town and there'll be plenty to keep you busy, as you can see.'

'Were you with her when she died?' Suzanne asked.

'It was very peaceful.' Emily remembered the thin frail hand in hers and the movement of Miss Thurston's eyes as they had rested on a picture of England. 'She died in peace.' The light from the opening shutters spread like gold dust over the room. 'There! It's better already. Katinka! Come to me, child.' She held out her hand and the young girl skipped towards her. 'I want you to go upstairs with Rosita and see if you can find a package in the bedroom. It's in the kist under the window.'

'What's in it?' Katinka asked excitedly as her imagination rippled with the promise of a paper parcel.

'Bring it down and you'll see.'

'Come on, Rosita.' Katinka took Rosita's hand and pulled, Rosita looking back at Emily helplessly.

'I'm coming,' she laughed.

Emily waited until Katinka's running footsteps, taking two stairs at a time, stopped at the top and Rosita's slower steps followed them. Suzanne stood still, looking out of the window, and Emily felt a deep sadness.

'You can't keep running, Suzanne.' Emily watched her neck stiffen and her head tilt back defiantly. 'You don't know that Thys has married. Prudence simply said he had a child with him.'

'A black child.' Suzanne's voice was flat and she turned to Emily coldly. The light in her eyes had gone and every day of her years was written in them. 'And I do think Katinka should be prevented from spending too many hours in the sun, for her own sake.' Suzanne took the corner of a sheet and tugged it off a chair, looking down at the empty seat. 'I will find my own life.'

'Suzanne.' Emily propelled her chair towards her. 'You look at Katinka as though she's unclean. She's our blood and you know that. But because Thys is . . .'

'Don't talk to me of Thys!' Suzanne cried. 'Do you imagine that at my age I still hold out hope for love? It's dead!' The clattering footsteps of Katinka rushing downstairs trod over Suzanne's words and the small girl bounced through the door holding a petticoat in front of her.

'Is this it? Is this what you wanted?' Katinka held it out to Emily. 'Is it yours?'

'Agh! The cobwebs in that room. I think I must stay and help Miss Suzanne clean up.' Rosita brushed her large bosom down.

'I will be fine,' Suzanne said, turning away.

Emily pulled Katinka towards her and fitted the petticoat against her. Katinka looked down at it as the petticoat hung to the floor.

'Stand up, Katinka! I want to see how much you still have to grow before this will fit you.' Emily's mind ran back to the day of Eva's wedding to her father. The day when, as a child Katinka's age, she had been given the petticoat by Eva.

'What is it?' Katinka's large puppy eyes were puzzled.

'Is it beautiful?' Emily asked.

'Yes.'

'Then what does it matter what it is, child. It's yours!'

'Mine?'

'How old are you now?'

'Ten, nearly eleven,' Katinka said proudly.

'Then it's yours.'

'Mine?' Katinka's green eyes shone like emeralds. 'It's like a wedding dress.'

'Then it's hardly for me!' Emily glanced at Suzanne, who had moved into a corner of the room, cutting herself off.

'It's very old,' Katinka said seriously as she fingered the

material. 'Is it as old as you?'

'Indeed. Almost as old as me.' Emily looked up as Suzanne turned to her. Very gently she led her back into the past which she knew she must face, if she was to find the future. 'This petticoat was made for me when I was born. Made by the woman who brought me into the world.'

Suzanne closed her eyes at the sudden image of her dead mother, and the dark threatening memory of Eva holding the newborn baby, Emily.

'But the past is over,' Emily said directly to Suzanne. 'It is gone and we are here.' Emily turned away from Suzanne to Katinka. 'And shall I tell you why we are here now, Katinka?' The small girl nodded as she fingered the petticoat but she wasn't listening. Her imagination had twirled her around a ballroom at her own wedding. 'Because there was love.'

Suzanne's eyes had settled on Emily. Love was nowhere to be seen in them.

Stringer's face was set and his jaw moved in a fast angry motion as it pressed tobacco between his teeth. The ageing madame of a brothel had outwitted him and his anger was heightened by her manner. As he rode beside Charles Marsden in the direction of Tshepo's land all he could think of was Mrs Audsley's farewell. She had stood at the window of her room gazing out at the empty water barrels outside the bordello. She had smiled, amusement teasing her eyes.

'It would appear Mr Bothma smelt you coming, Colonel Stringer.' She had lifted her head high and looked down her nose as he moved to the door. 'I think you would have been wise to have taken the bath I offered you.'

'That woman's no whore!' Stringer spat the ball of chewed tobacco ahead of him and his horse trampled it into the ground. 'She's a woman of breeding! She has the sharp mind of a gentlewoman!'

'Isn't that why she's the madame?' Charles was unable to hide a smile as he looked at Stringer. His anger amused him but he tried to defuse it by changing the subject. 'Did you know that the Cape diamond is as bright and clear as glass and its angles more accurate than the Brazilian diamond?'

'Did you manage to pocket one?' Stringer looked at him with

irritation as he stuffed more tobacco into his mouth.

'Unfortunately not.'

'Then I'm not interested in hearing about Cape diamonds!' Stringer heaved his body back in the saddle to stretch his thigh muscles. 'That woman's not a whore, I tell you!' Stringer's eyes suddenly narrowed. He had spotted the slightest glint of metal miles to the west of them. Charles saw it at the same moment and swung around on his horse, signalling to the men behind. Without a word the entire group split and rode fast in different directions.

As the dust from their horses' hooves settled there was no sign of man anywhere on the deserted plain.

'Colonel Stringer?' Geoffrey called across the plain as his eyes searched among the aloes and scattered rocks. 'Colonel Marsden?'

His saddle squeaked in the silence around him and a small spiral of dust sprung up from nowhere, pirouetting towards him. Crickets grated noisily and the earth buzzed in the midday heat. The rhythm of Africa, held deep in the land, pounded inside Geoffrey's body.

He looked around at the foreign sound of metal on rock. A rifle pointed at him from the flat edge of a bare rock just beside him.

'My name is Geoffrey Marsden,' he shouted at the glinting mouth of death aimed at him. 'I come on Her Majesty's business.'

The steel barrel moved and Geoffrey tensed as a man's face appeared from behind the rock. He spun round sharply as another man stood up behind him, his legs spread wide over the bush behind which he'd been totally hidden.

'Who are you looking for?' Charles Marsden yelled at the young intruder who had ridden straight into the trap.

'Colonel Marsden.' Geoffrey looked from Stringer and back to Charles. His heart raced. He was unable to recognize either and felt threatened by both.

'Then you've found him!' Stringer walked towards Geoffrey's horse. Though he smiled, his gun was aimed from his hip straight at Geoffrey's head. 'Colonel Marsden at your service.' Geoffrey's eyes followed the rifle. 'What do you want with me, boy?' Stringer went on.

'I'm looking for my father.'

Stringer's eyes shifted a little and Geoffrey was aware of Charles standing beside him. His rifle was held limply at his side. He was staring at him.

The piece of meat held on a stick over the fire sizzled and drips of fat sparked the blaze. Stringer peered in amazement at Charles Marsden, heedless of whether the meat burned.

'He need never have found you, Charles. How long have you been looking?' Stringer turned his eyes on Geoffrey. 'I tell you, you would not have found us if that whore hadn't disturbed me!' He felt suddenly insecure.

Charles stood up and moved from the light of the fire into the surrounding darkness. Geoffrey watched him constantly, and Stringer watched them both. An owl hooted into the blackness, as if to check it was not alone, but nobody heard it.

'To hell with them, Charles!' Stringer glared at his burnt meat and dropped it into the fire. 'Do you imagine *I'll* walk back to re-tirement like a lap dog when my time comes?' He joined Charles. 'To hell with them, I tell you. Nobody tells us when to retire!'

'I'm going back.' Charles's voice was firm but quiet. He allowed the flames of the fire to dance in his vision between him-self and Geoffrey for a moment, then moved to him. 'Your orders will have been carried out.'

'Why?' Stringer followed him in frustration. 'They'll never find you. They've missed your retirement by two years!' He laughed. 'Let them keep their damned pensions and spend them on the Governor's house! Better still, let them spend them in that whorehouse!'

'I'm going back.' Charles kept his eyes on the young man who represented so much of his own failure. 'I think you should stay with Colonel Stringer.'

'Why?' Geoffrey felt that in some way he'd come to the end of his lifetime's journey.

'You told me why they sent you to look for me.' He remem-bered the day he'd spoken to Jack and reached out to touch Geoffrey's shoulder. 'There are wars to be fought which the British army is unprepared for. Wars they know nothing about.'

'I'm coming back with you.' Geoffrey looked keenly into the eyes of the man he'd worshipped all his life but never seen before. 'I will come back to England with you.'

'No!' Charles turned away, unable to accept the respect he saw in Geoffrey's eyes. 'Your place is here,' Charles said firmly.

'My place is with my father.' Geoffrey moved in front of him determinedly. 'All my life I have waited for you and you can't walk out of it again.' Charles felt suddenly lost as Geoffrey's cry touched a part of him that he had thought was dead. Yet, from the midst of his confusion, his dignity rose and he snatched at it. He lifted his hands and placed them with great care on Geoffrey's shoulders, looking into his eyes from a face which had regained its pride.

'It's a father's place to guide his son in the ways he sees as right.' Charles spoke with a warmth he'd imagined long dead. 'Your place is with Colonel Stringer, as mine is in retirement.' Geoffrey looked down in refusal but Charles gripped his shoulders, forcing him to look back up. 'I will ride back in accordance with the orders you were given, Geoffrey. I will wear the uniform I have worn with pride for as long as I care to remember, and I will obey the orders given to you.' He paused. 'My pride will be in the knowledge that my son is fighting for his country.' He looked at Geoffrey keenly. 'For your country is Africa.'

Charles moved to his horse and Stringer's eyes narrowed as he saw his hand move to the roll strapped to his saddle.

'When you see your brother Jack, tell him.' Charles felt the gold epaulettes of his jacket press hard against his fingers. 'Tell him that you carried out your last orders with the dignity of a Marsden.' He glanced over his shoulder at Geoffrey, while his hands held on to the comfort of his uniform. 'Tell him, you took your father's advice.'

Geoffrey's body was rigid as he watched his father walk proudly in the early-morning light towards his horse. Stringer chewed the inside of his cheek. Charles Marsden was dressed in his uniform.

'It's suicide, Charles,' Stringer said, as his eyes raged against the bright red which the first glimmer of dawn had revealed vividly.

'What was it you said about my desk?' Charles called back. The stiff collar of the tunic rubbed his chin and accentuated the sardonic lines which had returned to his face. His eyes moved to Geoffrey and he smiled. 'You carried through your last orders, son; and your superiors will know that.' He swung his leg over his horse and sat erect in the saddle. The horse backed away from the rising sun as if it had heard and understood Stringer's last words.

Geoffrey took a step after him in panic. Stringer's hand gripped his arm and held him back. His mind had leapt ahead to the only way he had of protecting Charles from himself and his eyes moved quickly to the group of sleeping men curled around the embers of the fire.

'Wake them,' he whispered, as Charles Marsden rode out without looking back.

The sun stretched tentative rays towards the two flat-topped mountains, spreading a faint glow before them. A drop of dew clung desperately to a razor-sharp blade of grass, its short life threatened by daylight.

Bare black feet trod the ground leaving only a silent trail of dusty puffballs behind them. Tshepo's people walked through the dark mist of dawn, led by a man whose mind had been misled by suspicion and who concentrated only on Thys.

'You have a problem, Thys Bothma?' Tshepo called back as he watched Thys riding behind him. His dark suspicious eyes looked at his son, who leaned against Thys asleep, the tight black curls of his head rubbing against Thys's white chest. 'My people don't disturb you? My son does not touch your heart?' he called.

Thys had run out of arguments. His white skin condemned him, and they had judged him by it. 'Your people need a home, Tshepo, but that is not what you're looking for!' Thys felt the child's body lean to the right and he held him back with his arm. 'Your child needs a home.'

'It's been taken from us, Boer!' Tshepo's eyes narrowed and he peered accusingly into Thys's face. 'We have no home!'

'Then you must find another.' Thys met his accusing look and held it without flinching.

'With you?' Tshepo's eyes rolled in mock humour. 'It is the white man who will choose our home for us now? Yes?'

'The British gave you land in compensation! Take your people to that land!' Thys argued.

'That land? Tell my child about that land which the white man does not want!' Tshepo's eyes ran over the trail of people moving up behind them. 'Tell my people they have a piece of land! Land stalked by death. Tell them that they and their children must first die on that land that their blood might feed it so the white man can take it from them again!'

Thys dropped his head forward in despair as Tshepo's words touched the truth he had tried to fend off. The truth which fenced him in, kept him from Suzanne and trapped him in Tshepo's mistrust.

'Can you explain that to my people, Boer?' Tshepo leaned forward over his horse's neck. 'Tell my people *what* God has told the white man to make marks on pieces of paper and claim the land of our forefathers.'

'They have taken the land of my people too, Tshepo.' Thys fought to stay calm in the face of Tshepo's prods and tried again to concentrate his mind on Suzanne. He looked towards the two flat-topped mountains which stood ahead of them. 'We must fight their claims in a court of law, as they have said.'

'Law?' Tshepo's face crumbled into a pathetic smile. 'The white laws? They know about me?' His voice reached for the high note of bewilderment he felt. 'How can white laws draw boundaries across the land on which rain falls and the moon gazes without boundaries? No, Boer.' Tshepo's voice dropped to the low whisper of the wind. 'The law knows nothing of the land of our fathers and our children. We must fight for that land!'

The futility of Tshepo's words stirred the frustration which had tracked Thys as Tshepo had tracked him, and raised the memory of his own futile screams for revenge against the British.

'There is no point.' Thys looked into the gleaming dark eyes and felt the familiar trap of hatred tighten around him. 'We must make our lives together.' He pushed against the trap. 'We are all one people.'

The sudden movement of Tshepo's hand silenced Thys. His hand had lifted with the quick movement of an animal sensing danger. With an easy swing a man slipped off his horse and ran forward, low to the ground. His body melted into the shallow mist swirling just above the surface and vanished into the deeper shadow of darkness cast by the mountains.

Tshepo's son Adam stirred against Thys's chest as he woke, and Thys pulled him closer. An unknown danger had crept towards him through the silence and threatened him.

Charles Marsden looked towards the two flat-topped mountains and the sun bounced back at him as it hit the silver granite. He lowered his eyes against the glare and wiped his silk handkerchief across his forehead. Sweat poured from his body but was quickly soaked up by the heavy material of his jacket.

He was unaware of Stringer and his men, spread out behind and in front of him at a carefully measured distance.

He was blind to the black men and a Boer who crouched low at the base of the mountains, melting into its shadow.

Tshepo's eyes darted to Thys where he lay on the rocks beside him. Neither had seen Adam lying flat in a narrow gap between the rocks. The quick rattle of his gun ensured Tshepo had caught Thys's attention – and Adam's. Tshepo nodded towards the red-coated soldier they had spotted.

'He is yours!' He glanced at the gun between them. 'One for your father.'

Thys closed his eyes as he saw the British soldier riding towards them.

'You won't shoot him?' Tshepo leaned closer. 'The red coat is your friend?' The accusation in his voice jabbed at Thys. Tshepo pulled the gun back towards him. He gripped the barrel and his finger curled around the trigger as he took aim. Thys threw himself across the rocks towards Tshepo but the blast of the gun drowned his shout and Adam saw Thys's body in the air for a split second before it dropped on to his father's. He saw Thys grab at his father's shoulder, saw the burning hot metal of the gun Tshepo held press against Thys's throat.

'Your British friend is dead.' The glint of betrayal showed clearly in Tshepo's dark eyes as the gun dug deeper into Thys's neck. 'Your life is mine!'

Tshepo hauled Thys up and forced him to look. A horse galloped away into the distance with its empty stirrups swinging and a red heap of British uniform lay absolutely still.

'Bastards!' Geoffrey's voice rang through the still air and stirred the pot of simmering hatred which had been heated to boiling point. Adam peered from his hiding place. Men on gal-loping horses were drawing closer in a tightening semi-circle. The soldier's death seemed to have signalled a bloodbath and the small boy's mind spun in confusion.

A black man leapt over the rocks and whistled a warning to Tshepo's people. White men on horses raced towards them, scat-tering them in a fleeing mass. They were surrounded. Adam looked round quickly as Tshepo pushed Thys aside with his gun and raised it towards the man who had shouted as he rode in from the other direction.

A barrage of bullets volleyed back from the granite wall of the mountain disguising their source and burst into a series of hol-low echoes. Adam looked up as his father's face exploded in front of him.

'White bastard!' Thys dived low at Geoffrey's voice. It was suddenly very close. Adam pushed himself deeper into the crack in the rocks and closed his eyes. The rock under Thys's feet cracked as a bullet tore a path across its surface and Adam felt the reverberation. Gunshots and the screams of women and chil-dren mingled with his shock and confusion.

Thys crouched to make a run towards the people, but dropped with a kick in his back as a black man leapt over him. Thys reached up at the hurtling black body but it was too fast for him, and he saw the dark metal of a spear plunge into Geoffrey's chest. The black body curled, encircling Geoffrey under it as he pulled him off his horse. The spear dug deeper into Geoffrey and they somersaulted to the ground together.

Adam's small terror-filled face peeped out of the crevice at Stringer's voice. He was shouting at his men to stop. His horse reared as he fired his gun in the air while all around him black women and children fell in bloody heaps from the blind reprisal of his men. Stringer fired again in an attempt to stop the killing. But he couldn't. His men were out of control.

Adam watched Thys in terror. Thys had pulled Tshepo's gun from under his body and lifted it as the black man stood up over Geoffrey. The short wide blade in his black hand flashed and he ripped it across Geoffrey's neck, slitting his throat wide. The man raised his arms high and called in short sharp yelps as Geof-frey's blood dripped from the blade. Adam felt his stomach heave. He ran to Thys for relief from the nightmare.

But Thys was narrowing his sights on to the black chest swelled with the pride of Geoffrey's death. He pulled the trigger and the stock of the gun slammed against his shoulder. The body spun with the force of the blast, turned low to the ground in a slow pirouette; then rose, turning back to Thys. The dark eyes were filled with surprise and his chest was blown apart. Adam watched the blade in his hand slide down the rocks leaving a trail of blood behind it and the man's body curled forward in a ball rolling after it.

Adam looked round anxiously at a sound. A white man stood behind Thys with a gun in his back. Thys's head snapped back as a fist cracked across his jaw. A trickle of blood ran from the corner of his mouth as he looked at Stringer in silence.

'Haven't you heard what the British do to people like you, Bothma?' The fresh blood of women and children tasted in Stringer's mouth as the black child looked up at him. 'You've seen what we do!' Stringer's voice shook with rage at the stupidity of the massacre he'd been unable to stop. 'Why?' he demanded, gesturing at the bodies.

'You took their land.' Thys held his head up as he felt the child's body press against his legs. 'His father's land.'

Stringer looked down at Tshepo's son who stood protectively in front of Thys, but all he saw was the blood of black bodies pouring out at his own feet. The body of Charles. The horror-filled eyes of Geoffrey staring at him from a mutilated body. He could feel their eyes on him, both the living and the dead, and all of them looked from the eyes of one black child.

'Was it the only answer?' Stringer turned away from Thys. Beside the bodies of Charles and Geoffrey lay the bloodied corpses of Tshepo and many of his people. The sun beat down and flies buzzed in a hovering mass. 'Was your revenge worth this, Bothma?' Stringer pointed at the body of Charles Marsden. The red uniform was still immaculate. 'Will the blood of innocent people ever wash off your hands?' He returned to Thys and stopped in front of him. 'Will that child ever forget?'

Thys leaned back against the hard wood of a tree. He was still in the midst of the horror which had unleashed itself so suddenly and completely. He could still hear the screams of women and children and he could still see Tshepo's face as it exploded in front of him. But over it all, he saw Charles Marsden and the irony of what had happened.

'Take the child,' Stringer's voice broke into his thoughts. 'I will spare your life because through that child you will live with what has happened. As I will.' Thys felt the rope snap that bound his hands as Stringer slid a knife through it. 'We will all live with it!' He turned his back on Thys and shouted an instruction to his men as they dug graves further away.

'But will we learn from it?' Stringer's words hung in the air and settled on the sand falling from spades into the graves.

Katinka Westbury's constant chatter was hardly noticed by Jack as he studied the flow of pure white liquid which ran from the mouth of the coiling copper pipe into the gleaming tray below.

'Is that brandy?' Katinka asked and caught her breath against the vapours. 'What is it?'

'Pure spirit.' Jack moved past her and back to the glowing pot still. 'To *make* brandy.' His pride in producing a brandy of quality was bolstered by her fascination. But Katinka's constant attention and admiration was something he'd still not grown used to. She followed him wherever he went. Whenever he looked round he met her smiling face and adoring green eyes.

'My father says you saved Bonne Esperance.' She tipped her weight back on her heels. 'He said that without you it would be dead.'

'Did he?' Jack turned to her with a smile. 'Did he also tell you that without his guarantee I could not have done anything?' He held her by the shoulders and moved her out of his way. 'And that the cellars are not the place for a little girl?'

'I'm not a little girl.' Katinka flushed with the touch of his hand. She couldn't understand why he didn't know how she felt. That just being near him was more important than anything else. She wished she was a woman. She'd seen Jack with women. 'I'm nearly twelve!' she said with pride and looked at his reflection in the copper pot still rather than look directly at him.

'Murderer!' The word pierced the warmth of the cellars and Clara's distorted image appeared in the copper curve in front of Katinka. 'You bloody murderer!' Clara screamed, and Katinka felt the hard bone of Clara's arm push her to one side as she launched herself at Jack. Her hands reached for his face, and her eyes darted accusation as she screamed again: 'Murderer!'

Katinka drew back into the dark between the vats and her hands went to her ears in an effort to block out the screech of Clara's voice. It was a reminder of the growing arguments between her parents, but she knew this was different. Her small shoulders hunched and she hid her eyes as Clara struggled with Jack and her shrill voice broke through the protection Katinka had tried to build for herself.

'The knife that slit my son's throat was in your hand, and the spear that plunged into his body was yours!' Clara's nails slashed at Jack's cheeks. The violence and death on a lonely plain spilled from her mouth and on to Jack. It seeped into every part of his being and laid waste the innocent joy of past moments. Katinka peered between her fingers and her heart banged inside her as she saw the man she worshipped crumble.

Clara swung back on him from the cellar door, her face a hideous mask of contempt and her body rigid with bitterness. The clean shaft of daylight streaming in from outside silhouetted the black of her taut body, casting an ugly shadow across her face.

'The only justice is that your father died with my son, and you will wear his title with the shame it represents.' Clara turned into the light and darkness swallowed her as the door closed behind her.

Katinka's fingers opened and she looked between them at Jack. He hadn't moved. Blood streamed from the scratches on his face and his eyes gazed blindly at the cellar door. She made a move towards him but stopped as his legs buckled and he fell forward on his knees. He rocked backwards and forwards as his body heaved with silent grief. The small girl didn't know how to comfort him. She wanted to hold him, to wipe the blood from his face, to tell him it wasn't true. Instead she stood silently beside him and her hand reached tentatively to his shoulder. There was nothing she could say.

*

The grubby hand of the begging child tugged at Suzanne's skirt as she walked down the street with her head held high and her ears closed to his cries. The news of Charles' and Geoffrey's deaths had hardened her heart further and killed any small hope she might have had.

'Hungry, missy. I thirsty.' The child's voice tracked her closely.

'Go away!' Suzanne swung round and pushed the clinging black hand off her skirt. 'I have nothing to give you!' She blinded herself to the need of the near-naked child and walked away, a full basket of fruit and vegetables swinging on her arm.

'But I hungry. Want food!'

'I told you to go away!' Suzanne slapped his hand as it reached again for her skirt. 'Leave me alone!' Distaste filled her eyes as she saw the open sores on the child's dark arm which reached out to her so persistently.

'I hungry, missy,' he called desperately as she swept away, 'I thirsty.' His voice chased her as she walked faster down the street and began to run. A tomato fell from her basket and exploded behind her in a mess of red flesh. She ran up the steps of Miss Thurston's house, struggled to push the key into the lock and her hands shook as it turned uselessly unable to find its way. She leaned her head against the door to calm herself but the voice came after her again.

'I hungry.' The small black hand reached for her arm, the key turned in the lock and the door swung open with her weight against it. She pushed her way inside and the small boy tried to squeeze in after her. He jumped back in fright as she screamed at the black Africa he represented which had pushed its way into her life again.

'Get away from me!' She slammed the door shut against him. Tears of anger and guilt filled her eyes as the door handle rattled. 'Go away!' she screamed. She banged on the door, her emotions in turmoil and her anger directed at an unknown source of fear. Fear which leapt out at her each time she saw a dark child. She pushed herself away from the door, tossed the basket of fruit carelessly aside and strode towards the sitting-room.

'I hungry. I thirsty,' the child's voice followed faintly after her.

Suzanne slammed the sitting-room door behind her and breathed in the silence. Then she looked up. Rev. Phillip's voice filled the room suddenly, leaping out at her from nowhere.

'. . . whosoever takes one of these children . . .'

'No!' Suzanne's eyes darted across the room and fixed on Miss Thurston's bible. It lay where it always had, on a small table under the window. Suzanne had done no more than flick a duster over it, but now, as she looked at it, it was as if Rev. Phillip's voice had come from among its pages. She strode towards it, snatched it up and hurled it across the room.

'Leave me alone!' she yelled as the bible smacked against the wall and fell broken-backed on to the floor. The wafer-thin pages fluttered for a moment then fell open. Suzanne swelled with rage as it lay wide open before her; challenging her; calling her.

'Keep your God away from me!' she heard her own voice cry as she backed deeper into memory. 'Keep Him away!' she shouted aloud as a page turned over gently. She felt suddenly afraid. She moved towards the bible and bent down carefully as if trying to catch it unaware. Her hand gripped the leather binding to snap it shut and the words on the open page leapt out at her.

'For I was hungered and ye gave me no meat: I was thirsty and ye gave me no drink.'

She pushed the bible away as though it had burned her fingers and it slid across the gleaming wooden floor. Tears streamed down her face and her body bent double, curling into a broken ball. The pain she'd held back for so long poured out as though her heart had broken. She heard the pages flutter and glanced at the bible. Her breath caught in her throat as the words came at her again, sounding in her head, shaking her like a rag doll.

'I was hungry and ye gave me no meat.'

'Liar!' Suzanne screamed and lunged across the floor. A small splinter from the floor buried itself in her hand but she didn't feel it. She snatched the bible and the words on the open page stood out clearly, sounding in her head again.

'Whosoever shall give to drink unto these little ones a cup of cold water.' Her eyes closed and stinging tears washed away the words. Her hands tore at the fine paper as her tears fell among the turning leaves.

'I was a stranger and ye took me not in: naked and ye . . .'

She slammed the bible shut. Her body swayed and she felt herself break into a million small fragments. She could no longer see herself, she had come to the end of herself. She looked up as she felt a great weight descend on her shoulders, but it was lifting her.

'Let me go.' She raised her face and whispered, 'Leave me alone.' Suddenly she knew she was not alone. Her hands gripped the bible and every part of her shook, she was aware of being surrounded. Engulfed by a supernatural presence.

'Read it,' a still small voice prodded her.

Suzanne's fingers felt their way around the hard edges of the bible.

'Read it.' The still voice touched her again.

She looked up as the room seemed suddenly filled by light. Everything glowed. The furniture shone and shafts of light twisted through the air and spun in front of her: all round her. She felt herself falling. She was falling through space, but she was held, surrounded by power, flame and intense heat. She felt absolutely secure.

'Fear not them which kill the body but are not able to kill the soul: rather fear Him which is able to destroy both soul and body.'

She dragged herself backwards across the floor as the unspoken words followed her. She was dragging the bible with her, holding it firmly.

'He that dwelleth in the secret place of the most high shall abide under the shadow of the Almighty.'

She pulled her feet under her and tried to stand. She couldn't.

'Read it,' the voice commanded again and her eyes moved to the bible clutched in her hands. The leather back cracked as it fell wide open.

'Behold, I have taken out of thy hand the cup of trembling, even the dregs of my fury; thou shalt no more drink it again.' Suzanne's eyes ran on over the words of Isaiah as each one touched her soul and spoke only to her. 'I hid my face from thee for a moment; but with everlasting kindness I will have mercy on thee, saith the Lord thy redeemer.' The trembling in her body had eased and she drank in the words. 'For ye shall go out with joy and be led forth with peace.' She felt the peace. A peace she had never known before had settled deep inside her, filling the furthest reaches of her being. 'Fear not: for I have redeemed thee, I have called thee by thy name; thou art mine.'

Though tears ran unchecked down her cheeks, though her heart had been split in two and bled, Suzanne knew she had heard the voice of God.

He had spoken to her directly and had claimed her as His own. She had discovered the length and breadth of God's love in a moment of total despair and the Holy Spirit had filled her with the sweet perfume of His son, Jesus Christ.

Thys held Tshepo's child in the crook of his arm as he rode, using his body to shield the sleeping boy from the blazing mid-day sun. His dreams of finding Suzanne had died in the mas-sacre. All he was searching for was a place to take the child.

He looked into the far distance at the blue folds of mountains which rose majestically from a mist of hazy cloud. His home had been behind those mountains and Suzanne was behind them now. But he felt no joy. He was exhausted and the years weighed heavily on his shoulders. Only the light weight of the child's head on his arm reminded him he was alive.

'Cape Town?' Thys looked down at the child's voice and the sleepy face peered up at him with absolute trust.

'Not yet.' Thys shut his eyes and the swaying movement of the horse rocked him but didn't comfort him. He saw again Charles Marsden's gun as it was buried with him. And he saw Charles Marsden's son, Geoffrey. Looking into the open grave of his memory he saw his mother and father lying beside them, and the grave opened wider as countless black bodies fell on top of them, sucked down ever deeper into the African soil.

The soil moved under his eyes as his horse tramped it in slow strides. Stones and jagged clumps of grass lanced at the horse's hooves and for the first time he understood Suzanne's fear of the land. He felt as if a large part of him had been sucked into the earth with the blood of the innocent; that the part of him which had belonged to Suzanne had died with them.

'I can hardly believe it!' Emily looked around as a small coloured child ran with shrieking delight as he was chased by others. The comfortable armchair which she remembered Miss Thurston sitting in with such pride was covered by tumbling dark bodies as they bounced on it, hitting one another with cushions.

'You're not going to refuse permission are you, Emily?' Suzanne hauled the children off the chair. 'After all, Miss Thur-ston always wanted her house to be a school.' She pushed the children through the door. 'Now run along and wait outside till dinner's ready.'

'A school?' Emily looked at Suzanne in amazement. There was something different about her. 'As Miss Thurston was too old, so you're too old, Suzanne.' She watched her as she moved back into the room. Her face was alive and her eyes shone with a joy Emily could hardly believe. She wasn't older, she was younger. 'Besides,' Emily refused to be taken in, 'where has the woman gone who cringed at the touch of a black hand?'

'Emily! I promise you I will take care of the house. I'll even call it "Miss Thurston's School".' Suzanne knelt in front of Emily's chair and held her hands. 'And I assure you I will not offend the neighbours. The children will soon be as well-mannered as we are.' Suzanne smiled. 'Better, I hope.'

'You really do intend carrying this through?' Emily looked into Suzanne's face intently, aware of a strength she'd never seen in it before. 'Where will you get the money?'

'People's consciences are quickly silenced by digging their hands into a purse.' Suzanne stood up and looked at the door as a small dark face peered round it. 'What is it, Johannes?'

'We outside.' Johannes Villiers smiled expectantly. 'We outside and we waiting.' The small boy who'd appeared on her doorstep, having run away from a Catholic orphanage, ducked out of the room again.

'What are they waiting for?' Emily turned back to Suzanne. 'Manna from heaven?' she said with slight suspicion.

'Or a bowl of hot soup, whichever should arrive first.' Suzanne turned back at the door. 'They're street children, Emily. Some of them have never had a home and others have run from the one they had. Somehow I don't believe you would have me turn them away.'

Thys dismounted at the top end of the street and led his horse, holding Adam's hand. He had been told there was a woman in the street who cared for lost children. Tshepo's son tugged to free his arm as Thys led him forward into an unknown world; an English world which threatened Thys as it did the child.

'You can't stay with me, Adam. You need to be looked after properly and you need to learn.' Thys knew Gerrit would not accept the black child as he had. He no longer even thought of their land as his home.

'No.' The small boy dug his heels against the cobbles and

leant back. The long row of terraced houses terrified him. The solid white walls leaned into him and the gleaming windows were like spying eyes. 'No.' His mouth turned down at the corners and his eyes pleaded with Thys. 'I stay with you.'

Thys bent down and held him firmly by the shoulders. He could feel the small body trembling and he looked into his eyes, forcing the child to look at him.

'There is nowhere for us to be, Adam.'

'You be with me!' the child argued.

'No.' Thys held his shoulders tightly. 'There is no place for me!' He turned the child's body and pointed him towards the house. 'That is your place.' He pushed the child gently in the back and he lurched forward. 'Go on.' Thys stood up as the child looked over his shoulder. 'I don't want you!' Thys saw in the child's face that his words had hit home and turned quickly to his horse. The child moved forward in panic as Thys mounted and rode quickly back down the street. He took a step to run after him, then he stopped. He turned in a small circle and looked up at the white houses trapping him in the narrow street below. The wide blue sky had gone, cut into strange strange shapes by sharply pointed roofs. Solid dark shadows reached out over the hard cobbles under his bare feet and his body shook with terror as the sound of Thys's horse died away.

'What's wrong?' Adam felt a hand touch his arm and looked around in wide-eyed fear.

Suzanne smiled and moved her hand away from him. 'It's all right. I won't hurt you.' She watched the child curiously as he backed away from her down the cobbled street. 'But I have food if you're hungry.' She'd grown used to the terror of children who were left on her doorstep, and walked after him quietly. She looked up the empty street, and then the other way. Nobody was in sight. She bent down to him. 'Who brought you here?' She leaned towards him as he backed away. 'What's your name?'

'Tshepo's son,' the small boy said quietly, as his fears warmed in her eyes.

*

Thys sat quite still on his horse. He had waited just around the corner at the far end of the street. He knew he had to leave the child but his heart ached, and he couldn't go until he was certain

Adam had been taken in by the woman he'd been told about: the strange woman people talked about quietly and secretly, as though she was not quite real.

He slid off the horse's back and moved against the wall of the corner house. He leant on it for a moment, afraid to look, in case he saw Adam standing abandoned and crying as he'd left him. He pushed himself off the wall and turned into the street. He stopped and the world stopped around him.

A woman was leaning over Adam, pulling him close in her arms as the small boy looked up into her face.

Thys found himself moving towards her.

She stood up and turned away from him, taking the child's hand in hers, and he found himself walking faster up the street behind them. Suddenly he was running behind them. He was shouting.

'Suzanne!' His voice ran ahead of him, careless of everything but her. 'Suzanne!'

Suzanne stopped and looked back at him. Neither moved. Slowly she walked towards him. She was smiling and her face was radiant. She stopped a few feet in front of him, her eyes moved over his face gently and her mouth widened in a smile.

'It's you.'

Tshepo's son stood and watched as the man he'd grown to care for as a father moved to Suzanne. He wondered what was happening in the curious world he'd found himself in. Why was Thys reaching for her?

Suzanne felt the familiar touch of Thys's hands on her shoulders, smelt his warm breath brush her face, and she closed her eyes as he pulled her into his arms.

'Suzanne!' he breathed. Their bodies met and it was as if they had never been parted. The lost years melted between them. 'I was told you might have room for the child.' He held Suzanne tightly and felt her body shudder as her warm tears spread against his cheek.

'I have room.' She tightened her arms around him and hung on as her love reached out, surrounding him.

Suzanne tied a towel around her waist and looked from Adam, who stood in a corner, to Thys, who sat in a large steaming bath-tub.

'I don't know which of you looks more glum!' She whisked an enormous scrubbing brush off a hook on the wall and waved it. 'Where shall I begin?'

The small black face of Tshepo's son looked up at her nervously and he backed deeper into the corner, but his eyes watched Thys in excitement. The scrubbing brush was moving towards him.

'Hey!' Thys shouted as Suzanne scrubbed his back and Adam giggled. He looked on anxiously with his hands clasped between his knees as Suzanne held Thys's shoulder with one hand and the long hard brush scrubbed its way up and down his back.

'I don't think I've seen so much dirt on a man in all my life!' She ducked her face in front of Thys. 'When you sold that water to Prudence I think you should have used a little of it yourself.' She scrubbed his back and looked at Adam. His small shoulders lifted in terrified glee. He knew it was his turn next.

'As for you!' She flicked her brush at him and small drops of soapy water landed on his ebony skin. 'I presume you really are black underneath that dirt!'

'Look!' Adam moved to the bath and held up his arm to Thys. The frothy white bubbles on his arm burst and melted. His face was puzzled as he peered at where the bubbles had been.

'Soap,' Thys said seriously. Suzanne's hair dropped over his shoulder and his hand ran through it. 'It's darker.' He remembered the shining gold of her youth and twisted a thin strand of her hair through his fingers.

'And yours is grey. It suits you.' Suzanne ran her hand over the top of his head, dipped it in the water and ran a handful of water over him. 'Except it's grubby like the rest of you.'

'Mine?' The small boy pointed to his tight black curls and grinned. He leaned over the bathtub, ducked his head under the water and popped up with a wide grin, displaying his magical hair. It had stayed totally dry. Suzanne laughed and Adam's small body curled forward with pleasure as he looked from her to Thys. He was held by the silent love flowing between them; and although he didn't understand it, he wanted to be a part of it.

'Feet.' Suzanne looked at Thys and their gaze met in longing. The child grabbed Thys's foot, lifting it high as Thys slipped back in the water.

'A little lower perhaps.' Suzanne pushed Thys's foot down. 'We're not all young and supple like you, young man.'

'And not too old either,' Thys said quietly in Afrikaans. He sat up, his skin squeaking against the enamel tub.

'No.' Suzanne glanced at him as she scrubbed the sole of his foot and rubbed soap between his toes. 'We will never be too old, but a little crowded perhaps.'

The child's puzzled eyes darted from one to another as their strange language excluded him.

'I love you.' Suzanne looked at Thys and her voice dropped to a whisper. 'I do.' Her eyes clouded a little as she remembered Pieter. Then she smiled. 'Our son looked exactly like you.'

'Foot!' The small boy pushed his way back into the warmth between them as he yanked Thys's other foot out of the water and Thys fell back in the tub.

Suzanne opened the bedroom door and moved towards the small bed in the corner beside which Thys sat. Her face glowed from the warmth of a bath and her hair was wrapped in a soft white towel. Thys looked around as he heard the door and put his finger to his lips to silence her. His eyes ran over the outline of her body where the soft silk of her gown clung to her.

'He's asleep?' she mouthed across the room and Thys nodded, looking down at the child. One eye was shut and the other flew open as if the small boy had been caught by surprise.

'Where the moon?' he asked defensively, looking up at the white ceiling as if it would fall on him at any minute.

'Go to sleep.' Thys held his hand against the child's cheek and instinctively the small boy turned into it, closing his eyes.

'Suzanne?' Thys breathed quietly as he felt her move towards him before he heard her. The soft skin of her hand ran down the back of his neck and he reached behind him, pulling her knee against his back. Suzanne looked down at his broad shoulders as they curved over the child protectively and her hand ran on down his spine. His head tilted back as she leaned over him.

'Where are the stars?' the small voice piped and two large eyes fixed on them firmly.

*

Suzanne's head was tucked into Thys's arm and their naked

517

bodies lay quite still side by side, as the child's gentle snores rose and fell with his slow breathing. Every part of them touched. The familiar warmth as his smooth skin pressed against hers ran through her body and her fingers stroked gently through the greying hairs on his chest as she looked up at him. His eyes were on her and she was aware he'd never stopped watching her.

Carefully his hand plucked at the towel on her head, slowly unwinding it till her long damp hair fell across his face.

'Where've you gone?' Suzanne pulled her hair back off his face. Thys held a thick strand between his fingers and turned his cheek against it.

'Do you know how I've dreamed of you?' He stroked her wet hair. 'What it was like when I thought that the dream was dead like everything else.'

'You told me.' She pushed herself up on her elbows and looked down at him. His warm eyes held hers with the same demand they had always had; but behind them, the years of lost hope were clearly counted. 'We will go to your farm,' Suzanne said suddenly. Her face moved down to his lips and she gently touched them with hers. 'We will live with Gerrit as we planned long ago, and Adam will come with us.'

'What about your school?' he asked. He lowered his voice to a whisper. 'What will happen to your children?'

'I'll find someone.' Her eyes moved on to the sleeping child and her lips tentatively brushed across his mouth. 'Perhaps there are other children who need help.'

'There are plenty of children in Africa.' Thys turned his head away as he spoke Tshepo's words. 'Suzanne,' he breathed her name, and the years which had laughed at them melted.

Thys pulled her down to him and his firm dry lips pushed her mouth open as the familiar surge of desire rose inside her. The longing was still there, she was moist and wanting. His hand ran down her naked back and her body pushed against his as if trying to bury herself in him. Nothing had changed but their feelings. For the first time the threat which had always been there had vanished. In its place was the calm of a deep and abiding love.

Chapter Twenty-nine

The rhythmic squeak of the rocking chair never faltered as the frail body moved backwards and forwards and Mr Westbury stared straight ahead. Katinka stood with her back pressed flat against the wall of the house and watched him. She wondered if he had the answer to the growing tension between her parents. Fine white hair curled over the back of his shirt collar, his bony hands gripped the wooden arms of the chair and his neck bent forward as though he was peering at the cause. But he didn't move as Sarah's voice reached him from the house.

'I'm begging you not to go, John.'

'Why?' John Westbury was calm but the edge to his voice ran a shiver through Katinka's body. 'Have I reason to listen to your fears? Tell me!'

'Because I love you!'

Katinka closed her eyes as her mother screamed back at her father. She pushed herself off the wall and ran in leaping strides away from the house towards the stables.

'It's you I'm afraid for!'

Katinka pulled the stable doors closed, shutting out her mother's voice. She breathed deeply and allowed the warm smell of fresh hay to calm her. The Arab filly snorted a welcome and she held her hand under its nose. Its warm breath filled her palm, she leant her head against its head and the huge dark eyes watched her.

'Shasaan,' she whispered and the horse pushed its soft nose into her hair.

'Then tell me why I shouldn't go to the meeting.' John Westbury's eyes were alive with anger as he faced Sarah. 'Why is it that every time I'm due to address a public meeting you try to stop me?' Sarah turned away, keeping her silence, and he moved after her quickly. The frustration of not understanding what had happened to change Sarah rose in sudden anger. 'Tell me what you're afraid of.'

'Lies!' Sarah pulled her head back and her eyes sparked with resentment. 'Your life is a lie and every word you speak out there is a lie!' Tears of rage swelled in her throat.

'What lie is there in the justice I'm fighting for?' John's anger was roused further by the truth behind her words. 'Wouldn't the lie be if I was to turn my back on my own people?'

'Your people?' Sarah swung round on him, tears burning in her eyes. 'What do you know of your people? What do you know of what it's like to be coloured in this country when you live like a white man! When you enjoy the privileges of a white man: pretend you *are* a white man!' The tears broke and ran down her cheeks. 'Have you ever wondered what would happen if your apparently white skin vanished? Do you think those people who support you from the comfort of their white liberalism would still be there?' Sarah's emotions had broken through the corset in which she'd bound them since the birth of her child. Her last attempt to control her feelings had snapped and the truth blurted out. 'Our son was price enough!'

John felt his body sway as if he'd just seen the precipice he was standing on.

'Son?' The word crept out of his mouth and he looked at her in disbelief. His head spun with questions which had always been there but he'd never dared examine before.

Why had she insisted on going to Cape Town for the birth of their last child? Why had James Robertson seemed so ashamed when he'd told him his son had been stillborn? Why had the Robertsons suddenly returned to England? And, most of all, why had the wound he'd felt in Sarah not healed with the passing years?

'Tell me.' He held her tightly by the shoulders and looked into her face. 'Tell me the truth.'

'Our child was not stillborn.' She looked at him, searching for the courage to go on. 'Our son was alive.' She saw again the small baby between her legs and her heart cracked. 'But he carried the truth in the colour of his skin.' She paused. 'I gave up my child because he threatened you.'

'What have you done?' John's voice was no more than a

whisper but it threw Sarah into confusion.

'Don't you understand?' Her voice broke with the hurt she'd carried alone for so many years. 'I gave him up to protect you!'

'Where is he?'

'I don't know.'

'You must know!' His grip tightened and he shook her. 'Where is he?'

'He was put in a convent. But I don't know. I don't know!'

'Where?' He pulled her suddenly towards him. 'Tell me!'

'I can't!' She pulled away and backed across the room as the price she'd paid was suddenly more than she could afford. 'He ran away from the orphanage he was put in! He's lost! He's one of the people you fight for but don't know! He's out there!' She pointed outside wildly. 'Our son is the sacrifice demanded by white politics!'

The points of the labourers' reed hats bobbed up and down among the green of the vineyards. The Raisin Blanc and Ugni Blanc cultivars, which Jack had imported from France, had yielded well. The brandy ordered by the anonymous sponsor was a success and Jack had become an expert in the slow process of distilling. But his face reflected no pride. A large part of him lay buried somewhere on a dusty plain with his father and half-brother and his inner self was held under close guard. It was as if he was afraid the fragile shell he'd built around himself might crack if it was disturbed by emotion.

'Who's she?' Katinka Westbury looked at a young black woman leaning against a tree further away, sucking on a piece of long grass. The woman was watching Jack. 'Is she waiting for you?'

'No.' Jack glanced back at the woman as if he'd never seen her before and led his horse beside Katinka's along the edge of the vineyard.

'You're different,' Katinka said quietly as she looked at him. Her Arab horse, Shasaan, nudged its nose into her back and she laughed, turning back to it. 'No.'

'I've grown older.' Jack glanced at her and for the first time he noticed her eyes were a little sad. It was as if she knew she would have to say goodbye to the child she was, before she could become a woman. 'Like you.' He looked towards the house in the distance as a carriage rolled away.

Katinka watched him carefully. Though she'd been near him constantly, neither had ever talked of that day in the cellars.

'Is that your mother?' She looked after the carriage as it drew away, and he nodded. 'Where is she going?'

'I have no idea and less interest.' Jack swung his leg into the saddle and watched as Katinka hauled herself up on to the bare back of her filly. Her long suntanned legs gripped its white body and her head lifted as she rode. He could see Eva's dignity combined with a generosity of spirit in the young girl who had become almost a part of himself. 'How old are you now?' he asked casually.

'Nearly fourteen.' He noticed that the joy he'd heard in her voice when she'd told him she was nearly twelve wasn't there. 'Is what my father's doing right?' she asked suddenly, pulling Shasaan in as she turned to him. 'Do you think it's right?'

'Of course.' Jack watched her curiously as their horses walked side by side. 'Why do you ask?'

'If it's right, why does it frighten my mother?' She turned her face away. 'For it does.' Her chin tilted up and the curve of her long neck tensed. 'Do you know why?'

'Perhaps anything we do that's worthwhile is frightening.' Jack shrugged. Although he sensed her need for answers, her questions disturbed him. 'Is there something wrong at home, Katinka?' he asked carefully.

'My mother once said my father's life was in your hands.' Jack looked down at the warm brown neck of his horse; he felt her eyes on him, demanding an answer. 'Is it true?' she asked. 'That his life's in your hands?'

Jack lifted his eyes and looked at her. The first traces of the young woman which he'd seen earlier had gone. A child looked back at him; and the child was begging for an answer.

'If it was, would you trust me with it?' His horse rubbed its head against the Arab's white neck. 'Would you?' he asked again as she looked at him without answering. 'Then perhaps I should tell you something. Do you know what self-respect is?'

'I think so.'

'What is it?'

'What my father's fighting for.' She frowned. 'For the coloured people?'

522

'Your father gave me mine.' He looked away. 'And he had no reason to.'

'Perhaps he cares about you.' Katinka smiled for the first time. 'As I do.'

'Wait!' he shouted as she raced away. Katinka swung round and her auburn hair flew wildly behind her.

'Will you be at the meeting tonight?' she called. 'It's very important, Father says!'

'Of course I'll be there.'

Katinka pulled her reins in and Shasaan danced in a circle as her slim body leaned back. 'So will I!' She spun Shasaan and galloped away towards the Westbury farm.

Only as the last trace of the Arab horse carrying Katinka disappeared over the horizon did Jack realize he had been unable to take his eyes off her. He wanted to race after her. He wanted her and he felt suddenly ashamed. She was a child, young enough to be his own daughter. He turned his horse and looked back at the waiting woman. She pushed herself off the tree, spat the grass out of her mouth and moved towards him. Jack dug in his heels and rode towards the cellars, away from her.

Katinka rode like a gypsy, her hair streamed behind her and her body moved as one with the horse. She pushed Shasaan on faster, trying to leave her thoughts behind her. But still Jack was there. She longed to touch him. To lean her head on his chest, feel the touch of his firm broad hand on her. She could feel his breath against her skin and imagined his hands running over her body. She shivered, pulling Shasaan in on a tight rein, as if pulling in her thoughts.

She leapt off the filly's back and ran to a tree, pulling her skirt between her legs and tucking it into her belt. She lifted a slim brown leg, found a foothold on a bulging knot of wood and began to climb. She stretched up as she reached an arc between two high branches and looked back towards Bonne Esperance.

She could see Jack moving into the cellars. He was disappearing into that world which always excited her. Even when he wasn't in the cellars she often waited there; somehow she could feel him in the moist dark air.

Her hands moved to her small breasts as they tingled. The bodice had grown too tight, like all her clothes, but she had not yet dared to tell her mother. She was afraid that as her body changed so would her life; that she would be prevented from running wild, or seeing Jack.

She couldn't breathe and looked down at her dress where deep creases ran between the buttons as they were pulled apart by the swell of her new breasts. She undid the buttons and looked around; secretly; a little afraid. Her high silky breasts gleamed in the sun. It was the first time the sun had touched them or the air breathed on them. She didn't know why but she imagined Jack's mouth on her breasts. She felt a sudden heat between her legs. Her mouth was dry. Shasaan grazed quietly under the tree and Katinka felt guilty.

She pulled her bodice together and quickly did up the buttons. Her hand moved between her legs and pushed against the throbbing mound, trying to quieten it. Only then did she realize she was crying. She closed her eyes and leaned back against the bark, as her body heaved with the confusion of sexual awakening and the guilt which had accompanied it. She could feel beads of perspiration on her forehead and she could hear her own short breaths. At last her body had stilled and her breathing found its normal rhythm. Her eyes opened and moved to Bonne Esperance in the distance. She knew that what she had felt had something to do with being a woman and everything to do with Jack. She lowered her head as a wave of shame swept over her.

Jack looked up as the young black girl stood in the cellar door expectantly. He waved at her abruptly and turned away dismissing her. He tried to concentrate on the pot still as he prepared the fire underneath it. He would work and drive out the thoughts of Katinka which had caught him by surprise. It was as if he'd come face to face with the darker desires of his own nature and proved that the evil his mother constantly accused him of was right there inside him.

His thoughts of Katinka had changed, in one brief moment, from caring affection for a young child to passionate desire. He would not give into it. He could not. The only person who had ever truly trusted him was John Westbury. Nothing would destroy that trust. 'Katinka is a child', he told himself again and again.

The flame under the pot still licked at the chips of wood

around it and glowed into life. It would be a good brandy, a special one. He caught his reflection in the warm curve of copper and assured himself that the brandy he made tonight would be better than any he had ever made, no matter how long it took.

He had completely forgotten his promise. The public meeting which Katinka had made him promise he would attend, and which John and Sarah seemed so nervous about, had slipped his mind.

Emily looked at the single place laid in front of her on the large dining-table and turned to Rosita as she came into the room carrying a soup tureen.

'It's your favourite,' Rosita announced with pleasure as she held it high. 'Lentil.' She set the tureen in the centre of the table proudly. 'I'll serve it for you.' She lifted the lid and turned her face away as steam rose in a cloud. 'Hot. Just the way you like it.'

'Why am I eating alone?' Emily asked, her eyes on the empty place in front of Clara's chair.

'Master Jack say he is going to a meeting. No time to eat, he say.' Rosita tutted her disapproval. 'He work too hard.'

'And Clara?' Emily said casually. The empty place threatened her and she couldn't take her eyes off it. 'Where's my sister?'

'Lady Marsden gone out.' The haughty note Rosita gave the title was the one she only used in Clara's absence. 'That's why I made soup. She don't like soup!'

'Where?' Emily asked as Rosita moved past her to the door. 'I had no idea Clara was going out tonight.'

'She gone.' Rosita shrugged and her large bosom dropped lower.

'Where?' Emily demanded, pushing her chair after Rosita.

'I don't know.' Rosita stepped back in surprise as Emily wheeled her way past her in the doorway. 'Your soup will get cold!' she grumbled, remembering the care with which she'd made it. 'It will spoil!'

Emily stopped her wheelchair in front of the rosewood chest, slipped her fingers under the delicate brass handle of the smallest drawer and pulled it open. Loose papers filled it. Years of papers had been pushed inside. Emily panicked as she realized it was the first time she'd looked for the document since Geoffrey had died. Until then she had constantly checked that the document relating to John Westbury was there. She'd spoken to Jack, and they had decided it was best to leave it forgotten since the only threat it held was to Clara.

The bundle of papers shuffled through Emily's hands quickly. She tossed them aside and her face paled. The document was not among them.

'Oh!' Rosita huffed. 'What are you doing, Miss Emily?' She moved beside her and began picking up the discarded papers in irritation.

'Where's Jack?' Emily took Rosita's hands to get her attention. 'Has he left for John Westbury's meeting yet?' She pushed her chair towards the door.

'What is it?' Rosita was confused. Her enormous behind swung from side to side as she waddled after her. 'You stay. I'll go see.' Rosita stepped into the doorway and shrugged as Jack stepped through the front door. 'See!' she said reassuringly, not knowing why she had felt any panic in the first place.

Jack walked quickly through the hall past them both. He glanced back at his aunt as she pushed her chair after him.

'Has your mother gone out?' Emily demanded.

'I'm late.' Jack moved on. 'Excuse me, Aunt Emily.' He turned back with a smile. 'I promised I'd be at John Westbury's meeting.'

'Jack!' Emily shouted and he stopped at the shrill note of his aunt's voice. He'd never heard it before. She stared blankly ahead like a small trapped animal and Jack went to her immediately.

'What is it?' It was the first time he had seen his aunt as a helpless cripple. 'Aunt Emily?'

Emily laid one hand on his and the other reached out to his face, touching his cheek. 'Go quickly, Jack.' A tear rolled down her face as she looked at him. 'Go.' The tear clung to her chin and then fell, leaving a broad wet track down her cheek. 'The document's gone,' she said, and her hand clenched his, betraying her fears.

Streams of brightly coloured bunting stretched from the peaked roof of the village hall to the ground, fluttering in the breeze as a brass band played happily and gloriously out of tune, their instruments gleaming red in the rapidly setting sun. Skinny black youths leaned against the side of a small trading store and watched the ceremonies blank-faced.

A small black girl stood in front of a tree and looked at the picture of John Westbury which was pinned to it. Her finger carefully traced the outline of his face and her head tilted to one side.

'I do not believe there can be a separation of the people in this country, and as your elected Member of Parliament I will stand for an undivided nation,' John Westbury's voice inside the hall rose above the brass band. 'If we should even consider removing the franchise from some of the people in this country, as is being talked of already in Parliament, we will do no more than sow the seeds of discontent.' John's voice was clear and strong. His eyes moved over the crowd as though he were speaking to each one personally.

Sarah glanced over her shoulder as she sat listening to John. Clara was six rows behind her. Katinka looked at her mother as she caught the sudden tingle of her nerves and squeezed her hand.

'He'll be here soon,' she whispered and her heart urged Jack to come quickly. But as it did she blushed with the memory of her own shame. Even as she'd looked at his empty seat the same strange excitement had stirred inside her and she concentrated on her father quickly to hide from her own feelings.

'The present multiracial franchise, introduced in the province over forty years ago, has been discussed at some length by many of my fellow parliamentarians. There's talk of increasing the qualifications of fifty pounds' income and twenty-five pounds' occupation. Talk of raising the qualification for franchise out of the reach of the man of colour.'

Katinka glanced at the wooden door. The flush of excitement as she waited for Jack to walk through it burned her cheeks. She felt immediately guilty as her mother nudged her. Her father's face was as strong and handsome as always but seemed somehow different. There was a touch of pain in his eyes and she remembered the argument between her parents.

'Please come, Jack,' she said in her head as she felt her mother's body stiffen with tension beside her.

'They talk of excluding the possession of a perpetual quitrent allotment from qualification for the franchise. Do you understand what that means, my friends? It is a deliberate ploy to take the franchise out of the hands of the black people of our land. The so-called "blanket vote" is seen as a threat to our people. But which of our people? Our white people?'

Katinka pulled back in her seat as her father leaned towards his audience and she sensed a threat building around her. The people in front of her and behind her fidgeted with unease. She glanced at her mother and her fear rose; she hardly seemed to be breathing. Katinka looked up at a quick movement from a man beside her father. He appeared to be trying to attract his attention. Her father turned to him and the man shook his head.

'You don't agree that the ways of Imperialism are insidious, James?' John Westbury smiled and turned away from the man, running his eyes over the crowd in front of him. 'Will you allow humiliation to be used as a weapon in your own country and against your own people? Will you allow the dignity of our black and half-caste African brothers to be trodden under the marching boots of a foreign Empire? Will you allow the dignity of the African people to turn to shame as it's bred into them by politicians? And why? Why do our politics demand humiliation? They demand it to gain a firm hold on the new-found wealth of this land! Greed will be used to oppress our people. We have reason to be proud of this land and greed has no roots in honest pride! Those who have lost that pride must search for it in their own hearts or among those people out there!' John pointed his finger sharply towards the door. Sarah closed her eyes. The glimpse she'd caught of Clara sitting just six rows behind her flashed into her head. Why was Clara there?'

'Why is Jack late?' Sarah whispered to Katinka, but her voice was drowned by the swell of a suddenly uncomfortable and volatile audience.

'Those people are our brothers! Many of those people carry our blood and we theirs!' John Westbury shouted over boos and jeers as the roar of disapproval rose.

Clara's fingers felt the stiff parchment of the folded document and her gloved hand pulled it out of her bag.

'You question what I say? You refuse to believe me?' John Westbury leaned over the wooden pulpit which had been removed from the church and placed in the hall by the local people. Mr Cloete, whose idea it had been to borrow the pulpit, shrugged his shoulders to loosen the tension in his neck. John's words went against the words of God which he'd carefully selected for himself and had heard preached every Sunday from that pulpit.

'But it is not just for the black people that I will fight from within the government as your representative. It is also for the Boer, whose land is being taken from him again as the British annex it: the Boer whose language has been forbidden in parliament. For the Boer and for our half-caste brothers and sisters. All of us!'

John Westbury looked down at the gathering. His eyes passed over them slowly and settled on Clara as she sat straight-backed in her chair. A piece of paper flicked nervously in her hand. The deep lines on her face accentuated the bitterness in the woman he'd sworn would never cross his path again; yet her presence drove him on.

'For they are our brothers and sisters, friends.' John turned towards the door and pointed at it aggressively. 'Somewhere out there a child is homeless and lost. A child with nowhere to go and no land to call his own. Somewhere out there every one of us has walked past that child with no more than a glance of pity.'

'Mr Westbury!' Clara's voice rang sharply through the hall and the crowd fell silent. 'May I ask you a question, Mr Westbury?'

John's mouth tipped in a faint smile as he looked at her. He knew the question she was about to ask.

'Yes, Lady Marsden?'

Clara stood up and the heads of those in front of her turned back, looking at her curiously. Except one. Sarah Westbury's head didn't turn but her daughter's did. Katinka watched Clara with terror and her eyes darted to the door.

'Is there some reason why it is only after you have secured your place in Parliament, on the votes of these very people, that you should pledge yourself to the cause of men of colour?' Clara's dark, narrow eyes pinned him down.

'Yes, Lady Marsden, there is a reason.' John's hands gripped the wood of the pulpit in front of him. 'The dignity of man is reason enough and is personal to each and every one of us.' He looked at her directly. 'It is I myself who would be insulted by a change in the laws of our land, because it is my country as it is yours.'

'I challenge that, Mr Westbury!' Clara's voice was shrill. 'I challenge you on the grounds that you have personal reasons for the stand you take!' Clara's hand raised the document. She was fully aware of the damage its contents would inflict on herself but she no longer cared. Her mind was filled with revenge, her blood boiled with hatred and she no longer even heard John as he answered her.

'I challenge you with this, Mr Westbury!' Clara shouted over him, waving the document. 'This document swears to the coloured blood which runs through your veins! It swears to the blood which you have denied in order to achieve your position as our white representative!' She pushed the document at the man in front of her and held her head high. 'I accuse you of falsehood, Mr Westbury. You have lied to the very people you represent and that document challenges every word you have uttered.'

John watched the crisp document as it passed from hand to hand over the heads of the crowd and towards him. He looked up as the door pushed open and Clara stepped outside. He felt suddenly free.

Katinka looked into the black night which had fallen outside as the door remained ajar behind Clara. She didn't understand what was happening and turned to her mother. Sarah's chin trembled and Katinka turned quickly to look at her father. People were standing all around her. She couldn't see him.

'Father!' she shouted over the noise, trying to peer above the crowd, but he was lost behind moving heads and waving fists.

John Westbury felt the cold eyes of his supporters and heard the low bubble of their whispered conversation as they studied the document. The angry shouts of the crowd began to quieten as the doorway filled with people pushing out of the hall like sheep. A woman glanced back at him and her contempt reached out, touching him. For the first time he knew what Sarah had meant as he experienced the isolation of colour in his own country.

Jack looked at the crowds as they jostled their way out of the village hall. His horse reared as a carriage flew past him and he recognized it as his mother's.

'What's happened?' he shouted as his horse tramped the

ground nervously and people streamed past in the dim light of the lamps. The bunting running in a square around the hall snapped as Mr Cloete pushed his wife ahead of him and through it. He was too busy wondering what he would do with the sullied pulpit to care as the brightly coloured triangles fell limply, trailing across the ground through the dust.

Jack stopped as he reached the doorway and the last of John Westbury's supporters pushed past him. He looked towards the pulpit and saw John Westbury. His hands gripped the wood in front of him and he stared at Sarah and Katinka sitting in the crooked line of hurriedly emptied seats.

'Hello, Jack.' John Westbury turned to the door and smiled. 'You're late.'

'I'm sorry. I was busy and I didn't notice the time.' Jack stopped as he saw Katinka watching him from just behind her mother, and his guilt rushed back at him.

'Time?' John shrugged. He climbed down the three wooden steps of the pulpit, moving to Sarah. 'I think it's time to go home.' He held his arm out to Sarah over the tilted backs of the chairs. She took it and they walked with the jagged line of upturned chair legs between them. Katinka sat still in her seat and watched her mother and father as they moved towards Jack at the door. Somehow she felt she deserved to be excluded.

'A little fresh air has been breathed into politics tonight, Jack!' John looked at him as he reached him. 'Your mother was kind enough to speak for me.' He wrapped his arm around Sarah's shoulder and moved past Jack in the doorway, then stopped and looked back at him. 'Don't blame your mother, Jack. I think perhaps I have something more important to find than a political answer.'

As her father and mother moved through the door Katinka's eyes remained on Jack, watching his back. He turned to her and she lowered her head. He moved slowly through the chairs and sat down beside her.

'He was right, wasn't he?' she asked.

'Yes.' Jack took her hand in his and patted it as he would a small child. 'He was right, Katinka.'

John stood back as he held the carriage door open for Sarah. 'Katinka!' he called towards the hall as Sarah climbed the step.

'I'll get Katinka,' he said and moved away. He stepped back as a group of men moved towards him and stopped in front of him. 'Yes?' He smiled at them politely; but he felt suddenly angry as he recognized the same ugly face of prejudice he'd confronted in the courtroom many years earlier.

'What she said.' A lean white face peered at him and the others moved forward a little. 'It's true, isn't it.'

'It's true.'

John had seen a flash of steel before the words had left his mouth and he felt a sudden prick between his ribs. The solid bone of a forearm pressed hard against his stomach and he looked at the lean white face in surprise.

'Keep to your own kind, kaffir!'

The words sunk into John Westbury's body as the knife did, and he looked down slightly puzzled. A short wooden handle stuck out of his waistcoat and pushed a brass button to one side. The button fell off and he saw the loose black threads stretching out as if to snatch it back. He felt warm liquid swell up into his throat. It tasted bitter. He felt pain: terrible pain. His hand gripped the wooden handle sticking out of his waistcoat and his knees buckled. His hand was wet. It was dripping. He saw Sarah's face as she leaned over him, reaching out to him as he fell backwards, and he wondered why she wasn't smiling any more.

The bunting swung above him as it stretched down to the ground in a canopy. He saw another long string of bunting. A black child held one end and was walking towards the other end lying on the ground. She lifted it and held the ends together. She was on the other side of the bunting. A picture was pinned to the tree. It turned slowly and he thought he recognized the face.

Sarah was crying. She was talking to him but he couldn't hear her and tried to say 'pardon', but his mouth wouldn't move. Something was running over his lips and he tried to close them to stop it. He couldn't.

'Katinka,' he said in his head as his daughter's face looked down at him. 'Don't shout, Katinka,' he thought as her mouth opened in wide silent screams. 'Your mother doesn't like you to shout.'

He looked for Sarah but she had gone. Everyone had gone. Where had everyone gone? Where had the lights gone? Why was it dark?

'He's dead.' He heard Jack Marsden's voice somewhere near him.

'Who's dead?' John Westbury wondered.

Chapter Thirty

The only sound was Clara's even breathing as she slept. Her head lay comfortably against the enormous feather pillow and her long grey hair fell in an immaculate plait over the crisp linen sheet. A sudden stream of light shone across the bed and over her face. A man's hand moved through the light and cast a shadow on the pillow. The shadow pulled back as the linen sheet flew through the air.

Clara woke with a start as the sheet was pulled off her and Jack's face glared down at her, his anger like a burning wind in her face.

'What are you doing in here?' she screamed. 'Get out of my room!' She pulled her head back as his hand reached for her. She scratched at his arm as he pulled her forward, flinging her off the bed.

'Jack!' Clara shouted as he moved over her, gripping her arm and dragging her across the bedroom floor. 'No!' she screamed as he pulled her through the open door. She tried to hold on to the doorframe but was dragged away and her nails broke on the wood as she struggled to pull free. Her body was hauled across the cold red quarry tiles of the hall and she reached for his hand as he pulled her on relentlessly. Her nightdress ripped as he dragged her through the open front door, and the cool night air closed round her. She pushed her feet against the ground, trying to pull her body back.

'Help me!' Her arm pulled free and she swung away, crawling back to the door, but Jack's hands gripped her shoulders and hauled her after him again across the ground. The front of her nightdress fell open as it ripped wider and her once full breasts hung like empty sacks.

'No!' she screamed as she turned her head and saw the

cracked white walls of the slave quarters coming closer. 'Let me go!'

'I am!' Jack yelled, kicking the small wooden door open with his boot and flinging his mother forwards into the slave quarters. Her body slid across the grimy mud floor and hit the solid wall on the other side. She fell back against it and forward again with the impact. Like a cornered animal she crawled towards the dim light coming through the low door. The smell of damp stale air suffocated her. Through the open door she could see space, there were lights moving towards her and she could hear African voices in a bubble of nervous alarm. They were coming to help her and she reached out to them.

The door slammed against her hand and the small flickering lights disappeared. She pulled her weight up, clinging to the rough wood of the door and banged on it with her fists.

'Jack!' she screamed as her fingers tore at the hard wood. The damp stench and total darkness wrapped itself around her and she knew he would show her no mercy.

Emily shivered as Clara's screams and shouts reached through her subconscious and woke her. She had slept fitfully since Clara had arrived home. There had been a curious satisfaction in her eyes, almost sexual, and although Clara had said nothing, Emily had sensed everything was different. She didn't know John Westbury was dead.

'She will remain in the slave quarters until she dies!' Jack's voice tore through the lace curtain at Emily's open window like a gust of angry wind. Emily's mind leapt to discover the source of the distress in Jack's voice, but her body held her back. Never in her life had she felt so trapped by her crippled legs. She leaned over the edge of the bed, balanced herself on her hands as they reached the floor, lowered her body and allowed her legs to drop behind her. She crawled towards the window, dragging her limbs.

'Jack!' Emily shouted as she pulled herself up on the sill. 'Jack!' She could see Rosita with Sunday as they stood away from him. Their eyes were lit with fright in the flickering of the lamps they carried. Jack had his back to Emily. His arm swung back and forth as he hammered nails into a wooden beam across the door of the slave quarters and Clara's screams redoubled.

535

'What are you doing? Jack, what's happening?' Emily shouted, banging her hands uselessly on the windowledge.

'My mother will be fed gruel and water!' Jack turned and faced the terrified servants. His eyes blazed with an insane fury which neither Sunday nor Rosita had seen before. 'Nobody will go to her but me. If anyone helps her I will kill them myself. Do you hear me?' Jack's voice rang through the vineyards. 'The blood of John Westbury is on my mother's hands and she will remain where she is until hers is on mine.'

Jack swung back to the barred door of the slave quarters as Clara screamed from inside and Emily felt herself slip to the floor at the news of John Westbury's death. Her body hung limp and her legs slid uselessly across the floor as she tried to hang on to the window sill. Her mind spun with sudden memories of Jean Jacques. He was crying as he held a blond curly-headed baby. Now that baby was dead. In the dark Emily could just make out the outline of her diary as it sat where it always did. The words she'd written when the news of Geoffrey and Charles Marsden's deaths had spewed vomit from Clara's mouth over Jack sprang to mind; and she could hear again Jack's cries as he appealed to Clara for some understanding. He had wept openly for the loss of his brother: for the loss of his father, whose death Clara tossed aside as retribution. She could remember the words Jack had spoken as he tried to reach his mother, and their argument raged in her head once again.

'Geoffrey was the son of the only man I truly loved!' Clara's words had been slow and deliberate. 'The man your father chose to have executed. That is the truth you prevented me from telling my son. And it was you who allowed him to die for a man who had murdered his father.'

'What truth?' Jack's words had been as confused as the emotion he'd bottled up for years, and had poured out, one on top of the other at his mother's feet. 'The truth is I loved you, Mother! When I was a child . . . that peculiar child. "Kissed by the devil" . . . isn't that what you said? "Kissed by the devil"? No. It's you he kissed. I've listened to people who remember your past and they've told me the truth! Do you remember Titus, Mother?'

Emily was unaware of Rosita lifting her on to the bed as Jack's voice ran in circles inside her head.

'You must remember Titus! Everyone remembers him! And

his son remembers a girl. A girl Titus cursed with death! A girl who tried to kill Jean Jacques and his mother. A girl who grew into the woman that is you! You are the legend the people frighten their children with. You!'

Emily's head spun with Jack's last word as she looked up and saw Rosita's gentle face looking down at her.

'You all right? You? Miss Emily?' Rosita's words echoed with Jack's until Emily's mind finally cleared and the nightmare of jumbled words faded away.

'What's happened, Rosita?' she asked.

'The young master Westbury is dead.' Rosita shook her head. 'There's no way now for that boy and his mother. Sunday say there no way any more, Miss Emily.'

The lamp flickered on the desk as Emily wrote her diary. Clara's cries still reached into the room and Jack's anger still haunted her.

'We are in the very darkest hour.' Emily looked away at the light of the lamp for a moment. 'Clara's own hatred fell over her like a shroud, as Jack turned his back on her for ever.' Emily looked up with a thought, and then wrote carefully, 'Why is it that men speak abusively about things they don't understand?' Her mind had gone back to the constant gossip in the winelands surrounding John Westbury's life and death; back to the distaste she knew Sarah would live with for the rest of her life. She still wondered why Sarah had elected to stay in Africa instead of returning to England and remembered the face of Pauline's father as he had sat beside his grandson's grave. A man who couldn't understand why he was still alive, when everyone he cared for had gone. She remembered Katinka's dignity as she had stood silently beside her father's grave, and she thought of Eva.

'And why is it that those things men do understand,' Emily wrote, 'they instinctively seek to destroy.'

Although her full stop was clear and decisive, Emily added one word, 'But.'

Katinka's eyes moved over Emily's hunched body beside her as the carriage bumped over the rough road. She knew Emily's mind was elsewhere.

'I don't think it's right!' Rosita's worried voice broke through

Emily's thoughts but she kept her eyes away from her as they drove into the small Malay fishing village. 'But.' The last word she'd written stuck in her mind.

'Come, Katinka.' Emily ignored Rosita's grunt of protest and waited as the driver lifted her chair off the roof of the carriage. 'You asked to meet your great-grandmother.' Emily turned and Katinka held her hand tightly. Her eyes were still red from days of weeping and her usually smooth white cheeks were puffed.

'My father knew her, didn't he?' She glanced towards Eva's small house and her eyes settled on the old Malay woman standing erect inside a bent body. 'Is that her?'

'Yes.' Emily held her arms out to Rosita and allowed her to lift her from the carriage into the chair. She smiled as Eva moved carefully towards her. Rosita kicked out as a small yellow dog snarled at her ankles, and she turned away from the coloured faces staring at her.

'It's not right,' she whispered to Emily in shame. 'Not right the child should come here.'

Katinka stood on the step of the carriage and looked down at Eva.

'Hello,' she said. 'My name's Katinka.'

Eva straightened her tiny body and peered up into Katinka's face. Though her own face was hollow and criss-cross lines crinkled her skin, they were the warmest dark eyes Katinka had ever seen. 'I have heard,' Eva said very quietly. 'I am sorry, child.'

Katinka bit her lip and looked down. Emily held out her hand to her. She paused for a moment, took Emily's hand and moved down the carriage steps. Rosita turned away as Katinka reached Eva and tears filled her eyes. Katinka had run to Eva and held her tightly.

'But,' Emily mentally wrote the word in her diary again as she watched Katinka's young body bend into the fragile age of Eva's,' . . . there is love.'

'I will go to him!' Emily looked at Rosita's rigid shoulders as she sat in her wheelchair outside the black cellar door. Strange music came from inside and the stranger sound of Jack singing added to the horror Rosita felt.

'It's shameful, Miss Emily.' Rosita looked towards the slave quarters. Although there was no sound coming from them now she could still hear Clara's pathetic wails which had haunted her every night for a week. 'His mother will die in there!'

'Rosita!' Emily said sharply. 'I want to talk to him.'

'You want to talk?' Rosita's arms lifted at her sides in astonishment. 'Through the drink he will listen to you? No!' A sound of shame crept from Rosita's mouth. 'Sunday went in there. It's the devil, he say!'

'Then go away!' Emily shouted, and Rosita stepped back in surprise. She turned slowly; then stopped and looked back, watching Emily push the wooden wheels of her chair towards the cellar doors. She saw her push the door open and ran to her quickly, aware of Emily's sudden determination. Silently Rosita bumped the wheelchair down the cellar steps.

'Be careful, please,' she whispered, backing away from the door. Everything that had happened to the family she had served all her life, and her mother before her, was from the devil himself.

Jack turned bleary-eyed towards the door as he saw the eyes of the black men playing a strange assortment of musical instruments look towards it. His tuneless singing stopped and he smiled. He was slumped on a pile of sacking, with a bottle of brandy held lopsided in his hand.

'Aunt Emily!' he called drunkenly and tried to stand up. He fell back immediately and laughed, pulling a young black girl closer. He wrapped his arms across her breasts as he held her to him. 'Have you come to join the revelry, Aunt Emily?' He looked up at the strange orchestra as the music petered out, and shouted, 'I didn't tell you to stop playing! Play on! Mozart! What do you think of that, Aunt Emily? Mozart was debauched too, wasn't he?'

'I wish to speak to you, Jack.' Emily's voice was calm as she looked at him from the door. 'Would you ask these people to leave.'

'Why?' He hugged the girl closer to him. 'Do they insult you? Were you ever like this, huh?' He pulled the girl's dress open. 'Was my mother ever like this?' he asked.

'You insult that girl,' Emily said. 'And you insult John Westbury.'

'But he's dead!' Jack shouted and leaned forward, peering at her as he fell forward on his elbows. 'John Westbury is dead!'

The brandy slurped up the neck of the bottle and tipped over his arm. 'Ah!' he said, looking at his wet sleeve. 'My drink has spilled.'

'You have spilled John Westbury's memory like drink, Jack Marsden! Let your mother out of those slave quarters immediately, or I shall order the servants to do so!'

'Do that.' Jack pushed himself back and whispered as he looked at her, 'Do that, and I shall kill them for obeying your order.' He wagged a finger at her. 'I told you, didn't I!'

'What are you trying to prove!' Emily felt useless in the face of his drunken bitterness. Although pain screamed from his face as his head wavered back and forth, trying to see her clearly, she knew she couldn't help him. 'What good is there in your revenge?' she said.

'Are you crying?' Jack pushed the black girl away and crawled towards Emily's chair. 'Are those tears, Aunt Emily? Are they for me? For my mother? For you?'

'Have you no small spark of manhood left?'

'None!' Jack sat back and looked at her wide-eyed. He waved his arms around the cellars. 'All this?' He laughed. 'Grandfather told me to take it and lick it off the floor! Did you know that!' he exclaimed suddenly, as if he could see Jacques leaning against the vats as he died. 'But I don't want it!' He reacted as Emily swung her chair round and pushed it towards the door. 'Leave my mother where she is!' he yelled after her and fell back. 'Leave her to die like a slave,' he muttered.

Rosita stood with her head bowed at the door of the dining-room and watched Emily as she stared at her untouched plate of breakfast. Clara's faint voice reached them through the silence. Each day her cries grew weaker.

'Sunday says he will do it, Miss Emily,' Rosita said quietly.

'No.' Emily closed her eyes. 'Take this away!'

Rosita carefully took the plate and looked down at Emily's useless and helpless body. She remembered the young girl who had run through the grounds of Bonne Esperance with her, and Rosita made up her mind.

'I will tell Sunday he is not to let Lady Marsden out,' she said and moved to the door with the plate of uneaten food, carrying with it the courage she had just found.

Katinka looked down on Bonne Esperance, dug her heels into the flanks of the white Arab, and raced towards the cellars.

The sun was rising in a golden arc over the low white building and she remembered the excitement she used to feel every time she saw it. The excitement had changed. It was now an ache for someone she cared for deeply and was in danger of losing.

Sunday nodded, his head held low while Rosita whispered to him urgently at the back door of the house. He glanced up towards the slave quarters nervously. Clara had stopped crying but he was still afraid to go near the building. He felt the iron crowbar Rosita pushed at his hand and looked into her face. She smiled encouragement, and turned back into the house.

The slave quarters seemed a long way away as Sunday moved towards them. His attention was fixed on them and he didn't notice the slight figure of Katinka Westbury as she slipped into the cellar further away. He tried to remember Jack as he had been: the small white boy who loved to hear stories from the past, and was always somewhere near him, asking questions. The boy whose eyes held a curious detachment which Sunday had never understood, but had recognized somewhere deep inside himself as rejection.

Sunday reached the barred door and slipped the crowbar underneath the beam nailed across it. A cold sweat broke out on his forehead. On the other side of the door was the white woman whom his father Titus had talked of with such fear, and behind him, in the cellars, was the white man he'd watched grow from a strange child into an angry man who had threatened to kill anyone who let the white woman out.

'My mother told me I must never come here again. That I must never see you again.' Katinka spoke quietly. Jack was leaning against the cellar wall and his eyes were screwed into narrow slits as he peered at her. She saw the shape of a young black girl slip past her through the open cellar door. She felt nothing but sorrow as she looked at him, and quickly filled her mind with love to smother it. 'I loved my father,' she said quietly, 'but he wouldn't have wanted this, Jack.'

'Go away.' Jack pushed himself off the wall and turned his back on her. 'Your mother's right.'

'No.' Katinka's voice was firm.

Jack looked at her over his shoulder. He felt dirty and suddenly deeply ashamed as her clear fresh beauty gazed at him.

'Go home!' he shouted and waved his arm behind him. 'You're a child.'

'I'm not a child.' Katinka tilted her head up and moved towards him. She touched his back and he pulled away quickly. 'Will what you're doing change anything? Will it bring back my father? Or Eva's son?'

'Your father was right,' Jack suddenly shouted. 'And your mother is right! I'm bad for you.'

'No,' Katinka said again, very firmly, and Jack's eyes moved to her delicate hand on him. He wanted to push it off, but he couldn't.

'What do you want?' he asked, searching her face as though the answer would be there. 'Do you pity me?'

'I love you.'

Jack's head was suddenly empty. The words which had never been spoken to him in his life had swept it clean, but he couldn't remember what she'd said and he peered at her curiously.

'I love you,' Katinka repeated.

The past was summoned by the ringing slave bell as Jack pulled on the rope and it sounded throughout Bonne Esperance. Sunday stepped back from the door in fright as the last piece of wood came away in his hands and he saw Jack striding towards him. He stopped beside Sunday and looked at him. Sunday's eyes darted away nervously. He saw Rosita at the back door of the house and he moved away towards her. He was confused when Katinka Westbury ran past him calling, 'Make food for Lady Marsden, Rosita. And her bed. Is her bed ready?'

Katinka looked up into Rosita's face as she reached her. 'Where's Aunt Emily?' Her eyes followed Rosita's to the side of the house where Emily sat in her chair, watching Jack go into the slave quarters.

Daylight from the open doorway shed a dim glow into the dark room and found Clara. She was curled in a heap in a corner of the tiny room, her hair hanging over her face in grey matted knots. Her bare arms were white, with dark-brown spots of age spread over them like a disease. Her hands stretched out across the grubby floor as if reaching for a way out.

'Mother,' Jack said quietly as he moved towards her. He hardly breathed and his steps were wary. She looked dead. He moved faster and his feet trod on the tattered garments which had lain untouched since Eva and Jean Jacques had left. He bent down to his mother quickly, his hand moving to her face. Her eyes stared blindly at the ground in front of her, and, as his hand touched her, he pulled back. Clara's eyes had turned on him and a trickle of blood ran from the corner of her mouth.

Rosita tucked the linen sheets carefully under the edge of the mattress. Clara lay quite still, her hair plaited and lying neatly across the pillow. Her face had been washed and Rosita lifted her limp arms over the sheet, as she had her father's.

'You can go now, Rosita.' Emily's voice was calm and collected. 'Tell Master Jack he can come in.' She pushed her chair towards the bed and looked at Clara's dry cracked lips. They parted as she snatched each short, even breath. Emily dipped a piece of soft white wool into a bowl of water beside the bed and held it to Clara's lips. Her head turned away and her mouth pulled down. 'You must drink, Clara,' Emily said quietly with Miss Thurston's tone of command. She watched the water from the wool drip on to the pillow. 'We don't want a mess on the bed, do we, and you need liquids to bring your temperature down.' Emily rubbed at the drops of water. She was trying to keep her mind off the death which faced her yet again and felt suddenly tired. She wished she was not always alone when it came.

'Come along, Clara. Drink.' Clara's eyes darted at her in accusation. 'That's right.' Emily put the wet wool on her lips and thought of Suzanne instead of what was happening. She remembered the joy in Suzanne's face as she'd said goodbye: the care she had taken to choose the couple, a Mr and Mrs Davies, teachers who now ran her school. It had been called 'Miss Thurston's School'. Emily could still feel the love which flowed between Suzanne and Thys, and she envied it.

'And when you've had a little drink, Jack will come to see you.' Emily noticed the sharp movement of Clara's eyes but ignored it. She smiled as she remembered the small black face of

'Tshepo son', as Adam insisted on calling himself. He'd looked back at her from between Suzanne and Thys as they'd driven away to Gerrit's farm; and then she thought of the last letter she'd had from Suzanne.

'Adam didn't mind when Gerrit insisted he live with the other black people on the farm but I still cannot pretend to understand. Gerrit's a warm loving man. How can he object to him living in the house just because he is black? He cares for the boy and I believe he might even grow to love him, but he separates himself from his own feelings.'

'If you won't drink I shall get very cross, Clara. Jack will be in to see you soon.' Emily refused to give in to the tramp of death that came closer and thought back to Suzanne's letter.

'Do you know what Gerrit said when he saw me? "I think you are as beautiful as Thys said. I think it is a good thing he did not marry the widow Heunis's daughter. She has grown large on her own cooking. Yes, my sacrifice of the widow herself was worthwhile".' Emily could hear Suzanne's laugh from among the words.

'And Thys? Yes, Emily, Thys is happy at last and his roots have taken in this piece of land. He's a true man of Africa. And me? I'm Afrikaans now. Writing in English is becoming quite foreign to me. Peace and love be yours in abundance, as they are mine. Suzanne.'

Emily had detected the only unspoken sorrow in Suzanne's life. It was the part of her that was missing. Their son, Pieter.

'I told you, Clara,' Emily said as Jack stepped into the room. 'Jack's come to see you.' She pushed her chair back as he approached the bed. For the first time Emily felt the real pain of Clara's approaching death. She'd seen it in Jack's eyes as Clara's turned away.

'Forgive me, Mother.' She heard his voice and kept her look down. She wished she wasn't in the room. She wanted to fly away as Suzanne and Prudence had.

'Do you remember this?' Emily looked up at Jack's question. She saw the old key which had been missing for years. Jack was holding it out towards Clara. 'One day I will return to France with this key as you always wanted, Mother.'

Clara's hand moved suddenly and knocked the key to the floor. Emily saw Jack's back tighten as he pulled away. She knew his look without seeing it. It was the look of the rejected child she remembered well. Clara's lips moved as she tried to speak but all that could be heard was her defiant breathing.

'Don't go, Jack,,' Emily said. 'Please.'

Jack put his hand on the round brass door handle and turned it, walking out without looking back.

'Clara!' Emily turned to her sister. 'Jack is trying to say sorry.'

Clara's eyes closed and her breathing fell back into the familiar rhythm of short determined gasps.

Katinka looked through the sitting-room window and watched Jack as he moved away from the house. He stopped beside the slave quarters. Even at this distance Katinka could see something she'd never seen in him before. The man she'd worshipped since she was a child, the man she had since grown to love as a woman, was a child himself. Her eyes moved around the room as if searching for something. They settled on the family bible and she picked it up, moving out of the room with it.

Rosita stood outside Clara's bedroom door. She was waiting to prepare the body. 'What do you want, child?' she asked as Katinka came towards her. She placed her large body in front of the door protectively. 'She's dying, child. You not go in there.'

'I've got to see her.' Katinka's eyes dipped to the bible in her hands and she whispered, 'Please.' Her hand moved to the door tentatively and Rosita didn't stop her.

Emily looked up as the door opened. Katinka stood still with the large bible in her hand.

'You're his mother,' she said and moved towards Clara without looking at Emily. With relief Emily propelled her chair to the door, pleased it was not she who would sit and welcome death into their house again.

'It's your bible, Lady Marsden. Your family bible.'

Emily pushed the door open and it swung closed behind her. She looked at Rosita. 'Please take me outside,' she said. 'I would like to look at the mountains.'

Katinka looked at the bible in her hands and her bottom lip drew in under her teeth.

'Jack needs you, Lady Marsden,' she said. Clara's eyes opened but didn't turn to her. 'I don't know why everything's happened that has happened, but I know he needs you.' Katinka felt a rush of tears which quickly found the path of those she'd shed for her father and she looked down, holding them back. 'If you don't forgive him, if you can't find it in your heart to show him that you do love him . . .' Katinka stopped as her voice choked but she held the tears back and looked into Clara's cold grey eyes as they fought both death and love. 'I love him. I love your son, Lady Marsden. But if you die now . . . if you die without forgiving him,' Katinka's tears rolled in great silver balls down her cheeks, 'don't you understand what will happen? If you don't give him some sign that you love him? Just a little. Please tell him somehow that you do. Even just that you care. You see, if you don't forgive him he'll never be able to love anybody. I'm begging you, Lady Marsden. Please show him, somehow.'

Clara's arm moved beside Katinka and her eyes stared into hers. The coldness was still there, but there was something else.

'What is it?' Katinka asked desperately as Clara's breaths came a little louder. 'I don't know what you want.' Clara's face was a death mask but her eyes bore into Katinka's, then moved to the bible. 'You want me to read the bible?' Katinka opened the pages. She jumped as Clara's arm hit out and knocked the bible out of her hands. 'What is it?' Katinka panicked as Clara's eyes stayed pinned on her. Then her eyes moved and Katinka followed the look. It had moved past her and on to the floor. She was looking at the key on the floor. Katinka moved to it quickly, pushing the bible to one side.

'Do you want the key?' But Clara's eyes had moved back to the bible. Katinka broke down. 'I don't know what you want.' She opened the bible and looked at it. 'Is it the bible?' She glanced at Clara. 'Do you want me to read the bible?' She looked back at the page and the words swam behind her tears. She brushed the tears away quickly and looked again. 'I can't read it.' Katinka looked back at Clara, who was staring straight at the bible. Her breathing was agitated and Katinka was terrified. 'I can't read French.'

Clara's eyes moved slowly up to Katinka's and held them.

'I understand,' Katinka said very quietly, and the tears rolled freely down her cheeks.

Rosita pulled the new brocade curtains closed and moved to the next window. As she went she glanced at the empty hook on the wall from which she'd removed the old key for the little boy Geoffrey so many years before. The day he'd hidden that key was one that Rosita had never forgotten. It was the importance such a useless key held in a child's mind which had disturbed her and the intense determination he'd had to get rid of it. But that young child Geoffrey was dead, as his father was dead, and still Rosita didn't understand the significance of the key. She pulled the last curtain closed on her own questions.

'Go to bed, Rosita,' Emily said wearily. 'It's late.' Rosita turned, opening her mouth to argue. Her job was to wait until Clara died, and then to prepare her body for burial. 'Jack's with her,' Emily said quietly. 'And there's no need for us any more.' Emily watched Rosita as she left and remembered the way that Katinka had stepped outside and led Jack confidently back into the house. She'd led him as though he was the child, and the moutains around her had seemed to rise on a breath.

Emily pushed her chair through the door towards Clara's room. She could hear Jack's voice but she couldn't understand what he was saying. She turned the handle and pushed the door slightly ajar.

Jack sat in a chair beside his mother at the head of the bed and Katinka stood beside him with a hand on his shoulder. Jack was reading Isaiah: 40, in French.

Chapter Thirty-one

The room was small, dark and crammed with papers and parcels. Mr Harrison, a thin man in a peaked cap, sat behind the grubby counter in a round-backed chair. He looked up at Prudence from squinting eyes and his finger stopped its run down a list, stabbing its stubby end at the paper.

'Fifteen shillings,' he said, pushing the list across the counter at Prudence.

'Fifteen shillings!' Prudence tried to focus her eyes on his. 'It's daylight robbery.' She blinked. In all the years she'd known him she had never got used to looking into his eyes.

'Then send your message by postcart, Mrs Audsley.' He pulled the peak of his cap down and rolled himself away across the floor in his chair.

'How many words did you say?' Prudence asked the back of his bald head. The strap of his cap had moved up and a white line ran across his shiny scalp. It marked the spot the sun had been prevented from burning.

'Twenty.' He didn't turn to her. 'Including the address.'

'Very well.' Prudence held out a piece of paper. 'I wish to send a telegraph, Mr Harrison.'

'Address?'

'Farm Bonne Esperance, Cape Province.'

'The telegraph only goes to Cape Town.'

'Then how would my message reach its destination?'

'By postcart!'

'With all your modern advances, messages still finally depend on the horse and buggy!' Prudence straightened her shoulders as he rolled his chair back to her. She knew he had little respect for her; but more than a little fascination.

'Do you wish to send a telegraph or not?' He pushed his cap

back and rubbed his bald head before replacing it. He wondered what went on in the bordello he had never entered, on his wife's orders.

'Why else do you think I'm here?' Prudence pushed her piece of paper at him.

'There's twenty-one words,' he said without looking at her.

'Then remove the word six! I shall quite simply arrive on twenty February and not twenty-six February! And I shall count my change as carefully as you counted my words, Mr Harrison, I can assure you of that!' She slammed a bank note on the counter. He slid it towards him, slapped it into his open palm, and laid a pile of coins in its place.

'Your change.' He disappeared into the corner on his rolling chair, and pushed her back into his secret world of fantasy.

Prudence wasn't sure what had annoyed her most. The fifteen shillings, Mr Harrison's wandering eyes, or the fact that the telegraph was already being tapped out by his stabbing finger. It meant she couldn't change her mind.

Dust rose around her feet and powdered her neat ankle boots. It caught on the hem of her skirt, clung to it and rose in a fine white cloud as she walked. The sign over the bordello creaked ahead of her in the still hot air and the sun burned down on the flat horizon. A single squatting tree was the only reminder that the earth produced anything but diamonds.

All around her, koppie wallopers traded keenly and noisily and the wide Du Toit Span street was lined by trading stores. They bulged with fancy goods in an effort to prise a diamond from the rough hands of the diggers. Everything about the bleak land, where nature had been uprooted by greed, offended her senses. She stopped under the creaking sign and looked up at it. She remembered Jim Audsley's reaction when he'd first seen it, and realized how much she missed him.

Her arthritic hands ached inside the gloves which tried to hide them and reminded her that the ends had not justified the means. She had not been left untainted, and she wanted to go home.

'Do you imagine a bordello was ever my dream, Marianne?' Prudence turned the wine glass in her gloved hand and the dark-red liquid tilted in a smooth line across the bowl. 'It simply kept my dream alive.' She moved the glass under her nose and breathed deeply. She could smell the sweet air of Bonne Esperance, which held the mystery of wine close to its heart. '"Mrs Audsley's Parlour" saved Bonne Esperance; but now,' Prudence laid the glass on her desk, 'now I will call in my debts, and claim my dream.'

Marianne raised her eyebrows as she peered at Prudence from her arrogantly tilted head. Her face was layered in heavy make-up and her hair piled high. Her breasts, pushed tightly together, bulged over the low line of her bodice and there was no trace of the frightened young girl who had first stepped into the bordello. Looking at Marianne, Prudence realized, was like looking at herself: without her husband and without Bonne Esperance.

'I can hardly imagine you on a farm.' Marianne's voice was as brittle as everything else about her.

'There was a time I could not have imagined myself here, Marianne.' Prudence narrowed her eyes as she tried to see Marianne clearly. 'Now it is yours. I believe perhaps you've earned it.'

Marianne's face grew puzzled. Prudence shrugged and looked around the dark room which had depressed her suddenly as she'd read Emily's letter that morning.

'I have all I wanted from it.' Prudence looked at the glass of wine, and lifted it to Marianne. 'When Mr Audsley returns, tell him where I am. Bonne Esperance!' She wondered when the telegraph announcing the date of her arrival would reach home.

'You think Mr Audsley will be coming back?' Marianne could hardly conceal her amusement.

'Yes, Marianne. He'll come back.' She lied even to herself. 'Tell him his fifty per cent is with me, in the wine farm we subsidised.'

'And you are giving me the bordello?' A little of Marianne's past innocence showed in the amazement in her voice.

'You have made it more yours than it was ever mine.' Prudence's eyes moved from her glass to Emily's letter and she read the words again, although she remembered every one clearly.

'Katinka is sixteen now, and she and Jack are to be married on the second of February. I can hardly believe the joy I feel.' Prudence could hear that joy. 'It's as if Clara's death has lifted the shadow she cast on Bonne Esperance, Prudence. Even the tragedy of John Westbury's murder has somehow allowed light to shine into the darkness. But I wonder how many Claras there are in the world whom we have not yet met.'

'Bonne Esperance wine will, of course, no longer be served in the Parlour.' Prudence turned her attention back to Marianne. 'It has served its purpose and its purpose was never to inebriate the clients of a bordello.' Her eyes returned to Emily's letter.

'Jack has found his roots in Africa as our father never did. "The mother that never dies" has claimed him.'

Prudence knew what Emily meant. In all the years she'd been away from Bonne Esperance, its claim on her had not diminished.

'Love has come full circle; and our heritage has returned to its rightful heirs, as if a little of ourselves has fed the thirst of Africa.'

'Yes, Marianne. The bordello is yours.' Prudence folded Emily's letter and closed a chapter of her own life.

The small church was filled with the scent of cut flowers, while a circle of light from the church window shimmered around Jack and Katinka. Emily caught a glimpse of the petticoat under Katinka's delicate white lace wedding dress. The fifty years which had passed since Eva's nimble fingers had stitched it at Emily's birth wove a circle of love around the bridal couple.

Jack's back was straight and his eyes were on Katinka as they stood in front of the altar before the priest. She held his hand in hers and followed the priest's words in a sweet echo.

'I, Katinka Westbury, take thee, Jack Marsden, to my wedded husband; to have and to hold from this day forward, for better, for worse, for richer, for poorer, in sickness and in health; to love, cherish and to obey, till death us do part, according to God's holy ordinance. And thereto I give thee my troth.' The warmth that flowed from Katinka's eyes confirmed the sincerity of her words and Jack could feel her love pouring over him.

Sarah Westbury looked down as emotion rose in her throat. Jack had taken Katinka's left hand and slipped a simple gold ring on to her third finger.

'With this ring I thee wed; with my body I thee worship, and with all my worldly goods I thee endow: in the name of the Father, and of the Son, and of the Holy Ghost. Amen.'

Sarah felt as though John Westbury was in church beside his

daughter and giving her away to Jack himself. It was as if he had never died and none of the ugliness which had led to this moment had ever been, as if it had been he who had said, 'I do,' when the priest had asked who gave Katinka in marriage, and not she.

She glanced at old Mr Westbury as he sat silently in the pew beside her and she knew he was thinking about Pauline and Jean Jacques. Although he could no longer hear or speak; although he was waiting at death's door, he was at peace. It had been his wish to join their farm to Bonne Esperance as a wedding gift. The union of the land, as the borders were wiped out for ever, was the physical sign of a divided family reunited by love.

But somewhere in the streets of Cape Town was Sarah's son. All she could hope was that a little of the love in the air around them at that moment would fall on him: that, in some way, he might know he was part of a family, and a country that was his, as it was theirs.

Jack held Katinka's face between his hands, and kissed her. Rosita's warm face glistened as she stood beside Sunday in her finest clothes. Their small grandson, Titus, couldn't understand the emotion around him, and drew a circle on the stone floor with his bare toe.

Emily looked at the cross above the altar: the same sign which marked the graves of so many people she loved. For the first time, it no longer commemorated death, but the promise of life.

Laughter and chatter from the wedding party inside the Westbury house chased Jack and Katinka as he took her by the hand and led her running towards the waiting carriage.

'But we can't leave now, Jack.' Katinka glanced back at her home nervously, but she laughed as he pulled her after him. 'I'm supposed to change my dress. My mother wants to . . .'

'Shh!' Jack helped her into the carriage and signalled for the driver who was sitting under the shade of a tree nearby to come quickly.

Jack looked back at the house through the small window of the carriage and pulled the door shut. The driver climbed on to his seat and glanced down with an impish smile as Jack rapped the carriage side to move him on quickly. Katinka fell sideways against him as the carriage pulled away. She looked into his eyes and her hand ran up his face.

'Why are we running away?' Her eyes sparkled and Jack pulled her closely to him.

'For the first time in my life, Katinka, I am not running away,' he said.

The lace canopy over the four-poster bed stretched wide before falling in delicate folds, held back at each corner by plaited silk cords. Katinka stood beside the bed, still dressed in her wedding dress, and looked up at the click of a lock. Jack leaned against the door with his hands behind him, holding the key.

Katinka's eyes moved to the bed and away from him. Her neck curved and her hair fell forward, before her eyes turned on to him with the innocence of the small girl who had once asked him to wait for her. She faced him across the bridal suite he had secretly organized for them at the village hotel in Stellenbosch.

She moved to him; stopped in front of him. She felt the firm touch of his hands on her shoulders, and moved her body into his as he curled himself around her. He wanted to protect her, even from himself. The innocence and trust in her eyes pulled hard on his desires. Her supple young body pressed against his. The love he felt was deeper than anything he had known but was as delicate as Katinka herself. He was terrified of bruising it. Instinctively, he pulled his body away from her.

'I am a woman now, Jack.' Katinka's eyes searched his face for the source of the trepidation she felt in him. 'I'm your wife.' She reached up to him and her lips met his gently. As if he were a child, Katinka led him towards the physical union of their marriage. She slid the shoulders of her wedding dress down, and turned her back on him. The long line of small silk-covered buttons reached under her auburn hair and hid amongst it. Her slim hands moved under her hair and lifted it away from the buttons as they reached up to the nape of her neck, and Jack closed his eyes.

The white lace of the dress so neatly buttoned down her back had dared him to touch the purity it protected.

'I want you, Jack,' Katinka said.

Her body shivered as she felt his fingers push the first white button under the twisted silk loop which held it, and the dress loosened its hold on her body. With each cancelled fastening, her heart beat faster, until the last button slipped loose and the wedding dress fell to the floor. Katinka could feel Jack's eyes running down her bare back and let her hair drop loose as she felt his lips touch the small of her back. Desire bubbled inside her like a freshwater spring and she turned towards him, pressing her body against his.

'I love you,' she whispered.

Jack held her back as her true beauty touched him for the first time. Her skin glowed with a satin sheen, and her perfectly shaped young breasts tightened as the delicate pink nipples stood erect under his gaze. The petticoat made by Eva spread out from her tiny waist, and reached in soft folds to her slim bare ankles.

'You're beautiful.' Jack's voice was filled with awe at her beauty and, for the first time in her life, Katinka knew she was. Her head tilted back as his hands pushed their way through the mass of her hair. Holding her face gently, his mouth moved to hers and she felt again the wave of longing in her body as their lips met; but there was no guilt.

His hands ran gently over her shoulders, around her breasts in a caress and on down to her waist. The drawstring of her petticoat loosened and it fell to the floor among the silk of the wedding dress at her feet. Her body slowly drained of its strength as his hands slipped on down her thighs, and his mouth moved gently between her breasts, down along the line of her stomach, until his lips touched the throbbing mound between her legs. Her head jerked back and her slim body arched forward in a curve as gently his tongue stroked her, promising he wouldn't hurt her.

'The wedding was simple but beautiful, Suzanne; and the union of Jack and Katinka seems to have rekindled the spirit of Bonne Esperance. It's almost as though a deep wound has at last healed. He is so like Thys. Jack is a man of Africa. His heart is in the land, and it's as if Katinka is a part of it too.'

Suzanne smiled as she read Emily's letter against the background sound of children's voices chanting the two times table. She looked across the African land Emily had written of, and into the distance. She watched Thys herding the plump grazing cattle as tick birds fed on their backs, swaying with the movement of the cattle but somehow never falling off.

She turned back to the group of black children she was teaching. Some sat up in the tree and others hung upside-down from its branches as their chanting rang out, conducted by Adam's waving arms.

'And now three times.' Suzanne pushed Emily's letter into the pocket of her brown skirt and smiled at Adam, raising her arms. Adam lifted his in imitation and his face spread in Tshepo's wide grin.

'Three ones are three,' he announced.

'Three ones are three, indeed,' Suzanne repeated, and thought of the one that was missing from her life. 'Cover our son with your love, O Lord; but your will be done.' Her spirit lifted with the silent prayer she offered every moment.

Thys glanced towards Suzanne as the children's voices floated towards him. The earth was red and healthy, the pasture rich from the good rains of the last few years. He looked up the sky. It hung dark and heavy with more rain. Gerrit had been right. Even the land had needed the tread of a woman's feet.

Gerrit looked up from his comfortable position on the bench, towards the distant sound of a horse; a sound his practised ears had plucked from apparent silence. He banged his clay pipe against the gleaming wood of the bench and crushed the burnt tobacco under his boot, kicking it between the slats of wood. He replaced the empty pipe in his mouth and held his hand up against the sun. It burned strongly through the small gap it had found in the dark rainclouds above.

A horse and rider shimmered in the distance. A silver shape dancing in the shadows of clouds that stretched across the land between them.

Gerrit stood up and moved to the edge of the veranda. His arm curled around the broad, twisted trunk of the bougainvillaea and a mauve petal fluttered down on to his sleeve. He removed his pipe, blew the petal off his arm, and his eye settled on the bustling activity on the ground in front of the veranda. Fat-bodied flying ants were crawling out of holes and quickly took to the air in a cloud of whirring, transparent wings. To Gerrit they were a clearer sign than the dark clouds that more rain was on its way.

He looked back at the horse and rider, and his eyes formed

them into a solid shape as the sound of galloping hooves drew closer.

Pieter Pieterse glanced up at the dark clouds overhead as a distant roll of thunder rumbled among them and he pulled his horse up a short distance from the house. The square shape of Gerrit was moving towards him through a cloud of flying ants, and the horse blew a rubbery breath at him as he reached it.

'Can I help you?' Gerrit asked in Afrikaans, his eyes searching the young man's face for a clue to his occupation, as his teeth clenched the clay stem of his pipe. 'Are you lost?' Gerrit could tell the young man was a farmer and changed to English to discover his language. 'You're a stranger in these parts. Do you have trouble?'

'I am looking for someone,' Pieter said in Afrikaans and twisted his body to see Gerrit, as his horse turned away. 'I was told Suzanne Pieterse lived here.'

'Who?' Gerrit's eyes opened wide in innocence and he held the halter on the horse's head to keep it still. He pushed his pipe to the centre of his mouth with his tongue and his eyes suddenly caught the clear resemblance to Thys in Pieter's face. 'Pieterse? Suzanne Pieterse?' Gerrit asked as if he'd never heard the name before, and scratched his beard with his pipe stem. He looked into the distance. He knew Suzanne was where she was every day, attending to her tree school of black children. 'I know nobody of that name.' Gerrit turned back to Pieter Pieterse.

'Perhaps she calls herself Bothma now.' Pieter gripped his saddle and climbed down. 'Mrs Suzanne Bothma?' He wiped the bright red scarf around his neck over his face.

'Bothma,' Gerrit said slowly, and chewed on his pipe.

'Do you know her?' Pieter's face lit up with the hope of an end to his journey.

'You look tired.' Gerrit put his arm around his shoulder, turning him towards the house. 'You've travelled far, I think.'

'I'm looking for my mother.' Pieter felt the warm hold Gerrit had on his shoulder. 'I was told in Cape Town she was here. They say she came to these parts with a man called Bothma, Thys Bothma.'

'A drop of peach brandy will see you right.' Gerrit moved on towards the house but stopped when Pieter shrugged free of his arm. 'You're in a hurry? All the way from Cape Town?' Gerrit winked. 'I make fine peach brandy.'

'I don't drink.' Pieter took hold of his horse's reins. He was ready to move on to the next farm. 'I must go.'

'Why?'

'There's little reason to stay since you don't know my mother.'

'There's always reason,' Gerrit interrupted him. He could see Thys looking at him from Pieter's face. His eyes were tired but the determined expression was the same as his father's. 'You'll like my peach brandy.' Gerrit pinned him down with a challenging look. 'Or do you say it comes from the devil?' He rubbed his eyes and waited till a roll of thunder had passed and he could hear himself again. He remembered what Suzanne had told him about the Pieterse family and he recognized the rigid corsets of Calvinism around Pieter. 'Does the devil frighten you, boy? Is it him you fear or God?' Gerrit pushed his pipe forward with his teeth till it pointed straight at Pieter. 'For if it's the devil you fear, he's already won. He'd surely not need my peach brandy to do it.'

Pieter frowned as the old man looked at him with his pipe hanging impossibly from his lower lip. He was exhausted and wanted to move on to find his mother; to get her forgiveness and gain her acceptance before he could make a decision about his future with the rising band of Afrikaners. But there was something in the old man's eyes that held him where he was.

'I've money to pay for a bed,' Pieter said.

'You think money will buy what you're looking for, boy?' Gerrit glanced in the direction of Suzanne and Thys to ensure they were still out of sight. 'Come,' he said to the young man he knew was treading in the long line of Thys's footprints. 'Challenge the devil, boy!'

Pieter pressed his back against the hard wood of the bench and rolled his head to ease the muscles in his neck. His journey hadn't yet come to an end and every mile he'd ridden to find Suzanne ached through his body. The heavy clump of bougain-villaea rustled above his head as the wind, heavy with rain, lifted it.

'If you can tell me how the devil made anything as good as this I'll give up drinking it myself.' Gerrit pushed a mug of peach brandy against Pieter's shoulder. 'He spread the rumour, that's all!' Gerrit chuckled as he peered into his own mug of golden liquid and anticipation loosened his tongue even before he tasted it. 'I knew someone like you once.' Gerrit glanced at the horse which Pieter had knee-haltered exactly as Thys did. 'What did you say your name was?'

'Pieter Pieterse.'

'Taste it.' Gerrit nudged him and waited for the reaction he enjoyed more than the peach brandy itself.

Pieter lifted the mug to his lips and drank. His cheeks pulled in smartly and he let them out with a smack. Gerrit grinned and indicated for him to move up as he sat down beside him. He took his own first mouthful of the glorious sweet liquid and his body warmed as it ran smoothly down his throat.

'He went searching for his mother too. That man I was telling you about.' Gerrit looked at Pieter from the corner of his eye. 'For many years he searched. And do you know why?' Gerrit waited in the silence left by his question. 'Because the woman he loved was English.' Gerrit leaned back. 'He travelled all over, just like you.' His arm moved in a wide expansive gesture. 'All over. Looking for his mother to forgive him because the woman he loved was English.'

Pieter watched Gerrit curiously. He was aware he was trying to tell him something. 'Did he find her?'

Gerrit nodded, looking at Pieter strangely. But he said nothing. He was remembering the day Thys had come back without Suzanne.

'You were telling me a story,' Pieter said.

'He was like you.' Gerrit looked at him. 'But not like you. He only *thought* he had reason to seek his mother's forgiveness.' Gerrit paused. 'Do you have reason, boy?' Gerrit stared down into his mug as he spotted a fly land in his peach brandy and begin to swim. 'Do you think you have the right to ask your mother's forgiveness, Pieter Pieterse?' Gerrit's lips pursed and he dipped his finger into his peach brandy. The small black fly struggled on its back, stuck to his finger. 'Do you think she would forgive you?' He wiped the fly on his trouser leg and looked at Pieter keenly. 'Or is what you did unforgivable?' Gerrit's eyes filled with warmth. 'If you've come to your mother with love . . .' Gerrit's shoulders lifted in a small shrug and he paused. He didn't hurry the pause as he filled it with a long slow drink of peach brandy.

'If that's true, Pieter Bothma, if it's with love you've come, then time will not have stepped between you.' Gerrit had placed his firm belief in love between them like a winning card.

Suzanne looked up at the familiar bird call to see Thys riding towards her. She waited for him to reach her and climb off his horse. Thys opened his mouth to speak but thunder drowned his voice.

He looked towards the house as she did, and saw a man sitting beside Gerrit on the veranda. Suzanne's eyes moved from the man to his horse. A knee-haltered horse. A horse which had been haltered as she had taught her son. As she herself had learned from Thys.

Pieter Pieterse stood up as Suzanne and Thys approached, and he ran to meet them.

'Hello, Pieter,' Suzanne said very quietly and looked into his face. She saw the spread of freckles and a small boy riding an ostrich, wringing a chicken's neck, driving a cart. Then she saw the young man who had stood rigidly in front of her at Rev. Phillip's mission. She heard again the bitterness with which he had rejected and condemned her. His words had been carried on the breath of hatred. The same young man stood before her now; but this time only love breathed in the man he'd become.

Thys's face was puzzled as she raised her arms to the young stranger who had moved between them. He felt suddenly alone as Suzanne's body melted into the strong arms of the stranger.

A streak of lightning lit the darkening sky and a loud clap of thunder hung on its tail. A heavy blob of rain fell on Suzanne's shoulder and she pulled away from the young man.

'There's someone here I think you should meet,' Suzanne said and watched her son's eyes rest on Thys. 'This is your father, Pieter.' She turned to Thys, as the heavens opened and rain poured over them in a solid sheet.

Gerrit laid one hand on the bougainvillaea trunk and with the other he raised his mug towards the three people in the distance. The rain gleamed silver in the still bright ray of sun, and he saw Thys stretch out his hand to Pieter. Gerrit chewed on his pipe and turned away.

The transparent wings of the flying ants were falling off as they struggled against the suddenly drowning rain. Their short magical moment of flight had come to an end with the rain they had promised.

Titus was just six years old and had no idea why his grandmother Rosita had hurled him out of the house even before day had dawned. But he wasn't sorry.

Bonne Esperance was not the usual wonderland his imagination inhabited. For the last four days, leading to February 20th, 1878, it had been a hive of frantic activity. Everything which didn't move was scrubbed, swept and polished. His grandmother had even polished his face. For some unknown reason his nose and ears had suffered the same treatment, as she pulled, poked and cleaned with the twisted end of a wet rag. They still hurt and he wasn't sure they would ever be the same again.

He looked down at the starched white linen trousers he had been dressed in, and his heart sank with the certainty that nothing could ever be the same again. He squatted on a flat rock and his toes curled against the cold surface which had not yet been warmed by the sun. He wondered why there was something else in the air today in place of magic.

His grandmother Rosita had 'explained': but hadn't explained her sudden insistence on his cleanliness, or the new suit of clothes which meant he couldn't even sit down on the rock. She hadn't explained why his grandfather Sunday had also been hauled out of bed before dawn, and ordered to tidy the vineyards. Titus had never heard of the vineyards being tidied, and wondered if each grape would receive the same rough treatment as his nose and ears. He smiled at the thought of his grandfather trying to wipe the blue mist from the plump grapes. He'd tried that himself and solved the problem only by eating them.

His large dark eyes solemnly watched a long line of black ants as they scurried in a neverending journey backwards and forwards. He looked up through the first glimmer of daylight at the dirt road which wound its way through the mountains towards Bonne Esperance. The carriage he'd been sent to watch for was nowhere in sight, so he returned his attention to the ants.

Pushing his knees wider with his elbows he peered between his legs at the long moving line which wound its way around his bare black feet. He noticed one stray ant climbing over his big toe. It scuttled on up the arch of his foot and ran in panicking circles around his ankle. He licked his finger and held it in front of the minute body and rippling legs. The ant ran on to his finger in surprise, over his hand and up his arm.

Titus watched it for the briefest moment, then flattened it with a sharp slap of his hand. He peered at the smudge on the dark skin of his arm and then carefully examined the squidgy brown remnants in the palm of his hand before wiping it down his trousers. His eyes opened in horror as he saw the long brown streak on the starched white linen and his interest in ants vanished.

He stood up and twisted his body around, peering at the offending streak. He aimed and spat on it, rubbing the material together in a desperate attempt to wipe it out. The result was a larger mess than before, and a more certain promise of disaster. His small bottom twinged in anticipation of Rosita's beating hand, and in fury he stamped his bare feet down the long line of fleeing ants.

Jack Marsden stopped at the cellar door and looked back at the house. The air was crisp with the cleanliness of a new day, and the house stood silent in the warm cocoon of morning. The curve of the gable was lit in the palest of yellow as the first rays of sunlight reached out to touch it.

A window flew open, a duster flicked through it and Rosita's black hand automatically rubbed the pane of glass before pulling the duster back in. Jack looked away and stepped into the warm dark air of the cellar. The copper pot glowed gently with the first light creeping through the open door. The vats stood in dark, silent rows, and the smell of wood and fermenting grapes filled his nostrils. This was his world; the world in which he'd found Katinka and proved himself.

Jack couldn't remember Prudence, but he remembered his grandfather talking of her great love for Bonne Esperance, and her instinctive feeling for the vines. When Jacques had talked, he'd blamed himself for the fact that Prudence had gone; but always it was like a warning to his grandson that one day she would return: that when she did, her love for Bonne Esperance would still be there; that she would accept nothing from it but the best, and no excuse for failure would satisfy her.

That day had come.

Rosita stood up and her hand pushed at the small of her back. The days of scrubbing and polishing had left their mark, and still she had little idea why she was making such a fuss over Prudence's return. She remembered that her mother, Maria, had never been able to make Prudence brush her hair, let alone tidy the house.

'Is there any sign of the carriage yet?' Emily asked as she wheeled her way into the open doorway. Rosita shook her head, letting her breath out in a short blow.

'Little Titus let us know she here before she know she here!' Rosita waved the polishing cloth at Emily and coughed as the strong smell of wax blew back at her. 'You been up fussin' before even that cockerel I serve for dinner tonight, he woke!'

'Of course I have, Rosita.' Emily's eyes moved over the room quickly, checking for any unnoticed spots of dirt. 'You don't know how much Bonne Esperance means to Prudence.'

'Huh!' Rosita glanced at her own reflection in the rosewood desk as she spotted a small dull patch and polished it yet again. 'The house she won't see, but the grapes she will count.'

'And I sincerely hope Sunday will see that they are in order.'

'Miss Emily,' Rosita placed her hands on her wide hips and the polishing rag dived between the folds of her skirt, 'if Miss Prudence find one thing she not like, then perhaps it good she go away again!'

'Rosita,' Emily pushed her chair towards her and took her hand. She had seen the hurt in Rosita's eyes and tugged at her hand. 'I know how hard you've worked to prepare everything, but you don't understand.'

'I do.' Rosita knew very well why even her small grandson had to be spotlessly clean. 'I can polish. All day and all night I can polish, sweep and scrub, but I cannot wipe away what is in there.' Her hand indicated the rosewood desk. Rosita knew that once again the desk held the threat of impending disaster in its drawer: the pile of IOUs against Bonne Esperance, which the lawyers had informed them were about to be called in by the unknown sponsor.

Titus had spotted the smart carriage rolling its way down the dirt road while it was still many miles away. He'd heard the sound of iron wheels crunching the stones as he heard all sounds, by pressing his ear against the ground. The carriage was piled high with gleaming yellowwood trunks. Titus had never seen so much grand luggage in his life and his heart missed a beat in sudden fright. Perhaps there was a reason for the flurry of preparation. A white lady with so many possessions had to be very important. He put two fingers in his mouth, closed his lips around them, and a shrill whistle sailed through the air towards the vineyards and his grandfather.

Sunday looked up from the vines as he heard the whistle and waved to Titus in the distance. He could remember Prudence as a young girl. His father had always said she was a good girl, not like Clara. But she'd been away from the small world of Bonne Esperance he'd lived in all his life; and even he was a little nervous. Nobody who'd gone deep into that outside world had ever returned. Not his father, Titus; or his daughter, Marissa. She'd gone out there to look for work, after the birth of her son; and she had never come back. He looked towards the house and whistled.

Katinka smiled up at Jack as they stood side by side outside the house and heard Sunday's piercing note. Jack's arm was around her shoulder but she could feel the tension in him.

'It'll be all right,' she whispered, although she knew he had reason to be nervous.

'Are you finished yet, Rosita?' Emily called towards the house as she straightened her hair.

'Nearly, Miss Emily.' Rosita raised her eyes to heaven as she slid her feet backwards and forwards over the red quarry tiles of the hall. A large wooden-backed brush was strapped to the sole of each foot and her bosom and bottom swayed in opposite directions, threatening to spin her in an eternal circle on the shining tiles she was polishing with her feet. She reached the front door, disappeared behind her own rear end as she pulled the brushes off, and stood up.

'Nobody step on that floor!' she ordered.

Prudence had heard Titus's shrill whistle but though she looked hard through the carriage window, she could see nobody. The broad green leaves rustled in the slight wind and the smell of ripe grapes, which she had never forgotten, wafted in to her. She looked down at the gloved hands curled in her lap, and knew that the ache she felt was not from her arthritic joints. The carriage was driving her back into the past.

She could see the house in the distance at the feet of the mountains. Nothing had changed; yet everything had. Most particularly herself. Would she find herself again among these vines, she wondered, and inexplicably felt the loss of her father for the first time. It was as if he'd simply disappeared. When the news of his death had reached her many years ago, she had not allowed herself to mourn.

Her father had died without ever telling her that she did indeed understand the vineyards: that her love for Bonne Esperance was not unnatural. The day she had left and set out on her own seemed like yesterday. She could feel the sharp edge of the razor as it shaved her eyebrows, and her hand moved quickly to adjust her hair under the smart hat she wore. She remembered her terror as her long blonde tresses had fallen to the floor with the snip of the scissors. Her hair was long again, but not blonde. It was grey. The soft silky texture had stiffened as her joints had and she felt sad.

The house was closer now and seemed smaller than she remembered; then it disappeared as the carriage rounded a corner. In the brief moment it was out of sight, Prudence realized what it was that frightened her most. After all that had happened in her life, the driving force was still her love for Bonne Esperance. Perhaps it *was* unnatural.

'There!' Rosita pointed down the road as she spotted Sunday waving his arms towards them before he ducked back among the vines. 'She coming now.'

The carriage swung round the bend in the road and the two smart black horses lifted their feet high in a stylish trot.

Emily fingered the telegraph in her hands and looked down at it. 'Congratulations Jack Katinka stop arriving home twenty February stop.' The strange telegraph language told her nothing of Prudence, but reminded her that Prudence would be seeing her as a cripple for the first time.

'Come now!' Rosita knew what Emily was thinking and patted her on the back. 'We all older, Miss Emily. She older too.'

'Whoa!' The driver pulled his horses in and the carriage stopped behind him sharply. The pile of trunks slid forward and then back again on the roof of the carriage, before settling with a slight groan from the leather straps.

The horses stood still, looking straight ahead in their blinkers as the driver climbed down, nodding politely to the people outside the house. He wondered why they stood so erect as they waited for the occupant of his carriage. He hadn't noticed anything special about his slightly elderly passenger. He opened the carriage door, and dropped the steps down with the flourish that seemed to be demanded.

Emily realized she was holding her breath and forced herself to relax as she watched the open carriage door.

Rosita brushed away a persistent fly and concentrated more keenly.

Katinka looked at Jack and saw the ripple of muscle in his jaw.

'Are you ready, lady?' the driver asked Prudence as she sat quite still in the carriage, her eyes shut and her mouth drawn in a firm straight line.

'Your hand, please.' She held her gloved hand out to the driver, and bent her head low as her stiff body moved through the open carriage door. A brown ankle-boot reached for the first wooden step, and Emily watched carefully.

'Prudence,' she whispered, and Rosita's mouth opened in silent amazement as the full finery of Prudence's clothes made their impact. Her eyes moved in fascination from the gentle upward curve of her brown velvet hat, down the length of its short veil, and on to the smartly tailored silk bodice. The waist was ferociously tight and Rosita cringed at the thought of fitting into anything so small. The skirt was long and full at the back. The bustle Prudence had delighted in as the madame of a bordello was gone, as fashion now demanded, and instead a long flowing train dragged down the carriage steps behind her.

When Prudence reached the ground she turned and looked at the waiting family. Emily swallowed as she saw her face clearly. The delight in life, the bright determined smile she remembered, had gone. There was something brittle just under the surface of the smartly dressed grey-haired woman who stood facing her.

'Hello, Prudence.' Emily smelt a powerful scent as Prudence

moved to her chair, bent down to her and kissed her on the cheek. Her skin was wrinkled and powdery pale, as if it had never seen the sun and fresh air that Prudence had once loved.

'Emily!' Prudence smiled as she looked down at her; but even her smile had lost its sparkle.

'Brandy?' Prudence held her head back and looked at Jack accusingly. 'And who requested brandy?' She turned to Emily and raised her shoulders in a gesture of total loss. 'First you tell me you allowed some unknown person to finance Bonne Esperance in order to produce the wine they had purchased from you; then you tell me you borrowed more to produce the brandy they requested.' She narrowed her eyes and lowered her voice. 'I'd have expected a little more common sense from you, Emily.'

'I didn't agree.' Emily was embarrassed and uncomfortable as she remembered the day Ralph Saunders had arrived. 'I was the first person to question becoming involved in such a curious arrangement.'

'But you allowed all these debts to mount?' Prudence held a pile of IOUs in her hand, and her eyes ran from Emily to Jack in disbelief. 'These debts are more than the entire value of Bonne Esperance. Is your arithmetic that bad, young man?' Prudence was enjoying her moment of authority, knowing they had no idea that she was the creditor in question.

'Not now the Westbury farm is part of Bonne Esperance,' Jack retaliated quickly.

'Oh? Because John Westbury's guarantee must now be called in?'

'Because it is a part of Bonne Esperance. Because the families are united!' Jack's voice rose through the cloud of failure she had laid at his feet. He felt Katinka's hand slip into his, and her fingers curl around his own. 'I did what I thought was best.'

'That isn't what you did, Jack.' Prudence moved to him. 'You tried to prove yourself.'

'Perhaps.' Jack's honesty took her by surprise.

'And to whom were you proving herself?'

'Prudence, please!' Emily pushed her chair between them. 'Jack did what he had to do. Bonne Esperance had been killed by the British taxes, and without Jack it would not be here now! You would not have been able to announce by telegraph that

566

you were returning "home", because there would have been no "home" to return to.'

'Didn't I warn you and Father years ago that it would happen? But did you listen?'

'What is this, Prudence?' Emily was suddenly angry. 'Have you come back to gloat?'

'Just a little, my dear.' Prudence turned away to hide a smile and moved to a chair. Her gloved hands tried to keep hold of the IOUs, but some slipped to the floor. 'It's good for the soul to prove one's worth.' She looked at her hands in her lap. 'Can you graft as well as you distil brandy, Jack? For I will tell you something else before it happens. Phylloxera will spread here from Europe and devastate our vineyards as it has theirs – unless we graft now with wild vines from America. Can you graft?' Her eyes moved from her useless hands and on to Jack. 'Can you feel the life in a vine?'

'Grandfather said there was no one who could feel the life in a vine as you did.' Jack didn't notice her reaction to his words, and went on, 'He said you were at one with Bonne Esperance, as if you were the fruit of the vines themselves.'

Prudence felt her breath catch in her throat with the shock of hearing the words she had longed to hear all her life. They washed over her and swept away the protective shell she had built around herself.

'Did Father say that?' Her voice was soft and slightly nervous as she turned to Emily for confirmation. The brittle spark in her eyes had melted.

'Yes.' Emily had seen a little of the Prudence she remembered. 'Father understood why you loved Bonne Esperance, Prudence.' She nodded. 'He said it was natural.'

Prudence felt herself flush with pleasure and tried to control the emotions welling inside her. She winced as she bent down in vain to pick up the IOUs from the floor and pushed them away with her feet in a sudden fit of irritation.

'Let them stay there. But learn from this, Jack Marsden.' She looked at him keenly. 'Learn, if you want those debts forgotten!'

'I have never had any intention of forgetting them.' Jack bent to pick up the papers. 'I shall pay back every penny according to the agreement made. Even if it is at the cost of Bonne Esperance.'

567

'Please don't.' Prudence touched his shoulder as he knelt in front of her collecting the papers. His eyes were puzzled as they met hers. They were warm. 'I wouldn't want that, you silly boy.' She turned from him to Emily. 'It's taken me many, many years and a great deal of hard work to subsidize you.' Her eyes stayed on Emily and she shrugged with a sudden flash of the old Prudence. 'How else was a woman to control Bonne Esperance but to buy it!'

'It was you!' Emily's voice was a whisper.

'You don't imagine I ran a tea parlour because I like tea, do you?' She looked down at her dress. 'At last I can get out of these ridiculous clothes and back to work.' She glanced up at Jack. 'How nearly you spoiled an old lady's fun, young man.'

Chapter Thirty-two

The vineyards were filled with labourers and rustled with activity as Jack rode among them, with Katinka riding beside him. Shasaan's long white neck contrasted with the dark coat of Jack's horse.

'He went north to the goldfields, the last I heard of him.' Prudence kept her eyes on Katinka and Jack in the distance as she walked beside Emily's chair. It was pushed by the small boy, Titus. 'I loved him.' Prudence had felt the love between Jack and Katinka, and Emily's questions about Jim Audsley had stirred her own feelings; but still she kept her secret about the bordello. 'He was a waster and a scoundrel, perhaps; but he had certain other qualities: a strange honesty born of total dishonesty!'

'Then perhaps he wasn't,' Emily said, and Prudence glanced at her curiously. 'You said you loved him.'

'You are such a romantic, my dear.' Prudence pushed her feelings down as she stopped beside a vine and bent to it. She was dressed in a cotton skirt and pantaloons. The ankle-boots had been replaced by rough working shoes, and her grey hair was held back untidily in a gaudy African scarf. But still she wore her gloves.

'And you were right again,' Emily said.

'About what?'

'Phylloxera.' Emily reached out to the vine. 'Have the grafts taken yet?'

Prudence slapped her hand back quickly. Though Jack had done the grafting, it had been under her strict supervision and every scion was hers. 'Must you keep touching them, Emily? Look at them with your eyes, not your hands!'

'But I can't help touching them. It's magic.'

'And therefore we must keep our hands off them so that the

magic may continue!'

'You're like a mother hen clucking over her chicks!'

'I assure you I did more than sit on a clutch of eggs to achieve what I have!' Prudence quickly changed the subject before falling into the trap of admitting what else she had achieved in her tea parlour. 'The sooner we get you back into the house and away from the vines the better. Before I know it, you will have fingered them to death – even after the long journey from America which they survived.'

'Oh, Prudence, you do enrage me! All I want to do is look!'

'And look you shall, from the confines of the house.'

Titus's face spread in a puzzled grin as the elderly ladies argued. He wondered again why so much preparation had been made to greet this odd old woman, Miss Prudence. She was untidier than he was.

'Push Miss Emily back, little boy,' Prudence nodded to him. 'What did you say your name was again? I keep forgetting.'

'I Titus.'

'I Titus,' Prudence repeated.

'The child's name is Titus, not "I Titus".'

'How would you know, Emily? After all, it is I who remember the original Titus. Not you! Go on, I Titus, push!'

He turned the chair with a flourish and Emily glanced towards Katinka and Jack. 'Katinka makes a fine mistress of Bonne Esperance, don't you think?' she said out of the blue.

Prudence knew that the name Titus had swung them both from the present to the past: but like Emily, it no longer hurt. 'Though what she sees in Jack escapes me entirely.' Prudence looked towards the family graveyard as they walked back to the house. 'Perhaps the only thing I'm sorry about was not being at the wedding. What rumblings there must have been from Clara's grave that day. Have you heard from Suzanne?' she asked, almost too casually; as though there might be one grave missing. The chair wobbled on to the rough ground at the side of the path. 'Wake up!' she said to the small boy, who gazed at her as if he were part of the conversation. 'Look where you're going, or you'll have my sister in the ditch, I Titus!'

'I have heard from Suzanne.' Emily looked at Prudence with a serious note in her voice. 'She says there are rumours of war: that the Afrikaans people are talking of resisting British domination.'

'Pooh!' Prudence pulled her shoulders back and glanced over the vineyards. 'You shouldn't listen to rumours. There's a rumour the world is flat, too!' She glanced at Titus and concentrated her mind on him, to avoid the shadow creeping towards Bonne Esperance with the threat of war. 'The world is round, little boy. You remember that when they try to tell you otherwise.' Titus nodded. He knew the world was flat but he wouldn't argue.

Suzanne pulled the soft new wick through the base of the lamp and lit it with a twig from the fire. Thys and Pieter had been arguing all night, and though the sudden stillness outside heralded the birth of a new day, she knew the argument would continue into it.

'Passive resistance to the British as they annex our land has become futile resistance, Father.' Pieter's eyes were alight with the same flame she'd seen in Thys's eyes after the British had hanged his father. 'We are one people, the Afrikaner people; and we must unite to fight the British before we lose our country and our language for ever. Already they are forbidding us to speak in our mother tongue. What will they do next? Kill our mothers?'

'No, Pieter.' Thys looked away, shaking his head. He felt the familiar pain of facing his father many years ago. 'What good will there be in bloodshed?' His mind leapt back to the bodies of Charles and Geoffrey Marsden being buried alongside those of Tshepo and his people, then back again to his father's body as it swung for the second time and his neck was broken. 'Do you think bloodletting will ever make a nation of our people?'

Colonel Stringer's words rang in Thys's head: 'But will we learn from it?' Thys gestured at Suzanne. 'Your mother is English. Will you kill her too, Pieter?'

'Suzanne is Afrikaans, Thys.' Gerrit's words were quiet as he looked at her. 'Am I right, Suzanne?'

She nodded, and cleared away the empty mugs in front of them. Although she knew a moment was coming when her new family would divide her from her old, she was calm.

'But,' she said, 'vengeance is not ours.'

'Then what are the English doing? When they take our land, they take our lives.'

'I have packed you some food,' Suzanne said quietly and

571

turned away, picking up a bag and handing it to Pieter.

'He is not going!' Thys moved to Suzanne. 'Fighting is not the answer.'

'No.' She looked at Thys directly. 'Fighting your son is not the answer either, Thys.'

Thys knew she was right. He was dividing himself from Pieter as he had from his own father; but he went on. 'If you leave this home and go to fight, Pieter: then it cannot be your home and you cannot be my son.'

Gerrit watched the look of determination settle in Pieter's eyes as he faced his father.

'My heart will sing its own song,' Gerrit said quietly, and looked up as he felt their eyes on him. The bright blue of his own eyes had faded to an almost luminous white and he glanced towards the open door as the sun crept cautiously across the dark earth. He wished he had died and been under it before this day had dawned.

Tshepo's son, Adam – tall and lean with the gawkiness of a teenager, but still with his father'a wide spreading smile – looked up at Pieter and held out the reins of his horse to him.

'You go now?' he asked. He had no idea why his Afrikaans family had to fight the English.

'Yes.'

Adam glanced at the gun Pieter strapped to his saddle, and a disturbing memory stirred inside him, but he couldn't place it. He looked at the house and saw Suzanne as she stood alone at the window watching Pieter leave, and wondered why Thys wasn't there.

'Take care of them,' Pieter said to Adam, as he looked at his mother outlined against the window. Pieter mounted his horse and pulled it in as it reared, aware of the long journey ahead.

'Yes, master,' Adam nodded as Suzanne raised her hand against the windowpane. He knew she was crying though he couldn't see her clearly, and turned away to watch Pieter and his horse until they faded into the blue of the horizon. He wondered whose side he was on and felt suddenly isolated. When he turned back to the house Suzanne emerged with Thys. She seemed to be comforting him and Thys looked suddenly old as they walked together across the land their son had gone to fight for.

'Adam!' He turned at Gerrit's secret voice, calling from the house. He was glad to be called away to Gerrit's world, which he understood clearly.

'You want more peaches from the widow Heunis's yard?' he asked with Tshepo's wide smile. 'She kill me if she catch me again.'

'Better than the jam she'll poison us with if she gets the peaches first.' Gerrit beckoned Adam with his little finger, and they escaped together into a world which offered the delights of outwitting the widow Heunis. 'When I go to the front door,' Gerrit put his arm round Adam's shoulders as they walked towards the old cart, and the beginning of a long trek to the widow Heunis's house, 'when I have knocked and given her my greeting . . .'

'I say, "Hello".'

'Sometimes you're a very stupid kaffir, Adam.' Gerrit held on to his arm tightly as Adam helped him into the cart.

'Sometimes, I not a stupid kaffir.' Adam grinned, and climbed up beside him. Gerrit looked at him, puzzled, as he stretched forward and gathered the old leather reins. 'She know the last time you knocked, I stole the peaches. This time, maybe she will send her daughter to watch, if I not with you at the door.' Adam flicked the reins across the back of the old mare, disturbing the flies.

'Then how will you get the peaches?' Gerrit huffed at him, pushing his empty pipe into his mouth.

'If I at the door with you, she will tell you to send the kaffir boy away from her door. She will not want to see where I go because kaffirs are not to be seen.' Gerrit laughed. 'Clever kaffir?' Adam grinned, bringing the reins down on the horse's back as he drove them both towards their private world of mischief.

Suzanne stopped at the front door of the house, turned and looked the way Pieter had gone. Her son was long out of sight, on his way to the war he believed in, a war against her own people. She could see Gerrit and Adam in the cart, rumbling away. She could see Thys riding towards the herd of cattle in the distance, and she could hear his words, 'He is not my son!'

She felt suddenly alone in the vast and sprawling land which had become her home, and for the first time she felt her age. But although it had limited her movements, it had not limited her hopes. She moved on to the veranda and sat on the carved wooden bench. Her fingers ran over the smooth seat, rubbed even smoother by the polishing of tired bodies, and she pressed her back against the curve of the wood, looking up at the large clump of bougainvillaea above. The mauve of its petals became the mountains of Bonne Esperance and she wondered if she would ever see them again.

Then, from the purple shape of the mountains drawn by the bougainvillaea, a tiny black spider suddenly dropped down on a silken thread. Its legs curled under its body as it hung for a moment, then it swung itself through the air towards another stalk of bougainvillaea. Suzanne watched for hours as the spider swung backwards and forwards, spinning its fragile thread in a perfect web. She was tired but totally at peace and fell asleep as if held still by the web God's word held her in.

'He maketh wars to cease unto the ends of the earth.'

She knew there was hope. There was God.

Jim Audsley sat uncomfortably in the formal chair and looked across the stylish sitting-room of Bonne Esperance at Prudence. He could see she was angry and knew he could no longer win her round as he used to. He wasn't quite sure why he had come. The surroundings had only confirmed the fact that he had never truly known the real Prudence.

Though Emily had given him a warm welcome, and an immediate cup of tea had been produced by Rosita, he felt entirely out of place.

'I was on my way to Cape Town and thought I'd come and say goodbye,' he said as simply as he could.

'Goodbye!' Prudence's voice reached for the heavens and she pushed her untidy grey hair back as she looked at him. She still hadn't got over the shock of finding him drinking tea with Emily, and wasn't sure how much he'd told her of their past. 'There's somewhere else you have yet to travel? Or are you afraid of the coming war?'

'Perhaps I'm simply too old.'

'You are that,' Prudence added, trying to combat the age she'd felt in herself when she'd suddenly come face to face with him again. He looked as out of place as little Titus had made him sound. All the way back to the house Titus had described his gold brocade waistcoat and large brimmed hat, as if he'd come from another planet. 'Isn't it that I am simply too old for you to have your way with any more, James Audsley?' Prudence said, wishing she'd had time to straighten herself a little: brush her hair perhaps.

The crooked smile reached out, touching her as it always had. 'I remember our goodbyes well.' He paused. 'And our helloes.'

'You never were an accomplished liar, James.' Prudence turned away to hide a smile. It gave away the fact that she remembered the helloes and goodbyes herself. 'I don't know why you bothered to come here at all if it is only to say goodbye.'

'So that I can come back?' She turned and looked at him in surprise. He looked older and a little lost, but at least he no longer looked like a pimp, Prudence thought, and realized quite suddenly that love didn't age. It simply changed. She cared for him deeply.

'Where are you going this time?'

'Australia.' He looked at her, twiddling his hat on his knee. 'To catch the boat I missed: the boat you know nothing about.'

'You imagine I don't know about that boat? Huh! Do you think I haven't known all along that you were no more than a common thief being shipped to Australia?'

'Then you'll be glad to see me go.' There was a sad question in his voice.

'Of course not.' Though she didn't want him to go, she knew, as she always had, that she had merely borrowed him. 'I shall look forward to the pleasure of you, the day you come back, James Audsley.'

'Yes,' he nodded, and touched her gloved hand as it patted him warmly on the back. He held one gloved finger and looked into her eyes with a twinkle. 'I might be away a while,' he said. 'Can you wait that long?'

Prudence smiled, knowing that it was the last time she would see him.

'I'll wait,' she said.

Rosita's eyes were rounder than ever as she listened to Emily while peeling the potatoes. The long thin ribbons of potato skin curled into a spiral before dropping into the bowl of water.

'But Miss Prudence she must not know you know, Miss

Emily.' Rosita was clearly against Emily's plans and dug into a black mark on the white peeled potato with her knife. 'What's a bordello?' She dropped the potato into the pot with a plop. 'Is not a tea parlour?'

'Hardly.' Emily had not been at all surprised when Jim Audsley had appeared out of the blue looking for Prudence. He was exactly as she had imagined him to be. All that had surprised her was his talk of Mrs Audsley's Parlour. She had decided to keep her new-found information to herself and had left the moment Prudence arrived in the room. She remembered Prudence's letters, and suddenly she laughed out loud at the grand talk of the clients who attended her tea parlour: her boasts of the fine tea shipped all the way from England, and then up-country to the diamond fields.

'Tea parlour, indeed!' Emily pushed her chair towards the kitchen door. The pots hanging from the wall with their gleaming copper bottoms reflected Rosita's large frame as she ran after her.

'Miss Emily!' Rosita had spotted the note of triumph in Emily's voice. 'You bad!'

'I am simply enjoying being in possession of a weapon of sorts.'

'A weapon?' Rosita had gathered that a bordello was not exactly a tea parlour, but couldn't understand the glint in Emily's eye. 'What are you going to do?'

'Don't you think I deserve a little fun after all this time, Rosita?' She looked into her eyes. 'Do you remember the day Prudence came back?' Rosita nodded. 'She made me feel quite the country bumpkin.' Emily straightened her back. 'Besides, she's become very autocratic with age, and I shall enjoy having something up my sleeve when her behaviour as a "madame" in this house exceeds itself.'

'Miss Emily.' Rosita's large bosom bounced with laughter, although she wasn't quite sure what she was laughing at. 'You bad!'

'Then let me enjoy it.' Emily grinned and pushed her chair through the kitchen door. Rosita shook her head as she picked up another potato to peel. Emily had at last regained a little of her sparkle. She felt quite young and slim again herself as her knife ran an energetic circle round another potato.

Emily stopped her chair as she saw Jim Audsley moving towards the front door with Prudence on his arm. She could see why Prudence loved him. Humour bubbled in his eyes.

'Thank you for the tea. I shall be back.' He moved to Emily and took her hand, kissing it gently. 'After all, fifty per cent is fifty per cent. Goodbye.'

'Goodbye, Mr Audsley.' Emily felt suddenly sad as they moved away and Prudence turned to James quickly.

'Did Emily ask you any questions?' Her voice was casual.

'Yes.' James walked with her towards the young boy, Titus, who held his horse for him and plonked his hat on his head 'I assure you I told her no lies.'

'You didn't?' Prudence looked back uncomfortably at the house and Emily.

'The tea came from India, I said. Not England.' He lifted his leg preparing to jump up on to his horse as he used to. He stopped and looked at Prudence. 'Do you have a stool?'

'A stool?' Prudence smiled and turned to Titus. 'Bring my stool, I Titus.' She turned back to James. 'We all need a little help upwards nowadays.'

They stood in silence as they waited for the small boy to return with the stool and their eyes met in a warm acceptance of one another.

'Thank you,' he said as Titus placed the stool beside his horse. 'It's strange how horses do grow taller each year.' Titus removed the stool and stood back beside Prudence. His small face looked up at her. He knew the old lady he'd grown to care for was sad.

'Where he going?' he asked as Jim Audsley rode away.

'Why should that matter, I Titus?' Prudence rubbed his head and turned away. 'He'll be coming back.' Titus watched the old man riding away from Bonne Esperance and wondered.

'Well?' Prudence said, as she reached Emily, tossing her head back and looking at her accusingly. 'Is there some reason you are sitting in the doorway like that, my dear?'

'I can see why you love him.' Emily had changed her mind about the secret weapon.

'And?'

'What is it, Prudence?'

'It's you who should answer that, Emily.'

'I beg your pardon?' Emily looked at her in innocence.

'Come now, Emily!' Prudence pulled her chair round to push it back into the house. 'He told me all he'd told you.'

'Oh, about your tea parlour,' Emily exclaimed. 'It sounds very nice.'

'Nice? You know perfectly well it wasn't a tea parlour, Emily.'

'Isn't it you who knows perfectly well it wasn't a tea parlour, Prudence?'

Titus bent down and picked up the stool. So long as he lived he would never understand how two old women managed to talk so much.

'Is the world flat or round, I Titus?'

He looked round in surprise. 'Flat,' he said.

'Exactly!' Prudence disappeared through the door with Emily. 'That's obviously what my sister thinks too, and I have no reason to explain myself to you, Emily. None at all!'

Johannes Villiers pulled the cloth to and fro over the shiny black toe cap in front of him and looked up at the old man whose shoes he polished every Monday morning.

'Right?' he asked.

'Can I see my face in it?' Colonel Stringer peered down at his civilian shoe. 'Yes.' He saw the clean-shaven face which greeted him every Monday morning in the shine of his shoe leather. 'That's good enough.'

'Look!' Johannes Villiers stood up at the sound of horses coming down the cobbled street. 'Where they going?'

Colonel Stringer looked blankly at the troop of red-coated British soldiers riding through the town. 'To a massacre,' he said, as he remembered the day on a dusty African plain when he had decided to retire. The red jackets and gold epaulettes gleamed in the sun and he shook his head. He knew that very few of the young soldiers would ever come back from their apparently simple mission: 'to keep a little Boer rebellion down.' Stringer had failed in his attempt to teach the British army how to fight in Africa, and the failure was his own. He had had to face it the day he had found himself in the centre of a bloodbath. Now he was the old soldier with nothing but stories to tell; and nobody who cared to listen to them.

'You were a soldier.' Johannes Villiers flicked his cloth over the shoe with a flourish. 'I want to be a soldier, too. Tell me more.' Stringer looked down and lifted his other shoe to the one person who ever listened to him. A half-caste street child in Cape Town. A child who had no idea what the coming war was about.

'What do you want to hear today?' Stringer rested his eyes on the small brown hands as they brushed black polish on to his shoe. He didn't want to think about what had gone wrong in his life. 'You still haven't told me about you.'

'Nothing to tell.' Johannes Villiers shrugged. He would never tell anyone that he had run away from a convent and then from 'Miss Thurston's School'. 'You tell about you.' He wondered if today he would earn enough to eat before he settled down to sleep in a doorway. 'I listen.'

Colonel Stringer needed no more to loosen his tongue, and allowed his mind to travel back over the road of glory, the only one he chose to remember. He looked after the soldiers as they rode away, leaving him to dream about what might have been.

'I haven't told you about Major Charles Marsden, I believe. Would you like to hear about him?'

'Mmm.' Johannes Villiers nodded, picking up his cloth and holding it over the shoe ready to shine it. He had long since worked out that the more stories the Colonel told him, the more he paid him for shining his shoes. It was the only interest he had in the old man's stories. 'You tell me about Major Charles Marsden,' he encouraged Colonel Stringer. He had no idea that the story would be partly about himself.

Katinka had never felt such pain. Her back ached as if a red-hot poker was being held against the base of her spine and every muscle tightened with a contraction. She screamed as her mother and the midwife encouraged her to push the baby to life. She tried to think of Jack; to picture the warm brown eyes and remind herself that the pain was for his child. Her voice rose in a long agonized wail. It was as if her body was being torn apart as the baby pushed further down the channel between her legs. She couldn't bear the pain and tried to think instead of the previous night and the excitement as she had felt the first twinge of labour. She had seen Jack's bewildered face as she'd woken him. He'd laid his hand on her stomach and gasped as he'd felt the pull of a contraction under his palm. He had looked at her with such tenderness and care that she could still feel his comfort around her. But the pain had grown fiercer and more frequent. She was exhausted and had begun to hate the small baby who seemed determined not to be born.

'No!' Katinka screamed. 'I can't go on!'

'Just one more.' Sarah held her daughter's hand tightly as the midwife worked between her legs. The tiny head had just appeared.

'It's coming,' the midwife said excitedly.

'Where's Jack?' Katinka asked her mother before her face contorted with pain and her body gathered itself in one last effort.

'He's outside.' Sarah looked at her daughter, whose own birth she could remember as if it were yesterday. She could feel each agonizing contraction with her, and wished she could take the pain on herself. 'I suggested he kept himself busy.'

Katinka's pain suddenly vanished and she felt something warm and wet moving between her legs.

'It's a boy!' the midwife exclaimed proudly and gave the slippery baby to Sarah, going back to Katinka quickly. 'Just a little more work now, my girl.'

Katinka peered around the midwife and over her own shaking spread knees as she watched her mother holding her new baby close to her face. Her body was trembling with exhaustion.

'Is he all right, Mother?' she asked, without realizing what those words would mean to Sarah.

'Oh yes, Katinka. Your son is all right.'

The baby opened its tiny mouth and yelled. The little pink arms and legs kicked and its spread fingers grabbed at thin air, as Sarah wrapped it in a white sheet and handed it to her daughter. Katinka looked down at the bloodied bald head resting on her arm. The small mouth was still open wide in screams of terror at the world it had been pushed into, and its face was creased with rage.

'Call Jack.' Katinka looked from the baby to Sarah.

'One last push,' the midwife interrupted.

'Come on. One more, Katinka,' Sarah encouraged her as she remembered pushing out the afterbirth with no son as a reward. Katinka pushed and felt a swell of liquid between her legs before peace came.

'I want to see Jack.' Katinka's green eyes turned to her mother as the pain in them disappeared. Though her face was damp with sweat and her hair stuck in loose strands, she looked beautiful. 'I want Jack to see our son.'

'I'll tell him.' The midwife moved to the door, covering the enamel bowl in her hand with a cloth.

The midwife's message passed quickly from a bubbling Rosita to Titus; from Titus to Sunday, as he rushed from the vineyards; and finally to Jack as he stood among the vines, looking away towards the moutains as though they might calm him.

'It's a boy!' Sunday cupped his hands and called over the last short distance to Jack. He looked round and his mouth moved silently as if he was unsure he had heard.

'What?' he called back, and his voice tripped over Sunday's as it came back at him quickly.

'It's a boy!' Sunday yelled for the entire world to hear.

Prudence pushed Emily's chair across the lawn on the other side of the house and a grasshopper jumped away before the wheels flattened it.

'What did he say?' Prudence shouted to Titus as he ran back after delivering his part of the message. She saw Jack on his horse racing towards the house and a bubble of excitement skipped through her veins.

'It's a boy!' Titus called as he reached them, and Prudence looked down at Emily in her chair.

'I believe it's a boy,' she said quietly.

'So I heard, my dear.' Emily closed her eyes and her body curled in warm satisfaction. 'It's a boy,' she repeated the only words she would write in her diary that night as she remembered Eva's body being delivered to its grave only two months before.

Sarah stood in the small bedroom in which Pauline had given birth to her dead husband and stroked the fine white hair of Mr Westbury's head. He lay quite still on the bed, and she wasn't quite sure he could hear her, but she went on.

'They have called him John Geoffrey, and he's a fine healthy baby.' Sarah saw that his filmed eyes were looking at her intently, as if questioning her. 'What is it?' She leaned towards him and listened. 'Yes.' She smiled and stroked his forehead gently. 'I think it's a good name too.'

Mr Westbury closed his eyes, and Sarah knew he had heard what he was waiting to hear. It would not be long before the last breath slipped out of him and she hoped the child's birth would release him soon from the punishing grip of life. She stood up and moved to the window, looking out at the tree under which John Westbury had always shaved.

'I promise I will never stop looking for our son, John. Even though I don't believe I will find him, I will look.' Her silent pledge was like a wreath at the foot of the tree.

Sarah turned back to Mr Westbury. He lay absolutely still. The room was so quiet she thought she could still hear Katinka's cries of pain. But they were Pauline's cries: ringing around the silent house as if death had released the pain Mr Westbury had held to himself for so long.

Rosita placed her hands on her wide hips and turned to Sunday in fury as they stood together to one side of the house. Dust rose in a cloud over Bonne Esperance, creeping through the windows, as horses trampled the earth. Red-coated soldiers wheeled them about the courtyard as their commander, Major James Fitzpatrick, dismounted and moved to Jack and Katinka as they came out of the house.

'What those soldiers want?' Rosita demanded of Sunday. His eyes were narrow and his forehead was drawn in lines under his grey hair. Both clearly remembered the day Major Charles Marsden had ridden in with Thys many years before. 'Agh!' she shouted, as she remembered the washing on the line which would be covered with dust, and her body shook with anger as she marched round the house to attend to it. She turned back to Sunday. 'You watch the cellars! Or they take off all the wine they can carry.'

Sunday moved quickly to the cellars, ensuring he avoided the soldiers' eyes. Although the coming war they talked of did not concern him directly, the swords and guns glinting in the sun unnerved him. He glanced back to the house as Jack stood talking to the British major. It could have been Jack's grandfather, Jacques Beauvilliers, talking to Charles Marsden, with Thys one of the soldiers.

'We might need to utilize your house should there be trouble in the area; though I doubt it will come to anything.' Major Fitzpatrick smiled at Jack. 'We'll quell the unrest among the Boers soon enough. They've simply been stirred up by troublemakers from outside.'

'Are you so certain of that?' Jack asked quizzically and felt Katinka link her arm tighter through his. He knew his father and brother had died at the hands of blacks led by a Boer. He had no idea who that Boer was. Jack had never met Thys. The only mention of his name was as 'Aunt Suzanne's Afrikaans husband'. He had little time for the Boer himself, he still remembered the ugly faces of those Boers whose ignorant prejudice had led to the killing of John Westbury, but Jack found the pink-faced young Englishman equally ugly and dangerous.

'Perhaps they imagine they have a cause,' Jack said simply. 'And will not easily be put down.'

'The Boer?' The English major's face lit with amusement. 'I doubt we will have much problem. They're animals who have learned to walk on their hind legs.'

'And myself?' Jack asked with a smile.

'You are British.' The major's voice had a note of congratulation.

'And French,' Jack smiled. 'But I learned to walk in Africa.'

Rosita tugged the washing off the line with grunting huffs and puffs, then glanced into the distance where she knew her grandson Titus had gone with Emily, Prudence and the baby. She could just make out the silhouette of Titus on the river bank, and waved to him.

Titus waved back at the distant figure of his grandmother and then continued tossing flat stones across the water. Each one sank immediately, and he wished one of the two old ladies knew how to make a stone bounce. Nobody knew secrets like that any more and all grown-ups talked about was war. Even if they pretended to ignore the soldiers trampling their land, as Prudence and Emily had.

'So you're telling me you still believe there is hope, Emily.' Prudence looked at her over the baby carriage between them. She sat on the chair Titus had carried for her, and watched Emily cautiously.

'Yes.' Emily could see the far-off red of the British soldiers in the grounds of Bonne Esperance, and looked away to the baby, then to the river. She saw again the washing on the white stones the day she had run to fetch Thys for Suzanne. She remembered jumping from stone to stone and could hear the singing of the women as they scrubbed on the river bank. 'But Titus would have more hope with his stones if you taught him how to skim them.' Emily nodded towards Titus. 'Or don't you remember how to skim a stone?'

'Huh!' Prudence shot a glance at her, then went to Titus who was holding up a stone hopefully. 'You throw it like this, I Titus.' Prudence tried to show him how to hold it while keeping her mind off the soldiers who were invading the land she loved.

'That is entirely wrong, Prudence. A stone must be thrown like this if you want it to bounce on the water.' Emily curled her hand back as if about to throw a stone.

'No wonder Bonne Esperance nearly came to nothing. You know as much about throwing a stone as you do about wine. One throws a stone like this, my dear.' She tried to show Emily the correct way to do it and the two old ladies started their banter again. Titus wished he'd never thought of throwing stones.

'I doubt you had much chance to practise in that tea parlour of yours,' Emily said, turning her head away obstinately.

'You know what they say, Emily! One shouldn't throw stones at all if one lives in a glass house.'

'I didn't live in your house, Prudence. Indeed, I know nothing about Mrs Audsley's Parlour except the tea you didn't serve.'

'Then consider one thing, my dear. Your righteousness has stayed intact thanks to that wheelchair!'

Titus noticed the two old ladies had fallen silent, and saw a ray of hope in the silence. He bent down, found himself another flat stone and moved to them. The moment he did their voices started up again.

'I notice you kept silent at that, my dear!' Prudence said to Emily with a wry smile.

'I was thinking.'

'What about?'

'Suzanne.'

Prudence looked away at the small boy. He turned, disgruntled, and flung a stone. It dived straight under the water. 'Somebody will have to teach that boy how to throw,' she said, and Emily looked at her across the baby between them as she stroked its face gently. 'Don't wake him! We were asked to mind him, Emily, not play with him!'

Emily reached out, touching Prudence's gloved hand. 'Whatever happens, this baby is most important. Am I right, Prudence?'

'Yes.' Prudence rubbed her thumb on Emily's hand as she held it, but her eyes were cast down. 'If there still is a country by the time he grows up: then, yes; he will be most important.'

'There will be.' Emily looked at her. 'Oh, yes.' She turned to Titus, held out her hand and smiled. 'Bring me a stone and I will show you how to skim it.'

Titus snatched up a flat stone, wiped it on his trousers and ran to her. He moved from foot to foot in anticipation of a lesson at last.

'Suzanne's son, Pieter, has joined the Afrikaner band to fight, you told me.' Prudence watched Emily as she curled the stone in the palm of her hand, drawing her arm back to throw.

'Yes.' Emily threw the stone and it bounced twice on the still brown water. Titus shrieked with delight and ran to find another quickly. 'Suzanne said he was just one of some ten thousand Boers who have sworn to fight the British,' she added quietly.

'And you see hope?' Prudence looked at her in amazement.

'As Suzanne does,' Emily nodded.

Prudence watched suspiciously as Titus held a stone out to her. She turned her suspicion on to the small flat stone.

'What is this, a competition?' She looked into Titus's bright grinning face.

'Yes,' Titus said firmly. He'd found his way between them at last and tipped backwards and forwards on his heels with pleasure.

'Very well, I Titus!' Prudence pulled her gloved hand back and threw the stone. It bounced three times before disappearing below the surface. Prudence's head lifted with pride and her shoulders straightened as she looked at Emily.

'What is it, Prudence?' Emily asked, as though she hadn't noticed the stone bounce.

'It's your turn to throw.' Prudence looked away. 'Suzanne, I believe, has a vision.'

'Yes.' Emily hadn't missed the note of derision in Prudence's voice as she took the stone Titus handed to her. Her eyes moved from his bright black face to the peaceful sleeping face of the baby. 'Where there is no vision, the people perish.' Emily ran her fingers over the smooth warm surface of the stone. 'Or if love waxes cold,' she said quietly, pushing the stone into the palm of her hand with her thumb. Titus wished she would throw it.

'The hope for this land is in the people.' Emily glanced at the baby between them. 'As it is in our family. I have faith.'

Titus wondered why the baby interested her more than throwing stones, even more than talking of war. He decided that if he ever learned how to skim a stone, he certainly wouldn't teach the baby.

'There!' Emily exclaimed with delight as the stone bounced over the water in endless loops.

'What's to be so excited about that?' Prudence held her hand out to Titus and he placed a stone in it. She drew her arm back and threw it. The stone bounced higher and further than Emily's as it skipped over the surface of the water and Titus quivered with pleasure.

'When he be seven?' he asked as he looked at the sleeping baby.

'Eighteen eighty-six,' Emily said with little interest as she held out her hand, anxious to compete with Prudence's challenge.

Prudence watched carefully as the small flat stone passed from Titus's hand to Emily's. Her eyes moved to the water, ready to count the bounces.

'Huh!' she said as Emily's stone nose-dived into the water.

'I wasn't holding it quite correctly. Another one, Titus.'

'Wait your turn, Emily. Come along, I Titus, I need a stone!'

Titus ran around to collect as many stones as possible as the competition began in earnest. He had come to a decision.

When the baby was seven he would teach him to throw stones. He might even teach him to fish, as his grandfather, Sunday, had taught him.

ROWAN BESTSELLERS

OLD SINS
Penny Vincenzi

An unputdownable saga of mystery, passion and glamour, exploring the intrigue which results when Julian Morell, head of a vast cosmetics empire, leaves part of his huge legacy to an unknown young man. The most desirable novel of the decade, *Old Sins is about money, ambition, greed and love... a* blockbuster for the nineties.

GREAT POSSESSIONS
Kate Alexander

A wonderful saga set in glamorous between-the-wars London that tells the story of Eleanor Dunwell, an illegitimate working-class girl who comes quite unexpectedly into a great inheritance. Her wealth will attract a dashing American spendthrift husband – and separate her from the man she truly loves.

LOVERS AND SINNERS
Linda Sole

Betty Cantrel is about to be hanged for the murder of the only man she ever loved. Once a lowly housemaid, she is now one of the most glamorous nightclub singers in London. Two men have figured in her life: the dark and enigmatic Nathan Crawley and the cool and suave James Blair. Which one of them does she truly love – and why does she kill him?

THE QUIET EARTH
Margaret Sunley

Set in the Yorkshire Dales during the nineteenth century, this rural saga captures both the spirit and warmth of working life in an isolated farming community, where three generations of the Oaks family are packed under the same roof. It tells of their struggle for survival as farmers, despite scandal, upheaval and tragedy, under the patriarchal rule of Jonadab Oaks.

FIELDS IN THE SUN

Margaret Sunley

Continuing the saga of the Oaks family set in the Yorkshire Dales. As the children grow up, Jonadab Oaks finds his patriarchal authority diminishing. Facing tragedy, upheaval and bids for independence, especially from the wild Tamar with her illegitimate child, Jonadab learns a new wisdom which will keep a new generation heartbound to the farm.

THE SINS OF EDEN

Iris Gower

Handsome, charismatic and iron-willed, Eden Lamb has an incalculable effect on the lives of three very different women in Swansea during the Second World War that is to introduce them both to passion and heartbreak. Once again, bestselling author Iris Gower has spun a tender and truthful story out of the background she knows and loves so well.

THE DIPLOMAT'S WIFE

Louise Pennington

Elizabeth Thornton, beautiful and elegant wife of distinguished diplomat, John, has everything. Until Karl – dangerous, ruthless and passionate – turns up in her life again. Under the glittering chandeliers of Vienna, 'City of Dreams', her past returns with a vengeance and she must choose between the safe love she shares with John and the heady passion she feels for Karl.

THE ITALIANS

Jane Nottage

A contemporary international novel capturing the very essence of the fabulously rich D'Orsi family. Wealthy, passionate ex-playboy Alberto D'Orsi has everything – including the memory of the woman he loved and lost during the Second World War. Now an old man, he must decide who will inherit his vast fortune: his aristocratic wife or wayward son and daughter? His decision shocks everyone.

THE RICH PASS BY
Pamela Pope

How could Sarah have foretold the bitter destiny she was choosing for herself when she vowed to reclaim her illegitimate child. But she survives – fighting to remain true to her vow and to hide the passion she feels for the father of the child. Set amid the contrasts of Victorian London, Sarah's tempestuous story is inextricably linked to that of a harsh, unequal society in this moving story of endurance and love.

ELITE
Helen Liddell

Anne Clarke was a ruthless, politically ambitious, beautiful and brilliant woman... passionately committed to the underground workers' militia of Scotland. But did her seemingly easy rise to the post of Deputy Prime Minister and her brilliantly orchestrated, perfectly lip-glossed public face conceal a sinister secret?

ANGEL
Belle Grey

After the death of her Hungarian father in a duel, Sylvie is left to the mercy of her unscrupulous mother. Throughout her career as an actress in late-Victorian London and her involvement with Pre-Raphaelite artist, Will Mackenzie, who paints her portrait, Sylvie is seeking to avenge her father's murder and confront the ghosts of her past.

OUR FATHER'S HOUSE
Caroline Fabre

A subtly crafted saga spanning three decades, charting the slow disintegration of a family which salvages hope from the ruins. The rich and powerful Sir Edward Astonbury is betrayed by one of his children for tax evasion. To understand why, the youngest must trace back over a lifetime of manipulation, deception, and mingled love and hate that has made each of them what they are.

FOLLY'S CHILD
Janet Tanner

Top sixties model Paula Varna died, with her husband's business partner Greg Martin, in a yachting accident twenty years ago. Or did she? When Greg is found living a new life in Australia, Paula's family is devastated by old wounds and memories. Harriet, Paula's daughter, determines to learn the truth about the mother she lost when she was four, but is torn between family loyalty and her feelings for private investigator Tom O'Neill...

ALL ON A SUMMER'S DAY
Judy Gardiner

On the morning of her birthday, Miranda's dream brings the past painfully back to life – from her childhood in pre-war Liverpool, to the guilt of a baby's accident, to the Nazi invasion of Paris when her childhood Jewish friend is captured. Only after the liberation of Europe is there a chance for atonement when Miranda's Red Cross unit comes to a halt outside a silent place guarded by watchtowers and barbed wire.

SPIRIT OF THE SEA
Georgina Fleming

Kerry Penhale knows heartache: her childhood love has left her; her father and brothers were lost at sea; her family faces ruin; even her mysterious friend Missy has abandoned her to face alone her marriage to the squire of Trewen. As the waves crash onto the Cornish coast, a story unfolds of smuggling, witchcraft, and a tormented love that has lasted to the grave and beyond...

FRIENDS AND OTHER ENEMIES
Diana Stainforth

Set in the sixties and seventies, the rich, fast-moving story of a girl called Ryder Harding who loses *everything* – family, lover, money and friends. But Ryder claws her way back and turns misfortune into gold.

SANDSTORM
June Knox-Mawer

It is 1913 and the newly married Rose sets out for Arabia. Tied forever to a man she barely knows, she watches his charm changing to vicious neglect, his real desires becoming a mystery. In Aden the ideal love she longs for sweeps her away: away from the British, into the heart of this seductive land. But the scandalous affair between an English wife and a young Arab prince seems fated to destroy them both.

THE LAST SUMMER OF INNOCENCE
Linda Sole

For Kate Linton, 1913 is the last summer of innocence. During this summer she learns the joy of love, and the agony of betrayal. When she discovers that her mother has rewarded her love and trust with only lies and deceit, she leaves Cambridge for the bloodstained battlefields of France, only to realise that the past cannot so easily be left behind.

A WOMAN OF STYLE
Colin McDowell

Born Constance Simpson in rural Northumberland, she became Constance Castelfranco di Villanuova when she married the charming but penniless Italian aristocrat, Ludovico. Determined to succeed, she founded a fashion industry which became a major force in international fashion. But with fame comes heartbreak and emptiness... and Constance is forced to make a choice.

TOO MUCH, TOO YOUNG

Caroline Bridgewood

They are the baby boomers, a generation for whom anything is possible: to live together or to marry? to choose a career for personal gain or to benefit society? to be gay or to be straight? They are the generation of post-war babyboom Britain, where virtue is boring and corruption and greed are sexy. They are the generation who had too much, too young.

OTHER ROWAN BOOKS

Prices and other details are liable to change.

ARROW BOOKS, BOOKSERVICE BY POST, PO BOX 29,
DOUGLAS, ISLE OF MAN, BRITISH ISLES

NAME _____

ADDRESS _____

_____

_____

Please enclose a cheque or postal order made out to Arrow
Books Ltd. for the amount due and allow the following for
postage and packing.

U.K. CUSTOMERS: Please allow 30p per book to a
maximum of £3.00

B.F.P.O. & EIRE: Please allow 30p per book to a maximum
of £3.00

OVERSEAS CUSTOMERS: Please allow 35p per book.

Whilst every effort is made to keep prices low it is sometimes
necessary to increase cover prices at short notice. Arrow
Books reserve the right to show new retail prices on covers
which may differ from those previously advertised in the text
or elsewhere.